new Worlds Wake
ERI LEIGH

New Worlds Wake

Eri Leigh

This is a work of fiction. Names, characters, places, and incidents are product's of the author's imagination or are used fictitiously and are not to be construed as real. Any resemblance to actual persons, living or dead, events or establishments is solely coincidental.

New Worlds Wake. Copyright © 2024 by Eri Leigh and Delphi Publishing, LLC.

All rights reserved. No part of this book may be reproduced, scanned, or distributed in any printed or electronic form without permission of the publisher. No part of this book may be used or reproduced in any manner for the purpose of training artificial intelligence technologies or systems.

Paperback: 979-8-9852409-4-8

Ebook: 979-8-9852409-2-4

Cover designed by Books and Moods.

Layout by Books and Moods.

Maps by Eri Leigh.

Eri Leigh asserts the right to be identified as the author of this work.

Scan the QR code below for a digital copy of the maps and glossary.
www.authorerileigh.com/the-world-of-new-worlds-wake
The World of New Worlds Wake

Author's Note

The following are the content warnings for New Worlds Wake. Each has been thoughtfully included with care and respect, without any intention to shock or sensationalize.

Abusive relationship (on screen), including emotional abuse, physical abuse, and sexual abuse (non-graphic). Alcohol and alcoholism. Anxiety. Blood. Death, including death of a parent. Drugs. Genocide (mention). Kidnapping. Sexually explicit scenes. Violence. War.

If you have any specific questions or concerns about the content, please feel free to contact Eri directly.

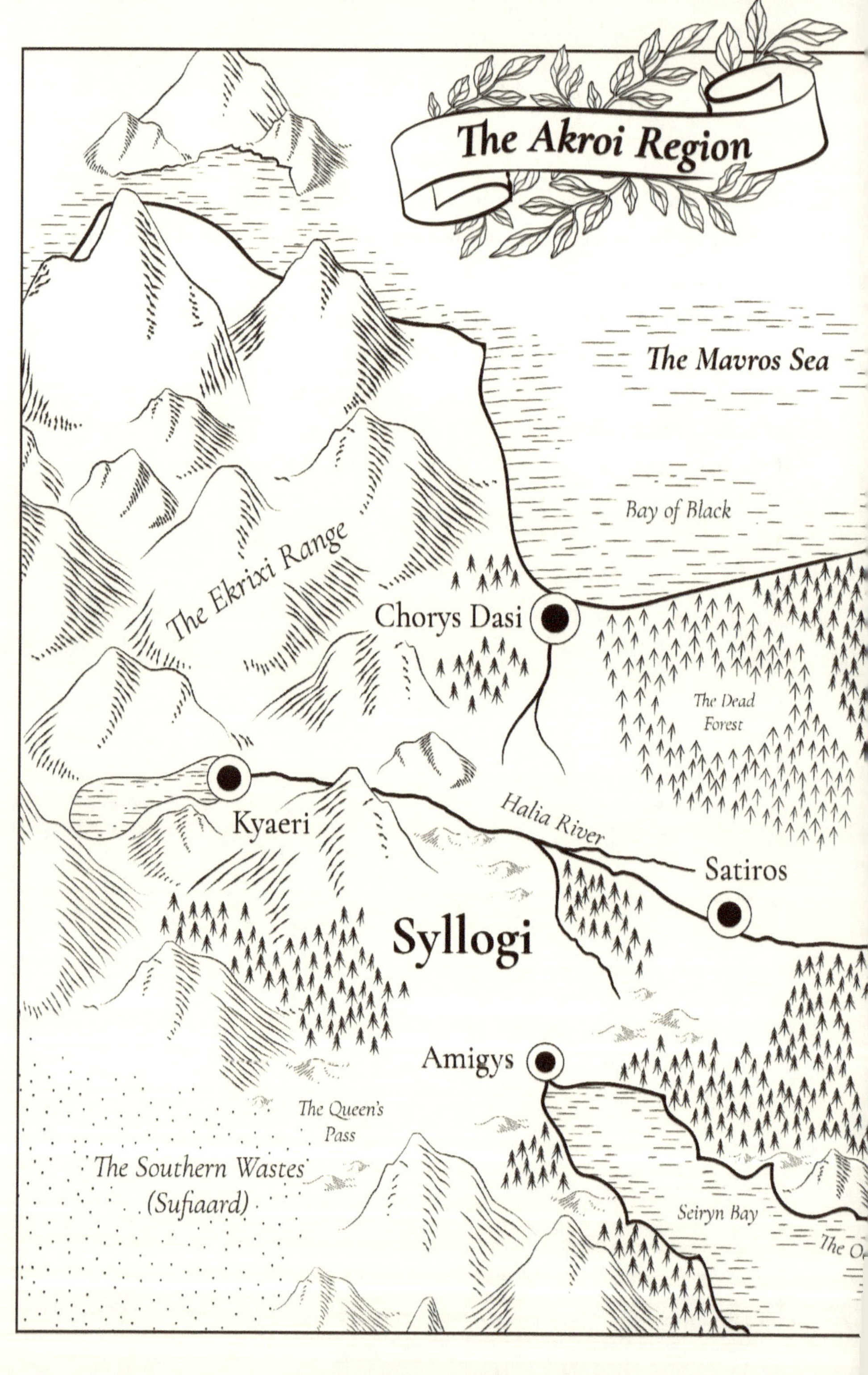

The Akroi Region
The Mavros Sea
Bay of Black
The Ekrixi Range
Chorys Dasi
The Dead Forest
Kyaeri
Halia River
Satiros
Syllogi
Amigys
The Queen's Pass
The Southern Wastes (Sufiaard)
Seiryn Bay
The O

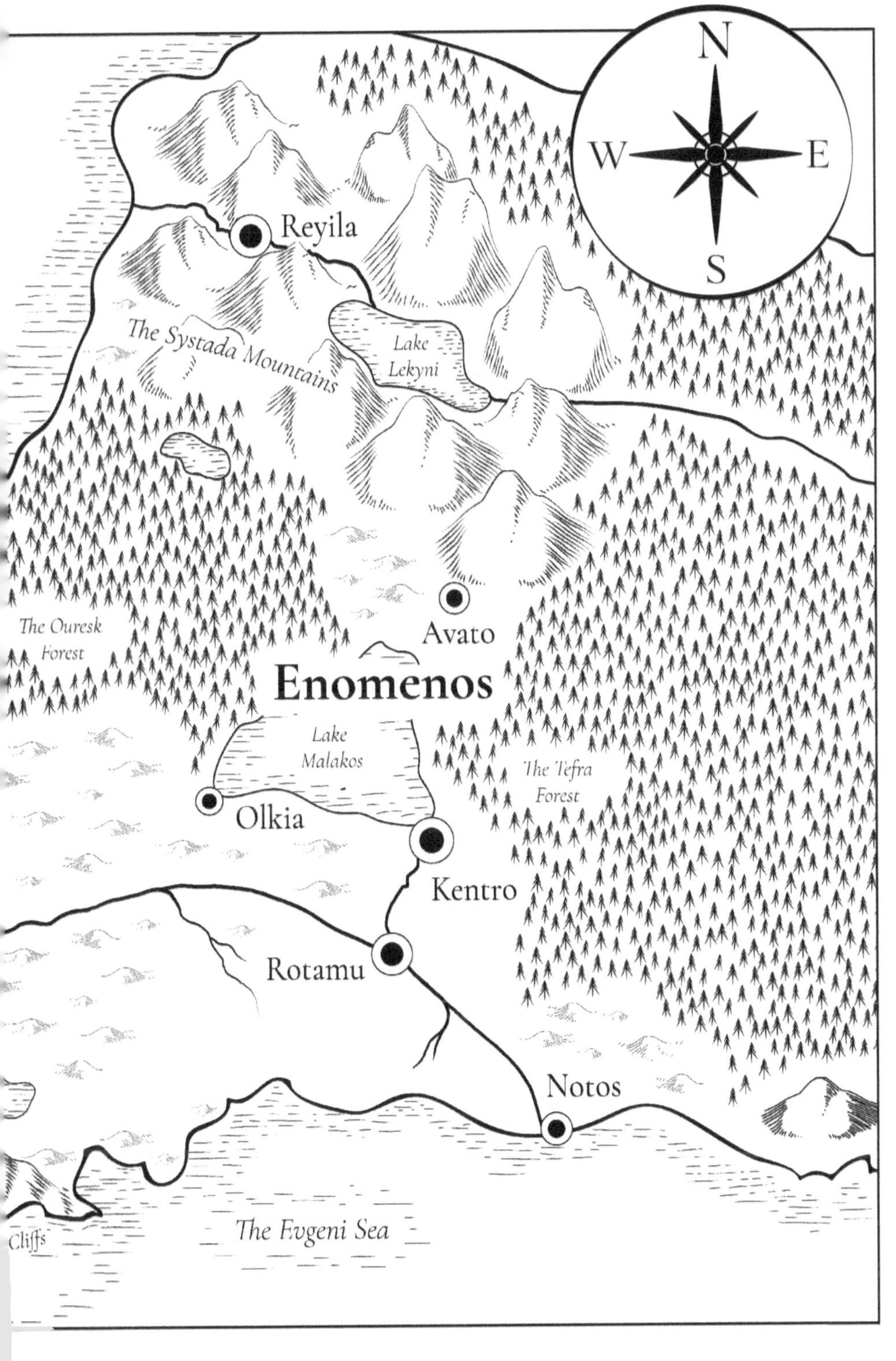

N
W
E
S
Reyila
The Systada Mountains
Lake Lekyni
The Ouresk Forest
Avato
Enomenos
Lake Malakos
The Tefra Forest
Olkia
Kentro
Rotamu
Notos
Cliffs
The Evgeni Sea

Satiros
ELVEN CITY-STATE
N
W
E
S
Upper Fronds
Petal Row
Blooming Borough
Palace of Satiros
Greening Juncture
Acorn Hill
Blossom Center
Wisteria Heights
Wooded Ward
Bud Town
Rambler Grove
The Weeds
Key
1. Temple Row
2. Amryth's Apartment
3. Honeysuckle Tavern
4. Ladybird Inn
5. The Silts
6. River's Bottom
7. Oakwood Academy
8. Amryth's Parents' House
9. Randylph Theater
10. Acorn Hill Park
11. The Ash Gardens

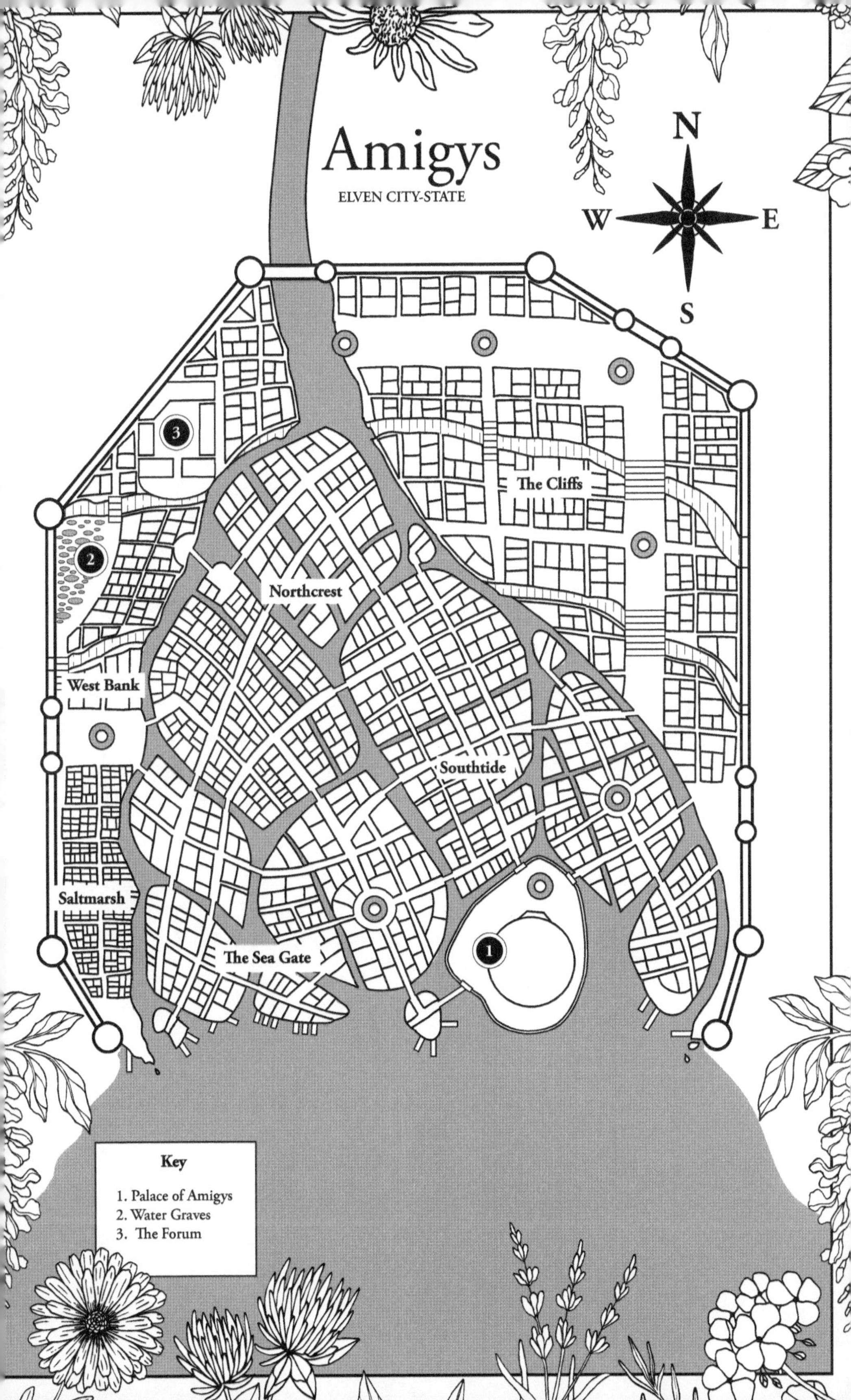

Amigys
ELVEN CITY-STATE
N
W
E
S
The Cliffs
Northcrest
West Bank
Southtide
Saltmarsh
The Sea Gate
1
2
3
Key
1. Palace of Amigys
2. Water Graves
3. The Forum

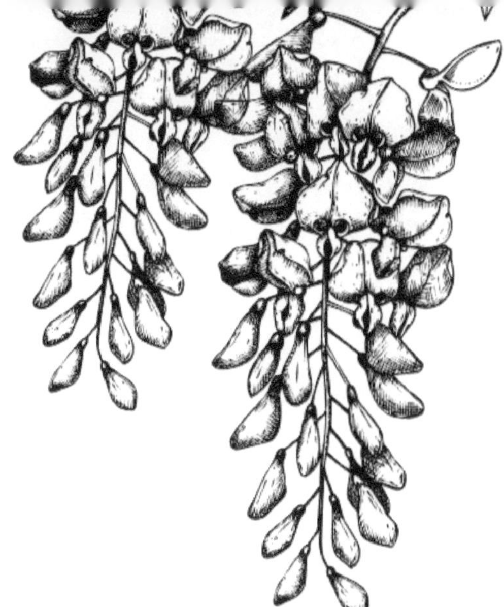

Part One

"Tending to your emotions is like tending to a
garden. No matter how meticulously you care for it,
weeds will still grow."
-

Lyken's Fourth Principle

Chapter One

MARIETTA

As restless voices echoed from the throne room, Marietta couldn't help but contemplate how a crown would be, undoubtedly, a heavier burden than bread. Mere months ago, she was more likely to be covered in flour than gemstones; kneading dough, not alliances. But life once again proved surprising. She was never just a baker.

Her palms grew clammy, her head dizzy. The sound reminded her of the riots—when Keyain had dragged her through the streets while his guards slaughtered innocents.

"Breathe," Wyltam said, his hand finding her lower back.

Marietta inhaled through her nose and held as long as she could before slowly releasing it. She directed her gaze toward the throne room's antechamber, adorned in the greens and golds of Satiros—her colors now, too. Her throat tightened. "I've never struggled with crowds, people, or speaking."

Wyltam shushed her and pulled her close. "The guard has checked and approved all attendees."

"Is that supposed to calm me while Keyain remains their leader?"

"Would you rather oust the leader of our army as two city-states intend to march on our borders?" Wyltam shook his head. "Unfortunately, he's the most qualified to lead."

"I don't agree with that decision."

"It's the decision, regardless if you agree or not."

"Apologies," she said, her voice tightening. "I forget the part I'm supposed to play in all of this. Was it the quiet symbol of unity, or were the ministers hoping for a more 'rags-to-riches' angle?" She focused on her dress, its deep lavender satin pulling tight across her ribs with each strained breath. "It could let pilinos know they, too, can come into wealth and strut around in fanciful frocks. Inspiring hope, or whatever it is you all are planning me to be."

Wyltam remained quiet, causing her to glance at him. A mourning sash made of navy brocade and edged in silver adorned his usual black ensemble. The fabric had come from Valeriya's wedding dress and served as a constant reminder of her sacrifice. Marietta's fingers twitched as the memory of Valeriya's death replayed in her mind, as it often did. Most nights, her dreams twisted into nightmares of rioting crowds and the late queen falling with a crossbow bolt through her chest, bleeding out to save Marietta.

"Having you by my side is a joy," Wyltam said, "but this isn't how I intended to unite Satiros with Enomenos. I never wished this for you. A crown is a burden. A shackle. A magnifying glass. You can no longer be just you."

"A queen can be whoever she wishes," Marietta said dryly. "Isn't that the power of the position?"

"Look where it got Valeriya."

The mention of her name made her recoil.

"Not her death," he added quickly, "but her favor was lost among court. She had no allies who would've supported her in usurping me. How you speak, how you dress—even how you eat—will come into question. Especially because you are a pilinos in an elven-dominated society."

"Not for long."

"No, not for long." Wyltam brought her hand to his lips and pressed a kiss into the back of it. "The price of change is losing a piece of who you are."

Marietta's grip tightened on his hands before she pulled away. "A cost I'm willing to pay, but I need you to promise me something."

"Which is?"

"The ministers of Satiros won't silence me. I want to have a voice and be involved in every aspect—the treaty, the laws. All of it."

Wyltam tilted his head. "You're a consort to the crown. While I have confidence in your ability to make choices for the city-state, it's unusual for someone not from the Grytsier line to assume that responsibility."

"Make it happen," she said. "Because I don't trust the Council of Ministers to have the best interest of pilinos on their mind."

"Already making demands?"

Marietta lifted her chin. "Is that a problem?"

"Yes, but I'll see what I can do." Wyltam's mouth twitched into a smile.

A short man appeared in the doorway, his brown skin slightly flushed. Minister Rymos, the head of all court affairs, said, "We are ready for you, Your Graces."

With Wyltam's steadying hand at her back, Marietta approached the entrance and caught sight of the crowd. Rymos called the throne room to order, a hush falling over the attendees.

"Introducing King Wyltam Grytsier, First of His Name, Sovereign of Satiros, and his bride, Lady Marietta Fulbryk."

The surname caused her to stumble, her father's hidden lineage still unfamiliar and unsettling. As if being the leader of the Exisotis—the militia he had founded to aid the pilinos in Syllogi—wasn't enough, she had also learned during her trial he had once been a Satiroan lord named Anthys Fulbryk.

As they crossed the threshold, a sea of eyes stared back at them. Marietta's steps slowed, the suffocating silence triggering a rare moment of self doubt. Then, all at once, came the eruption of cheers. It echoed off the marble walls and the stained glass window behind the thrones. Loud. Deafening. Marietta caught the gaze of a young pilinos boy screaming as he clapped his hands. Seeing him there, in that throne room with elven nobility, reminded her of her purpose.

Slowly, Marietta and Wyltam walked to the dais and stood with the thrones at their backs. Guards lined the walls, their presence a stark reminder of the danger. Stretched before them were a sea of elves and half-elves and humans, all coexisting, all within the palace. Whatever apprehension had weaseled into her heart was forcefully removed by the sight.

Wyltam stood tall, but with a hint of tension in his posture. One hand remained in a fist behind his back, the knuckles white. The other brushed against Marietta's, as if she were grounding him.

"People of Satiros," Wyltam called out, his voice steady but distant. The room fell silent, anticipation hanging thick. "We gather today in a time of great change. Today, I introduce to you Lady Marietta. She is to be my queen."

A ripple of murmurs passed through the crowd. The weight of their stares bore down on Marietta, a mix of curiosity, doubt, and expectation. She lifted her chin and met their gazes, observing the tight expressions of the elven nobility and their stark contrast to the eager eyes of the pilinos.

"I know the loss of Queen Valeriya is still fresh," Wyltam said, his voice softening. "Her memory will forever guide us. Yet, we must focus on what lies ahead.

Marietta stepped forward, her heart pounding. "I stand before you as a bridge between our peoples," she called out. "Not just between Enomenos and Satiros, but pilinos and elven. I am committed to fostering unity and understanding among us all. We will face challenges head-on, united with strength and compassion. Together, we'll create a future where every voice is heard, and every life is valued."

Applause started as a tentative murmur before swelling into a resounding cheer, gradually filling the throne room with a cautious optimism. Her minister-approved speech had worked its magic, the tension melting away with each clapping hand.

She glanced at Wyltam, whose eyes softened as they met hers.

"My queen," he murmured, his voice meant only for her.

His words left a flutter in her chest that lingered as the citizens drew near, each eager for their own blessing from her and Wyltam. A basket was placed at Marietta's side.

"For you," she said, handing a loaf to the young half-elven woman that came forward. Therypon's symbol of twined snakes hung at her throat. "A recipe of my own, made by my hands."

She glanced at it briefly before accepting. "May the goddess Therypon ever shine upon you."

As the next individuals approached, whispers broke out over the crowd and grew louder as they surged forward. Many called her name, a few mentioned 'bread.' Guards appeared at once, stopping the citizens. Tension heightened across the sea of people, Rymos's men guiding them onward with stern expressions.

Some citizens brought gifts—a handful of flowers, trinkets, small tokens from their lives. Following her and Wyltam's request, they prioritized inviting the less wealthy. Although nobles and influential families were there, the majority donned simple, yet well-made clothing.

Many pilinos gazed at her with reverence as they approached, requesting to kiss her hands or their children. Though physical contact wasn't allowed, Marietta couldn't resist smiling. Others, however, came with cautious expressions—mostly elves who made her uneasy. She tried to brush off their disapproval until a mother with a baby in her arms stepped forward.

The elven woman trembled as she lowered her gaze. "Your Graces. An honor to have your time."

"The honor is ours." Marietta tilted her head toward the infant. "And who do we have here?"

"My—my son. Daryus, named for his father who—" Tears welled in the woman's eyes. "Who recently passed away."

Marietta placed her hand on her chest, knowing the grief.

"We apologize for your loss," Wyltam said.

Marietta took a step toward the mother, the guards jolting forward. Even Wyltam's fingers reached for her own. She held up a hand to them. "Don't raise swords against a grieving wife left to raise a child all alone. "

"Th-thank you," the woman managed, fumbling with her son as Marietta leaned over to see his face.

The bundle fell, and Marietta instinctively reached out for the baby, realizing her mistake too late. The glint of a silvered blade caught her eye, flashing in her peripheral vision. Marietta moved to grab the assailant's wrist while summoning Therypon's ever-present energy from within. Her fingers closed around the woman, but not before the knife sliced across Marietta's upper arm. As pain surged through her, the black crackling energy of the goddess erupted from her fingertips.

Screams cried out. Wyltam had an arm around her waist as the guards surrounded the woman.

"Take her away!" a guard commanded, as they surrounded her and Wyltam and hauled them from the room.

Above the cacophony, Marietta noticed a pattern to the crowd's voices. They were calling upon the goddess, chanting Marietta's name with a similar veneration. She hissed as she tried to get one last glimpse at the crowd, imprinting the eyes of the holy staring at her in reverence.

In the antechamber, Wyltam began barking orders and calling for a healer. The wound, while not deep, burned. A scream tore at her throat.

"It's all right. You're going to be all right." Wyltam lowered her to the floor, brushing back her strands of hair. He glanced over his shoulder. "I said find her now!"

Marietta's vision edged in black as seconds stretched into minutes. Finally, the palace healer arrived, accompanied by a familiar face. At their arrival, the guards raised their swords.

"I'm the head of the Temple of Therypon," Nosokyma said. "I can heal her."

The palace healer rushed to Marietta's side and hissed. "Your Grace, I'll need a second set of hands. Nosokyma has assisted us before and I trust her."

Wyltam answered with a single nod. The guards allowed the temple acolyte to approach, her face weathered by many years, the tattoos on her skin showing signs of age alongside them.

Pain shot up Marietta's arm and into her chest, making her bite her lips to stifle a cry.

Nosokyma turned to the healer. "We need to treat the poison before I heal the wound."

The healer pulled out a kit with vials, wetting a cloth before holding it to Nosokyma.

"This will sting," she warned.

Marietta gripped Wyltam's hand, her nails digging into his skin as fresh waves of agony coursed through her arm. She panted through gritted teeth, silently cursing herself for not reacting faster, for falling for the trap in the first place.

"It's all right," Wyltam continued to murmur, his hand clutching hers back.

After a minute, the burning sensation eased. Sweat clung to her skin as she leaned against Wyltam for support. Nosokyma placed her hand over Marietta's arm, emitting a soft white glow.

"It won't even scar," she said as she rose, wincing slightly. "The poison has been removed, but keep a healer nearby in case of complications. You're lucky, Lady Marietta." She bowed her head. "It could've been much worse if any organs were damaged."

As Nosokyma and the healer continued their quiet discussions, the reality of surviving not one, but two assassination attempts, made her grow quiet. She focused on steadying her feet as she stood and keeping her head held up high.

Guards escorted Marietta and Wyltam back to the Royal Suite—her new residence since the trial a few weeks prior. She found herself alone in Valeriya's room, now designated as her own. Her breath came in sharp gasps, and she leaned against the bed frame of the deceased queen. Her trembling hand traced the spot on her arm where the blade had cut, then moved to her chest, where Valeriya had been struck. It would continue to happen. Therypon had told her that death would be a known friend, but it wasn't a friend at all— more a relentless nightmare she couldn't outrun.

Marietta imagined her assailant. Her trembling hands. Her baby that had been nothing more than cloth. She expected Marietta to look at the child and used it against her.

Marietta's hands clenched into fists. How dare she? How dare she try to strip this city-state of the fragile unity she and Wyltam were striving to build?

After all, it was her marriage to Wyltam that united her homeland of Enomenos to Satiros. It was her marriage that promised aid from her father's militia group. Only with their help could they hope to beat Reyila and Chorys Dasi. Marietta knew they would meet opposition from elves, but she hadn't expected them to choose their tradition of oppressing pilinos over surviving a war.

A knock sounded from the door. Marietta flinched, her body tense, ready to fight or flee. Wyltam appeared in the doorway, his face pale and expression strained. "I brought something to help you sleep. Do you mind if I come in?"

Marietta nodded and sat on the edge of the bed, pressing her palms together to steady her hands. "I understood the crown is a burden, but I didn't think—" Her voice caught with emotion.

Wyltam placed a vial on the nightstand with a decisive clink, then knelt before Marietta, his hands enveloping hers with a firm grasp. "You endanger their power, their old ways. They are desperate to preserve their control."

"I know," she whispered. "I'm a threat because I embody a future outside their authority." She tightened her grip on Wyltam's hands. "Twice, they've tried to kill me. Twice they've failed, though I hadn't expected them to strike so soon. I'm trembling with fear, but I understand the risk. I'm willing to take it."

"There will be no more attempts—"

"You can't promise that."

"No, but—"

"I'm prepared to sacrifice everything if it means bettering Satiros."

Wyltam's silence was thick as he tightened his hold on her hands. "Together then," he said with a quiet fierceness. "We will face this together."

Their eyes locked, and a surge of determination tempered Marietta's fear. The cost didn't make a difference; what mattered was that they would fight, that they would carve out the future they'd dared to dream of, regardless of the challenges ahead.

Chapter Two

AMRYTH

"**I** had forgotten how strikingly feminine you appear without the armor."

Amryth quickened her steps through the echoing palace halls, tugging at her shirt sleeves with a grimace. "Not today, for the love of peace."

Ryder matched her pace, his smirk unwavering as he glanced at her. "What? I can't remark on an acquaintance's new look?"

"Are you saying I'm not your friend?"

"Friends don't turn their backs on each other, and they sure as hell don't hide truths, like the fact that our friend's wife wasn't actually pregnant."

Amryth swallowed her frustration. The thought of Keyain still holding his position despite his deceit only fueled her resolve. She patted the pocket where Deyra's journal rested—her sole tangible link to her late wife. The truth about Keyain was the final blow she needed to leave.

"It might be best if I accompany her," Adalyn's voice cut through, a welcome relief as she appeared beside Amryth.

"The king commanded me," Ryder snapped.

"He asked for someone to escort Amryth, with no particular preference," Adalyn countered, stepping between them. "But if you value your limbs, you'll let me handle it."

Ryder muttered something incoherent and stalked off. Amryth had only been gone a week, yet it felt like a lifetime, seeing their usual disgruntled dynamic.

"Thanks, Addie," Amryth said as they turned down a new hall, far from his sight.

"Ryder ought to be thanking me."

Amryth chuckled, the sound mingling with Adalyn's. There was a bittersweet quality to it, one that spoke of shared memories and lingering loss.

"But honestly, I did it for myself," she continued, her tone softening. "I missed you. It's not the same without you and Deyra. The three of us …" Her voice faltered, the weight of unspoken grief hanging between them.

"I know," Amryth said, hoping to steer them away from the raw wound.

"I told Keyain," Adalyn confessed, her gaze steady.

Amryth eyebrows lifted in surprise.

"I told him it was all his fault. I tore into him for sending us to die for a cause we barely understood. We trusted him, and we expected him to honor that trust." Adalyn glanced toward the two guards as they passed, then resumed in a low voice, "He said things will change."

Amryth's throat closed, making it difficult for her to say, "I can't come back—"

"I understand." Adalyn nodded. "But don't disappear on me again, all right?"

Amryth nodded, absorbing the image of her friend—one she might not see again for a while. Then she turned and headed toward King Wyltam's public office.

The afternoon light spilled through the windows, casting long beams of light across the room, and illuminated the king's solitary figure behind the desk. "Illustris Amryth," he greeted as she entered, "thank you for coming."

The former title stung—years of hard-won respect now reduced to a name she no longer held. Amryth bit back the urge to correct him, settling instead for a measured, "Your Grace."

"Please, sit."

As she crossed the room, Amryth's gaze fell on Wynn, slouched casually against the wall. His lazy smile didn't quite mask the sharp edge of vigilance in his eyes. Her practiced scrutiny took in the gleaming armor—rich green accented with a gold royal sigil—an upgrade from the worn leather he used to don. It signaled the king's favor, a reward for the days he'd spent safeguarding Marietta and Elyse.

As Amryth sank into the chair, she observed the unchanging presence of King Wyltam. Despite the recent assassination attempt on Marietta, his appearance remained as unyielding as ever, his inscrutable calm as familiar as his dark hair and pale complexion. The weight of yet another failed assassination must be pressing heavily on him, even if he wore his impassivity like armor.

"I find your resignation from the guard troubling," the king said. "You've served the crown for decades, quickly rising through the ranks because of your skill as a guard and your aptitude for leadership." He flipped through a stack of papers as he read. "You've had the highest-performing and best-trained units for multiple years. Nothing but praise from fellow soldiers." He glanced at her. "Though you are at the height of your career, you resign."

Amryth stared right back at the king. "There is no future for me in the Satiroan Guard."

The king's eyes narrowed slightly. "I disagree," he countered before she was able to speak. "We're forming a Queen's Guard, and I want you to lead it. Marietta's safety is crucial to the future of Satiros, especially after another assassination attempt. Right now, you are the person I trust most with her protection. Given Keyain's history with Marietta, the Queen's Guard will report directly to me."

Amryth leaned back, her breath escaping in a slow, measured sigh. The offer provided a rare honor, an opportunity to protect Marietta with the limited allies she could rely on. The king's trust should have made the choice straightforward.

But the palace revived the pain of Deyra's death, her ghost lingering in every hall, whispering from every corner. Their relationship had been tied to this place, and walking away had been like stepping into open air after suffocating for months. But now, as she sat here, the past loomed large and her words faltered, trapped in her throat by the gravity of what she left behind.

"I will take the position if Your Grace forced it upon me," she said, pausing. "But if I have the freedom to choose, then I decline the offer. My life calls to elsewhere."

What little expression the king held iced over as he tapped his fingers slowly and shifted in his seat. "I do not force anyone to do my bidding." He looked past her, his eyes darting back and forth. "However, I do not trust anyone else with Marietta's life."

Amryth let out a long breath. "For the late Queen Valeriya, I would have a handful of suggestions. But because of Keyain, Marietta is unfavorable among the guards."

Her circle of people all swung from his coattails. The right fit would be someone who had no affiliation with Keyain whatsoever. Amryth hesitated as a ridiculous idea came to her. "Coryn Niershade might not be a guard, but his training at the Temple of Therypon is no less rigorous. He's never served under Keyain, is a pilinos, and his concern for her well-being is already driven by her new role as an iros."

King Wyltam sat back with his brows raised. "An interesting choice. You would choose a citizen over the guards you've worked alongside for decades?"

"I would choose someone outside of Keyain's influence." Amryth moved to the edge of her seat. "I can name a dozen people who'd be a good fit for the Queen's Guard, even if they could not be its captain."

The king handed her a quill, and she jotted down a list, remembering the years and accolades of each person. She slid the paper back across the desk. "While I'm in no position to tell you what to do, may I suggest a change to the guard, Your Grace?"

King Wyltam studied the list in his hand. "You may speak freely."

"Integrate pilinos into the guard. There's no reason for them not to be, especially with a war on the horizon."

"We're steps ahead of you in that regard. Keyain and Leyland are negotiating the details." He set the list down. "Adalyn? You'd recommend one of Keyain's Elite Guards?"

"Yes, Your Grace. Adalyn is …" Amryth closed her eyes and sought the right words. "Complicated, but dedicated. Less blind in her loyalties. She would also help to bridge the Queen's Guard with the army, showing a united front."

The king shook his head as he sighed. "And there's no amount of gold I could use to persuade you?"

"Perhaps a guilt trip from Marietta?" Wynn offered in the corner.

A smile tugged at the king's lips. "She can be quite persuasive."

Amryth gnawed on her lip, her hand absently going to the journal in her pocket. "If you would, Your Grace, please let Marietta know I'm sorry. I wish I could be there for her, but I can't—I can't stay here anymore."

The king eyed Amryth, his stare searing. "If you're still inclined to help her, there's something I could use your help to investigate."

Amryth spotted Deania in the temple gardens, bent over a cluster of calendula, her shears poised in a practiced grip. "Oh, you're a pretty one. A shame I'll have to snip you."

"Talking to the plants again?"

Deania cut the bloom and placed it in her basket. She turned to Amryth, her face lighting up with a smile that revealed a set of dimples, her eyes sparkling. The summer sun dulled in comparison. "Only the plants I like."

Amryth chuckled, settling on the edge of the retaining wall. The temple attendants moved with purpose, some gathering herbs, others finding respite beneath the trees. A gentle breeze stirred the air, cutting through the day's heat and bringing a quiet calm. This was the pull of the temple—its peace, its rhythm, a balm for the restless. It was why Amryth returned, again and again.

"I met with the king."

Deania raised a brow and turned back to the plants. "After he demanded your presence," she replied under her breath.

"I couldn't refuse him." Amryth plucked a flower from the basket and spun it between her fingers. "He offered me the position of captain of the

Queen's Guard. No oversight from Keyain."

Deania whipped her head toward Amryth. "That's … good. I'm happy for you." She turned away, though her hands didn't move. "I'm happy that you'll—"

"I didn't take it."

Deania sighed. She moved to the next stem and snipped. "Why would you pass on such an opportunity?"

She had worked tirelessly for decades to attain exactly this kind of position. And yet … "It didn't feel right, not with Keyain still in power and … everything else."

"If King Wyltam were wise, he'd strip him of his rank. You're not the only one who's left the guard. Maybe if enough of you walk away, he'll have no choice but to oust Keyain."

"I wished for the same before I left, but now my hope has shifted."

Deania shot her an incredulous look.

"War is coming," Amryth explained. "Keyain is a symbol of victory and strength. Removing him would mean displacing the hopes of many, and I don't wish for that. The king had another offer for me, though."

"Hopefully better than serving."

Amryth swatted at her. "He asked me to dig into the pilinos murders."

Deania dropped her shears and turned to Amryth. "This is about Jory."

"How did you know?" The king had been clear the information wasn't out to the public.

"It's not exactly subtle when the guard storms into someone's home and drags them away, only for them to disappear for an entire week." Deania trembled all over as she took a seat next to Amryth. "Do they truly believe a pilinos was behind it?"

"I think King Wyltam shares your skepticism. Why else have me look into them?" Amryth smoothed the fabric of her pants. "He's paying me. Gave me a list of places and leads to follow up on. I even have notes from the guard."

Deania's hand slipped into Amryth's. "You have to save him."

"I will—"

"They're going to make an example out of him—a public execution,

Amryth." Deania's round eyes turned glossy. "There's already been too much death. We can't …" Her voice faltered, choked by emotion.

Amryth pulled her into a hug, reveling in the scent of her hair. "I'll clear Jory's name. We'll find out who did this. I promise you, D."

As Deania clung to her, Amryth felt purpose surge through her. Investigating these murders and exonerating Jory wasn't just about justice; it was a chance to unravel a piece of the very system she had upheld for too long.

Chapter Three

KEYAIN

Seated among his peers and the king, Keyain's fingers tightened around the edge of the table, knuckles whitening. "You want to wait how long?"

"Indefinitely. Until either Reyila or Chorys Dasi make a move." Wyltam reclined in his chair, his dark eyes hardening with his stare.

Keyain's grip intensified, and his jaw set like iron. "It would be best if we strike quick before their troops could rally. If we hesitate, they'll have a chance to gather their forces. We should strike now, before the snows or spring thaw. Time only serves our enemies."

"Would it not serve us as well?" Wyltam's posture shifted slightly as murmurs arose from Walyn, the commander of the Guard, and Hastyrn, the Army's general. "If we wait, the forces from Enomenos will have time to join us. Minc and Marietta's marriage will secure their aid, and it's not slated to happen until the winter solstice."

Keyain's blood surged with a fiery rage, his vision blurring, and his hearing dulled by the thunderous pounding of his heart. The marriage. The fucking marriage.

Marietta had been his. For weeks, he believed she carried his child. He had endured the headaches and public humiliation, willing to overlook it all for a chance at the one thing he had ever truly wanted with her: a family. But when he discovered her betrayal, Dyeiter, the minister of law, had swayed him to vote for her execution. The decision had left a hollow ache in his chest. Voting for her death had saved his position; however, Keyain no longer wanted it. But war loomed ever closer, and he would be damned to let anyone else control the Satiroan army.

Keyain took a steadying breath, focusing his gaze on the map of Akroi spread across the table. "Last I recall, I'm the only one here who has ever fought in an actual war." Keyain's voice became clipped. "I hold the minister of protection title because of it. Because I know the cost." Keyain looked at his king. "We should strike sooner than later."

"Do you truly know the cost?" Wyltam leaned forward, his expression impenetrable. "Because you're rushing into this foolhardily. If you march on Reyila, who defends us from Chorys Dasi?"

"We have the guard stationed within Satiros."

"Yes, only half of our forces. Please tell me when the full brunt of Chorys Dasi is on us and our strength is divided, how will we win? You seem to know something I don't. Do you have Chorys Dasi's military numbers?"

"If we give them time—"

"Minister Keyain, answer my question."

The title was an insult, a barrier. But Wyltam understood Keyain completely. Acting as if nothing had transpired between them was the most effective way to twist the knife.

"We don't have their numbers," Keyain ground out. "But Reyila called for this war."

"And we banished the Chorys Dasian prince from the palace. How well do you think they took that?"

"None of us knew." Keyain leaned forward on the table and hung his head, remembering the prick who had gone by Brynden. "He still deserved his banishment."

"It doesn't matter what he deserved. Doesn't matter that we didn't know his identity. What matters is that they have a reason to march on us beside their alliance with Reyila."

Keyain cracked his neck and looked at Wyltam. "If we wait, their forces will only gain strength."

"So will we," Wyltam said. "Enomenos supported by the Exisotis."

"Bodies are one thing," Keyain countered. "But our enemies have mages. If they consolidate their power, we'll stay outmatched."

Wyltam's stare was a blade, cutting through any pretense. Keyain's jaw tightened, and he turned to his subordinates, dismissing them with curt efficiency. "We'll reconvene this evening."

As the room emptied, Keyain's gaze shifted back to Wyltam, the distance between them like a chasm. The urge to upend the table and seize Wyltam by the collar thrummed beneath his skin, but he stifled it. He couldn't bring himself to hurt the male he once loved, and he knew better than to test Wyltam's formidable mage abilities.

"How many mages?" Keyain demanded once the door sung shut behind the last person.

"The Circle of Mages declined my request for aid, but a few answered my call. Some will arrive by week's end. The rest are heading to Chorys Dasi to find our ambassadors and tamper with their court."

Keyain's eyes closed, his jaw clenched as he recalled the two teams he'd sent to Chorys Dasi, who had vanished without a trace. "They know about the others?"

"They do," he said. "Being Chorys Dasian, they'll navigate their own city-state more effectively."

Keyain's fingers drummed on the table. "And the ones coming here? They could help train our service mages if we're delaying the attack."

Wyltam pinned him with a stare. "No. Even if they would train them, carriage drivers and light globe enchanters need years of training before they could stand their own in a battle."

Keyain's fists clenched at the condescension. "Then what's their purpose? A few will do nothing against their armies."

"Marietta's Queen's Guard."

Keyain's his body went rigid. "Her what?"

"Queen's Guard. I've been working on selecting the right guards to protect her."

Keyain smacked the tabletop and swiped the papers from the surface. He took a seat and tried to control his breath. "Why? That's—I'm—my guards?"

"A group of Satiroan guards, yes." Wyltam's voice remained even, as if he wasn't ripping out one of Keyain's duties from underneath him. "Amryth was more than happy to supply a list after she declined my offer to be its captain. How you lost such a dedicated soldier speaks volumes about your ability to push people away."

The rage in Keyain extinguished, his limbs and head heavy. Amryth resigned not long after the trial. *Fuck you and fuck the guard.* Her last words, the resounding fury, continued to haunt him.

"Part of her list included a member of your Elite Guard."

Keyain's nails dug deeper into his palms. None of them had mentioned this. "Who?"

"Adalyn. Given her background, I believe she would fit wonderfully. She was notified yesterday, and if she is selected, I think it would show unity between you and the crown." Wyltam raked his gaze over him. "Something you desperately need, especially after arresting a pilinos for the murders."

Keyain locked his muscles before forcing himself to relax. The dismissal of the arrest stung, as did the name he had dropped. But what kindled his rage was the tilt of Wyltam's head and the casual curve of his mouth. Wyltam relished delivering the blow. "Adalyn would leave the Elite Guard?"

"She'd split her time between protecting Marietta and her current duties. You need all the help you can get right now."

Keyain fought to keep his expression neutral as he considered his next words. "I want Ryder included too." The thought of Marietta's disdain for him brought a grim satisfaction, a way to tip the balance in his favor.

Wyltam studied him for a moment. "Can you afford to lose another Elite Guard member, even part-time?"

"It's a matter of unity," he said, quickly adding, "Your Grace."

Wyltam made a note on the paper in front of him. "I'll add Ryder to the list. For the captain of the Queen's Guard, I'm choosing Coryn Niershade from the Temple of Therypon," he continued. "His appointment will be contingent on a physical assessment of his skills, which you will conduct alongside the others."

The pounding of blood deafened his hearing as he asked, "You have the audacity to put the other male she was fucking as her captain?"

"You never bothered delving further into that, did you?" Wyltam raised a brow. "I question your ability to find the actual murderer if you couldn't disprove such a flippant rumor."

Keyain thought of the pilinos male in the dungeons below the palace. The evidence had been clear. "You don't think I found the murderer?"

"I don't believe this is as straightforward as you think. All guards are to halt their investigation and redirect their focus to the war effort."

"You ordered me to continue searching for the murderer."

"I instructed you to uncover the killer, yet you've presented me the bastard son of a minister." Wyltam stood, his gaze becoming shards of ice. "Since you failed at that, I expect you to concentrate on your strengths and secure this victory. And this time, I'd prefer if you avoided slaughtering the innocent."

Keyain closed his eyes at the jab, remembering the truth all too well.

"As for the Queen's Guard, your role is limited to evaluating the candidates. After that, they will report directly to Marietta and me." As Keyain went to speak, Wyltam held up his hand. "Evaluate Coryn. Verify he meets the standards of the rest of the guard."

Keyain stood, his muttered response barely a whisper. "He won't."

"You might be surprised. Go, you're dismissed."

Keyain rolled his eyes as he headed toward the exit.

"Try to get some rest," Wyltam said. "Don't let your guards see how poorly you're coping."

Keyain wrenched the door open, slamming it shut with a force that would have cost anyone else their position. The fact that Wyltam wouldn't enforce such a penalty only fueled his ire further. Pity was the last thing he needed— least of all from him.

Chapter Four

KEYAIN, BEFORE

The sharp tang of copper stung Keyain's nostrils as he yanked his sword free. Blood bubbled and gushed, smothering the green-tinged skin of the fallen orc. He wiped the sweat from his eyes, scanning the battlefield. The only green remaining upright was the Satiroan armor. More had survived today than the last. Yet, the victory felt hollow, tainted by an unsettling question—where were the rest of the orcs?

Keyain spat blood beside the lifeless orc sprawled at his feet—a creature with elongated ears, jutting tusks, and crimson irises. Inhaling deeply, he swung his sword toward the thundering approach of footsteps behind him. Steel rang against stone as Keyain parried the orc's weapon. As the hammer slid past, he dodged nimbly, then slashed at the creature's ankles. An ear-piercing scream tore through the battlefield as the orc crumpled. Without hesitation, Keyain drove his blade into its heart, silencing it.

A thud sounded nearby. Keyain turned to see Peryn dispatch the last orc in their vicinity. The sunlight gleamed on his captain's bald head, a stark reminder of the scorching heat enveloping the day. Their plan had been to strike at dusk when the heat subsided, but these orcs, hardened by their nomadic life in the deserts of The Southern Wastes, seized the chance to ambush them. Keyain cursed inwardly at their vulnerability to such a simple trap.

Surveying the shallow valley, Keyain noted the remaining Satiroan guards, their worn-out expressions exposing the toll of the battle. At their feet were the putrid green of the orcs, armored in boiled leathers and dressed in ragged fabrics. Barbaric and a waste of Satiroan resources. The sooner they rid the creatures from The Queen's Pass, the sooner these messy clashes with the orcs would end.

Keyain nodded at the battlefield. "Make sure none of them makes it out alive."

"Yes, Illustris." Peryn sprang into action, his voice carrying over the heated land and followed by the whoosh of swords plunging into the bodies littering the ground.

Keyain sprinted up the hillside to join the remaining Satiroan forces locked in combat. General Mylax had selected Keyain and his legion for the vanguard, the most perilous military position on the battlefield. Despite the inherent danger, Keyain held his head high as he cast a proud gaze upon the resilient soldiers behind him. This was precisely why General Mylax trusted his legion.

At the summit of the hill, Keyain halted, his eyes locking onto the scene below like a punch to the gut. The Satiroan Army, now a mere fraction of its former self, faced an overwhelming tide—twenty to one odds. In the distance, reinforcements from neighboring city-states trudged forward, their approach seeming little more than a futile gesture against the decimated Satiroan ranks. The earlier ease of their victory took on a bitter clarity; he had been blind to the enemy's trap. With a sharp motion, he retrieved a glass globe from his pocket, pressing it to his lips. "Every able-bodied soldier, rally over the western hill now!"

Without waiting for a reply, Keyain sprinted down the hillside, eyes fixed on a group of orcs surrounding a young soldier.

The first hit landed true, slicing deep into an orc that crumpled to the ground. Keyain spun, unleashing his fury upon the next creature foolish enough to face him. The young soldier smiled through the blood marring his face. "Illustris Keyain, I knew you'd come. I—"

A rock collided with the side of his head with a spray of blood, silencing him forever. Suppressing the bile burning at the back of his throat, Keyain channeled his disgust into a fiery rage as he searched for the source. An orc shot another rock from its sling, the crude projectile sailing toward Keyain. He dodged and lunged at the orc, his sword slicing a brutal line from groin to shoulder. The orc's body fell apart, spilling its dark, pulsing blood onto the ground.

Keyain silenced his thoughts, ignoring the carnage and viscera his sword brought, and advanced toward the heart of the battle where General Mylax stood. He only noted the tension in his shoulders, the razor-sharp blade meeting its next target, and the thud of carcasses trailing in his wake. He dared not glance at the sea of Satiroan green surrounding him, or the lack thereof.

Only upon reaching the central rear did he let his gaze wander beyond his immediate surroundings. The Satiroan Army had disintegrated, soldiers scattering in disarray, their movements lacking any semblance of order or direction. To his left, a cluster of soldiers stood encircled by a larger horde of orcs. Keyain tightened his grip on the hilt, a primal yell escaping his lips as he charged forward. The bodies fell, the green flesh serving as mere obstacles in his path. As he neared the group's center, he glimpsed which soldiers were surrounded.

His heart ceased as General Mylax used both hands on his sword to push back against an orcish hammer. Keyain screamed as he neared, cutting down each creature standing in his way. He had to reach him, had to help. The soldiers' disorganization suddenly made sense. The general's death would disrupt any semblance of order that remained.

Keyain sliced through another orc and turned as General Mylax slipped, losing his footing adjacent to his foe. Before Keyain could blink, the hammer was through his skull. Not even the sight of his superior being bludgeoned to death stopped him from surging forward, relentlessly pursuing the savage creature to exact his vengeance.

The orc dodged Keyain's strike, its hammer crashing into his left bracer. Waves of agony pulsed through his arm, leaving behind a mangled and dented piece of metal. Inhaling through the pain, Keyain harnessed it, using it to sharpen his focus and tighten his grip on his weapon. The orc swung its hammer once more, falling for Keyain's feigned maneuver to the left. Keyain's sword met its heart, and he twisted the blade. The weight of the orc fell onto him. With a scream, he lifted the body and tossed it aside.

He didn't need to check General Mylax's pulse to know if he lived. The hammer had done its damage and had done it well. Bile rose again and that time Keyain let himself purge at the sight. Around him, his soldiers kept fighting, kept pressing on.

Keyain wiped his mouth and scanned the battlefield. From his vantage, he could see the colors of the other city-states nearing, though most of them were blotted out by the growing number of orcs. Even with the mages flaring their magic beyond, it was nothing compared to the sheer number they were up against.

The Satiroan Army needed to regroup and press forth as one if they had any hopes of surviving. His gaze shifted to the lifeless form of General Mylax and the badge adorning his chest. The general was more than a symbol; he embodied invincibility. However, that fateful day shattered the illusion of the infallible, proving even the best soldiers fell.

Keyain cut the badge from General Mylax's chest, carefully securing it in his pocket. His sacrifice would not be in vain; none of their deaths would go without meaning. He pushed aside all emotions, his mind working best when he allowed himself to feel nothing.

Keyain took the general's glass globe and raised it to his mouth. "All soldiers regroup in the valley of the western hill. We're making our final push."

With a sharp command, he rallied his soldiers with a fierce cry. They became his weapons, his body another tool. For his queen and for his city-state, Keyain raised his sword and charged back into the fray.

Chapter Five

ELYSE

Wind tousled the stray strands of Elyse's hair, which had escaped from her neat knot. Her eyes were closed, brows pinched. She shut her mind to the surrounding noise. A bead of sweat dripped down her forehead as she pulled aithyr into her body, letting it release with the same steady flow.

Amid the verdant embrace of the Central Garden, two men lounged in a shaded nook, seeking refuge from the late-morning heat. To an ordinary observer, their conversation would have dissolved into a mere murmur. But Elyse focused her magic to sharpen her hearing. The whispering rustle of leaves, a muffled sniffle from one of the males, the distant cadence of footsteps from passersby. She wove through the ambient noise, focusing intently on their exchange.

"And you're dead."

Elyse jumped at the voice that came from beside her, now much too loud for her sensitive ears. She glared at Wynn. "I was trying to concentrate."

Wynn rocked back on his heels as a bemused smile slid to his lips. "Concentrating is important, but not when it leaves you unaware of your surroundings. Unfortunately, Marietta set a good example of what happens when you don't pay attention."

"Can't I learn how to strengthen my magic before I also have to pay attention?" Frustrated, she rubbed her ears. Elyse wanted to excel past the expectations Wyltam had set for her. She couldn't be *any* mage—she had to live up to her title. She was the King's Administrator: his eyes and ears at court, his mage in secret, and she needed to prove herself deserving of such trust.

Absently, she thumbed the broach pinned to her chest. Though it marked her new status, it also brought her back to the moment she pricked her finger with its needle. Not only had she defied Wyltam's directive to keep Marietta's birth a secret, but they had also unearthed evidence of the fey's existence— evidence that branded her own bloodline as fey.

Allegedly, she kept reminding herself. Until they found more proof of her heritage, Elyse had begged Marietta to tell no one for fear she would lose everything. The incident with her father and losing control of aithyr had nearly cost her just that. Until they had further confirmation, her discovery would remain a secret from Wyltam. How would he react to the revelation that the fey were real? He might judge her as unstable, and she couldn't fault him for that.

Elyse exhaled, sinking her awareness back into the currents of aithyr. Her thoughts stilled as she reached out to the ceaseless flow of energy, grounding herself in its silent, pulsing rhythm.

"Are you still worried about Marietta?" Wynn's voice was gentle but insistent.

Elyse kept her eyes shut, trying to maintain her focus. "I'm concentrating on the lesson."

There was a pause, and then Wynn's question cut through the stillness. "Or is it him you're thinking about?"

"I don't know what you mean," she snapped, the taste of the lie bitter in her mouth.

Wynn hummed with disbelief, a tuneless sound that Elyse tried to shut out. Az had a way of creeping into her mind during the quiet lulls, between lessons or just before sleep claimed her. The dreams were the hardest to shake, leaving her with a hollow ache in her stomach. She missed him, hated him, and loved him all at once. A part of her clung to him, even knowing he was a monster in every possible way.

She often caught herself reaching for the copy of *Lyken's Guide to Chorys Dasi*. She couldn't say if she wanted to see his face again or if she needed to remind herself of his fey form. So far, she had managed to resist the urge to open the book.

"It's understandable if you still think of him," Wynn said, his tone softening. "You didn't know the truth."

Elyse opened her eyes, releasing her hold on aithyr.

"Be kinder to yourself," he added, his hand settling gently on her shoulder.

Elyse drew a shallow breath. Wynn didn't know the extent of the truth she uncovered. Fey existed, and they raised the Chorys Dasian banners for war. Her throat tightened, and she pulled away from Wynn's touch, heading for the path.

Wynn grasped her arm. "I won't mention it again if you'd prefer. Just remember, you deserve so much more. You have centuries ahead and countless people to meet. He may have been your first love, but he won't be the last."

"I don't love him," Elyse said quickly, her voice too sharp.

Wynn's smirk accentuated the twisted scar across his face. Before, such a look from Wynn would have made her nervous. Now, she found it equally endearing and frustrating.

"Love is not aithyr; it does not bend to your control." Wynn stepped past her. "Lie to me if you must, but at least be honest with yourself."

Elyse swallowed, noting the amusement in his eyes and the relaxed set of his shoulders. Wynn trusted her, genuinely wanted to help. Guilt twisted her insides. Maybe she should tell him everything. "It's just—" She faltered.

"Come on." Wynn nodded toward the path. "We should grab something to eat before your meeting."

Elyse paused, trying to steady her racing heart. Was it that obvious she had loved their enemy? He was a murderer, a fraud, a liar. Nothing Az had shared with her could be trusted, yet an inexplicable pull gnawed at her whenever she thought of him. Nightmares of his face and voice haunted her sleep. Sometimes, it was as if she could hear him calling, and she wanted nothing more than to shut him out.

She pressed her hand against the satyr statue beside her, grounding herself in the cool, smooth stone. A fragile sense of peace began to form, and she hoped the path ahead would be clearer without Az's shadow lingering over her thoughts.

After a quick meal and a change into fresh clothes, she stood outside the meeting room, jaw clenched in frustration at not taking more time to prepare. She adjusted her stance, straightened her spine, and steeled herself for the task ahead.

"Remember to breathe," Wyltam's voice came from her side.

Elyse pulled at the cuffs of her sheer sleeves, her stomach churning. Despite dressing in pants and a blouse to stand out from the average court lady, she remained unsettled. At the other entrance, males Elyse had known since her childhood filed into the room.

"You're here to observe how I function in meetings and to learn about the current events of our city-state. You only have to speak if addressed, which would be a few words at most. A scribe will take notes for you. Remember to collect them before you leave."

She swallowed hard and nodded. Easy enough, she could do this. Unless they questioned her attendance, or why Wyltam had named her his administrator. She grabbed the broach pinned to her chest, absently rubbing the metal.

"And try not to fidget." He glanced at her hand. "Don't let them know you're nervous."

"I'm all right," she said, offering a tight smile as she dropped her hands.

Wyltam huffed a small laugh. "You are more all right than you realize. This populace meeting will be an easy introduction."

"Why?"

"Minister Leyland has been advocating for the recent changes in our city." Wyltam straightened the navy mourning sash draped over his chest. "He sees you as part of that change, given your connection to Marietta."

There were rumors that Minister Leyland Fedyr had an affair with a pilinos and even had a bastard child. At least, it's what she overheard from other courtiers when they questioned why his wife stayed in the countryside.

The murmuring behind the entrance ceased abruptly, replaced by a muffled voice before the door swung open. Elyse followed Wyltam, her movements deliberate and calm.

The room swirled as she focused on her chair, avoiding the faces of the males around the table until she reached her spot. Standing next to her seat, she clasped her hands tightly, quelling their tremors. Wyltam waited beside her, surveying the table. After a pause, he signaled for everyone to take their seats.

As she sat, she noticed the male sitting on her right. He was the father of the relentless flirt who had been a constant nuisance at gatherings. Elyse quickly turned her attention across the way and locked eyes with a male she had known in her younger years. Once troubled by a severe drinking problem, he now appeared to have moved past it. She shifted her focus to her lap, deliberately avoiding further eye contact. Digging her nails into her palm, she reminded herself that she had every right to be here. Wyltam believed in her.

Minister Leyland brought the room's attention to him with a sharp clap of his hands. In the light, the shadows under his eyes deepened, and his warm brown skin appeared paler.

"My King, thank you for attending today's update. Given the recent developments, we have much to cover. Before we proceed, I'd like to introduce Lady Elyse Norymial, the King's Administrator." He paused, gesturing toward her.

Elyse tightened her hands into fists and cursed her heart for its fretful pounding. She parted her lips to offer a thanks, but the words stilled, trapped within the hollow of her throat.

"For your awareness," Wyltam said, breaking the deafening silence, "Lady Elyse is an extension of my crown. Any information held in meetings I'm unable to attend will be delivered to me through her."

Elyse squared her shoulders and drew in a calming inhale, her gaze sweeping across the table. Confusion flickered in the eyes of several males, their glances shifting uneasily among one another.

"Then we will treat her with the respect we give you, Your Grace," Leyland said before diving into his report.

Elyse wrestled with her racing thoughts, anchoring herself in his words. She learned that a significant number of elven citizens were abandoning the city-state to settle in the countryside after announcing their new queen. He went on to mention their opposition to granting pilinos full citizenship or aligning with Enomenos. The representative from the Wooded Ward revealed a document from his district, expressing fears that integrating Satiros might sever their elven heritage ties to Syllogi.

Courtiers only ventured as far as Greening Juncture in the city, never south of Oak Boulevard into the Wooded Ward, deeming it unsafe. It was a statement she had grown up hearing and had never questioned until recently. Her throat tightened at how she had remained quiet when she hadn't shared those beliefs. She had done so when Az had slipped the same sentiment into their conversations, and not once did she question it. How did she not see he was no better than them? Why didn't she ever push back?

As her mind reeled, she struggled to concentrate on Leyland's monotonous drone.

"Following the failed assassination attempt on Lady Marietta, we've seen another surge in the pilinos population. Many have claimed asylum with the Temple of Therypon."

Elyse studied Wyltam's response—or rather, his lack of one. Despite the unfolding revelations, his face remained an inscrutable mask, responding only with a nod or a brief query. She suppressed any emotion that threatened to surface in her own expression. His mastery over the room lay in his ability to remain unaffected, allowing no hint of his inner state to escape. Perhaps this control was something she could harness as well.

As the topic turned to the temples, Elyse remembered a bit of her notes Wyltam had prepared for her before the meeting, that the minister of vassals oversaw the relationship with the temples after Wyltam's mother dissolved the minister of religious affairs position.

A new figure rose, one Elyse didn't recognize. "The other temples are restless. Lady Marietta's affiliation with the Temple of Therypon has caused their numbers to swell beyond what seems fair. The temple heads now suggest that Lady Marietta familiarize herself with all the gods to avoid any hint of favoritism."

Wyltam acknowledged this with a curt nod, scribbling a note. "We should consider alternatives, as Marietta will have her hands full. Coordinate with the temples and ensure they grasp that this is a matter of timing, not of preference."

The speaker nodded and took a seat.

"That leaves only one last manner of business," Leyland said, sliding Wyltam a document.

Wyltam's gaze raked the paper, his brows pinching as he slid it toward Elyse. "How did you come about this knowledge?"

Elyse read the transcript from a conversation. Her heart sunk as the details of Queen Valeriya's death were described in detail, down to the weapon that ended her life.

"A district delegate caught wind of it a few days ago," Leyland said. "At first, he thought it was only a disgruntled worker angry about having to use magic, but he asked a few questions. They're saying an aithyr-infused arrow killed Queen Valeriya. Someone had leaked the true details surrounding her death."

"Work with Minister Keyain to launch an investigation," Wyltam said, sitting forward. "Start with that individual. They have a likely reason to spread this information about Valeriya, and we need them silenced.."

"It will be done, Your Grace."

As the meeting concluded, Elyse noted the cornicular in the corner, his horn-shaped badge catching the light, and approached. His swift, precise handoff of the notes and the tightness of his lips went unnoticed; her thoughts were preoccupied with darker concerns.

Once in the hallway, Elyse reached out to the aithyr, allowing its energy to envelop her. The touch was profound, a melding of her physical and mental being that promised peace. She knew better than to believe that such power was innocuous; its potential for destruction was ever-present. Yet, a shiver coursed through her as she considered the possibility of wielding such force for harm, for death. In that moment, a silent oath formed in her mind—a promise to herself that she would never give in to such darkness.

Chapter Six

KEYAIN

Keyain's gaze lingered on Ryder and Adalyn, a few of the first to arrive at the training grounds. Laughter mingled with the clinks of sparring weapons. Keyain stood at the other end, papers in hand, all too aware of the barrier between him and the Satiroan guards. It was good, he supposed, that they had friends that weren't their superiors, yet the familiar pang of isolation twisted in his gut. He masked his unease, silently observing their inside jokes and easy smiles.

Looking for a distraction, he watched as Coryn jogged across the green to their group, muttering an apology for being late. Keyain said nothing, letting the others judge him for his tardiness. He turned back to his list, looking up once more when he heard a round of laughter. Coryn addressed the guards and got another laugh. The sound made Keyain's fists clench.

"Since we're all here," Keyain said, "we can begin. You have all been selected to defend the future queen of Satiros on her Queen's Guard. After the tragic events that led to the death of Queen Valeriya and the second attempt at an assassination, it is of most importance to protect our new queen." Keyain avoided using her name, a deliberate choice that kept him emotionally distant. He maintained a semblance of control until his gaze fell on Coryn and his half-smile. Keyain cleared his throat. "Coryn Niershade is here on behalf of the Temple of Therypon. Given the future queen's status as iros, they wished for the person overseeing her training to be placed in close proximity to her." He left out the part where Wyltam chose him to be the Queen's Guard captain. After all, there was still a chance he could fail.

One guard stepped forward and Keyain gave him permission to speak. "Will it be ill-received if we have a pilinos serve on the Queen's Guard if the integration doesn't go through?"

"It will go through." Keyain adjusted his sleeves. "Any other questions?"

Silence greeted him. Keyain clapped his hands, setting the pace for warm-ups before shifting to group drills.

"Unity is crucial," he instructed as they gathered around him. "You must—" A hand on his shoulder interrupted him, halting his words.

He turned to find Wynn grinning. "Apologies for the late arrival." Behind him stood Andyr and two other people he didn't recognize, an elven female and half-elven male. Wyltam's mages. Keyain jerked his chin toward the rest of the group, waiting for the newcomers to join.

Keyain ground his teeth as Coryn greeted Wynn as if they were old friends. Wyltam had been very busy, it seemed. "We're already behind schedule," he snapped. "Get into groups of three. Mages, don't shy away from using magic in your attacks, but be mindful that this is just a training. No permanent injuries, please."

At all times, three guards would be required to shield Marietta. They had to move and operate as a single unit, and this drill was designed to evaluate their cohesion. One trio would shield a wooden target, while another trio would engage them in combat. This exercise revealed the defensive capabilities of the protectors and the offensive prowess of the attackers.

Adalyn was paired with another guard and the orange-haired mage. Their coordination was precise, while the defensive team struggled with communication. The mage conjured a gust of wind into one of the defenders' faces, giving Adalyn a clear opening to incapacitate her opponent. Keyain gave a nod of approval as they shifted to another target.

He made his way over to Coryn's group, noting that he defended against Wynn. Coryn barked orders at the unfamiliar female mage and Ryder.

Surprisingly, Ryder listened. Wynn had always been quick on his feet, but he moved much faster than the guards he was paired with. His attacks hit harder than they should have. Keyain's eyebrow rose, recognizing the telltale sign of a mage using aithyr to enhance strength. Wyltam had often employed this tactic during their sparring sessions, much to Keyain's irritation.

Wynn slipped through their defenses, twisting low to hit the target. Coryn used the momentum from his swing to carry it through against Wynn's sword, knocking it from Wynn's grip. In the next moment, Coryn's weapon was ripped from his hands as Wynn rushed him. Unfazed by the magic, Coryn grappled Wynn and pinned him to the ground. Their bout ended when Ryder and the mage took down the other two. Keyain moved onto the next group but heard the low tone of Coryn's voice followed by a bark of Ryder's laughter.

As the first hour turned into the second, Keyain maintained his steady demeanor, leading the soldiers through rigorous strength and teamwork drills. Approaching the third and final hour, Keyain chose to test their endurance to the utmost. Despite their exhaustion, the Queen's Guard candidates were tasked with carrying a dummy representing Marietta within a strict time frame. To simulate a real scenario, they had to navigate around other candidates posing as obstacles, ensuring the dummy remained unharmed and was swiftly evacuated.

Keyain sent Ryder first. Ryder easily dodged the other guards, reaching the end of the obstacles with the dummy unscathed. Next was the female mage, whose slight frame belied her strength; she maneuvered the dummy with agile steps, evading foes. Keyain thought she was cornered when two guards trapped her, but a translucent dome materialized, deflecting their swords. Before they could recover, she dashed forward, completing the course.

Coryn stepped up next. Keyain masked his irritation and shouted, "Go!"

Coryn sprinted with the dummy on his back, spinning to evade Ryder's charge. The half-elf sidestepped and continued. Andyr pursued, using his magic to trip Coryn. Coryn tumbled, the dummy falling with him. He rolled back to his feet, pulling the dummy along. As he slung it over his shoulder and sprinted, a white light radiated from his hand onto the dummy's limb.

Of course, that's why Wyltam wanted him near Marietta—the bastard could heal her on the spot. The logic of it somehow made Keyain more annoyed. When Coryn crossed the finish line, Keyain swore. Despite the hiccup, he still had one of the fastest times.

When the last guard finished, Keyain had them gather around, announcing that they'll end the test with sparring one-on-one. Keyain pulled Coryn to the side. "You'll be against me."

Coryn wiped sweat from his forehead, still wearing that damned smile. Keyain's hand twitched toward his sword. Coryn wouldn't last a minute against him.

As soon as they were in position, Keyain darted forward with rapid swings, Coryn scrambling to defend himself. He smirked as he swung his sword in a wide arc. Coryn parried the attack and responded with a swift strike of his own, surprising Keyain as he barely dodged the blade.

Irritated from being caught off guard, Keyain stepped forward, slashing his sword in a flurry of attacks. Coryn blocked each one with precision, though he pushed him back a few feet. If in a room, Keyain would have cornered him by now.

They broke apart, circling one another. Coryn spit onto the ground, wiping his mouth as he drew his blade up again with a smirk. Despite the exhaustion that should have weighed him down, he appeared more energized than Keyain had anticipated.

A wave of frustration washed over him as he charged Coryn, spinning and thrusting his blade. Coryn moved to counter Keyain's attack, but the half-elf was too slow and the dulled blade connected with his arm. He stumbled back, catching himself as Keyain pressed his advantage.

Coryn maintained his footing as Keyain drove him back, but Keyain carried a different motivation—one honed by a need for reprisal. For every person who asked Keyain if he knew about the rumors. For every person who said they were surprised his wife would even cheat on a minister. For Coryn's refusal to let him take Marietta home after she disappeared for hours. Rage overtook him as he pressed Coryn back. The cultist struggled to deflect the onslaught, but Keyain's fury made every strike land with fierce precision.

Coryn stumbled and crashed to the ground. Keyain surged forward, blade raised for a decisive strike. In the blink of an eye, Coryn spun on his feet, still crouched. Keyain's swing connected, sending Coryn's weapon clattering away.

Coryn, quick to recover, drew a dagger and hurled himself at Keyain. Keyain raised his sword to deflect the attack, twisting his blade to dislodge the dagger, but not before feeling the sharp sting of a cut.

Keyain laughed, lowering his blade. "A neat trick, but not good enough—"

Coryn tackled him to the ground and held his hand before Keyain's face, crackling black energy surrounding his fist. "One of a few neat tricks I have at my disposal."

Keyain ground his jaw as he shoved Coryn off him. "The fuck was that?" he managed as he brushed the dirt from his pants.

Coryn offered to help Keyain stand, his free hand slipping to Keyain's forearm as a white light flashed. "I figured if this were a test and I was protecting Marietta, I would do everything in my power to win." He held up a hand, wiggling his fingers as the black light surrounded it. "Benefit of being an iros of Therypon."

Keyain went to call him a cultist but noticed the surrounding silence. The guards and mages had gathered to watch their fight. Amid them stood Wyltam and Marietta, the latter possessing an infuriating smile.

"Have you seen enough?" Wyltam asked. "Or should I announce it for you?"

Keyain tightened his grip on his sword's pommel, struggling to keep his anger in check. If Coryn hadn't aligned with a cult, he could have become a formidable fighter within the guard. The decision was inevitable. "Congratulations," Keyain said, extending his hand to Coryn and forcing a genuine smile, "you're appointed as the captain of the Queen's Guard."

Chapter Seven

KEYAIN, BEFORE

"**G**eneral Keyain." A court lady greeted him with a curtsy. Her name eluded him, but the memory of her body didn't. "It's been a while since we last shared *tea*."

Keyain's smile broadened as he dabbed at his face with the hem of his shirt, noting her gaze fixed on his abdomen. "Are you free tomorrow?"

"For you, I could make the time."

"Send the details to my cornicular," he replied, resuming his brisk pace. "I'm off to meet the queen."

He left her standing alone in the corridor as he hurried to the far side of the palace. Fortunately for him, he had *tea* most nights. Females, males. Anyone who piqued his desire. A satisfied smile crept across his face. What a life indeed.

Months had passed since their victory over the orcs, driving the savages back through The Queen's Pass and out of elven lands. The horrors of war still haunted him, but the triumph made it worthwhile. Satiros was secure, and his loyalty had not gone unnoticed. Queen Olytia had elevated him to general, a mantle he took up after his fallen leader.

As he navigated the corridor, people waved or sought his ear. He acknowledged them with a casual promise of "Another time." His family's wealth and his father's standing at court had always attracted attention, but it paled in comparison to the prestige he currently possessed.

With his rise in position, his parents eagerly arranged matches with various respectable females, but he refused each offer. Why settle now, with his career on an upward trajectory? Minister Tryke had perhaps a century before age would force him to step down. Keyain saw a clear path, through careful maneuvering, to surpass Commander Walyn and claim the ministerial title for himself.

He neared the Royal's Wing, navigating the familiar gilded halls. Memories tugged at him, as they often did with thoughts of Wyltam. His absence weighed heavily, a constant, suffocating fog. Shadows and social fringes felt emptier without his presence. Wyltam had left court, and the void was palpable, yet unnoticed by others.

He didn't need Wyltam. He especially didn't need his sympathies for the orcs—the same orcs responsible for the deaths of his comrades.

Pushing the prince from his mind, he approached the queen's suite, as requested. The guards outside nodded as he passed, their acknowledgment quick. Likely, they would spread word of his summons to the queen's quarters, amplifying his significance. The thought added a spring to his step.

A servant ushered him inside and led him to an ornate sitting room. At its center sat Queen Olytia. Her gaze raked over him slowly as he approached. Keyain flashed a smile and dipped into a low bow, glancing up to catch the red smirk on her lips.

"Your Grace."

"General, thank you for making haste in joining me. Please, have a seat."

Up close, the queen was more beautiful than he remembered. Her black hair was glossy, her skin flawless and alabaster in color. The dress she wore matched the recent styles of court, the neckline dipping to the top of her breasts.

"May I offer you anything? Wine? Spirits? Something stronger?"

Keyain laughed and ducked his head. "If anything, Your Grace, water should suffice."

"Ah, yes. You've just come from training." Her dark eyes roamed over his body. After a cup of water was delivered, Queen Olytia clapped her hands. The servants and guards vanished from sight.

"Much better. General Keyain—may I call you Keyain?"

"You may call me whatever you wish, My Queen."

Her smile sharpened. "Keyain, then. The new role I granted you is fitting, I trust?"

"Beyond fitting, if I'm allowed to be so bold. Thank you for entrusting to me the Army of Satiros. I promise to make you proud."

The queen let out a soft laugh. "I know you will, for you already have. The greatest Satiroan warrior of all time deserves a suitable position, no? It just makes perfect sense. Strong, talented," she paused as she leaned forward, exaggerating the swell of her breasts. "And handsome. You have the makings of someone special."

Heat rose to he's cheeks as he ducked his head again. "You are the most gracious queen to say as such. But is you who is deserving of such compliments. A vision of unmatched beauty and charm, which leaves me captivated."

Her dark eyes practically glittered. "Are you pandering right now?" Her laugh was bright and high. She stood and walked toward Keyain, her long legs peeking through the slit in her skirt. "I love when handsome males pander to me. Continue." She crossed her arms as she stared down at Keyain.

He felt small with her standing above, making the heat in his stomach lower. "I'm at a loss for words, for none can encompass what it's like to be in your presence."

"Then use your actions." She snapped her fingers. "Stand."

Keyain didn't hesitate before jumping from his seat.

"Take off your shirt."

Keyain lifted the wet fabric over his head. When he refocused on the queen, her red lips were hooked into a smirk, her gaze smoldering. "Such a loyal subject."

"Consider me your most loyal, Your Grace."

"Good. Now take off your pants."

Keyain's heart pounded in his chest, thrilled by the demand. He unfastened his pants, dropping his underclothes with them.

"Touch yourself."

The effects of her words left his cock partially hardened. As he wrapped his fist around himself, he matched the queen's gaze.

She reached out and cupped his chin, Keyain's stomach tugging hard with the gesture, and he gasped. "You will be perfect," she purred. "Come along."

Keyain trailed after her to her bedchamber, his gait measured and deliberate. He knew each step drew him closer to earning the queen's favor. As he kneeled before Queen Olytia, the weight of the moment settled upon him, a mix of ambition and reverence. Here, in the heart of power, he felt alive like never before.

Chapter Eight

MARIETTA

On the veranda in the Royal's Wing, Marietta sipped her tea with the elven nobility, more out of obligation than desire. Tryda had been relentless in her insistence on assembling the Queen's Court sooner rather than later, leaving Marietta with little choice but to comply. As she settled at the round table, she reminded herself this was not her court—merely an opportunity to learn the faces and voices of those who held power for so long.

Elyse sat quietly to Marietta's side, having arrived late from a meeting and needing to leave early for another. She picked at the fabric of her skirts and kept glancing at the door. Marietta shared the sentiment—she didn't want to be here, either.

Marietta tore her gaze away to look at Lady Ymorea, the perky wife of the minister of conduct. "How long have you and Rymos been married again?"

Ymorea clinked her spoon against the side of the cup, making Grytaine next to her flinch. "I think twenty-six years now. No, wait—twenty-seven. Where do the decades go?" She giggled into her cup as she took a sip. Her tight, black curls were pulled back into a puff, making her round face appear more youthful than the near two centuries of her age. She turned to Tryda. "You and Dyeiter have been together for three centuries now, right?"

The older elven woman sat back, her rich brown skin glowing in the afternoon light that drifted in past the balcony. "A decade shy of three."

"So exciting," Ymorea continued. "Many examples for you to learn from, Lady Marietta."

Marietta forced a cheerful expression and set down her cup. "While I appreciate the encouragement, I have been married before."

A heavy pause held the room, the silence filled with birds chirping from the Queen's Garden. Grytaine hid her smile behind her tea as Tryda cleared her throat. "Grytaine and Royir have had luck in the past few years together." She reached across and placed a gentle hand on Grytaine's swollen stomach. "Have your aversions gotten any better?"

Marietta stilled at the change of subject, not missing Tryda's deft hand. While not a topic Marietta wished to discuss, she wanted to make that call for herself.

Grytaine pushed her tea further away, her features becoming more pinched as she grimaced. "I can hardly eat. All I can stomach is a few sips of water at a time."

Despite the growing life inside Grytaine, she looked leached of it. Hallowed cheeks, dark circles under her eyes. Her pale blonde hair hung limp. Even her normally thin frame appeared exceptionally frail with the swell of her belly.

"It'll be worth it once they're here," Tryda said.

"Tell that to Royir—" Grytaine snapped her mouth shut at a glance from Tryda. "Apologies. That isn't proper."

Marietta leaned in. "If you wish to share your thoughts, know that you're welcome to. No one should face hardships alone."

Grytaine's gaze shifted to Tryda, who forced a thin smile.

"While your concern is appreciated, such matters of marriage are not discussed over tea." Tryda then bent close to Grytaine, murmuring words that slipped past Marietta's hearing.

"Oh! Lady Marietta, I meant to ask." Ymorea dabbed the corners of her mouth, her eyes gleaming with curiosity. "I read that temple followers once possessed abilities granted by their deity. Is that true?"

Marietta's lips curved at the question. "Many still do." She gestured to the twin snakes coiled down her neck, vanishing beneath her dress. "As an iros, I wield both of Therypon's domains."

Marietta raised her hand and pulled at the goddess's energy under her skin when Tryda spoke up. "Elyse, have you found any new suitors? You've been spending a lot of time with the branch officers. Dyeiter mentioned a few of his subordinates have expressed an interest?"

Elyse choked on the tea she was drinking, coughing suddenly as she set down her cup, sloshing some of it onto the table.

Ymorea smiled conspiratorially and leaned toward Elyse. "You didn't tell me you're courting again! I have a cousin in the education branch who is quiet and a touch odd like you. Poor guy is too shy to make a move, but I'd be more than happy to connect you."

"Oh, I'm not—I haven't." Elyse took her napkin and wiped the spilled liquid. "Sorry," she muttered.

"Nothing to apologize for," Marietta said. "And I think what she was trying to say is that she's focused on her role as king's administrator."

"Playing hard to get." Ymorea giggled into her teacup. "They will love chasing after you."

Elyse's mouth moved, yet no sound emerged. Sensing the falter, Marietta said, "She'll be assisting Wyltam more closely as his responsibilities increase— particularly during our journey to Olkia for the treaty signing at month's end."

"I—yeah. Yes." Elyse sat up straighter. "It's been a lot to learn."

"Regarding the treaty," Tryda said, redirecting the group's focus, "We should schedule a meeting this week for wedding preparations."

"We?" Marietta blinked and drank her tea. "Wyltam and I will start when we return."

"As customary, the ladies of your Queen's Court help plan the wedding. Though we are rather sparse these days." Tryda glanced around the room with a sigh.

"I don't have a Queen's Court," she said.

"Then what are we?" Tryda's back remained pin-straight, her gaze locked onto Marietta. "We are the wives of the ministers, or daughters in Elyse's …"

Tryda trailed off and cleared her throat. "Such is tradition to have us help guide your reign."

Marietta studied Tryda. Tea was a mere pretense; this woman was no ordinary noble. Tryda had maneuvered her way to the royal's side with rigor, and no simple dismissal would remove her from that position. She was a force, an obstacle that wouldn't easily be moved.

Marietta lifted her chin in defiance. "That won't be necessary."

"Oh, but it will. Valeriya knew no one when she arrived. Ymorea and I helped her to find other worthy candidates to support her. Getting a place on your Queen's Court will nearly be a competition among the ladies. Many are looking forward to it. I know I was."

"As was I," Ymorea said with a sigh, her expression wistful. "I was hoping you'd show us a few of your traditions from home when the search began. I'm still dreaming about that dance Valeriya had taught us. Oh! Maybe you could teach us about your goddess!"

Tryda's calm demeanor slipped.

"I'd love to know myself," Marietta said. "We could learn together."

"You don't know?" Ymorea leaned forward. "I thought all pilinos belonged to a deity."

"Perhaps it'd be better to serve a pastry from Enomenos," Tryda interjected, her voice heightened.

Marietta dismissed her with a slight wave. "Not all pilinos. I'm rather new to the faith myself. I could invite someone from the Temple of Therypon to join us for our next tea." The image of Coryn or Deania seated among the ladies brought a smile to her lips.

Tryda's hand tightened around her teacup. "If I may, the temples will be ill-suited for such a gathering."

"Why is that?"

"Surely you don't believe they sacrifice people, Tryda." Ymorea laughed, reaching for a biscuit. "The book I'm reading mentions offerings of seeds or water, not people. The closest they come is blood. Occasionally, there are—"

Grytaine's face paled further as she retched.

"This topic grows inappropriate," Tryda snapped, leaning forward to steady Grytaine. "Please, Ymorea."

"If I have to hear one more comment about their cultist sacrifices, I will be sick." Grytaine held her head in her hands.

At Marietta's side, Elyse stood abruptly from the table. "I have to leave. Lady Marietta, Ladies." She curtsied and hurried from the room so quickly that Marietta didn't have a chance to say goodbye.

Sighing, she turned back to the ladies. "I would appreciate if you didn't call them cultists."

"Olytia stripped them of their power for a reason," Tryda said under her breath.

Marietta tilted her head. "Did she now? Care to elaborate?"

"Perhaps this was enough excitement for the day." Tryda stood, helping Grytaine.

"Isn't it the queen's place to dismiss her own court?" Marietta's gaze was steady, unyielding.

"It either is or it isn't a Queen's Court. You should decide, and soon." With a subtle nod, she guided Grytaine to her feet. "You too, Ymorea."

The other lady dipped her head and took Grytaine's hand. Marietta, arms crossed, watched as Tryda lingered. Influence was familiar to her and she wielded it with ease.

"If having a court means more than just tea, then I would consider gathering one." She didn't have time for routine idle gossip.

Tryda sighed as the door clicked shut behind Grytaine. "At least tea time can only get easier from here. Valeriya's entrance to court was rough as well."

"This isn't my entrance."

"It is as queen, not as—" She waved her hand, dismissing the thought. "Valeriya wanted the Queen's Court to fencing at first. Said it was a special interest of hers."

Marietta tried and failed to imagine her wielding a sword.

"Thus, we landed on a traditional dance from Reyila, as Ymorea shared. I suggest something simple, normal even, such as tasting desserts from Enomenos."

"Opposed to learning about my deity?" The words hung between them, their weight as tangible as the symbol of Therypon inked into her skin. Despite this, it felt foreign to name the goddess as her own. "Perhaps there might be more interest among the ladies."

Tryda exhaled slowly. "If you insist, though I advise against it. The temples are dangerous. You only sought yours when you felt the need for freedom."

"Keyain abducted me and locked me in a room. You might be like a second mother to him, but do not twist the truth of what happened." Marietta drew herself up straight. "If there's nothing more, you may leave."

Tryda's gaze hardened. "Very well, Your Grace. But there is one more thing. Has the prince returned? It's been too long since I last saw him. The poor child." Her lips pressed into a frown.

"I didn't realize you were close with him."

"Both his mother and grandmother were dear friends to me," she said, swallowing hard. "All I have of them is Prince Mycaub. I would like to see him when he returns, if that would be all right."

Marietta eyed her. Valeriya hadn't mentioned her closeness with Tryda, but that didn't mean it wasn't true. "I'll talk to Wyltam."

"Thank you, Your Grace."

After the lady departed, a familiar face stuck his head in the door. "Do you want us to wait out here or come in?" Coryn asked, his smile bright against his dark brown skin. Fitted in his metallic green Queen's Guard armor, she could almost forget that he had belonged to the temple.

"There's leftover sweets I'd rather not go to waste."

"If only Deania were here," he said, holding the door for Wynn and Adalyn behind him. "She'd be stuffing her pockets."

"We could arrange for some to be brought to her," she suggested as they drew near. "Or perhaps she and the other temple acolytes could visit?"

Coryn's laughter cut off as he caught the shift in her demeanor. "And where did that notion come from?"

"Lady Ymorea asked me a few questions," she said, crossing her arms. "I had few answers, and it got me thinking. Perhaps I should invite them to tea."

Adalyn snorted a laugh as she approached the table. Marietta narrowed her eyes, still wary despite the guard's apology. The sharp edge of Adalyn's disapproval had been clear to Marietta—Adalyn did not support elves who claimed pilinos as their spouses without their consent. If she had realized Keyain had done just that, then Adalyn stated her actions would have been kinder.

"I bet Tryda love that," she said, eyeing a biscuit before popping it in her mouth. "She and Keyain were always weird about the temples. The countryside folk were used to them."

Marietta turned to Coryn. "Any idea why court thinks the temples had human sacrifices?"

"There were several disappearances," Coryn explained, rubbing his chin. "Queen Olytia tried to blame them on the temples, though they had no connection. It was her way of undermining their influence. She didn't succeed entirely, but it led to a public reluctance toward magic. That happened well before my time here."

Marietta looked at Adalyn for an answer, who responded with a shrug. She turned to her last guard, who looked over the edge of the balcony to the garden below. "Do you know, Wynn?"

He turned to face Marietta and shrugged. "I was still in Enomenos at the time. Didn't get here until after magic was regulated to service mages."

"How did I not know you were from Enomenos?" She planted her hands on her hips. "What city-state?"

"Doesn't matter." He turned back to the garden, an uncharacteristic frown forming on his lips. "Not fond of my days there."

Coryn pulled out an aithyr clock. "We're going to be late for your appointment with the tailor."

"Before that," Marietta said, holding out her hand as she thought. "Could you extend an invitation on my behalf to the other acolytes of Therypon? Perhaps it's time I undo the hate sown into the city-state, starting with my court."

Chapter Nine

AMRYTH

Amryth kept her head low as she nursed an ale at the curved bar that wove from the back wall to the heart of the bustling room. With subtle glances, she eyed the patrons of the Honeysuckle Tavern.

Cheers erupted from the brightly lit side of the floor, where elves and pilinos sat in groups at the wooden tables scattered across the space. A performer on stage strummed their lute to a jaunty tune. Some patrons danced to it; others traded cards and words.

From what she gathered, the folk sitting next to her at the bar were longtime regulars, needing only a gesture to receive another drink from the bartender. Unsure if it was the rowdy groups or simply a dislike for her, Amryth had to try three times before finally getting his attention. Not that it mattered. She wasn't there for the drinks.

To her left sat an older pilinos male with an elf who was presumably the same age. Even before hearing their conversation, their oil-stained clothes and hunched backs revealed they were factory workers as her father had once been.

"I'm telling you, once they start producing that shit, they're going to use it to replace us." The half-elven man threw back his ale and singled for another.

"That's not how *aithyr*" — the elf pronounced the word in a nasal tone

—"works, though. You heard the bosses."

"Say that to my cousin who made a living off of lighting gaslights." He chuckled and spun his glass between his fingers. "If *elves* find a solution to replace their grunt labor, then what happens to my kids? What will they do for work?"

Amryth turned away, remembering her father having the same conversations when globe lights replaced most of the street lighting in Satiros. Some recruits she enlisted with were former lighters who needed alternative sources of income, and joining the guard was one of the few employment options.

A sudden evening breeze swept through the tavern, carrying with it the mingling scents of pipe smoke and spilled ale. Amryth's gaze shifted toward the door as it creaked open. Two pilinos stepped inside, their presence cutting through the haze of the dimly lit room. One locked eyes with her—a man with a barrel chest, dark hair, and olive skin. He narrowed his eyes before slipping into a low-lit section of the tavern. The newcomers joined a group at the corner booth, and while Amryth could no longer see him, she felt his searing gaze.

To remain inconspicuous, she watched the elven female who left the same section and headed toward the bar. Her rich brown skin shined in the light as she approached the open spot next to Amryth, tray in hand. She glanced at Amryth as she waved to the bartender. "I don't think I've seen you here before." Her gaze worked down Amryth's body, then returned to her face. "I would've remembered."

Amryth offered a smile and said, "Just moved back to the Ward."

"You have a name?"

"Amryth. And you?"

"Tanaly." The bartender came over and Tanaly rattled off a list of drinks. Her puff of black hair pulled back from her face complimented the angular features. She then turned to Amryth. "Then another one of what she's drinking."

"No, that's all right." Amryth waved her hand in dismissal.

"Nonsense. It's on me. Not every day I get an attractive new customer such as yourself." She nudged Amryth. "Gotta keep you around, even if it's just to admire from afar."

Amryth coughed into her drink to mask her surprise. "Kind of you."

Tanaly leaned onto the bar with her one hip, her arm crossed. "You staying late? I could use someone to walk me home."

Amryth's cheeks heated, and her pulse thumped wickedly in her ears. After years with Deyra, she became unaccustomed to such advances. "Not sure I can do that."

"Oh." Tanaly stood. "I'm sorry. Is someone waiting for you at home?"

A cold sweat broke over her skin as the lie slipped out of her mouth. "I have a partner who'd be with me tonight but she's stuck at the temple."

Tanaly's lips curled into a smile. "We love elves who support the temples around here."

"She's half-elven."

Her brows raised, and she glanced over Amryth once more. "Even better. Which temple is she from? What's her name? Tell me about the lucky female that gets to call you hers."

Amryth took a sip, willing her heart to cease its erratic beat. "Deania from the Temple of Therypon."

Tanaly's brows furrowed as she slapped the countertop. "That rascal! She didn't tell me she was seeing anyone." As the bartender set down a few tankers of ale, she turned to him and said, "Fern, did you know Deania was seeing someone?"

"Seriously? Who?" He slid a tankard toward Amryth.

Tanaly gestured to Amryth. She nodded her head and lifted her nearly empty mug, wishing she could sink into her seat. What were the chances that these people knew Deania?

Before Amryth could grab her fresh drink, Fern replaced it with another. Amryth went to comment about it when he added, "Glad to see she's finally settling down."

Tanaly laughed as she loaded her tray. "About damn time. Amryth, next time you come to the Honeysuckle, make sure you bring Big D with you. She's been working too much lately. We miss her dearly."

Before Amryth could reply, she slipped into the crowd of people. Amryth glanced down at her drink, then back at the bartender, who moved onto the next patrons. Peculiar, but perhaps she was reading into it. She pushed her fresh drink away and turned her attention back to where the pilinos had sat earlier, only to find the booth empty. More peculiar, considering the door hadn't opened again. To her knowledge, there wasn't a second floor either. Taking the signs that something had happened though she was unsure what, Amryth threw some coin onto the counter and stepped into the late summer evening.

The Honeysuckle didn't strike Amryth as an establishment that would house a pilinos murderer, which left her wondering its place on the guard's list. Perhaps they also experienced the same weird behavior and stares. There had to be a connection.

Letting those troubling thoughts go for now, Amryth instead focused on a more immediate problem—Deania.

Chapter Ten

ELYSE

Wynn stood, his arms crossed, wearing an unimpressed expression directed at Elyse who once again opened her eyes. "I have a question."

"Does it pertain to your lesson?" he asked.

"It doesn't but—"

"Tell me what's in the first bucket, and then you can ask."

Elyse sighed, redirecting her focus to channeling aithyr into her body. She drew in through her nose, letting the magical energy flood her nasal cavity, and she concentrated. She imagined a tendril of aithyr slithering from her body to the buckets, but it would dissipate before fully reaching its destination. Old paper, dust, and a hint of something delicate—the same things she'd been smelling all week.

Frustration gnawed at her as she relaxed her shoulders and refocused. Instead of pulling energy into her body then sending it out, she considered how much easier it would be if the aithyr stream carried the scent to her. In her mind, Elyse tugged the stream toward the first bucket. For a moment, it gave into her efforts, then it snapped back into its current.

"You're forcing your magic," Wynn said. "Release the energy as you inhale while focusing on the target."

Elyse had tried that already. Yet she attempted his method again, releasing all the aithyr stored in her body. The scents of the room bombarded her. Sharp tang of lemon. Warmth of leather. Something floral, perhaps roses? Sweat mixed with pepper, which she knew was Wynn. She stumbled backward as her nostrils burned.

"Too much. Try to trickle the aithyr out—"

"That is what I'm doing!" A sneeze tickled back by her sinuses, and she tried and failed to hold it in. "It would be easier to move the aithyr over the scent and bring it to me."

"Again, that isn't possible." Wynn walked to her. "This is the first thing you've struggled with since we started training. Normal students would still be attempting to heat spoons. Getting frustrated now that you've discovered something that's difficult for you won't help you grow." He handed her a handkerchief for her nose.

The issue wasn't her inability to enhance her sense of smell; it was that she couldn't control it. She sighed, clenching her fingers into a fist.

"Take a break." Wynn clasped her shoulder as he passed. "What was your question?"

Elyse followed him as he plopped down into a chair, and she leaned on the desk across from him. As she settled into her position, she noticed her feet rested in between his, his posture relaxed and legs spread. "Wyltam mentioned there were new mages."

Wynn's mouth slid into a lazy grin, the scar that forked across his face curled with it. "I'm going to need you to be more specific."

"For Marietta. Her guard?"

"Ah." Wynn sat back further in the chair. "He called in a favor from some members of the Circle of Mages."

Elyse's pulse fluttered. Her mother had belonged to the Circle of Mages. "Do you know them?"

"Andyr is healed, and he brought a group of mages back with him." Elyse went to ask who that was, but he beat her to it. "He was injured in an altercation with another mage—severe burns. An attendant of Therypon stabilized him and then he went back to the Circle for a few weeks to rest and finish healing."

"The Circle of Mages is a place?"

"It's an organization that has a place. And before you ask, I cannot reveal the location."

"And you know it because …"

"I'm a member."

Like her mother. Like Sylas.

"I knew your mother only in name," he said, his grin softening as he took in her expression. "When I joined, she had already returned to Satiros, taking her family's place since her brother had disappeared."

Elyse remembered the stories her father had told her, about how her uncle left court to never be heard of again. He also shared that her mother refused to take her family name, only using her father's surname once they married. Elyse never had it in her heart to ask about that side of her family. Anything pertaining to her mother was still too raw.

"No need to worry about that." He stood and guided her back to the buckets. "I'm sure you're buzzing with questions now, but I want to get scent training down before you meet them." He caught her question once again before she could ask. "There's pride in teaching another mage. You're supposed to be Wyltam's pupil, yet he's preoccupied with his duties, which makes me your teacher for the foreseeable future. I'm already proud of the progress you've made and I can't wait to show them how talented you are."

A tingling sensation cascaded through her cheeks and fingertips. Determined to make him proud, she focused on the pull of energy again, this time closing her eyes as she exhaled through her nose, then inhaled deeply. Aithyr trickled from her body, her mind imagining it being a thin string, no wider than her smallest finger. As she pulled it back from the bucket, she picked up on a scent—a rose.

She opened her eyes, excited to tell him what it was when something hit her in the face. Startled, she jumped back with a yelp, finding a balled-up paper at her feet.

Wynn laughed as he grabbed another sheet and crumpled it in his hands. "I could tell you got it, but you forgot your surroundings. What if you were in a fight?"

She threw the ball of paper back at him, missing completely, which earned another laugh from him. "I'll know if I'm in a fight."

His laugh sobered. "Not always. The chance of being attacked is always present. It's something I learned the hard way at the Circle of Mages."

"How ... how did you learn?"

He shook his head and ran a hand over this hair. "Wyltam said he didn't have plans to send you there but now I'm second-guessing it. Although ..." He paused to crumple another paper. "I think I finally found the perfect training method for you."

Elyse laughed as he rearranged the scents for her to continue training. As he did, she tried to imagine what the Circle of Mages was like. Perhaps it was similar to the university, or so she had heard. Lecture halls with hundreds of seats. Students swapping notes and testing each other on what they learned. A piece of her yearned for it, but then again, she had Wynn to train her. Taking in the curve of his mouth and the fluid way he moved, he had become a part of her normal and she wasn't willing to let that go.

As dawn broke, Elyse rose early and made her way to weapons training with Wynn. The Mage Pit, a hollow deep beneath the palace, held the familiar scent of earth and sweat, its sparring mats and weapons waiting in the dim light. An entire space carved out for mages, hidden away with a secret passage barely twenty feet from her favorite library alcove. The first time she stepped into it, the sheer existence of such a place had been a revelation.

Her body had trembled under the strain of those early sessions, every swing and lunge with a dagger becoming a trial. But within weeks, her muscles responded, her strikes landed harder, her movements sharpened. Yet the discomfort lingered—the sweat clinging to her skin, the labored gasps for air, the ache that settled in her limbs long after she'd left the Pit. After those initial weeks with Wynn, she remained convinced it would never get easier.

Elyse was halfway through her last miserable warm-up lap when she noticed three strangers lingering near one of the tunnel entrances. Wynn clasped the shoulder of a male marred with molted scars. Andyr, she recalled. Next to him stood an elven female with brown skin and long, silky black hair streaked with silver. Her full lips were marked with a scar similar to Wynn's. She noticed Elyse and nudged the half-elven man beside her. He turned, his orange hair and beard also silvered with wrinkles pulling at his skin when he smiled. Catching their stares, Wynn called her over.

"This is her?" The elven female's intense gaze roamed over Elyse.

"Elyse Norymial, in her full glory." Wynn slung his arm around her shoulders. "This is Sibylla and Tolis from the Circle of Mages."

Elyse had thought members of the Circle of Mages would exude power or wear special outfits to signify their status like in her books. Instead, they wore training clothes similar to her own sweat-stained ones. "Nice to make your acquaintance."

Tolis, the half-elven man, gestured with his hands. Andyr nodded and said, "Tolis thought Wyltam would train her."

"Wyltam already has a lot on his plate, so I'm here to make sure she doesn't fall behind." Wynn pulled her closer, forcing a smile from Elyse. "Though I don't know if we'll need to worry about that."

Sibylla's eyes widened. "Anthylia's daughter then, without a doubt."

"You knew my mother?" Elyse asked, furrowing her brows.

Sibylla and Tolis exchanged glances. "I knew her for a time, though at a distance. Tolis was young in the Circle but did meet your mother. She's a legend."

Tolis made another gesture with his hands. Andyr and Sibylla both nodded.

"Like her father as well," Sibylla added.

Elyse's brows furrowed further. They knew her father? He was far from being considered a legend.

Before she could ask her question, Wynn said, "We should finish training. Andyr, I'm glad you're better. I'll find you this evening to fill you in on what you've missed."

The group of mages departed, leaving Wynn and Elyse alone as he guided her to one of the mats. "They're pleasant enough," she remarked, drawing a hidden dagger and sinking into her starting stance.

"Tolis is the pleasant one. Andyr's got an edge, but we appreciate that about him." Wynn drew his own dagger and positioned himself across from her. "Sibylla, though ... she's something else."

"You know her well?"

A smirk played on his lips, causing her heart to falter in its rhythm. "Better than most. She's my mage mentor. Friendly, sure, but ... intense. I'm a far gentler teacher than she is."

Elyse rolled her eyes. "If that was true, then I could beat you in a spar."

His smirk sharpened. "This is me going easy on you."

He jutted forward suddenly, his dagger swinging toward her body. Elyse stepped back in time, leaving her weight on her toes. She lowered an arm and swung at him. Wynn sidestepped and spun, tapping his dagger against her collarbone. "Stop dropping your arms."

"How am I supposed to hit my target if it's down low?"

"Like this." Wynn came to stand behind her and his boot slid between her feet, forcing her stance to widen. Dizziness washed over Elyse and not from physical exertion. He pushed down on her shoulders, forcing her knees to bend. "Use your legs for movement. You're trying to pivot at your waist and arms. Your full body should be moving. Got it?"

As he went to move away, Elyse considered asking him to show her again, but thought better of it. "Got it," she answered, slightly out of breath.

Wynn crouched into position again. "That's my girl. Again."

Following his instructions, Elyse stuck with her whole body. She swung, parried, and returned to her starting position, over and over. When she'd make a mistake, Wynn's hands would guide her shoulders, each touch a spark lingering in her mind.

Toward the end of their session, Wynn eyed her with a smirk. "Ready for something more challenging?"

She nodded despite her tired limbs. "Depends on what it is."

"I'm going to use aithyr to hit harder, faster," Wynn replied. "Every mage channels magic into their fighting, so you need to learn how to deflect and move against that power. Channel aithyr and let it flow with your movements."

Elyse closed her eyes for a moment, her mind reaching out to the tendrils of energy around her. She pulled them into herself, like water soaking into dry soil, feeling her muscles hum with power.

When she opened her eyes, she focused the energy to her legs and darted toward Wynn. He stepped back and narrowly dodged, laughing as he deflected her dagger. He recovered quickly, his strike a blur. She barely intercepted it, the force of the impact reverberating through her arm, but she held her ground.

"Good," he said, a hint of pride slipping into his voice. "Now, counter."

She let the magic guide her, pushing her to be faster. Her blade whipped toward Wynn, and though he parried with ease, she felt the aithyr thrumming through her, urging her forward.

Wynn pressed his assault, his strikes testing her limits. Elyse met each one, their daggers ringing out in the cavern's stillness. The strain in her muscles built, the burn deepening, but she pushed through, unwilling to falter.

"Excellent," Wynn said. "Now, add the wind. Push me back."

Elyse imagined the aithyr whipping into air, gathering it in her grasp. With a flick of her wrist, she sent a gust hurtling toward Wynn. He staggered, his feet skidding against the stone, but his smile was one of approval.

"Impressive," he said, "but I know you can do more."

Elyse grinned, feeling a spark of confidence. She gathered more air, channeling it into a swirling vortex. Wynn's eyes widened slightly, and he braced himself as she unleashed the full force of the wind at him. He slid back several feet, his boots scraping against the stone floor.

"There it is," Wynn said.

He closed the distance between them with a speed she had yet to see. Elyse barely had time to react, her dagger clashing against his and holding. He leaned in close, his breath warm against her ear as he whispered, "Don't hesitate. Trust your instincts. Use magic to your disposal."

She parried his next strike, her aithyr-enhanced strength giving her the edge she needed. With a swift motion, she knocked his dagger aside and pressed her blade to his chest, her breath coming in heavy gasps.

Wynn looked down at the dagger, then back at her, a proud smile on his face. "About damn time. Again—use more magic."

Elyse's heart still pounded from the victory as she returned to her starting position and launched her next assault. Aithyr coursed through her veins, the intoxicating rush that came from channeling her magic. Wynn's words of praise lingered, feeding her rising confidence with every heartbeat.

But then, in the next instant, she made the mistake of wanting more.

She swiped at Wynn. Her control over aithyr erupted, hot and insistent, and without thinking, she summoned fire. It licked along the edge of her blade, a searing, brilliant orange that flared too high, too wild. She swung the dagger. The fire blazed in a furious arc, too close to his face, and Wynn had to break his movement, stumbling back to avoid the flames.

Panic seized her, the dagger slipping from her fingers and clattering to the ground. She stared at it, horrified, the flames sputtering out as quickly as they had come.

"Wynn, I'm sorry—" Her voice trembled, the words catching in her throat. "I didn't mean to—"

Wynn held up a hand, his expression unreadable. "Elyse, it's okay," he said, but his voice was measured, careful. "But this is training. Fire isn't something you can toss around lightly. You could've hurt me. Seriously hurt me."

She shook her head, her cheeks flushing with shame. All that praise, all that confidence, and she'd nearly turned it into a disaster. An idiot. A fool playing with power she didn't fully understand, trying to impress him and instead ...

Wynn exhaled, long and slow. When he spoke again, his tone had softened, the edge gone. "You've got so much raw talent, Elyse," he murmured. "Sometimes, I forget that. What you just did—there are full-fledged Circle members who don't have that kind of strength. It caught me off guard."

She lifted her eyes, catching the way he watched her, hands on his hips, an easy smile slowly spreading across his face. But she couldn't return it, not when she trembled, not when the memory of that fire was still too close.

"Hey," Wynn's voice gentled further, and he took a step closer, the tension of a moment ago easing into something warmer. "It's a good thing. You'll need to be mindful of it, though. I'm not trying to lose any hair."

Despite herself, a nervous laugh bubbled up, shaky but real. Wynn reached out, clasping her shoulder, the touch grounding her, pulling her out of her spiral.

"We're done for the day," he said, his smile widening, the warmth of it reaching his eyes. "We'll pick up where we left off next time."

Elyse nodded, the tension in her chest unraveling. She could still sense aithyr hovering near, as if it wished to be inside her once more. And she knew that as long as Wynn was there to guide her, she'd learn to control it.

Chapter Eleven

MARIETTA

"It's too unorthodox."

Marietta bristled on Tryda's arm, turning to gaze into the Central Garden. The shade did little to quell the heat. "It's simply different. Besides, I meet with them this afternoon. It's too late to cancel."

"I know you're eager to change things with your rule," Tryda said, pivoting toward Marietta. "However, if you turn the ship too quickly, you risk capsizing. Ease us into the idea of temples and gods before you integrate them into our world."

"Perhaps the ship should've been sailing in the right direction all along." Marietta laughed dryly. "Care to know what I think?"

"I believe you're going to tell me regardless, Your Grace."

"I think the root of Queen Olytia's discontent for the temples stemmed from her hate for pilinos. The temples harbor pilinos from all of Syllogi." Marietta leaned closer, her tone remaining cheery as her anger seethed. "They had the power to protect them, and Queen Olytia didn't approve of that power. It wouldn't surprise me if she made the sacrificial rumors herself."

Red plumed on the lady's cheeks. "I suggest you don't speak ill of your predecessor."

"Then she shouldn't have been such a vile woman." Marietta released herself from Tryda's arm and faced her guards. "Change is coming, Tryda."

"Alienating yourself won't lead to change," Tryda warned. "Support goes a long way."

Marietta gave her lady-in-waiting one last look before dismissing her and strode down the garden path. Perhaps she should have tempered her words, but it was frustrating when this should have been their goal all along. From what Marietta gathered, Queen Olytia had ruled by fear. While Valeriya attempted to undo the late queen's efforts, there was still much work to be done. Marietta's resolve hardened with each step, knowing that true change was an uphill battle she was ready to fight, but she couldn't do it alone.

Back in her suite, Marietta went to nestle down with a book when she noticed a stack of papers on her desk. Walking over, she found a note on top.

As you demand, so shall you receive.
- W

Marietta furrowed her brows as she read the first paper. Wyltam had left her a copy of the treaty, or rather an abbreviated version. With a laugh, Marietta scooped up the papers and got comfy on the couch to work through it.

Preamble. Definitions. Parties involved. She paused at the Principles and Goals section, reading that her and Wyltam's union would promise both parties unity and peace, mutual prosperity, cultural exchange and respect. The last included a caveat about the full rights and citizenship of pilinos upon their wedding day.

She smiled to herself. They were only a few short months of making sure it would become a reality.

Marietta turned the page to the following section—Obligations of the Parties. Its sections contained support and protection, which included the war efforts. Economic contributions to promote trade. Training and education, which granted Enomenos access to magic. Her heart stopped as she reached the next section.

Offspring and Succession.

The more she read, the more her temper simmered. By late afternoon, Marietta's fury had only intensified. When she joined the temple acolytes on the veranda, anger still clung to her, stubborn and unyielding.

Nearly a dozen were in attendance, some she knew, others she didn't. Coryn sat with Nosokyma—the Temple of Therypon head—and another familiar face.

Deania was the first to approach, throwing her arms around Marietta. "Oh, how I've missed you," she said into Marietta's shoulder.

Nosokyma cleared her throat, Deania going stiff before stepping back. "Apologies. I suppose it's not proper to hug a queen."

"I'm not queen yet. And I've missed you."

"Amryth sends her love," she said, hesitating. "At least she had when we last spoke, but …"

The mention of her friend's name caused Marietta to frown. Amryth had abandoned, refusing to take the captain's position of her guard. While happy to have Coryn, she couldn't help but be disappointed when it wasn't her. After all they had been through, she walked away as if it was nothing—as if Marietta meant nothing.

Tea was promptly brought out as Marietta took her seat. Coryn, Deania, and Nosokyma sat to her left, adorned in Therypon's blue. Beside them was an iros from Seidytar, the goddess of order and chaos. Rafayl, as he introduced himself, said, "I never thought I'd be able to see the palace, Your Grace." He smoothed the fabric of his taupe tunic embroidered with jagged lightning bolts that spun out in a circle. "I heard there used to be a temple here at some point."

Marietta smiled. "If that's true, then it's the first I've heard of it."

"It's been defunct for some time."

Marietta turned to the iros from the Temple of Zontykroi, the god of life and death. "You've seen it, Moira?"

"Unfortunately, no." She tucked the white blonde of her hair behind her rounded ears, the white irises still a shock to Marietta. "But my mother spoke of it often. The way she described it was reverent, as if the memory of the place too was holy."

"I heard it was small." Cyrus, the iros from Kystrorgiste, leaned in closer with a rough voice. "Hardly could be called a temple."

"Didn't your temple offer to build a grander one?" A half-elf named Izzy tilted their head, their eyes shining and framed by their delicate curls. They pulled up the sleeves of their golden yellow robes, the color of Oramytiz, deity of reality and deception. "Don't tell me you're still bitter."

"How small do you think it is?" Marietta asked, setting down her teacup. "Surely a palace this size could boast an impressive temple."

"The only way to know is to see it ourselves," Moira said with a faint smile.

"Wish that we could."

Coryn cleared his throat. "But we could, if you wished it."

Marietta turned to her guard. "See it?"

"Reopen it even. It would help with your iros training."

Nosokyma leaned forward. "Which you should start sooner than later."

Marietta had forgotten she would need to train for that. She thought back to Tryda's warning. "I don't think it would be well-received."

"Perhaps not within the palace," Izzy said. "It would only bolster your popularity outside of it."

Marietta went to question when Cyrus spoke. "That popularity has served the Temple of Therypon well."

Deania rolled her eyes. "You're only bitter because we've gained more followers. Yes, Marietta has helped us, but a win for one of us is a win for all of us."

As he went to counter, Marietta raised her hand. "I don't know what you're speaking of."

"You used Therypon's power to stop the attempt on your life," Nosokyma said. "Many of the attendees went on to spread your story. They say your ruling is a blessing of the divine."

While accrediting her ascension to the power of a deity didn't sit well with Marietta, it did start to unravel her glaring problem in the treaty. If she had any hopes of opposing the ministers, she would need alliances. Marietta put on a thoughtful expression then said, "Then perhaps it's the deities who push me toward reopening the temple."

As tea with the acolytes ended, Marietta found herself still agitated over the treaty, but the time cooled most of her anger. She had a plan. Grow her relationship with the temples, and in turn, get their support.

After a meager dinner, Marietta took her wine on the balcony overlooking the Queen's Garden. Sunlight lingered in the sky, slowly giving way to night. The intricate garden below filled with tangling wisteria and sweeping trees with wafting scents of floral and woodsy alike should have brought Marietta peace, yet she felt none of it. When she offered her hand to Wyltam, she didn't mean to offer her womb too.

Lost in her head, she missed the suite's door opening for Wyltam until he knocked on the balcony's doorway, startling her.

"It's as if my thoughts summon you," she said, leaning onto the railing.

He took the spot beside her, his hands clasped behind him. "Thinking of me, are you?" He glanced at her with a twitch of his brows. His amusement made her stomach swoop, the sensation only adding to her frustration.

Marietta swirled the wine in her glass. "I was speculating whether you'd be good in bed."

Wyltam became unnaturally still before turning to her.

"After all," she continued, "the Satiroan government deemed it necessary that we breed like livestock until they have a substitute heir to use at their whim."

He exhaled slowly. "I wondered when you'd read that section of the treaty."

"You knew and you're okay with this?"

"There are worse fates than having you in my bed, Marietta."

In any other conversation, she would have entertained such a flirtatious reply, yet instead she sipped her wine, trying and failing to hide her anger. "I suppose the bedding part is all you care about," she said heatedly as she pinned him to the spot with her glare. "I couldn't expect you to care about the resulting child, considering you're willing to toss your current heir to the side as if he's nothing."

A plume of pink appeared on his cheeks as he slowly blinked at Marietta. "Don't speak of things you know nothing about."

"I know the treaty would remove him as your successor. He'd be out of the picture. The only lasting memory of Valeriya—"

"Enough."

"Did you enjoy that part of your marriage with Valeriya, too? Was 'sharing a bed' with her also not the worst fate you could conjure?"

"Neither of us wanted to have a child," he snapped, turning away from Marietta. "Valeriya saw it as her duty and—" His voice faltered. After a moment, he took a steadying breath. "Mine and Valeriya's relationship is not for discussion.

"The circumstances merit a conversation, at least." She emptied her glass. "Let's discuss your intimate relationship with Keyain—why he would believe that you were with child?"

Marietta turned and grabbed the carafe of wine, needing more alcohol to get through the conversation.

"No, you wouldn't want to speak about it. Nor would you want to answer the same questions about Tilan."

Her hand fell from the vessel, guilt twisting her heart. Silenced fell between them. Relationships were complicated enough without political strings that pulled their limbs. She set her glass to the side and turned to Wyltam. "You've made your point."

"When you agreed to our marriage, I thought you understood having an heir would be a part of it."

"A glaring oversight."

Wyltam ran a hand through his hair, pushing back the black locks that shifted into his face, the action causing a fluttering in Marietta's stomach. "We'll postpone it for as long as we can."

"The treaty states within the first decade of marriage, we need to produce an heir." Marietta gripped the railing and sighed. "Someone to rule in case we don't live the full twelve decades—which, being a half-elf, I won't."

Wyltam hushed her. "It took a few years to conceive Mycaub. Such things can be tricky. We'll lie and tell them we're trying, but claim issues with …" He gestured with his hand.

"I don't think you understand." Marietta paused, her voice soft but steady.

"There shouldn't be a postponement because I refuse to have a child.

I'm allowed that right."

The corner of his mouth ticked up as he raised his hand to her cheek. "May I?"

Breathless, she turned to face him.

The cool tips of his fingers brushed past the arch of her ears as he tucked her curls behind it. "Then we won't. I would never force you, and I will not allow the ministers to pressure you into it. We'll tell them you're incapable of conceiving."

"They'll check for that."

"The doctor will agree with what we tell them, I assure you that."

"The doctor would still know the truth."

"If I thought they'd share the truth, then I'd kill them."

Marietta jerked back her head. "You'd kill a person for doing their job?"

"No," he said, lowering his face to hers. His finger tilted her chin, angling her face toward his. "I'd kill a person if they ever posed a threat to you."

Marietta ignored how her body ached to lean into his. But killing someone? She shook her head. "No more death," she whispered. "Please."

Wyltam looked at her from eye to eye, searching for something, though she wasn't sure what. "No more death," he repeated.

"I'm sorry for pushing the subject." Marietta turned to face the garden once more.

"Such marriages are stressful," he said after a moment. "We're still navigating the boundaries of ours." His hand slipped to her waist as he stood behind her, hyperaware of his touch.

Marietta's throat tightened at the threat of tears as she turned the problem over in her mind. "Enomenos won't accept the transition time they're proposing. Half of the pilinos don't have a lifespan that long—I don't have a lifespan that long. Let alone if they'll accept our child to rule if something happened to you or I."

Wyltam furrowed his brows. "What do you propose?"

"The transition is complete upon my death. You and I will be the last queen and king of Satiros."

The proposition hung between them, Wyltam's eyes darting back and forth as he thought. "It could motivate someone to attempt another assassination to speed up the transition."

"The most likely people to murder me are the ministers who are trying to prolong the transition. They won't kill me."

"It would give Enomenos or the Exisotis reason to then."

"Not if I'm a symbol of change and peace." Marietta turned to rest a hand on Wyltam's chest, his heart beating wildly beneath her touch.

Wyltam placed his free hand over hers. "It could work."

"And what of Mycaub?"

"We'd be saving him from an ill fate."

Marietta tilted her head. "You never wanted him as your heir."

"I would never wish this burden on anyone."

Most people would kill to have the power Wyltam possessed, yet he tossed it away at every turn. Ever the enigma, Wyltam proved once again to be a puzzle where she didn't see all the intersecting pieces. At least, not yet.

Fireflies sparked around them as twilight settled over the garden. "I'll present your proposition to the next treaty planning meeting." Wyltam stepped away and part of her wished he had lingered.

Chapter Twelve

ELYSE

The hushed atmosphere of the library embraced Elyse as she trudged toward what she now considered her office. Pain still shot from every muscle as she walked.

Thankfully, Wynn moved her training to this evening, which meant she had a chance to sleep in. But another troubling dream of Azarys, which felt all too real and unsettling, cut her rest short. Having woken up earlier than expected, she had the entire morning to herself, and decided to search for Sylas's books again. He had sent her to find them for a reason, one containing the secret of the fey. Somewhere on that list included more proof—the proof she needed to bring to Wyltam. She checked the slip of paper.

Goodnight Feyries: Bedtime Stories from Feyrie Tales.
History of the Fey.
Statues and Sculptures of Syllogi.
Beyond the Tefra Forest: An Outsider's Guide to The Disputed Lands.
Aithyr and Air.
~~Lyken's Guide to Chorys Dasi.~~
Myths & Legends of the Akroi Region

After dropping her notes at the office, Elyse made her way to the top floor of the library, recalling where she had found *Fulbryk's Guide to Chorys Dasi*. While she didn't expect to find more fey books in the same place, she considered it her only starting point. Perhaps if she combed it again, she'd find one she had missed.

She scanned the titles gracing the spines of books in the low light, the soft pattering of her steps her only sound. Lost in her thoughts, she turned the corner and bumped into someone.

"Oh!" cried a woman, dropping her tomes. The golden quill brooch pinned to her chest signified her position as a librarian.

"I am so sorry," Elyse quickly said, bending to help pick up the mess. "I didn't realize anyone else was up here."

"Usually, I'm the only one," she said with a quick laugh, the lines around her eyes creasing with her smile. "Did you need help finding something, Lady Elyse?"

"No, thank you," she said at first, then thought better of it. It's been months since she found the last book. The librarian's help could speed up her search. Elyse mentally went through the list of titles, choosing one that would raise the least suspicion. "On second though, do you know where I could find books on the statues of Syllogi? I want to note which sculptures I should see for some upcoming travel."

The librarian nodded and motioned for her to follow, making small talk as they ventured to one of the librarian desks. She wrote down a section number and handed the note to Elyse. "Don't hesitate to ask for help if you need something, Lady Elyse. You're one of the few nobles who values this place as much as us librarians."

Elyse ventured back into the bookcases, considering the librarian's final swords. Due to the copious amount of time Elyse had spent in the library over the years, they knew who she was long before her rise in station. At one point, becoming one of them would have been a dream. Now, with the knowledge of magic and fey, she couldn't imagine her life being confined to the library.

Her mind dwelled on the thought as she searched, and she saw it halfway through the second location: *Statues and Sculptures of Syllogi*. Her heart flipped in her chest as she rushed back to her office.

She first checked for blank pages at the center, her heart sinking when she found none. All pages were accounted for and from a quick glance, there were no notes in the margins. Knowing she had some time before her meetings that afternoon, she dove into the book.

While the other titles in the section focused on specific statues throughout Syllogi, this was entirely different. The first chapter proposed a theory of where the statues originated, stating that they were not made by a living person's hands—human, elven, or otherwise. While she had heard of the theory prior to this, she never gave it much thought. The statues were akin to any part of the palace; she never thought of who built it. They always existed.

A few weeks ago, Elyse would have dismissed the book altogether. Yet with the truth of Chorys Dasi coming to light, she knew the book had to have some validity. It noted that these statues would remain in pristine condition, citing other sculptures carved by artists deteriorated over the years due to the elements of nature. No one knew why the statues remained unmarred, but many believed it was due to aithyr.

The most popular belief was that the stone was naturally rich in aithyr. However, many mages and geologists over the years couldn't prove if the magic originated in the rock or if it retained it. Another belief was that a mage enchanted the statues. Whether mages used aithyr before they were carved or after remained unknown. However, none of these possibilities covered the level of detail in the sculptures.

Her heart stopped when she got to the last theory, reading once. Twice. A third for good measure. With the belief that all elves descended from the fey, the elven held an old notion that the feyries gifted statues to their descendants as a reminder of their origins. While this explained the statues consistent theme of fey beings, there was no written history of this occurring. But then again, there was also no written history of the fey ... unless Elyse uncovered it through her fey blood.

Her mind reeled as she gathered her notes and departed for her afternoon meeting. She had enough time to visit her favorite statues in the Central Garden.

Elyse made her way through the paths, ensuring that no one followed. She stepped into the bed of yarrow, anemone, and oleander, coursing her way to the small clearing that sat beyond a row of lilac bushes. A gentle breeze blew a strand across her eyes, and she tucked it behind her ear as she ducked to inspect the five tiny statues of winged pixies. Their limbs were of delicate stone, thin and fragile, with nearly translucent wings protruding from their backs.

Moments of her childhood came flooding back. In her youth, she had named them all and had created stories of adventures they would go on together. There were five in total, and each one had their own personality. She tried to recall any further details but her memory fell short, as did most things did from that period of her life. It had been around when her mother's illness worsened.

Elyse touched the head of a pixy as she pulled aithyr into her body. The energy coursed into her and flickered under her skin. As she went to drop it, a single pulse tapped into her fingertip. Curious, she focused on the aithyr and imagined pulling it through the body of the pixie. And …

Nothing happened.

Elyse released a long, slow exhale, her shoulders sagging. Despite expecting it, she couldn't rid herself of the sting of disappointment.

The sensation lingered as she made her way to her meetings, her mind circling on the statues and the possibilities of what each theory could mean if proven true. Why had Sylas added this book to his list? He clearly wanted her to search for *The History of Chorys Dasi* because it gave her the truth about Azarys. What did the statues have to do with any of it? The answer remained elusive, as if she possessed many of the pieces but not enough to solve the mystery. The statue hadn't reacted to aithyr, so why involve these theories?

As her current meeting concluded, Wyltam stood and asked, "Do you have a moment? There's something we need to discuss."

Her heart stopped at his words. "Of course, Your Grace," she said, expecting him to continue.

"Not here."

The king spun toward the door, and Elyse followed him through the halls to his public offices. Was it that obvious that she wasn't paying attention? Perhaps he noticed her mind wandering while Minister Gordyn discussed the maintenance details of the north river gate. In her defense, he once again went into excruciating detail about what masonry needed repair.

As she settled into the chair in his office, Wyltam finally glanced at her, drawing his brows together. "You're panicked and for what reason?"

"It won't happen again," she said, rubbing the sweat from her palms into her lap. "I promise next time to keep my mind focused on every meeting—"

Wyltam laughed, his expression forming an uncharacteristic smile. "Minister Gordyn is zealous about infrastructure and often forgets that his audience is not. You were not the only person he lost during that meeting."

Elyse sighed with relief. "Then is something the matter?"

"Less of a matter and more of an inquiry." Wyltam moved to stand by the window behind his desk. "With the war, I've been devising strategies to benefit our soldiers and those from Enomenos." He turned to her. "Both Chorys Dasi and Reyila will have mages on their side. Because of my mother's fear of being overpowered, Satiros has a small reserve of magic users for the guards that I have not been able to grow during my reign. As for the Enomenoan soldiers, it's safe to assume that they have no mages."

"While time is not on our side, I want to create a team that focuses on special projects around aithyr-infused objects." Wyltam pulled a light globe from his pocket and set it adrift in front of him. "Instead of domestic items, I'd like to develop objects that can either diffuse the enemy's magic or indicate which soldiers are mages."

Wyltam lit the light globe as Elyse stood and crossed the room to him. "Aithyr objects as weapons?" Her stomach twisted at the thought.

"Only if necessary, but we're quite far from resorting to those types of tools. For now, I want my team to focus on simple prototypes, then that you'll develop into tactical arms. The first project is a set of glasses that allows the wearer to see aithyr streams."

Elyse hesitated. "Like when people take Mage's Eye."

Wyltam nodded. "Without the harmful addiction properties."

"Has anyone done that before?"

"I have an artificer who has already made headway in infusing glass with aithyr in a way that makes it visible to the wearer."

Her mind reeled. "I want to see that for myself."

"You will if you accept my invitation to be on this team."

"I can barely use aithyr to enhance my senses," she stammered, heat rising to her cheeks with the admission. "Has Wynn not told you about my latest practices?"

"You wouldn't be aithyr-smithing." He leaned against the window frame as he met her gaze. "I need someone I know I can trust involved in the conversation. The artificer will believe you're there to help draw the prototypes. What you must covertly do is keep me updated with your progress and ensure they don't stray from the items I request."

Elyse glanced at her hands as her excitement hedged. Between mage training and her responsibilities as the king's administrator, when would she have time? "Are you sure you want me for this? What about Wynn?"

"Wynn and the other mages will be busy with other tasks in the coming months. Your schedule is also quite full, so please take on the workload you can handle. Declining this project will not cause me to hold any grudge against you."

Elyse nodded. She could do actual magic work with a real mage, not just basic lessons and dreadful training. Between sessions with Wynn and her meetings, what free time she had remaining was to hunt down the books from her list. Didn't that take precedent over everything?

Yes, but she could learn a great deal from this artificer. Perhaps growing her understanding of aithyr would fill in the missing pieces.

"You don't have to decide now—"

"Yes, I accept."

With the extra responsibility on her plate and the book search leading to more questions than answers, Elyse found herself thankful for her evening training session with Wynn. Sweat stung in her eyes as she lunged, her thighs burning and knees threatening to buckle. She gasped as she ran for her last lap around the Mage Pit.

Wyltam continued to put more trust into her, but doubt lingered. Could she live up to the expectation? What happened if she failed? Her mouth dried at the thought. She had never drawn for anyone except …

Az willed his way into her head like an unwanted visitor, her already-tired body becoming heavier as she stumbled and came to a stop. Did he save her drawings as she had with his letters? They were hidden. But sometimes, in the quiet hours of the night when she couldn't shake thoughts of him, she read them in the safety of her bed.

Guilt tightened her throat as her stomach lurched. She could imagine his deep, rolling voice calling her goddess as if he had actually been there. She hung her head in shame, resting her hands on her thighs.

Wynn jogged to her side. "Getting tired?"

"I'm all right," she answered, her voice shaking.

Elyse stood and took an unsteady step forward. Wynn's hand caught her wrist. "Let's take a break."

Elyse shook her head. Quitting now wouldn't help her. Since Wyltam had placed his trust in her, her life had grown full. It's why she knew she could never become a librarian. A quiet life was as damning as it was enticing.

As she went to move again, Wynn gripped her shoulder. Conceding, Elyse lowered herself to the floor, falling onto to her back. She stared at the rocky ceiling, blinking back her tears.

Wynn sat next to her. "Something on your mind?"

Elyse shook her head and closed her eyes. She couldn't share her thoughts with him. Who would understand that she still thought of Az when he was a murderer? Except Wynn didn't know that—he believed Az was the disguised prince of their enemies. Tears trailed down her cheeks.

"There it is," Wynn said, wiping one away. "Are you overwhelmed? We've put a lot on your shoulders."

Elyse drew a deep breath, calming herself. "I'm fine."

"You aren't, but you don't have to tell me everything."

Elyse opened her eyes, her vision blurry from the welling emotion. Hesitantly, Wynn stroked her hair back from her face, his touch gentle and welcoming.

"But holding it in doesn't help," he said. "The amount that you've taken on in the past months is impressive, you know. If it's too much—"

"For the first time in my life, I have purpose." Elyse swallowed hard. "Please don't take it away from me."

"I won't," he murmured. "Are you thinking about the Chorys Dasian?"

An ache formed in the back of her throat, silencing her lie.

"For what it's worth, you can do better."

Elyse gawked at him, surprised.

"Prince or not, he was a heartless, arrogant prick who went out of his way to be trouble." He shook his head. "You are talented and kind. You make choices that will better the world. He is actively making it a worse place for people to live."

With each word, Elyse's tears eased and her guard dropped little by little. He hadn't scorned her for still having these feelings for him. Would he if he knew the truth? That he had brutally murdered pilinos?

Wynn stood and offered her his hand. She grasped it and rose, holding his hand longer than she ought to have as she appreciated the roughness of his palm, the connectedness to him. Elyse hesitated, then threw her arms around him and buried her face into his chest. "Thank you," she whispered.

"Anything for you." He cupped the back of her head as he embraced her back.

Standing there in the middle of the fighting pit with only the sound of Wynn's heartbeat, a sense a peace washed over her. Az didn't deserve her, which she already knew, but hearing it from Wynn cemented the idea in her head.

Chapter Thirteen

AMRYTH

"I heard her acting was atrocious."

"You must have heard that from someone kind."

Amryth's parents' friends laughed at the joke, the male continuing.

"Zoi clearly didn't possess the required skills to carry such an impertinent character to the story."

"They set her up to fail. I've heard that story a hundred times over at this point."

Amryth absently nodded along with the other guests, half-listening as they discussed the most recent play at the Randylph Theater. She almost forgot how much she hated these gatherings.

She usually left when the drinking got out of hand, but without commitments the next morning, she had no excuse to leave early. Thus, she endured her parents' wealthy acquaintances, who only befriended her parents to bolster their status. For years, her parents basked in Amryth's success, ignoring their own humble origins. Alcohol often dulled the truth for them.

One of their friends went on a rant about the costume designs. Amryth stifled an eye roll, turning her focus to the other room where her parents sat with other guests, hoping it would be more interesting.

"They forget their place!" someone yelled.

Another shushed them

"You suddenly have a gentle heart for them?"

A few chuckles sounded.

"Amryth will get upset and I want her to stay," her mother said, her voice dropping.

A cold sweat broke out over her body as she excused herself from the table, feigning going to the restroom. She paused in the hallway, having an easier spot to listen.

"Too bold for my liking, asking for more money for the same work they've always done." There was the clinking of glass. "Ever since that *pilinos* arrived at court, our society has been declining."

"And making her our new queen, right after the gracious Queen Valeriya was murdered?" There was a murmur that went through the room in agreement.

"Let alone the treaty with the mixed cities and that anti-elven group," a new voice added. "Do they expect us to be comfortable with that?"

"I don't mind it, honestly," someone said. "But will there be a loss of pride when it comes to King Wyltam, our *elven* king? Now that I fear."

"They keep forcing it in our faces that she'll be a *pilinos* queen. The more they point it out, the more the pilinos will get riled up."

Amryth forced her jaw to unclench as she leaned against the wall. These were all arguments she had heard whispers of in the palace but never spoken so plainly.

"Hopefully she follows in the steps of her predecessors, if you know what I mean." The chatter in the room died down.

After a brief silence, Amryth's father steered the conversation in a new direction. By the time the topic changed, Amryth had reached the door of their townhouse and stepped into the late summer evening.

Part of her longed to go back inside and unleash her frustration at their narrow-mindedness. Her parents had welcomed pilinos into their lives for years, but now, their circle had grown closed. Trying to reason with them would be akin to teaching a cat to swim—an arduous task that might cause more harm than good if they even grasped the concept at all.

Amryth stepped out into the night, her mind heavy with the divide between elves and pilinos. She shoved her hands into her pockets and took a slow, deep inhale. The tension between the groups simmered, fueled by Jory's arrest, and with the war approaching, internal conflict seemed unavoidable.

Silence now served no one; inaction would only deepen the wounds. Taking King Wyltam's directive seriously meant securing the release of an innocent pilinos before more blood stained her hands.

Yet one obstacle stood in her way: Deania. Small and bubbly, Deania would likely be upset after what happened at the Honeysuckle. How many elves had betrayed Deania's trust in the past? She might now see Amryth as another disappointment, or worse, someone who used her.

She sighed as she crossed Oak Boulevard and cut through a park, pausing at the griffin statue that divided her path home. Regardless if Deania thought Amryth was too assertive or controlling, she at least deserved an explanation.

Amryth fidgeted with Deyra's notebook in her pocket. While it had become a source of comfort the last few months, it did nothing to ease the dread coiling in her gut. She imagined Deania's tear-filled eyes, envisioning her expressing to Amryth that she was disrespectful and had no right. Even though it would be difficult to sit through, Amryth waited quietly outside the tea shop for Deania, hoping there would be some way to fix this.

"Hey you."

Amryth spun at the sound of Deania's voice. Instead of Therypon blue, she wore a blouse with a wild array of oranges and yellows.

"Thanks for meeting me," Amryth managed as her mouth went dry.

"About gods damn time," she said with a pout. The wind caught the dark loose strands of hair that fell from her knot. "Care to explain why you suddenly decided to ignore me?" She looped her arm through Amryth's and led her into the shop.

The earthy and floral scents hit them as they approached the circular bar at the center of the building where patrons could order. Small tables dotted the first floor. The second overlooked them with the sound of soft chattering falling over its edge. They ordered and found a seat.

Though the chairs were plush, Amryth shifted uncomfortably under Deania's unusually serious gaze. She said nothing, as if she waited for Amryth to speak.

"How have you been?" Amryth asked.

Deania fidgeted with Therypon's symbol hanging from her neck, her only sign that she was an attendant. "Not much to complain about. Had tea with Marietta. She sends her love, though she mentioned you abandoned her."

Amryth cringed and went to speak, but Deania continued.

"Besides that, the only thing is that you've been avoiding me."

She took a second to breathe as guilt twisted her stomach. "I didn't mean to."

"But you did—avoid me, that is."

The shop worker placed a tea set before them. Amryth thanked him and poured Deania a cup. Deania nodded, tipping an excessive amount of sugar into the tea—far more than Amryth deemed reasonable. Usually, Amryth would have chastised Deania's sugar-laden diet, but the words wouldn't come.

Why couldn't she speak?

"I did hear something interesting, though." Deania paused, taking a sip. She scrunched her face and stirred in additional sugar. "Someone stopped by the temple this week." She batted her lashes, drawing more attention to her large brown eyes.

Amryth nodded as she drank, savoring the earthy richness on her tongue before swallowing.

"Old friend of mine, actually."

Amryth's stomach dropped. "Wait."

"She congratulated me on my new relationship."

Amryth set down her cup. "I can explain."

"Imagine my confusion, considering I'm not in one."

"I'm sorry—"

"And they told me that my partner, Amryth, seemed delightful."

"I wasn't in the right headspace," Amryth said. "I shouldn't have said it."

Finally, Deania broke into a smile as she tossed her head back and laughed, a dimple forming on her right cheek. Amryth couldn't break her stare. "I don't think I've ever seen you distraught over something as ridiculous as that."

"You aren't mad?"

"I'm mad that you ignored me!" Deania leaned forward, her eyes gleaming. "I don't care about you telling people we're together. I mean, I would want to be with me too. Although I would prefer an explanation."

Amryth hesitated. "I was at the Honeysuckle."

"Gathered that." She rested her chin on her hand as she propped herself on the table.

"A potential lead into the case I'm investigating. I thought I'd check and see what I find."

Deania shook her head.

"I know it's ridiculous … "

"What's ridiculous is that you're doing it alone."

Amryth furrowed her brows.

Deania savored her tea and sat back with a smile. "Where do we go next?"

"*We* don't go anywhere." Amryth crossed her arms.

"I don't need protection," Deania said. "For all I've been through, a little investigation is nothing. Plus, I owe it to them."

Amryth's gut said no, not wanting to involve Deania getting any closer to the person who killed pilinos. However, there was logic to it. Deania could find her own closure and having a pilinos to talk to witnesses in Rambler Grove could help. The notes King Wyltam sent contained the names of victims, their friends, and their last known whereabouts. What the guards had struggled to get was additional information on the victims themselves—what had they done for work, where they went in their free time. Unsurprisingly, none of the pilinos wanted to talk to the guard.

Amryth sighed. "Only if you promise to not look into anything without me." So she could keep her safe. So no one would hurt her, too.

"Same to you." Deania added another spoonful of sugar to her tea. "We're partners in this, both for the investigation and while we get information from my friends."

Partners. The word left her heart thudding a little too fast, her head a little too dizzy. Amryth nodded, knowing they were terms she could accept. "Deal."

By the time Deania left Amryth's apartment, the sun had long set. After going through the notes, they took a break for the night and agreed to reconvene the following afternoon. That's how Amryth found herself in Deania's office, moving a stack of books to a different cluttered heap so she could sit on the overstuffed couch. She shook her head, not because of Deania's typical disarray with her belongings, but because of the reckless idea she had. "*You* want to go talk to him?"

"I sure do!" Deania plopped a pile of papers onto the coffee table, swearing under her breath as they fell to the floor. She shrugged and sat across from Amryth. "Dyadic Tapya is one of our only leads."

"And he could be a murderer. You want to go to his house and—"

"Not his house—his place of employment," Deania said. "He should be at the brothel as soon as the sun sets."

"Tonight?" Amryth wiped her face, her limbs feeling heavy. "Can we think about it?"

"I've already asked around about where he works. Better to go before he hears we're trying to find him."

"And there's no way I can talk you out of this?"

Deania flashed her a grin. "Not a chance."

That evening, they ventured to the south side of Bud Town near the river. While brothels could be found in every district, the ones in Bud Town didn't attract the best characters. What else would she expect from a murderer?

While the rest of Bud Town quieted for the evening, Fully Street came alive. Tonight was no exception. Deania had convinced Amryth to walk with a slouch. Dark makeup covered her eyelids, her lips painted into a bright red slash. Gaudy, but necessary. She blended in with the crowds. Even with such precaution, lingering stares pressed into Amryth as she and Deania as they made their way to the brothel, River's Bottom.

Outside the establishment stood two burly males who watched them as they approached, the one placing a hand on the hilt of a sword. "Evening. Do you have an appointment?"

"I do, with Dyadic," Deania said, trying and failing to hide the eagerness in her voice. She was almost as bad at lying as Marietta.

The enforcer eyed them before leaning toward the door and knocking. It cracked open, and he covered his mouth with his hand as he spoke to someone indoors. He shrugged, then ushered them in.

The humid air in the dimly lit interior was a shroud hanging around Amryth's head, heavily perfumed with jasmine and musk. Grunts and whispers came from darkened corners as they made their way through the first floor. A worker dressed in gauzy clothing slipped past them carrying a tray of drinks and other objects she didn't want to look too closely at. She caught Deania's grin at her reaction. Amryth glowered and followed their escort to another room thick with pungent smoke, stopping at a drawn velvet curtain.

While she had never visited a brothel, she'd heard enough stories. Rich silks in the hot months, luscious furs in the cooler ones. Companions who provided emotional and mental comfort, helping guards gain a calm and focused mindset. They must have never set foot in River's Bottom.

A disheveled elven male with greasy blond hair lounged at the center of the alcove. His rough face appeared puzzled as he eyed Amryth and Deania when they stepped through.

"You're not my usual type of client." He gestured them to sit. "Makes me wonder why two lovely females scheduled an urgent appointment on my busiest evening."

"Thank you for taking the time," Deania said as they took a seat. "We aren't here for your services."

"But paying?" he asked with raised brows.

"Paying, of course."

"Then why come?"

Deania glanced at Amryth and said, "You might be of some use to us."

Suspicion flickered in his eyes as he sat up straighter. "I won't sell to pilinos."

Clearly offended, Deania went to snap back when Amryth shushed her. After decades of being in the guard, she knew what he meant by 'won't sell to pilinos.'

"Drakon root?" Amryth asked.

Dyadic licked his lips. "I don't sell it, but if I did, I wouldn't sell to you either if you're together."

"We're not interested in getting high." The type of mandrake root was outlawed in Satiros. Elves could get a strong high except the margin of lethality was slim—and was even slimmer for pilinos.

Deania settled back but Dyadic's gaze narrowed on Amryth. "If not root or sex, then this meeting is even more odd. You have a minute before I take your gold and throw you out."

Amryth weighed her choices. If Dyadic cared enough to not sell a dangerous drug to pilinos, there was a chance he wasn't involved in the murders—or he used it as a convincing cover. Most likely, he didn't appreciate his clients dying from his goods. Being that he was their only lead, Amryth considered the risk of being up front with him.

"We're looking into the pilinos murders," Amryth said, Deania going still at her side.

Dyadic cocked his head. "Two civilians digging into the biggest blight on our city-state in recent years … how noble. Why are you *here?*"

Amryth recalled the notes. "Someone mentioned you may have seen something related to them."

"They must have been lying."

Amryth leaned forward. "I don't think they were."

Dyadic toyed with the drink in his hand. "I can't recall talking about the murders with anyone."

"We'll double what we're paying," Deania said, her eyes ablaze.

Amryth went to shush her again when Dyadic said, "Fine. Around the time of the murders, I had a customer searching for substances I definitely didn't deal, and he asked about a friend named Berlena. Told him nothing, sold him less. She disappeared two nights later, and they found her body a day after that."

"I'm sorry for your loss," Amryth said, blood thumping in her veins. "Did you catch your client's name?"

"Did I ask you for yours?" He pulled out a pipe that was already packed. "I don't ask for details of my clients; I use discretion."

"Understandable. Did you see anything that would distinguish him? Anything we can follow up on?"

Dyadic lit his pipe and inhaled, waiting a moment before blowing out the smoke. "He kept his face covered. I only know he was an elf because I made him show me his ears. If I did sell root, I wouldn't have sold to—"

"Pilinos, yes. I got that," Amryth said. "What he was wearing? His height? Hair color?"

He shrugged. "Hard to tell height when I'm sitting. Didn't see his hair, and he wore a cloak that obscured his frame."

"Do you remember what it was made of?" Even knowing a material could be another clue.

"Why in all the hells would I remember that?"

"A no would suffice," Deania chimed in.

"And his voice?" Amryth asked. "I'm assuming he talked."

Dyadic nodded. "He did, though briefly. He had a slight accent that I couldn't place."

Amryth sat up straighter with that. "What kind of accent? A Chorys Dasian lilt? Or more angular, like a Kyaerian accent?"

"More restrained, as if he hid his accent. And you're out of time." He clapped his hands, and an enforcer appeared to pull back the curtain. "Don't come here again."

While his voice remained cheery, the warning was clear. Deania and Amryth paid and made their exit from the brothel.

"That was a complete waste. Why did the guards even have him as a suspect?" Deania crossed her arms as they made their way back toward the temple.

"Because he sells drakon root. They've been trying to eradicate from Satiros for a few years," she said. "It wasn't a total loss of an evening. We did learn something."

"What? That a guy with maybe an accent asked for a pilinos who ended up dead?"

Amryth shook her head. "That the murderer searched for specific pilinos—he went and asked for her by name, meaning the victims from Chorys Dasi were selected for a reason." Amryth paused, meeting Deania's gaze. "We also have our first lead that proves an elf had been searching for one of the victims in the days leading up to her murder. Even if Jory's ears could pass as an elf's, Dyadic is the type of person who pays attention, if only to cover his own ass. Now, we have an unnamed suspect with no facial details."

"That's assuming the male was one of the murderers."

"Regardless if he was, why would someone go to the lengths to disguise his body, hide his face and voice to ask about a person who died two days later?"

Deania sighed. "Too many what ifs."

"What ifs are better than nothing. We can follow this. I'm just not sure what our next move will be."

"I think I do." Deania turned to her abruptly. "How well can you act?"

Chapter Fourteen
MARIETTA

Marietta pressed a single key on the piano, gasping with delight when the deep, rich note echoed through the room. "I haven't seen one if these in years." She turned to her guard, who trailed her through the Royal's Wing. "Do any of you know if Queen Valeriya played?"

"Unsure, but Wyltam does," Sibylla, one of the mages, answered as she inspected the scrollwork on the side of the instrument. "One of his more princely traits I would tease him for."

Marietta frowned, her fingers tracing the keys. She hadn't known he could play. "When did you get to know him? Did you two grow up together?" Curious that she referred to it as princely instead of kingly.

Tolis walked up and gestured, Marietta only catching a few of the words despite trying to learn hand speak. Sibylla laughed and said, "He is a graceful dancer, if you can convince him to do it. Also wicked fencer before he left court, though we only saw the remnants of that."

Marietta's frown deepened. She longed to see Wyltam play the piano, to hear the style of music he played. The realization formed a knot in her stomach. "I find that hard to believe."

Coryn joined her side and ran his finger along the instrument's smooth surface. "He doesn't strike me as a musical type."

Sibylla's smile was playful as she glanced at Marietta. "Wyltam has a way of surprising people, especially when he lets his guard down."

If he ever let his guard down. Wyltam could kiss her hand or make a flirtatious comment, but he could never share a piece of himself. The thought was troubling.

As they left the music room, Marietta couldn't help but wonder what else Wyltam hid, not that she expected him to reveal much.

Sleep eluded Marietta that evening. She lay awake on the floor, her back aching. The shadowy silhouette of Valeriya's bed canopy loomed in the dim room, a reminder of who should have been there. Her thoughts wandered to Wyltam—imagining him wielding a rapier, playing the piano, and interacting with his mother. It was startling how little she knew about the man she was about to marry.

Marietta rolled onto her side, her body resting uncomfortably on the hard floor. She sighed again and shifted to her back. The cold stone leached through her thin blankets, leaving her skin chilled despite the late summer heat.

A faint creak and footsteps echoed from within the suite. Was Wyltam returning this late? Curious, she padded out to the hallway and knocked once before pushing open his office door.

Wyltam blinked slowly at her arrival. A band held his hair away from his face as he glanced up from the contents on his desk. His jacket hung over the back of his chair, the top buttons of his shirt left open in a casualness she had yet to see from him. Wyltam's stare darted down her body, then sharply returned to her face. "You should be asleep."

Marietta's stomach fluttered as his gaze met hers, but she couldn't ignore the shadows deepening beneath his eyes. She crossed the room, toying with a curl that escaped her silk scarf enwrapping her hair. "Same to you."

She took one of the overstuffed chairs before his desk, nearly groaning at their softness. This was a chair she could fall asleep in.

"There's much to work on," he answered after a moment, his stare lingering more on her than the book in front of him.

"What could possibly be more important than sleep at this hour?"

Wyltam lifted the book, Marietta only getting a glimpse of the title. *The History of—*

"History books hardly count as work."

"It's for something I'm working on when I have the time which I have little of these days."

Marietta nodded in acknowledgment, letting the silence wash over them. Peaceful, enjoyable even. Her lids grew heavy as she tucked her legs up onto the seat, her mind drifting. Fighting back her exhaustion, Marietta channeled Therypon's pain domain and sent a small crackle of energy into her arm to jolt her awake. She closed her eyes at the murmuring voice in her head, there a moment and gone the next.

"The Council of Ministers agreed to your change," Wyltam said at last, drawing her attention. "There's no need for an heir."

"They can think logically."

Wyltam offered a small laugh. "Mycaub will be returning to the suite after the treaty. Apparently citizens fear we'll harm the child since he's Reyilan, which we would never do."

Her shoulders tightened at the thought of Valeriya's mourning son. He'd become another constant reminder of her death, as if replacing her in all other aspects of life wasn't enough. "Did all the ministers voted in favor of my proposal?"

"More than I had expected."

Marietta pinned him to the spot with a look. "You didn't think my idea was good enough?"

"I'm surprised at some of the ministers who were in favor. Few were open to the idea of us being the last royals definitively. At least it kept us from having a tie since we still haven't named a new minister of foreign relations."

"It seems ill-fated that the position is open amid treaty negotiations."

Wyltam glanced away, a sign that she prodded a sore point. "I'm aware. The role needs to be filled, yet we are still investigating the branch. It's tough to know who partook in Gyrsh's betrayal and who's innocent."

Marietta nodded her head. It was a position she didn't envy given all that happened.

"I think the ministers and I have agreed on a person, but they may have aided Gyrsh's treachery."

Marietta watched as he furrowed his brows as he concentrated on the documents. "Fear fuels indecision," she said, pulling his attention. "Are you unsure, or are you afraid to decide?"

"Perhaps both." Wyltam's lips ticked downward. "You'll excel at being queen if you possess such intuition."

"If I'm allowed to have such a say. Not all your ministers will agree with me."

Wyltam leaned forward, his voice low and thoughtful. "What's intriguing is that I had intended to offer a place at court if your trial had ended differently," he said. "Before you intervened on your fate."

Marietta arched an eyebrow, meeting his gaze evenly. "You know as well as I do they would have never accepted me willingly."

"The Shepherd's position would have helped, but even then, you stood for more. Since the moment Keyain announced you were his pilinos wife, you've been a symbol for change." Wyltam's expression softened. "I was not going to let you go."

Marietta offered a returning smile. "You're getting your symbol then."

He nodded. "Provided we get a crown on your head."

"You'll have to ensure that happens then."

"You'd have to be dead for it not to."

"How about I don't die, because I quite enjoy living."

Wyltam chuckled. "Trust me, I've grown fond of you and would prefer if you lived."

Marietta wouldn't meet his gaze, instead focusing on the paper on his desk. It was too late to discern if he was flirting to keep her complacent or if it was something deeper.

"Elven citizens are split on your ascension. Those who are devout to the temples support you. Many are indifferent and don't see it as a threat, nor see it as a boon. There's also a group campaigning against your reign, gaining more followers than what's comfortable."

"I'm more surprised that people are in favor." Marietta rubbed her eye, wishing her tiredness would clear.

"There's also the added complication of the pilinos murders."

Her heart stopped. "What do you mean?"

"We found the murderer," he said, his dark stare landing on her. "He's been arrested."

"You found..." The room begun to spin.

"A pilinos born and raised in Satiros."

Marietta tried to mask her surprise. "A pilinos?"

It had to be a lie. They had an eyewitness state people with horns and wings attacked them, then they found that exact depiction in *Lyken's Guide to Chorys Dasi*. It couldn't be a coincidence. Suddenly, the list of books Elyse wanted to find seemed ever more important.

"Allegedly. I have my doubts. Many do."

She examined Wyltam, trying to read his face. His expression remained carefully blank, leaving her uncertain of his thoughts. She didn't think he was lying, but his words still left her uneasy. Narrowing her gaze, she asked, "When will they go to trial?"

"Not until after the wedding. Given the unrest in the city, I thought it wise to hold off until your crowning. No need to add another layer to the mess."

Marietta bit the inside of her lip. She could tell him now, about Azarys and the portraits of fey, breaking her promise to Elyse. An innocent man could go to prison, or worse. But would Wyltam believe her?

"I know that look in your eye," Wyltam said, drawing her back. "We have too many fires to watch. Please refrain from getting involved." She opened her mouth to argue, but he cut her off. "I'm on your side. Though things aren't great for him with what they found in his home, I am working to have a more thorough investigation in the situation. So please, for the sake of my lack of sleep, I ask you to not add to my worries."

At the sight of him rubbing his eyes, Marietta relented. For the moment. "I won't but it's hard to believe the right thing will be done, your promise or not."

Wyltam sighed and stood and crossed the room, opening one of the cabinets lining the back wall. He removed an unmarked glass bottle filled with clear liquid. A set of glasses clinked in his hand as he returned, uncorking the bottle to pour the drink then handed one to Marietta.

The sweet scent of the liquor brought her back to holidays spent with her parents. To chilled winter nights surrounded by neighbors. To milestone celebrations over the years with friends. Marietta blinked, trying and failing to hide her surprise. "Firewater? How and why do you have this?" It was more than a spirit—it was an Enomenoan ritual.

"I have an old friend who distills it." Wyltam sunk back into his seat and kept his eyes on her. "Trust that I'll find a way to save Jory because I don't believe he's the murderer." He raised his glass.

Marietta wanted to raise hers, wanted to believe he shared the truth, but an uneasiness formed in her chest.

Wyltam lowered his glass with a frown. "Satiros will become like every other city-state in Enomenos. You and I will still rule, but I fully intend to follow the laws and regulations of Enomenos early on. As soon as we sign the treaty, every Satiroan pilinos will have all the freedom as those from your home." He swirled the liquid in his glass. "I never wanted to be a king, to rule. I'm not cut out for it, nor do I enjoy it. But for the first time, I see myself appreciating it because you will be at my side." Wyltam took a sip of his drink.

Marietta tried her firewater, the burn chasing away the sensation in her chest. In her gut, she knew he was telling the truth, or at least partially. "That's all fine and well, but it's hard to trust someone I know nothing about."

"What would you like to know?"

Marietta glanced down at her glass. "Fencing? Piano? What other *princely* traits do you possess?"

Closing his eyes with a sigh, Wyltam said, "Sibylla talks too much. Playing the piano helps me think through my problems. Fencing was a requirement of every royal."

"I can hardly imagine you wielding a sword."

"Enlighten me." His lips twitched into a smirk. "What do you normally imagine me wielding?"

Marietta's pulse quickened as she imagined his insinuation and threw back her drink. "Don't deflect, even with entertaining innuendos."

He huffed a laugh into his glass. "Fencing influenced my fighting style after leaving court." Marietta waited for him to speak further, but when he didn't, she motioned for him to continue. "I left around the time of the Orc Skirmishes to train under a mage mentor with the Circle of Mages. The Circle is an organization committed to teaching future mages magic in an ethical and moral way."

Marietta furrowed her brows. "You just left?"

"My mother was grateful to have me gone. However, I did miss playing piano."

"You're going to go back to piano after admitting you left court to be a mage?" Marietta laughed. "No offense, but knowing more about your time away at court is more interesting."

"Perhaps." Wyltam sat down his glass and leaned forward. "But you wanted to know about me. Piano clears my head. There's a finite beginning and end to music. A set of rules and instructions to follow. A system. Playing helps when I can't solve a problem or my mind is restless."

She clung to the explanation, her precious reward, and stored it to memory. "I'd love to hear you play sometime."

"I don't perform for people."

"Nor would I expect you to. But you get this look in your eye when you're thinking. I wonder how it changes when you play."

Wyltam grew silent as Marietta shifted in the chair, her sleepiness edging back in. Not wanting to nod off, she reached for the goddess's energy under her skin and sent pain through her arm once more. For a moment, her vision went hazy and her head fell back to the chair.

"What's that about?" Marietta glanced up at Wyltam, who raised a brow and gesturing to her arm. "You've done it twice now."

"A little trick I learned to keep myself awake."

"How does it work? Is it a single jolt of pain dependent on duration? Or can you control how painful it is?"

"Honestly, I don't know how it works. I haven't had a chance to train formally." Marietta stared at her hands. "Coryn said there was a palace temple at some point?"

"It's been closed since the start of my mother's reign."

"I'm going to reopen it."

Wyltam lifted a brow. "Oh?"

"Seems fitting for an iros queen. Plus the temples and pilinos are so closely related. It'll be good for court to have exposure to both."

Wyltam sat back and regarded her for a moment. "I heard you had the temples here for tea. Bold decision. You don't strike me as devout."

"I have this connection to a goddess I know nothing about. Somehow I'm her chosen?" She rubbed Therypon's mark tattooed on her neck. "At the very least, its garnered some positive attention from citizens."

"I've heard." Wyltam grew quiet a moment, then said, "Be careful. Explore what you need to explore, but remember they are organizations with their own agendas."

Marietta placed a hand over her chest. "Aw, you do care about me."

His expression turned tense. "Deeply."

The air between them thickened, and she swallowed hard.

Wyltam frowned as he finished his drink and set it down with a thud. "You should go back to sleep."

Marietta stood with a stretch, the skin of her stomach showing as her shirt rose. Wyltam's eyes locked onto it. "Only if you promise to get some sleep too," she said, drawing his attention.

"I will soon. There's just one last thing I'd like to do." His stare dipped momentarily to her body before returning to her face.

Marietta's smile sharpened as her stomach heated. "And what would that be?"

Wyltam's fingers twitched as he raised his hand, and she imagined them gripping her thighs, his head straddled by her legs. He tapped the open book on the desk. "Finishing the notes on what I was reading prior to your visit."

"That's all?"

Wyltam's smile made her want to melt into a pool of herself. "Goodnight, Marietta."

She lingered another moment, refusing to adhere to his dismissal before turning for the door. When she glanced back at the doorway, catching his stare rising up her body. "Good to know that I'm still not at the top of your to-do list."

She could hear his chuckle as she closed the door behind her, only adding to her smile.

Chapter Fifteen
KEYAIN

Sunlight streamed through the tall windows, casting long shadows across the polished wood table. Keyain's fingers drummed a silent rhythm as he scanned the recruitment record once more, his jaw tightening with each disappointing line. The numbers remained stubbornly low, a stark reminder of their faltering efforts.

Around the table, the guard's leadership exchanged uneasy glances, their concern mirroring his own. Wyltam leaned back in his chair, his eyes narrowing as he considered the figures before him. Elyse, ever composed, sat with her hands folded, her gaze shifting between Keyain and the rest of the room.

Commander Walyn's fist hit the table with a dull thud, rattling the few untouched goblets of water. "We need them in the countryside," he insisted, his voice a low growl. "If we lose control of the outskirts, it won't matter how fortified the city walls are."

General Hastyrn shook his head, a sneer curling his lips. "But if we can't hold our army units together, we're defenseless against our enemies. Two fronts, remember? Those recruits belong with us."

Keyain knew this argument; it had played out countless times before. He glanced at the sparse recruitment ledger on the table, the stark reality of their dwindling forces staring back at him.

"Enough." Keyain's voice cut through the heated exchange. "We need a solution, not more bickering."

Keyain had witnessed the savagery of Chorys Dasi's fighting style during the Orc Skirmishes. Describing them as brutes hardly did justice to the havoc they wreaked—relentlessly hacking down enemies and leaving a trail of carnage in their wake. Fighting them on the battlefield would be no different, which was why Keyain wished to get any edge they could. Getting eyes on their inner workings had always proved challenging, considering their royals had always been secretive. The queen had never shown her face in public, a tradition that other ruling city-states had accepted with little question.

He shifted in his seat, rubbing the back of his neck. Time was running out to figure out how to confront Chorys Dasi without suffering a swift defeat. They needed more information about the queen and her court.

"Place new recruits with the inner city guard," Keyain finally said. "Pull some of the experienced inner city guards to the army." A good in-between that defended the city-state while also giving them a fighting chance. The external army units have dwindled since Keyain's days in the Orc Skirmishes. Not long after that, Olytia wanted bodies to protect the city-state fortifications, always the paranoid ruler.

"My soldiers will quit if they're transferred," Walyn said with a glower. "Too many are upset about going against Syllogian city-states and they won't want to kill fellow elves."

"When our enemies annihilate our army and our only defense is them on the walls, they will have no other option than to kill. They will not hesitate," Keyain said. "Tell them that and if anyone still resists, they can come talk to me." He left the threat hanging in the silent room. No one dared to utter a word.

He met Wyltam's unyielding gaze that burned as it raked across him. Keyain checked his temper and added, "What is your plan for recruitment, then?"

"A draft is an option," Walyn offered.

"That is a last ditch effort." Keyain's anger threatened to rise. "It'll show that we do not have citizens who want to fight for us. Both our enemies and allies will see that weakness." He turned to Hastyrn. "I hope you have a better idea."

Hastyrn exchanged glances with one of his marshals. "The pilinos want to fight in the war. We've been approached numerous—"

"I must have somehow missed Minister Leyland passing that legislation," he said, his tone dripping with sarcasm. "Please, I'd love to hear how we're going to blend the army. I suppose you know how recruited pilinos will gain rank? The detail that's kept it in a bureaucratic standstill for weeks?" Keyain tried to reign in his temper, but he felt his grip on it fray.

Hastyrn ground his jaw. "I apologize for not having a better solution while trying to train soldiers who have never witnessed a real fucking war."

"The soldiers were prepared for war when I held that position. Enlighten me with what happened when they were under your leadership that changed that?" Keyain pinned him with a stare.

The air between them grew taut, and no one dared to make a noise. Did they not understand what position they were in?

"I'll follow up with Minister Leyland on the pilinos law, see where it stands," Adalyn said, earning a relieved look from Hastyrn. "While we await that outcome, I suggest heavier recruiting in the countryside. They're more likely to want to fight in the external forces when it's their towns that could be hit first. From what I've heard, many don't want to move behind the walls."

Keyain blew out a slow breath. "Finally, a good fucking idea."

Hastyrn considered this, his fingers tapping thoughtfully on the paper before him. "We can't guarantee the numbers. It's risky."

"So is doing nothing," Keyain countered. "We're arguing over scraps when we need results."

The room fell into a tense silence, the weight of the decision pressing down on them. Keyain's eyes flicked to Wyltam, sitting calmly at the far end of the table. A familiar, knowing smile hinted at Wyltam's lips, making Keyain's stomach twist. He recognized that expression—it always preceded something unpleasant.

"Don't tell me you let another detail slip."

Chapter Sixteen

ELYSE

Elyse glanced between Wyltam and Keyain. The king had shifted in his seat, his attention locked on the other end. Keyain's jaw twitched, his eyes narrowed. All she wished to do was crawl under the table and escape whatever was transpiring between them.

"What detail, Your Grace?"

Wyltam let the silence stretch for a moment, then said, "The mages I sent to Chorys Dasi."

Elyse's lips pursed. She hadn't known about that.

"Do you have an update?"

"I do, though perhaps it would've been helpful at the start of the meeting."

Keyain's jaw tightened, his eyes narrowing into cold, precise slits. Elyse leaned back and bit the inside of her cheek. This was a side of him she hadn't encountered before, save for that morning at the Chorys Dasian townhouse.

"Well, we're all still gathered, Your Grace."

Wyltam stood slowly, gesturing to Elyse. She slid the report she held onto over to him.

"They have eyes on the Chorys Dasian army. Sixteen legions have been accounted for."

Keyain's face drained of color. The general and commander shared nervous glances. Adalyn, in stark contrast, sat serenely, her posture impeccable, her gaze unwavering. Elyse marveled at her composure, feeling a pang of envy. She mimicked her posing, stilling her expression.

"That's eighty thousand soldiers." Keyain took a seat, his gaze focused through the windows.

"The mage I've been communicating with believes another four legions are unaccounted for, mainly composed of magic users. Unfortunately, the Chorys Dasians have tight security around their castle." Wyltam slid the paper to Adalyn. "Though they did catch Prince Auryon arriving on a merchant ship from Reyila. Your suspicion of Reyila discreetly moving their people about was correct."

Keyain swore under his breath and ran a hand through his hair. "We're nowhere near that number."

His head snapped toward the king, his eyes widening.

"Leave us," Wyltam demanded. "Elyse, wait for me in the hall."

Elyse rose on unsteady legs, following the others to the door. She glanced back as Wyltam walked to Keyain, his voice low. She lingered a moment, then shut the door.

The king had asked her to wait. Knowing him, there must have been a reason. As the others took off down the hall, Elyse leaned against the wall, her mind finding the tendrils of magic around her and pulling them into her body.

"—disappointing. We need to figure out who," Wyltam's muffled voice said.

"I'm spread thin as it is."

"Have Adalyn keep an ear—"

"Lady Elyse?"

She jumped, losing her grip on the aithyr. Before her stood a male with a bright smile. "Yes?"

He drew his shoulders back and puffed out his chest. "How's your day going?"

Elyse glanced at the meeting room door. "Um, fine."

He nodded. "I'm Felyx, in case you didn't remember."

"I don't," she snapped. "I mean, sorry. I don't know who you are."

"We met at a party a few years back?" He brushed back his glossy blond hair. "Thought you were with Minister Keyain at the ..." He cleared his voice. "We've met."

Elyse moved her mouth, but no words came to mind. She glanced at the door again, her heart pounding. "I'm sorry. You caught me at an inconvenient moment."

"Apology accepted. Though perhaps I could help you remember who I am?" He offered his arm. "I could escort you to wherever you're heading."

"Oh, no. Sorry. I'm waiting for King Wyltam."

He lowered his arm. "Perhaps another time then."

"Perhaps."

The male went to speak, then closed his mouth and promptly walked away. Elyse shook out her sweaty hands.

"Gracefully done."

Her head jerked at the voice, finding Adalyn standing with her arms crossed over her chest armor. "Excuse me?"

She sighed and walked across the hall. "He didn't deserve an apology."

Elyse shut her eyes, wishing her heart to still. "He caught me off guard."

Adalyn hummed. "Learn to assert yourself or this position will chew you up and spit out the scraps."

The door opened, cutting off her answer as Keyain and Wyltam strode out. The king gestured for her to follow. Elyse stepped in line with him, leaving behind Adalyn's frustrating smirk.

"How much of that did you hear?"

Elyse tugged at her sleeves. "Only a small bit. I was ... disturbed."

Wyltam nodded. "Hate when that happens. At least you tried."

He guided her through the labyrinthine garden, thick with the scent of jasmine and roses. He stopped abruptly on a narrow path, closing his eyes. A shimmering dome enveloped them, muting the world beyond.

Her pulse quickened as Wyltam spoke in a hushed whisper. "I need you to head to the Crystal Gardens right now. Minister Royir, Grytaine, and their visitors will be there. You must hear what they discuss. Wynn and the other mages are tied up.”

Elyse's stomach tightened. She opened her mouth, but Wyltam's hand on her shoulder stopped her.

“I trust you,” he said, his eyes locking onto hers. The dome dissolved, and with a nod, he turned away, leaving her standing there, heart pounding, with the weight of his words pressing down on her.

She watched the Wyltam disappear around the bend before she inhaled slowly, rubbing her palms on her thighs. He wanted her to spy. On Grytaine. Right now. Mustering whatever courage she had, Elyse made for the Crystal Gardens.

The sun shone through the crystal orbs hovering overhead, creating rainbows in the mist rolling of the fountains. Statues and shrubbery dotted the indoor gardens, giving objects to dart behind as she channeled aithyr. Once out of sight, she closed her eyes and pushed the energy toward her hearing.

The noise of the room was nearly overwhelming. Elyse furrowed her brows as she imagined her hearing reaching closer to the main fountain. Then she caught the soft pitch of Grytaine's voice.

“How's the university?”

Elyse heard a deeper tone, but couldn't make out the words.

She dropped her magic and turned toward the fountain. They were likely in one of the seating areas adjacent.

Carefully, Elyse left her spot and edged toward it, seeing the massive rock face of the fountain come into view. Mimicking the side of a mountain, at its base sat a cave with a statue of a hauntingly beautiful female figure. She followed the edge of the pool, nearly reaching the first row of shrubs when she heard the tapping of shoes coming from the other direction.

Elyse swore. The only time she had managed to turn invisible was aided by Mage's Eye, and she didn't feel confident in her ability to hold it long enough. She could either retreat and go back the way she came but risk being seen or …

She turned toward the fountain. A pair of satyrs frolicked before a large outcropping, one that could hide Elyse. She sighed and stepped into the water.

It soaked her shoes and pants through to her flesh, leaving her skin prickled as she hurried into a raised bit of rock to get out. As she ducked down, she saw Royir.

Elyse channeled aithyr once again and focused on the group beyond the hedges.

"Apologies for being late," Royir said.

"Not a problem," the unknown voice answered, his tone rich and each syllable precise. "Your wife entertained me with her innocuous questions."

Royir barked a laugh. "She's good for that." She heard some shuffling, then a sigh. "How have the lectures been?"

"Sparse, though growing every week. Your channels are garnering interest."

"I'm glad my family has time for you." Grytaine's tone came clipped.

"Grytaine, hush."

"She's fine, my friend," the unknown voice said. "Though I'm curious. Where are Dyeiter and Tryda?"

Elyse's heart leaped as her foot slipped on the slick stones, plunging her back into the cold water. Gasping, she scrambled to her feet, her soaked clothes clinging to her. As she wiped droplets from her eyes, she found Royir and Grytaine standing at the pool's edge.

"Lady Elyse?" Royir shook his head. "May I ask what you're doing?"

"I'm, uh, inspecting at the statues." She peeled back the hair sticking to her face.

Grytaine glared and said, "More like swimming with them."

"Clever," Elyse murmured to herself.

Royir offered her a hand as she climbed out and onto the path. Glancing at where they were seated, she saw an older elven male with a hooked nose and a sharp widow's peak. He eyed her with open curiosity.

"Oh, you have company." Her lie came smoothly. "I should've checked the bushes before I did something ..."

"Odd?" Grytaine offered.

"Yes, odd," Elyse said with a bite. "Sorry—" She stopped herself before saying the full word. "I'm going now."

Elyse darted off before they could answer, her steps quick as she headed to the Central Garden once more. Without bothering to dry off, she moved quickly and discreetly to the Royal's Wing, her clothes sticking to her. Her hair was still damp when Wyltam arrived.

He took one look at her and said, "What happened?"

"I can explain, just not—" She exhaled sharply, closing her eyes.

"Come."

She followed Wyltam into the suite, her eyes sweeping the rooms for Marietta only to find them empty.

Once in his office, he gestured for Elyse to sit, then stood across from her, arms folded.

"I know you said to be discreet."

Wyltam's gaze held steady.

"I found them, but I couldn't hear from where I was, so I went into the fountain to get closer." Elyse's fingers picked at the skin around her nails. "I caught part of their conversation before … before I fell into the water."

"What did you hear?"

"They were meeting with someone who teaches. Grytaine mentioned the university. The male asked about Dyeiter and Tryda, but didn't use their titles."

Wyltam's brow arched. "Did you see him?"

Elyse described the male, watching as Wyltam's brows climbed higher. He remained silent for a moment, eyes darting as thoughts churned. "Thank you. You're dismissed."

She rose, hesitating. "I apologize for not following orders."

"You collected enough information that it was worth it." Wyltam sighed. "Perhaps I threw you into it too soon."

Elyse's lips wobbled, unable to defend herself. He was right. She couldn't turn invisible, couldn't remain aware of her surroundings while using aithyr. Despite all her training, she still failed in the end.

Chapter Seventeen

MARIETTA

Marietta focused on the motion of her hands and fingers as she and her guards came to a stop in the hallway. "Friend."

"Good," Tolis signed back with a smile.

Marietta's gaze shifted from her guard to the ornate wooden doors before them. The surface told stories of the sun and moon, swirling winds, serpents winding through flames, water rippling along the edges, and lion heads melded with goat bodies peering from between. "More intricate than I imagined," she murmured, her fingers tracing the carved patterns. "And well-preserved."

Coryn gave a nod. "They must've had someone maintain it all these years, though …" He pushed open the door, releasing a curtain of dust that settled around them. Golden light streamed through a row of tall, narrow windows, casting sharp lines across the floor. Statues of deities stood guard between each window, imposing and silent.

"Wow." Marietta stepped inside, a flood of sensations washing over her—heat and heaviness, both uneasy and warm, a restless stirring. She smiled, her chest tight. "There's something about this place."

"Are you sure?" Wynn quipped from the doorway, half-hanging from the frame.

Her eyes swept over the small, circular chamber, divided by worn benches and an altar. Dust blanketed every surface, the air thick and musty. "A thorough cleaning wouldn't hurt," she said, wiping a finger across a bench.

"It's not fit for prayer today," Coryn agreed. "We could have someone clean it before we return."

Marietta waved the thought away. "We just need a few rags and some water. Soap. And a broom." She planted her hands on her hips and spun around the room.

Wynn's laughter rang out as Coryn scoffed. "You can't be serious."

She turned to him, a hint of a challenge in her voice. "I used to clean kitchens twice this size, and with twice the mess. Every night, sometimes even more often." She stepped forward, each footfall tapping sharply against the stone floor. "It's far from impossible."

Coryn followed, his armor thudding in time with his steps. "You're a queen," he said in a lowered tone.

"Not yet."

"An almost queen, then. How many of those have you seen scrubbing floors?"

"Can't say I've ever laid eyes on one," she replied, spinning on her heel to face him. "But don't tell me an iros has never cleaned before."

His gaze didn't waver. "I've done my share at the temple."

"Then this temple should be no problem."

With the cleaning supplies gathered, Marietta set Coryn to work. Wynn and Tolis grinned as they left to guard the hallway, closing the door behind them. She took a damp cloth and approached the first deity statue, a figure of a handsome god with short-cropped hair. "Zontykroi," she murmured, wiping the fabric over the carved lines of his face. "God of life and death. You'd expect him to be scarier."

From across the room, Coryn glanced up, his arms filled with jars. "Death isn't always scary. Sometimes it's peaceful."

Marietta hummed in agreement, her focus returning to the statue. "True, but that doesn't make it easier. I enjoy being alive."

The glass clinked as Coryn set them down. "Glad to hear it. I'm putting my life on the line for you, after all."

Marietta's hand stilled. "I don't like it phrased that way."

He met her gaze. "It's the truth."

"Yes, but ... " Her arms crossed defensively. "I don't want you to die, either."

A bright smile spread across his face. "Ah, so you do enjoy my company. Perhaps that's where those rumors started."

She scoffed, tossing the rag at him.

He laughed and said, "It's a joke."

"I'm glad you find it amusing."

His smile faded slightly as he inclined his head. "Apologies. I suppose you were on the worse end of it with Keyain and all."

"Worse would be accurate." She muttered as she retrieved the rag from the floor.

Coryn bent down at the same moment, his hand brushing hers aside. "Let me. It's bad enough you're doing this."

"Now I can't even pick things up?"

"You're an almost queen—"

"We've covered this."

"But you're also a pilinos. An iros. I know you can clean, but you also need to strive for your title."

She snatched the rag from his hand. "Cleaning this temple will be beneficial for both my queenship and my reputation with the temples."

He eyed her carefully. "I understand, but remember, being the voice of the pilinos is a ... delicate matter."

Marietta's expression hardened. "For elves, sure."

Coryn shook his head. "You're half-elven, but not Satiroan. You're not from Syllogi. The life you had in Enomenos isn't like ours."

Her lips pressed into a thin line. "You're right. I don't know what it's like to grow up in Syllogi. But I do understand what it's like to have my freedom stripped away by an elf. To be at their mercy. That doesn't equal a lifetime of hardship, but it's enough for me to refuse to let it happen to anyone else."

Coryn closed the space between them, taking her hands gently in his.

"They won't, at least not in Satiros. And afterward, maybe you could extend that change to our western allies."

He released her, and she turned back to the statues. "I want to make things better," she said. "And yes, I'm leveraging my connection with the Temple of Therypon. I suppose I should learn more about the deities."

Coryn gestured to the statue of the goddess she had been cleaning. "Seidytar, goddess of chaos and order. Therypon stands at the center, as you know." He moved down the row, pausing at the next figure. "Oramytiz, deity of reality and deception." The veil draped over their face was carved with such finesse that Marietta almost believed she could see through it.

"And lastly, Kystrorgiste."

Marietta shifted her gaze to the stern visage of a man, his long hair ending in billowing, carved flames. "God of creation and destruction," she recited, recalling her friends in Enomenos who had worshiped him.

"You should learn them all—not just their names, but their rituals, their followers."

"Shouldn't be too hard with an excellent teacher." She nudged him playfully with an elbow.

He chuckled, ducking his head. When he lifted his gaze, the light caught his eyes, turning them into pools of gleaming umber. "I can share what I know, but my knowledge is limited to Therypon's rituals." He hesitated, then gestured to the altar. "There are still offerings here, if you're interested in trying."

Marietta nodded, following him to the raised stone. "Therypon governs healing and pain, both of which can be administered through plants. As there are many medicinal plants, there are also those that are harmful." He poured a dried substance into a depression on the altar. "This is rhododendron. Consuming its leaves or flowers can lead to confusion, stomach pain, and, in high doses, death."

He lifted another container. "And this is yarrow, known for its healing properties and ability to reduce inflammation. Both plants are common, each embodying the dual aspects of our goddess."

Coryn fetched a viscous liquid and a fire striker, pouring the oil over the dried plants. The flint sparked, igniting the mixture.

Marietta flinched at the sudden flame. "Is fire necessary?"

"The components align with Therypon's domains. The smoke carries the essence to her. Our goal is to capture her attention." Coryn knelt before the altar, closing his eyes.

Marietta hesitated before joining him. The cold stone pressed against her knees, discomfort intensifying with each passing moment. She shut her eyes, willing her mind to empty, focusing only on the serene visage of Therypon. For a fleeting moment, there was nothing but the rhythm of her pulse and the darkness behind her eyelids. Her mind drifted.

When she opened her eyes, a swirling fog enveloped her. Through the mist, stone structures emerged, adorned with detailed carvings and overgrown with greenery. Voices, muffled and distant, echoed around her. She strained to make sense of them. A figure loomed in the shadows, its presence palpable. Urgency radiated from the words, a mixture of concern and warning. Then, a whisper, delicate as silk, threaded through her thoughts.

"*Deirìmòd.*"

Marietta jolted, blinking away the fog as reality snapped back into focus. Ash lay scattered on the altar.

"About time you came to," Coryn remarked, a broom in his hand.

She steadied herself on shaky legs, the blood rushing back to her limbs. "How long was I like that?"

"An hour at least. Left me with all the cleaning."

"An hour?" Her brows knitted in confusion. "It felt like seconds."

Coryn caught her arm as she wavered. "Did you see Therypon?"

She shook her head slowly. "No. At least, I don't think so. I don't remember."

Returning to the task at hand, Marietta couldn't shake the lingering unease—a gnawing sensation that she had glimpsed something forbidden, something that she wasn't meant to see.

Hours later, Marietta stretched out across the couch in the sitting room, a book resting in her hand. The cushions beneath her were a far cry from the hard floor she'd been used to. As she delved deeper into her reading, the day's excitement weighed on her, and her eyelids grew heavier until sleep overtook her.

A hand jostled her from slumber. Marietta mumbled and turned over.

"You can't sleep on a couch."

She jolted upright at the sound of Wyltam's voice. "Says who?"

Wyltam sighed, his face illuminated by a soft glow from a light globe hovering between them. "You're going to be a queen."

"An almost queen can sleep wherever she pleases."

"Find a bed," he said, stepping away and entering the hallway. "That can't be good for your back."

"Want to rub it for me, then?" she called after him. Her only answer was his office door clicking shut.

Her back did ache but not nearly as much as being on the floor, meaning returning to Valeriya's room wasn't an option. And if she did, she'd be doing exactly what Wyltam wanted her to do, and she didn't take his demands lightly. After a moment, she had an idea.

Marietta crossed the suite and slowly eased open the door. Beyond revealed a sizable chamber that possessed a fraction of the furniture needed to fill it. The walls were bare, with no other personal artifacts decorating the room. So this was how Wyltam lived.

She moved to his bed and tested the mattress, finding it firm but with a good amount of give. Better than her other options. Marietta slipped between the covers and her skin prickled with the cool silk of his sheets. Gods, she would rest well if she could manage to fall back asleep. After adjusting to the new room, she must have dozed off, for she woke to a bright light.

Keeping her eyes closed, she sensed Wyltam pausing beside the bed and half-expected him to throw her out. Instead, his footsteps pattered deeper into the chamber, followed by the sounds of running water and other rustling. When he returned, she waited for him to leave entirely and find a new place to sleep. The room darkened and the mattress shifted as Wyltam eased himself next to her. Marietta turned to face him in the dark. She could only see the outline of him in the dim, his chest slowly rising and falling.

"Is there a problem?" he murmured.

"Not at all."

The sheets whispered against her skin as she rolled onto her back, every nerve attuned to Wyltam's presence beside her, close enough to touch. A thought flickered—did he consider reaching out, drawing her near, pressing his lips to hers?

Time drifted, each minute heavier than the last, the quiet broken only by Wyltam's steady inhale and exhale. The sound carried her, pulling her down into sleep's embrace.

Morning came too soon, with an annoying chorus of birds shrilling rudely just outside the window. Soft, diffused light crept into the room, stirring Marietta from sleep. She stretched, her back arching, and was met with the sensation of something solid against her. Awareness rushed in—an arm wrapped around her waist, the hem of her nightgown bunched above her hips, warm breath brushing her neck in steady waves. A shiver threaded through her at the realization, cursing her heart for its treacherous flutter at the intimacy of being entwined with Wyltam.

Maybe it was the haze of sleep, or perhaps the ache of loneliness she'd refused to acknowledge, but there was comfort in the weight of his arm. She wanted to pull it closer, to bask in the safety it promised. Each of Wyltam's breaths, deep and heady, traced her skin, and Marietta bit down on her lip, stifling the sigh that welled up. His body tensed, then relaxed once more, settling against her in a way that made her pulse quicken.

As she thought he'd drifted back to sleep, his fingers grazed her stomach, the touch maddeningly delicate. Heat flared, fierce and insistent, pooling between her legs. She should guide his hand downward, enjoy the depth of his fingers within her, or lower his head to feel the warmth of his breath between her thighs. To know the tenderness of his tongue against the most sensitive parts of herself.

But just as she moved to face him, Wyltam withdrew. The moment dissolved as swiftly as it had formed, leaving Marietta to wonder if it had been a dream or a fleeting taste of something more. A shift lingered between them, subtle yet undeniable, an understanding she wasn't ready to address.

Chapter Eighteen

AMRYTH

Upon entering the Honeysuckle, Amryth realized two things. One, that she definitely did not enjoy a tavern filled with strangers staring at her. Two, that Deania was more than a regular to the establishment.

The cleric's excited yell pierced through the lively atmosphere of the bar, eliciting an equally enthusiastic response from Tanaly. They ran to meet each other in the middle. Amryth approached while they were still embraced and squealing to one another.

When they peeled apart, Tanaly turned to Amryth. "You know how to take an order. Grab a seat and I'll be by in a moment."

Deania led Amryth to the dim side of the bar, selecting a booth away from other patrons.

"I didn't realize you were that close," Amryth said as she sat on the bench. She froze when Deania slid in next to her.

"Oh, we're friends, but surprisingly not that close." She scooted closer. "Quick, put your arm around me."

"What?" Her pulse grew louder in her ears.

Deania punched her in the leg as Tanaly approached them. "It's always a good night when you're here, D."

Amryth slipped her arm around her, her heart hammering as Deania settled into her side.

"Look at you two!" Tanaly leaned against the edge of the opposite bench with her arms crossed. "Having your usual, love?"

Deania nodded and added, "One for her, too."

Tanaly raised a brow and turned her attention to Amryth. "Well, well, keeping up with our dear Deania, I see. I'll be right back."

When she was far enough away, Amryth asked, "What's your usual?"

"When she returns, I'm going to ask her about one of the close friends, the one with the eyewitness account," she said, ignoring the question. "Adira used to drink here a few times a week. There's a good chance they'll be around."

"But will they talk in front of me?"

"I'll vouch for you."

"Will that be enough? They could recognize me from the guard."

"Or the temple," Deania said, her brown eyes wholly black in the low light, giving her a doe-eyed appearance. Amryth's arm relaxed along her shoulders. "If I say you are trustworthy, they'll believe me."

"Why though?"

Deania stared at her from eye to eye. "You really aren't aware of the temples' involvement with relocating pilinos."

The guard had never probed into it deeply, not wanting to provoke tensions. "What does that have to do with you, particularly?"

"I help create the channels to move people."

Amryth pulled back. She had known Deania for months and hadn't realized she was one of the individuals helping pilinos escape to Satiros. "I thought you did recruitment."

Deania gawked. "Yes, *recruitment*. How many refugees become attendants compared to the normal population?"

Tanaly approached and set two cups on the table. Amryth peered in to find the contents clear. She sniffed, getting hit with the overwhelming piney alcoholic scent. Tanaly laughed. "Deania likes a taste of home."

Amryth raised a brow. "Straight gin is your usual?"

"You'll see another side of her tonight," she said with a knowing smile.

"Let me know if you need anything else."

As she turned to leave, Deania asked, "Have you seen Adira lately?"

Tanaly furrowed her brows. "Why?"

"I haven't heard them in a while and wanted to chat."

The barmaid held her stare. "About what?"

Deania flashed a smile. "Just checking in."

"They're not interested in talking to anyone associated with the guard," Tanaly said after a moment, her gaze landing on Amryth.

"That obvious?" Amryth said, shifting in her seat.

"We did some searching after you left. Would've kicked you out today if you weren't with Deania." Tanaly crossed her arms again. "What is a guard doing snooping around here?"

"Former guard," Amryth corrected.

"Moot point."

Deania sighed. "If you won't give us information on Adira, will you at least sit?"

Tanaly glanced over her shoulder at the bar. "Marv, I'm taking a break!" A half-elven man waved in acknowledgment as he helped patrons. "What's going on?" she asked, dropping her voice.

"We're investigating the murders," Deania said, leaning forward and letting Amryth's arm drop.

Tanaly's posture went rigid. "You two are investigating ..." She trailed off, her eyes brightening. "You're trying to help Jory?"

"The guard had other leads they dropped when they arrested him," Amryth murmured. "I have the time, the resources, and the motivation to find the actual killer."

Tanaly's gaze burned across Amryth's skin under her cool assessment. "Why? You were one of them for decades. A few weeks out doesn't make a difference."

"The guard and I had different philosophies on what is morally right and wrong." Amryth pinned her to the spot, meeting her intensity. "I don't doubt they found the first plausible suspect they could find and apprehend him in order to toss it under the rug and be done with it."

"Why did you stay as long as you did then if you thought them so morally wrong?"

Amryth swallowed hard, the changing emotions from the past month overwhelming her. "Let's just say a particular half-elf needed my help because of those who control the guard. It changed everything for me—she changed everything for me."

A sly smile slipped onto Tanaly's lips. "Care to elaborate?"

She hesitated, not wanting to say anything that would reflect poorly on Marietta. But Tanaly was searching for information. Amryth sighed. "Minister Keyain made it clear that his morals and mine do not align, therefore I left."

Amusement danced across the barmaid's features. "Ah, the snatcher himself. Is it true you saved our future queen?"

A direct question about Marietta could breech her discharge agreement, meaning she picked her words carefully. "Perhaps once or twice."

Tanaly sat back with an indiscernible expression. "All right. I'll work on getting Adira to talk in exchange for your stories about saving our pilinos queen."

"There's not much I can say. I won't risk her reputation ahead of her reign."

"I don't deal in gossip but in stories," Tanaly said. "My goal isn't to shame her whatsoever, but I am rather interested in learning what truly happened to her. While Deania and the Temple of Therypon shared what they could, it's better to hear it from someone who was present."

Amryth worked her jaw. Was this too far? There wasn't a way for her to check if she was honest or not.

"You can trust her," Deania said, leaning into her.

Staring into her eyes and seeing her hope, Amryth conceded despite not trusting a stranger. With a sigh and a sip of her gin, Amryth shared how she saved Marietta.

Chapter Nineteen

ELYSE

Elyse spun the rings on her fingers as Wyltam introduced the artificer, a half-elf named Fig. Standing no taller than Wyltam's shoulder, Fig adjusted their glasses. The silver chains that connected them to their earrings glinted between their black, choppy hair as they clinked.

Wyltam gestured for them to follow him deeper into Elyse's office, where a table had been placed.

"You'll work here temporarily until we can build a better workshop," Wyltam said.

Elyse caught Fig's stare, and they flashed a smile, easing her nerves.

"The goal is to create prototypes to help both Satiros and Enomenos against our enemies," Wyltam continued. "Your first project being a pair of glasses that enable the wearer to see aithyr streams." He turned to Elyse. "This is something Fig has been working on for a few months and is close to solving. You'll start with a traditional glasses prototype, then design a more tactical version suitable for combat."

Elyse began to speak, then stopped, pulling at the cuff of her sleeves. Wyltam motioned for her to continue. "You've already made progress on it?" she asked Fig in awe.

"Some yes, but the lenses aren't perfect," they said, smiling. "I'll show you what I have thus far."

Elyse beamed at the thought.

"From there, we'll decide on what idea to tackle next. You both have free rein. Whatever material, whatever the cost. If you run into any issues, let me know." Wyltam stepped toward the door. "I'll check in periodically to see your progress, but ultimately, this project is yours to control."

As they fell into silence following Wyltam's departure, Elyse busied herself by rummaging through her belongings for something to draw with.

When she returned to the table, Fig commented, "Charcoal over ink? The sketch might get messy if the charcoal smudges."

"The, uh, charcoal is enchanted to not smudge." She drew a line onto the paper and ran her finger through it. "See?"

Fig flashed a smile. "I keep forgetting we have a royal budget. That stuff is expensive."

Cracking their fingers, they pulled out a flat glass disk, no larger than a date. "This is approximately the size of the lens we can use. Any bigger and it loses potency. First, we should decide who we are making the frames for." Fig leaned back in their chair, eyes cast to the ceiling as they braced their hands behind their head. "I'd prefer not to be the wearer because I'll only focus on the flaws. King Wyltam said that he wouldn't be able to wear them regularly to test, said something about 'public appearance.' I thought that we could have you wear them. The king mentioned you've seen aithyr streams before?" They raised a brow, their mouth tilting with a smile.

"A few times yes, though that was with …" She didn't finish the thought, unsure of how Fig would react to her using drugs.

"I remember the first time I saw streams," they said wistfully. "I had a friend with a potent mix of Mage's Eye. Mesmerizing at the time, and I haven't been able to recreate that experience."

"That's how I saw it."

Fig laughed. "Unsurprised. The lenses are crafted with an ash made from the substance. All aithyr-infused objects have the ash incorporated into their creation process. It's then on the mage to be capable of enchanting the object for its purpose. Enchanting for glass to emit light is easy—that's why light globes have become commonplace. Something like showing aithyr is a great deal trickier."

"The ash is… added in?" Elyse furrowed her brows.

"Yes! For metal, ash is part of the flux—a substance used in the smelting of ores to promote fluidity and prevent oxidation." Fig leaned forward, their words coming faster. "Surprisingly, it doesn't make the metal scale. Doesn't affect the soda ash in the flux whatsoever."

Elyse blinked, trying to decipher their words. "I'm not following."

Fig frowned for a moment, making Elyse want to recoil.

"King Wyltam wasn't kidding when he said you were green." Fig rubbed the lens of their glasses on their shirt before replacing them on their face. "Let's start at the beginning. Creating magical objects is similar to any trade—glass blowing, metal smithing, hells, even woodworking. Within those processes, a form of Mage's Eye is included to give the object an aithyr focus. Once the object is created, mages can enchant the item for a specific purpose. For globe lights, the Mage's Eye compound is added to the raw materials after it goes into the reheating furnace to melt down, becoming fused with the glass. After the glass is blown into an orb and fully cooled, a mage pulls aithyr into it while focusing on its purpose—light." Fig paused and took a long breath.

"How does it work with more complicated tasks?" Elyse retrieved a globe from her desk and set it afloat. "These don't just give off light, they hover." She touched her finger to the surface, and it began to emit light. "It can be ignited and extinguished."

"Takes more focusing and more aithyr," Fig said, finding their excitement again. "More aithyr and less longevity. Those need to be re-enchanted or replaced sooner than outside ones. See, you're getting it."

Elyse nodded, unsure how true that was. Until now, she had never thought about the application of aithyr in the objects she always interacted with.

"If the main goal of the glasses is to see aithyr streams," Elyse said, "and only that, shouldn't it be easy to enchant?"

Fig thought for a moment. "Emitting light or cold is much more straightforward than having it reveal one specific thing. Takes a lot of focus and aithyr. We can get into the crafting details later, but for now, we can grab your measurements and start the diagram."

Fig grabbed the fabric ruler draped around their neck and measured Elyse's head and eye placement. As they did, Elyse jotted down the numbers. From there, she drew a rough sketch of her head before moving onto the frames. When finished, she slid the paper to Fig.

"I think this will be fine for a prototype of this caliber," they said. "The metal will be pretty forgivable. We'll need to be more detailed and specific with future plans as the designs get more complicated."

"I'll get better," she said, vulnerability stinging across her skin. "I promise."

"You're already doing great." Fig clapped her on the shoulder. "I'll set a time with the jeweler to elaborate on the design—I'm guessing you'll want them to be fashionable—and from there we can go and be part of the process. I'll finishing making the lens with the glassblower, however. And we'll work together to get them in place and start the enchanting process. Sound good?"

"We'll go to the jewelers?"

"Of course."

Her gut twisted. "I can't leave the palace."

Fig gave her a wistful stare. "I think exactly what you need is a trip outside the palace."

That evening, Elyse received a knock on her door. Wynn waited on the other side.

"Busy?" he asked.

Elyse glanced over her shoulder at her copy of *Statues and Sculptures of Syllogi* opened on the couch among the pile of blankets. Her activity for the night until Wyltam summoned her. "Not at all."

"I don't mean to intrude," he said as she guided him in. "The Mage Pit is rather full these days, and I needed a break."

"Trouble with your friends?" Elyse closed her book and settling into her spot. She propped her legs up on the couch, tucked into her body. To her surprise, Wynn took the other end instead of a chair.

"Not enough quiet time." He closed his eyes and rested his head on the back of the couch. "I forgot how much Sibylla can talk."

Elyse laughed and took in the details of Wynn's face. Lines formed around his eyes when he smiled, the scar less menacing when it curved with it. His jaw was strong, his face angular. Handsome even, in his own intimidating way. After Az's attempt at abducting her, she remembered Wynn acting as her guard as they went through the halls. People steered clear of him and stared at her in awe. With him by her side, she became powerful.

He peeked open an eye, revealing the icy blue color. "Staring at me?"

"I like your smile."

"And I like yours. You don't do it nearly enough."

Her stomach fluttered as she nervously ducked her head.

"Continue reading, though. I'll enjoy the quiet." He closed his eyes again and folded his hands over the plane of his abdomen.

Elyse hesitated, then picked up her book and read, but she never lost her awareness of Wynn. Every few sentences, she would glance at him, noting how the smile hinting at his lips remained. She had many moments similar to this with Keyain, but Keyain had never made her heart race. Keyain had never made her stomach flutter or complimented her in a way that made her feel special. With Wynn, it was different, and Elyse had to force her attention back to her book unless he caught her staring.

When she was a few pages from the end, she heard Wyltam's voice in her head. *"I have one more meeting this evening. Can you stop by my office while I wait?"*

Elyse had yet to master the response to messages, but that didn't stop her from trying. Setting her books aside, she closed her eyes and focused on the aithyr around her, letting it slip into her body. She thought of Wyltam in his office, his black hair and dark eyes. *"Yes."* She panted at the exertion of her focus, unsure if her words reached Wyltam.

"My student passes another test."

Elyse jumped at the sound of Wynn's voice. "What?"

"Wyltam wanted to see if you'd respond through magic, and I was here in case you couldn't, but didn't doubt it for a second." He stood with a stretch, his shirt rising to display the taut muscle underneath. For a moment, she thought she saw some scarring, but he lowered his arms, holding out an arm to Elyse. "Ready?" She accepted, and they left her suite.

At that time in the evening, the lights were kept low in the Noble's Wing. Though some chatter and music arose from the common rooms, they didn't run into people. A small blessing for Elyse. A divide was prevalent between nobles whose family owned Satiroan land and those who worked for the crown. The nobles she grew up with had no responsibilities beyond managing their family's estate and the corresponding villages. That's to say they spent their days not doing as such. Some nobles, especially second siblings, trained for government jobs, often studying at the university and being away from the palace. The main difference between the groups were their motivations. From what she gleaned, politicians used their connections to move up within their position or to work seamlessly across branches. The nobles used their connections for popularity and clout at parties.

Wynn elbowed her. "You're quiet."

"I'm thinking."

They stepped out into the Central Garden. The clicking, buzzing sound of cicadas greeted them. Overhead, the globes flickered on as they passed.

"About him still?" Wynn stuffed his hands in his pockets.

"No. About some of the nobles I knew."

They reached the path. Elyse nodded at someone she knew from the health branch.

"Care to share?"

Elyse sighed. "There's not much to it. I grew up with the other nobles at court. Most of them drink until they pass out, party even harder, without consequence or responsibility. At least for their first century. After that, most of them search for prospective spouses, take a serious role in their family affairs, or study for a political position."

"What would you have done if you had gotten through a century without Wyltam taking you under his wing?"

"I was never going to make it to a century." Her throat tightened with the memory of being trapped, on how the palace had been her prison.

"You never planned that far ahead, then?" He glanced at her. "Never dreamed of what you could do?"

She had, but they were simply dreams, ones she knew would never be attainable. "This exceeds any dream I could have imagined."

"Working for a king is better than your wildest dreams?" Wynn laughed. "I'll have to tell Wyltam the extent of your devotion."

She shot him a look.

"I tease. You are full of potential that it's hard not to see you do something significant, you know?" He smiled at her.

Her head remained light the rest of their walk to Wyltam's office, with Wynn by her side. Wynn had always been kind to her, and she noticed that when he's around, she stands taller and holds her chin higher. As stars came into view in the night sky above them, she thanked whatever deity may or may not be listening. For once, everything felt right.

When they reached Wyltam's office, Wynn said he'd wait outside for her and walk her back to her room. She told him she looked forward to it.

Inside, she found Wyltam bent over papers at his desk. "Elyse, welcome. Take a seat."

"Busy day?"

He huffed a laugh. "Every day is a busy day. How did the rest of the meeting go?"

"Good, all of their projections are on track for the fall harvest." Elyse thought back to her note. "The only hiccup is in iron."

"Ah, unsurprised. Kyaeri has been cutting back on the amount they're trading in order to not pick a side."

"Minister Asyn did have a question for you."

"Go on."

"About the resources clause. He wants to know if the treaty will add in Enomenos supplying iron during the war."

"The meeting I needed to depart for discussed it." Wyltam took something out of a drawer. "The clause has been approved with the addition that we include enough food for Enomenoan soldiers when they arrive in Satiros for the war. Could you send a note for me?"

Elyse sat forward, patting her pockets. "I can if you have something to write with.”

Wyltam handed her the paper and ink, and she formed her note to Minister Asyn. When she finished, she caught Wyltam’s stare.

“How are you feeling regarding your administrator duties?” he asked.

Elyse reclined and picked at her nails. “I thought it would be more difficult, especially with how I struggle when talking to people.” She cursed inwardly at herself for admitting as such to the king. She quickly added, “Not that I’ve had any trouble. Everyone has been so nice, always answering my questions and speaking to me outside of meetings. A few have even invited me to their gatherings, though I declined those.”

Wyltam didn’t speak for a moment. “That’s interesting to hear. While I’m gone, I need you to attend those gatherings. It’ll be good practice for when you go to other courts.” Elyse’s heart dropped at the thought as Wyltam held something out. “There’s also this.”

Elyse took a ring from his hand. The band was crafted with vines and flowers onto its metal surface, ending in petals that formed a flower bud. On top of it sat entwined wisteria that matched her administrator’s broach with the letters *EN*.

“You’ve proven to be quite dependable, even with the minor hiccup with Royir,” Wyltam said as she inspected. “Before mine and Marietta’s wedding, I’m sending you to Amigys then Kyaeri to see where our alliances lie.”

Elyse dropped the ring. “I’m traveling to Amigys and Kyaeri that soon?”

“Before the wedding, yes.”

“By myself?” Elyse’s heart quickened in her chest. Wasn’t this what she wanted?

“With a few trusted members of the Foreign Relations branch now that we’ve settled on Sethyr Calsyn as your father’s replacement.”

If they decided on Sethyr, they had to go pretty far down the list to get a separation from her father. Sethyr was that annoying twat Kurtys’s direct superior. “That is surprising.”

“He’s one of the few people we knew with certainty that didn’t conspire with your father. He was on track to take a position higher up.” Elyse raised her brows at that. “He was cleaning up a lot of your father’s slack and made himself useful to other teams."

She nodded her head. "Will he be the one going?"

"A handful of other representatives will be going too. You won't be the only person on their first trip to a foreign court." Wyltam glanced up from his sheet. "Oh, and Wynn will be accompanying you in case you need help."

The lump in her throat loosened at the mention of Wynn. At least she'd have him to keep her calm.

"Are you upset that he's taken over your training?" Wyltam asked. "With everything going on, I cannot give you the proper attention."

"Though I could have learned much from you, I'm enjoying my time with Wynn. He's wonderful."

Wyltam nodded. "That's good then. You were able to send a message back. Wynn said that was your first success at it?"

"It was," she said, beaming.

"Interesting, considering you're struggling to balance concentration and awareness."

Elyse's momentary pride faltered.

"We all have things we need to work on." Wyltam stood and gestured toward the door. "Try to attend at least one gathering while we're in Olkia and prepare yourself for more when we return. I need you to be my eyes and ears, but remember: pay attention to what's not said. Use some of the skills you've learned to your advantage."

Chapter Twenty

MARIETTA

The sun dipped low on the horizon, casting long shadows over the palace hallway as the evening Queen's Guard took their positions. Marietta paused at the entrance to their suite, her gaze drawn to Wyltam, who stood at the doorway, engrossed in conversation with Coryn.

Marietta stepped up behind him, her presence announced by the whisper of her gown against the marble floor. "We make a matching set," she said, spreading the gauzy black skirts that flared out from her waist. Her eyes traced the fine lines of Wyltam's tailored black coat, the golden crown nestled in his dark hair.

Wyltam turned, words halting as his gaze landed on her. His eyes traveled down, catching at the neckline that plunged over her chest, the cut emphasizing the graceful curve of her neck and the intricate iros tattoo inked there.

She smoothed her hands over the sheer black bodice, the amethyst beads sewn into the fabric catching the fading light. "Is everything to your satisfaction?"

Wyltam swallowed, the movement betraying a flicker of something deep within him, before offering his arm. "You make me a frivolous man."

Her stomach gave a small, fluttering leap as she slipped her hand into the crook of his arm. They moved together, stepping out onto the pathway that led to the Central Garden. The evening air carried the distant clinking of glasses, the low hum of voices, and the soft strains of music, mingling with the rhythmic clank of the Queen's Guard's armor.

They came to a halt behind a row of cypress trees, their silhouettes stark against the deepening sky. The cacophony of cicadas droned in the background, mingling with the muted sounds of the gathering beyond. Wyltam leaned in close, his voice a soft rumble in her ear. "Ready?"

"As ready as someone can be when diving into the unknown," she said, her heart suddenly thundering. A voice came from behind the bushes as the party grew quiet.

Wyltam withdrew a slip of paper, handing it to her with a raised brow. "Your speech?"

She took it, her fingers brushing his, noting the official signature of approval from the ministers. "I'll manage without it."

A wave of anxiety threatened to crest, but Marietta pushed it down, drawing in a steadying breath as they were ushered forward. The crowd before her was a sea of faces, some familiar, others not, all of them turning as one to acknowledge their king and his future queen. They bowed and curtsied in practiced unison.

The Central Garden had been transformed into a setting of understated elegance. Drapes hung between the trees, creating private alcoves for conversation. Richly woven rugs softened the cobblestone paths, adding a touch of luxury to the natural beauty of the surroundings.

"Today, we celebrate new beginnings," Wyltam said, his deep voice projecting. "With our new queen and new alliances, we move Satiros into a brighter future where all can live peacefully."

"War may loom, but there is no need to fear," Wyltam continued, his hand slipping to the small of her back. "Tomorrow, we depart to solidify our union with Enomenos, securing our success. Tonight, we celebrate—for all we have prepared, for Marietta's ascension to the throne, for a new future. May we move forward with steadfast grace so that we remain ever blooming."

Applause rippled through the garden. Marietta's mind raced, the approved speech hovering at the edge of her thoughts—a polite, simple thank you to the attendees. It rang hollow, disconnected from the moment. Her eyes swept across the expectant faces, the rehearsed words fading into irrelevance. A pause lingered as she grappled with the urge to speak—to say something genuine, something that truly mattered.

"My journey to this moment has been anything but ordinary," she began, "and I am honored to serve as your queen and ally, uniting my home and my people with yours. One day, we will look back and wonder why this union between Satiros and Enomenos, and the inclusion of pilinos in the ruling body, did not happen sooner." She glanced at Wyltam. To most, he would look neutral, but Marietta knew better—he did not like Marietta's unscripted speech. A satisfying stirring sensation started in her chest as she walked to the edge of the platform.

"Our motto, 'ever blooming,' stands for many things—our thriving businesses, our prosperous relations with neighbors, our pride in this city-state. But it also represents what we will become, where we will go. It stands for change. So with my ascension as your monarch, it is my honor and pride to be the first pilinos queen and the last queen of Satiros."

Marietta lifted her chin as she took in the crowd. Half of them applauded, the others shared confused glances. Wyltam appeared at her side, his hand gently pulling her face toward his. He kissed her. The soft tenderness of his touch didn't match the fierceness of his grip. She tried to pull away, but he held her true. A thousand thoughts surfaced at once as the cheers from the party grew louder, her heart matching its thundering sound.

When he finally withdrew, he murmured, "You were running your mouth, so I gave it something else to focus on."

The music resumed, and servants carrying trays of food circulated through the garden. Marietta despised the heat that crept into her cheeks. "Apologies. I went with a gut instinct."

"Smile," he replied as he brushed a rogue lock from her face. "People are noticing."

Marietta's frown deepened. "It was a good speech."

Wyltam guided her through the crowd, leaning in close with a whisper.

"We will talk after."

They approached the dais, where two thrones stood amidst towering rose bushes, the blossoms heavy and fragrant in the evening air. A servant handed them each a cup as they sat. Marietta sipped and frowned at the lack of flavor.

"Water?" she asked, raising an eyebrow.

"A trick of mine," Wyltam said. "You keep your wits while they lose theirs."

"Practical but boring."

"Boring, perhaps," Wyltam said, his gaze shifting as the first guest approached, "but boredom means decorum isn't lost to alcohol."

Minister Adryan greeted them with a deep bow, an elven man by his side. Politicians of non-noble birth, free from the constraints of traditional family roles, often explored unconventional marriages. "My gracious king and his beautiful bride."

"Minister Adryan," Marietta said before Wyltam could speak. "A pleasure to see you and to meet your partner."

Adryan's smile was easy, practiced. "The pleasure is all ours, Your Grace. We bid you safe travels tomorrow and successful meetings in your time in Olkia."

"Your well wishes are appreciated," Wyltam answered.

"If you see Fabian Rodallis," Adryan added, turning to Marietta, "please send him my love."

"You know Fabian?" Marietta asked, her curiosity piqued. Fabian was the head of Olkia's Business Chambers, a man she had shared polite conversations with, though nothing more.

"Fabian inquired about your arrival in Satiros a few months back. He mentioned your tenacity for shrewd business deals." Adryan's eyes gleamed with something she couldn't quite place.

After they bid farewell and stepped away, Wyltam murmured, "He wants something."

"A favor?"

"Perhaps. Or he's extending one to us."

"Which would leave us in his debt."

"You catch on quick." Wyltam settled back into his chair.

The evening unfolded with ministers approaching to offer their well wishes. Even those who had opposed the marriage, like Minister Gordyn, extended an apology, eager to align themselves with the new order. Yet one minister lingered at the edge of the gathering, avoiding their gaze. Marietta meant to mention this to Wyltam, but a more familiar face caught her attention.

Elyse stood amidst a group of politicians, shoulders back, her smile warm and unforced. In contrast to the swirl colors around her, Elyse wore a simple black gown, the front buttoned like a blouse, the neckline elegantly slipping off her shoulders. The skirt clung to her form before cascading to her boots. Marietta found it difficult to reconcile this confident woman with the nervous girl she'd met months ago.

"Elyse's new role suits her."

Wyltam nodded. "Between that and separating her from her father, she's grown. But there are still hard lessons ahead."

"Does she not live up to your lofty expectations?"

"She exceeds them every day."

Marietta studied Wyltam's face, his focus unwavering, his brow drawn in a subtle crease. "You truly care about her."

"I do."

Marietta returned her gaze to Elyse, watching her throw her head back in laughter. "What lessons does she still need to learn?"

Wyltam's fingers curled around hers, bringing her hand to his lips. "The kind that teach her to read the unsaid, the truths hidden between words. A skill you've mastered."

Marietta's stomach sunk with the insinuation. "We should guide her."

"No." Wyltam's voice was firm, his eyes meeting hers. "Tough experiences ensure she never forgets the lesson."

Chapter Twenty-One

ELYSE

Returning from refilling her drink, Elyse approached her group, noticing their heads bent together in a whispered exchange. Drystan, a male she'd grown close to from the Resource branch, caught her eye and beckoned her nearer. Puzzled, she asked, "Is everything all right?"

Drystan's hand swept over his dark, tight curls, a nervous gesture she rarely saw. "We're ... surprised, that's all. Did you know they were the last royals of Satiros?"

She did know, but Wyltam wanted to keep it secret until after the treaty was signed. That was until Marietta broke the news. Wyltam had campaigned to give Marietta a voice, and her first act of using it sparked fear and suspicion. Elyse's gaze flicked to the dais, a grimace tugging at her lips. She rubbed the gold broached pinned on her chest then shifted her focus back to Drystan. "Perhaps."

Drystan's brow furrowed. "And you've been walking around with that knowledge? Without a word to anyone?"

Her voice remained steady, though the weight of his question pressed against her. "Why would I? It's simply a part of the treaty."

"Because it's monumental. An announcement of this magnitude—"

"It's a treaty, Drystan. Every detail carries weight."

He studied her in silence, the gravity of the situation clear in the furrows between his brows. "It's … jarring to hear." His serious expression melted away. "Not that there's any problem, of course. We all assumed the transition to Enomenos wouldn't change our administration. That King Wyltam would be the head of our government for years to come, not …" He gestured vaguely.

"Why? When Enomenos is based on an elected system?" she asked.

Aryk, who worked with Drystan, spoke first. "We all thought we'd hear about our positions being elected on in some future, you know? It's a shift that affects us all." He pinned Elyse with his stare. "Even you."

Elyse nodded, impressed that Wyltam predicted this reaction from his officials. The idea of needing votes from people outside their influence made them panic. "Treaties tend to come with big changes. I don't find it all that surprising."

"Without a doubt," Drystan said, draping an arm around Aryk. "She would know because she's *close* with the queen."

Aryk snapped his mouth shut after a glance from Drystan.

"I work for King Wyltam," she corrected. She was friends with Marietta, but their friendship didn't make her privy to that information.

"Of course. Enough of work!" Drystan nodded to Elyse's cup. "What's your poison for the evening?"

"My usual, wine." Elyse took a sip. "Drier than I prefer."

"If you had to pick your perfect glass of wine, what would it be?" Drystan asked.

Elyse had never considered such a question. Wine was a necessity to get through social gatherings and not something she sought out. "Um, I'm not sure. Something red and a little less sharp?"

"Good to know," Drystan said, nodding. "I'm hosting a small get together soon, and we could pull a rare vintage I think you'd enjoy. You should come. And before you say no, it'll be modest. Exclusive, if you will. I know you're not a fan of big gatherings."

Elyse's instinct was to refuse. An evening alone with *Statues and Sculptures of Syllogi* had been her solace on the horizon for days. But then she remembered her conversation with Wyltam. "I'd love to attend."

His smile widened. "Perfect. I'll introduce you to my other friends. They're eager to meet you." At her confused expression, he added, "Well, some of them already know you. Nobles from your youth."

Elyse choked on her drink. "Which ones?" she asked, her heart racing.

"I'll let it be a surprise."

"I'm not fond of surprises."

He chuckled. "A hint then—no one too close, but familiar enough."

Relief crept in at the thought of Lydia's absence. That she could manage. Elyse exhaled, tension easing from her shoulders.

"I wonder what details they're keeping hidden about trade," Aryk interjected. "There has to be something in there with what we're getting from Enomenos."

"This is a party, not a meeting," Drystan answered.

"Humor me. Maybe their ale will be—"

"It's nice to see you dry, Elyse."

Her stomach churned at the sound of the voice. She turned to see Grytaine smiling, hand resting on the swell of her belly, utterly unconcerned with interrupting.

Drystan bowed his head excitedly. "Lady Grytaine, it's—"

"There's a fountain on the other side of those bushes if you wish to take another dip," Grytaine murmured, her gaze darting to something in the distance.

Elyse bit back a retort and swallowed, her lips parting as she struggled to find the right words. The chatter and laughter mingled with the soft music, creating a chaotic backdrop that made it difficult for her to gather her thoughts, let alone formulate a response.

"What's this about fountains?" Aryk asked.

Grytaine's lips pursed in mock chastisement. "Your friends are unaware of your ... recreational pursuits, it seems."

Elyse's pulse quickened, the need to escape crawling beneath her skin. She shook her head, willing herself to retreat, but Grytaine pressed on, her voice teasing, though laced with an edge. "Our dear Elyse has developed a penchant for plunging into the water features and disrupting perfectly pleasant afternoons."

Drystan turned to her with a confused smile.

"I, uh. I'm—" Elyse stepped away, her foot catching the corner of a rug. She staggered backward into a passing tray of drinks. The delicate glasses wobbled on their perch, then toppled off, spilling across the ground in a cascade of cracking and splashing. She gasped and scrambled to steady herself, heart pounding in her chest.

Drystan and Aryk's hands reached out, but Grytaine was quicker, extending a hand to Elyse. She paused before accepting. As she stood, Grytaine drew her in, whispering with an annoyed expression, "Aim higher, will you?"

Chapter Twenty-Two

KEYAIN

Keyain watched Marietta and Wyltam on the dais, his fingers tightening around his glass as he tried to block out the sight of them leaning close, their heads bent together. Their words were muffled, but he could see their mouths moving. The same black outfits, the matching expressions. Keyain took a sip of his drink, a knot forming in his stomach as he witnessed his peers congratulate them. Those same fucking people congratulated him on saving his wife a few months prior. And now look at her. A queen, or soon to be.

"Ready for Olkia?" Dyeiter asked.

"Hmm?" Keyain tore his gaze away as the sound of shattering glass resounded through the party.

"The treaty? Olkia? You never got to visit after you conquered the city."

Keyain took a long sip of the drink. Conquered was a strong word. He had spent the better part of the past month approving an exit strategy ahead of the treaty. "I hate that place." He glanced back at the dais, to the female he associated with the city-state.

Dyeiter stared a moment, then sighed. "I forget you *traveled* so much."

Keyain caught the irritation in his voice.

"Hope it was worth it while things were good. Now she's our biggest security risk."

At the sound of Marietta's laugh, his gaze darted to her once more.

"Get over it, son." Dyeiter placed his hand on his shoulder. "Better things will come."

The mere thought of Marietta becoming Wyltam's wife made him want to drink himself into a stupor. Still, he couldn't deny his strange satisfaction, knowing her greatest weaknesses were now Wyltam's problems. It was a bitter irony.

Time altered everything yet, in some ways, nothing changed at all.

"You'll have to congratulate them at some point." Dyeiter took a sip of his alcohol and nodded toward the dais. "Do you have a plan?"

Keyain raised his glass, swishing the contents. "Drink until shame eludes me."

Sighing, Dyeiter stepped closer. "You are a warrior—a leader. You don't need substances to give you strength." He lowered his voice, his gaze landing on a group of individuals that Keyain had also been avoiding all evening. "Approach with the Exisotis. Let's see how the future queen handles the pressure of her past."

Keyain gripped his glass tighter, throwing back the remaining drink. Not a bad plan, but one that would invoke the wrath of Wyltam.

Dyeiter patted his shoulder as he turned to leave. "You're more than capable of handling this. Use tonight to your advantage."

More sage advice from Dyeiter that left Keyain wanting to pull out his hair. If he could focus on planning a war without court scheming in the background, maybe he could fully fill his lungs with air again. Keyain flagged down another servant for a drink.

"It's hard to watch, isn't it?" Tryda's voice cut through his thoughts as she approached.

"Marietta?"

Tryda shook her head, indicating another direction. "No, Elyse. She's turning into Wyltam's little puppet."

Keyain's gaze tracked the path of hers until it settled on Elyse, dressed in black, mirroring the attire of Wyltam and Marietta. An unsettling bitterness crawled through his mind, the unity in their appearance a silent affront he could neither dismiss nor swallow.

"She could be useful," Tryda mused, her tone light yet edged with intent. "Rekindling that union might be worth considering. Both of you are young, influential, attractive—there's power in that."

Keyain's shoulders tensed. A marriage between them had never been part of the plan.

"Handsome couples hold influence at court."

His response came out dull, hollow. "I'll consider it."

Tryda's smile widened. "Some matters aren't left to thought. Speak to her tonight, before you're gone too long."

Every bit of his being wanted to say no, but the harsh reality of his position clamped it down. He understood the price of maintaining his status, the cost of remaining a minister. Dyeiter and Tryda had altered their approach since the truth surfaced—his secrecy had costed him and now he was firmly in their debt. He raised his glass, letting the liquor burn its way down, a moment of bracing heat before he could gather the resolve to make his way over.

Elyse chatted with a few of Minister Asyn's stewards. When Keyain drew near, their conversation halted abruptly. They exchanged furtive glances before slipping away, leaving Elyse with a faintly furrowed brow as she turned to depart.

Keyain stepped up and asked, "How are you?"

Elyse pivoted toward him, her stare hardening. "Fine."

"It's been a while since we last spoke." He cleared his throat, the sound sharp in the heavy silence. "You appear to be well."

"We've both been busy." She fidgeted with the rings on the fingers holding her glass, her gaze unwavering from the party.

"When I return from Olkia, we should get together." He took a sip of his drink to bolster himself. "Like we used to."

"As in, when we were betrothed?" Globe lights rose from the garden beds, their gentle glow turning her eyes into pools of melted gold.

Keyain shrugged. "I always enjoyed the time we spent together. We could see where it leads."

"You can't be that dense."

"What do you mean?" His pulse quickened as he surveyed their surroundings. The spacious distance between them and the nearest listener brought a momentary relief.

"I think you know." Her eyes darted over his shoulder, toward the dais.

Keyain's anger surged, the alcohol pushing it into a white-hot blaze. "Marietta turned you against me," he snarled, his grip tightening around the glass until the crystal threatened to shatter. The thought of it breaking under his hand had a twisted appeal.

Elyse shook her head. "Leave me alone, Keyain."

"You were my friend," he pressed, the words heavy with accusation.

She exhaled sharply, turning to walk away.

Before she could take more than a step, Keyain's hand closed around her wrist, holding her back. "After all this time, you—"

"She asked you to leave her alone." The voice, low and cold, was in his ear before he could finish. Keyain turned his head to find Wynn standing uncomfortably close, eyes dark with warning. "Wyltam won't hesitate to make an example of you if you cause trouble tonight. Go on, give him a reason."

Keyain's gaze flicked around the garden, the realization dawning that others had started to notice. He dropped his hand, releasing Elyse. His lips curled into a sneer. "Always playing the king's whore, aren't you, Wynn?" He spun on his heel before the insult could fully land, walking away before the urge to strike overtook him.

His heart pounded in his ears as he navigated the crowd of guests, seeking out Tryda. But when he spotted a cluster of Exisotis members moving toward Wyltam and Marietta, the anger flared up again. Now? Of all times? His pulse hammered as he fought to steady himself, a slow inhale, then another, before he forced himself to join the approaching group.

Keyain's gaze settled on the man standing directly in front of him, an older human with brown skin—a tactician named Josse. A few decades back, several nobles vanished after visits to Enomenos, and whispers of Josse's involvement had lingered ever since. He leaned closer to a second male with a shaved head, murmuring words that reached only the intended ears.

Keyain's eyes narrowed as he recognized the other male—Tilan. Gone was his matted hair, now shaved to his scalp. "I can't do it," he said, his voice thick with emotion.

"Not surprising," Keyain cut in. "How do you face the woman you conned into marriage when she sits beside her new husband?"

Tilan spun around, his expression twisting into a snarl. "At least ours was her choice. Unlike you, I respect the concept of consent."

A slow smirk tugged at Keyain's lips. "I didn't realize she consented to her father handpicking one of his lackeys to wed her." He took a deliberate sip of liquor, savoring the moment. "But then again, you never truly understood her."

Red plumed on his cheeks as he stepped forward. Keyain's smirk deepened when Josse caught Tilan's arms, restraining him.

"No need, Josse," Keyain's voice dripped with mockery. "It's not as though he could hit me with those hands."

His momentary win soured when his gaze locked onto Wyltam's. His expression echoed that night, the one when he learned Keyain had gone into the dungeons and shattered every joint in Tilan's hands. Keyain glanced at the reason he had gone down there in the first place. Marietta sat Wyltam's side, her smile serene as Pelok droned on about glasses. His drinks threatened to come up as his stomach churned.

"I suppose I can pay for thrice as many now," Marietta responded with a laugh.

"I'll remember to follow up on that when we reach Olkia. Though with your new position as queen, you'll likely be too busy for a drink at the Dog."

Keyain's eyes narrowed in disbelief. Of course, Wyltam would never allow Marietta near an Exisotis stronghold. It was laughable, really, the idea that she might want to go. Despite her fury at Keyain's lies, she seemed perfectly content with the Exisotis' grip on her life—a grip they'd held for years. What did Keyain know? He'd only tried to free her.

His attention snapped back as Tilan approached, his voice low enough that Keyain couldn't hear. Marietta's face betrayed nothing—either the words were rehearsed, or she had mastered the art of masking her emotions, a skill likely learned from Wyltam. What a charismatic pair they made.

Marietta didn't even offer her thanks, instead nodding her head as Wyltam accepted it for her. His heartbeat quickened, hopeful it'd be more of the same. For once, maybe Marietta would fade into the background.

As the last Exisotis member said their piece, Keyain approached with a deep bow. When he picked up his head, he saw Marietta's glower. Whatever peace he had hoped for vanished, instead replaced with irritation prickled by alcohol. Even now, she hated him more than Tilan. The least he could do was give a genuine reason to be angry. "I am humbled by the appearance of Your Graces," he said, keeping the bite of sarcasm buried beneath his words.

"We're grateful for the work you've put toward protecting our city-state, with both the war and the treaty," Wyltam answered, Marietta quiet at his side.

"I'm pleased my efforts to protect our city are recognized. Amazing, really, what losing a burden can accomplish."

Wyltam's expression turned to stone, but his voice lanced through Keyain's mind. *"You'll come to regret those words."*

Satisfaction rippled through Keyain, a quiet victory against months of silent suffering. The taste of defiance was sharp, almost intoxicating. He raised his glass. "To the new queen. May her reign break the curse upon the throne."

He didn't wait for a response, draining his glass as the hum of conversation swelled into a fervor. He rejoined Dyeiter and Tryda and retreated at the fringes of the party. Keyain shot a glance toward the dais, his eyes seeking Adalyn's. He greeted her with a nod, only to be met by a cold, dismissive stare. The satisfaction he had taken in slighting Marietta dissolved under the weight of her disregard. Elyse wasn't the only one deluded by Marietta's charm.

Royir clapped Keyain on the shoulder and guided him over to Dyeiter. "A cursed throne, indeed. Come, there's much to discuss."

Keyain forced a smile and glanced at the exit, the gathering now too loud, too suffocating. "Unfortunately, I have work to finish before we leave in the morning."

As he went to excuse himself, Dyeiter patted the seat next to him. "I insist you stay. There are some people I'd like you to speak with before the night is over."

Though the desire to escape gnawed at him, Keyain forced a smile and ordered another drink. The glass clinked against the table, the sound distant in the haze of forced laughter and empty nods. Words circled him, meaningless chatter that couldn't cut through the fog settling in his mind. The conversations meant nothing; the faces around him, even less.

As evening dragged on, Keyain's thoughts unraveled, pulling him back to those early days of military ascent when ambition blazed brightly, casting long shadows of promise. Now, those flames had guttered, snuffed out by the relentless press of reality.

It was as Olytia had promised. Regardless of who held the power, he would be nothing more than a pawn. No true friends. No true allies. In this suffocating realization, the finality of his position became unbearable. He was nothing more than a piece on the board—easily moved, easily discarded.

Chapter Twenty-Three
MARIETTA

The door to the suite clicked shut behind them, the soft sound swallowed by the thick, muffling silence that followed.

"At least tonight is over," Wyltam muttered, dragging his fingers through his hair. He paused in the entryway, where the dim evening light washed the colors into deep greens and blacks. The moon's glow seeped through the balcony doors, tracing the edges of the living room's furniture in pale silver.

"Worse than you anticipated?" Marietta rolled her shoulders, the weight of the wisteria headpiece pressing against her skull.

Wyltam's gaze flicked to her, but his answer was in the weariness lining his face. "Well, you were the first to declare that we're the last of the Satiroan royals."

"What?" The room stilled. Her pulse quickened. "How is that possible? It's written into the treaty."

"Yes," he said slowly, "but that particular detail was never meant to be known outside the drafting committee."

Marietta's cheeks burned. "You conveniently left that part out. How could I have known?"

Wyltam's hand moved to his collar, fingers working to undo the top button of his shirt. "Perhaps I should've said something."

"You absolutely should have." She stepped closer, the distance between them shrinking into nothing. "How am I supposed to succeed when you withhold information?"

"It was an honest mistake."

A wave of unease suddenly pressed onto her chest, threatening to steal her breath. She didn't trust his easy dismissal. "Was it?"

Wyltam's fingers paused their work for a brief second, then he offered, "Of course."

As the unease in her chest twisted, she knew at her core that he was lying. Marietta turned away, conflicted. Until now, things had been good—she believed Wyltam had been working with her, not against her. She hesitated, then asked, "You don't want me involved, do you?"

Wyltam tilted his head, a gesture too calculated, too measured. "I want you by my side, to advise—"

"I have trouble believing that."

She moved to leave, frustration driving her steps, but his hand closed around her arm, halting her. "You will have a voice. A powerful one. But only after you've grasped the intricacies of Satiroan politics. Your speech carried a good message, but it will lead to multiple meetings during our journey to Olkia. There will be last-minute additions that must be addressed before we depart."

"That's a bit dramatic."

Wyltam's expression sobered as he turned Marietta to face him. The cool touch of his hands slid up her arms, cupping her elbows. "Until the treaty is signed, until we're officially married, nothing is certain. Between now and then, there's a potential for everything to all fall apart. I want you to be present in every meeting, and I want you to lead. But until you sit on that throne, everything you say and do will be scrutinized and potentially used against you."

Marietta opened her mouth to speak, then paused, silence slipping into the space where words had been. She had known better—the elven nobility would always dissect every word that passed her lips. It's why the ministers insisted on writing her speech in the first place. But those details had slipped her mind when she stood before the people she would come to govern, once again speaking without considering the consequences. She drew back from his touch, the cool air rushing into the gap between them. Her headpiece became unbearably leaden.

"We're treading a delicate path between the familiar monarchy our government knows and the foreign concept of a republic," Wyltam continued. "Those in power will do anything to retain it, and they see the treaty as a threat to their control."

Marietta's fingers fumbled with her hairpins, each one clinging stubbornly to her curls as if conspiring with the headpiece to prolong her torment. The weight dug into her scalp, sending a dull throb across her forehead. "I can't apologize for what I said tonight." Another pin surrendered, falling to the hallway table with a soft click. "No one warned me it was a secret."

"I'm not here for an apology," Wyltam said, his voice softening. "What I need from you is trust."

Her hands fell to her sides, her voice barely a whisper. "You are a tough person to trust."

"I've done everything within my means to earn it, Marietta." He closed the distance between them, his gaze intense. "Every decision, every action was guided by consideration for you and your needs, even when it went against my own better judgment."

Marietta inclined her head, brows arching. She had longed for a voice in her role as queen, but not at the cost of diverting his focus toward her happiness. A shiver traced her skin at the notion, and she pivoted toward the bedroom. "Save your 'better judgment' for the throne. While my trust in you is lacking, I believe you'll make a good king. But a king with divided attention is a dangerous one. I'll do my best to remain silent and out of your way if that's what fits into your plan, because you, above all, cannot afford distraction. Focus on the crown, not me."

In an instant, Wyltam blocked her path, halting her movement. With a gentle touch, he tilted her face to his. In the dim light, she traced the hard angles of his face, the shadows gathering in his dark eyes. "You say that as if it's easy, as if I'm capable of staying away. You are gravity—everything pulls toward you. My whole being is hopelessly drawn to *you*."

His lips found hers, hungry and desperate. Marietta's breath hitched, her fingers curling into the soft fabric of his shirt as she pulled him closer. It was months of longing and unspoken tension coming together in one sweet, aching moment. She deepened the kiss, her tongue finding its way into his mouth. The low groan that escaped him made something inside her shift, and she tugged him closer, urging him toward the bedroom.

"Wait." His voice strained, his cheeks flushed pink and eyes glossy. "There have been emergency meetings called. I have to attend. Leaving you is the last thing I want to do."

She stepped back, her hand going to her lips where his phantom touch lingered. "What's the emergency?"

He glanced down, then back at her. "About your speech. Concerns about the future government." He kissed her cheek. "Don't wait up for me. I'll see you when we leave in the morning."

Wyltam departed, leaving Marietta alone in the hallway, the silence heavy around her. The heat of their exchange ebbed away, and clarity crept in, sharp and unwelcome. He had lied—without flinching, without hesitation—and yet, she had been ready to cast that aside, to let the pull between them drag her into his bed.

As she moved to prepare for sleep, her thoughts refused to settle. The man she was destined to marry called her gravity, yet he was the storm, a force that tore through her resolve. He engulfed her, unyielding, searing through every defense she tried to muster. And as she lay down, the question gnawed at her: how long could she withstand a storm without being shattered by it?

Chapter Twenty-Four
MARIETTA

With the Queen's Guard by her side, Marietta stepped out of her carriage and became immediately overwhelmed by the vibrant sights and sounds of Olkia. It was a welcome respite after a week confined within a cozy but monotonous wooden box that offered little distraction from her restless thoughts.

Olkia stretched out before her, a patchwork of pink, orange, yellow, and blue, forming the city she considered home. The whinnies of horses and the clatter of hooves on cobblestones reached her—sounds she hadn't heard in months. The wind played with her curls, carrying with it the damp scent of Lake Malakos, stirring memories that were both comforting and bittersweet.

This city had once been theirs—hers and Tilan's. Now, the final remnants of their marriage were about to be severed, leaving them both to forge separate paths. Marietta shut her eyes, recalling their wedding on the lakeshore. The nights at the Lonely Dog Tavern, where laughter flowed as freely as the ale. The languid afternoons spent meandering through market stalls. Moments of shared joy, the kind that lingered in a smile long after the joke was forgotten. Her heart clenched at the illusion of what had been. She swallowed against the thickness rising in her throat.

Wynn signaled from the inn's entrance, and Wyltam slid his hand to her lower back, guiding her into the building and to her room on the top floor. The door clicked shut behind them, a sharp sound that cut through the fading echoes of the guards' footsteps outside.

After spending countless of nights at inns, she concluded none of them compared to this suite. Lush rugs, silk furnishings, intricate wood details on the bed and wardrobes. She wandered toward the sitting area, finding crystal glasses and a matching pitcher for water. No inn in Enomenos had ever matched this level of luxury. Did the inn always offer a room like this, or had they furnished it for her new royal status? The thought coiled uncomfortably in her gut.

Despite her overly opulent surroundings, Marietta's thoughts drifted to Wyltam. This was the first moment they'd been truly alone since leaving Satiros. Her lips tingled with the memory of his kiss, searing and unforgiving, while her body ached for more than it should have. She turned, eyes searching the door where he stood, his face a mask of inscrutable calm.

"How does it feel to be home?" His voice, rich and deep, dragged her mind from its wandering.

Marietta continued toward the bed and let her hand drift across the fine covers, fingers tracing the intricate patterns. "This is ... strange, but I'm managing."

"If you're comfortable sharing, I'm here to listen."

She sank into the bed with a sigh. "It's as if I'm a stranger in my own home. Everything is familiar, but it no longer feels like mine."

Wyltam nodded and approached her. "Mind if I sit?"

Marietta hesitated, nervous to be close to him again, but conceded with a nod. The surface dipped beneath his weight, her arm tingling with his closeness.

"I faced something similar when I returned to court."

"And why did you leave again?"

Wyltam's laugh came softly, a slight smile pulling at his lips. The sight drew her in, a haze settling over her mind—equal parts infuriating and soothing.

"So nosy," he murmured. "This isn't about why I left, but what happened when I returned. Decades of my life were spent behind the walls of the palace. The marble, the gardens, and the luxury filled my every day. When I returned, I had remembered those things, but they didn't feel the same. It took me a while to realize why that was," he said. "Nothing had changed, but I had."

The revelation made her frown. Marietta had left Olkia as a baker and came back a queen. The days ahead promised little more than endless meetings, each one erasing any hope for time to herself. At first, she had wanted to see more of the city-state, to reconnect with old friends. Now, the idea of being consumed by obligations was almost a solace. At this moment, she couldn't bear the weight of seeing her home through unfamiliar eyes.

"At least there's comfort in knowing I'm not the only one who has gone through this," she said.

"We're partners. Distractions and all." Wyltam brushed a few strands behind her ear, his gaze darting to hers before returning to his hand. "In the same vein as being partners, we also need to remember to be a united front."

"Any treaty details I shouldn't talk about?" She arched an eyebrow.

"I'm telling you this because your father might do something ... unexpected."

Marietta pulled away from him. "My father will be excited to see me."

"He will," Wyltam agreed, voice steady. "But he would also go to any lengths to keep you safe—even if it means drastic measures." He let the weight of his words settle. "But we need to stand together, show everyone that I see you as my equal, that we're on the same side."

"Do you, though? See me as your equal?"

His answer was swift. "I do."

"Me, who was a baker mere months ago?"

"You, a courageous woman who finds joy in helping others and has a long-standing history of doing so."

"Dug into my past?"

He averted his eyes, the fall of his hair obscuring his expression. "Pelok and the other Exisotis members shared your previous work. You were never merely a baker or a bookkeeper. You were hope to some and a friend to many."

Her lips curved into a sardonic smile. "None of that places me on equal footing with a king."

"No, it makes you far more worthy than I to rule." Wyltam stood and made his way to a door on the other side of the room. "I'll let you rest and get ready for our meetings this afternoon. If you need anything, I'm in the adjoining room."

As he departed, Marietta's handmaids swept in with a flurry of excitement. They spoke in hushed tones, their hands moving deftly as they guided her through the rituals of preparation. The bath was a refuge, its warm waters and faint aroma of herbs cocooning her as she wrestled with her emotions.

The impending meeting and her reunion with her father hung heavy in her thoughts. No words could capture the depth of the betrayal searing within her. While Tilan's deception had been painful, her father's had been cruel. Despite it, a flicker of genuine eagerness remained when she thought of reuniting with her parents.

The handmaids worked around her, their expertise transforming her from a woman of contemplation into one of regality. They adorned her in garments that whispered of nobility and elegance—rich, flowing fabrics in deep purple and green jewel tones that seemed to shimmer with every movement. Their hands moved with practiced precision, arranging her hair and applying makeup with the same grace. As the gilded wisteria wreath settled upon her head, her reflection shifted in the mirror. The queen gazing back at her was a stark contrast to the baker she once was in this city-state. Until that very moment, it had felt like a distant concept, a duty to be checked off from a list. The actuality of her position rested heavily on her shoulders.

The subsequent silent dinner failed to provide any comfort, as she returned to Wyltam with the weight of her responsibilities still on her mind. Together, they made their way to Olkia's civic building. The wake of the recent attack was barely visible; the damage was less extensive than she had expected. As Marietta craned her neck for a better sight of the surrounding buildings, she caught a glimpse of what appeared to be a scorched structure before her view was blocked. Their guards formed a protective ring as they disembarked from the carriage and guided them through the corridors to the meeting room.

The moment they entered, Marietta could sense the shift in the space.

Before the gathered attendees, her regal attire cast her as an anomaly—her gown better suited for a ball than an official assembly. Her eyes swept across the room, searching for familiar faces amidst the sea of curious stares. City-state representatives. Members of the Enomenos Unionization Council. Arlo, her local butcher. Gods, even he knew about the Exisotis, given that he sat among their members. Pelok leaned over to say something to Arlo as someone stood, drawing her attention.

His brown wavy hair hung loosely around his head, his tawny skin more lined than the last time she saw him. When his stern eyes met Marietta's, a fleeting softness emerged. Marietta slowed her pace, Wyltam and her guards falling into step beside her.

The room hushed as her father drew nearer. "Marietta." His voice rasped, his expression slackening with awe. As he moved closer, her guards tensed, shifting into a defensive stance.

At that moment, she didn't care about the rules. She tried to push past Coryn, but Wyltam slipped his hand into hers and held her back. His voice slithered into her head. *"You are the queen of Satiros right now. Show unity."*

Exasperated, she wished for the ability to snap back at him with her mind. Instead, she paused, dipping her head. "Father." A flash of pain showed in his expression as she turned with Wyltam.

In the heart of the meeting room, three tables curved in a grand horseshoe, their dark wood gleaming under the light of flickering chandeliers. At the open end, a podium stood poised, its surface meticulously polished and waiting. Of those who were already seated in the high-backed chairs, they murmured softly to one another as they waited for the session to begin.

Golds and greens draped the center table, with the crest of Satiros gleaming in gilded detail. Marietta took her place beside Wyltam at the heart of the room. To Wyltam's right sat Minister Sethyr Calsyn, the newly appointed foreign relations minister. The chair next to Marietta was claimed by another high-ranking diplomat in the foreign relations branch. Keyain, stationed at the end near the podium, remained conspicuously distant.

She leaned over to Wyltam and nodded toward him. "Your doing?"

He took her hand in his and brushed her knuckles against her lips. *"Don't be too obvious. Your every move is being watched."*

Marietta steadied her smile as her gaze drifted, registering the weight of countless eyes upon her. Her father came into view, returning to his seat with an expression as impenetrable as stone. Marietta's smile softened, a silent gesture hoping to reassure him of her well-being.

As someone called the assembly's attention, Marietta recognized some of the Enomenoan officials, the most notable being the human woman well into her decades. She had last seen Elector Alora Lunalis at a gathering celebrating commerce in Olkia a few years ago.

Introductions began with members of the Enomenoan Union Council. Marietta's eyes flickered across the faces of the Assembly representatives, noting the one she had voted for from Olkia. It seemed the council had sent only the leading representatives from each city-state. Following them were the Advisory members, elected officials who offered counsel to the elector on various committees like education and health. Their names rang unfamiliar to Marietta, the last election having been years ago. The final group consisted of Judiciary members, tasked with interpreting Enomenoan law.

As they proceeded to the Exisotis, Marietta grew restless. She shifted in her seat, her leg shaking beneath the table. Wyltam's hand settled gently on her thigh, a silent reminder to still herself.

They introduced her father as their leader, notably using his moniker—the Shepherd—rather than his real name. Tilan stood next and was announced with his official title: Head Artificer.

Her father gestured to Tilan. "Though Tilan has recently rejoined us, he opted to stay in Satiros to strengthen our ties with their court."

Tilan's nod was minimal, a brief acknowledgment. Marietta stifled the urge to ask Wyltam about the implications as they moved through the list of names. Pelok garnered the title Head Diversionist, her butcher named Quartermaster. Her chest tightened, each title a new shard of betrayal. How could she have been such a fool?

Wyltam's hand, still resting on her thigh, squeezed. The only thing that helped was when she finally called upon Therypon, the goddess's warmth soothing the tightness in her chest.

Half an hour passed as the introductions dragged on. The Satiroan officials were presented one by one, starting with Wyltam and then Marietta, who was recognized as the future queen. They meandered through the agenda for the week's meetings, a process that left Marietta puzzled. The endless discussion of coming plans instead of addressing the immediate matters seemed pointless to her.

As her patience waned, a representative from Enomenos finally stood. "Before we proceed with the negotiations, we must first dissolve the marriage between Tilan and Marietta Reid," he announced. "This will begin first thing tomorrow morning." His words were accompanied by a display of enthusiasm for forging new connections. Marietta, however, felt the weight of expectation press heavily upon her shoulders as she met Tilan's gaze across the room.

As she and Wyltam made for the exit, her father approached once more. "Your Graces," he said, the sound coming forced. "Allow me a few minutes with my daughter, please."

Wyltam opened his mouth to respond. "Unfortunately—"

"Go on ahead," she said, turning to him. "I know you have much to do, and I'd hate to delay you with our reunion. I'll join you shortly."

Wyltam held her gaze for a moment. "For you, I can postpone it," he said with a tight smile. "I am equally eager to meet the man who raised this wonderful woman." He signaled the guards to move aside.

Her father cleared his throat. "Ah, I was hoping to speak with her somewhere more private." He gestured to the room. "And alone."

"We can step into another room, I'm sure," Wyltam said as he grabbed the attention of one of the functionaries, who motioned for them to follow.

"I meant just Marietta and I. A moment for a father and his child to be reunited."

Wyltam kept his back to her father. "That won't be possible."

Her father's jaw flexed as he glanced at Marietta. She offered a small smile of comfort. "I don't mind. I have nothing to hide."

He responded with a low hum, his grimace easing.

They were led to a narrow room off the main walkway. While her guards waited at the door, she guided her father to the couches, Wyltam trailing behind. Marietta cleared her throat and leaned toward Wyltam expectantly. "Could you find me a drink?"

He hesitated, his gaze drifting briefly before he nodded and crossed the room to the water pitcher.

Marietta turned to her father. In that moment, all the anger dissolved as she threw her arms around his neck. He pulled her close, cupping the back of her head.

He leaned away and examined her face. "Are you okay? You look thinner." His brows knitted together as his gaze fell on her neck, catching sight of the visible end of her iros tattoo.

"I'm as healthy as I've ever been, but I need answers now." She withdrew from his embrace, keeping her strained voice low. "Where's mother?"

"In an undisclosed location ever since you were—" He stopped himself and glanced at Wyltam and her guards. "Since you left Olkia."

"Did she know?" she asked, her rage building. "About the Exisotis?"

"Yes, but—"

"I'll need to be furious with you two and Tilan then."

"Tilan followed my orders."

"That makes it worse." Marietta clenched her teeth, folding her arms tightly around herself.

"We hid it from you to protect you."

"Protect me?" Marietta's laughter cut through the room, sharp and disbelieving. She shook her head slowly. "Was I truly born in Satiros?"

"Unintentionally—"

"Why were you in Satiros?" Her father glanced at Wyltam again. "Don't look at him," she snapped. "I'm the one who wants answers."

Her father sighed and rubbed his face. "My sister. Word had gotten back to me that she needed … support. And your mother went into labor early," he said, his voice tight. "You were so small, so not ready for the world. We had no choice but to seek help, which led to the city-state recording your birth. Yet," he paused, a heavy sigh escaping him, "I had it scrubbed from the official records."

Anger surged with panic, tightening around Marietta's throat. "You kept all of this from me." She turned away, her hand pressed over her mouth as she struggled to grasp the weight of the truth.

"Marietta—"

She raised a hand to silence him.

"While we're on the topic of your sister," Wyltam said, drawing her gaze, "they're friends."

Confused, Marietta turned to Wyltam and then her father.

Her father paled. "Enough of this. I need a *private* moment alone with my daughter before she leaves. Queen or not, she is my blood."

An uneasiness settled onto her chest as he walked to the door, letting it slam behind him.

Marietta turned to Wyltam as he approached. "Care to explain?"

"It should come from your father."

She laughed, exasperated. "You see me as your equal but you hide information from me once again."

"It needs to come from him."

Marietta lifted her chin and turned to Coryn. "Take me back to the inn."

"Mar—"

"Alone," she snapped without looking at Wyltam.

For all his talk about unity, he once again kept truths from her. Her emotions unraveled, her thoughts a tangled mess. As she stared ahead, the weight of the day's events pressed down, leaving her to wonder how she would endure the upcoming week if this was only the beginning.

Chapter Twenty-Five
MARIETTA

As evening draped itself over Olkia, Marietta paced through her room, her steps slow, her appetite sated by the feast held in their honor. She had spoken little during the meal, offering polite smiles and measured laughter when expected. The dishes—eggplants stuffed with onion, garlic, and grated tomatoes; spiced lamb kofta with yogurt sauce; rice laced with cinnamon, cumin, and cardamom, studded with almonds and dried apricots—should have stirred something within her, perhaps comfort or even a trace of longing. Instead, an unfamiliar weight settled in her stomach, heavy and unmoving.

The dessert lingered in her mind. Semolina flour, roasted and steeped in a milk syrup, embedded with chopped pistachios, shaped into a perfect dome. The delicate hint of rose water intertwined with the nuts and dried rose petals dusted atop. When she cut into it, a sweet cream had flowed from the center—a precise touch, one she had spent years perfecting.

Had someone stolen her recipe book? Perhaps one of her apprentices had moved on, opened their own shop? Such thoughts should not have been troubling, but the uncertainty nagged at her. The fact she couldn't ask, couldn't know who had carried this piece of her, left her restless, pacing the confines of a room that grew too small.

Lost in her thoughts, Marietta didn't notice Wyltam's arrival until the door swung open, startling her. "I knocked," he said, his tone carrying a trace of apology without conceding the word. "You were upset earlier."

She waved him off. "I'm fine."

"That's a lie." He slid his hands into his pockets and leaned against the doorway.

His infuriating habit of keeping information to himself extended her frustration. Yet, over dinner, she had accepted her new life. Wyltam played his games, and she would have to navigate the maze of half-truths and fragments he handed her. Instead of dwelling on it, she focused on her new fixation: her recipe book.

"I'd like to visit my bakery tonight." She needed to see if it still stood, if anything remained of the life she once knew. Today had marked the end of one chapter—one that closed with revelations of her father's secret dealings and Tilan's shadowy involvement.

Wyltam's gaze held her. "I'll have to accompany you."

"Why?"

"There have been two attempts on your life."

"Tilan should be the one to come with me. Anyone else would be … wrong." She refused to meet his eyes, even as the silence between them deepened, pressing against her like a physical weight.

"Your life isn't something I'm willing to gamble with. If you wish to go, I'll remain discreet."

"Very discreet, then. If you must."

Marietta stepped into the hallway, where her guard had already assembled—Coryn, Sibylla, Ryder, and a few others, each standing at attention. She acknowledged them with a slow nod.

"You're still on duty, Coryn?"

He shrugged, the quiet clink of his armor breaking the silence. "I'm assigned to stay close whenever you leave your room while we're in Olkia."

She studied him, arching her brow. "And why is that?"

"If you were injured, I could heal you immediately." Coryn raised his hand, a soft white light pulsing from his fingertips.

"While I appreciate the caution, you need rest as well."

Coryn's shoulders lifted in another shrug. "It's an opportunity to see the city."

Following Coryn down the narrow stairs, the inn's wooden steps creaked under their combined weight. Soldiers in gleaming Satiroan armor awaited at the bottom, their presence a silent but heavy reminder of her new reality. Behind her, Wyltam's low voice murmured to Wynn, the sound barely audible over the clink of metal.

Marietta bit the inside of her cheek, the sensation grounding her amid her whirling thoughts. The sheer number of guards surrounding her made her meetings for the week all the more inviting. Walking through her home city-state with this retinue created a stark contrast to the carefree exploration she once enjoyed.

As they stepped onto the cobblestone street, another set of guards merged with their ranks, closing in around her. "My evening stroll has turned into a parade," she muttered under her breath.

Coryn's lips twitched, almost breaking his stoic facade, though his gaze never stopped scanning their vicinity. "You could have worse company."

"Gods, don't tell me you're bragging about yourself."

"I don't know if I should be amused or insulted."

"If we were alone, it'd be different." Marietta glanced between the onlookers and the uneven path beneath her feet as she walked the familiar hilly streets toward her old home. Some Olkians greeted her with bright smiles and friendly waves, while others met her with a more cautious stare, mirroring her own unease. "I can't escape the sense that I'm both home and a stranger here."

Coryn hummed thoughtfully. "I imagine I'd feel that if I ever set foot in Amigys again."

"Would you ever?" she asked.

"I'm not sure I'd be able to." His eyes lingered on the coral-colored building they passed, a flicker of something unreadable crossing his face. "Technically, I broke the law in Amigys by fleeing to Satiros. If I returned, they'd have every reason to arrest me, and that would spiral into a political mess. We're not exactly in need of more of those right now."

"Could your family come here?" she asked, rounding the corner. "I'm sure your father and brothers miss you."

He smiled at her. "Maybe I'll invite them. Though my youngest brother would have a jealous fit if he saw where I live. He always had a taste for the finer things."

Marietta looped her arm in his. "Let's find the nicest inn in Satiros, then. Give him something to talk about."

Coryn chuckled, and their conversation flowed into easy banter. She pointed out familiar buildings and landmarks as they strolled, the comfort of sharing her memories filling the space between them.

The lamplighters were making their rounds along the street as they neared the bakery. How many times had she gazed upon this scene? How many times had she set off to meet Tilan at the Lonely Dog? How many times had she walked this same stretch of road? It resonated with familiarity and nostalgia, tying her stomach into knots. This was the place where people knew her as Marietta Reid, a name she would soon surrender.

Rise Above stood out among the surrounding buildings with its golden yellow exterior had now dulled, and the bright white awning had grown grimy. Several guards broke away from the group, entering the building before Marietta. Along the front of the store, there lay a collection of old flowers and trinkets, as if it had transformed into a makeshift shrine. She pressed past the guards, her curiosity piqued by the signs.

"We love you, Marietta!"

"To our favorite baker."

"Justice for Marietta and Tilan."

Her hands trembled, and she couldn't bring herself to read further. Wyltam had called her hope, but she hadn't expected such grief. She raised her gaze to the boarded-up windows that were painted over. Squinting, she deciphered the words beneath: *"Fuck the Pig-Eared Bastards of Satiros."* As Marietta turned to speak with Coryn, the sight of Tilan standing alone off to the side caught her attention. She nodded, and Tilan echoed the gesture.

They both moved toward the door, only for Tilan to halt abruptly.

Marietta sensed the presence behind her, and she turned to Wyltam. "What happened to 'discreet?'"

"I'll be trailing a room behind you," he said, taking her hand and brushing a kiss against her knuckles. She didn't miss his glance toward Tilan.

"He's harmless."

"I wouldn't use harmless to describe him," Wyltam said. "Though he and I have an understanding."

Marietta's brow arched, her eyes narrowing. "An understanding?"

"I'll be here if you need me." Wyltam stepped back, joining Wynn, his hands sliding into his pockets.

Her mind churned with questions, trying to grasp the nature of their exchange. She studied Wyltam's profile, searching for hidden motives. The lines between her past and future blurred, a knot of anxiety tightening in her stomach. Taking a breath, Marietta entered the bakery.

The shop front appeared as it always had with its tables and display case. She wrinkled her nose as she inspected the moldering food left inside.

Tilan approached slowly. "Pelok shared no one had the heart to reenter the building after their initial sweep to see if we were ..." He trailed off, his voice quiet.

Marietta didn't respond, instead letting her hand glide across the countertop, leaving a trail in the dust. Her steps were heavy as she made her way to the kitchen.

The counters were how she left them except for the surfaces caked in debris and the faint fetid stench of old food. Tears pricked behind her eyes to see the place she considered a sanctuary in such a discarded state. She covered her mouth as she wandered. This kitchen should've been filled with laughter and gossip, heavy with the scent of yeast and sugar. Her apprentices should've been rolling out dough and helping Marietta decide new recipes. Her chest ached, and she absently reached for the warmth of Therypon, her presence easing Marietta's sorrow but not enough to wipe it away.

"Do you know if Genna and the others are safe?" she asked, her voice low as Tilan hovered in the doorway.

"I don't know," he answered, hesitating. "But the dessert tonight—it was yours, wasn't it? I remember you developing that recipe. Pelok only spoke of my apprentices."

"And they're unharmed?"

"Yes."

She turned toward him, a bitter edge creeping into her tone. "I suppose that's one advantage of being part of the Exisotis, then."

"Not all of them were."

"How long were you a member of the Exisotis?"

Tilan's eyes dropped to the floor, his silence heavy. "We don't have to talk about it."

"But we do." Marietta hastily wiped away her tears. "How long?"

The muscles in Tilan's jaw tightened, a grimace crossing his face. "A decade and a half."

"For half your life, then?" Her laugh rang out, cold and hollow. "And my father arranged for us to marry?"

"I love you, regardless of how our relationship began." His blue eyes met hers, intense and unwavering. "The Exisotis placed me in that position, but I was not ordered to fall in love. That part is real."

Marietta shook her head as she ducked below the counter. "As real as it could be, at least."

She sifted through the small pile of recipe books, her fingers brushing against the worn spines until she found the one she wanted. With a sigh, she stood, placed it on the countertop, and then flipped through the pages.

"Did I ever make you question it?" he asked, his voice growing sharper. "At any point, did I make you doubt I loved you?"

"Not once while we were married." Marietta paused over the dessert recipe, her fingers tracing the inked lines. A sense of gratification arose as she pictured one of her apprentices preparing the dessert for something as important as their dinner. Content, she closed the book. "Since I've discovered your hidden talent for lying, I've questioned it often."

Silence settled thickly between them as she focused on the cover, tracing the letters embossed across it.

At last, Tilan said, "Shep won't agree to any terms with Satiros."

"Shep?" Marietta repeated incredulously. Her anger relit anew. "The first time you met my parents, I was elated you and my father bonded so quickly. Foolish me," she said. "You two already had pet names for each other. What did he call you? I'm curious about how 'man I ordered to marry my daughter' shortens."

"Marietta—"

"If my father was concerned about my well-being, he would've told me the truth years ago."

"Your father loves you."

"Then why does he not want to see his child succeed in ways the Exisotis never could?"

"You're a baker and a businesswoman with a heart vast enough to hold the world," Tilan said, his gaze piercing hers, "but you are no queen."

His words struck, bitter and burning, cutting deeper than any insult. Tilan, the one who had been her rock, her unwavering belief. But now, to hear him cast doubt on her worth after all she had fought for—it stung worse than any lie he had slung. Had he only supported her because it kept her busy? Because it was part of his task?

The answers didn't matter. That seed of doubt, once planted, would forever twist in her mind, questioning what had been true between them.

She crossed her arms defensively. "What would you know about queens?"

"I know places like the palace and dresses like yours, are not you. You belong here" —he hit the countertop— "in Olkia. You belong with your people."

Marietta raised her chin, her gaze settling on Tilan. "If you had a chance to change the world, would you do it?"

He laughed, the sound harsh, matching the bitterness in his twisted smile. "I was changing the world. Look where it got me." He choked on his words as he stared at his hands. The knuckles were puffy and their movements stiff.

She furrowed her brows. "Were they not fixed?"

"They could reset the bones, but there was too much damage to the cartilage between the joints," he said. "I won't smith again, let alone hold a fucking spoon. I can't even smoke without ..." He took a deep breath as his voiced heightened.

Marietta closed the space between them, taking Tilan's hands in hers. "The Temple of Therypon could heal this."

He moved from her grasp. "They wasted my time and hope."

"They tried?"

Tilan nodded. "They can't regrow what was lost, only heal what is broken." His gaze dropped to her neck, to the tattoo of Therypon that crept out of her neckline. "Wouldn't you know that?"

"There hasn't been much time for training."

Tilan tore his stare from the tattoo to her face. "All of this is wrong."

Silence fell over them again.

"We should …" Tilan's voice trailed off as he glanced back at Wyltam, waiting in the shop's front.

Marietta didn't respond. Instead, she turned and made her way toward the hallway leading to the stairs. Her steps faltered at the sight of the dark reddish stain marking the bottom landing. Tilan appeared at her side with a sharp inhale.

"Keyain said I fell down the stairs, but I didn't realize this." She placed her hand over the area where the bandage had once been, a faint memory of pain lingering from her awakening in Satiros. "I thought he exaggerated the severity." Marietta stepped over the spot and climbed to the apartment.

The living room lay in disarray, furniture scattered and upended. Marietta's gaze swept over the wreckage, landing on the bookcase now stripped bare. Someone had been in here to pilfer what they could take. So much for no one entering.

"Are any of your things missing?" she asked.

Not hearing a response, she left and found Tilan standing in the doorway to their bedroom, his stare fixed upon another patch of old blood below the window. The mattress teetered precariously off its frame, and the sheets were mussed and stained. Their last moments together were frozen in this room at the moment everything had changed. The shambled state was a poetic fit to their end.

After all they had endured, one question burned in her mind. "Why return to Satiros? You should remain in Olkia."

Tilan stood motionless, tears spilling freely as he blinked rapidly. "If I'd been honest about the Exisotis from the beginning," he asked, his voice trembling, "would it have made a difference?"

Her voice was a whisper. "I would've never given you a chance."

Beside her, Tilan's chest heaved with each uneven inhale. Marietta's throat tightened as she remembered her first visit to his blacksmith shop. From that moment, their relationship was doomed to a bitter end, with Tilan's secrets inevitably crashing down on him.

The impulse to hold Tilan's hand or offer a comforting touch arose within her, but it was a kindness that was no longer necessary. Today marked the conclusion of their relationship. They were not partners, and in truth, they never should have been.

Tilan's voice cracked as he cleared his throat, the sound harsh and raw. "Could we go to the shore where we were married? It would be more fitting …"

His voice faltered, letting the unspoken words hanging between them— fitting for an end to their shared history. Marietta's eyes hardened as she caught his meaning.

"I never want to see it again," she murmured, her voice barely audible but laced with finality.

Without another word, Marietta turned, leaving as Tilan's emotions overcame him. She passed by Wyltam and Wynn, her gaze fixed straight ahead, her silence cutting deeper than any confrontation. Outside, she joined Coryn and her guards, the cool night air drawing her away from the painful memories she wished to leave behind.

Wyltam appeared at her side. "Are you all right?"

"I would like to be alone for the evening," she said, her voice thick. "That includes you."

He nodded and said nothing more as her guards took their positions around her. The sky had darkened, leaving the flickering orange of the gas lamps to light her path away from her past and into the future.

Chapter Twenty-Six

KEYAIN

Sweat gathered along Keyain's back in the stifling heat of the meeting room. Wearing a jacket in the late summer proved to be a poor decision, but he clung to it as a shield against the faces staring at him. He always found comfort in a uniform, and these days he wore more jackets than armor.

The Shepherd's face revealed nothing, a veneer of calm that mirrored the unreadable expressions of the Exisotis around him. Tilan's absence heightened the tension, sharpening Keyain's gaze on their leader. How many lies had the Shepherd fed Marietta throughout the years? How many Exisotis agents had he dispatched to pursue Keyain? The title 'Shepherd' was ill-suited. While he claimed to aid pilinos seeking refuge from Syllogi, the flock he tended were not docile sheep but a pack of wolves, lying in wait for the opportune moment to strike.

Steadying Keyain were General Hastyrn to his left and Wyltam on his right. The latter hadn't spoken a word to Keyain since his congratulations at the treaty send-off party, likely still upset. Let him be angry. What difference would it make?

As the meeting continued, Keyain rose to contribute, only to be forestalled by Enomenos's Head Defense Councilor. A moment of annoyance flashed across Keyain's face, but he chose silence, settling back into his chair as the councilor began detailing the aid promised for the war. The councilor's tone was measured, purposefully downplaying the previously reported legion numbers. Keyain lifted his hand, hoping to interrupt, but the councilor's gaze remained fixed, ignoring the gesture.

When the discussion turned to records of their enemies' armies, the councilor shifted his attention to the Satiroan side. "What was your last recorded sighting of Chorys Dasi's troop movements?" he asked, his voice steady.

Keyain and Hastyrn started to answer simultaneously. Keyain glanced at his subordinate, noting the confusion on Hastyrn's face as he struggled to keep up with the conversation.

"The question was for General Hastyrn."

Hastyrn cleared his throat, leaving Keyain confused. Had he missed something?

"A week before we departed, we still have seen no troop movements from Chorys Dasi. However, we found a contingent of soldiers leaving Reyila, heading south through the mountains. We have an informant keeping eyes on them."

The councilor nodded. "We're aware of them and have sent soldiers in Avato to the north to keep an eye. What of your spies within Chorys Dasi?"

"They've confirmed sixteen legions, though we suspect more," Keyain said, drawing the glare of the councilor.

Wyltam's voice sounded in his head. *Let Hastyrn handle this.*

Before Keyain could respond, Hastyrn spoke again. "We suspect at least five more legions dedicated to magic, but our sources can't confirm it. They keep their mages locked away within the castle. No one has infiltrated their court."

A councilor paused, the scratch of their pen cutting through the tense silence. "No eyes on the Chorys Dasi mages, no reports on troop movements. This is … troubling. Please tell us you have something more."

Hastyrn hesitated, the brief pause an invitation Keyain seized. "As General Hastyrn was about to say—"

Elector Alora leaned forward, her gaze sharp over the rim of her glasses. "Let General Hastyrn speak. You were permitted in this meeting under the condition that you remain silent."

A low hum buzzed through Keyain's thoughts, his pulse quickening, his ears ringing. "Pardon?"

"Minister Keyain, you have committed several serious crimes in Enomenos that we are overlooking on behalf of your king. The agreement is you are here to boost morale for Satiros but cannot collaborate in this meeting." She turned back to Hastyrn. "If you could, please continue."

Keyain ground his jaw and began to stand.

"*Stop talking, Keyain. Do not make me remove you from this room.*"

Keyain snapped his gaze to Wyltam, who remained focused on the meeting. They had conspired behind his back, excluded him from this planning. A cold wave of dread crept through him as he scanned the room. His eyes locked with the Shepherd's, who offered a sly, knowing smile. Fuck.

Fuck.

Fuck.

Keyain dug his nails into his palms, the sharp sting a warning that his skin might split and bleed. This was what it had come to—a minister stripped of power, helpless as his city faced negotiations that could break them.

Marietta's return had unraveled him, thread by thread, leaving him a frayed rope on the verge of snapping. His work had once been the knots holding him together, but now those knots had loosened, slipping away with each passing day. It wouldn't be long before there was nothing left, nothing to hold him together, and when the final thread snapped, he knew there'd be no one to pick up the pieces.

Chapter Twenty-Seven

ELYSE

As her first week without Wyltam ended, Elyse found herself secluded in her office with a stack of drawings spread before her. Acting as Wyltam's stand-in had seemed like it would be the greatest challenge, but as she scratched out yet another failed attempt, she realized how wrong she had been.

"Easy there," Fig murmured, their eye pressed to one of the lenses as they scribbled a note. "You're tearing yourself apart over some charcoal on paper."

"None of these are right." Elyse plopped back in her chair, chewing at her lip. She'd been so eager for their second project, designing jewelry with hidden compartments, but the excitement had faded as soon as she tried to sketch the details. "We should've waited before diving into the rings. I can't figure out how to make the hinges disappear on paper. I wish we could just tell the jeweler to hide them."

"That might work for now," Fig said, "but as the designs get more intricate—like the spike ring—we'll need precision. If it's not exact, we can't guarantee it'll function as intended."

At Elyse's exasperated sigh, Fig handed over the lens with a measured calm. "This one is the strongest of the set, if you're interested. The aithyr lines are still faint, but I believe I've found the right mix for the next batch."

Grateful for the diversion, Elyse brought the lens to her eye and drew in a sharp breath. "These are faint to you?" Through the glass, wisps of aithyr swirled gently through the room—barely distinct but undeniably present.

Fig sat up straighter. "Are they clear for you?"

"They're fainter than what I've seen with Mage's Eye," Elyse replied, her gaze fixed on the streams. "But I can still make out several patterns."

Fig fumbled for their quill, eyes bright with anticipation. "Please, count them and note their positions. If you can see this much, comparing it to the next set of lenses could be very telling."

As Elyse described the placements of the aithyr streams, a question she had grappled with since her scent training with Wynn surfaced in her mind.

"I know Fulbryk states that aithyr streams are fixed and can ebb and flow with their concentration of aithyr," she said to Fig, "but *can* they move? Is that a thing?"

"Not that I'm aware of. Fulbryk may have laid the groundwork for our understanding of magic, but his rules aren't the final word." They leaned back, pondering for a moment. "If you're up for it, we could dig through the library for other references."

Elyse's pulse quickened at the mention of time. She shot out of her seat. "How late is it?" she asked, hastily gathering her things.

Fig pulled out an aithyr clock, their eyes widening. "Damn, nearly ten o'clock."

"I forgot about the party." Elyse groaned, her belongings spilling from her hands. An hour late already, she had no choice but to head straight there, skipping a return to her suite. She glanced down at her button-down shirt and pants, frustration welling up. No time to change, either.

"Like a fun party or…?" Fig waggled their brows.

"More like a room full of politicians and nobles, drowning in alcohol and gossip."

Fig stretched with a grin. "Have fun with that special layer of hell."

Elyse's second groan earned a chuckle from Fig as she hurried toward the Noble's Wing.

The gathering was already in full swing when Elyse arrived, slipping through the doorway unnoticed. Drystan stood nearby, a sheet of paper in his hands—something blue marred its surface. He quickly folded and tucked it away into his pocket as his gaze met hers. "I won't lie—I thought you might skip tonight." Drystan's hand brushed through his curly hair, a gesture both casual and deliberate. "It worried me, actually. There's someone here I'd like you to meet."

He took her arm, guiding her through the crowd in search of a drink. The weight of countless eyes pressed upon her, a silent scrutiny she knew all too well. The gowns and suits around her shimmered with opulence, each one finer than what she wore, a reminder of her lateness and the long hours spent at work.

He offered her a smile, bright and disarming, his eyes drifting over her outfit. "I should've known the King's Administrator would work late while His Grace is away. Apologies for not considering your schedule."

Elyse swallowed down the nausea that threatened to rise and nodded, keeping her voice steady. "I decided not to change. I didn't wish to be any later than I already was."

"Oh, don't concern yourself with that." Drystan led her into an adjoining sitting room, the lighting low and intimate, drawing them into the center where groups of people watched with careful eyes. The air hung thick with pipe smoke as a glass of wine was pressed into Elyse's hand. She took a sip, hoping to steady her nerves, and was surprised by the taste—fresh fruit at first, deepening into a smoky blend of tobacco and blackberry. "My brother hand-selected that wine," Drystan said, watching her expression.

"You'll have to thank him for me; it's lovely."

A voice, smooth and unexpected, came from behind her. "I suspected you'd have a refined palate, Lady Elyse."

She spun and came face to face with a male almost identical to Drystan, but with twisted locks instead of curls.

"There he is," Drystan said. "This is my brother, Lord Myron."

Myron took her hand, his grip warm, and pressed a lingering kiss into the back of it. "Lady Elyse, what a pleasure to have you with us tonight. I don't believe our paths have crossed in the usual circles."

Elyse had spent most of her years at court with her head down, focused on her small group of acquaintances, never caring to venture beyond them. His handsome face, however, sparked a faint recognition. She offered a curtsy, only to falter when she remembered she wasn't wearing a skirt. "The pleasure is all mine."

Myron's questions about her position were easy, casual, as he mentioned his brother had spoken of her. His smile possessed a warmth, the kind that coaxed a rare laugh from her, an unexpected ease in a setting she usually found stifling.

As she finished her wine, he offered her a fresh glass. "Another unique find. Collecting them has become something of a passion." He leaned in closer as she took a sip, his voice dropping to a soft murmur. "If you enjoy this one, you must visit my manor before summer's end. My wine cellar is overflowing with priceless vintages, and I've been waiting for someone special to share them with."

Heat came to Elyse's face. "Oh, um. Unfortunately, I won't have time."

"That's an interesting proposition." The new arrival's voice made Elyse inwardly groan. Kurtys avoided Elyse's glare as he nodded at Myron. "Kaderyn mentioned your courtship with her had a similar proposal early on." Kurtys lifted his glass, taking a measured sip, the curve of his lips a mockery of a smile that never touched his eyes. "A pity you broke off the engagement officially last week."

The wine in Elyse's stomach soured, realization dawning like a dark cloud. Her gaze flickered from her glass to the lord, searching for meaning in the spaces between words.

Myron's glare shifted to Kurtys. "I don't recall inviting you this evening. Perhaps it's time you leave."

"I'm escorting Lady Elyse."

Elyse scoffed. "You are—"

Kurtys's hand discreetly tapped her thigh, a sharp, sudden gesture that silenced her. "I was merely waiting for her arrival. If you'll excuse us."

Before Myron could respond, Kurtys took Elyse by the arm, steering her firmly into the adjoining room. Once they reached a secluded corner, he turned to face her, his expression shifting. "Apologies. He's a prick. The moment I heard you agreed to come, I guessed his intentions."

Elyse wiped her damp palms against her pants, her thoughts tangled. "Why would you know that? Why would you even help me?" The last time they spoke, the king had threatened him to leave her alone.

"We'll be working together in Amigys and Kyaeri," he said, a brief smile flashing as he waved to someone over her shoulder. It dropped when he focused back on Elyse. "The worst people crawled out tonight after Drystan boasted about getting you to attend. After being on the receiving end of your persistent refusals, I figured I could at least keep you from being cornered by him and his brother."

"Kurtys, what are you talking about?"

He sighed, drawing her deeper into the corner where the noise fell away to a muted hush. "Word's been going around," he said, leaning closer. "Drystan's been telling people he's been softening you up for weeks, all to get his brother a chance to court you. They're aiming for a spot in the royal family."

She shook her head, her brows furrowing. "Royal family? I *work* for Wyltam. Gods, that's why he's been so nice?" Her cheeks flushed with a heat she couldn't ignore, her gaze flitting to the room where more and more eyes seemed to linger on them.

"Want to get out of here?"

The question cut through her rising panic. "Yes, please."

Elyse kept her stare fixed straight ahead as she made for the door. Drystan's voice called after her, but she caught the faint sound of Kurtys intercepting him. They left the Noble's Wing and stepped into the cool night air.

Her fists clenched at her sides. "I feel like an idiot."

Kurtys shook his head. "Don't. You're one of the rare few who doesn't measure their worth by the weight of their family's fortunes."

"And you don't? You asked to court me how many times?"

His cheeks stained bright pink. "I was trying to get your father's attention.

Worked out, however. Amigys and Kyaeri will be interesting."

Elyse pivoted to face him. "Why did you help me? And don't say because we're traveling together."

"Your reputation. Myron is a speck compared to you. Plus, I heard his family is coming due on some debts." He rubbed the nape of his neck. "The last thing we need is Myron pushing for a rushed wedding when we should be focused on our coming travels."

Elyse frowned, trying to grasp the meaning. "Why would it need to be rushed?"

His brows drew together, the tension in his expression mirroring the knot tightening in her stomach. "So he can claim the title of your husband before the royal wedding."

"Again, not following."

"The prestige of sitting with the royal family on the most historical wedding of our lifetime?"

Confusion sharpened her tone. "But I work for Wyltam, not—"

"It's not the king I'm talking about."

Elyse's confusion only deepened as she struggled to piece it together. Kurtys sighed, his eyes softening with a mixture of frustration and sympathy. "Oh, Elyse. Don't tell me you don't know."

Chapter Twenty-Eight

MARIETTA

The week passed in a whirlwind of legal speak and tense negotiations as Satiros and Enomenos, with the aid of the Exisotis, worked to form the treaty that would bind them together. After the first meeting, Marietta ensured her morning teas were brewed strong. In her naivety, she had imagined days filled with impassioned speeches, only to be confronted by law councilors obsessing over grammar and precise wording.

When the meeting paused for a recess, Marietta resisted the urge to stretch—a gesture she deemed too unqueenly. As Wyltam pulled General Hastyrn aside for a private word, she took advantage of his temporary distraction to stand as well. Her gaze swept the room until it settled on Fabian Rodallis. Recalling Minister Adryan's words, she decided to approach him.

"Fabian, it's good to see you again," she said. "Even under these peculiar circumstances."

Fabian's smile was restrained, his eyes darting over his shoulder before he spoke. "Your Grace, 'peculiar' seems to be the word of the week."

Next to her, Coryn made a low, disapproving sound.

"Minister Adryan asked me to send you his love."

For a moment, Fabian's stern mask softened, a flicker of something almost fond in his gaze. "Adryan—always the charmer, even when he's meddling.

But tell me, how are you finding your new surroundings?"

"Unfamiliar," Marietta said. "But I'm finding my way."

"You navigate these unfamiliar waters with a grace that seems almost too practiced." His eyes flicked to her dress before meeting hers again, his voice lowering to a murmur. "It does make one wonder who might be steering the ship. Yet, our new allies would never deceive your homeland—after all, they have no real sway over you. If there were any hint of that, the treaty might not hold as firmly as we believe." His smile was thin and insincere, sending a chill through her. "But surely, that's not the Marietta everyone remembers so fondly. You're guiding your own course, so there's no cause for concern."

She kept her expression calm, even as her mind raced to unravel the layers in his words.

"It's been a pleasure, Your Grace," Fabian said abruptly, his tone shifting. "Tell Adryan that we still have unfinished business." With that, he turned and left.

Uncertain how to respond to the abrupt dismissal, Marietta looked at Coryn, who simply frowned.

Fabian's words lingered in Marietta's thoughts throughout the day and deep into the evening. In the meetings that followed and during the formal dinner, she caught the glances of the Enomenoans—pity etched in some faces, a quiet anger in others. By the time she returned to her room, the silence felt like both a comfort and a curse.

Sleep refused to come, and she paced restlessly, replaying Adryan's warning and the new attitudes she had seen. Unable to endure it any longer, she opened her door and found Adalyn on duty in the hallway. "Can you find Coryn?" she asked quietly. When he arrived, one of her handmaids entered the room as well.

"What's this about?" Marietta asked.

Adalyn gave her a sideways look, her voice a low murmur. "It'll help with the rumors." Her gaze darted to Coryn before she shut the door.

Annoyance flickered across Marietta's face, but she couldn't help but appreciate Adalyn's foresight as she guided Coryn into the sitting area. For the first time since he took the role as captain, he was unburdened by armor, dressed in simple clothes that clung to his muscular frame with an unspoken ease.

"I'm sorry if I woke you," Marietta said, her voice softening. "I needed someone to work through this with."

"No trouble at all," Coryn replied, settling into the couch with a relaxed posture. "I was down at the tavern, having a drink. You caught me as I was heading back. Though, I have to admit, you had me worried for a moment."

"It's just …" Marietta's voice dropped, the vulnerability threading through her words. "Did you see them at dinner? I think Enomenos is considering backing out of the treaty. Of all the ways this treaty could have failed, I never considered that they might not trust me—an oversight on my part."

Coryn tilted his head, considering. "Perhaps there's a reason the obvious slipped your mind. What made you certain they would trust you?"

Marietta's fingers drifted to a loose thread on her nightshirt, picking it absentmindedly. "My father, to start. But I suppose his distrust of Wyltam has seeped into how they see me—as if Wyltam is 'steering the ship,' or however Fabian put it. I don't blame my father for thinking that." She shut her eyes, picturing her father's wounded look when she'd brushed him off that first day. "Wyltam asked me to show solidarity with Satiros, and in doing so, I've sacrificed unity with my own people. But they're my community. I am who I am because of them. I dedicated my life to giving back, and now it's as if they believe a few months in Satiros have turned me against them. No matter how Satiros has changed me, I'm still the Marietta they knew, aren't I?"

"I think you've changed more than you're willing to admit," Coryn said gently. "You walked in with a king at your side."

Marietta's foot tapped restlessly against the floor as she wrapped her arms around herself, sinking deeper into the couch. "I need them to understand that beneath all these changes, I'm still the same person. Just with more …"

"Trauma?"

A bitter laugh escaped her. "Yes, trauma. But I chose this path. I was the one who proposed marriage to Wyltam—to secure the alliance. This treaty has to succeed. Coming this far only to fail … I won't allow it."

Coryn's steady gaze remained on her. "What do you want to do?"

A thought flickered to life, growing until it burned with clarity. She met Coryn's eyes. "Do you ever follow your instincts?"

"Frequently," Coryn answered. "Why do you ask? What are you planning?"

Marietta's boots struck the tile floor with sharp precision as she walked beside Wyltam, each step reverberating with a heavy resolve. Wyltam shifted his gaze sideways, breaking the silence between them.

"You're still not going to explain the pants and tunic?" His voice carried a mix of curiosity and irritation.

"No," she replied, adjusting the folded fabric in her arms.

"Or whatever that is—"

"You asked me to trust you, and I did," she said, her tone unwavering as her gaze locked onto his. "Now, I need you to trust me."

Wyltam opened his mouth to protest, but no words came. Instead, he nodded curtly and resumed his stride beside her.

"Back me up on whatever I say in there," she continued, voice low, her hand gripping his biceps to pull him closer. "If we want Enomenos to sign that treaty, it's necessary."

He halted, his frustration cutting through the mask he usually wore. "What have you heard?"

"Nothing—"

"Marietta, we know they're skeptical of the terms. What do you know?"

Her hand lifted to his cheek, a touch both soft and firm. "Trust me. I have it under control."

Wyltam's jaw tensed, thoughts visibly churning behind his eyes. But he turned away, muttering, "I trust you."

Marietta's gaze found Coryn's, and he gave a reassuring nod.

Together, Marietta and Wyltam stepped into the meeting room. Conversations ceased abruptly, a stillness falling over the chamber as eyes turned toward them. Marietta seized the moment, stepping forward with a calm yet commanding presence.

"Before we start today's discussions," she announced, her voice steady and clear, "I request a private audience with the members of the Enomenos Unionization Council and the Exisotis—without the Satiroan representatives."

A murmur rippled through the room. The ministers of Satiros exchanged sharp glances, and Wyltam's stance grew tense beside her.

"Except for my guard, Coryn, given the recent threats on my life," she added.

Elector Alora traded a brief look with the man next to her before responding, "We have time for this, if you would."

Marietta glanced at Wyltam, expecting him to intervene, perhaps even to use his magic to halt her. But instead, he inclined his head with a slight nod. "You heard our future queen."

The Satiroan ministers and officials reluctantly moved toward the exit. Wyltam lingered, casting a narrow-eyed glance back as he shut the door behind them.

The remaining members of Enomenos and the Exisotis took their seats. Marietta approached her place at the table, removing her wisteria headpiece and setting it down. She then unfolded the cloth she carried—a simple apron embroidered with "Rise Above Bakery." She placed it beside the crown, meeting their eyes with unyielding resolve.

"You have doubts. I'm alone now, without them. They did not know I'd call for this meeting. Ask whatever you need to."

Silence stretched tight across the room, every breath held in anticipation. Her father, after a long pause, stood. "Are you under any coercion?"

Marietta's voice remained steady. "No. I understand the skepticism, but it's the truth. I proposed the marriage to Wyltam during the trial to save myself, yes. But I also saw the potential for change. Uniting Enomenos with Satiros opens the door to freedom for their pilinos. Believe it or not, Wyltam has sought this change for decades."

Her father scoffed. "If that's true, he'd have changed their laws as king."

"And risk the reprisal from his court and ministers? Wyltam prefers not to rule with an iron fist. Over the years, he has actually empowered his ministers more while easing restrictions on pilinos. I'm sure you have records of these changes."

Before her father could respond, Elector Alora stood, her presence commanding attention. "Forgive my bluntness," she began, "but the significance of your marriage is unclear. In Syllogi, political marriages are common, but not in Enomenos. If this union has any meaning, why you? Your father may have influence, but you hold no power over our laws. You are an ordinary girl with no authority. If Enomenos is open to a treaty on its own terms, why is this marriage needed as a shroud for diplomacy?"

Marietta's smile held steady, her eyes clear. "You're right. I'm not of any great importance—a half-elf from Kentro, an ordinary Enomenoan who lived and worked among you. It's my ordinariness that makes me significant."

She let her words linger, allowing their impact to settle over the room. "While this lacks legal weight, it carries meaning for the people—not just here, but for the pilinos in Satiros who need reform. By standing at Wyltam's side, I'm not his Enomenoan bride securing a treaty; I am a symbol for every pilinos in Satiros longing for a different life. A symbol of hope, a promise their voices might be heard. I am the link between their dreams and your actions. It's not about the marriage; it's about an ordinary pilinos—someone like me—leading the way for change." She paused, hands clasped behind her back, grounding herself in her conviction. "It is precisely my ordinariness that gives me weight."

Silence settled over the room again. Marietta steadied herself, holding Alora's gaze, refusing to waver. Doubt crept in slowly. And then, at last, Alora took her seat with a nod of her head.

"Do you love him?"

The question caught Marietta off guard. She couldn't see who asked it, but the surprise made her laugh softly. "Love has no bearing on this. It's about aiding the pilinos in Satiros."

"That wasn't a yes or no."

Marietta's heart stopped when she saw who it was—Pelok, her old friend, Tilan's closest companion. His expression was unreadable.

She didn't hesitate, meeting his eyes. "No."

Pelok exchanged a glance with her father, and a murmur of uncertainty rippled through the Enomenoan side. Marietta let the whispers fade before she spoke, her voice steady. "If there are no further questions, I would like to offer my perspective. My love for Enomenos is not just a sentiment—it is woven into every fiber of my being. This land, our people, the lives we've built together—I want to see it flourish, grow stronger. I believe that our true strength lies in our unity. By embracing Satiros, by drawing them into our fold, we reinforce our own strength and honor a deep, long-held dream. The pilinos in Satiros have waited far too long for the freedoms we cherish. They deserve to be part of the community we have built together. This is our chance—our defining moment—to extend our hands and bring them into the light. It is your duty to seize this opportunity and ensure it does not slip away."

Alora's nod was measured. "You've given us much to consider. Inform King Wyltam and his delegation that we'll require time to deliberate."

Marietta inclined her head, her voice steady. "Of course."

She placed the wisteria headpiece back on her head, gathered the apron into her arms, and moved toward the door. The moment she stepped into the hall, Wyltam's hand clamped around her arm, pulling her into a room across the corridor. The door slammed shut behind them, and whispers erupted among the Satiroans outside.

Wyltam pressed her gently against the wall, his hands firm on her shoulders. A translucent dome formed around them.

"You're reckless." His voice was a low, urgent whisper that sent shivers across her skin. "Brash. You could have jeopardized everything."

"But I didn't," she replied, her voice soft and laden with a hint of defiance as she tilted her face closer to his. "I saved it."

Wyltam's gaze dropped to her lips, his breath ghosting over her skin. Then, catching himself, he pulled away, clasping his hands behind his back. His eyes flicked to her arms. "What are you holding?"

A faint smile touched her lips as she handed it to him. Wyltam unfurled it, a low chuckle escaping him. "Reckless."

"They suspected you were manipulating me," she said. "Thank you for listening, for stepping away as I asked. They needed to see that I had control. I was able to bring up the pilinos who—"

"I heard every word."

Marietta flinched. "Oh."

He returned the apron, and the barrier between them evaporated. As he moved toward the door, he cast a final glance over his shoulder. "You may have my trust, but theirs is gone. Brace yourself for their interrogation."

Wyltam's warning proved accurate. The politicians of Satiros weren't just angry. Their faces bore a deep-seated suspicion of her actions. Keyain's silence weighed heavily, contrasting with the relentless inquiries from General Hastyrn and Minister Sethyr. They demanded detailed recounts of her words and those of Elector Alora, their expressions clear in their apprehension that the treaty might be lost.

General Hastyrn drew Keyain aside, their hushed exchange thick with urgency. Marietta caught fragments of their discussion—about stretching their forces thin and the strain of proceeding without Enomenoan aid.

Marietta stood resolute, her demeanor unwavering despite the possibility that she had misjudged their new allies' concerns. The Exisotis, intent on aiding the pilinos, opposed the stifling elven oppression. Enomenos valued Satiros for its fertile lands and transport routes along the Halia River, with the added benefit of supporting the pilinos reinforcing their position. She hoped her words had illuminated their common purpose and demonstrated Satiros's readiness to align with their cause.

As the meeting resumed, Marietta and Wyltam led the Satiroans to their places and faced the representatives of their homeland. The speaker at the podium unraveled the treaty's details, outlining the gains for each side. Marietta noted with satisfaction the inclusion of provisions for the well-being of the pilinos in Satiros among the treaty's benefits.

The Enomenoan official's gavel struck with deliberate authority. "Today, we carve a new chapter in history. This treaty marks the addition of Satiros into the Enomenoan city-state collective. It heralds the start of new alliances against our adversaries. We seal this accord not only with ink but with marriage. Are there any final words before we proceed with the signing?"

Marietta held her breath, bracing for any objection from Elector Alora or her father. The room remained silent.

The official raised the treaty, her voice firm. "By signing today, you affirm your commitment to this agreement and acknowledge your review of the terms." She placed the document on the podium and signaled for the Enomenoan Unification Council to sign first.

In a symbolic act of unity, each member lined up with quill in hand to inscribe their signature at the bottom of the document. The Exisotis members signed next, followed by the Satiroans.

As Marietta approached the podium, her gaze settled on the extensive list of names, each one representing a collective agreement to a shared future—one where she would marry Wyltam and Satiros would become an Enomenoan city-state. With steady resolve, she added her signature beside Wyltam's.

With the stroke of her quill, her destiny was irrevocably bound by paper and ink.

Chapter Twenty-Nine

MARIETTA

After the treaty signing, the celebratory dinner had marked her farewell to her father. He would be present at the wedding, providing an opportunity for her to seek answers in private.

In her room, Marietta paced, her thoughts tangled with the day's events and the ire she had stirred among the Satiroans. Doubts emerged—had she already compromised her reign before it had even begun? Yet the transition to a republic remained the ultimate goal, and her and Wyltam's influence would inevitably diminish with time. For now, the treaty's completion was the true triumph, overshadowing any personal setbacks.

She dimmed the oil lamps, allowing the solitary light globe to cast a faint, uneven glow. As shadows filled the room, she settled into bed, her gaze fixed on the ceiling. As she reached for her light globe, a soft tapping broke the silence. Marietta turned toward the door connecting her room with Wyltam's, her heart quickening with anticipation.

Her excitement turned to dread as the unmistakable noise of a window sliding open sliced through the quiet. She sprang from the bed, her instincts screaming. As she opened her mouth to call out, a cold, firm hand clamped over it, silencing her. Panic gripped her as she struggled.

"Marietta, it's me."

Relief washed over her at the sound of her father's voice. When his hand withdrew, she pivoted toward him, the last remnants of fear still coiling in her chest. "What are you doing?"

"I couldn't let you leave Olkia without speaking to you alone." In the low light, his eyes were dark, unfathomable pools.

Marietta examined his face, seeing only the earnest concern of a father. She threw her arms around his neck, and he gripped her back with the same love that had enveloped her throughout her life. She inhaled the sweet clover scent mixed with smoke—the smell of her childhood. "Did you have to be so dramatic about it?" she asked, pulling away.

His lips twisted into a worried frown. "Was this truly your decision?"

A shiver crept down her back, like tiny needles pricking at her skin. What would Wyltam do if he discovered them like this? "You shouldn't be here."

"I can make you disappear right now." His eyes flickered toward the window, his grip unyielding on her arm. "Don't do this."

Marietta twisted away, trying and failing to break free. "It's too late for that."

"But it isn't. I never wanted this for you. All my life, I've kept you and your mother out of harm's reach."

"Do you think I'm unaware of the risks? This isn't just about me. Becoming a pilinos queen is a symbol to all those your organization claims to help."

"It makes you a prime target, and I will not compromise your safety. Not again." He pulled her toward the window. "We need to leave now."

Marietta placed her hand over her father's, drawing on Therypon's energy. As the crackling black encircled her fingers, her father flinched and pulled away. "I've already been a target," she said, her voice steady. "There have been two assassination attempts, and there will be more. But this is my choice. I choose this willingly."

"Is that proof enough for you, Anthys?"

Marietta spun around to see Wyltam standing in the doorway between their rooms. Even in his nightclothes, he exuded an aura of command.

"Don't call me that," her father growled as he grabbed Marietta's arm and jerked her toward the window. As silent as a cat, Wynn slipped through the opening, his face twisting into a scowl.

"Stay a moment, will you?" Wyltam's voice was honey laced with iron, his steps deliberate as he crossed the room. His gaze never wavered from her father, whose eyes darted around, searching for escape. "And perhaps release your daughter."

Marietta wrenched herself free from her father's grasp, putting distance between them. Wyltam moved to her side, his presence a dark shadow at her shoulder. She looked up at him, her tone steady. "I didn't know he would attempt this."

"I know," he said, slipping an arm around her waist. "I'm relieved that your choice remains unchanged even after signing the treaty."

Her father's eyes locked onto Wyltam's touch, his gaze sharpening onto Marietta. "He's lying to you, Marietta. His intentions have always been in pursuit of power."

"Power?" Marietta shook her head. "I haven't quite figured out what he wants yet, but it isn't power."

"Would you truly know that?" Her father stepped forward, his voice a low growl. "You've watched his every move for the past few decades to know more than I?"

Marietta's pulse quickened, his accusation heavy between them. How deep did their shared past run?

Wyltam's expression hardened. "Would you like to share the truth about Anthylia, or shall I?"

Her father's head snapped up, eyes blazing with fury. "Don't you *dare* say her name!"

Marietta's gaze darted between them, the silence pressing in on her. "Who is Anthylia?" Her voice barely breached the quiet.

Wyltam's response came slowly, a cold edge to his words. "No? That's unfortunate. I was offering you a chance to be honest with her for once.

Anthylia Fulbryk was your aunt—your father's sister. He abandoned her to rot away with Gyrsh Norymial."

Marietta struggled to grasp his meaning. Her father's sister had been married to Gyrsh Norymial. Norymial, which was … Marietta's limbs went numb, her mind spiraling with the stories her father had told her as a child about her aunt in Satiros—Elyse's mother.

Her father glared, his hand twitching toward his side. "That information is irrelevant."

"I wouldn't reach for your weapon," Wyltam warned as the door to their suite opened. Adalyn and Andyr entered with their hands on their swords. From beyond the doorway, she could see other guards gathering.

Marietta's father cast a final, urgent look at her before leaping toward the window. His fist connected with Wynn's gut, driving him back. Wynn staggered, but his reflexes were sharp; he gripped her father's arm as he neared the windowsill, pulling him away from the ledge.

"Marietta has become close with her," Wyltam said. "They need to hear the truth of their family ties from you, not from the court. She deserves that much."

Her father met her gaze, his breath coming in ragged bursts. "Are you going to let me go, or hand me over to the authorities?"

"I'm sure my guards would be more than happy to escort you out of the building," Wyltam said, nodding his head toward him.

Adalyn and Andyr approached, each putting a hand on her father's shoulder and guiding him to the door.

Marietta shook off her shock and darted after them. "Wait! What does that make me?"

Her father twisted, his gaze locking with hers in a moment of raw bewilderment.

"She knows what she is—what you are," Marietta's voice broke through, frenzied. "What does that make me?"

Her father's face drained of color as he fought against their hold. "Our blood is not yours," he choked out, before Coryn shoved him from the room.

Marietta stared at her hands, unsteady, turning them over. If their blood didn't run in her veins, what did that mean? Her breath came in sharp gasps as she moved toward the bed. Was her father truly fey, while she was not? Did that mean he wasn't her father at all?

Wyltam came to her side. "I'm sorry this is how you learned the truth."

Marietta pressed her palms together, willing them to cease their trembling. Her father had confirmed fey existed, that he and Elyse shared that blood. If she hadn't known about her aunt being Elyse's mother, she wouldn't have been able to figure that out. Her gaze hardened as she directed it at Wyltam. "You've known this for a while and kept it secret."

His brows furrowed. "Yes."

"How long?"

Wyltam addressed the remaining guards. "Leave. Ensure he returns to their organization." He turned his attention back to Marietta and studied her for a moment. "My suspicion started in the sculpture garden when you mentioned your aunt's reputation for her plant displays. That was Anthylia's hobby. She loved plants and flowers, and they loved her back. It was its own kind of magic."

"How would you know that?"

"Because she was my mentor. She taught me how to become a mage."

Marietta pressed the heels of her hands into her eyes, trying to ward off the impossible reality. This couldn't be happening. It had to be a mistake. "How did we not know?"

"You wouldn't, but Elyse should've recognized the name. After I started introducing her to magic through your grandfather's books and she didn't recognize the name Fulbryk, I realized she had no clue."

Marietta's gaze locked onto Wyltam as she let her hands fall to her sides. "I don't understand what you're saying," she said sharply.

Wyltam reached out to touch her cheek, but she pulled away, her expression unyielding. "You're angry," he observed.

"Sharp as ever."

"The information doesn't change much," he said calmly.

Her eyes shut tight, as if to shut out the world. "Maybe for you." The weight of his words crushed her: the man she had called father was not her true parent. Fey were real and tangible. She had to find Elyse and face this new reality before the truth unraveled everything.

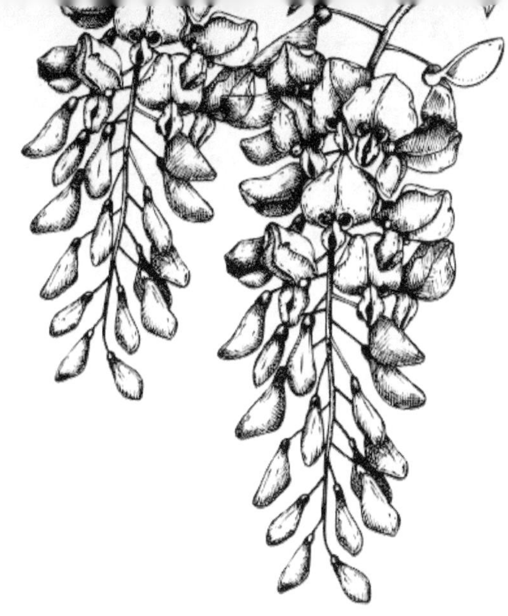

Part Two

"At some point, you will reach your limit. Don't ignore the signs; brushing them aside risks diminishing your strength—or worse, your control."

-

Lyken's Eighth Principle

Chapter Thirty

MARIETTA

Marietta had hoped that returning to Satiros would ease the weight on her chest these past weeks. With the treaty signed, only her marriage to Wyltam and her ascension to the throne remained. She had imagined the wedding would happen swiftly, but reality took a different turn.

Instead of the quick ceremony she had pictured, Satiros was amidst a major transformation. Laws needed rewriting, infrastructure required adjustments, and royal weddings, as she soon realized, demanded months of careful planning. The date was set for the winter solstice, and as summer's heat faded into autumn's chill, Marietta felt the days slipping away.

She moved through the palace corridors, absorbing the frantic energy around her. Servants darted past, arms full of trays and bundles, their footsteps a constant rhythm on the marble floors. In shadowed alcoves, politicians whispered urgently, their conversations half-hidden. Courtiers fluttered about like jeweled moths, their words veiled behind delicate fans. The palace itself seemed to hum with anticipation.

When she entered her suite, she found Wyltam waiting, his presence tightening the knot in her chest. "Do you have a moment?" he asked.

Suppressing her annoyance, she nodded. She hadn't forgiven him for hiding the truth about her connection with Elyse. What kept her attitude tempered was that she held a secret far more damaging. She and Elyse needed to share their fey discovery, and soon.

Wyltam guided her to Valeriya's bedroom, where a new bookcase now stood in the corner, laden with books. Marietta moved closer, sinking to her knees to examine the titles. *Strange Tides. Touch in the Dark. His Gentle Rose.* She pulled the last off the shelf and opened it, finding her name written on the inside with a handwritten note from a friend. She thought back to her apartment in Olkia, where she'd noticed her books had gone missing. Now she knew who to thank. "I didn't realize you had a knack for thievery," she said, glancing up.

He shrugged. "I didn't think you'd want to return, so I had someone fetch your things beforehand."

Marietta flipped through another book, trying to keep her voice level. "That was thoughtful of you."

From the corner of her eye, she caught him tilting his head. "Which is your favorite?"

"Are you asking out of genuine interest or just to be polite?"

"Part of being in a partnership is taking an interest in each other's passions."

"Does that mean I should start note-taking?"

"I enjoy more than only that," he said, his tone amused. "I'll find something suitable for you to explore. In the meantime, I'd like to read your favorite book."

Marietta's fingers lingered over one of her more explicit novels, entertained by the thought of him reading those particular scenes—and his likely reaction to them. But after a moment's consideration, she chose her true favorite: an adapted fey tale of two lovers separated by a river, with the man swimming across each night to be with his beloved. The original story ended in tragedy, but this version offered a much happier conclusion. She handed the book to Wyltam.

"*Beneath the Summer Moon*," he read. "I'll report back my thoughts."

Marietta held Wyltam's dark gaze, the moment stretching between them. She felt their relationship, fragile yet insistent. Even now, with all the frustration between them, she wished to hear what he thought of the book. And that, more than anything, unsettled her.

The palace temple gleamed, refreshed and renewed after being restored from its neglected state. "It only took an afternoon to clean," Marietta said to the gathered acolytes. "With Coryn's help, of course."

Rafayl from the Temple of Seidytar raised an eyebrow. "You handled the cleaning yourself, Your Grace?"

"Indeed, with my own hands."

The iros from Kystrorgiste muttered to his companion as he examined the deity's statue with a critical eye.

"Fortunately, the dirt was minimal, and the damage was slight," she said, moving toward the statues. "It only required some muscle and a rag."

Nosokyma took a seat with a smile. "The results are evident, Lady Marietta. Your dedication to the Deities of Duality is deeply appreciated, and I believe I speak for us all."

Moira, from the Temple of Zontykroi, settled beside the Therypon elder, a bright grin on her face. "I thought our first meeting might have been an anomaly. It's been two centuries since a royal showed any interest in the temples." She twirled a strand of her white hair and glanced around the room. "It's refreshing to be acknowledged."

Izzy, the iros to Oramytiz, nodded as they examined the altar. "Will the temple be open to anyone in the palace?"

Marietta's gaze flickered to Coryn before responding. "I suppose so. It doesn't seem right to keep it closed off from those who might be curious."

Izzy raised an eyebrow. "How will they learn about the deities?"

Marietta considered this, her stare wandering over the temple's freshly polished surfaces. An idea formed. "I'd be glad to help bridge the gap between the Deities of Duality and the palace. We could keep the temple open to discuss the deities and their teachings."

A murmur of agreement rippled through the group, followed by Cyrus's gruff voice. "We'd need someone present when the temple is available."

Nosokyma nodded. "We could arrange shifts. Each temple could have a designated day, allowing visitors to explore the deities."

Cyrus rubbed the dark scruff on his chin. "Could work. Although, it would be fitting for Your Grace to visit our temples as well." He quickly added, "I'm sure you're curious about all of us, given your interest in building a relationship."

Marietta studied their expectant expressions, a tightness settling in her chest, as if the option to say no had already been stripped away. "I would be delighted."

The promise lingered in her mind, its burden following Marietta into the evening hours. She walked the quiet hallways of their suite, finding a faint glow spilling from Wyltam's study. The scent of parchment and ink greeted her as she found him buried in a sea of papers, his brow furrowed in concentration.

She tapped on the door frame. Wyltam's eyes softened as they met hers, and he waved her in. "How did unveiling the temple go?"

"As good as I expected."

"Now you'll have a place to direct them when they visit." His focus shifted back to the papers scattered across his desk.

"More than just that," Marietta said, lingering in the doorway. "We thought it wise for temple acolytes to be present during the day in case those at court showed interest. But don't worry—I'll be overseeing the arrangements."

Wyltam's pen halted mid-scratch. "What?"

"Nobles and politicians will probably be curious about the religious practices," she continued, her head tilting as she noted his confused expression. "The temples are rotating to ensure someone is always available to assist newcomers."

"Marietta, that's a promise you can't make."

"Who else was going to?"

"The Minister Leyland and the vassals branch, as they have since the minister of religious affairs position was removed." Wyltam abruptly opened his draw and pulled out a fresh piece of paper.

"The temples weren't happy with the attention they received from him," she said, taking a step into the room. "They've been dismissed by court for so long."

"That was for a reason." His quill scratched along as he continued. "They are like any other organization hoping to scrape power where they can."

Marietta rolled her eyes. "You sound like your mother."

Wyltam's head snapped up, his expression darkening. "For the sake of our relationship, never compare me to her again." He folded the paper with sharp, deliberate movements and rose to his feet.

"I just meant she accused the temples of sacrificing people."

Wyltam crossed the room and paused before her. "All rumors contain some truth. The temples favor you, Marietta, for what you offer them—power."

"The power is mutual."

Wyltam tilted his head, a challenge in his gaze. "Explain."

"Do the people not love me because of my connection with Therypon?" She placed a hand on his arm. "Developing a relationship with them only strengthens support for me."

"You are playing a dangerous game you do not understand."

"Then help me understand it." She placed a hand on his chest, toying with a button. "I'm an iros. I'm tied to a deity regardless if I seek out their support. At least this way, I can control it."

Wyltam shook his head, lifting her hand to his lips. "Once again, you've promised something you had no right to offer."

He turned and strode into the hallway, Marietta quick on his heels. "Where are you going?"

"I'm drafting a note for the King's Council of Ministers. They need to hear about this first thing tomorrow morning." He glanced back at her. "I'd prefer Leyland learns of it in a formal setting to mitigate the repercussions."

Marietta stopped short. "I didn't think this would be a problem."

Wyltam continued to the exit of their suite. "Everything becomes a problem in government."

Chapter Thirty-One

ELYSE

Wynn grunted, setting down the last crate with a thud. "How many books did you have in there?"

"Just a few," Elyse replied, weaving around the elegant furniture of her new suite in the Royal's Wing, a few floors below Marietta and Wyltam. The plush rugs and opulent tapestries contrasted with her old quarters.

Wynn straightened up, wiping his hands on his pants. "That's more than a few."

She peeked inside the crate, her fingers brushing the spines of her cherished collection. "I used to have more."

He shook his head, a smirk tugging at his lips. "Next time, I'm making you use the palace workers."

"I would've, except they always want to talk."

He faked being a surprised. "Gods no, not talking! What a horrible fate."

She swatted at him. "I never know what to say."

"You never have issues when it's me."

Elyse paused, her gaze lifting to his face. The soft light cast gentle shadows, easing the tension that had been haunting him as of late. "I don't."

"Does that mean you like me?"

She rolled her eyes, a smile tugging at the corners of her mouth. "Don't start with that."

"Does that make me your favorite?"

Elyse made for the bedroom and he followed.

"Your silence is making me think it does."

She turned abruptly, colliding with Wynn. His hands shot out to steady her, gripping her arms firmly. His eyes flicked to her lips, then he cleared his throat and stepped back, breaking the contact.

"Guess I'm your favorite for all this heavy lifting," he said, his voice carrying a teasing edge. "Could've made you use aithyr. Build a muscle or two."

She laughed softly, the warmth of his touch still lingering on her skin. "I'll keep that in mind," she replied, her tone light despite the flutter of anticipation in her chest.

A knock echoed through the room, followed by a familiar voice. "Where is she?"

Elyse emerged from the bedroom, Wynn trailing closely behind. Marietta stood in the doorway, her eyebrows arching in surprise. The expression quickly shifted to confusion before settling into a smirk.

"By all means, don't let me interrupt," she teased, turning back toward the hallway.

Elyse rolled her eyes. "Get in here, will you?"

She laughed and ran across the room, throwing her arms around Elyse. "Oh, how happy I am to see you," Marietta murmured against her. She turned to Wynn. "Could we have some privacy?"

"Leaving you two alone is asking for trouble," Wynn answered.

"You can help me unpack after," Elyse said. "We just have some, um … things to talk about."

"Like?"

Marietta crossed her arms, the smirk still playing on her lips. "The scintillating details of my night with Wyltam."

Wynn snorted. "As if that's happened yet."

Marietta's expression tightened. "What's that supposed to mean?"

He shrugged and gave a lazy salute, then slipped out the door without another word.

"What did he mean by that?" Marietta turned back. "Never mind—do you know? I'm guessing you know."

Elyse twisted the rings on her fingers. "About your father and my mother?"

Marietta nodded.

"You don't look like my mother."

"There's a reason for that." Marietta's brow furrowed as she moved to the couches. Elyse followed, settling across from her, listening intently as Marietta recounted what had happened in Olkia. When Marietta confessed her father hinted he wasn't her birth father, her voice wavered. "I don't know what to think."

Elyse paused, then spoke. "Was Lyken Fulbryk fey?"

"I suppose he was," Marietta replied.

"I'm still wrapping my head around the fact that my mother was a Fulbryk. My father never told me, and I was too young to understand when she passed." The old memories constricted her throat. "If he was fey, why would Lyken write a book on magic?"

Marietta shook her head. "There are so many questions without answers. We'll ask my father when he arrives for the wedding—if he's still allowed, considering. Until then, we'll keep digging through those books. Have you found anything useful?"

"Not much, but I managed to find *Statues and Sculptures of Syllogi*." Elyse stood and dug through her crate, pulling out the book. "Apparently, aithyr is why the statues never deteriorate."

Elyse set the book aside and pulled out *Lyken's Guide to Chorys Dasi*.

"May I?" Marietta asked.

She handed it over, and Marietta opened Lyken's Guide to Chorys Dasi to the blank pages nestled in the center. "Are you planning to do something?" Elyse asked, curiosity piqued.

"Hand me something sharp, please."

Elyse rummaged through her crate, retrieving a letter opener and passing it to Marietta. She watched intently as Marietta drew the sharp edge across her palm, allowing blood to seep onto the blank pages.

A sudden burst of light flared from Marietta, filling the room. Elyse's eyes widened. "Your hand!"

Marietta wiggled her fingers nonchalantly. "Just one of the benefits of being a deity's chosen."

"I've never witnessed deity magic before. Does it happen by itself? Actually, how does channeling a deity's magic feel? How does it work?"

Marietta's attention remained fixed on the book. The blood saturated the page, spreading into a vivid red splotch.

"Here." Elyse took the book, hesitating before she pricked her finger. The droplet absorbed into the page and spread into the swirl of portraits. Azarys's smirk leered up from the center. Elyse's gaze darted away, avoiding his image. She focused instead on the words scrawled at the top. "What does beastial mean?"

"Do you know anything about feyrie tales?"

Elyse shook her head.

"My father described four distinct types," Marietta began, her stare steady on the book. "Botanical fey, with traits of plants and fungi—vines for hair, bark for skin. They wield influence over plant life to a certain degree." She turned a page. "Then there are elemental fey, able to take on the form of various elements and shape them—fire, water, and the like. Azarys, for instance, embodies the beastial type, adopting features of animals or insects: horns, claws, tails, antennae. The fourth type is more ambiguous. Ethereal fey possess qualities tied to their domain but lacking physical form— shapeshifting, sound, light manipulation. They often resemble typical fey, marked by their elongated ears and sharp fangs." Marietta's finger traced the illustrations, highlighting each type.

Elyse struggled to keep up as she spoke, her mind racing to catch the details. "Wait a moment," she said, rummaging through two crates in search of paper and charcoal. "Could you go over that again?"

Marietta nodded and began again, detailing how every sort of fey wields influence over their own domain. "I always enjoyed the botanical fey. My favorite childhood story was about an arch fey who controlled plant movements and played tricks on the cruel or guided the lost in her forest, all without having to interact herself."

"But do people like that exist? Is that what …" Elyse trailed off, her heart racing.

"We have to tell someone, Elyse."

"I know but—"

"By the wedding."

She met Marietta's gaze. "That's too soon."

"There's a war happening with or without us sharing that information," she said, her brows furrowing. "The sooner we tell Wyltam, the sooner we can make a plan on how to stop fey."

"I—okay." Elyse bit the inside of her lip. "I'll try to find the remaining books by then, but I should tell you about what I had found. What do you know about the statues?"

"No one knows where they came from or who made them."

"That's true, but there are theories surrounding the stone and aithyr," Elyse said, opening the book. "Some think that the stone is rich in aithyr, yet there hasn't been conclusive evidence to support it. Another more popular theory is that a mage protected them through an enchantment. The issue with that is aithyr infusions degrade over time. The theory that stood out the most is one I've never heard of—that the statues were gift from the fey to their descendants."

"Gifts?" Marietta asked. "Some feyrie tales mention skilled weavers and smiths. Sculpting could fit into that tradition."

"But why would they be specifically fey gifts to their own bloodline?" she asked. "Sylas wanted this book for a reason. I suspect it's a clue."

"A clue to what? Do you think they're hiding things?"

Elyse shook her head. "I don't know. A few weeks ago, I tried channeling aithyr through a statue I was familiar with, but nothing happened."

"I'll take a guess that the book didn't have any secret pages in it?" Marietta's tone was laced with skepticism.

"None that I saw. But Sylas must have sent me after these books for a reason—they hint at evidence of fey. We need to locate the others; perhaps then we can persuade Wyltam."

Marietta nodded, her gaze distant. "Let's see what we can uncover by the wedding."

Elyse moved through the halls with purpose, shoulders back and gaze fixed ahead. Kurtys walked beside her, his presence steady. Since uncovering the true motives behind her peers' sudden interest, Kurtys had become invaluable. He guided her through the ruthless social terrain, steering her away from unbecoming circles and guiding her toward more tasteful gatherings. It almost made him tolerable. Almost.

Despite Wyltam's return from Olkia, Elyse found herself engulfed in meetings on his behalf, stacked on top of her already overflowing schedule. As if that weren't enough, she still had to unpack. With everything going on, she gratefully accepted Kurtys's help when it came to social functions.

"Will you be there?" she asked. "To help deflect, of course."

"I can if you wish," Kurtys said with a shrug.

Elyse nodded. "I'll see you tomorrow then."

With his departure, she made her way to the bottom floor and channeled aithyr into her body. *Meet in the same spot?*

She waited a moment, then heard, *What if I told you I'm already here?*

A smile hinted at her lips as she pushed past the exit and into the evening air, finding Wynn leaning against a column. "You think I wouldn't wait? I'm crushed," he said.

"I never want to assume."

Wynn nudged her with his elbow. "You can rely on me, El."

Her heart skipped a beat as they made for the garden path. The evening sun painted him golden, his smile radiant and eyes alight. Wynn had a rugged nature about him, with his hair tied into a messy knot and the forked scar curving with his lips. Even the way he walked and held himself alluded to someone deemed *unrefined* by the court, and Elyse couldn't break her stare. When his smile turned to her, it was as if any problem she had never existed

"Ready for your surprise?" he asked.

"I need to know what we're doing to be prepared."

He looped his arm through hers. "Then it wouldn't be a surprise."

"Then how can I be excited about it?" She laughed and followed him into the gardens, quickly making their ways through the paths. They came to a new section of the palace, Elyse pausing as he held open the door. "The surprise is inside, then."

Wynn tsked as she passed. "Enjoy it, will you?"

"I am enjoying it!" She glanced at the floor, then at him. "I'm with you."

With a grin, Wynn took her hand and led her up the stairs to the top floor. They emerged into a long hallway, its length lined with rooms Elyse had never entered. He paused halfway down and opened a door, gesturing for her to enter the darkened room. As Wynn closed it behind them, the darkness deepened, illuminated only by the windows overlooking the garden and a solitary dormer window above.

Elyse nodded enthusiastically. "A dark room? Wonderful surprise."

"Love the sarcasm on you," he said as he pushed a table to the center of the room. "Glad you learned a new skill while I was gone. Now, come here."

As she approached, Wynn placed his hands on her waist. Breathless, Elyse began to ask what he was doing but stopped herself. His grip on her sides, his scent enveloping her—alone in the darkened room, she wondered what his kiss would be like, a thought that had crossed her mind more than once.

"On to the table," he said, lifting her up. He joined her and pointed to the window above. "You'll have to unlock it using magic like I taught you, then crawl out. I'll be right behind."

"We're going to …" She shook her head, backing up. "Up there?"

"Yes."

"One the roof?"

"Yes again." Wynn pulled her close to him the hoisted her above his head. Elyse drew magic into her body, releasing it slowly into the lock. Unlike the ones she had practiced with, there were no pins she could sense inside. Instead, it possessed layers of rotating disks, each needing to move in different directions to unlock. She concentrated, envisioning the metal spinning in her mind until she heard soft, distinct clicks. After a few minutes of focus, the last disk slid into place, and she opened the window, crawling onto the roof.

The Central Garden stretched out below, a patchwork of deep greens and sharp bursts of color. The late sun painted the edges of the blooms in amber light, while shadows crept along the narrow paths and still ponds, hinting at the approaching night.

A laugh, light and carefree, slipped from her lips as she gazed down the roofline, her eyes following the graceful rise of the palace's higher towers. Each turret and spire stretched skyward, their silhouettes etched against the evening light as if the fingers of a colossal hand reached out in silent aspiration. When Wynn pulled himself up, she said, "I've heard of people getting up here, but I thought they were lying."

Wynn stood and brushed off his pants. "They likely were. This is the only window left open, per Wyltam's orders. It's one of many useful mage entrances."

"Many?" Elyse shook her head. Turning to the Central Garden, she experienced a familiar sight at a whole new angle. With the sun about to set, light globes glowed above the paths below, resembling stars that hung above the greenery. "It's beautiful."

"It is." She turned to find Wynn staring at her. He extended his hand. "But that's not why we're here."

He led her up the slope of the roof toward its peak, ducking down when they neared the top. "We'll have to remain invisible until the sun sets. Guards on duty don't take kindly to people walking on the palace roof. Think you're up to it?"

She rubbed her hands against her legs. "Is this a surprise test?"

"Every day is a test."

"Wynn."

"We're going to miss it if you don't hurry." Then Wynn disappeared. "Hold my hand and we'll go down together."

Elyse exhaled, drawing in aithyr with deliberate calm. She imagined herself as the surrounding wind, as lighter than air. When she opened her eyes, she saw exactly that.

She blindly grasped for Wynn's hand and stood with him. From the other side, Satiros sprawled with twisting paths and veining greenery. Wynn pulled her down, and she felt him take the seat next to her.

As the sun dipped below the horizon, the light globes of the city state rose and flickered to life. If the garden had mirrored the stars, then these were a galaxy scattered above the silhouettes of buildings. Slowly, the sky faded from indigo to inky black, the lights burning brighter as night took its hold over the world. Sitting there, she watched Satiros and discovered a newfound appreciation for her failed dreams of escaping this place. The city-state was beautiful and alive.

"I should scold you for dropping your invisibility," Wynn said, startling her. "But I'm happy I got to see your reaction."

Elyse glanced down at her herself, seeing her body in the low light. "I didn't even notice." She turned her wide eyes to Wynn. "Does this mean I failed?"

She noticed a new tenderness in his gaze, with his brows slightly furrowing. "It's only you and me right now, Elyse."

A gust of wind sent prickles across her skin. Wynn lifted an arm and tucked Elyse close to his body. She gazed up at him and her stomach fluttered. In his arms, she felt safe. Protected. Cared for. Deep down, she was certain he would go to great lengths to protect her or make her happy. He already did every day.

He glanced down, his lips tilting into a smirk. "I didn't bring you up here so you could stare at me."

Elyse wished herself to make a quip back, to laugh, to do anything other than think about his mouth on hers. She failed miserably.

Her hand trembled as she raised it, tracing the curve of his jaw with a delicate touch. Her fingers lingered along his lips, feeling their warmth and the pulse beneath. Within the last few weeks, she stopped dreaming of Azarys. Now she knew why.

The moment hung heavy, almost tangible, and Elyse could nearly taste it on her tongue. A pull deep within her urged her forward, and she surrendered to it. She leaned closer, her lips grazing his with a tentative kiss. The contact was light, a fleeting caress that sent a ripple of emotion coursing through her.

Wynn jerked away. "It's getting late," he said, breaking through the charged silence.

"Oh. I'm—" Elyse's voice faltered, her cheeks burning with a rush of heat. The ghost of his touch lingered on her skin.

He stood abruptly and ran a hand over his face, his expression tense and closed off. "We should get you back to your room. Come on, I'll walk you."

His sudden withdrawal cut deep, a piercing ache twisting through her chest. Words formed on her lips—a hollow, meaningless apology. She'd believed he wanted this, let herself think his actions hinted at something more. But that warmth had chilled in an instant, replaced by a cold distance. He hadn't welcomed her kiss. He hadn't desired her. The truth stung, a sharp realization that she had reached for a part of him that was never hers to claim.

Chapter Thirty-Two

KEYAIN

Keyain lay in the dark, sprawled on a couch in his manor. The emptiness of the house mirrored the dismissal Wyltam had delivered—Keyain had been temporarily relieved of his duties and removed from the palace for some 'much-needed time' to himself.

If his housekeeper Irys was still here, she would've had every room lit and dinner prepared. Instead, Keyain sent her and her pilinos daughter away. He couldn't stand to see the look on young Emlyn's face when she realized the half-elven hero Keyain had always talked about wasn't coming home.

A bottle of liquor balanced on his chest. The only effort he'd bothered with in the past day was lifting his head high enough to take a swig. The thought of food was distant and irrelevant; he knew he wouldn't bother.

Months had passed since he last visited his countryside manor. While the village leaders always sent updates to the palace, Keyain couldn't be bothered to check in with them in person. Couldn't be bothered with reports or paperwork. None of it really mattered and it would likely slip from his grasp, too, as all things did.

The couch beneath him still bore dust covers, which Keyain had rolled onto. Days had passed since he was last sober, but it didn't matter. No one was here to see him in his stupor. At least here there would be no more shame. It struck him how different it was from his youth, when visitors—friends and politicians—came and went in a steady parade. It was a stark contrast to the dark, empty rooms haunting the place now.

Keyain sighed, rolling into a sitting position with his limbs and head heavy. As he stood, his weight swayed beneath him and he steadied himself with the couch. He held the bottle to his face and squinted. When did it become empty? He tripped over a forgotten bottles at his feet. The walls were his support as he stumbled to the cellar. Grabbing the first bottle he found, Keyain unstoppered it and took a swig, noting the alcohol no longer burned. Soon he'd pass out, which was the goal. He couldn't think if he was unconscious.

He wandered through the manor, his movements growing slower and more sluggish with each mouthful of alcohol. As he made his way to the third floor toward his bedroom, he stopped at one of the few rooms not covered in dust cloths. But that didn't mean it was ever used.

Keyain lumbered in, triggering the room's globe lights, blinding him so that he needed to shield his eyes. The room that came into view was one of the largest in the manor. Marietta would have had all the privacy and space she needed here. She could've been free from the Exisotis, from Wyltam's grasp. Irys could've been her friend. And though Marietta didn't want children, he knew she would've loved Emlyn. Over time, she could have helped the businesses in the village, bolstering their lands and helping people as she wished. She could've had a community here. But it was all just a ruined dream, one that left Keyain alone and in an empty room with nothing but shame.

The tension at the base of his neck snapped as raw emotions surged. He hurled his bottle against the wall, the glass shattering into sharp fragments as the last of its contents dripped slowly down. Marietta could've had a life she always wished for. His chest heaved as he grabbed a chair, hoisting it above his head and smashing it into the ground. If he had listened, if only he had acted sooner, then perhaps he could've saved her. Driven by rage, he destroyed anything within reach, each broken piece mirroring his own sense of devastation.

When the room lay in ruins, he fought to draw in enough air, his lungs resisting. He caught sight of his reflection in a fractured mirror: tear-streaked, reddened, and unrecognizable. Stumbling backward, he struggled to make sense of the broken image before him. His gasps came unevenly as he sank to the floor, folding his head between his knees.

He had lost everything. Lost everyone. Not even alcohol could drown out his emotions. He needed something stronger.

He staggered his way to his room, digging through his bag for the bottle of a milky white substance. Why suffer any emotion when he could experience nothing at all? Keyain withdrew the cork and took a few gulps.

Collapsing onto his bed, he stared at the ceiling, counting the panels of scrollwork. If he could revisit his old self, he would tell him to stay with Marietta, to leave his position and his city-state behind, for there was nothing worth more than her. Keyain could have changed his name, lived a different life. He could've convinced the Exisotis that he had a change of heart. He could've saved Marietta from marrying Tilan, and Marietta could have lived forever in ignorant bliss. At the very least, he wouldn't have to watch her marry Wyltam. The most depressing part was that he had no one to blame but himself. Not Wyltam. Not Marietta. Not even Tilan. It was his decisions that led him to this moment, and now he had to deal with it. Dealing with it meant drowning himself until it all passed, if it ever did.

His throat tightened, and his eyes watered as he struggled to remain calm. With a sob, his control slipped, and he shut his eyes tightly as hot tears streamed down his face. His body grew hazy, his head suddenly light as Choke began to take its affect, but it didn't stop his mind from spiraling.

Marietta being with Wyltam echoed the same suffocating dread he had known with Olytia. The days spent in the late queen's bed started as a dream, but twisted into an unrelenting nightmare. He recalled the betrayal etched into Wyltam's expression when the truth of Keyain's actions came to light. Olytia's laughter, sharp and jarring, had grated against every nerve, a reminder of the torment that had followed.

As Choke took hold of his remaining thoughts, Olytia's voice cut through his mind like a blade. *I always knew you'd amount to nothing.*

She was right. She was always right. He was nothing.

Chapter Thirty-Three

KEYAIN, BEFORE

"**I** tell you, the new fighter from the south is unstoppable."

Keyain nodded absently as one of his peers chirped on. The grand hall thrummed with energy, lights casting a warm glow over the lavishly dressed guests. Laughter and the soft murmur of conversation mingled with the strains of a lively waltz.

"I put a hefty sum on him in the pits last week, and he didn't disappoint."

Keyain kept his pleasant smile as another lord offered his opinion. He took a sip of his wine, trying to ease his nerves. Did she know? She had to know.

"You wouldn't believe the odds on that last match," the lord added, swirling his drink with a dramatic flourish. "A hundred to one, and the underdog still managed to win!"

Keyain's gaze drifted past the sea of silk and velvet to where Queen Olytia stood, surrounded by a throng of admirers. Her smile was radiant, her laughter a delicate chime that pulled the entire room into her orbit. His fingers tightened around his glass as he tried to focus on the conversation.

"He's got a fierce reputation." Keyain closed his eyes when he heard Cedryc's voice, not realizing he joined their gathered group. "Though I wonder how long he can keep it up. The pits have a way of breaking even the strongest."

The other lords laughed, one clapping Cedryc on the back. "You're too cautious. Sometimes you have to take risks to win big."

The tension in Keyain tightened, teetering on the edge of shattering. He turned to Queen Olytia, her dark eyes locking onto his with a precision that echoed the sting of her slap. She knew.

Keyain's breath hitched, his fingers drumming an erratic rhythm against his thigh. The conversation shifted to a new topic, but the words were lost on him. His gaze flickered to the queen, his heart pounding. Did she recognize him? He conjured every possible scenario in which they would've met, each more nerve-racking than the last. His palms grew damp, and he swallowed hard, forcing a smile as he nodded along to the lords' chatter. The weight of her potential recognition threatened to crush him.

Maybe she didn't recognize his face. Maybe …

"Are you all right?" Cedryc's hand on his arm felt electric, the low hum of his voice making his skin prickle.

Keyain jerked away, the memory of Cedryc's touch etched sharply in his mind. Nights with Cedryc had always been his favorite until—

Queen Olytia's stare burned like a brand on the side of his face.

"I'm fine," he said.

"You've been on edge lately." Cedryc leaned closer, his voice dropping. "I haven't seen you in months."

The queen's emerald gown shimmered each time she moved, a beacon that drew Keyain's eyes no matter how hard he tried to concentrate.

"I've been busy."

"Busy." Cedryc sighed. "If you say so."

Keyain downed the rest of his drink, the liquid burning its way down his throat. He mumbled an excuse and slipped away from the group, seeking refuge in another glass, then another. Each sip blurred the edges of his anxiety, but his thoughts still raced. He hurried to the hallway, the silence a stark contrast to the ballroom's din. Leaning against the cool wall, he gathered his resolve. Queen Olytia loathed reminders that she wasn't his only desire. She had to know about Cedryc. She always seemed to sense when his past threatened to catch up with him.

He steadied himself. There was still time to make things right.

Keyain took off and headed toward the Royal's Suite. Queen Olytia enjoyed making him wait. It could ease the sting.

An hour past midnight, she finally arrived. The queen marched into the room, a smirk hooking her lips. "Waiting for me like a faithful hound, I see."

Keyain exhaled sharply, forcing a smile. "How did the rest of the night go?"

"I finally got Minister Lyonell to admit the news from the cultists to the north are a problem." She laughed to herself as she removed an earring. "The minister of religious affairs admitted it in front of Dyeiter, nonetheless. We can finally make the case to remove his position and stick the temples under vassals."

Keyain nodded, stilling his expression. Perhaps she didn't notice. "Diminishing the temple's influence."

Olytia smiled as she glanced at him. "I thought closing the palace temple would've done more. No matter. I'll kill them off, starting with the head."

Years earlier, a pilinos had wielded the powers bestowed by their deity to assault guards during an arrest. They escaped, but their display of such formidable strength marked them for retribution. Since then, the queen's wrath had remained fixed upon them.

She had already outlawed magic in public spaces, despite warnings from other ministers. With city-states in Syllogi still allowing its use, they stood at a distinct disadvantage. Yet Queen Olytia continued unfazed. Power and control were her true pursuits, and both magic and the temples jeopardized them. Keyain needed no further explanation; it was clear that her ultimate aim was to eradicate the temples from Satiros entirely.

Under Queen Olytia, crossing her meant losing power.

She walked toward Keyain and pushed him back onto the bed. "Tell me about your evening."

Keyain's pulse quickened. "Not nearly as exciting."

"No?" She brushed her fingers through his hair, then gripped it tightly, yanking his head back to force his eyes onto hers. "Nothing you want to apologize for?"

Keyain hissed through the pain as his stomach dropped. "He came up to me. I didn't think—I wasn't trying—" He closed his eyes. "I'm sorry."

She released him and stepped back. "I warned you. Do not make a fool of me by entertaining your past affairs."

He flinched at the sound of her voice. "I'm sorry."

Her hand met his cheek in a resounding crack. "If you're going to grovel for forgiveness, get on your knees and beg."

Keyain noticed the spark in her eyes as she sank into the chair beside the bed, her anger clear but not overwhelming. The tension in his shoulders eased; she was upset, but not beyond reconciliation. Slowly, he lowered himself to his knees.

"Forgive me. I didn't mean to insult you."

She hummed to herself. "Forehead to the floor, General Keyain."

His skin met stone. "Please, forgive me."

She made him wait a moment, then her laugh came soft, amused. "Now crawl to me like the big, important male you are."

Chapter Thirty-Four
AMRYTH

Amryth ran a hand over her braids as she inspected the side street next to the park in Wisteria Heights. While Tanaly worked on convincing Adira to talk, they sought out other leads from the investigation notes. Amryth scanned the surrounding buildings, reconfirming that there was no obvious correlation between the sites where the pilinos' bodies were found. After she and Deania had checked every scene, they were no closer to answers.

She thought that maybe businesses nearby would be similar, or maybe a type of housing. Even the streets and where the sites fell seemed arbitrary, leaving her and Deania with the same amount of questions and growing frustration.

What they did know was that the murders weren't random. Every victim had been from Chorys Dasi and the murderer had been searching for them. Given that Jory was a Satiroan native, that specific detail made his arrest even more puzzling. As Amryth approached the park, the sharp edge of angry voices yelled from just inside the entrance.

"I don't care what you think you were doing," snapped a voice. "You have no business being here!"

"I didn't realize that sitting in the grass was a crime." Deania's voice—

gods, she was pissed. Amryth hurried her steps, finding an elven female wagging her finger at a glaring Deania.

The female took a step toward her. "You weren't just 'sitting in the grass—'"

"You dense fucking cabbage!" Deania closed the space between them and lifted her chin, the tiny half-elf barely reaching the female's shoulder. Though small, she could be vicious.

A bright spot of pink bloomed on the apples of the elven female's cheeks. "How dare you call me a cabbage?"

"What's the problem here?" Amryth interjected.

"There was none until she started heckling me." Deania crossed her arms.

"You were trespassing!"

"This is a public park and we're here during park hours," Amryth said lazily. It was as if she were on patrol duty from her early years in the guard, often having to deescalate interactions between the elven elite and pilinos minding their own business.

"I've never seen her before and I walk here every day."

"People are allowed to visit parks at different times as long as they remain open."

Amryth moved to Deania's side, the other woman retreating with a stammering protest. "You're in league with her! I'm going to get the guards!"

"And tell them what?" Amryth shook her head. "I was a guard, ma'am. I know the laws and know we aren't breaking them."

"Well, I'd still like to—"

"Oh, my gods!" Deania yelled, tossing her head back. "Is this what people do when they have somebody doing all their work for them?"

"The new clip in charge is making your kind too bold!"

"Excuse me?" Whatever patience Amryth had withered away.

The female gestured to Deania. "Mouthy and won't listen to anything we say! Back in my youth, they would have never thought they were equals because we didn't blur that line."

Deania went to respond, but Amryth placed her hand on her shoulder and cut her off. "Why do you think pilinos are not equal to elves?"

"Their lives are a fraction of ours," the lady responded incredulously.

"What they experience is a blip to what we will amount to."

"Have you known anyone who has died too early, before they reached a century? Maybe even two or three? What about a child?"

"That has nothing to do with this."

Amryth shook her head, watching the lady try to re-rationalize her thinking even though part of her likely agreed. "If they died young, then clearly their lives were inferior." Amryth turned away. "You know your logic is flawed. Have a lovely day."

The woman kept yelling, but Amryth blocked it out. She could've been one of her parent's friends, blinded by their own logical fallacies.

Deania slipped her arm through Amryth's as they made their way back to her apartment. "I had it handled back there," she said.

"I know but—"

"Thank you, though." She glanced at Amryth, her eyes containing earthy tones that ranged from deep chestnut to hints of amber that shifted in the fading light. "For standing up for me. For trying to prove that Jory is innocent. Have I ever told you that you're a good person?"

Amryth huffed a dry laugh, suddenly needing to stare anywhere else. "Anyone should want to do what I'm doing."

"But they don't. Many people have good intentions and the right mindset, but never put them into action." She grew quiet for a moment, then added, "You're much better than most people, and I'm glad I have you in my life."

The words became jammed in the back of Amryth's throat, wanting to say she felt the same, that Deania has been the brightest part of her life for the last few months. Instead, she asked, "What do you want for dinner?"

Amryth left the confectionery, carrying Deania's requested Chorys Dasian treat—sweet cheese curds pressed with caramel and cloaked in chocolate. It wasn't a meal, but she wasn't in the mood for a lecture. Plus, she intended to visit a few more places to find more substantial options.

Entering the nearest bakery in Greening Juncture, she found the baker speaking softly with the sole other customer.

"They're a new group," the baker said, dropping his voice as he eyed Amryth. "I think they're going to do something about this problem." His shoulders were tense, and he turned to keep his back to Amryth as he continued talking to the elven female.

With feigned disinterest, Amryth perused the sparse selection of baked goods, her ears straining to catch bits of the conversation.

"About damn time," the customer said. "Consider me interested in joining, though."

"You free midweek?"

"I can be."

"Ladybird Inn, an hour after sunset." The baker slid something across the table. "Bring this."

The other customer said her thanks before quickly leaving the store.

As Amryth ducked down to examine the remaining loaves, she pretended not to hear him when he asked, "Do you need help finding anything?" She heard his steps thud across the floor and grow closer. "Excuse me, miss?"

Amryth jolted, her surprise carefully staged. "Oh? What was that? I'm torn between these two. Which do you suggest?"

The baker's expression softened as he gestured toward the sourdough. "We're fortunate to have a loaf still. It's my specialty."

She purchased the bread and left, her mind circling around their conversation. The baker had been riled up, the women intrigued. The meeting at the Ladybird Inn piqued her interest, and she was determined to find out the reason behind it.

Chapter Thirty-Five

MARIETTA

Marietta guided the acolytes through the palace's winding corridors, her stride more steady than the racing beat of her heart. She hadn't meant to invite them; it had slipped out that today she'd be reviewing the plans for the royal wedding. But when the acolytes asked if they might attend, hoping to offer their aid, Marietta hadn't refused. A whim, perhaps, but also a chance to show goodwill between the crown and the temples—a part of her new role after Wyltam had brokered peace with Minister Leyland.

The acolytes trailed behind her, their colorful robes bright against the stone walls. A few representatives from each temple walked together, their voices hushed. Now and then, Coryn's laughter broke through the murmurs as he eagerly pointed out parts of the palace he now called home. Marietta noticed Tolis's hands moving in swift, subtle gestures to Sibylla. "Strange."

She tsked under her breath, drawing their attention, and gestured back. "Not strange."

They exchanged a look, then Sibylla said, "You're picking things up fast, Your Grace. Didn't think you could read hand speak."

"You didn't want me to?" Marietta added a smile to mask the irritation in her expression.

Sibylla hummed softly, a note of amusement. "We're simply staying vigilant, is all."

Marietta's patience wore thin as they approached the throne room. She released a slow breath, trying to steady herself, her guards trailing in her wake. The grand doors, etched with vines and flowers in intricate detail, swung wide. She stepped inside, the acolytes close behind her. Sunlight poured through the stained glass windows, casting a kaleidoscope of green and gold across the polished stone floor and towering columns. At the center of the room stood Minister Rymos, his aides, Tryda, and Wyltam, all turning to face them as they entered.

Rymos's lips parted when the acolytes followed her into the room. "Ah, we have guests," he said, a forced politeness in his voice. "Welcome." He motioned for them to join the circle.

"I thought it might be wise to have them participate in the wedding plans." Marietta felt Wyltam's gaze burning into her.

As she approached the group, his voice slid into her mind, sharp and unimpressed. *"A little warning would've been appreciated."*

She slipped her hand into Wyltam's, giving it a light squeeze, hoping to soften his mood.

Rymos glanced between them, his smile taut. "Very well," he said, clearing his throat. He opened a booklet he held. "As you all know, due to the recent security threats, the wedding will be a more controlled event. No public processions, no large gatherings outside the palace grounds."

He outlined the plan with brisk efficiency: a series of small receptions as different allies arrived in Satiros, a contained ceremony in the throne room, followed by a feast, and a final ball to close the celebration. All carefully planned, every moment accounted for, every potential threat minimized. The acolytes listened quietly, hands folded, heads bowed, respectful.

But then Nosokyma stepped forward. "Minister," she said, her voice calm but firm, "I see no mention of a religious bonding ceremony in your plans."

Marietta blinked, unable to hide her surprise. Religious bonding ceremony? She hadn't heard of this.

"I wasn't aware that the royals were interested in one?" He turned to

Marietta and Wyltam.

"Consider it a recent addition," Marietta said.

Wyltam stiffened beside her.

"Indeed," Rymos said, gesturing toward the acolytes. "How long will the ceremony last?"

"The temples have discussed it," Nosokyma replied. "To honor all five deities, it will require at least half a day."

"Oh." Rymos peered over his glasses at Wyltam, then turned his gaze to Nosokyma. "This is unexpected. We'll have to add in an extra day, work around the welcome gatherings." He then faced Wyltam. "Will that be acceptable, Your Grace?"

"Of course."

Marietta didn't miss the tick in his jaw when Wyltam answered. She squeezed his hand again as if it would mean an apology.

Tryda cleared her throat and stepped forward. "If I may?"

"By all means," Rymos said.

"While we value the presence of the temples today and the added weight they lend to this historic wedding, we must consider how it will be perceived by the public." Her violet gown shimmered as she turned to face Marietta. "Lady Marietta has graced a temple before and received the favor of a deity, yet she is not an active member of that community. This is an arbitrary addition."

"Then she should be seen at the temples more frequently." Nosokyma stepped forward. "The temples would be greatly honored if Lady Marietta and King Wyltam made regular appearances."

Marietta hesitated; Wyltam had made no such promise. His eyes flicked to hers, and then he spoke. "We'll see what can be arranged in the coming days."

Tryda gave a nod, her glance skimming over Marietta with a cool detachment.

"Now that we've addressed that," Rymos said, "let's move on to the details we've planned."

Rymos's aides moved about the throne room, speaking of draping new silks from the ceilings and walls, a vision they intended to replicate in the ballroom. Marietta's lips tightened. Silk in that quantity would be costly—thousands in gold, at the very least.

As they stepped into the ballroom, one of the aides gestured to where a new portrait of her and Wyltam would hang for all to see. The crown would surely commission only the finest painters; another thousand in gold, easily.

The discussions continued, and a sheen of sweat gathered on Marietta's brow. Invitations gilded with gold, additional guards for security, performers from across the region for a week of celebrations—thousands more. Delicacies from the far corners of the Akroi Region and beyond, gifts for dignitaries from other city-states, favors for every guest. Each detail seemed more extravagant than the last.

They passed through the doors into the Central Garden, standing atop the steps that overlooked the verdant expanse. "To crown the evening," Rymos announced, snapping his book shut, "we have enlisted a master craftsperson specializing in aithyr displays—fireworks, guided by magic, to illuminate the skies above the Central Garden."

Marietta bit her tongue. She knew well enough the costs associated with Enomenoan craftsmanship; their wedding would drain a fortune in gold before even accounting for their attire—a sum that could have matched her earnings from her most prosperous years helping others with their businesses.

As Rymos droned on, Marietta leaned over to Wyltam. "It's a bit irresponsible to pay this sum for our wedding as we go to war."

The minister quieted at her murmur. Wyltam nodded and said to the group, "What was the budget your team decided on?"

"No budget, Your Grace," Rymos said. "After consulting with Minister Royir, we were given the directive to spend as we saw fit. Considering the unprecedented significance of this union, we believed no detail should be overlooked."

"A royal wedding can still carry great weight without draining the Satiroan coffers dry," Marietta countered. "We're going to war. We should be more responsible with what we spend."

A soft murmur rippled through the gathered assembly. "Your Graces, if I may?" Lady Tryda inclined her head in a respectful bow.

"Continue," Wyltam ordered.

"While it may appear wise to curtail expenses in a time of conflict," Tryda began, "consider the message it sends to our enemies. To spend sparingly on a wedding of this magnitude could be perceived as a sign of weakness."

Nosokyma's frown deepened, a low sound of disapproval escaping her lips. "And what will your people think if they see their rulers squandering gold while war is certain? They'd rather see steel than silk from their leaders."

Wyltam's gaze moved between Tryda and Nosokyma, then settled on Rymos. "I share Marietta's concerns. While I understand that this wedding must rival, if not surpass, all that came before, it seems unwise to spend resources on a mere celebration with the coming war. Find places to cut expenses without losing the grandeur."

A tense silence fell over the group, broken only by Rymos's anxious sputter. "But Your Grace, this could delay us by weeks. Do you wish to change the wedding date?"

"The date stays," Wyltam said, his tone leaving no room for argument.

The silence that followed was damning. Marietta sighed, stepping forward. "If I may offer a few alternatives?"

"We welcome any insight, Your Grace," Rymos replied, his voice tight.

"Instead of sourcing rare delicacies, let's focus on dishes that reflect both Satiroan and Enomenoan traditions. Firewater is essential—it symbolizes camaraderie in Enomenos. We could also import ale from Rotamu. Surely, it wouldn't cost much to bring it up the Halia."

Rymos nodded slowly, then snapped his fingers. His aides quickly began jotting down notes. "We can make those adjustments, Your Grace."

Feeling confident with his acceptance of the idea, Marietta continued with a momentum she hadn't felt since she was working at her bakery, throwing out ideas that spurred better ones from the minister of conduct's team. At the end of the meeting, they had decided on musicians from both Satiros and Enomenos. Settling on Satiroan flowers as the focus for decorations, Marietta used it as inspiration for her own attire, feeding the team rough sketches and ideas.

By the end, Marietta's pulse raced. Wyltam's hand had settled at the small of her back again, his touch a steady reassurance. She leaned into it, drawing strength. "With all the gold we save, we could put it toward recruitment," she suggested, recalling the figures she had seen in the reports. "Especially for the guards who've volunteered for the front lines. And let the people know—this is where the wedding budget went. We chose them over indulgence."

"Such a gesture would go a long way," Nosokyma murmured to the other acolytes.

"Another excellent idea," Rymos said, pausing to check his aithyr clock. "We've gone over. Let's plan to reconvene the same time next week."

As the group dispersed, Wyltam pulled Marietta to the side. He kept his voice low as he leaned into her. "The temples? Really?"

"Wasn't on purpose. I was meeting with them then mentioned where I was heading next." She wrapped a curl around her finger. "One thing led to another and I felt like I had no choice."

"Do you understand what religious ceremonies entail?"

"Don't say sacrifices."

"But they are sacrifices—of our bodies and our blood." His hand brushed the side of her neck where her tattoo inked her skin. "It'll involve the permanent altering of our bodies in some way."

She closed her hand over Wyltam's. "Maybe we could change parts of it?"

He sighed and pressed a kiss into her palm, his expression disappearing as he glanced over her shoulder. "It's a pleasure to see the temples represented," he said.

Marietta turned to see Nosokyma approaching.

"The honor is ours, Your Grace," Nosokyma said, bowing her head. "We were hoping to arrange dates today for when you could visit our temples."

Marietta tightened her hand in Wyltam's. "We're busy most—"

"We can make time for a temple this week," Wyltam said. "And perhaps spread them out between now and the wedding. I can have a cornicular send you the details."

"That would be much appreciated."

She bid her goodbyes with the other acolytes, Marietta turning to Wyltam with a question at the tip of her tongue.

"This is what you asked for," he said, his voice clipped. "Next time they join us, please warn me."

"Of course."

Wyltam turned to leave, but Marietta's hand halted him.

"I'm sorry," she said quickly. "I didn't realize the full extent of the ceremonies, nor that you would."

"I know you don't know." His gaze shifted past her to the group departing, a subtle tension in his shoulders. "They know it too. Just don't promise them anything until we talk about it. At least for the foreseeable future."

Marietta opened her mouth to argue but stopped herself, picturing Wyltam marked with ink he hadn't chosen. "I promise," she said softly.

Marietta rubbed her temples as she closed the suite door behind her. The brief tea with the Queen's Court had been a trial; Tryda's presence had only added to her mounting headache. As she turned, she heard a childish voice.

She found Wyltam in the sitting room, his posture stiff and hands clasped behind his back. A boy no more than a few years old stood at his side. The resemblance between them was undeniable: dark hair, pale skin, and sharp, defining features. Behind them hovered a woman with a rounded face, her expression pinched.

"Remember when I said we'd have a new person in the suite?" Wyltam's voice, deep and unyielding, had not softened for the child.

The prince nodded, his eyes wide and serious.

Marietta noted how little Prince Mycaub resembled his mother as he turned to face her. His gaze held a mixture of awe and shyness. She crouched to his level and extended her hand.

"Hello, Prince Mycaub. I'm Marietta," she introduced herself, her smile warm.

Mycaub hesitated but took her hand, his grip firm. "It's a pleasure to meet you," he said clearly.

Marietta's smile grew. "You speak with such composure for someone so young. How old are you?"

Mycaub held up three fingers and shied away.

"Three? That makes you the same age as my friend's son. I'm sure you two would get along well if you ever met," Marietta said, her voice gentle.

The boy glanced at Wyltam, then back at Marietta, his interest piqued.

"Perhaps one day you'll meet him. Would you like that?" she asked.

Mycaub blinked, then gave a slow nod.

Wyltam cleared his throat. "This is Keya, the governess. She's nearly always with Mycaub, so you'll see her often."

Keya dipped her head in a respectful bow. "It's a pleasure to meet you, Lady Marietta."

"And the same to you," Marietta replied, rising. "I hope we can become well acquainted."

Keya's gaze softened, though her lips remained pressed together. "The honor would be mine. But the prince should eat soon and keep to his schedule, Your Graces."

Marietta observed the shift in his demeanor as Wyltam dismissed his son and the governess—his silence and the inscrutability of his expression.

"Not the fatherly type?" she asked. "Not even a hug for your son?"

Wyltam's gaze met hers, flat and unyielding.

"Just a joke," she said. "Though a touch of affection might benefit the child."

"How was tea?"

Marietta's lips curved into a wry smile. "Changing the subject, are we?" She walked to the pile of notes waiting for her on the low table before the couches. "Tea was as you would expect. If I have to hear one more piece of gossip about court, I will tear my hair out."

Marietta picked up the first note, breaking the seal and quickly reading the inside. Another dinner party invitation. She sighed and let the paper fall back onto the table.

"This is getting ridiculous." She held up the remaining notes.

"They thin out after a while," he said, hovering behind the couch. "We can have a cornicular assigned to open yours."

"Do you ever accept these invitations?" Marietta asked.

"Not once," he replied, a smile hinting at his lips. "That's why they stopped coming for me."

"I suppose I'll have to wait it out then." She held his gaze for a moment, feeling his eyes soften as they traced her features. Marietta ducked her head and tucked a stray lock of hair behind her ear. "If you had to choose between tea with the Queen's Court or dinner with a noble family, which would it be?"

"And I had to choose?"

Marietta nodded.

"Honestly, tea. Takes less time. And from what I've experienced, Ymorea does a fine job filling the silence."

Marietta's eyes grew wide. "She talks so much! I thought I was bad. It's not that I mind her company, but endless tea sessions with the same stories she has to share …" She sighed. "I wish tea wasn't mandatory."

"Who said you had to?" Wyltam walked to the doorway and paused. "Your Queen's Court is what you choose it to be. Teach them to bake if you are so inclined."

Marietta considered that. Watching Tryda do something unorthodox sounded rather enjoyable.

"I have something I want to show you, if you have a moment," Wyltam said, pulling her attention. "Unless you'd rather read through all the invitations first."

"Not in the slightest," Marietta answered, following him.

Wyltam led her to his office. "I finally completed what I'd like to share with you in return for reading your favorite book." With a flick of his hand, the lock clicked open, and he pushed it aside.

"Mine involved work?" Marietta trailed him into the office, intrigued.

"It didn't need to, but I thought some notes would make it easier," he explained, crossing the room to rummage through a drawer.

"Gods, it is note taking."

His eyebrows twitched as he glanced up at her, his mouth ticking toward a smile. "That I wish."

Her stomach tightened at the sight as she approached. "You're unusually excited about this, for you at least." His momentary smile faltered. Quickly, she added, "What I mean is that you look happy. It's nice seeing your smile."

Wyltam ducked his head as he showed her the title of the book he procured.

"*The History of Lyken Fulbryk?*" she said incredulously. "You want me to read my grandfather's biography?"

Wyltam came around the desk and leaned against it, crossing one leg over the other. "It's quite a bit more than that. Lyken had an odd sense of humor, one that I think you'll be familiar with. He used accounts of his own life to teach the ten principles of magic."

Her smile faded as his words sunk in. "Don't tell me you want me to learn magic."

"Only the basics."

"I'm a bit too busy to casually learn a new skill at the moment."

"Do you think I had an abundant amount of time to spend reading?"

"There's a big difference between reading a book and learning magic."

He handed her the book. "Just read it. Tell me what you think."

Marietta sighed and tucked it under her arm and made for the door, pausing before she exited. "You said there were notes?"

His lips ticked into a smile as he followed her. "Turn to the first page."

Marietta eyed him before opening the book. The top was titled *Measuring Mental Mettle,* followed by neatly printed lines of text. In the margins, she found Wyltam's handwriting.

"I left notes where they correlated with the passage. Nothing too detailed, only basic references. Though if you prefer something more detailed—"

"Gods, no." She read the scrawl of his handwriting in the margins. *"Mental strength meaning how well you can control emotions and attention, unlike your books where only the men were strong."* She snorted a laugh. "That's a little obtuse," she said, glancing up at him. "The women were strong too."

"Do you like it?"

His dark eyes practically sparkled with the question, a rare openness that made her stomach flutter. The task shifted from an assignment to an opportunity. "I love it."

"If you enjoy it, we could dive further into you learning magic."

Her smile lessened. "I'm not sure I have room to learn something else."

"What about protecting yourself?" he asked as they made their way down the hall. "If we're going to be making regular visits to the temples, there will be more opportunities to harm you."

"Isn't that why I have guards?"

"Magic is a useful tool that can enhance your life," he said. "Imagine being able to message me back."

She paused at that, knowing that she very much wished to snap back at him with her mind. "Fine, but only if you come bake a pie with me some—"

As they turned the corner, they stopped abruptly at Mycaub and Keya walking toward them, the prince dressed in his sleeping clothes.

"Pie?" he asked in his small voice.

Marietta crouched to meet his gaze. "Did you know I used to be a baker?"

He shook his head, eyes widening with interest.

"I baked cookies for children just like you," she continued, smiling warmly. "Do you like cookies?"

His face lit up as he nodded.

"I could use a helper to bake something special with your father. Would you like to help us? You can have as many sweets as you like when we're done."

He nodded more enthusiastically.

Marietta smiled and turned to Wyltam, who seemed to close off his emotions once more. "Perhaps you could read him a bedtime story?"

Wyltam cleared his throat. "Not tonight, unfortunately."

"Nonsense."

"Marietta," he warned.

She turned back to Mycaub, who tucked himself behind Keya's leg.

"Good night, Mycaub," Wyltam said, kneeling before his son and pulling him into a hug. The prince repeated the phrase before Wyltam walked to his office and shut his door.

Marietta sighed and turned to Mycaub. "How about I read to you tonight?"

His nod was much less enthusiastic that time.

They settled into his room, Marietta sitting in a chair next to the bed and the prince tucked into the covers. Unlike his father's room, the walls were covered in colorful art. "What book should we read?"

"The feyrie one." He pointed to the book on the table beside his bed.

"My father used to read similar stories to me when I was your age! My favorite was always …" Her voice tapered off as she read the title. *Goodnight Feyries: Bedtime Stories from Feyrie Tales*. Marietta stared in disbelief. The book in her hands was one from Elyse's list. Her breath caught as she read the author's name, the shock of recognition freezing her in place.

Lyken Fulbryk.

Marietta cleared her throat, trying to steady her racing pulse. "And did you have a favorite feyrie tale you'd like me to read?"

Mycaub helped Marietta flip to a page that had a drawing of a young botanical fey falling through the sky with wings slipping from his back. Marietta turned the book to the prince and read.

On waxen
Wings bound with twine, he shall fly
Despite odds.

A fey youngling with a big dream
Soared too high.
A letdown due to his kind.

Far he fell.
Though not from height, but from
His nature.

Mycaub reached to turn the page as Marietta sat motionless. She knew the tale of Icarys, but this version was unfamiliar to her. The original had a lesson of being proud of oneself and not trying to envy other people. Her father had said it was a favorite of his father, who she now knew was the author of this odd children's book.

The next page revealed another feyrie tale written with the same stilted stanzas. By the time she made it through a few more, the prince had fallen asleep. Careful to not wake him, Marietta made her way to the door with the book hidden beneath the one Wyltam had gifted her, keeping it out of sight as she wished the governess a goodnight.

Though stealing a book from a child might not have been the most ethical action, she couldn't resist the opportunity. She promised herself she'd return it after she and Elyse discovered why Sylas wanted it. Perhaps this could be the very thing that convinced Elyse to finally confide in Wyltam about the fey.

Chapter Thirty-Six

ELYSE

Since that night on the roof, something had shifted between Elyse and Wynn. Their training sessions continued as before, but a new tension hummed beneath the surface. Wynn remained unchanged—his jokes as frequent, his smile steady as ever. He corrected her with a familiar, sure touch, guiding her wrists, adjusting her stance. But his touch was different now, his fingers brushing her skin fleetingly, as though mindful not to stay longer than necessary.

They moved through a series of hand-to-hand drills, their bodies close, steps synchronized. Elyse's mind should have been on the movements, but she kept noticing the way he withdrew too soon. Not avoiding her, but careful—measured. He still leaned in, close enough that she could feel his breath, still murmured instructions in that same low tone. Yet he always pulled away quickly, his gaze steady and unreadable.

She matched him, strike for strike, their silent exchange carrying more weight than before. When he placed his hand on her arm to demonstrate a maneuver, his touch was precise, deliberate—never lingering. It wasn't the discomfort she had feared, but something more subtle, an unspoken acknowledgment that things had changed. She tried to focus on the drills, the rhythm of their steps, but the charge between them made it difficult.

The session ended, leaving Elyse with a tightness in her chest. Her muscles ached, and she craved the distraction of her morning routine—a stack of paperwork and a few quiet hours before Fig arrived. But as she approached her office, she saw light spilling from beneath the door. She pushed it open to find Fig hunched over the table, papers scattered around, hair disheveled.

"Fig?" Elyse said, closing the door behind her.

Fig glanced up, eyes wide with frustration. "We're behind schedule," they muttered. "The schematics for the goggles—those should've been finished weeks ago."

Elyse moved to her desk, spotting a sealed letter on top. She broke the seal and read the note inside.

I miss you. Can you make time this evening to see me? I want to tell you about the latest <u>book</u> I've been reading.

- Marietta

Elyse slipped the note into her pocket, hiding her expression despite the unease tightening in her chest. She hadn't found any other books and had no new updates to share. Swallowing her anxiety, she seated herself at the table.

"I took a stab at the design," they said, sliding a set of rough sketches across the table. "But the parts aren't fitting together as they should. And … I went to King Wyltam without speaking to you first."

She paused. "You spoke to the king?"

Fig nodded, eyes darting away. "I needed guidance, and you were preoccupied. Before he left for Enomenos, I asked him to look over my plans. And I convinced him to consider a … different approach."

"What do you mean?" Elyse furrowed her brows.

A knock sounded at the door. Elyse turned in her seat to find a male with a shaved head, plain clothes, and hands that no longer appeared ruined. Confused, Elyse turned to Fig. "Him?"

Fig waved him over. "Tilan Reid is an ingenious inventor. Heard of his work. Never thought I'd get the chance to work alongside."

Tilan approached, his scowl etched deeply into his features. Elyse struggled to picture Marietta ever marrying such a man. He cast a glance her way, revealing his discontent, before shifting his gaze to the drawings on the table. Fig slid the papers toward him.

Elyse leaned over to Fig and whispered, "Shouldn't he have guards? He's a criminal."

"The charges were dropped with the treaty," Tilan said, still concentrating on the papers. He lifted his hand to trace the sketch lines of the rings, his hand stiff and fingers unmoving. "Then Wyltam wanted to employ me, so here I am. Who did these?"

"I did this rough sketch," Fig said, sliding it aside. "Elyse drew these."

Tilan nodded and studied Elyse's designs for the glasses and the rings. "Not bad. You should add in more detail if you're working on something such as those goggles. The more components, the higher the chance that pieces won't align. Got something to write with?"

Elyse retrieved her charcoal and handed it to Tilan. He stared at it, then glanced at her. "I can't draw anymore."

A sudden warmth came to her cheeks. "Oh, I'm sorry—"

Tilan ignored it and gestured to the paper. "Let's redraw these with more detail, then we can move onto the goggles."

Fig's eyes lit up with a hint of relief. "This is more like it."

With Marietta's note weighing on her mind, Elyse sat through her meetings, counting down the moments. She had hoped a few might finish early, giving her a chance to slip away to the library to continue her search. Better to uncover anything than to meet empty-handed. But as the hours crawled by, that hope withered. And even if she went now, there was no certainty she'd find the books from the list.

On the walk back to her suite that evening, she practiced her apology to Marietta. They had little time to gather more knowledge on the fey before meeting with Wyltam, and Elyse was already stretched thin, barely managing her duties, even with Fig and the skilled help she'd enlisted. By the time she reached her rooms and sat for dinner, her nerves twisted her stomach. The unease only deepened as a knock came at her door.

Taking a steadying breath, Elyse answered it, bracing for Marietta's disappointment. Instead, she swept in with a warm smile and a stack of books teetering in her arms. As Elyse moved to close the door, Wynn wedged his boot in the gap, blocking it. "I need to check the rooms before you're allowed to be in here alone."

Marietta tsked. "Do you really think Elyse is going to harm me?"

"Not one bit," Wynn said, palming his sword. "But that doesn't mean someone can't sneak through the window."

"Then have someone guard the windows from outside."

Wynn lifted an eyebrow, unamused.

"It's about girl stuff, unless you'd like to know the details." She examined him from head to toe. "Maybe you do."

Wynn sighed and asked Andyr to take watch outside their window as he stepped into the hall. "At the first sound of distress, I'm coming in."

"Don't use magic either, please," Elyse added as he went to close the door. "Some of this is … embarrassing."

Marietta whipped her head to her. "What do you mean 'use magic?'"

"To enhance his hearing."

As the door swung shut, Marietta gripped its edge. "You've been using magic to hear what I'm doing?"

"Enjoy your chat," he said with a smirk, the door clicking shut.

"That's incredibly invasive and terribly upsetting." Marietta turned her attention to the room, motioning for Elyse to follow. "This is much brighter than your last suite! Great light for reading all these books."

Elyse frowned, catching Marietta's meaning, and guided her to the office, closing the door behind them.

"Wow, and that view!" Marietta signaled to Elyse for something to write with as she continued her empty banter.

Retrieving her charcoal and a spare page, she handed them to Marietta. She quickly wrote, "How far can Wynn use magic to enhance his hearing?"

"Honestly, I'm not sure," she murmured. "I think he got the point to, uh, not listen." Elyse caught Marietta's quirked brow. "He tends to honor my wishes."

"While I'm dying to know the details of your relationship, they'll have to wait. I found something." From the stack, Marietta pulled out a book and held up the cover.

Goodnight Feyries: Bedtime Stories from Feyrie Tales by Lyken Fulbryk

Elyse's breath caught. "You found it."

"And you'll never guess where." She flipped through the pages, glancing at Elyse. "Mycaub had it, though the stories are written … in an unfamiliar way."

Elyse took the book and turned to a page where a fey male with foxlike features lay slumped on the ground, gripping his stomach. Underneath, the text said:

*A fey who
Only wants what served him best
Sought a tree*

*Belonging to an archfey
Of hunger
And satiation, no less.*

*Ignoring
The warning, he chopped it and
Became starved.*

"That's the story of Erysichthon, but I've never seen it so simplified," Marietta said. "*All* the stories are simplified like this."

"And you're sure they're the stories that you know?"
She nodded. "My father said they were his father's favorite, which makes sense, considering Lyken wrote this book. Feyrie tales are always accompanied with a moral lesson, but that's absent here."

Elyse bit the inside of her cheek and searched the margins, finding nothing. "What do you think this means? Writing a children's book is vastly different from writing about magic. Did you know our grandfather was the one to establish the principles of magic?"

"Gods, you sound like Wyltam," Marietta said under her breath. "I did, but I was focused on the stanzas and how they alternate between three and seven syllables. It makes sense for a fey book; the numbers are usually prominent in feyrie tales, but does it take on another meaning because Lyken might be fey?"

"I think he has to be fey if I'm fey, right?" Elyse frowned. "How many of Lyken's favorites are here?"

"*All* of his favorites are." She paused as Elyse reached for her administrator broach. "Are you going to …"

Elyse struck her finger with the pin. As soon as her blood soaked into the page, two symbols appeared. One depicted a bull, while the other illustrated a quadrangle with two non-parallel sides, fragmented into three triangles that resembled an inverted crown.

Marietta tilted her head to see. "The first is from the cover of *Lyken's Guide to Chorys Dasi*, right?"

Elyse nodded, her hands trembling. She pulled out the book and set it on her desk, the symbol embossed into the leather matching the symbol in *Goodnight Feyries*. Elyse bit her lip as she dripped another bit of blood into the pages.

Marietta peered over her shoulder. "How are they connected? Why would they be?"

"I don't know," Elyse said.

Marietta took *Chorys Dasi*, leaving Elyse to reach for *Goodnight Feyries*. Curious, she flipped to another feyrie tale and let her blood drop to the sheet. A new symbol appeared next to the upside-down crown. Elyse went through each page, dripping her blood onto each one. Her heart stopped when she got to the last symbol.

"What are the chances?" She dug out another book. A matching outline of a head on the cover of *Statues and Sculptures of Syllogi*. "But why? Where's the connection?"

"Lyken didn't write this one," Marietta said, tilting the book to read the cover.

"No, but he did contribute to one of the chapters."

"That means something, then. How many symbols did you find in *Goodnight Feyries?*"

Elyse flipped through and counted. "Seven." Her skin prickled as realization settled over her, frantically going back to each symbol to examine their shapes. Bull. Statue. Spiral. Tree. Broken chain. A set of wings. A rune she didn't recognize.

"That number again," Marietta murmured as she started pacing. "It has to mean something."

"Sylas gave me a list of seven books. Does that mean ..."

Marietta's eyes widened. "But *Goodnight Feyries* was on that list. Do we need another book by Lyken?"

"If we follow this theory, yes. But he wrote eleven books on the principles of magic that I know about."

"One of those then." Marietta leaned against the desk with her arms crossed over her chest. "There's something here with these symbols. Sylas had to have known that. Why else would he give you the list? He must have forgotten about the last book."

Dread snaked its way through Elyse's stomach. "Unless they already have that book. Who knows where any of the rest of these books are? *Goodnight Feyries* was with the prince. There was never a chance I'd find that on my own."

"You're giving up too easily." Marietta squatted before Elyse, taking her hands in her own. "This is more than proof that fey are real. I think this is something bigger."

Elyse shook her head and hesitated. "But this isn't proof. It's coincidences and I don't think Wyltam will accept it."

Marietta considered her for a moment. "All right, we dive deeper into what these symbols are. But whatever we find between now and the wedding will have to be enough. Understand?"

Elyse nodded as a sense of dread washed over her. In a few weeks, she'd be traveling to Amigys, then Kyaeri. She wouldn't be in Satiros again until the wedding. Whatever she was going to find, she needed to uncover it now.

Unearthing the symbols had at least given her a direction. But why were there symbols in the books in the first place? Elyse's mind wandered to the statues once more, as if they could command her attention.

The day she captured her father, she'd been inexplicably drawn to a statue in the Central Garden. With what she knew now, Elyse wondered if it was more than luck that led her there.

Chapter Thirty-Seven

AMRYTH

Amryth smiled as she dug into her cart, keeping an eye on the Ladybird Inn across the way. It was nearly an hour after sunset and people had been trickling into the establishment since she arrived. Deania persuaded a friend to lend their cart to Amryth for the evening, allowing her to gather more information about the meeting she had overheard. She scooped zucchini fritters into a paper cone and handed it to the young elven male, whose gaze kept straying toward the inn.

"Busy night, huh?" She kept her eyes down and her face covered with a kerchief as she collected the coin. As he rearranged the items in his hand, she noticed a slip of paper with a patch of blue colored onto it. So that's what they were showing at the door.

"We're having a gathering," he said, turning away. "Nothing more than community matters."

Amryth nodded and said no more as he crossed the street and joined a couple walking up. When he gestured toward Amryth's cart, her stomach twisted. Why were her parents' friends here? She pretended to drop a coin and crouched beside the cart, not rising until she heard the inn door close again.

Her parents' friends were hardly the type to engage in community matters. In fact, they're the kind that preferred to complain and do nothing. Why were they meeting with a baker, a kid barely into his second decade, a prominent lector from the university, and at least another dozen people?

Over the past few days, she dug for more information on the Ladybird Inn. The owner bought the building a few decades back, renaming it after centuries of it going by another one. According to the old newspapers she'd found, he'd stirred up trouble by claiming it was among the first structures in Satiros. The city had its share of historical landmarks, but the Ladybird Inn wasn't one of them—despite the owner's best efforts.

With fewer new faces arriving, Amryth pushed her fritter cart down the street, determined to keep selling. She still had at least an hour before it was due back. If anyone was watching, she'd complete the full shift without question.

Making her way, she heard a voice echo from down a valley. "Leave me alone, will you?"

"Don't walk by my house then."

"I'm heading home from work."

"Likely fucking story."

A pilinos male rounded the corner, his curly brown hair still damp, his shirt marked with the river canal workers' sigil. Trailing behind him was a spindly elven male with a scowl.

"My neighbor's house was broken into not even two weeks ago," the elf spat. "Bet was you and your lot who—"

Amryth pushed the cart in front of the elf, putting a barrier between him and the pilinos. "Is there a problem here?"

"Yeah, that fucking clip was acting suspicious outside my house."

The pilinos male rolled his eyes. "I'm tired. Let me go home."

The elf still addressed Amryth. "I bet he doesn't even have a job."

"Yes, the male in the river workers' uniform with damp hair doesn't have a job. Stop heckling him."

He appraised Amryth coldly. "As if you could even afford to live in this part of town. How about you both get out of here or I'll make it a problem?"

She flexed her fists on the handle of the cart, half wanting to fight the prick to prove a point. The pilinos male glanced over his shoulder and shifted back and forth. She sighed and asked him, "You want me to walk you home?"

He nodded once, and they took off down the street, ignoring the yells of the male they left behind.

She learned his name was Nyk, and he was one of the maintenance workers for the river gates. Nyk agreed to a quick stop to lose the cart and continue on to Rambler Grove.

Amryth walked with her hands in her pocket, her fingers tracing the edge of Deyra's leather notebook. "Stuff like that happen often?"

Nyk shrugged. "More lately. The last few months have been shit. Ever since the pilinos arrived at the palace."

"Right," Amryth said, choosing her next words carefully. "Did that make it harder?"

They paused for a carriage to pass, then crossed the street. "Yes and no. At first, it was exciting. Then some elves got it in their heads that we all think we're noble. Now that we'll have a pilinos royal and have better opportunities, most nights are worse than tonight. I've had friends leave that job even though it's a good gig. It's not worth the walk through Greening Juncture or Petal Row. Hells, I've considered leaving."

He fell quiet, the silence between them punctuated by the chirp of cicadas. Amryth's stomach knotted with guilt. Though she hadn't personally harassed the workers, she couldn't shake the feeling of responsibility. After all, she had enforced the very laws that emboldened such behavior.

"What if," Amryth said, then hesitated. "What if I walked you back from work? And to work, if that's an issue as well."

He huffed a laugh. "Every day? I don't have that kind of money."

"For free."

Nyk eyed her. "Why?"

"Because I want to."

He grew quiet a moment, then said, "It's fine. Don't worry about it."

Amryth frowned. "Would it help if I said I'm a frequent visitor to the Temple of Therypon?"

"It would." He paused with a tilt of his head. "Are you?"

"I am. I can come in the morning with someone from the temple if that makes you feel more comfortable. And we'll come get you in the evening."

Nyk's steps slowed as they approached the border between the Wooded Ward and Rambler Grove. "Are you sure? It's a lot to ask for."

"Good thing you're not asking. I'm more than happy to help." Not to mention it gave her a good reason to be in the area to check in on the Ladybird Inn, though that wasn't the point.

She and Nyk parted ways, but as she replayed the evening's events, a nagging unease settled in. The surge in harassment against pilinos since Marietta's ascension, the covert gatherings of elves in a district hostile to pilinos—Amryth sensed a connection. Now she just needed to uncover how it all fit together.

Nestled at the cross section of Petal Row, Blooming Borough, and the Upper Fronds, Oakheart Academy's campus seemed like a world unto itself. Although Amryth had been required to take the university's classes as she advanced through the guard ranks, she had never truly belonged among the scholars. Now, even under the guise of one of them, her presence stood out sharply.

Students meandered through the lush green lawns and tended gardens, their faces alight with the enthusiasm of learning. Amryth, in contrast, moved with the purposeful stride of someone accustomed to a different kind of discipline. Her steps faltered as she noticed a group of pilinos passing by. That was new.

She pushed through the heavy oak doors of the main hall and located the room of Daniyar Yanovich's lecture. The prominent lector had attended the meeting at the Ladybird Inn, which meant she had a new thread to follow— one that wasn't interacting with her parents' friends.

Most of the seats in the hall were filled with chatting students, ink and papers ready. As Amryth scanned for a spot, she noticed a female standing at the front of the class writing on a chalkboard. She came to pause on a landing, letting other students slip on past. This was the correct hall; she must have misjudged the date or time.

"Looking for Professor Daniyar?" A young elven male beside her asked.

"Yeah, thought this was his class."

"I wish I lived in whatever hole you've been hiding in," he said, his friends laughing with him. "The board relieved him of his position a few days ago. It's been all anyone has talked about."

Amryth furrowed her brows. "What for?"

The male frowned and said, "For barring pilinos from his lectures. Seriously, where have you been?"

"Preoccupied," she murmured as she walked back up the steps and into the hallway.

Amryth paced outside the lecture hall door. The professor had been dismissed for his beliefs, only to be spotted at a covert meeting not long after. While his beliefs might not align exactly with those of the group at the inn, she suspected their interests were intertwined.

"You're not a student, are you?"

Amryth turned to an elven female, likely not passed her third decade, and eyed her warily.

"I heard you in the hall," she added quickly, her hands fidgeting with the strap of her bag. "You're not the first person who's come to Professor Daniyar's lectures not as a student. He gives private lectures now, if you're interested."

"Perhaps I am."

The girl reached into her bag and pulled out a slip of paper, its size and shape resembling what she had seen at the Ladybird Inn. She passed it to Amryth.

"There's a salon around the corner from here—the Athenaeum Society. Show this at the door and they'll let you in, even if you aren't a member."

A bright blue flame marked the center of the paper, Amryth turning it over to find nothing else. "And you don't need it?"

"I have multiples. Told us to give them out to people who would benefit from hearing him speak." The girl glanced over her shoulder. "I have to head back in, but it's tonight, an hour after sunset." She slipped back inside the hall.

Amryth stood frozen in the hallway, her eyes fixed on the blue flame depicted on the paper. It was another lead, albeit a convenient one. She could try trailing another attendee from the Ladybird Inn or return to the site itself, but neither would offer the same directness or ease. She intended to go after she escorted the canal workers back to Rambler Grove.

Shortly before sunset, Amryth positioned herself in an alley across the street from the Athenaeum Society, observing those who came and went. Elves clad in fine clothing and exuding an air of superiority paid no mind to the doorkeeper. As dusk settled, the first person flashed a paper in order to enter. She waited a while longer until a small group congregated at the entrance, slipping in alongside them.

They were ushered into a side room, spacious enough to accommodate a few more arrivals. Amryth gravitated toward the back, avoiding any engagement in conversation. The audience was a mix of elves spanning various ages. Some seemed to be regular members of the Athenaeum Society, treating the lecture as another social affair. Others stood in stark contrast to that affluent lifestyle. There were those dressed in laborer's attire, their clothes still bearing the marks of their profession, while others appeared to be students from the academy.

An elderly man with a pronounced widow's peak, his hair graying at the temples, and a prominent hooked nose, entered the room. He focused on the board rather than the assembled group. "I'm Daniyar Yanovich, historian and lector of elven heritage." Each syllable, crisp and precise, echoed with the rich tones of Kyaerian natives.

"In the year 2,580 PD, Sepeia was founded by pilinos radicals who refused to yield to their new elven rulers," he began, facing away from the group as he wrote on the board. "Situated between Satiros and Chorys Dasi, on the border of the Ouresk Forest, the settlement bore witness to one of the bloodiest chapters in the history of the Akroi Region. Today, we shall delve into how the kings and queens of old successively eradicated this settlement in the Battle of Sepeia."

Amryth's blood ran cold. She was well-versed in the history. Most knew it as a dark day that signified the largest mass execution of pilinos in Syllogi. She instantly understood the kind of person Daniyar was, and a wave of nausea swept over her.

The professor continued, recounting the skirmishes that led to the pivotal clash between the pilinos defending the city and the elven forces determined to displace them. These pilinos were the last of their kind to resist the elven advance on the region.

In the climactic Battle of Sepeia, the elven army set the city ablaze, reducing it to cinders. As pilinos fled into the Ouresk, the elves pursued. They lured their victims out with false promises of peace, only to take sport in striking them down. Gradually, the pilinos realized the treachery and refused to leave their hiding places, forcing the elves to resort to fire as their method of execution.

"Legend says that the flame burned blue through the trees and encircled where the six thousand pilinos hid." Daniyar finally turned and faced the assembled group. "Every last one of them was vanquished. The fire is believed to be responsible for the formation of the Dead Forest, permanently altering a portion of the Ouresk, although historical records are inconclusive."

The pulse in Amryth's ears drowned out the professor's voice. The blue flame motif should have been a clear sign, and she cursed herself for missing the link when she first saw the paper. Maybe she had lost her edge since leaving the guard. The choice of fire as their symbol made her fists tighten, a faint tremor rippling through her. Flame had killed the pilinos then, and they planned to kill pilinos now. And, perhaps, they already had.

Marietta's ascension must have given these people a newfound confidence, allowing them to gather formally. Satiros was already a kettle simmering over the fire, and soon it would boil over. If she were still in the guard and assigned to monitor these individuals, it might have been a different story. But too many people with these beliefs had been arrested over the years, and Amryth had no intention of joining their ranks.

As the professor called for a break, she slipped into the hallway and headed for the exit. She would inform the king of what she had uncovered but couldn't sit in on these meetings or join them in any capacity for his sake. However, Amryth was certain Jory was innocent. In fact, there might not have been one single murderer, but rather a group of them.

She was about to reach the door when an arm wrapped around her biceps and pulled her into a hallway. Panicked, Amryth grabbed their wrist and twisted, forcing their grip to release.

"Fuck, Amryth."

Her heart skipped a beat as she turned to find Peryn dressed in civilian attire. It had been months since she last saw him, not since their last Elite Guard meeting. He stood before her, rubbing his wrist with an irritated expression. "What are you doing here?" she asked.

"I could ask the same of you." He eyed her cautiously. "Please tell me you aren't poking into matters that should be left for us guards."

She kept her expression neutral, not wanting to jeopardize the king's confidence in her discretion. "I was handed a flyer and curiosity got the best of me."

"If you wanted to play detective, then you shouldn't have left," he hissed. "Don't come back, all right?"

"Trust me, I won't."

Amryth turned on her heel and exited without a word. The oppressive humidity of the evening wrapped around her as she trudged south toward the Wooded Ward. The guard's investigation into the group was a glimmer of hope. The sooner they dismantled the organization, the sooner the city could breathe easy.

As she approached her apartment, a plan took shape in her mind. She would compile everything she had uncovered and draft a formal request. The time had come. She finally had enough to meet with King Wyltam.

Chapter Thirty-Eight
MARIETTA

Marietta's days blurred into a whirlwind of meetings, afternoons with Iros, and endless wedding preparations. Of all these, the wedding plans were the most tedious. The elegant simplicity of her bridal gown hid the countless hours spent in fittings, where the seamstress draped swathes of cream fabric over her and scrutinized each one under varying lights. Together, she and Wyltam attended dozens of tastings for each course of their wedding feast, right down to the desserts. While she wasn't one to be overly critical, the chosen Enomenoan pastries left Marietta less than satisfied. It may have prompted her to slip a few of her own recipes to the kitchens—though she preferred to keep that a secret.

While having breakfast one morning, Marietta thumbed through *The History of Lyken Fulbryk*, her thoughts wandering to what type of person Lyken must have been. Eccentric, sure. But he also hid information about the fey in plain sight.

Wyltam glanced up from his plate and smiled at the book. "Are you enjoying *Lyken's*?"

"As well as I can."

"What do you mean?"

"I'm having the same problem I did when I was a child," she said, popping a grape into her mouth. "When I sit down to read, I get distracted by my own thoughts. Then I get to the end of a page and realize I haven't read a single thing."

Wyltam frowned and went to speak, but Marietta quickly cut him off.

"I do find it fascinating, trust me. But there's a lot going on in my head."

"I can imagine that it's a loud place."

Marietta rolled her eyes. "Thanks. With the temples and meetings and Queen's Court, my head is full."

Wyltam nodded slowly and returned to his food, the breakfast becoming uneasy.

His silence lingered in her mind despite her busy schedule. When she finally had a moment to herself that evening, preparing for sleep, she recalled the downturn of his lips and his lackluster tone. It wasn't that she didn't want to read the book—she appreciated his notes. Yet, his reaction gave her pause. As she carefully separated her damp curls, she replayed the interaction.

A scuffle sounded from outside the bathroom. "Wyltam?" she called.

He appeared in the doorway, his gaze finding hers before flitting away. "I know you're busy but …"

Never one to hedge his words, Marietta dropped her hands and turned to him. "What's wrong?"

He took a few controlled breaths as if he struggled with his words. "I'm … distracted."

She lifted a brow. "Distracted?"

His gaze landed anywhere but on Marietta. "Yes, distracted."

"By me or—"

"Anyone could be a mage, and with a mere blink, they could hurt you. If you don't know what to expect, how can you protect yourself?" He shook his head.

"I trust my guards," she said, raising her hands to her hair as she turned back to the mirror. "And you. You'll keep me safe."

His steps echoed off the stone walls as he approached. When he appeared over her shoulder, it wasn't Wyltam's reflection she saw. Jumping back, she swatted at Coryn. "What are—"

It was Wyltam's voice that responded. "Mages can appear as anyone." The next moment, Wynn stood before her. "They can impersonate your guards, your friends, and even me."

She swallowed hard as she took in the realistic edges of Wynn's scar and his electric blue eyes. "I somehow doubt that the basics will teach me how to defend against that."

Wyltam's touch was icy as he took her hand and brought it to his face, still appearing as Wynn though what she felt didn't match what she saw. Soft skin that should've been scarred. Full lips where there should've been thin ones. "It's an illusion," he said. "Enemy mages would know how to be convincing. They will try to lure you close and hurt you." All at once, Wyltam's appearance returned, and he pressed a kiss to her knuckles before dropping her hand. Marietta's pulse thumped wickedly at her throat. "The thought of anyone touching you—harming you—is all I can think about at the moment, and it's distracting."

"Hence why you're doing this now as I …" She trailed off and gestured to herself in her sleep clothes, her curls half set.

"It's an all-consuming thought."

She glanced down with a laugh, her head light at the thought of him being so anxious he couldn't wait another moment. "What would ease your mind right now, Wyltam?" She drew out his name like it was honey on her tongue.

Wyltam swallowed hard. "Making you understand why it's important to learn magic."

"All right," she murmured. "Show me more, then."

He nodded once, then moved faster than she thought possible. His voice came from over her shoulder. "Aithyr can quicken a mage's movement."

She turned to him, only to find the spot empty.

"Can turn them invisible," he said from behind her once more. "I'm sure you remember that." As he reappeared, Wyltam stepped into her, forcing her back into the counter as a translucent dome formed around them. "They can create barriers that mute noises so no one can hear you scream."

"I can think of a few uses of that one," she said, her gaze fixed on him, half expecting him to retreat.

Instead, he reached for her hands. "May I touch you?"

"I was hoping you would."

The moment hung between them, the iris of his eyes dilating before he grabbed her wrists and pinned them back on the counter, his body dangerously close to becoming flush with hers. "Try to break out of my hold."

A pleasant, deep ache formed in her lower abdomen with his touch and proximity. "What if I don't want to?"

"Humor me," he said, his voice rough.

Marietta tried to pull away, but his grip remained firm.

"Harder."

With the full force of her body, he still wouldn't budge.

"Mages can use aithyr for strength," he said, finally stepping away as the dome disappeared. Marietta tried to move but found her body frozen in place. "And some can hold you still without touching you. They can control you without lifting a finger."

Understanding washed over her as she took in his stare. "Come here," she said, her body still restricted. "I wanted to see something."

Wyltam stepped forward, leaving a space between them.

"Closer. You can touch me." He hesitated for a moment before pressing his body flush against hers, sending a shiver that left her knees weak. Marietta angled her mouth to his, finding the soft curve of his lips. "Kiss me," she whispered against him.

All at once, his magic dropped as his mouth found hers, gentle and curious. Expecting that reaction, she raised her hand and summoned the energy under her skin, sending the black crackling pain of Therypon through Wyltam. Unexpectedly, he groaned and pressed his mouth harder into hers—a sensation she welcomed eagerly with parted lips. She slipped her fingers into his hair and pulled him closer, each swipe of his tongue sending electricity shooting through her body and left her desperate for more.

Wyltam pulled back abruptly, his eyes wide and panting heavy. His hair, usually perfectly coiffed, became disheveled from her touch, sending a sinking satisfaction through her. Before she could narrow the space between them again, he turned and left without another word.

"Wyltam?" she called after him, hanging out of the door of the bathroom. The only response she got was the door to his office slamming shut.

Confused, Marietta hurried finishing her hair and trudged through the suite. She checked his office, but it was empty. A thorough search of the rest of the suite yielded no sign of him, either. Stumped, she went to bed wondering where he went. And though she lay awake for hours waiting for him to join her to figure out what the hells happened, Wyltam never came.

The next morning, Wyltam sat across from Marietta in the carriage, acting as if the night before had ever happened. He never came to bed. He offered no explanation. When she tried to breach the subject, he skillfully avoided the topic.

It left Marietta quiet as she watched the thickening crowd through the gauzy curtains covering the windows. "Gods, this is going to take a while," she said, breaking the silence. "Please, entertain me."

"'Her presence, with the ability to captivate my heart and stir my soul, became the sweetest refuge from the mundane.'"

Marietta jolted at his words, her heart pounding. Had she marked her favorite quote from *Beneath the Summer Moon*, or had he noticed it too? "I'm dying to know your thoughts."

"I enjoyed it. Personally, I didn't think I'd be drawn to romances, though I haven't read many stories with them included. I found myself pleasantly surprised with each book I picked up."

Her eyes widened. "You've read more?"

Wyltam leaned over, his deep voice reverberating through her. "'I want to ravage you until you're begging for mercy, until you're a quivering mess beneath me,'" he quoted.

A delighted laugh passed through Marietta's lips. "I see you've read the most scintillating ones."

"I've read seven, and I'm halfway through my eighth. I hope you don't mind that I borrowed a number of them."

"If you keep quoting them to me, then not at all. Did anything surprise you?"

A smile hooked Wyltam's lips. "I think I've learned a few new things. Others invoked some rather salacious memories."

"By all means, feel free to elaborate on those details."

His laugh was deep and rich. "Why do you want to know?"

Because she wanted to know the extent of his experience, to be on the receiving end of it. What kind of life had he lived before taking the throne?

"I'm often told I'm a nosy person."

"I'm shocked." He turned to stare out the other window, appearing perfectly pleased to not provide an answer.

As if she'd let the conversation end there. "If you don't tell me, I'll have to guess. You had a secret affair with a tavern mistress who wished to be a singer?"

Wyltam's laugh was rich and velvety like a fine wine, one she very much would intoxicate herself on. It only encouraged her to continue.

"You once were a stablehand who captured the heart of a wealthy woman who had a love for animals?"

"If only," he murmured.

"You had a secret affair with a servant who opened your world to dubious sexual relations? You had a whirlwind romance with another couple after spending a summer in their manor?"

With each scenario she listed from her books, Wyltam's smile and laugh continued, and gods, would she do anything to bottle the sight and sound.

By the time they arrived at the temple, Marietta was intoxicated by his amusement. As she took his hands and stepped from the carriage, she found herself unprepared for the cheering crowd that surrounded them. A cacophony of voices called her name. Others whooped and cheered as they made their way up the temple steps with her Queen's Guard flanked around them.

The attention spun her head, blurring her vision at the edges. Her legs stiffened, and her throat tightened as if caught in a vise.

Wyltam appeared in front of her, his cold touch on her chin, his dark eyes searching her face. "Stay with me," he murmured right before he kissed her.

The cheers began with a new fervor, Marietta suddenly pulling out of her thoughts and into the sensation of Wyltam's lips. As with every kiss with him, it ended too quickly.

"Was that necessary?" she asked as they continued up the steps toward the gray banners that flew lazily between the temple's columns. They matched the fabric of her dress, made of something airy and light that captured the gust that blew past them.

"You froze and people noticed. I thought it might give the impression you were waiting for a kiss, or at least shift focus from your obvious anxiety."

"I would never wait for a kiss."

"I would never make you wait."

Marietta blinked, wishing to ask him to elaborate further on that, but her attention was pulled to the towering statue of the goddess as they approached. As the deity of air and earth, she was perfectly depicted with her hair twisted into a spiral above her head. She stood perched on the edge of the base, which was fashioned to resemble crumbling rock. A stirring started in her chest as they drew closer, Marietta focusing on the sharp angles of her face and the keen eyes that seemed to follow her.

At the entrance, Rafayl ushered them into the building. "Your Graces, apologies for the crowd. We didn't anticipate such a large gathering for the royals' visit." His smile said otherwise.

As the doors swung shut, the cries from the street below muffled.

"Let me be the first to welcome you to the Temple of Seidytar." Rafayl walked through the temple backward, facing them as he explained more about the goddess. "Air is known for its anarchic movement. Earth is the solidity beneath our feed. They embody that of our goddess, her nature of chaos and order."

Marietta nodded along, offering a question here and there as they wound their way through the twisting halls. The contingent of her guard followed closely, the sound of ringing metal echoing off the marble floors and walls.

At the heart of the temple, they arrived at a cavernous room with a disorienting swirl of stonework racing up columns, past a set of balconies, and swirling into the ceiling. At the room's apex was a circular window that the design spiraled into. From its center point struck a lightning bolt to the ground, its shaft held by an even more prodigious statue of Seidytar. The sight triggered the stirring in her chest once more.

"Impressive detail," Wyltam said. "I read that the iros of Seidytar used her gifts to construct such stonework."

Rafayl cheerfully elaborated on that history, Marietta too enraptured by the room to listen. Where the Temple of Therypon had brought comfort, Seidytar's was overwhelming to the senses in the most joyous way. She could spend hours inspecting the details, noting how often the lightning bolt motif was incorporated around doorways, some being inlaid with precious stones. Her gaze shifted back to the statue, and a sense of awe swept over her.

"The lightning bolt connects the sky and ground," Rafayl explained. "While it is neither made of air nor earth, it bridges both while remaining true to her essence. Lightning strikes in chaotic patterns yet branch in familiar with …"

Marietta disregarded his words, though she should've been listening. Her gaze kept being drawn to the statue. It was as she was at the center of something bigger than herself. A breeze swept past, a chill rushing over her body. Without thinking, she stepped toward it.

"What do you think, Your Grace?"

It took Marietta a moment to realize Rafayl spoke to her. "There's so much to take in, and I don't think my eyes would ever grow weary of it."

"You are more than welcomed to come and see our temple whenever you wish." He bowed his head and gestured to the rows of benches before the statue. "Would it be too much to ask Your Graces to pray with me?"

"That won't be necessary—" Wyltam started.

"Of course," Marietta said over him as she slid onto the bench. Wyltam cast her a sidelong glance. She simply slipped her hand into his and made an expression that hopefully said it was rude to say no. It would've been much easier to convey if she could use magic to speak to him privately as he did to her.

With her eyes closed, Marietta settled into the ritual, her breaths slow and steady. The process was almost second nature now, the familiar steps guiding her toward stillness. Yet, as her mind cleared, the faint whine of the wind cut through her focus. It grew louder with each moment of near-emptiness, an insistent, nagging presence that pulled her back from the brink of peace.

It reminded her of the cold gusts that would whip over the Olkian hills in winter and rose goosebumps over her body. An itch crawled up her leg and she resisted reaching for it at the same time the sharp, clean scent of ozone assaulted her senses. She fought to focus but when light arced behind her lids, realization settled over Marietta. Instead of fighting it, she sunk herself into the chaos.

A voice echoed in the back of her mind, a shadow of a voice that she urged forward. *"Do you remember?"* it asked.

"Remember what?"

The voice giggled as if delighted. A gust blew into Marietta's face and the memory came rushing back.

There was a fog, thick and rolling. Muffled voices. A place of ruins and rich plant life, things she couldn't begin to conceptualize. What in the gods had she seen when she prayed with Coryn?

Marietta opened her eyes, finding herself hovered over a mountain top. Wind ripped past her, tangling her curls back from her face. In front of her flew an ethereal being, slim and bony, with a mess of ashy brown hair swirling above her head. Her skin had the same gray undertone, her smile sharp and frightening. Despite the wind, Marietta could hear her perfectly. *"Hello, chaidhleh sithfaielph."*

Marietta blinked. "Seidytar."

The goddess laughed, her voice sharp and sudden, echoing like a crack of lightning. *"It is true."*

"Why am I here? Why did you return my memory?"

"Why anything?" Branches of lightning arced behind the goddess, the landscape a blur of rippling shades of gray. *"The world has a natural order to it; things happen for reasons beyond mortal understanding. And you, through it all, remain an agent of chaos."*

Lightning struck the ground before Marietta, causing her to jump back as Seidytar laughed again. The thick smell of ozone made her believe she was actually there with the goddess, not in a vision, which would be impossible.

"Your world has been stuck in its ways for far too long," Seidytar said. *"I've been waiting for a catalyst like you. You seek power, do you not? Influence? Think of how much more you could have if you were my iros."*

"Your iros? As in instead of Therypon's?"

"Ah, but I cannot break that bond. That is a deal you made. What I offer is something new—be my iros, take my follower's influence."

"Make a deal?"

"Precisely."

"What do you get from me being your iros?"

"Chaos, sweet child. And a balance to it. Growth of those who worship me. Need you only accept, and my abilities and blessing will be yours."

Having the status as an iros to another deity would be unprecedented, from her understanding. It would bolster her reign. She could have more influence than she ever dreamed of. With it, she could better help the pilinos. And if it came to it, she could rally the temples to support them in the war.

That thought sparked an even grander idea that dawned on Marietta. "I accept under one condition."

"Oh? You make demands of a deity?" Her sharp feature formed an amused expression.

"I do. I don't want to be an iros to two deities." She lifted her chin. "I want to be an iros to all of them. Tell the other deities I want to be theirs as well."

Seidytar threw her head back in a laugh, lightning arcing across the sky behind her. When her gaze landed on Marietta again, her eyes had an unnatural glow, as if the electric energy cracked within her irises. *"Deal. I can't wait to see what you do now that you're free."*

A question formed on Marietta's lips, silenced by the sudden bolt in chest. She flew backward with a scream, the intense burning shooting through her, leaving a whirring as it fled.

Marietta groaned and opened her eyes. She stood before Seidytar's statue, the lightning bolt glowing brightly.

Wyltam tugged at her sleeve. "Marietta?"

"My King, she is—how is—" Rafayl approached with wide eyes, his hands trembling. "Lady Marietta, you're an iros to Seidytar. This doesn't make sense."

"I was sitting," Marietta said, the sudden pounding in her head making her dizzy.

Wyltam slipped his arm around her. "You stood and started walking. You wouldn't answer—I didn't know what was happening."

Excited whisper sounded from behind them. She turned to see the entrance crowded with people pointing at the statue.

Rafayl stepped up. "May I introduce Seidytar's newly claimed iros—Lady Marietta, future Queen of Satiros!"

Chapter Thirty-Nine
MARIETTA

"**B**ut how can we be sure?" Cyrus asked yet again. The iros from Kystrorgiste crossed his arms over his chest, still in denial.

"The king and Lady Marietta also saw the lightning bolt come alight, not only our attendants." Rafayl hit his hand on the tabletop. "I'm telling you, she's an iros to Seidytar."

"I'm not going to repeat myself," Marietta said, silencing the acolytes gathered in the meeting room. "I saw the Goddess Seidytar, just as I saw Therypon. I'm her iros. What I'm asking is if it's possible that I could be an iros to the rest of the deities as well."

"We've never heard of such a thing," Nosokyma said with a frown. "Not in any text I've read, at least."

"Nor I." Moira sat quietly in her muted colors of white and black. "I extend an invitation to Lady Marietta to perform the iros claiming test at the Temple of Zontykroi."

"The Temple of Oramytiz also extends this offer." Izzy reclined in their seat, their expression emotionless.

All eyes turned to Cyrus. He threw up his hands. "I'm not going to deny my future queen the opportunity. I just ask that you visit our temple first."

Rafayl glared at Cyrus with a scowl, and Marietta silenced him as she stood.

"Thank you for believing me. I don't know why I've become this chosen to multiple deities," she said, half lying. "But I look forward to visiting all your temples soon. Decide the order of the remaining temples and send the schedule. Now, if you would excuse King Wyltam and I."

Marietta clasped her unsteady hands together as she and Wyltam left the room and walked through the halls. The next step was to confront the other deities and persuade them that she must be their iros. Easy. Because making herself valuable to an otherworldly being of great power was simple. Definitely not her once again biting off more than she could chew in an impossible time frame. The wedding loomed ever closer, as did the war. She was no closer to solving the fey puzzle with Elyse. And now she'd have to navigate what being an iros to multiple deities meant.

Marietta's vision blurred with tears, her chest suddenly too tight.

Wyltam pulled her into an empty hallway and cupped her cheek. "Take a breath."

"I'm fine," she said, pulling away from his touch.

"You're a terrible liar." He sighed and placed his forehead against hers for a moment. "I don't trust this with the temples. You being an iros to more than one is too convenient."

"I know."

"First the religious ceremony, now iros claiming." He shook his head. "If you want out, we can do that, Marietta. It's never too late."

She pulled back from his touch. "The temples are my allies. Being their iros only helps me bolster my future position as queen."

"But you'll always owe them something. Those relationships are give as much as they are take."

"I understand how deals work, Wyltam."

He sighed and clasped his hands behind him. "If you're determined to dive into this religious endeavor, I'll support you. But take a moment to consider your choices before making any decisions."

"Like the religious ceremony?"

His grimace deepened. "I only agreed to it for you."

"I know," she whispered. "And I appreciate it."

Wyltam sighed. "We'll be quite busy, but it's something we can manage. One day at a time, all right?"

Marietta met his gaze. "What if there isn't enough time?"

He pressed a kiss onto her forehead. "Then we'll get through what we can, starting with the first task—the Temple of Kystrorgiste's ceremony."

Following the meeting with the temple acolytes, Marietta had planned to go to a number of fittings for her wedding week outfits. Instead, when she returned to the suite alone, she found a note sent by Wyltam.

Your meetings are canceled for the day. Enjoy your time.
- W

Beneath it sat her copy of *The History of Lyken Fulbryk*. She smiled with a laugh, wondering what excuse he gave for Marietta to not take part in wedding plans or tea.

She brought the book to the couch, where she curled into a ball and read the first chapter. It covered how magic was a measurement of mental strength. She had never considered that it could be a measurement, nor was she expecting the message of self-compassion in order to become a better mage. Even her grandfather's words lingered with her on how he not only enhanced his magic but improved as a person by learning to love himself. It was enough that she continued reading.

At the end of the second chapter, Marietta had learned more than she cared about aithyr—that it could take over a person. When Elyse shared Wyltam thought aithyr would impair her mind, Marietta hadn't thought it physically took control. She had likened it to a high from drugs or the effects of alcohol. Wyltam's notes in the margins, however, painted a different picture. Mages worked diligently to prevent such incidents among their peers. The community's collective support played a crucial role, vigilantly watching over their well-being and maintaining their safety.

Forcing herself to stop, Marietta went and readied herself for bed early, expecting to read her own book again. Yet as she wrapped her hair, her mind lingered on the details of the book. She eased into Wyltam's bed with *The History of Lyken Fulbryk* in her hands and continued reading.

The following chapters explained aithyr followed the Conservation of Equilibrium, which stated aithyr couldn't be created nor destroyed. Aithyr was an energy that converted from one form to the other, similar to wood burning and its flame creating a heat.

Similar to how someone couldn't create wood from nothing, aithyr couldn't be created either. Aithyr was the wood of magic and mages converted into their flame—apparently sometimes a literal flame, according to Lyken's stories. Wyltam's handwriting was scribbled into the margins at the end of the paragraph.

This is the foundation of all magical theory. Let me know if you have questions.

It wasn't too difficult to understand. She may not have been the best student, but she knew enough, though it made her wonder about the source of aithyr. Trees grew from sunlight and people converted food into energy, both used to chop wood. The energy could be traced back to another source, but aithyr couldn't. Marietta wrote her own question next to his, so she wouldn't forget. *Where does aithyr come from?*

Chapter four shared how mages must control their emotions while practicing, and Lyken's life example was of having to deal with difficult people while practicing magic. In his anecdote, he attempted to focus on the water he tried to control and instead dumped it on the person annoying him by accident. In the margins, Wyltam wrote:

Perhaps I'm fortunate you're not interested in magic. I believe I'd be doused often.

Marietta snorted with a laugh and imagined doing such a thing to Wyltam, finding the image surprisingly satisfying. Much of Wyltam's comments were similar, Marietta not realizing he could be funny. With each page she read, she raced to get to his handwriting in the margin. As she reached the end of the chapter, she noticed a change.

Marietta would do this.

The note referenced Lyken making his annoying companions leave before channeling aithyr, which to his point was something she would do. But what stuck out to her was that until then, Wyltam hadn't referenced her by name.

Curious, she continued onto the next chapter, her eyes skimming to the first note. *How Marietta views the world.* The paragraph stated Lyken saw the world as a stew and each person was an ingredient in it that made it heartier. Not a poor comparison, though entertaining. He went on to explain some people are the meat in the stew, others are the parsnips—not good enough to be a carrot but a suitable alternative in a pinch. While the analogy was ridiculous, she held a similar belief and shared such with Wyltam at one point. Did he truly remember that?

She flipped to a random page to see how far his notes go. Could she read through them all before falling asleep? She stopped and read the first note she found: *M has the most stubborn mind, wouldn't have issues. Would love to see her try.* Scanning the paragraph, she discovered the chapter focused on strengthening the mind to prevent aithyr from taking over. She wasn't sure if stubborn was a compliment or a criticism, but regardless, he had a point that she couldn't debate.

She flipped to another page. *When did M become this?* The passage referred to something called 'restorative practices' and having someone be an emotional anchor. Her heart faltered, and she continued to read the paragraph.

My wife is my anchor. When life grows chaotic, her calmness helps me find peace. Her touch, her words—they ease my worries, giving my mind a break so I can be a better mage. Being held by her pulls me back to myself, offering a new beginning. It is her love that heals me. <u>Seek this for yourself, and you'll never be empty</u>. **M**

It felt as if the world tilted. Marietta reread the passage and reexamined the last line. He wrote M next to it.

Marietta jumped out of bed, pacing as she chewed at her nail. M couldn't be anyone else, right?

She chased the thought away. Until that point, he had been writing Marietta's name in the margins—it had to be her. What did she do with this information? Was this his way of telling her that he cared?

The door opened without warning, Wyltam pausing in the doorway at Marietta's frazzled state.

"Is everything all right?" His eyes flicked toward the bed, catching on the abandoned copy of *Lyken's* resting on the blanket. A quiet chuckle left him as he crossed the room, reaching for the book. His amusement vanished in an instant. He snatched it up, skimmed a few lines, then snapped it shut. "How much did you read?"

"I need you to explain what it means."

Wyltam studied her face for a moment, then tucked the book under his arm. "I gave you the wrong copy. Let me get the correct one and forget what you read."

Marietta moved to stand in front of him. "I want you to explain, Wyltam. What exactly does this mean?"

His jaw worked, his body tensing. "It doesn't matter. You were never supposed to read it."

"I won't let this go until you tell me."

His dark eyes searched her face before he whirled toward the door.

"Please don't leave this time." Her voice was edged with more emotion than she intended. "Don't keep walking away."

Wyltam paused with his back still turned to her, his shoulders tense and rigid.

"In the stairwell when Keyain caught us, you wanted to kiss me, to possibly do more. Then that day in the infirmary, you kissed my hands and promised that I wouldn't be harmed. You kept that promise. Now we're here living together and when I made a move, you were too busy. You held me when you thought I was asleep. You're always flirtatious with me. You gave me one of the best gods damned kisses of my life, then walked away as if nothing happened. And now this?" She gestured to the book. "One moment you're affectionate, the next you're indifferent. Don't walk away again unless you mean it."

Wyltam glanced over his shoulder. "What do you want it to mean, Marietta?"

"I need clarity on the relationship we're heading into." The blood pumping in her ears nearly drowned out his response.

"I have always desired you," he said, his voice stripped bare, "but only if you felt the same."

Marietta swallowed the lump that formed in her throat. "I thought I made it quite clear."

He pivoted to meet her gaze. "You were pushed into this marriage. Is your attraction genuine, or a result of obligation?"

"No one can dictate my choices. This isn't about me—it's about you," her voice quivered. "Be honest about your feelings."

He stood there, jaw slack, hands clasped behind his back. The stormy mask he usually wore fell away, revealing all he had kept hidden—fear, anxiety, and doubt. It was as if she could glimpse the battle within his mind. Finally, he spoke. "You're all I've ever desired in a partner."

The knot in Marietta's throat loosened. "Please elaborate on 'partner.' Like a business partner, or like a partner to help run an entire city-state?"

As she continued talking, Wyltam closed the space between them.

"I'm a great dancing partner—"

He hushed her rambling with a kiss, a blend of tenderness and intensity, his hands cradling her cheeks. The book landed on the ground with a muted thud. When he drew back, he murmured, "I want you as my *partner*—my wife."

"Oh," she managed between breaths, her mind grappling to comprehend the implications. Seeing him move as if to withdraw, she held him fast by his belt loop, pulling him flush.

His kisses unfolded unhurriedly, each one a deliberate exploration. He tasted of black tea and impulsive decisions, a daring blend that lingered with the sweet thrill of overdue abandonment. There were no more questions in that moment, only the surety of his skin on hers.

Grasping the front of his shirt, Marietta led him back toward the bed, their lips never parting. The mattress pressed against the back of her thighs as Wyltam lowered himself over her, his knee sliding between her legs. Marietta made quick work of the buttons down his shirt. The plains of his abdomen were firmer than she'd anticipated. Her hand traced his muscles, and he shivered under her touch.

Marietta brushed back his silky hair, getting a clear look at his face. She met his gaze, wholly soft and curious, his subtle expressions given way to full emotions, and she drank in the sight of him. All at once, his mouth claimed her, the silk of her nightgown sliding up her body.

"Wyltam," she moaned into him.

"Is this all right?"

She nodded and pressed her hips forward.

Wyltam slipped a finger under her chin and tilted her face toward his. "Use your words."

"Yes," she answered breathlessly.

With a low laugh, Wyltam slowly removed her nightgown, his lips caressing her skin as he moved from her neck to her chest. He gently grazed his teeth along the sensitive curve of her breast, teasing at the tip. Marietta arched her back, her body yearning for his touch, wanting to surrender herself completely.

Wyltam lifted himself off the bed and onto his knees, sliding Marietta to the edge with him. He pushed the skirt up higher, taking off her underclothes while planting soft kisses on the inside of her legs, and his eyes locked with hers. She trembled with desire as she beheld him kneeling before her, her stomach constricting with excitement. The intensity in his eyes matched the firmness of his grip on her hips, his mouth exploring the delicate skin right above her pelvis. She rolled her body, aching for him to go lower.

A pleasant heat came to her belly as Wyltam's mouth descended, and he paused, his gaze lingering on every curve of her body. As Marietta threaded her fingers with his soft strands of hair, she pulled his head closer to her, causing a smile to form on his lips.

She sensed the heat of his breath first, and then a surge of pleasure coursed through her as his tongue teased her most sensitive spot. She let out an embarrassed whimper, but any lingering apprehension vanished as Wyltam responded with a low, rumbling groan. His tongue flicked against her with such desperation, it was as if he were a starved man and she was his source for satiation. Moaning his name, she sunk deeper into herself, her back arching in pleasure. His touch was a sacred invocation, sending stars to her vision as her body wound tighter.

The edges of her mind blurred as he sensually traced his fingers along her entrance. "Wyltam," she murmured through the fog, her voice rough with desire.

The feeling of him filling her was so intense that her thighs quivered, her throat catching. Wyltam groaned between her legs and she broke. She was free falling, her head sinking into the mattress as her legs trembled around him. The sensation enveloped her completely, washing away all her tension and leaving her consumed by the moment.

When her breaths evened, he stood and undid the buttons on his pants, his intense gaze fixed on her. When he pulled out his cock, Marietta sat up and grasped the hardened length of him. His mouth clashed with hers, the taste of herself strong on his lips and tongue, stoking her desire as she continued to stroke. He hissed and grabbed her wrist.

As he went to guide her back to the bed, she made him pause. "Lay down," she demanded.

"Marietta—"

She stood and pushed him onto the mattress, his dark hair sprawled around his head. Straddling him, she bent over and kissed him once more. "I need to be in control."

"You are always in control," he murmured. "Unless you tell me otherwise."

As she lifted herself over Wyltam's cock, his rough hands pressed against her chest, their touch contrasting with the sensation of his length gliding deep within her. "Marietta," he moaned, half between a prayer and plea. "You feel like the first time I ever touched aithyr. You feel incredible."

Watching his face, she couldn't help but smile at the unexpected and intriguing expressions that flickered across it. Enamored, entranced. Marietta lowered herself fully, sighing deeply as she rocked her hips. Wyltam's fingers grazed her core, causing her to tighten around him involuntarily while emitting a soft whimper.

As Wyltam's thumb continued its tantalizing touch, waves of pleasure coursed through her body, causing her to quiver. With the other hand gripping her hip, he assisted her as she slid over his cock.

Her body wound tighter, her chest expanding further. She lost herself in him, with him, for him. Pleasure welled and snapped through her, and she fell forward onto him. As she braced herself above Wyltam's body, he thrusted up into her as she continued to pulse, her mouth pressed into his shoulder as she cried out. When she could no longer hold herself up, Wyltam flipped her onto her back and eased himself back in.

"Fuck," he groaned, his fingers rubbing against her. "Give me one more, Marietta."

Her name slipped from his lips, dripping with reverence, and she began to further unravel. Quick, intense—she moaned his name, gripping onto him as he thrust deeper. "Wyltam," she murmured, her voice far away. "Wyltam."

Her feet numbed, her vision going white as she cried out, her body tensing as he broke her into pieces. Wyltam kept thrusting, kept moving his fingers until he grabbed her hips and pulled himself deeper into her. She rode the high of his touch, her body ready to crest and fall again as he gave a shuddering moan. His cock spasmed inside her as he finished, his dark eyes locking onto her.

He lowered his head to hers, the black strands tickling her skin as he kissed her deeply.

After a few minutes, their breaths eased and Marietta asked, "I'm your emotional anchor?"

"You are much more than that." He kissed along her jaw. "As long as you will have me."

She cupped his cheek to bring attention back to her. "No more running away."

"There is no place I'd rather be than right here with you." Wyltam brought her hand to his mouth, pressing a kiss into her knuckles. "If you're nervous about conceiving, I've been taking something for prevention since we deemed an heir was no longer necessary in the treaty."

"And did you presume you'd need it?" she asked, quirking a brow.

"Call it wishful thinking." He cradled her cheek in his hand and kissed her with a fervor that spoke of everything left unsaid.

Chapter Forty

ELYSE

Elyse slinked through the halls, avoiding the few palace dwellers awake at the early hour. A linen cape cloaked her frame, the hood pulled low over her face. Wyltam had told her to be discreet today, and she intended to follow his instructions to the letter.

As she rounded a corner, a pair of servants passed nearby, pushing a cart down the adjoining hallway. Quickly, she channeled aithyr, making it sound as if someone called out to them from behind. The servants turned to look, and she slipped into a shadowed alcove just as they continued on, oblivious to her presence.

Nearing the servant entrance, Elyse slipped into a normal walk while keeping her face hidden. Even with the hood pulled slightly back now to appear less conspicuous, her hair hung in her face and she kept her head tilted low. If she did all of this correctly, then there was no way that someone would have recognized her as she exited the palace, which was important. Today, she, Tilan, and Fig were picking up the glasses in Rambler Grove. Her new title drew too much attention and apparently her name and relation to Marietta had been noted by the public. When she asked Wyltam if she should go, he insisted she needed to see the city-state beyond the palace walls. It was exactly what she had hoped for.

Elyse entered the courtyard and walked toward the gate, her heart thundering in her chest. She had managed to remain unrecognized—

"What are you doing?"

She spun around and came face-to-face with Tilan, lounging against the palace wall. "Are you trying to blend in," he asked, his eyes sweeping over her, "or stand out even more?"

"I was being discrete, thank you."

"You were acting as if you had something to hide." A smile curled to his lips. "Why?"

"Wyltam said to not let anyone see my face so …"

"So this getup. The trick to hiding is to hide in plain sight." He pushed off the wall and headed to the gate. "C'mon. We're going to be late to meet Fig."

Elyse drew herself up straighter and adjusted her hood again. She wasn't that obvious, was she?

The further they ventured from the palace, the more crowded the streets grew. Elyse bit the inside of her cheek as they paused, not recognizing where they were. "Oak Boulevard should be here," she muttered.

Tilan swore under his breath. "You don't know your own city?"

"I've only left the palace a handful of times."

"Then why don't we have a guide?"

She gestured to her cloak. "We need to be discrete."

Tilan held her stare for a moment, then laughed. "Right, well. Do you have a general sense of where we need to go?"

Elyse hesitated a moment, then drew back her shoulders. "Let's try this way."

Elven folk darted between the shops and stalls of Blooming Borough, weaving through the crowded market. Some refused to step aside, jostling Elyse as they passed, their shoulders knocking into hers. Those who did acknowledge them did so with wary glances, suspicion etched into their expressions.

"I didn't realize people were this rude," Elyse said under her breath.

"It's because you're with a pilinos." Tilan met the glare of an elven man as they passed. "They assume you're one of us just for walking together."

Sure enough, she noticed the elves' expressions shift—cheery at first, then turning to wary glances or outright scowls as they passed. They quickened their pace, finally reaching Oak Boulevard where the larger crowds helped them blend in. As they waited at a corner for the trolley to pass, the heat from the surrounding bodies pressed in around Elyse.

The walkways grew less congested as they crossed over the Halia. Overhead were the broad leafy canopies saving them from most of the day's heat. As a light breeze threatened to pull back her hood, Elyse deeply inhaled the fresher air. While she was excited to see her city-state, it didn't mean she enjoyed the crowds.

They approached a park, finding Fig waiting near the gate. They quirked a brow at Elyse. "What's with the cloak?"

"She's playing spy," Tilan answered before Elyse could reply.

Elyse shot him a glance. "Wyltam said to be discrete."

"I'm glad you're as odd as the rest of us." Fig shook their head and turned into the park. "Honestly, I was nervous when Wyltam said I'd be working with a court lady."

Elyse fidgeted with the tie of her cloak. "Understandable. They're the worst."

"You're included in that, you know?" Fig tossed their hair as they glanced over their shoulder. "How often do you think court ladies interact with pilinos? How many of them interact with people outside the palace in general?"

"Some of the politicians do," Elyse said, hesitating. "Well, the politicians who aren't noble do."

"Precisely. I expected a noble lady with her head shoved so far up her own ass that she would ruin the project," Fig said.

"I honestly thought the same," Tilan said, "when the king told me who I'd be working with. Fig just put it more politely than I would have."

For a moment, Elyse was tempted to defend herself but decided against it.

"Instead, we get you," Fig said with a smile. "Quirks and all."

They came to a statue at the center of the park, a bird-like creature with its wings spread wide and beak opened with a silenced cry. She thought back to the pixie statue in the Central Garden and how she had pulled aithyr into it.

As they passed, she rested her hand upon the stone and channeled aithyr. As expected, it didn't react. Her eye caught a bronze plaque on the side.

Griffin in Mid Takeoff.
Griffins Pass, Kyaeri.

"Isn't it taboo to move statues?" she asked no one in particular.

Fig gave her a look. "As if that would stop an elf from doing what they please."

She didn't need to reply. Her mind wrapped around that thought as they walked along a leafy path that spat out onto another street. Gone were the white-stoned buildings of Oak Boulevard and Petal Row. Red-bricked structures stood one after the other, only broken up by the occasional alley and the shade of trees overhead. Fig explained that they were in the Wooded Ward.

Elyse took in her surroundings. Despite court gossip labeling the district as rundown, the buildings stood well-kept, balconies adorned with plants, and the scent of fresh bread drifted from open windows. People bustled about—vendors haggling, children darting between carts, and neighbors chatting on doorsteps. Elves were still the majority, but as they ventured further south, the presence of pilinos grew more noticeable.

Fig was the first person, apart from Marietta, to voice criticism of how the court treated pilinos. While it was understandable given their own experiences as a pilinos under an elven system, hearing such open disdain from Fig eased the tension in Elyse's shoulders. She was thankful to find other people who disliked courtiers as much as she did.

Laughter drew her attention, her gaze finding a group of mostly pilinos standing outside a tavern. As they passed, the strangers nodded in their direction, Elyse finding herself returning it—something she'd never do to another member of court. These were strangers, yet Elyse experienced a greater sense of acceptance from them than from her own peers. Why did she find herself more at ease among those she barely knew?

Because they weren't trying to get something from Elyse by saying hello. They did it to be kind.

It was the same kindness she had experienced from Fig. And while Tilan didn't possess the cheeriest demeanor, she didn't suspect he was using her. They were a team, though an eclectic one.

The metal adorning Fig's ears clinked, their long hair secured in a loose half knot, and glasses held in place by chains attached to a hair clip. Their low-cut shirt was tucked into a pair of billowing pants, a whimsical figure beside Tilan with his shaved head and a simple white shirt that revealed a hint of chest hair. Elyse rounded out their group with her amorphous cloak and half-hidden face. Despite their quirky appearance, they attracted little attention beyond the briefest of acknowledgments.

They reached another broad street that stretched from east to west, the absence of traffic allowing them to cross without pause. On the other side, cobbled stones met the dirt streets of Rambler Grove. Fig turned and walked backward toward the buildings, their arms outstretched. "Welcome to the Weeds."

Tilan's eyes grew wide as he took in the district. "A fitting name for such a shit hole."

Elyse flinched, partially because of Tilan's harsh tone, but mostly because he was right. Dirt clung to the sides of buildings, which were narrow stacks of mismatched bricks and wood and metal. The street beneath them was pockmarked with holes they had to dodge, and plants hung unruly from the balconies lining the streets.

Fig laughed. "Don't worry. Satiroan pilinos can make the most beautiful things out of shit. We had to in order to survive."

Elyse drank everything as if she were in another world. Tall poles with cages on top lined the streets, which she knew from reading were gaslights but had thought they were out of use for over a century. Elyse nearly collided with a pair of males hauling a cart burdened with barrels and crates. She quickened her pace to catch up with Fig, casting a glance back at the males. "Why are they pulling that?"

"How else do you think they move stuff?" Fig lifted an incredulous brow. "No magic. No beast of burden—besides pilinos, of course."

Tilan leaned over as they continued their walk. "Fig is somewhat of an anomaly because they know magic."

Elyse hadn't considered that. If Fig could enchant glass to see aithyr streams, then they must've had excellent training. Where would have Fig gotten such a mentor? From what she knew, they weren't a member of the Circle of Mages.

Her attention settled on a tangle of gardens nestled between the buildings. Humans and half-elves alike emerged, their baskets overflowing with freshly harvested fruits and vegetables. Darting around them were children—more children than she had ever seen in the palace.

A memory surfaced from some dinner party a number of years ago, of someone saying pilinos multiplied like rabbits. At the time, Elyse was young enough to not quite understand what they meant. Staring at the elated faces of children as they play a game, her hands grew sweaty, which she desperately wiped onto her cloak.

The feeling continued as they arrived at a nondescript building. A sign that read *JEWELRY* hung above the door. A bell rung as they entered the small space cluttered with neat rows of shining objects. A half-elven man appeared from the back. "You're late, Fig."

"Can your most loyal customer ever truly be late??" They approached the back room and patted the jeweler on the shoulder. "I shall be but a moment, you two," they said before disappearing through the doorway.

"I knew it was bad," Tilan said, drawing Elyse's gaze, "but not this bad." He nodded to the window.

Though Elyse had always considered it unfair to confine pilinos to one section of the inner city, she hadn't grasped the full extent of their hardship. No magic, no open spaces—gardens replaced parks, and carts were pulled by hand. "I should have known," she murmured, the reality hitting her with a new intensity.

"At least you're acknowledging it now, which is more than most elves can say."

A heavy silence settled as their gazes followed a pair of women walking past the window.

"Marietta can't do it alone," he said after a moment. "She will need elves like you, who are willing to understand. The pilinos need you to change."

"But what could I do? I'm only—"

"—the closest person to the king and queen? You have power with your position. You have influence at court. Pilinos were never going to change elven minds because they already discounted us. But you—" he turned to her "—you are their peer. Half the burden of change is on you. You have to challenge them for people like Fig, for children we passed on the street."

Elyse picked at the hem of her cloak. "I don't know what good fighting people will do."

Tilan shook his head, turning his back to her. "It's that mentality that made even the most reasonable elves complacent. Believing the laws against Pilinos are wrong means little if you don't act to change them. Beliefs are empty gestures without action; they mean nothing unless you be part of that change."

Could she truly make a difference with her position? All her life, she assumed she'd be sold to the most affluent bidder to her father's benefit. She never saw herself in a position to do anything. At most, she had hoped to evade marrying altogether and live a peaceful life somewhere beyond Satiros. Yet here she stood with countless opportunities, this one included.

Tilan's silence drew Elyse's gaze to the jewelry displayed in the cases below. One necklace caught her eye, the make and design simple but stunning. The silver band was twisted into detail and dotted with delicate beads in an intricate pattern.

"If their metal work is this good," Tilan said, peering over the case, "then the glasses should be of a similar caliber. You're lucky Fig knew someone this talented." He leaned closer, his brows furrowed together. From this close, she could see the stubble along his jaw. "Glass beads, well-crafted. I bet there are a handful of expert craftspeople hidden in here." His lips tugged into a frown.

"Have you always had an eye for this sort of stuff?"

He nodded. "Talent of mine. I know good work when I see it."

Elyse hesitated. "Should I buy it?"

"If you have that palace coin, then you should buy the whole collection. Consider it a donation to Rambler Grove."

While his voice carried a hint of sarcasm, Elyse found herself contemplating the idea. The other pieces of intricately crafted jewelry were equally striking.

"I'm telling you, this was way worse." Fig entered the room with a laugh, the jeweler at their side.

They gestured for Elyse to come over as they continued the conversation. The jeweler procured the frames, the metal possessing delicate details of scrolling vines down the arms, curving elegantly around the lenses. Elyse took them and slipped them on, hearing Fig's voice as she did. *"Be subtle."*

The warning came with enough time for Elyse to stifle her gasp with a cough. Thick strands of aithyr rippled into view, weaving through the shop and seeping through the walls. She turned to Fig, catching the faint threads of energy drawn into their body, so subtle she might have missed it on Mage's Eye. Elyse's gaze shifted to the jewelry, noticing the same swirling currents of energy pooling into several of the pieces.

"How are they fitting?" The jeweler appeared in front of her, fiddling with the frames. Without a word, he slipped the glasses from her face, adjusted the arms, and carefully set them back in place. "Your measurements were accurate."

Fig clapped Elyse's shoulder. "We're nothing if not accurate. Are you happy with them, Elyse?"

"More than happy." Watching the flow of energy around her, a tension that had been coiled in her chest loosened. If they could craft goggles of this kind and replicate them on a larger scale, it would open up the possibility for countless people to learn magic. Ordinary soldiers could finally stand against mages on the battlefield. The idea of being involved in something this transformative, something that could shape the world, something she rarely—if ever—felt.

"Let's go then."

Fig wheeled her around when Elyse turned back to the jewelry, remembering her conversation with Tilan. "Could I buy some stuff first?"

With a smirk, Fig glanced back at the jeweler. "See, elven money. I was worth the risk."

The jeweler smiled and asked which pieces Elyse had her eye on. With Fig's helpful fashion advice, she left with three new sets—some for herself, others for Marietta.

As they stepped back onto the street, Elyse barely registered Fig's voice. Her attention was fixed on the thick stream of aithyr curling through the air, leading her gaze down a nearby alley.

"Hello? Elyse?" Fig snapped their fingers in her face. "Thoughts?"

"They work." Elyse laughed. "This is incredible—Gods, Fig, it's like I took Mage's Eye."

Fig spun with a gleeful whoop, keeping pace as they rejoined the group. "The formula has been perfected then. At this rate, we could finish the first goggles in a few weeks' time. Now that's cause for celebration!"

Their steps grew lighter as they made their way to the edge of Rambler Grove, eventually finding a tavern. The thick scent of musk hit them as they stepped inside, greeted by the clamor of voices and the shuffle of bodies. Over the din, the barkeep shouted orders, his voice barely cutting through the noise. Elyse's gaze followed the aithyr trails as they wound their way across the room and through the walls.

Discomfort knotted in Elyse's throat as Fig guided her through the crowd and up to the bar. Fig turned to place an order, and Elyse clenched her hands to steady herself, trying to focus on individuals rather than the chaotic room around her. Nearby, a human woman with furrowed brows gestured animatedly at a half-elven man. Intrigued, Elyse tapped into the faint stream of aithyr beside her, honing her magical senses to eavesdrop on their conversation—a perfect chance to practice her skills.

"It meant nothing!" The male shrugged, spreading his hands wide.

"It did and you know it! You've been eyeing my sister this whole time!"

Pilinos weren't that different from courtiers after all.

After they received their drinks, Fig directed them to the far side of the bar where the crowd thinned. Elyse took the opportunity to focus on both random conversations and her surroundings, recalling Wynn's lessons. The thought of him sent a flutter through her chest, making her push farther.

In the corner of the room, two males sat with heads close together and their hands covering their mouths. Elyse pulled aithyr into her body and focused all her energy toward the pair.

"—been asking too many questions."

"She's been walking me through Greening Juncture. It's nothing to worry about."

"An elf with her background wouldn't be involved in charity work," he said, pausing to swallow. "If she inquires about our visitors from out of town, keep silent, understood?"

As she concentrated on their conversation, a male stepped into her path. Elyse reacted too slowly, stumbling into him. The male swore as his tankard slipped from his hand. Without thinking, Elyse caught it and used aithyr to keep the contents from spilling to the floor.

"Fucking leecher!" he yelled and threw the drink at her.

Elyse screamed and stepped back, tripping on her cloak and dropping to the floor. Her glasses slipped from her face and she scrambled to grab them.

"An elf, too?" someone else yelled.

Elyse placed the glasses back on her face and reached for her hood, which sat limp against her back. Fig lifted Elyse by her shoulders.

"We gotta go!"

Murmurs turned into angry yells as more liquids landed in their vicinity, Fig dragging Elyse through the crowd with Tilan at her back. Once they made it to the door, Tilan turned to her with a scowl. "You need to be aware of your surroundings. For fuck's sake, do you have no awareness?"

"I was trying," she said. "But it was so crowded, and I was trying to calm myself by using magic—"

"A working-class tavern with mostly pilinos is possibly the worst place to use magic—"

"Tilan," Fig warned.

He shook his head. "We're only a few years apart in age. There's no excuse for you to be an oblivious child."

Elyse recoiled from his insult, her emotions fraying. He was right. If she had stopped listening a second sooner, if she hadn't used magic to stop that drink from spilling, then she could've avoided all of this.

"Go easy on her, all right?" Fig turned to Elyse and clasped her shoulder. "Mistakes come with learning, and you'll make plenty more as your world widens."

Tilan went to speak then paused, shifting his weight. "I'm sorry," he said after a moment. "I didn't mean to lose my temper."

Elyse nodded at the apology, her breath unsteady and tears welling at her eyes. Without thinking, she drew on the aithyr, allowing its energy to weave through her emotions, easing her anxiety. The relief settled in, and she anchored herself in that feeling as they made their way back to the palace.

Chapter Forty-One

ELYSE

"Can you see it?"

Elyse blinked, her magnified vision watering her eyes as aithyr enhanced her sight. "You said 'something white' but there are a dozen things it could be."

Wynn sat at her side on a branch of an old oak tree at the heart of the Central Garden. "Are you looking in the right spot? Don't tell me you're distracted again."

Her cheeks heated at the mention of the tavern incident, but she brushed off his teasing. "Left of the clover fountain, between the library entrance and that pergola—"

"Other side, sweetheart."

All at once, the aithyr left her body, startled by the nickname. "What?"

"Other side of the fountain. Somebody was holding a white parasol, but I think they left now." He blinked his eyes and turned to Elyse. "What? What's wrong? It's just a game to practice."

"You—" She shook her head. The name had been an accident, clearly.

A raindrop landed on her cheek. She glanced up as dark gray clouds rolled in.

Wynn's thumb swiped the droplet away and tsked. "I thought we'd have more time."

"We should go before it—"

The sky opened up around them. Wynn laughed, taking Elyse's hand and guiding her down the tree. He left his hand in hers as they ran to the Royal's Wing.

Water dripped from her hair, her clothes, with droplets blurring the lenses of her glasses. Wynn shook his head and spread water across the marble floor.

"Ugh, you're like a hound," she said, shoving him aside.

"Hopefully you like hounds then."

"I've never been around them."

Wynn halted on the stairs. "Really? Not once?"

She shook her head. "Some ladies kept lapdogs, but they weren't permitted at gatherings. Too many complaints about …" She tapered off, noting Wynn's amused expression. "What?"

"You have so much to see and experience—it's almost infectious," he said, pulling her along. "But we need to get you changed, or you might fall ill."

They dashed to her suite, stumbling over the threshold. The crates were finally unpacked, and the space now seemed to embrace her as her own. Elyse took off her glasses and set them on the long, polished mahogany table capable of seating twelve. The chairs, upholstered in rich burgundy velvet, bore intricate carvings of mythical creatures along their backs and legs. She would never have a use for such space, but it was hers to do with as she pleased.

Wynn hovered by the stack of books left on the table. "Some light reading on Amigys and Kyaeri?"

Elyse walked toward her room, the light globe igniting as she entered. "Helps to know about the place we're going. Do you need a towel?"

"Please."

Elyse returned to find Wynn leaning against the table, his arms crossed over his chest with a smile on his lips.

"What?"

He shook his head. "Just you."

Her pulse fluttered as she handed him the towel. "That's not an answer."

"Being with you is the most fun I've had in years."

He reached for the hem of his shirt and pulled it overhead and tossed the wet fabric to the floor. Elyse couldn't tear her gaze away from the towel rubbing across his abdomen.

"Not that Wyltam isn't one of my closest friends," he said, forcing her eyes to his face. "But it's also not fun working with your friends."

"Aren't we friends that work together?"

Wynn paused, his expression thoughtful. "I suppose we are. Even though I'm mentoring you, this feels different."

Her only response was a quiet, "Oh."

She fidgeted with her rings and abruptly went to her room. She closed her eyes, inhaling once, twice. Wynn was her mentor. Mentor. Just a mentor.

The image of him shirtless flashed in her mind, stirring a deep ache of longing in her stomach. She undid the buttons on her blouse, hesitating as she reached for the silk to slip it off her shoulders.

Neither of them talked of what happened on the roof, the kiss that had nearly happened. Elyse often thought about it but brushed it away, remembering the sting of his rejection. Except their relationship *felt different.*

She glanced over her shoulder at the door. "Wynn?"

He entered, shirtless with the towel in hand, stilling when Elyse turned with her open blouse. His gaze darted to her chest, then to the ceiling. "Oh—"

She let the blouse drop from her shoulders, drawing his stare again. His eyes darkened, and he swallowed hard.

"Do you—" She cleared her throat. "Do you want to help dry me off?"

Wynn's jaw tightened, and he remained utterly still. His eyes didn't waver; he didn't blink. He was as unyielding as stone, rigid and motionless.

"Please."

The single word broke through his guarded expression, and he closed the distance between them. He took her hand and rubbed the cloth up her arm and across her shoulder.

"Lower," she whispered, her core melting from his touch.

His voice deepened with a rough edge. "Are you sure?"

"Yes."

He drew it over her breast and she moaned softly at the contact. Wynn moved it to her other one, his free hand tentatively cupping her waist.

A gasp escaped her as his calloused fingers drew down her sides.

"Is this okay?"

"More than okay."

Elyse grabbed the towel and took it from his hands, ignoring the shaking in her own. "I want—I want you to touch me."

"Elyse." Her name was a moan, a plea.

She grasped his wrist and guided his hand to her breast. He groaned softly and drew her closer, their bodies pressing together. As she tilted her head to meet his lips, the faintest touch sent a shiver through her. Wynn remained still, his silence hanging between them. Her stomach dropped along with her heart, realizing the mistake she made. But as she pulled away, Wynn cupped her cheek and kissed her deeper.

His lips moved against hers with a warmth and softness that stole the air from her lungs. Each kiss was tender, a gentle exchange that made her heart race. She surrendered to the moment, discovering a sensation she had never known before. His kiss transformed her understanding of intimacy, revealing depths she hadn't imagined.

Wynn kissed her as if he was drawing something out of her, as if he knew she held herself back with every spiraling thought in her head. She was kissing him and … everything was fine. Perfect, even.

It was always that way with Wynn—perfect. His lighthearted manner always brought a smile to her face, and his watchful eye never missed a detail. From the moment he entered Elyse's life, Wynn became the unwavering force that kept her moving forward. The steady presence t hat steadied her when everything seemed uncertain, a constant that made every challenge seem manageable. With Wynn by her side, she knew she wouldn't just make it through; she'd find her way.

She walked backward toward the bed, drawing him along. As she reached the edge, Wynn lifted her effortlessly, easing her onto her back with him hovering above. She drew him closer, wrapping her legs around his waist as his hips drove into her. She gasped as his mouth moved to her collarbone and then her breast. He drew her nipple between his teeth, biting gently.

"Fuck," he groaned, his hands moving to her pants.

Elyse aided him, sliding them off in a hurried manner. She feared that if they didn't act quickly, he'd stop again, just as he had on the rooftop.

Her pants were at her ankles when Wynn slipped a hand between her thighs. "Can I?"

"Please," she moaned, shifting her hips into his touch.

His fingers slid inside, her throat catching as he slowly moved them deeper. He slid them out and touched her at her apex, pleasure coursing through her with a whimper.

"I want you to come for me, Elyse." He lowered his mouth to her stomach, his fingers rubbing tantalizing circles between her legs.

The edge drew nearer with each pass of his fingers. "I will if you're inside me."

Wynn drew in a sharp gasp, his free hand pulling out his cock. Elyse kicked off her pants and repositioned herself on the bed, her body trembling as he got on top, nudging at her entrance.

He leaned back, his fingers touching her once again as the length of him filled her.

Wynn groaned her name and rested his forehead against hers and murmured sweet words as she felt herself stretch around him. "You are everything." He kissed her, his tongue slipping against hers. "You are perfect."

Her chest expanded as she arched her back.

"Come for me."

All at once, she reached that edge, her body falling as waves of pleasure coursed through her. She cried his name, feeling herself tighten. He hissed and pulled himself out.

"That's my girl," he moaned. "That's my girl."

She hadn't recovered when he dove back inside her, his movements growing frantic. She memorized the wild, unrestrained look in his eyes as he shuddered and cried out her name.

He lay there for a moment before shifting to the side and drawing Elyse close against him. He kissed her slowly, gripping her neck in a possessive way that marked her as his. She didn't want him to leave. She wanted to be wrapped up with him forever. "Stay with me tonight," she whispered.

Wynn tucked her hair behind her ear. "Are you sure?"

Elyse nodded and pressed a kiss into his jaw. "I'm always sure when it comes to you."

Wynn's face split with a smile.

Sleeping next to Wynn resulted in little sleeping. The night passed with teasing touches, their bodies twisted together. It led to Wynn being inside her again. He took his time, easing each orgasm out of her with his tongue and touch, until she was nothing but liquid when she fell asleep in his arms.

Her mind was hazy when she heard a voice—somewhere between a growl and a pained whisper. She caught the word 'goddess' before sinking back into Wynn, slipping into a dreamless sleep.

She woke when the bed shifted, finding Wynn sitting at its edge in the low morning light. He wiped his face with his hands before reaching for his clothes.

Elyse sat up. "Where are you going?"

Wynn faced her for a moment, his gaze darting to her chest. He abruptly turned back around.

His silence was damning, sending Elyse's heart into a staccato rhythm. "Wynn?"

"I'm so sorry, Elyse." His voice was pinched. "I should've had more restraint."

She crawled to the edge of the bed and grabbed his arm. "I want this with you."

He pulled out of her touch and shook his head. "It doesn't matter what you want. I was in the position to force that boundary, and I failed to." He turned to her, his expression agonized. "This was a mistake."

Elyse's breaths came sharply, her vision spotting. "You said I'm everything—that I'm perfect."

Wynn paused as he buttoned the fly on his pants, not meeting her gaze. "This can't happen again. Elyse, I'm truly sorry." He finished getting dressed, then left the suite without another word.

His rejection landed with the force of a slap, leaving her stunned with nothing else to do but give in to the tears threatening to fall from her eyes.

Wynn's departure had been harsh, but the real blow came when he acted as if nothing had transpired during her morning training. He pulled back the string on the bow, aiming it at the target. "The bow's length determines the range in which you can shoot. Some can be nearly as tall as me. When paired with using aithyr to enhance your sight, you could hit a target as far as triple the length of the Royal's Wing."

He handed the weapon to Elyse, the wood clunky in her hand and the string's tension difficult to pull back. "I'm never going to use this."

"You won't use any weapon," he said, not meeting her gaze. "But this is part—"

"I might need to. That's the point of all of this." Elyse gestured to the Mage Pit and its armaments around them. Her words came sharply. "At least teach me a weapon I could use at court, like daggers."

"Were the basic stances not enough?" He took the bow from her.

"Swinging at the air is different from swinging at a person."

"You shouldn't be so eager to attack someone with a weapon." He placed the bow on the rack.

"We are at war!" Elyse snapped. "Teach me how to throw a fucking knife. That's at least useful."

Wynn's eyes widened in disbelief, as though she had grown a second head. "First, the attitude is unnecessary. Second, you don't have the coordination nor the strength to have any impact with those yet. We do the bow first because it will strengthen your arms."

"Again with the patronizing," she mumbled under her breath as she reached for a dagger.

"If you want to be an adult, try enunciating your words."

She shot him a glare, then slowly inhaled. She threw her knife toward the target on the exhale. It clattered to the ground before it even reached the painted circles.

"You aren't strong enough."

Elyse tightened her jaw as she pulled aithyr into her body, the energy thrumming under her skin as she slid another dagger into her hand. She was faintly aware that Wynn still spoke. Her focus remained on her arm as she pulled back, releasing the aithyr as she threw the dagger again. The weapon hit handle-first, cracking the wood on the outer ring. She smirked and turned to Wynn. Her excitement died when she saw his expression.

"You are *not* ready to use aithyr like that," he growled. As she reached for another dagger, he swiftly took her hand, glanced at where their skin met, and then released it.

"But it worked."

"You are not ready."

"Then maybe you're the one holding me back!" Her chest heaved with her words, immediately regretting them as soon as they left her lips. She didn't mean them, not truly. Wynn had taught her so much, had helped her grow. The memory of that morning, the sting of his rejection, held back her apology as tears pricked her eyes.

He remained quiet for a moment, then said, "You're right. Maybe I am. We're done for today." He turned his back to leave, pausing to add, "For a while, actually. I'll talk to Sibylla. She'll take over."

Her throat tightened. "You're acting as if nothing happened."

"Nothing should have happened, Elyse."

"Look me in the eye!"

He pivoted, his blue eyes hardening as they met hers. "It was a mistake."

Elyse trembled as his words registered, the pulse in her ears near deafening.

With one last forlorn look, Wynn turned and said, "Sibylla will be harder on you."

Her breaths came sharp, her eyes stinging as tears formed and fell in hot streaks down her face. Suddenly, she was a child hiding in the Central Garden after her father's fit of rage. She was alone in the quiet halls of her family's manor, her skin still clinging to the scent of smoke of her mother's funeral pyre. She was broken on her bathroom floor, distraught over a male who made her dream of a better life. She was standing at the center of the Mage Pit, wondering if she would ever not be alone.

Chapter Forty-Two

AMRYTH

Kings preparing for their weddings, it turned out, rarely had time for murder investigations. Though she longed to wash her hands of the case, she appreciated that he'd sent Wynn to gather her notes, promising to meet once the dust settled. It gave her the opportunity to pause, to reconsider where her life was headed.

The quiet of the temple brought clarity to Amryth's thoughts as she paced the bright halls, walking in a familiar loop while Deania finished her work. While she had no interest in joining their ranks, she'd grown fond of the acolytes. Whether they were a basic attendant learning poultices, a cleric who could use magic to heal, or a paladin tasked with guarding, everyone welcomed her. Even the iros, who could do it all, made her feel at home.

Perhaps it was because they, too, thought she and Deania were partners. Tanaly enjoyed pointing it out whenever she visited, quite loudly at that. It led to people making comments on how cute of a couple they made, or invites to dinners with other couples. Apparently, their lie convinced everyone but themselves.

On her sixth loop of the building, she ran into a breathless Deania. "They're ready!"

"Who's—"

"Adira! Tanaly stopped by earlier. Adira wants to know what we've uncovered. They're willing to make a swap."

That afternoon, Amryth and Deania went to Rambler Grove. While she once had only a vague sense of navigation in that district, she now moved with confidence. Twice a day, she escorted humans and half-elves between their residences and workplaces. Since starting this routine, she had inspired more elves, especially those from the temples, to join in.

They arrived at a worn-down building and Deania slipped her hand into Amryth's as she knocked on the door. Before she could question the action, Tanaly appeared in the doorway, her smile bleak.

"Ah, the happy couple. Come in. Adira is in the back room."

Inside was sparse, besides a few pieces of threadbare furniture. The air was stale and stifling, with a hint of dampness that grew stronger the further they walked. The floorboards squeaked beneath their feet, the wood long having lost its luster with an unevenness that suggested the building's foundation sank to one side.

Tanaly guided them to a well-lit room where a half-elven person sat staring out the window, their bruised undereyes suggesting sleepless nights. When they turned at Amryth and Deania's arrival, Amryth caught the slight tremor in their body.

Deania hurried across the room, enveloping them in a tight embrace and murmuring words Amryth couldn't make out. Adira laughed, a fleeting smile momentarily easing the weariness from their face. Yet, when they acknowledged Amryth, the smile vanished, replaced by a solemn expression. "You're the guard?"

"Former guard."

They nodded. "Your former peers are pricks."

"That's why I left."

Adira's eyes became less guarded, having won them over at least briefly. They gestured to the seats across from them. As she and Deania settled in, so did Tanaly.

Amryth cleared her throat. "I thought this was between us and Adira."

"They want my support. Either I'm here or there's nothing to share."

Amryth met Tanaly's intense gaze, understanding the weight of the information they now shared.

With a deep breath, Amryth launched into a detailed account of their findings from Dyadic, with Deania filling in any gaps. She then delved into her discoveries about the group meeting with the professor and her growing suspicions. Throughout, Adira listened attentively, nodding occasionally but saying little.

As she finished, Adira let out a heavy sigh. "Do you think they were targeting specific people from Chorys Dasi, not just any pilinos?"

Amryth furred her brows. "What do you mean 'not just any?'"

They hesitated. "There aren't many of us native Chorys Dasians in Satiros—a couple hundred at most. For them to kill that many could mean they were looking for specific people, right? He asked for Berlena by name."

"We came to the same conclusion." Amryth considered her next question. "Is there anything you had in common with the other victims?"

"We're all from Chorys Dasi, which you knew." They sat back and cast their gaze to the window. "I've thought about this, and I have a hunch. Berlena and I were pretty close." Their eyes grew watery, and they swallowed hard. "We left Chorys Dasi around the same time. It could be the timing of when we fled, or it could be because we were both caught committing crimes."

Deania began shaking her leg beside Amryth, who tried to ignore it and give Adira her full attention. "Were you two convicted of the same crime?"

They shook their head. "I was involved in a robbery of an elven noble, and I was the only one to escape Chorys Dasi." They worked their jaw, pausing. "Berlena stole bread from an elven baker and was caught. She barely got away, only for her to ..."

She hadn't noticed her hand in Deania's until she clenched her fingers around Amryth's.

"The connection is you both committed crimes against Chorys Dasian elves though the acts were different." Amryth sat back, keeping her hand clasped with Deania's. Such crimes didn't warrant death, unless ... Icy dread washed over Amryth. "What crimes are punishable by death in Chorys Dasi?"

"Few for elves," Deania said, her voice quiet. "Punishments are much harsher for pilinos. Committing a crime against an elf is punishable by death."

"Could the murderer be some kind of bounty hunter?" Amryth bit the inside of her cheek and sat back. Foreign hunters weren't allowed to touch pilinos inside Satiros's inner city. "Maybe Chorys Dasi sent someone to find their version of justice?"

"But that doesn't explain what I saw." Adira hastily gathered their choppy golden hair into a tail. "Promise me you won't dismiss what I said."

"Never. We're here because you were the only person who had seen the murderer." Amryth let go of Deania's hand and leaned forward, resting her forearms on her knees.

"Murderers," Adira corrected. "There were two people after me that night."

Amryth gestured for them to continue.

"I was heading home from the tavern I worked at in the Wooded Ward. It was late, and I wasn't paying attention. Then I noticed a figure coming toward me from an alley. Immediately, I knew something wasn't right, so I ducked into another alley. But when I got to the end of that one, there was someone else waiting there. And when I turned back around, the first person was blocking my way out. That's when I saw them *change*."

They clasped their hands together and held them between their knees. "The alley was dark, but I could see clearly two very defined features appear from nowhere. Big, feathery wings. Horns erected from the other's forehead. I … I froze. But then my own self-preservation kicked in and I scampered up the building to the first window I could find. There was a flap of wings behind me and I wedged the window open. Two hands that gripped my upper arms to pull me back down. I flailed my one leg out, kicking the person. That's when I heard a masculine voice call me a 'stupid fucking clip,' and I slipped through his arms, finding myself in the hallway of an apartment building. One of the doors opened, and the person yelled at something … I don't remember. But when I turned around, I saw the two figures in the alley watching me before they took off running. And that's it. That's all I know."

If Dyadic hadn't been careful to not sell drakon root to pilinos, then Amryth would have assumed Adira was on it. The drug's hallucinogenic properties would craft similar memories for the elves she'd interviewed while working in the guard. Even now, as Adira lifted a glass to their lips with a trembling hand, water nearly spilling over the rim, Amryth saw this was more than just a drug trip.

"I believe you," Amryth said. "And I believe you saw wings and horns on these attackers. My mind is having trouble wrapping around what they could be."

Adira's grip tightened on their drink until their knuckles turned white. "Do you believe in fey?"

Amryth blew out of a breath. That was a loaded question. Some believed they existed long ago, but she always believed it was elves trying to differentiate themselves from pilinos. In recent years, the only person she had heard speak of fey was Marietta.

"An old Chorys Dasian folk tale that says fey walk among us," Deania murmured. "But even if they were, if they didn't have horns or wings at first, it means they'll conceal them when we search."

"Which is why I didn't want to share." Adira grew quiet for a moment, then said, "This was inevitable, but at least someone else potentially saw one of the males, even if it can't be confirmed. Berlena didn't associate with elven males when she could help it, so I doubt it was a friend. If you find anything else, please let me know."

Amryth and Deania walked in silence all the way back to Amryth's apartment, not uttering a word until they were seated. When Deania finally spoke, her voice was barely above a whisper. "Would you still like me if I had committed similar crimes in Chorys Dasi?"

"Not all actions define us," Amryth said, furrowing her brow. "Under desperation and hate, even the most well-hearted can show the darkest part of themselves."

Deania's smile was tight as she said, "You must really not be a guard anymore."

Amryth laughed and stood, knowing food was the best way to free Deania of any negative emotion. She sliced a piece of halva, a Satiroan sweet made from semolina, butter, and sugar. It also was one of Deania's favorite foods, which she always kept on hand. Amryth dwelled on her words. Few crimes were forgivable to her when she was a guard. With Marietta, that had all changed.

A small part in the back of her head nagged her, though. Had she truly believed that, or was she told to? Maybe the difference now was that she was surrounded by people who didn't need to uphold the law and instead could look at the nuances of the crime. Adira had tried to rob a noble, but they likely did it out of desperation. Berlena stole a basic necessity which didn't come close to warranting death.

When Amryth brought Deania her halva, her face lit up and reminded her of the journey she was on. There was much to atone for in her past life. This was just the start.

Chapter Forty-Three

ELYSE

Elyse drew in a long breath, trying to ignore the pain searing in her arms as the aithyr under her skin bucked against her control. A bead of sweat rolled down her temple as she channeled the energy into her eyesight, focusing at her target. It appeared larger, closer, and suddenly she could see the distinct rings painted onto its surface.

"And release!"

The bowstring snapped, sending her arrow soaring across the cavern and landing pitifully twenty feet from the target.

"That was closer," Sibylla said.

Elyse readjusted her slipping glasses, swallowing down the wave of nausea that washed over her as it did every time she used aithyr in her sight. Yesterday she had to take the meds Sylas gave her in order to prevent another day of head pains. "Not close enough," she murmured.

"As you said before, you won't be using a bow. The goal isn't to become competent with the weapon. Pairing bow work with eyesight is the natural progression of becoming a mage."

Elyse rubbed her biceps, wishing Wynn hadn't been right. Even without his presence, her irritation grew. "Does Wyltam know how to shoot a bow, then?"

Sibylla barked a laugh. "Not well. Wyl learned like the rest of us, but he never had a skill with a bow. Knives, however …" She shrugged.

She tried and failed to imagine Wyltam wielding a weapon against anyone.

"Wynn is an excellent shot with a bow," Sibylla said with a side eye. "Better with a crossbow."

She made a noise somewhere between a grunt and clearing her throat in acknowledgment. Hoping to ignore Wynn as a topic, Elyse raised her bow once more. With her glasses, Elyse focused on a thick aithyr stream to her left and pulled a strand of the energy into her body.

"I've been meaning to talk to you about him."

Elyse's focus faltered as Sibylla clasped her shoulder. "What about him?" Elyse asked.

"I know what happened."

She winced as she lowered her weapon. "He told you?"

"Sure did," she said, motioning for Elyse to follow her. "Came to me for advice. I was his mentor, after all."

"He mentioned that."

"Wynn also shared that you might not fully understand what happened."

Heat plumed across her face as she ground her jaw. "I've had sex before."

Sibylla turned with her brows furrowed, only for them to raise a moment later with a laugh. "Oh, gods. No, I meant with why relationships beyond camaraderie are prohibited for mentors and their apprentices." She made her way to a bench beside a rack of weapons and took a seat, motioning for Elyse to join her. "While he wasn't your permanent mentor, he was responsible for what you were learning."

Elyse nodded as she sat, wishing the conversation would end. The back of her throat burned, and she tore at the fabric of her shirt.

Sibylla grabbed Elyse's hand and folded it into her own. "When we take on apprentices, it's because we believe in them and want them to grow. The focus is on *you*. When the relationship between teacher and pupil is suddenly romantic and sexual, the focus is shifted. It turns into *us*. Healthy relationships, that is. We won't even begin to touch the unfair power dynamics." Sibylla sighed and sat back. "Simply put, it's unfair to your own learning."

Elyse fixed her stare on the far wall and asked, "What happens when the apprentice is done learning?"

"You're never done learning. Gods, I still learn new things all the time. Wynn even teaches them to me, but our relationship will always hold that dynamic. He can come to me with any question or concern." Sibylla patted Elyse's hand. "He was immensely proud to have you as his apprentice, and what happened between you is tearing him apart."

"I didn't realize." Elyse swallowed hard. "I knew we shouldn't, but I didn't think it would bother him so much. If I did—"

"Stop." Sibylla sat forward and faced Elyse. "You did nothing wrong. You aren't the first mage to fall for their mentor. It was up to Wynn to stop things before they progressed, and unfortunately he didn't. He needs some time away to process. For now, give him some space. I'm sure you'll be on friendly terms at some point. I think it's best for me to oversee your progress until Wyltam can take over. So, you're stuck with me for the next few months." She stood with a stretch and offered a hand to Elyse. "I hope you understand this is all to help you grow into the best mage possible. Wynn, Wyltam, and myself want you to succeed."

Elyse took her hand and rose, nodding solemnly. Her stomach soured at the idea of Wynn blaming himself. He had tried to prevent it, but Elyse had been focused solely on herself, convinced it was her decision alone. Despite the fact that he was supposed to intervene, it didn't negate how validated she had felt. How empowered. Part of her clung to that feeling as the most significant aspect, regardless of what Sibylla had to say. Yet, a larger part acknowledged they had crossed a line, and now they were facing those repercussions, for better or for worse.

Later that afternoon, Elyse sat in Wyltam's office watching the white energy flow around her fingers of her outstretched hand. If she concentrated, she could almost sense the silk-soft aithyr skate across her skin. In the corner of the office, Wyltam stood with his hands clasped behind his back, impressed with the glasses but not the sketches.

"He's holding back."

Elyse dropped her hand and stared at him. "How do you know?"

"I've seen his other designs." He gestured to her drawings left on his desk. "This goggle design is rudimentary for him. Perhaps I should have had you work on the braces first to win him over."

Elyse weighed her options, thinking about what she had learned of Tilan. "Do you think it would've made a difference?"

Wyltam turned to her. "Do you think it wouldn't?"

"I believe he's fully committed to the project." Wyltam went to speak and Elyse hurried her words. "Though he could be lying; I understand that. But he's seen Rambler Grove. He suggested that if someone such as me could alter the perceptions of my peers toward pilinos, it would be more impactful than a pilinos individual attempting to do so. I think … I think he cares about the city-state and the people here. Maybe it's not the best design because it's the first he couldn't draw himself?"

Silence stretched between them as Wyltam stared, his eyes darting back and forth. "Do you trust him?"

"He … Well." Elyse dug her nails into her palm. "There was an incident at a tavern."

Wyltam's gaze slid to her. "Explain."

"I, uh, may have been trying to listen in on conversations after we went to a tavern to celebrate the glasses." She touched the frames on her face. "I accidentally knocked a drink out of someone's hand and used magic to keep the contents from spilling. Apparently the tavern goers were not aithyr enthusiasts."

"Many aren't. Then what happened?"

"My hood fell back—I'm sorry. I tried to be discreet."

"It's all right. What did Tilan do?"

"As the crowd hurled their drinks at me, he and Fig hauled me out of there."

Wyltam nodded. "Did you at least hear anything useful?"

"Not really."

"A shame, but at least you tried." Wyltam walked to his desk and took a seat. "Before you go, I've been meaning to talk to you about Wynn."

Elyse sat straight in her chair. "Sibylla already did."

He nodded, then asked, "How are you doing?"

"I'm fine."

He exhaled slowly, his gaze softening. "When you're back from your travels, I'll have the time to truly be your mentor, if you're interested."

A flicker of relief spread through her chest. "Yes, please," she said, the weight of her earlier dread lifting slightly.

"Unfortunately, we've already arranged for Wynn to accompany your group. I had hoped your training would continue during the journey, but circumstances have shifted," he explained. Pausing, Wyltam added, "Whatever feelings you and Wynn share mustn't impede your tasks in Amigys and Kyaeri. Is that clear?"

Her cheeks burned at his assumption that she would prioritize her relationship with Wynn over her responsibilities. "Understood."

"Good. You're dismissed."

That evening, Elyse sat in the dimly lit common room, the soft music mingling with the low murmur of diplomats and their companions engaged in quiet conversation. Someone had thrown together a gathering of the representatives who would be traveling to Amigys and Kyaeri. Somehow, the list of attendees expanded beyond her travel companions, with a quarter of the Foreign Relations branch in attendance. Elyse, dressed in her usual meeting attire of pants and a blouse, had hoped it would signal that she was there as one of their peers. Unfortunately, hope was not enough.

"I heard the new play has a pilinos lead," a young male across from her said. He was one of the lower-level corniculars who sucked her into a conversation. "I'd like to take you before you all leave."

Losing her patience, Elyse swiped a wineglass from a passing tray and took a sip. "Do you invite all your colleagues to an evening at the theater?"

"If they were half as beautiful as you, I may consider it."

She forced a smile. "I don't have a free night."

"Spending more time together might make you reconsider." With a smirk, he raised one eyebrow in a confident, swaggering manner.

Elyse's eyes skimmed the room, her tone flat as she muttered, "Good luck with the rest of your evening."

Her jaw tightened as she took off in search of Kurtys. The liar had promised to interfere when their peers decided she was better on their arm than in a meeting. He'd missed two of them now. Had the gathering stayed small, she wouldn't have been so rattled. She'd attended enough without Kurtys now that she had grown comfortable in both holding a conversation and ending them. She spun in a circle, cursing under her breath as she didn't see him.

Flustered, she stopped short as an older male appeared in front of her. "Lady Elyse, I was hoping to run into you."

She blinked, easing the tension from her expression. "Minister Sethyr, it's good to see you."

"Just Seth outside of meetings," he said. "And I try to avoid these things like feybarb. Didn't take you as a person for one of these gatherings, either." He gave a conspiratorial smile.

"Honestly, I'm not," Elyse admitted. "It'd be less painful to catch feybarb."

He huffed a laugh. "Come, have a drink. I wanted to pick your brain."

As they settled on the couches, their voices dropped to a murmur, discussing the details of their trip. Talking to Seth was as easy as sharing plans with an old friend. They traded lighthearted jabs about the tiresome gatherings awaiting them in Amigys. Then Elyse learned he'd be joining her in Kyaeri afterward.

"Have you ever been?" he asked, taking a slow drawl out of his pipe.

"I've never been outside of Satiros."

"Ah, a green traveler," he remarked as tobacco smoke wafted with his words. "Though we're bound by the king's orders, steal a moment away for yourself, even if it's to aimlessly wander the city streets. You'll find Amigys and Kyaeri to be worlds apart from Satiros."

"Noted," Elyse said, smiling.

Seth pulled out his aithyr clock and smiled. "Thank you for keeping me company. I'm going to sneak out before I get dragged into another conversation." He stood and shook her hand. "I look forward to working with you more closely."

"As do I," she said as he walked away. Her father's successor proved more agreeable, though he hadn't set the bar particularly high. He gave her hope that they could stabilize their relationships with their allies.

Elyse kept to the edges of the party, her nerves surprisingly calm as she used her glasses to count the aithyr currents throughout the room. A maze only she could see. She noticed a few individuals had thin streams pulling into their bodies. As she went to get a closer look, she made eye contact with a male she sorely didn't wish to speak to.

Drystan forced a smile as he crossed the room. "Elyse, wonderful to see you. Couldn't help but notice you garnered the minister's attention."

"Unfortunately, I've garnered yours as well. If you'll excuse me." She went to walk away, but he stepped in her path.

"Makes sense why you didn't want my brother—trying your hand at a second minister."

Elyse went rigid. "Excuse me?"

"That's what I heard at least," Drystan said. "Especially with your upcoming trip. Whispers within court say you begged the queen to send you with Minister Sethyr, all because of your ... special interest." He shrugged. "Not as handsome as Keyain, but I understand the appeal."

Elyse tapped into her aithyr stream beside her, letting the energy cool her anger before she spoke. "Who told you this?"

Drystan smiled and glanced over his shoulder. "Lyd! Come here a moment."

What control Elyse had on the energy slipped away with the name. "You're better off trusting a fox in a henhouse."

A blonde head of hair appeared over Drystan's shoulder, his arm slipping around her. "Elyse," Lydia said in her grating, saccharine voice. "A pleasure, as always."

"It has never once been a pleasure." Elyse threw back the remains of her drink, desperately wishing for another.

"I heard it was a pleasure at least once between you two," Drystan said with a wry smile, gesturing at them.

That night flashed in Elyse's memory, of Lydia and whatever male she was trying to impress. Of her father's rage. Nausea rolled through her stomach.

Lydia tsked. "She's too shy to talk about that."

Beside her, a familiar voice spoke. "Weren't you trying to earn Orym's hand at that time?"

While relieved to see Kurtys, she still wanted to berate him for abandoning her in the first place.

"How did that work out for you?" he continued. "Chasing him for months, doing him favors. Most of them were sexual, weren't they?"

Drystan pulled Lydia closer to his side. "Elyse's lapdog joined in on the fun. Funny how you serve the female who rejected you … how many times?"

"It's actually an honor," Kurtys said, taking a sip of his drink. "Clearly, you haven't had the chance to work with Elyse in a meaningful way. Unsurprising, considering your position. She is among the most cunning, influential, and talented individuals I've ever had the privilege to work alongside. While you'll be here collecting notes during meetings, Elyse and I will be securing allies for a war."

"But won't you mind watching Elyse chase after another minister?" Lydia asked. "Regardless of whatever it is you're doing, that'll be difficult for you to watch."

Kurtys took a long look at Elyse before turning to Lydia. "Minister Sethyr is only interested in males. Your rumors are getting sloppy, Lydia." Kurtys looped his arm through Elyse's and asked, "Ready to leave?"

"I'm starting to get the worst headache," Elyse said sarcastically as they made their way to the door.

They walked in silence to the Central Garden, Elyse's mind reeling. No matter what she did, people would always assume her presence in court would always be for marriage. It didn't matter that Wyltam chose her to be at his side. It didn't matter that she worked to prove herself in her position. All people ever saw was the meek child she was under her father. A hand to be sold to the worthiest bidder.

As they stepped into the cool evening air, her chest tightened, each inhale carrying a sharp sting of memories—her father's scornful words echoing in her mind. The weight of her own inadequacy pressed down upon her, suffocating her with every step. Pathetic. Useless. Disappointing. These labels, etched into her subconscious, gnawed at her, leaving Elyse small and insignificant.

"Just take a breath," Kurtys murmured as he pulled her into a shadowed part of the courtyard. "Don't let her nonsense get to you."

"It's not nonsense if people are so quick to believe her." She tried to steady herself, to cease her shaking hands. "I appreciate your help, but I need to be alone."

Elyse dashed along the garden paths, half expecting Kurtys to follow, as he once would have. Yet, to her relief, she found herself granted a fleeting moment alone, allowing her mind to sink further into the dark spiral of memories.

Lydia had dismissed their encounter as Elyse's shyness, deliberately misinterpreting the situation. She had coerced Elyse into a sexual encounter with her and Orym, hoping to impress him. Elyse nearly gave in, not out of desire, but due to a sense of obligation to Lydia. The situation never escalated to that point; instead, Elyse left in tears. However, the rumor Lydia spread was far from the truth. When it reached her father's ears, his rage marred her skin for weeks. She had been confined to her room with no escape. It broke her, extinguishing any fight she had remaining.

Elyse's body led her to a familiar refuge, where the fragrance of sweet lilac wrapped around her, offering a sanctuary from the outside world. As she lay beside the four delicate pixie statues, her fingers traced the fragile contours of their wings, longing for the innocence of her childhood imagination. But now, her mind remained barren. She became hollow, a husk.

Loneliness descended like a suffocating shroud, punctuated by the ache of a solitary sob. There was no one to turn to. Marietta was absorbed in the preparations for her wedding and her religious duties, while Fig and Tilan remained unfamiliar. As for Wyltam, they didn't possess that kind of relationship.

Once, there was someone she could turn to, someone who had a way of drawing out her innermost thoughts and emotions. But she had pushed him away, trading his friendship for a fleeting moment of intimacy. If only she could turn back time, she would plead with herself to stop, to not indulge. One night with Wynn was not worth sacrificing a lifetime with him by her side.

Chapter Forty-Four
MARIETTA

While the Temple of Seidytar was airy and filled with intricate details that hooked Marietta's gaze, the Temple of Kystrorgiste existed as its opposite. Warm, muggy air made her tunic and pants stick to her skin. The dim passageways were narrow and lit by torches, an anomaly in Satiros.

The stone walls were plain but functional, adorned with hanging armor, weapons, shields, and other metal artifacts. Attendants in red tunics marked with a flame within a water droplet kept their heads bowed as Marietta and Wyltam walked by, glancing nervously toward them. They clustered around fountains, each with a brazier atop it, casting a warm, flickering glow.

"Smithing is a holy craft in the Temple of Kystrorgiste," Cyrus said, guiding them further into the temple. "The process is tied closely to our deity—Fire and Water, Creation and Destruction."

"A fitting craft, indeed," Marietta said as she kept a simple smile on her face, more than making up for Wyltam's quiet companionship. "Blacksmiths heat metal with fire and quench it with water. I had friends in Rotamu who were attendants to Kystrorgiste. I now understand their obsession with smithing."

They entered the prayer room, where a group of iros stood, their silhouettes outlined by a wall of fire. A bead of sweat traced down Marietta's back as she regarded the searing blaze, its heat mitigated by a narrow pool that edged the flames.

"For your test, Your Grace, you must wade through the water and navigate through the maze of flame. The flames shouldn't burn you," he added as Marietta and Wyltam both started. "Unless you are here for nefarious reasons."

Wyltam began to protest, but Marietta stepped forward. "Are you insinuating I'm here for the wrong reason?"

Cyrus smiled and dipped his head. "Never, Your Grace. Simply a warning."

Marietta lifted her chin, refusing to show signs of the panic that sent her heart racing. "What will I be doing in there?"

He ushered her forward to the edge of the pool. "You'll see."

Marietta grimaced as she slipped off her boots and strode into the water, the warmth seeping into the fabric of her pants. Ignoring the sensation, she pushed forward, refusing to glance back even as she reached the other side and stood before the entrance to the fiery maze. Twin braziers marked the threshold, casting a brilliant blaze. Marietta studied the dancing flames, hues of orange, red, and yellow swirling as if emerging from the very ground. Her task was clear: navigate the maze with no guidance and somehow contact a deity. Simple. Easy. Not a damning task at all. She took a moment to calm her nerves and stepped inside.

The heat clung to her, relentless, as if the air itself had turned solid. Sweat beaded on her skin, vanishing before it could cool her. Marietta slowed when the path split, hesitation creeping in as the maze closed in around her. She paused, first moving one way, then turning back, steady and certain. Trusting the pull, she pressed on, her steps more assured.

Her senses muddled, the shadows cast by the flames twisting unnaturally, distorting her vision. More than once, she believed she'd lost her way, until the crackling in her chest offered reassurance. Every step stretched on, dragging time with it.

The heat caused Marietta's eyesight to blur, but she could still make out a gap in the fire. Heart racing, she hurried toward it, relief washing over her as she found a tunnel cutting through the wall. Without a second thought, she plunged into its cool embrace, desperate to leave the oppressive heat behind.

The darkened tunnel opened into a space no larger than a sitting room, leaving Marietta to gulp down the cool, moist air as she surveyed her surroundings. The narrow ledge she stood on could barely accommodate a single person comfortably, jutting up against a sizable pool of water that dominated most of the space. Besides a solitary torch mounted on the wall, there was little else to see.

Marietta's breaths came in shallow gasps as her eyes scanned the stones, searching for any discernible pattern but finding none. She dropped her hand into the water, the coolness growing more unsettling as her fingers reached deeper. Her grip on the platform tightened, knuckles whitening as her hand dug into the stone. A swift realization sparked, cutting through her spiraling thoughts. She lowered herself onto the ledge and dipped her feet into the pool. She cleared her mind and focused on her slowing breathing. She slipped into the prayer's trance when the heat in her chest flared, along with the sudden urge to plunge into the water.

Without hesitation, Marietta dropped herself into the pool, immersing herself completely. Opening her eyes, she blinked against the flickering light dancing at the bottom. Bubbles escaped her mouth as she laughed. She broke the surface of the water and inhaled a lungful of fresh air before plunging back down, eager to explore below.

Marietta kicked hard, her legs burning as she plunged deeper, arms slicing through the water. Her chest tightened with each stroke, a desperate pressure building as she wriggled through the narrow gap. As soon as she emerged, a powerful current seized her, yanking her violently. A scream tore from her lips, swallowed by the rushing water, and panic surged through her limbs as she thrashed in the darkness. Her body was tossed and twisted before her head broke the surface. Gasping for air, she coughed up water.

Her heart pounded in her ears, thoughts skidding and colliding as she tried to piece together the chaos she'd just escaped. She swam toward a platform, eyes widening at the massive forge carved into the wall. Pulling herself onto solid ground, she shielded her eyes from the searing glow. A light mist drifted down from the ceiling, blending with the water that clung to her skin as she approached the ominous structure.

The heat rolling off the forge wasn't nearly as bad as the maze as she neared, enabling her to get close. Slowly, her eyes adjusted. Marietta blinked once, twice, and then the god appeared before her.

His long hair flowed behind him, resembling fiery waves one moment and cascading water the next. He tilted his head down at her with a frown.

"You." The word spat from his mouth like sparks from a fire.

His abrupt nature surprised her. "You've talked to Seidytar."

"A bargain with the deities is but a whisper in the wind unless both parties honor their vows. You come to me with a deal and yet you lack understanding of the terms."

The god began to turn his back on Marietta.

"You want followers, but not just any. You need makers—those who embody half of your domain."

Kystrorgiste paused.

"With me comes war. Is it not the embodiment of what you stand for? Mortals create weapons to destroy lives."

"Is war what you came to bargain with?"

"I come with an offer—claim me as your iros. As queen, I'll ensure that smiths dedicated to Kystrorgiste make the steel that will destroy our enemies."

"You speak boldly for someone so small." The god narrowed his eyes and turned toward her. His brows raised with realization. *"I haven't seen your kind in centuries. Not at your age."*

Marietta's confidence faltered. "A half-elf?"

Kystrorgiste slowly smiled, his chuckle reminding her of popping would in a fire. *"I ask, who are your enemies?"*

"Chorys Dasi and Reyila."

"Wrong." Suddenly he was towering before her. She resisted the urge to recoil. *"I ask again, who are your enemies?"*

Marietta bit the inside of her cheek. The war was between Chorys Dasi and Reyila. However, that was from their ruling government, Prince Azarys and his sister. Did that make the entire city-state her enemy?

She steadied herself and replied, "Those who wish to harm innocent people. The pilinos of Satiros, and all of Akroi, deserve to be free. My enemies are those who choose to use their power for suppression."

Kystrorgiste's lips parted with a smile. *"Not entirely correct, but not entirely wrong, either. I accept your offer. Find out who your enemies are before it's too late."*

Pain shot through Marietta's head and she fell to her knees. A cry left her mouth, and she glared up at the god, only to realize she was in the room with the maze. However, the fire was gone. The iros murmured to one another while Cyrus clapped slowly. At his side, Coryn held back Wyltam, whose eyes were wide with panic.

"Congratulations, Lady Marietta," Cyrus said. "You are an iros to Kystrorgiste."

Chapter Forty-Five

ELYSE

"We still have heard nothing from Kyaeri." Minister Sethyr spread out the papers in front of him on the table. "While they agreed to us visiting in a few weeks, they haven't given us a definitive answer on if they plan to attend the wedding."

"Perhaps they're waiting for an invitation in person," Wyltam said at her side. "Should that be the case, Elyse will extend it on mine and Marietta's behalf."

She nodded, glancing back at Sethyr, who moved on to the next point. Most of her days were filled with meetings, especially with the Foreign Relations branch. With Wyltam's support, she became well acquainted with the role she would assume when they traveled—orator of the king. With the little free time she had, she once again scoured the library, not finding any books from the list nor anything pertaining to fey. The routine, once helping her succeed, now weighed her down. It no longer served as the distraction she needed. Her father's long-forgotten voice screamed from the back of her mind. It grew louder with every meeting, every gathering, from the pang of loneliness that settled deeper into her bones.

She drifted through her days like a specter, visible yet distant. She thought of Wynn often. Of the jokes he would make, of how effortless his presence used to be. Even learning magic lost its luster, not for Sibylla's lack of talent but for the loss of Wynn. It became less about the possibilities of magic and more about pushing her body to its breaking point. Her only escape came through training, where each ache and fatigue provided a fleeting distraction from thoughts of him. She threw herself into becoming faster, hitting harder, and wielding aithyr with precision. It was her one true freedom.

By the end of the next morning's session, Sibylla stood with her hands on her hips, shaking her head. "Mentoring is a young mage's game. I can't keep up with you."

Elyse stretched the muscles in her arms, sore from sparring Sibylla for the past hour. "We could've stopped sooner."

"No, no. I don't want to hold you back." She loosened the tie on her hair and shook how the black and gray strands. "You're plateauing."

Elyse rounded her shoulders. "I'm trying—"

"Because of me, Elyse." Sibylla smiled. "You and Wynn will be traveling together, right?"

She hesitated. "Yes, for a few months."

"Might be good to work with one another again. He could keep up with you and continue your training while you travel."

A knot formed in her throat and she forced herself to swallow it down. "I'm not sure if he'd be comfortable with that."

Sibylla clasped her shoulder as she passed, heading toward the hallway with the sleeping quarters. "I'll talk to him."

The next morning when Elyse arrived for mage training, Wynn waited with a solemn expression. Her gaze traced the line of his scar, the angles of his cheeks and chin. Her father's voice echoed in her mind. *Ungrateful. Undeserving. He's only there because he has to be.* A shiver worked through her body, and she forced herself to walk toward him.

Wynn placed his hands in pockets and slowly approached. "Are you okay with this?" He cut through the thoughts, Elyse not realizing how much she missed the sound of his voice.

"I am."

"Right. Well." He took a deep breath. "We can do this with minimal talking if need be. Wyltam asked if we could speed along a bit of your training before we leave in a few weeks."

"All right," she said, reaching for the bow of the rack only to have Wynn's hand still her.

"We'll be working on knives now."

The irony wasn't lost on her. They had fought about knives the last time they stood in this room together, and that argument had ultimately pushed him away. She thought about voicing that fact, of making a joke about it. However, whatever truce settled between remained thin and fragile. She didn't want to make him leave. For the first time in days, her loneliness lifted.

Wynn guided her through the proper motion of throwing knives, his hands hovering close but never making contact, as she struggled to grasp his instructions. Eventually, he sighed and put her into position. Elyse jerked away from his touch.

He frowned. "I'm sorry—"

"It's fine."

"I know we said we didn't need to talk, but clearly, something is wrong."

"I'm all right."

He stepped in front of her. "You aren't."

Tears prickled at the back of her eyes as his concerned gaze pierced through her carefully guarded expression. She bit her trembling lips, fighting to hold back the flood of emotion threatening to overwhelm her.

Everything was wrong. She lost Wynn and couldn't form relationships at court without enduring ulterior motives. To them, she was merely an object of status, valued for what she could offer rather than who she was—a commodity to be traded like an expensive necklace or ring. The only people she could manage a civil conversation with were Kurtys, who had always managed to irritate her, and Sethyr, now a potential source of new rumors about her.

Her eyes fluttered shut as she reiterated. "I said I'm fine."

Wynn remained quiet for a moment, then said, "I know you better than most. If you don't want to tell me, I understand, but it's clouding your head, which interferes with training. Whatever you need to say, just say it."

Her voice was thick as she said, "I'm so sorry."

"Sorry? Sorry for what?"

She sniffled and wrapped her arms around her middle. "If I knew sex would lead to losing you, I would have never considered it. I miss you, Wynn."

He stayed silent for a moment, shifting from foot to foot. "I've missed you too. But there's no need to apologize—it happened because of me and I take full responsibility for that night. Sibylla already gave me an earful about it." He ran his hand over his hair. "I think it's best if we stick to training now, especially before leaving for Amigys."

Elyse nodded. "I'll take whatever part of you that you'll give."

Wynn held her stare. A quiet intensity bore within him with something she couldn't place. He cleared his throat, breaking the moment. "What else has been bothering you? And don't say nothing. Something else is wrong."

Burden. Selfish. Greedy.

"I don't want to talk about it," she whispered, and she grabbed her knife and got into position. Elyse focused on the target, ignoring Wynn in her peripheral.

"You need to talk about it. Pretend I'm someone else and let it all out— anything you need to say or do. Scream, for all I care." He lowered her arm that held the knife out in front of her. "But what you can't do is hold it all in."

Her breath caught, tears filling her eyes as she frantically blinked. She tried to speak and couldn't. Her grip on the knife tightened as she cleared her throat. "Why does everyone keep using me?"

"Go on."

"I try to be involved in court as Wyltam asked, but it always recoils in my face." She paused, sucking in a breath. "My entire life has been crafted by my father. Every decision, every action, was decided not for my benefit, but for his own. And now my peers treat me in the same way? I'm so sick of it all!" She moved to throw the knife but thought better of it. "I hate them—I hate them all so fucking much."

"Good." Wynn raised her hand that held the knife, helping her get into position. "Now take that hatred and channel it into fighting. Remember your stance."

Elyse let aithyr into her body, the sensation bringing clarity to her mind as she drew the knife back. She released it all at once, a scream tearing at her throat. She bent over, planting her hands on her knees as the energy left her body, her tears falling to the mat below.

"We'll need to keep you angry, it seems," Wynn said, his tone amused.

Elyse sniffled and looked up, finding the knife at the center of the target.

"Pretty neat, right?" Fig held out their arms wide with the goggles affixed to their face, jostling their head from side to side.

Elyse chuckled softly. Her session with Wynn had quieted her father's voice, allowing her to lift her chin a little higher, to find her smile again.

"The leather needs to be broken in, but I imagine they'll be quite comfy after a few wears. If costs are a concern, we could switch to a utility cloth instead."

"Let's stick with leather for now." Wyltam leaned in, his eyes narrowing on the device. "Down the road, we can switch to whichever is faster to process in the manufactories, though leather ensures stability."

As Fig discussed assembly and how fast they could produce it in mass quantities, they handed the goggles to Elyse. She slipped the leather over her head and secured the buckle. The main lenses were regular glass enchanted to resist fogging. She toggled down the first set of loupes, revealing the streaks of aithyr through the room. Elyse nodded at their potency. If they could maintain the lens quality while increasing production, then maybe they would have a chance against the fey and their magic.

She slid the remaining loupe over her right eye, the lens having the same effect as a spyglass. As she stared out into the library, she noted that the aithyr streams were harder to see from far away, but at last they could use them for scouting.

Wyltam took the goggles from her and slipped them on. He hummed and toggled between the lenses. "The scope is an unexpected touch, though we should work to make the arms less delicate. I could see guards struggling with their gauntleted hands."

Fig nodded eagerly, jotting down the note before diving into Wyltam's thoughts on other aspects of the design. Then they turned their attention to Tilan. Upon his arms were the prototype for the braces they'd been working on, though they still had a few issues to solve. The metal supported his arm, connecting to the fine but sturdy wires that were attached to hinges along each finger joint.

"Piano strings?" Wyltam asked with a frown.

"With treble-gauged sizing. Fine enough that they'll wind around the bobbins." Fig took Tilan's hand and bent his fingers, the wire pulling from the tiny spools on the back of his hand. "Aithyr eases the movement and keeps them attached at each joint."

"And the pain?" Wyltam asked, turning to Tilan.

He shrugged. "Still not the best on my joints, but we're working it out."

"Excellent, then. I have to say I'm impressed." Wyltam turned with a smile hinting at his lips. "Have you worked on anything else?"

Fig practically vibrated with excitement. "We've nearly completed ten designs altogether ahead of Elyse's extended absence. We should have enough to do with the prototypes that we won't lose momentum."

Wyltam chuckled softly. "Ten? Let's see what you have."

Fig retrieved a metal casing that housed a glass globe, the murky insides containing magicsbane. They described how the timer would trigger a mechanism that cracked the glass and released a fog. Fig had tested the vaporized magicsbane and confirmed inhaling it was as effective as releasing it into the bloodstream through a wound.

"Who tested it?" Wyltam asked, inspecting one go the globes. "And how?"

Elyse closed her eyes, remembering the day Fig had shouted, "Watch this!" and created a fog cloud for themself to inhale. It had been completely unprompted and unexpected. Fig was like no one else Elyse had met before, only adding to their charm.

"Myself," Fig explained with a grin. "I inhaled a bunch of it. Couldn't do magic for a couple hours. I have notes on the effects—"

"Perhaps another time we could go over that."

The next was Elyse's favorite—aithyr shields that deployed from a wrist apparatus. When the wearer activated it, a protective field of aithyr energy would deploy from a mechanical iris. The main issue was that the wearer needed to use magic to activate it in order for it to be hands free, a problem they were still solving.

Many of the prototypes still required refining. One machine pinpointed the location where a mage or magical device siphoned aithyr. Another hearing apparatus detected subtle sounds, such as an enemy's heartbeat. An ozone contraption forecasted weather patterns, while a tool projected directional light like a globe for better visibility in darkness. Lastly, a rudimentary stealth armor muffled sound and scattered light, though it was far from perfect.

As Fig went over the technical details with Wyltam, Elyse wandered to the table where the jewelry pieces waited. Selecting one of the many rings, she fidgeted with the closure, the tiny hinges almost invisible to the eye. As she flicked it open, she noted the reservoir wouldn't hold much liquid, but it was better than nothing. At least they crafted a set of seven for her specifically, allowing her to fill them with magicsbane and her supply of liquid Mage's Eye. However, Wyltam would never approve of the latter. Not after she almost lost control to aithyr. It was only if she needed the extra push, just in case.

Wyltam appeared at her shoulder. "Thank you for making quick work of these. We'll need them for the group heading to Amigys." Elyse turned to him with the question formed on her lips. "In the worst-case scenario, you and your peers must take a painless poison if captured by an enemy to safeguard our plans."

Elyse worked her jaw, staring at the jewelry. "Poison?"

"It's just a precaution," he said, a bit gentler. "Something to use only in the most dire of situations."

Wyltam asked how far they could continue without Elyse, but her mind remained stuck on the poison. It made sense, eliminating themselves as a threat to their own city-state because they held secrets their enemies shouldn't know. Elyse understood the alternative would be torture. She thought of being captured, of having to take poison in that moment. Could she even do it?

"Elyse," Wyltam said, garnering her attention, "if you could make a duplicate of each drawing, that would be appreciated. Minister Keyain will need to see these to add to his military plans." She didn't miss his pause before saying his name. "Also, please denote which ones Fig believes could be mass produced by winter's end."

"Is that when the war will happen?" she asked.

"It's difficult to move armies in the cold weather and snow, when exposure to both could kill a soldier. No, I don't think things will escalate that quickly, though that doesn't mean they couldn't attack sooner." He paused, his expression conflicted. "Our prediction is early spring."

"Are you interested in weapons?" Tilan asked.

"Not at this time," Wyltam said. "But we'll cross that bridge when we work through everything here."

Tilan rubbed his chin, the metal creaking with the effort. "We might need a mechanist for some of the larger concepts I have. I had a contact in Enomenos focused on vehicles, if you were inclined to pursue that."

Wyltam tilted his head. "What kind?"

"A coal-powered locomotive to expedite travel between Avato and Kentro, with the goal of expanding to other city-states."

"Consider me intrigued," Wyltam said. "You'll have to give me that name. And if you're interested in learning more about locomotives, we should have you meet with orcish artificers. You'd be surprised at what they could do with sand."

Tilan dropped his hand, his brows furrowing as Wyltam turned to Elyse. "Walk with me," he said, offering his arm.

Wyltam led her into the library, stopping near the shelves. "This will be my last opportunity to check in with you before you leave. Is everything settled between you and Wynn?"

Dread shot through her middle. Elyse went to apologize, then stopped herself. "We'll be fine working together again."

"I'm glad to hear it. Wynn is a good person, as are you." He cast his gaze to the ceiling, his eyes darting back and forth as he thought. "I've been thinking about you and your progress of late and I know one thing for certain: your mother would be proud of the person you've become, Elyse. You've grown not just as a mage, but as an individual. Thanks to you, the past few weeks have been less stressful, and you are more of an asset to me than you realize. I can rely on you to hold your own with court, and I know you will do so when in

Amigys and Kyaeri." He paused, his throat bobbing. "I don't know if this is the life your mother wanted for you, but it's what you want, and I think that is what would make her most proud. As long as you are happy."

Elyse wasn't sure when she started crying, unable to hide it in front of the king, but she hastily wiped them away. She cleared her throat. "I am. Thank you."

"And one last thing," he added. "I should've done this months ago. Legally, you renounced your father, forfeiting your rights as his heir. Now that he cannot rule your family's lands, it would pass to next of kin. That, of course, would be Anthys—Marietta's father—but he also relinquished his title decades ago, meaning it would go to Marietta. Being that she will be the queen, it's unnecessary." He pulled a rolled up paper from the inside of his coat and handed it to Elyse.

She unrolled it, finding it to be a land title with her name etched into the document.

"It's yours if you want it," he said. "And if you don't, it'll get passed to someone else."

Elyse pictured her childhood home, the manor tucked into the hills, surrounded by blooming flowers and towering trees. An old oak stood at the back of the property, one she had always loved to climb. How many times had she neared the top, only to tell her mother she could see the mountains on the horizon? Of course she hadn't, but her mother had played along and joined Elyse in her fanciful daydreams.

Those were the good memories, the ones she forgotten, overshadowed by her mother's death and her father's rage. Could it be hers? Did she want the manor with all its responsibilities and memories, both good and bad?

"I don't know how to run an estate or a village," she said, her stare far off. "We'll find a mentor to teach you. Don't discount the opportunity because of what you currently know." He placed a hand on her shoulder. "Anything you want, I will make it happen. That's my promise."

Elyse closed her eyes, imagining her mother's smile, her hand wrapped in her own. There were more good memories than bad. Perhaps, with Wynn and Marietta, she could begin making new ones again.

Chapter Forty-Six

MARIETTA

"You haven't found anything?" Marietta crossed her arms and watched a blackbird preen itself on the windowsill.

"I tried—I searched new parts of the library and still nothing has turned up." Elyse frowned while she picked at her nails. "I've had too much on my plate to look."

"Trust me, I understand." Marietta sighed, thinking of the trip to the palace temple she'd make that afternoon. Word had spread quickly that she was an iros to three deities now, and Cyrus wanted to utilize the excitement of her latest claiming to his temple's advantage. If she had to sit through one more prayer, she'd fall asleep. "Can you at least leave me what you have? I see what I can do while you're gone."

Elyse wrote down a copy of the list of books and gave her the three they had collected. After a brief goodbye, Marietta dropped the items off in the suite, then went to the temple.

It was late when she returned. Fortunately for her, only two dozen nobles had shown up for the prayer that afternoon, meaning she didn't have to stay as long to make small talk. Instead of praying, she focused on the books Elyse had given her.

The suite was devoid of both Wyltam and Mycaub. Not that them being present meant it would be any louder, but Marietta wouldn't need to hide what she was working on. Seated in the sitting room, she had the three books spread in front of her.

Goodnight Feyries: Bedtime Stories from Feyrie Tales.
Statues and Sculptures of Syllogi. (Statue)
Lyken's Guide to Chorys Dasi. (Bull)

Elyse had mentioned that *Statues and Sculptures of Syllogi* had a single chapter with Lyken, so she began her search there. However, she found no useful information. She then flipped through *Lyken's Guide to Chorys Dasi* and couldn't shake the sense that she overlooked something. Stumped, she returned to *Goodnight Feyries.*

The poems still caused her to pause. Her father had always said the purpose of feyrie tales was to teach a lesson to prevent falling for the same mistakes. These versions were so stifled that the meaning almost changed. The story of Aktayon involved respecting people's boundaries, especially when it came to one's body. However, the poem read:

Hunter fey
With feyhounds and spying eyes
Finds archfey.

He watches her naked swim,
With desire.
She discovers him hiding

Tells him, "Run."
Sends his own hounds to kill him
With same lust.

Marietta shook her head. It cut how the archfey was known for her privacy and kept herself hidden from everyone's eyes. No one had ever seen her face. In most versions, Aktayon followed her to a pool while pretending to be out hunting all in hopes to lay eyes on her. While the archfey had killed him, the story focused more on the importance of privacy and one's right to their body. Lyken's version broke it down to its nearest bones—a perverted man who died trying to get a glimpse of a naked woman.

Rereading a few other poems, Marietta came to a conclusion. There had to be a reason her grandfather chose this format. Because it wasn't about the content of the poem, but the number of syllables. The threes and sevens.

Inspired, she dug through the books at her disposal. In *Statues and Sculptures of Syllogi*, she turned to the third chapter, looking for the seventh word and its third letter. She wrote it down before turning to *Lyken's Guide to Chorys Dasi*. The letters she found were a G and an F. Staring at them, she shook her leg as she thought. Would there be a word at the end of this?

Perhaps it meant the third chapter, seventh line, third letter of a book. Or seventh chapter, third line, seventh word? Maybe it's only the letters?

Marietta wrote down a variable of possibilities, keeping track of them all on a separate paper. With only *Statues and Sculptures of Syllogi* and *Lyken's Guide to Chorys Dasi*, she could only find so much. The option that stood out to her the most was the third chapter, seventh line, third word. She stared at the two words that the key uncovered:

Where. Unroot.

The door to the suite opened. Marietta swore and gathered her notes and books. She was mid tucking them between the cushions when Wyltam appeared in the doorway. His gaze locked onto her hands and the books in them.

He nodded at her arms. "What're you doing?"

"Reading," she answered. "And books."

"You're behaving oddly."

"Don't I always?"

Wyltam held her stare long enough that she turned back to her books and placed them next to her body so he couldn't see. "What are you hiding, Marietta?"

She jerked upright. "Nothing. Just some light reading."

"What books?" He slowly crossed the room toward her.

Marietta slid them behind her back. "Something particularly filthy. You wouldn't want to know."

He stood before her, his dark gaze assessing. "Liar."

"I'm not—"

"If the book was as raunchy as you said, you'd be forcing it into my hands to read, would you not?"

She lifted her chin. "Not if it was between two women."

"Of all people, you know I have no room to judge. Enough of the lies."

Marietta closed her eyes, her pulse thrumming under her skin. "Books by my grandfather. They make me feel closer to my father. I miss him." She sniffled, pretending to be overcome with emotion.

Wyltam narrowed his eyes. "Why are you lying?"

"It's hurtful that you think—"

"You're a terrible liar. Mycaub has been asking for *Goodnight Feyries* for weeks."

Marietta started. "How would you know that?"

"I've been trying to read to him a few times per week. He doesn't seem to mind and I rather enjoy it."

Marietta blinked back her surprise. "Since when?"

"Since you confronted me about it."

"Why is your relationship strained with your son? He's so young, so I doubt it's anything he has done." Marietta stood with the books tucked into her arms. "Does it have anything to do with your mother?"

"Stop deflecting. Why are you reading a book you stole from a child, a book about your grandfather's anecdotes on our enemy city-state, and one on statues?" He closed the space between them, glancing from the books to her face. "Don't tell me it makes you 'feel connected.'"

She moved her mouth, failing to find something to say.

Wyltam's voice was a murmur. "What did you find?"

She shook her head. "What are you talking about?"

His gaze bore through her. In response, Marietta lifted her chin and took a step back. Icy dread shot through her gut as he took a step, closing the distance between them. He knew.

"What did you and Elyse find?"

Her breath came quick. "How did you know?"

"Wynn. He overheard your conversation when you refused to let him check Elyse's suite, said you two were already acting suspicious. Thus, he listened in to make sure you two weren't doing something reckless."

"That's incredibly invasive," she snapped.

"You had a choice. Wynn could've searched the suite and we wouldn't have known." Wyltam grabbed her hand. "What did you find?"

Marietta pulled her hand from his and squared her shoulders. "Do you have any idea how scared Elyse is of you taking her magic?"

"I wouldn't unless she showed signs like her mother."

"And does that include finding a series of clues Lyken left behind in his books?"

Wyltam blinked, his lips parting. "That is oddly specific. How did you know about that?"

Marietta paused, letting his words sink in. "What are you talking about?"

"What did you find?" he repeated more urgently.

They held each other's stare for a moment before she said, "If I show you, you cannot retaliate on Elyse. She's terrified that you'll take her magic away."

"I wouldn't do that unless she was at risk. I believe you about the clues. Just tell me."

She sighed, took his arm and forced him to the couch, and began with Sylas's list of books and finished with her discovery of the puzzle.

"In *Goodnight Feyries*, we found the symbols that correlate to other books that Lyken had worked on," she ended.

Wyltam's lips tugged downward as he grabbed the book and flipped the pages. He hovered his hand over the pages and waited a moment. "How did they appear?"

"Elyse's blood."

Wyltam stared at her. "Blood magic?"

"I don't know. You're the mage."

"Tell me what she did."

"When the pages received a drop of her blood, they appeared." Marietta mimicked the action with her hands.

"And how did Elyse discover this?"

She hedged. "You'll have to ask her. She's the one that had the list."

He eyed her, then nodded. "Do you have it still?" Marietta handed him the list. Wyltam read through the titles, then stood. "Come along."

She trailed behind him. "Where are you going? And don't lose that. It's the only copy I have."

They entered his office and moved to the bookcase beside the fireplace. "I swear if you had these books the whole—"

Her response was cut off by the fireplace sliding back. "Not in my office, no," Wyltam said, stepping through as he offered her his hand. "But I do have them."

Chapter Forty-Seven
MARIETTA

Marietta remained silent as she trailed Wyltam through the palace tunnels, her mind racing with countless possibilities. What if he had known about the fey all along? The question gnawed at her, offering a glimmer of relief from the guilt that had weighed heavily on her for months. If he was aware, did he also know about their enemies? Could it be that there was a plan in motion all this time?

After navigating through the labyrinth of paths, they came to a wall. Marietta slowed her gait, nearly pulling back Wyltam as he continued forward to smack into it. Except he didn't. Her heart leaped to her throat. She held out her hand, touching nothing as it passed through. Magic unlocked possibilities she didn't realize were there.

The path continued into an open cavern, a series of globe lights illuminating the spiked ceiling and trail around the top. Her eyes traveled down to the weapons and targets, to the two familiar faces sparring in a ring. Sibylla and Tolis stopped their training only for a second until Wyltam said to carry on.

"Are you going to explain?" she asked as they stepped into a small room. "Because what in the seven hells is this?" The space they entered was warm and lit with cozy lighting. To one end sat a modest kitchen and dining area, and the other held a couch and chairs, a fireplace, and a bookcase, which he walked toward.

"Mage Pit, where the mages train. Out of sight of everyone." Wyltam clasped his hands behind his back and looked at the bookcase. She followed his gaze and read the titles.

Beyond the Tefra Forest: An Outsider's Guide to The Disputed Lands.

History of the Fey.

Aithyr and Air.

Myths & Legends of the Akroi Region.

The History of Lyken Fulbryk.

"You had these," she said, holding up *Statues and Sculptures of Syllogi* and *Lyken's Guide to Chorys Dasi,* "but Elyse found them in the library. Your son had the last one?" Marietta shook her head.

"No, I only had a few. The others I retrieved from their hiding places when Wynn told me about your books."

"How—what?" She stumbled over her words.

Wyltam took the books off the case and brought them to the dining table. "The last time I saw Anthylia alone was the day she told me she was with child, already a few months away from giving birth." The books thudded to the tabletop, and she met his gaze. "I was shocked, confused. I didn't think she and Gyrsh would ever copulate, but that's another discussion."

"Gross."

He shot her a look. "Anthylia had insisted that I take these books and either finish 'the puzzle' or hide them. Scatter them all across Syllogi and never let people know of their existence." His gaze was far off. "She told me she checked the mountains and her home, but he left nothing there."

"You never scattered them?"

"They were well hidden," he said. "Hiding around the palace in places where no one would find them, save the few in the library."

"Why did she want you to hide them?"

Wyltam shook his head. "She wouldn't tell me why, but she gave me this." He walked back to the bookcase and came back with a small vial filled with a dark red liquid. "Her blood, magicked to not coagulate in a vial that keeps it from expiring. Said I could figure out what to do with it, and that I couldn't tell anyone." Wyltam rattled the vial, his throat working. "That I must do what she could not before it was too late. I was nervous about her sanity, especially since she was so close to giving birth, so I asked her who told her that this needed to be done. I asked her if it was aithyr. Anthylia swore it wasn't and proceeded to get irrationally angry when she could tell I didn't take it seriously. Her panic, her paranoia … I thought aithyr sickness had started, and I would've sworn that was true until today, until this moment. Show me everything, Marietta."

They worked together to add blood to *Goodnight Feyries*, showing him the symbols and how they matched the other books.

"I have a few variations of the puzzle I was working on, alternating threes and sevens between chapters, lines, words, and letter." She slid it over to him. "I think we should check all of them. I'll take these three" —she grabbed the top books— "if you could go through at the bottom two and write down the options."

They worked in silence, taking turns to jot down the letters and words they discovered. When they finished, they bent their heads together.

"I don't think it's letters," Wyltam said, jotting the two sets they had. "The words though …"

"I thought maybe it was the third chapter, seventh line, third word, but now that I'm seeing them … quietly I repose where my secrets unroot? Repose my secrets quietly where I unroot?"

"Unroot my secrets where I quietly repose?" While a pale man, Wyltam seemed to pale further. "Lyken's secrets. He left something for Anthylia to find."

"Why though?" Marietta sat back in her chair. "Why have all this to chase down? What's the point?"

"The royals of Syllogi were furious that Lyken made magic accessible to everyone five centuries ago. He broke it down to its simplest form and taught people how to wield aithyr. That kind of power is detrimental to those who rule with an iron grip. In retaliation, they all made laws to restrict who got to learn magic. When my mother took the throne, she enacted the strictest laws, banning practicing magic from the public because of her fear. She even celebrated his death, and I wouldn't be surprised if she orchestrated it herself."

Marietta sat quietly for a moment. "That's a lot to take in." The lengths to which these people would go to suppress others shouldn't have been surprising, yet it was. The realization was both enraging and frustrating.

Wyltam slid the paper in front of her. "Do you have any idea what this means?"

"I was hoping you would," she answered with a cough.

"No, not right at this moment." He sat back and regarded her. "I need some time to sit on it, to think of where Lyken would relax. Then we can potentially search in those places, but I don't know about the war. Did you ever finish *Lyken's*?" Marietta shook her head. "Finish going through it. See if you can catch anything I'm missing."

"I would, but I get distracted by all your notes."

Wyltam went still. "Apologies, I didn't mean—"

"No, Wyltam. I'm distracted by them because I like them." She placed her hand over his. "I like to know how you feel about me."

Wyltam's posture stiffened. "I apologize for not opening up more about my feelings. They're … confusing."

Her smile faltered. "It's all right."

"Confusing as in I've never felt this way before about anyone. About anything. You could devour all of my attention every day for the rest of my life and I would never grow tired of you."

Her heart fluttered. "Even when I'm being impulsive?"

"That's when it hits me the hardest." He leaned over and pressed his lips to her forehead. As they pulled back, their gazes locked, carrying the same intense connection they always shared. Wyltam's eyes drifted to her mouth, and he followed the impulse, kissing her softly. This kiss was different— unburdened by desperation, frustration, or lust. It conveyed a depth of emotion that she understood without words. When he finally pulled away, the lingering warmth left her breathless.

While sex with him had been enjoyable, it hadn't been *this*. Heady with sharp breaths, lasting stares as if either of them turned away, the moment would pass too soon. Sex was passionate, fiery, releasing. What she felt now staring into the depths of him was all-consuming, as thick and as sweet as molasses. It stuck to her soul, her heart, and she knew in that moment there was a change between them.

Her gaze drifted to *Lyken's Guide to Chorys Dasi*, to the hidden portraits that were there. She had to tell him, with or without Elyse.

"Before we go," she said, "there is one other thing we found."

"What is that?"

She slid *Lyken's Guide to Chorys Dasi* in front of her and turned to the blank pages. "I wanted Elyse to be the one to show you, given that she found this the day she was almost abducted. But after you grew suspicious of her mental well-being, she didn't think you'd believe her. So, she brought it to me because she didn't know who else to turn to, not understanding what she discovered."

He sat deathly still, his lips pressed into a thin line, waiting for Marietta to continue. She took the blood and smeared it into the pages. Marietta bit the inside of her cheek as the portraits appeared in red ink, the rows of fey with names.

Wyltam grabbed the book, his knuckles turning white with his grip. A range of emotions crossed his expression as he read the pages—rage, shock, betrayal.

"Fey exist," she whispered. "Elyse is fey. My father is fey. Anthylia and Lyken were fey." She swallowed hard and met his gaze. "And the Chorys Dasian royals are fey."

Chapter Forty-Eight

ELYSE

Summer's heat kept its hold on Amigys despite the turn of the season. Loose strands of hair stuck to Elyse's forehead as she climbed the remaining steps of the Palace of Amigys, leaving her panting in the humid air. It had been over an hour since they arrived by carriage, but halfway to the palace, they were guided into small push boats to traverse the rest of the way.

Unlike Satiros, Amigys sat half-sunken into Seiryn Bay with waterways dividing the city-state like veins. The east side—where they had entered—was hilly and solid, possessing wide streets that soon gave way to the watery canals deeper into the city.

Though they weren't far from Satiros, it seemed as if she had stepped into an entirely different world. The city thrummed with life as its inhabitants navigated narrow boats with long poles. Cafes and shops lined the canal banks, while crowded markets filled the occasional square. Through her glasses, she saw thick streams of aithyr dividing into thousands of small lines, flowing into buildings, the water, and statues alike. Marine animals thrived with crustaceans scuttling along the paths, starfish lounging partially out of the canals, and strange fish swimming alongside her boat. Even the birds were different—the air *felt* different.

Interspersed through it all were statues, similar to those in Satiros, but depicting unfamiliar creatures. Feminine figures with pointed webbed ears and the tail of fishes, birds with heads of beautiful females, and horses with two front hooves with a marine tail in the back. Everywhere she looked, there was something new to see, something new to experience. By the time they arrived at the palace, she thought there was nothing else that could surprise her. She was sorely mistaken.

The palace itself was of white stone, with ornamental details shining iridescent in the afternoon sun. The domed tops, mostly made of glass, had a similar effect that reminded Elyse of the Crystal Gardens in Satiros. Grand columns twisted toward the sky to hold aloft arch doorways, and as she passed underneath, she noticed the gilded pattern on them was crafted from individual seashells of more varieties than she thought existed.

Inside, the palace was equally impressive—bright and airy, with the scent of salt and sun. Tropical plants with their blade-like leaves flanked entryways while doors were adorned with pulls fashioned after fish. Kurtys leaned over to her and murmured, "They took the sea motif a bit seriously." Elyse ignored the comment, excited to see what each hallway revealed as they were escorted to their suits for the week.

A gentle breeze greeted her when she entered her room, finding the far wall open to the sky with a sizable balcony. Gauzy curtains blew lazily in the wind as she walked past, taking in her first uninterrupted look at Seiryn Bay. The water shone bright blue and stretched beyond Elyse's line of sight. In the distance, the sandy shoreline rose into jagged cliffs that embraced the bay as if they were arms.

While she had read about the Evgeni Sea, she hadn't grasped the sheer size of it. Seiryn Bay was only an offshoot, a fraction of its whole. As Elyse took in the expanse of water before her, she realized how large the world was and how insignificant it made her. Perhaps to anyone else, that feeling would be damning—to be so small and unimportant. For her, it was freeing. She wished to be a part of it, to lose herself in the water, to know what saltwater was like.

Turning back to her room, she tested her bed, finding it soft and luxuriant, noticing the headboard imitated a large shell. Across the way was a mother-of-pearl inlaid wardrobe, which she opened to find a single dress made of fabric that almost appeared wet in the way it pooled. The material was smoother than any silk she had touched before, the cloth cool on her skin. While pretty, the gown was something she would never wear with how little it would hide. Even by Satiroan court standards, it was flimsy. Hanging with it was a mask of matching fabric and a headdress fashioned with webbed ears that fanned out like a fish's tail.

"What do you think?"

Elyse turned to find Wynn leaning against the balcony doorway. "Not a fan of using the main door?" she asked.

He laughed and stepped into the room. "Not a fan of people thinking a Satiroan soldier spends an ample amount of time with you alone." He raised a brow. "Incredible, right?"

"By how excited you are, I'd assume you were from Amigys."

Wynn threw himself on her couch. "This place was always more like home. How are you doing? This is all very new."

The question caused her nerves to bubble below the surface. She was in a new court with new people; there was a new queen and king to impress—alliances to test. So much of this trip rode on her shoulders being Wyltam's proxy in a foreign land. She took a breath and latched onto the excitement that her unfamiliar surroundings brought and drowned out any worries. Those were later problems and were ones that a glass of wine and Mage's Eye could aid.

Elyse flashed a smile. "I think I'll manage."

He stood. "Send a message if you need anything, okay?" She nodded, and Wynn disappeared over the balcony railing.

As the afternoon slipped by, she paced the halls alone as she waited for her peers. With the additional Mage's Eye in her system, the aithyr streams became nearly opaque when viewed through her glasses. A light globe, much similar to the ones she has used all her life, hovered in a sconce with thin threads of aithyr pulling into it. Elyse peered over her lenses and could no longer see the streams.

Curious, she padded down the hall and stopped short when she saw a statue. The creature's body coiled with serpentine grace, its ridged back adorned with fins that fanned from head to tail. Its mouth gaped wide, revealing a menacing array of fangs. While the statue itself was frightening, it was the streams of aithyr that flowed into it that drew her near. Elyse rested her palm onto the carved scales, her mind focusing on the pull of aithyr around her. Her eyelids fluttered closed, and through the stone came a pulse.

"I've always found sea serpents terrifying."

She jumped at the sound of Kurtys's voice and quickly withdrew her hand. "Do you think they ever truly roamed the seas?"

He shrugged and leaned over to inspect the statue. "All I know is that they don't anymore."

"Are you sure about that?" Elyse teased.

He flinched at her answer and before she could comment, she heard the scuffle of feet and the murmur of voices behind them. She turned to find the remaining members of their party, Minister Sethyr nodding at her to follow.

An Amigyan official met them and directed them to the throne room. As she walked at the minister's side, Elyse found herself thankful for the Mage's Eye in her system and her all-black clothing that had become her uniform. Shining brightly on her chest was her administrator's pin, contrasting against the dark.

Upon entering the throne room, her gaze jumped from the glittering nobles to the iridescent walls. A set of grand thrones fashioned after shells sat at the far end, the occupants of them watching as her party entered. Water streamed through the floor, twisting through narrow channels that fl owed from the thrones to the rest of the room.

As they came to a stop at the center, the Amigyan queen stood, her brown skin glowing with the reflecting light and her voice booming. "Representatives of Satiros, we welcome you to Amigys. I am Queen Octavya, and this is my husband, King Ivyn."

As instructed in her meetings, Elyse bowed with Sethyr and her party. The royals were younger than Elyse expected, Queen Octavya being within a few decades of Wyltam's age.

"May our home be yours on this visit of friendship."

Thankful for her drug-induced assistance, Elyse stepped forward. "On behalf of King Wyltam and his bride, we thank you for your hospitality and alliance in these times. We hope that if you cannot attend their wedding personally, that he insists on arranging a time to meet Lady Marietta."

Queen Octavya's gaze raked over her as if she saw something the rest of the room didn't. "Lady Elyse, tell your king that we are gracious and accept the proposal for a future meeting."

Elyse bowed again and stepped back, her hearing muffled by the blood pounding in her ears. Sethyr spoke next, introducing himself and the remaining Satiroan politicians and commenting on the beauty of the city-state.

As Elyse's mind settled, she tried to focus but had this nagging sense on the back of her neck. She glanced over her shoulder into the crowd of nobles, locking eyes with a man whose tousled brown hair added to his rugged charm as he gazed intently at her. She met his challenge and took in the details of his handsome face, the expensive cut of his clothes, and the confident way he held himself. At her lingering attention, his lips tilted into a smile. Heat crept to her cheeks, but she gave no other acknowledgment to him and turned toward the royals.

After a few more minutes, Queen Octavya said, "And with this grand welcome to our city-state, it is our pleasure to throw a masked ball tomorrow evening in your honor. Fret not, we planned outfits for our Satiroan friends, already provided in your rooms." Elyse's heart jumped to her throat at the memory of the dress in her wardrobe.

As they were dismissed and turned to leave, Elyse sensed a strong pull toward the man, his gaze lingering on her until they exited the throne room. Just before turning the corner, she glanced back and instantly found him again. An unsettling sense of familiarity clung to her, as if she knew him from somewhere.

Elyse felt naked. The dress wrapped over her breasts but left open skin through her abdomen before draping over her hips and pooling down to the floor. Pearls and shells studded the fabric as if she emerged fresh from the sea.

To further the look, the royals had sent a team to help her ready, and they styled her hair to appear wet and her makeup dewy. Her hair wrapped around the headpiece that hooked onto the back of her ears with an iridescent fin, giving them a webbed appearance. A second part clipped in to make around her eyes. When she glanced in the mirror, she hardly recognized herself. She experienced a deep sense of vulnerability, not from the exposed skin, but from her inability to wear her aithyr glasses.

During the ball, attendees' attention stuck to her like a thick blanket on a hot summer evening. They were present when she greeted the royals and all throughout the dinner. While she ate, Elyse grew keenly aware that every move she made was watched, which made the menu even more difficult. Creamed cod smeared on pieces of grilled bread. Seared squid served with boiled cornmeal dyed black with squid ink. Whole soft-shell crabs fried, the curled legs and dark eyes churning Elyse's stomach before taking a bite. And a dozen other plates that contained some sort of marine animal, including clams, baby octopus, and grilled eel. Trying not to offend their host, Elyse tried every dish and washed them down with a dry, light-bodied wine with a smooth oily finish and a hint of saltiness. The alcohol rushed to her head faster than she preferred for her first public evening at the palace.

By the time tables were cleared and the ballroom floor open, Elyse had enough of the night. Her fellow politicians were expected to dance with the nobles of the court, but she made that her boundary. She would dance with no one, not wanting the added pressure of tripping over her own feet.

She clung to Kurtys's side, suddenly anxious at the thought of being alone. "Stay with me."

"I can't. I'm supposed to—"

"Kurtys, please."

He sighed and said, "I can't. But I have a few people who can meet you and I guarantee they won't want to dance, either."

"I don't do well with strangers."

"It'll be fine," he said, plucking another wine from a tray and putting it into her hand.

He slipped his arm through Elyse's and wove through the crowd. Curious eyes hidden behind scaled and shelled and finned masks followed them, Elyse suddenly aware of how little her dress covered. She gripped onto Kurtys, urging him to move faster.

At the edge of the ballroom, Kurtys stopped before a group of three people. A female with icy blonde hair watched Elyse intently, her blue eyes unnerving through a mask composed of shells, pearls, and sapphires. She leaned over and murmured something to her companion, a male with dark hair and a somber expression that his simple mask didn't hide.

"Layla, Assyl, wonderful to see you." Kurtys turned to Elyse and said, "They're the ambassadors of Kyeari and friends of mine."

Elyse stilled the surprise that surged through her.

"Since when are we friends?" The words rolled off Layla's tongue, each syllable precise. Kurtys stammered a moment before Layla slipped a graceful hand in his and said, "A joke. Do you still not have those in Satiros?"

"Their jokes are usually contrived," Assyl answered. "The point beaten into you so clumsily that you forget to laugh."

"Will you two hold it for a moment?" Kurtys said, clapping his hand with Assyl's.

As Kurtys turned to the remaining person, Elyse eyed the two Kyaeries. In the meetings leading up to their trip, they had spoken about the other city-state's ambassadors being present, but she didn't think she'd meet them so soon or so casually. She had no idea that Kurtys was on a first-name basis with them.

"This is Nyran, an ambassador from Chorys Dasi."

Elyse raised her brows as she looked at him for the first time. Nyran bowed his head, which only drew attention to his considerable height. Almost as if to compensate for that attention, his mask was simple, made of plain fish scales. "A pleasure," he offered.

She turned to Kurtys, the question wanting to form on her lips. He ignored her and asked Nyran, "Have you seen Dominykas? I thought he'd be with you tonight."

"Not since dinner."

"He's likely still sulking," Layla said, sharing an amused glance with Assyl. "Lady Elyse is more than welcome to make up his absence."

"Right, well." Kurtys placed a hand on Elyse's shoulder. "You already know that this is Lady Elyse Norymial, Administrator to the King of Satiros."

Elyse offered a smile and dipped her head.

"I have some obligations to take care of, if you don't mind keeping her company. She isn't one for dancing."

"An overrated art form," Layla said, eyeing Elyse. "You have more taste than the average Amigyan."

Kurtys slipped into the crowd, leaving her with the foreign dignitaries. "I'll assume that's a compliment," Elyse answered, taking a sip of her wine.

"More than you know."

"Have you been here long?"

"Too long."

Assyl placed a hand on Layla's arm. "It's been a few years since we've been stationed in Amigys. She gets surly when she's away from the mountains and winds."

"The weather makes me too sticky," she said with a glower.

Oh, are you from the lakeshore or cliffside of Kyaeri?" Elyse asked. Kyaeri sat on top of a two-tiered waterfall that backed a lake.

Layla smirked. "You've done your research."

"I'm excited to see it."

Nyran cleared his throat.

Assyl exchanged a glance with her and said, "Sure you are."

Elyse furrowed her brows, uncertain if it was their humor or an insult. An uncomfortable silence fell over them, making her turn her attention to the surrounding crowd. It was then that she noticed people circling their group.

Layla and Assyl complained about the recent weather, Elyse nodding along as she watched the three separate males pass by her multiple times, slowly getting closer. Her chest constricted. Her skin itched all over.

At last, one of them approached, a portly male with a crop of blond hair with a ruddy complexion. "Lady Elyse, your beauty knows no bounds. You look like a creature belonging to Amigys."

Elyse scowled and took a sip of wine, waiting a moment before saying, "I'm an official of Satiros, not a creature."

The male sputtered. "Apologies, I only meant—Would you like to dance?"

Elyse met his gaze. "No."

Layla snickered behind her and said something to her companions. Undeterred by the rejection, the two other males made their way directly toward Elyse.

The room became too small, the people too close. She turned to Layla. "I need air. Excuse me a moment."

Elyse dodged her way through the crowd, ignoring those who called after her or tried to get her to stop. It grew hard to breathe, the room humid with the crowd of bodies that pressed against her.

She inhaled deeply once outside, tilting her head back and closing her eyes.

"Lady Elyse, I was wondering if you'd do me the honor of having a dance with me?"

Elyse pivoted to find a male that had been circling since dinner standing behind her. "Unfortunately, I'm not in the mood for dancing."

"Are you sure? Perhaps then we could—"

She abruptly turned and darted down a set of stairs and into the garden, ignoring the male's voice calling from the balcony. When she accepted the position from Wyltam, she eagerly anticipated travel and exploration, unaware that the people she'd meet would be just as unappealing as the courtiers in Satiros. A glaring oversight on her part. All they wanted from her was the power of her position, meaning she wanted nothing to do with them.

She hurried through the garden, carefully descending the many stairs that snaked through the greenery. While the statues typically drew her attention, she had to put some distance between herself and the ball behind her. She raced to the bottom, coming to a low barrier that overlooked the bay. In the evening light, it remained a dark blanket rippling under the moonlight. Her heart beat in time with the waves crashing into the wall just below her.

For the first time in hours, her body calmed. Leaning onto the barrier, Elyse hung her head and watched the waves below. With a crash, she inhaled. Another crash, she exhaled. After a few minutes, she noticed dark shapes swimming in the water. She leaned over closer to get a better view, only for her foot to slip.

Elyse screamed as she fell forward, the jaws of whatever creature she stared at suddenly snapped up at her. Then she felt it, the hands holding her waist.

"Careful there," said a male voice, controlled and almost as if it were restrained. "You wouldn't want to swim with those."

He set Elyse back on her feet. "Thank you, I …" Her voice trailed as she raised her head and came face-to-face with a male wearing a mask made of tentacles. Despite the coverage, Elyse could feel that it was him, the male from the throne room, just as she felt his rough hands on the open sides of her abdomen. He quirked a smile as she stood there, unable to speak. Up close, he was impossibly handsome, with piercing eyes, a strong jaw, and a smirk that she found both infuriating and intoxicating. Her chest lurched, making her want to know everything about him. "What's in the water?"

"Trained sharks," he said, leaning in. "I hear the queen enjoys feeding them live prey. Makes them vicious."

Elyse eyed the water nervously.

"You're lucky I found you."

"Lucky indeed," she said, her blood thrumming in her veins. "Why are you out here and not at the ball?"

"I'm not one for dancing. But you're the guest of honor." He took a long drag of something that smelled similar to Mage's Eye cut with the richness of tobacco. "Why would the guest of honor be wandering the waterfront alone?"

"What if I told you I'm also not one for dancing?"

"Then I say we'd make quite a pair. That is, two people who want to be alone finding each other in the most dangerous of places."

"Most dangerous?"

As if on cue, one of the sharks came snapping out of the water. Elyse screamed and reached for aithyr before stopping. Gods, what was she even doing?

"Is everything all right? Besides the sharks." He gestured below.

"Yes—no," she said, her mood returning to sour. "I have no wish to be a guest of honor."

He nodded. "Means a lot of dancing."

"Or at least dance offers."

He laughed and glanced at his hand before holding out the smoke to her. "Need some help before going back in?"

"I think I'll manage."

He looked her eye to eye, his thin lips tilting with a smile. "I wouldn't offer if I think you could."

"Excuse me?"

"Manage, that is." He gestured with it. "It's Mage's Eye. I'm guessing a Satiroan royal is familiar? It's not frowned upon here."

Elyse stared at it, then stared at him, the offer tempting. "The legality isn't the part I'm questioning."

"Then what are you questioning?"

"Your character."

He barked a laugh, his lips revealing a bright row of teeth with his grin. "I don't remember the Satiroan politicians having such a bite." He stepped closer. "I hope you continue to question my character if it makes you this interesting."

Her head grew light even without his Mage's Eye. "That's assuming I'll see much of you after this." She took his smoke, inhaling deeply and releasing with a cough.

"Ah, not so familiar then."

"Familiar enough." Already she could sense the effects mellowing her more than her alcohol. And for the first time since she set aside her glasses, she could see the white wisps of aithyr—including the ones flowing into the stranger.

He watched her, his gaze darting over her face. "Aren't you going to ask me for my name?"

"I don't need to know it if I don't plan on seeing you again."

His frustrating smile remained as he said nothing.

"You truly expect me to ask." She laughed and rolled her neck. "Unfortunately for you, I can be quite stubborn. Thank you for the help. Have a good evening." She hurried away, keeping her back to him as she took the closest set of stairs returning to the garden.

"If it was a good evening, this wouldn't be the end of our conversation."

She glanced back only once to catch him letting out a puff of smoke, the aithyr strands curiously swirling into him. Once out of sight and out of earshot, she hid behind the bushes to catch her breath and ease her heart from racing. The bit of Mage's Eye would only help so much and she shouldn't be alone in the garden too long, especially with males she didn't know.

Except she didn't know the way back beside the path she came. Swearing to herself for not retracing her route, Elyse pulled aithyr into her body and listened to where she left the stranger.

There was the rhythm of his inhale and exhale, followed by a sigh. Then footsteps sounded, followed by a masculine voice. "Where the fuck have you been?"

"Nyran, my friend, I've been admiring the most beautiful night." A pause followed by a small laugh. "It's been quite some time since I've witnessed one so enchanting."

"I thought you were *eager* to be at the ball this evening."

"I was."

Nyran sighed. "You missed Kurtys introducing us to her. She was supposed to meet all of us, including you, Dominykas."

Dominykas hummed to himself. "I have a sinking suspicion she won't want to see me."

"Seriously?"

Dominykas laughed. "You need to relax."

"Will you at least return to the ballroom?"

"I could use a refresh of my drink."

Elyse let her aithyr drop as she heard them leave, Nyran hissing something back at Dominykas.

She had a face to the missing Ambassador of Chorys Dasi. She wished she'd never laid eyes on him. Her pulse thumped wickedly as she remembered his hands on her waist, the curve of his mouth when he smirked.

She stormed back to the ballroom, refusing to turn in his direction. She talked to Sethyr and the few Amigyans gathered around, but her eyes would start to drift to the corner. She'd get a glimpse of a tentacle from his mask before turning her gaze sharply to her drink. She wouldn't go through that again.

Chapter Forty-Nine

ELYSE

"The weather is lovely," Elyse responded to Queen Octavya's question, sipping her fish stew. The food surpassed what she had at the ball.

"Remains similar to this throughout the cold months," said King Ivyn, his dark skin glowing in the low light. "Perhaps you can stop on your way back from Kyaeri, stay a few weeks longer? I'm sure avoiding the cold would be nice. Plus, your limited amount of time is not sufficient to see everything we have to offer."

Elyse smiled. "No, not nearly enough time. Especially with most of my days being filled with meetings and nights with parties."

In Satiros, gatherings were kept small and exclusive. In Amigys, they were entire banquets turned into bacchanals. They poured their drinks heavy, the multiple meals doing little to dull the alcohol's numbing. From what she'd learned at these events, they were not just in honor of the Satiroan guests, but another reason to have them. Never in her life had she gotten such scant sleep, each night returning long after the moon reached its peak and having to wake at dawn.

Queen Octavya laughed. "Perhaps we should have planned something outside of the palace. We could ask them to make a few arrangements if you wished." She glanced between Seth and Elyse.

"No need to trouble yourself." Seth's eyes crinkled with his smile. "If we are able to return after our visit to Kyaeri, then we can plan to see more of the city-state. If not, then we have an excuse for a personal visit."

"True words," said the king. "How do you feel about them returning, Kryssida?"

The princess had been quiet up until then, her long, black hair twirled into tight braids embedded with shells and gems. She kept her head down as she said, "That would be most agreeable."

Elyse caught the slight downward tick in the queen's mouth, her disapproving gaze toward her daughter. Based on the information Elyse was given before her trip, she knew the princess was a decade younger than her.

"Perhaps if they make a habit of visiting, Lady Elyse could become a good friend?" The king laughed and took a drink.

"While that gesture is nice, please remember that Lady Elyse is an acting member of our court and an extension of King Wyltam himself," Seth said. His eyes did not match his smile. "With all due respect, perhaps with our visits, both present and future, she could remain on friendly terms with all politicians within your court, not only that of your daughter. Unless all of us are granted such kinship with your daughter?"

Heat rushed to her cheeks but she refused to look down, even if she hadn't caught that herself.

The king apologized. "No ill will was meant." He placed his napkin on the table and gestured Seth to stand. "I've heard you're a fan of spiced rum. I have an aged bottle that I've been wanting to share with the right company for some time. Come."

Elyse stood to follow, but the queen spoke up. "I'd like a moment alone with you, Lady Elyse, if you do not mind."

She lowered herself down to her seat, her pulse quickening. Even with Mage's Eye in her blood, it didn't stop her anxiety from flaring from the full attention of Queen Octavya.

She turned to her daughter. "Good night, Kryssi."

The princess stood and curtsied, delivering a rehearsed departure that

Elyse had given numerous of times during her father's parties. The princess probably looked forward to leaving, as she once had.

The queen's gaze bore down on her, its weight palpable in its scrutiny, yet revealing none of her thoughts. "Your father portrayed you as a pliant little thing, easily swayed and kept in line." Queen Octavya's mouth slashed into a smirk. "That's what I was expecting to see with your visit, wondering how a complacent girl came to be a king's most trusted. Now I understand. You've turned into quite the female. How did you manage that?"

Elyse dug her nails into her palm. "Perhaps I was never what my father intended."

Queen Octavya considered her for a moment. "Those who are stunted flourish the most once they are allowed to grow. Personally, I applaud you. Satiros doesn't treat females like you as they should."

Elyse swallowed her wine, the heat radiating down her chest. "King Wyltam and Lady Marietta are seeing to that."

The queen nodded. "Ah, yes. His new bride—your cousin. Was your rise due to that relation?"

Elyse set down her glass, her gaze wandering along the scrollwork of the tablecloth and toward the queen. "It was because I stopped my father from fleeing after he betrayed the king. I was given my position because of how close we were working together prior and rewarded for preventing a traitor from walking free. Those events and my rise in position occurred before Marietta's trial and before she was declared to be our queen."

Queen Octavya nodded along. "I've heard King Wyltam and his bride had an affiliation before they were to be married?" She raised a brow, leaning in.

"I, uh, don't deal in court gossip."
"Neither do I, which is why I'm asking. Curious times, Lady Elyse. I'm just trying to understand you better." The queen wiped her mouth and stood. "Walk with me."

Queen Octavya guided her out to the veranda, wandering to a landscape overlooking the bay. The moon painted a streak of white across the dark sea, the evening air comfortable. "You have pride and a sense of honor, Lady Elyse, one that you fight for. I admire that. Despite what nepotism that could have occurred to secure your spot next to King Wyltam, you believe you've worked to earn it and defend that position. A far cry from the weak girl Gyrsh loved to vaunt about."

Elyse nodded, wondering where this would lead to.

"And even so, what power do you have? The ear of the king, sure. But do you have influence?" She lifted her arched brow. "It's a shame that a female such as yourself has settled with being an assistant. What sway do you truly have in your court?"

Elyse went to counter, but the queen held up her hand.

"By the time you gain enough wisdom to advise the king, Satiros will no longer have a monarch. The city-state will officially be part of Enomenos and you without a position. Where does that leave you for the remainder of your life?" She shook her head. "On the other hand, you have a war coming. What happens if Satiros falls? I can't imagine being defeated in a war is advantageous to the cousin of the losing monarch.

She focused on the trail of terraces that led to the water below. "I have faith that Satiros will be victorious. As for my future ..." Elyse trailed off. She hadn't thought that far.

"It isn't in Satiros."

Her matter-of-fact way of saying as such made her flinch. How long had she wished to be free from Satiros? To never gaze upon its white buildings and greenery ever again?

"You know it to be true." The queen turned to face her. "When you find yourself sick of being another male's minion, return to Amigys. We'll see how we can grow you into a proper figure at court."

"You want me to abandon my king and my city-state?"

The queen drew her shoulders back, her dark eyes glittering in the light of the moon. "Don't think of it as abandoning but rather securing your future with a monarchy that has no intention of handing its crown to Enomenos."

"This offer is ... odd. I have no interest in leaving my home."

"I know," the queen said with a smile. "At least right now you don't. But remember that you have allies in Amigys even if your king loses them."

King Ivan called from the doorway. "Octavya, darling. Come hear the jest Minister Sethyr told me. It's a hoot!"

The queen turned with a bright smile toward her husband. "Coming, my love." She turned back to Elyse. "Consider what you want your future to look like."

When Elyse returned to her suite much later that evening, she sent a brief message to Wynn. *"Are you awake?"*

He appeared a few moments later on her balcony. "How'd it go?"

"Strange, to say the least. I would message Wyltam now, but it's late."

Wynn sat on the couch with his legs spread wide. "Talk to me about it."

"The queen made me an offer?"

"Oh?"

"To leave Wyltam's side and join Amigys' court." She threw herself back on her bed. "I declined, obviously. But she made a comment that I have allies here, even if Wyltam doesn't."

At Wynn's silence, she looked up at him. "That's deeply concerning and something Wyltam and Sethyr need to know."

"I know. I'll tell them tomorrow. But it wasn't hostile. Just … odd."

"I think stating anything as Wyltam losing an ally is considered hostile."

"Trust me, it wasn't."

Wynn stared for a moment, his gaze lingering on her. "Tell Wyltam, okay?"

She nodded. "I'm going to go to sleep, I think."

Wynn stood with a stretch. "Sleep well." He paused on the balcony and stuck his head back in. "And Elyse?"

"Yeah?"

"It's rewarding to see you work. As in, when you're in your meetings acting in Wyltam's stead. You've really come into yourself."

She smiled and pushed herself up on one arm. "That means the world coming from you."

Wynn held her stare a moment longer before disappearing into the night.

Chapter Fifty

AMRYTH

Amryth found arranging a meeting with the soon-to-be-married king more difficult than expected. The situation left her with a bitter taste. While the king had tasked her with helping clear Jory's name, he couldn't spare the time for a face-to-face meeting. Understandable, yet undeniably frustrating.

Although, her and Deania's discussion with Adira offered little clarity either, leaving them with more questions than answers. Did Adira truly see fey that evening, or were her attackers in convincing costumes? The only way to achieve the latter was with aithyr and a substantial amount of gold, which narrowed their search to a singular location.

The lobby lights blinded Amryth as she walked into the Randylph Theater with Deania on her arm. Attendees milled about in small social circles, waiting for the cue to take their seats. The crowd consisted of high elven society dressed in their best. And not for the performance they were there to watch, but rather for the spectacle they put on in front of each other. Not a hair was out of place, each wearing their most expensive outfit for the evening, hoping to prove who had the most wealth.

And Amryth despised all of it.

It was the same posturing as court, which meant it was unsurprising as she caught sight of a few nobles hanging in exclusive groups—a cut above the rest. Despite the mix of people that spread out before them, Deania was the only pilinos within eyesight. Clad in her formal Therypon attire, no one would dare speak a word against her. Amryth had no such uniform, resulting in her taking half the day to choose a simple dress with a practical jacket for the cool evening air. Dressing herself was not one of the difficulties she thought she'd face when she left the guard.

The goal was to blend in as much as possible, not drawing too much attention to themselves before finding the costume storage. If a feathered costume powered with aithyr existed, it would be here in the most prestigious theater in Satiros.

She didn't count on it. The chances were slimmer than a handkerchief, but at least still there. Deania, on the other hand, thought it was a simple solution.

Deania spotted the theater worker she was after and darted toward him. Amryth lingered nearby, observing as Deania effortlessly drew him in, his laughter coming within moments of her arrival. Her smile outshone the dozens of light globes suspended from the chandeliers above.

In the past, Amryth and Deyra had only attended the theater once at her parents' behest. Since then, nothing had changed. Rich elves surrounded by what they deem a proper setting. The columns were fashioned out of trees and gilded with gold, holding up a domed ceiling that mimicked the painted ceiling panels of the palace ballroom. They drank pouskyai, an expensive sweet bubbling wine that could only be fermented from its namesake village just outside of Satiros's city-state proper. From what she knew, even if people didn't enjoy the cloying sweetness of the drink, they consumed it anyway for the sake of status.

Keyain used to complain about the nobles to his Elite Guard. Over the years, Amryth had heard enough sickening stories that made her never want to interact with them more than she had to.

Now she was standing to the side of the lobby as a civilian, watching Deania help her clear an innocent male's name. Deyra wouldn't believe it if Amryth had foretold the event a year ago. But would she approve of it?

Deyra never spoke ill of pilinos; she never questioned Keyain's choice of wife when it came to the mission. But she also never spoke out against the laws. There were times when Amryth would have her moments of rants with Adalyn, but Deyra had always remained quiet. Did that mean she approved of pilinos being forced into marriage, or did she have other reasons to say nothing? Perhaps, like many in Satiros, she thought they were lucky to be here instead of the other Syllogian city-states.

Deania had shared some of her experiences growing up in Chorys Dasi. With the little Amryth did know, it was incredible that Deania approached each day with a smile. Her positivity was her armor that hid the anger and hurt lying underneath, much of which she had worked through with the help of Therypon. Amryth knew one day she would need to let out more, and she wanted to make sure she was there to help Deania when she did.

Staring at Deania's smile, Amryth's stomach curdled with guilt and she spun away. Cutting through the noise of the crowd, she heard someone call her name, and she inwardly groaned.

"Amryth, it is you! I told you, Lyon." Her mother rolled her eyes and patted her father's chest. "Never believes me, I swear. The other day when I got our delivery from the market—"

She sighed and pulled her mother into a hug. "Missing things from your order again?"

"Yes! And your father said it was my fault for not putting it on the list." As her mother carried on with the story, Amryth's attention drifted to the guests standing with her parents—a couple she held in clear disdain. The two males were theater regulars, wearing outfits that rival the cost of those who are noble, giving tight-lipped smiles and scrutinizing gazes. She leveled them with her own.

"Are you here alone?" her mother finally asked.

Amryth's mouth went dry. "I'm with someone named Deania."

Her mother's expression fell, and she exchanged a glance with her father. "You're *with* someone? Can we meet her?"

Amryth shrugged and swallowed the tightness in her throat. She wanted to say the truth, that they were here as friends, but the words never left her mouth. "Only if you promise not to make her uncomfortable."

Turning to find Deania, she jumped when the cleric popped up behind her. Before she had time to question, Amryth pulled her to her side. "Mother, Father, this is Deania."

Her mother's lips parted and her father's brows raised to his hairline. Behind them, their friends shared a conspiratorial smile with one another.

Deania noticed none of it and stuck out her hand. "It's lovely to meet you!"

Her father snapped out of his surprise first and shook Deania's hand. "Glad to meet you," he said in his rough voice. Her mother nodded her head, her eyes blinking rapidly as her mouth failed to catch up with her mind.

Deania pointed out the gold pin on the front of her father's jacket, the one he received for his years of service to the carriage factory. While he had loved that job, he chose the simpler life when Amryth paid for their living. Her father's eyes lit up as Deania asked a few questions regarding the production of carts and carriages.

"You didn't grieve Deyra very long," her mother said as she dug through her purse. "What's it been, only two months?"

"Mother—"

"After how many decades together?"

"How dare you bring this up *right now?*" Amryth hissed as her friends shared amused glances.

"It's only fair to Deyra. She was a daughter to us, too. Did you ever consider our grief?" Her mother dabbed her eyes with a handkerchief. "I suppose you wouldn't."

"This is hardly the time or place." Amryth exhaled slowly, suddenly noticing the weight of Deyra's notebook in her pocket. Beside her, Deania paid little attention to them, only excitedly nodding along to her father's story. "I didn't know you would be here tonight."

"If you bothered to stop by more, then maybe you would. And would it hurt to warn your parents that you're already starting a new relationship? This is entirely embarrassing."

"I never said we were in a relationship. And if we were, what would it matter?" Exasperated, Amryth cut off her father. "We have to get going if we're finishing before the show."

"Oh! Right." Deania smiled and said, "I'd love to hear more about the early days at the factory. I always found them fascinating."

Beaming, her father clapped her shoulder with a laugh. "We'll have you over for dinner sometime. How does that sound, Vyvienne?"

Her mother glanced down before offering a smile. "We'd love to have you. But where are you two going? The show doesn't start for another half hour."

"A friend of mine is getting us backstage!" Deania said, looping her arm through Amryth's as they walked off. She shot a playful wave at Amryth's stunned mother.

Thank gods her father acted reasonably. Deania must have noticed her mother's reaction yet said nothing, at least for right now. Amryth would have to apologize later.

The corridors behind the stage buzzed with frantic energy as Deania's friend guided them through. Actors and dancers flitted past, glitter and feathers swirling in their wake as they hurried to prepare for the show.

At the end of the hall, they stopped before a door. "You've got half an hour," her friend muttered, cursing under his breath. "This is everything from the shows that aren't running right now."

"Anything with feathers or horns?" Deania asked.

"Have you not seen any of the actors?" He sighed dramatically. "Feathers and horns are half of what they wear."

"Anything with wings?" Amryth chimed in. "That uses aithyr to help fly?"

The guy threw back his head and laughed. "That's a good one. You better start digging, though. There are a lot of racks and—" he pulled out an aithyr watch "—you only have twenty-eight minutes. This makes us even, D."

When the door shut behind them, Amryth took in the rows of costumes. Half an hour wasn't enough time, but she noted the determined gleam in Deania's eyes. With a resigning sigh, she began combing through the costumes as quickly as she could.

"He wasn't kidding about the feathers," Deania said from behind her. "There's an entire rack over here full of them, but none of them are wings."

Amryth hummed and continued along the rows until she discovered a section of props that were on stands in the back. A pair of gray wings stood out to her immediately.

"D!" she called as she inspected them more closely.

Deania came to her side with a hum. "Adira said they were white."

"I know, but in the low light, could gray be mistaken for white?"

She thought for a moment, tilting her head to the side. Deania's dark hair tumbled freely over her shoulder and Amryth wished she could run her fingers through it.

"Even with magic, are they big enough to lift a grown male?" Deania stepped forward and stood in front of them, holding her hands out to the side. The wings were much wider than her arm span.

Amryth examined the frame more closely, noticing narrow slots designed for arms to slip through. "See this? Adira said the attacker grabbed their leg while they were in the air behind them. Even if the wings could lift someone off the ground with aithyr, they couldn't have don't that while flying."

For a moment, Deania grew silent. "I thought we'd find something here. I know Adira isn't lying. I know they aren't crazy."

Amryth offered her hand and walked back through the racks. "The alternative is that they were actually fey, which is ridiculous."

"Is it though?" Deania stopped walking and forced Amryth to turn. "In Chorys Dasi, pilinos whispered that the fey existed. Many of those beliefs originated from the northern folk of Isvark, but they had since taken root among the pilinos of Chorys Dasi. We never spoke about it in the presence of the elves because it usually resulted in receiving their ire, but some of us believed. I think … I think it's possible they're real, Amryth."

Deania's mouth pouted, her round eyes glossy, melting the part of Amryth that was skeptical. "It could be possible. But how do we find out more about fey?"

"Leave that to me. I'll see what questions I can ask my fellow Chorys Dasians, but we can rule out costumes."

When they returned to the lobby, unease crept over Amryth. Fey being real? She couldn't exactly bring that to the king as proof. He'd likely stop listening to her altogether if that's the only new thing she had to report.

Perhaps they were overthinking things. The king had pointed her toward the Honeysuckle for a reason at the start of her investigation, a reason she hadn't quite unraveled yet. Maybe it was time for her and Deania to pay Tanaly another visit.

Amryth sat alone at a tavern in Greening Juncture, waiting for the canal workers' shift change so she could walk Nyk and the other pilinos back to Rambler Grove. As the evening crowd settled in, she kept her head low and listened to the surrounding patrons.

Many talked of the war. The prospect of having to fight other Syllogian elves rubbed them the wrong way. Some even insisted that Enomenos would stab them in the back.

The two males immediately next to her grieved about the surge in pilinos entering the city and how some had taken residence in the Wooded Ward.

"Any more north and we'll have to move to the river," one of them joked.

"Hopefully, most of them will die in the war," the other grumbled.

As they went on to talk about the pilinos in the army, Amryth lost interest. All of it was troubling, though she shouldn't be surprised. Most elves were going to have these opinions. For centuries, their lives have been secure and comfortable on the backs of pilinos. Now it wasn't just being threatened, but overturned. Still, she had hoped it would have been smoother in other parts of the city-state.

"Did you hear?" a female shrilled behind Amryth. "Another statue went missing and not from the palace this time. It was in today's issue of *Petal Revelry Review.*"

That got Amryth's attention. She took a sip and listened to her continue.

"Remember how they said that groundskeeper was suspected of stealing them?"

"I told you there was no way—"

"I know, and you were right. But you're never going to guess which statue was stolen."

There was a pause and a new voice said, "One of the dryads from the palace gates."

A round of laughter came from others at the table.

The original woman huffed. "This is serious—they took the griffin statue from Acorn Hill. A park in *our* neighborhood!"

Amryth knew exactly what statue she raved about, having passed it a few times on her way to visit her parents. The statue towered over a horse in size—surely someone must have seen it being stolen.

"Don't be ridiculous. Someone would've noticed," someone else said, echoing Amryth's opinion.

"That's the thing—it was there one day and gone the next. No one saw anything. Heard anything. It's a difficult statue to move and then hide."

A murmur broke through the group, Amryth losing where the conversation went.

As she finished her ale and tipped the barkeep, she couldn't help but compare that female to the pilinos she now left to go escort. Her biggest worry was a missing statue. The pilinos worried whether they'd make it home from their shift. Frustrated by the divide, Amryth swallowed her irritation and made her way to the canal.

Chapter Fifty-One
MARIETTA

Marietta's carriage rolled through the city-state, carrying Tryda, Grytaine, and Ymorea. The rest of her Queen's Court followed in a dozen carriages, their presence a mix of excitement and formality. Wyltam, who had been expected to join them, had chosen not to. Since learning the truth, he had become distant, avoiding her and barely speaking. Their shared bed remained empty, and their conversations grew scarce. Marietta swallowed her irritation and remorse, focusing instead on Ymorea to distract herself.

"I love seeing the city-state this time of year!" Ymorea proclaimed to no one in particular. "There's just something so comforting about it."

Tryda's blank expression rivaled that of Wyltam's. When Marietta had shared her plan for her Queen's Court and what she wished to do with it, Tryda had tried to talk her out of it. Marietta didn't heed her advice.

Grytaine looked utterly miserable, her lips set in a constant frown. Her hands rested over her swollen abdomen, cradling the child within. Between the relentless nausea and the baby pushing against her organs, she claimed she hadn't slept in weeks. Ymorea, however, had a completely different demeanor from her fellow ladies, that notion not being lost on Grytaine or Tryda as they shared glances.

With her face nearly pressed to the glass, Ymorea added, "Rymos tries to get into the city more, but it's hard with his schedule." She turned to the other ladies. "I'm sure you know how it is. I do get to see it though when we visit Randyl at our estate"—she redirected her attention to Marietta—"Randyl is our son. Usually I'll stay with him for a few months at a time, but court has been so … exciting. I know that isn't the best word with all the awful going on, but you have to admit the change is exciting!"

Her fellow court ladies remained quiet as they jostled along. Ymorea rattled off story after story, barely pausing for breath as they passed each landmark. While Wyltam had given Marietta the city-state's history in his usual dry tone, Ymorea's enthusiasm was contagious, making her smile despite herself. Even if no one else gained something from the outing, at least she had. She made a mental note to invite Ymorea to one of her temple visits.

When the carriages finally stopped, Ymorea gasped. "The buildings are taller than I imagined!"

Marietta smiled to herself as she stepped out of the cabin. She turned toward the district, feeling her plan coming to fruition. Anticipation thrummed through her veins, as if she had indulged in one too many cups of tea.

The Weeds, or Rambler Grove as Coryn had instructed her to call it today, contrasted sharply with everything these ladies were accustomed to. It was raw and unrefined, home to hardworking people who possessed only what they truly needed. The district stood in stark opposition to the excess they knew, offering lessons that would be valuable as the war loomed ever closer.

"Esteemed ladies and Your Grace," Alderan said by greeting, bowing his head. "An honor to have you today."

"The honor is mine." Marietta shook his hand, ignoring the murmur through the small crowd that gathered, held at bay by Marietta's guards. "Ladies, this is the District Delegate of Rambler Grove. Alderan will be our guide for the day."

Ymorea stepped up excitedly and took his hands, rattling off a dozen questions before Alderan could answer one. He shared a worried glance at

Marietta.

She smiled and turned to her court. "This is an excellent opportunity to see what it is like to be a pilinos in Satiros and to see why King Wyltam and I are implementing our changes. A chance to see the wondrous things they make in their little slice of our great city-state." She gestured for them to follow, and she took the historic first step into Rambler Grove.

From what Alderan shared, Marietta was the first queen—or almost queen—to set foot in their district in centuries, ever since it was deemed a location only for pilinos.

"We're going on foot?" she heard Grytaine grumble.

Anticipating her disapproval both because of the dirt streets and having to walk while pregnant, she had Coryn offer her his arm to escort her. The lady accepted it after some slight hesitation.

The entire outing was part of her plan for them to not only witness pilinos but to experience what they experienced, which meant no carriages in the district. Alderan explained Rambler Grove's rapid growth over the last few decades and pointed out a group of workers filling a pothole in the road. He described how they managed their own infrastructure that was vastly different from that of the rest of the city-state. Next, they came to a building that was under construction. Because of the lack of tools and materials available at the time of its creation, many of the structures from the last century were constructed haphazardly.

The ladies remained silent as they walked through the streets—all but for Ymorea. The questions never ceased, Alderan answering one only to be asked another. "How do the street lights ignite?"

"District workers go around every evening to light them and then again in the morning to extinguish them," Alderan answered.

Ymorea's face scrunched. "There has to be an easier way."

"Magic is usually the solution, but unfortunately not allowed in Rambler Grove."

"That should change. Light globes are inexpensive now with the new factories. It would be much more efficient and less expensive if you didn't have to light the streets manually."

Alderan's smile came forced, catching Marietta's eye. She looped her arm through Ymorea's. "We're working on that with the changes to the laws."

Her face relaxed. "Oh, that is so good to hear. That makes me happy."

Marietta glanced at Alderan, wishing she could convey that not everyone in the court was malicious—many were simply ignorant. If she couldn't shift their perspective, the backlash would persist.

Alderan led them past a bustling market, and Grytaine remarked that it looked much like any other in Satiros. The surprise in her voice made it clear—she hadn't expected it to be so organized or filled with people going about their business. When they passed a park next, Alderan explained they turned them all into food gardens a few years ago to lower the cost of fresh food for their district. One of the ladies asked where would they walk if the parks were used for gardening. Alderan had to share that pilinos spend most of their days walking since there were no carriages. He reminded them of a man pulling a cart that they saw a few blocks back. Everything in the district was on foot. A collective "Oh" came from the group.

They came across a group of children screeching as they chased each other in the street. The group kept moving, but Marietta caught Grytaine and Coryn remaining behind. Curious, Marietta excused herself and made her way over.

Grytaine had her hand on her abdomen, her eyes locked onto the children.

"Everything all right?" Marietta asked as she approached.

"She wanted to watch the kids for a moment," Coryn said, then he leaned in and whispered, "She said she has hysteria from her pregnancy."

"That's what Royir called it, at least," Grytaine said, her gaze fixed on the kids. "Coryn here informed me it's normal for pregnant people to be emotional. How many pilinos children don't have parents?" Her hand reflexively rubbed over her stomach.

"Roughly one in every five," Coryn said, frowning.

Grytaine's lips wobbled. "That's horrible. I could never …" She trailed off and let her hands fall.

Coryn's voice was gentle, more than it ought to be for someone such as Grytaine. "Most of them are placed in families. They all have something to eat and somewhere to go. They're safe."

He hooked his arm through hers again and wheeled her back to the group. Marietta stayed at their side.

"No offense, but you didn't strike me as a person who cared about children," Marietta said, keeping her voice low. "Let alone pilinos children."

"This pregnancy has changed me, Your Grace," she said, her expression twisting into a scowl. "You don't know what matters until it's staring you in the face."

"Your child is lucky then to have you and Minister Royir as their parents," she said.

Grytaine scoffed. "Royir doesn't care. He rarely sleeps in our suite, often choosing to—" She paused and shook her head. "Between us three, this baby isn't his." She sniffled and drew back her shoulders. "Only mine. His older son is to inherit his wealth, his lands. It was already decided."

"I'm sure he cares," Coryn said, trying to console her.

"Don't bother," she said. "I came to terms with it."

Her tone suggested she was done speaking about it, her chin lifted as if she were trying to control what fraying emotions she had remaining. As they rejoined the group, Marietta took her spot next to Alderan once more, her mind lingering. Perhaps what she said was true, that her pregnancy had changed her.

As a group, they continued onto several pilinos businesses—first to a cobbler, then a furniture maker, and a bakery before visiting a jeweler. Their last stop was a glassblowing shop, where Alderan mentioned they crafted the finest glass in the city-state. A few skeptical murmurs passed through the group until they entered the shop. Inside, an array of glassware stood on display. Bowls stretched into elegant, elongated shapes, their edges delicate with a shimmer of subtle hues. Plates featured intricate patterns, their designs twisting across the surfaces like wind over water. Vases rose gracefully, adorned with sophisticated details that made them appear more art than craft.

"A technique blended from Amigyan glassblowing techniques with influences from the lands outside Syllogi." He introduced the head blower, a woman who looked more human than half-elven. She shared her story of how her father was an expert glassblower back in Amigys and had worked with the most renowned blower in all of Syllogi. A few ladies murmured at the artist's name, having recognized it.

Ymorea wandered the storefront and discovered a set of lamp covers made of ornately worked multicolored glass on a brass stand. "I haven't seen one of these since I was a child! Back when light globes were first introduced. It's so beautiful!" She turned to the head blower. "Do you have to use gas in them, or could I put a light globe in there?"

The glassblower stumbled over her words. "I don't see why not, though I could rework the base so that it could cradle the globe instead, if you'd like."

Ymorea's face lit up. "Could you? I'd love to purchase them if you could!"

As the Ymorea and the glassblower worked out the details, Tryda pulled Marietta to the side, her voice low. "I hope you're happy with your outing."

"It's going quite well, is it not?" Marietta smiled, watching as the ladies examined the glasswork and began to reach for their coin purses. They had bought treats at the bakery and Marietta bought a few necklaces from the jewelers, inspiring others to pick up pieces. In many ways, it was working out better than she had hoped.

Tryda nodded toward the door, where a group of women huddled with frowns. "They're concerned about your lack of love for all businesses in the city-state," she explained. "Some even say that you're working to run elven businesses out of work in favor of pilinos. Something you should keep in mind."

Marietta bit her tongue and forced a smile. "From my understanding, elves already support elven businesses. By expanding their knowledge of ones here in Rambler Grove, it allows them to truly find the best work. If that's not by elven businesses, then so it shall be." She stepped closer. "They cannot imagine a world where they are not seen as superior to pilinos. Their worldview is threatened, but they will come around. As will you."

Tryda's smile was sad, though it never reached her eyes. "It's your grave, not mine, Your Grace."

Marietta left her, not wanting to spoil the success of the day. While she had been cordial and patient with Tryda, that well had dried up. It was time for her to align with the change or be left behind.

Chapter Fifty-Two
MARIETTA

Seated around a sizable oak table, Marietta sat in on her official first meeting with the minister of vassals, the district delegates, and Wyltam. She dug her nails into the fabric of her pants to not stare at the latter. A gaze of disappointment or anger would be preferred to his indifference. As if the last few months have meant nothing. As if she meant nothing.

Instead of focusing on him, she turned her attention to the ten representatives and how they depicted the perfect stereotype from the districts they oversaw. The Wisteria Heights official dressed in tailored clothing and slicked-back hair, where the man from Bud Town wore a plain shirt tucked into work pants. Marietta had spoken with Delegate Alderan before their start, discovering that, despite his decade-long tenure, this was one of his first meetings. He was also the only other pilinos present. She kept her eye on him throughout the hour, counting how often he pushed his glasses up his rounded nose. Seventeen times, to be exact.

"Lady Marietta," Leyland said, drawing her attention. "Do you have an update from the temples?"

She stood with a smile. "Recently, more people have joined, not only due to my connections with the deities"—Wyltam stiffened in his seat—"but also out of fear of the impending war."

"Do you have those numbers?"

"No, but I can get them for you."

Leyland nodded and moved on to the delegates. When Marietta took her seat, she glanced at Wyltam, noting his grip on the arm of his chair.

When Delegate Alderan stood to speak, he cleared his voice as the delegate from Wisteria Grove murmured something to the person next to him. "We're seeing an 8 percent growth in population for Rambler Grove in last month alone. If this stays as it is, we'll double in population by the end of the year."

"Troubling," someone murmured.

"But also expected with our new queen."

Alderan fixed his gaze on his elven counterparts. "I urge you once more to reconsider the stipend costs to help pilinos move beyond Rambler Grove. They may be able to relocate within the city, but affordability remains a barrier. Families are crammed into unsuitable living conditions, and panic is spreading. Each day, we see more newcomers being driven to the Silts."

"The Silts isn't officially recognized," Minister Leyland said, his chin pinched between his thumb and forefinger. "What of employment?"

"No improvement. Businesses aren't willing to hire pilinos."

Marietta sat forward, garnering the attention of the table as heat climbed up her stomach and settled in her chest. "Could you elaborate on that for me, Delegate Alderan?"

He glanced once at his peers. "While pilinos are free to work at any business in Satiros, we're seeing few businesses willing to hire them. Since the treaty, we've witnessed a drop in employment of pilinos by elven businesses."

"It's true, Your Grace," Leyland added. "Although, Minister Adryan reported many have joined the guard instead."

"While that may be true, it's often out of necessity of work rather than freedom of choice. It's the only job offered to many pilinos." Alderan placed his palms on the table and leaned in.

A small laugh came from Marietta as she digested his words. "Part of the agreement in the treaty was that we set plans for encouraging businesses to hire pilinos *before* the wedding, or so I thought. Am I wrong in thinking that?" She turned to Wyltam.

"You are not," he answered, his face devoid of any emotion.

She faced the delegates once more. "Does anyone care to explain why pilinos are not being hired?"

Alderan looked to Leyland, his jaw set. The minister sighed and wiped his face. "Potentially, the Commerce Council is slacking on their enforcement of that part of the treaty."

A stirring in her chest joined the heat as she regarded the men—and only men at the table, she noted, making the sensation more crazed. "I'm going to explain what I'm hearing. We have a group of people, whose population grows by the day, struggling to find work. The promises *we*"—she gestured to the table—"made to the people were a fair-handed opportunity to work like the elves in Satiros. Ensuring them *we*"—she gestured to the table again—"will make sure that they have those opportunities. Two months later, we not only have broken those promises *in a treaty*, but conveniently, the only job available is to join our guard while we were amid a recruiting shortage." The room didn't dare move as she stared them down, her pounding blood deafening. "Someone tell me, please. What do the recruitment numbers look like today compared to two months ago?"

"Your Grace," Leyland started, "I agree that something needs to be done—"

"Do not make me ask again." Marietta lifted her chin.

"Minister Keyain shared that recruitment numbers are up significantly," Wyltam said at her side. "That the pilinos recruits make up that majority."

Marietta hung her head for a moment, taking a steady breath to calm the emotions raging in her chest. "One month."

"Excuse me, Your Grace?" Leyland asked.

"One month," she said louder, raising her head. "You have one month to fix this. As the committee overseeing the people of this city-state, I'm putting the pressure on *you* to fix this. In one month, I want you to have an approved plan implemented. While we're at it," she said, letting her rage take over, "draft a plan on how to expand pilinos's housing into the rest of Satiros. They can live in more than one district now, so why was this not already done?"

"Our team has been overworked with—"

"Then find more people." She stared all of them in the eye, ending with Wyltam. "I expect to see this team expanded to include women and feminine folk alike. I'm tired of being surrounded by near-sided men who have done things their way for too long."

Wyltam held her stare as the silence stretched on. Finally, he said, "You heard our future queen." He stood and smoothed out his jacket. "We have one month."

The room scattered, delegates whispering as they gathered their things and hurried into the hallway. As Marietta turned to leave, Wyltam wrapped his arm around her waist, halting her movement. *We need a moment.*

She tried to pull out of his touch, but it held true. Anger roared like a thunderhead, her wrath sparking, her hands curling into fists. She lifted her chin.

"Leave us," Wyltam ordered her guard, his gaze fixed on her. "And shut the door behind you. No one comes in."

The door snapped shut as her guards locked Marietta in with him. As soon as they were alone, she turned on Wyltam. "Don't you dare be angry with me," she spat. "How could you let this go—"

Wyltam's mouth crashed into hers, his moan making her body freeze. He wrapped his arms around her and pulled her close, his hands digging into her as she tried to move away. Breathless, he raked his teeth across her lip, drawing out a whimper, and he pushed her back into the table. When his hands started to skate up her skirt, she came to her senses.

She pushed him away. "You haven't talked to me in days and you decide this is okay?"

"Oh, I'm still furious with you. And you still have a damning habit of making impulsive decisions based on emotion." His finger traced the curve of her ear to her jawline. "One month? Really?"

Marietta gestured between them. "Is this how you show anger?" Wyltam's hand slipped into her hair and pulled, tipping her head back so her mouth came closer to his. "This is how I show appreciation."

"Appreciation?"

"While your heart is in the right place, your methods are unskilled, ungraceful, and lack decorum. The rest of my day will be filled with cleaning up the mess you just delivered." His hand tightened on her hair and she arched her back, grinding her hips into his. "Yet you can hold a room and demand results, and it's never made me want you more."

He kissed her slowly that time, his tongue exploring, savoring. Marietta's fingers dug into his back, her breaths turning to moans as he moved down her neck. She went to lift her skirts, but he grasped her wrist. His forehead pressed into hers as he swallowed hard. "Decorum. We can't here."

Marietta gripped his chin, making him stare at her. "You can't form a sentence right now, can you?"

Wyltam untangled himself from her and brushed back his hair, the gesture stirring her desire more. Somehow, his hair combed away from his face made him more handsome, more approachable.

"A month is not a lot of time for this change," he finally said.

"Considering it should've been done two months ago, the time I gave them was generous."

"We've already expedited women through the universities. I can't just place them into the positions unqualified. It'll take longer than a month."

"Perhaps they need more of a hands-on approach to their learning." She crossed her arms and closed her eyes. "I'll oversee them myself if I have to. Enough is enough."

"Enough is enough," he repeated, humor hinting in his tone. Marietta opened an eye to find him smiling. Wyltam took her hand and kissed the back of it. "We can talk more tonight. Until then, I have to help our government determine how to reward businesses for hiring pilinos."

"And what's that supposed to mean?" Marietta trailed him as he made his way to the door.

"It means more than loose accountability is holding pilinos back. How will they be able to move outside Rambler Grove if they don't have the savings to support themselves? Will women pilinos join the government at the same rate as elven ones?"

"I … hadn't considered that."

"We'll figure it out. We always do."

Marietta sat at Wyltam's desk, mindlessly flipping through *The History of Lyken Fulbryk* as she waited for him to finish his meetings. A handful of hours had passed since Marietta read a bedtime story to Mycaub, assuming Wyltam wouldn't have been much later than that. She read the notes in the margin, wondering if the man who wrote them was the one she got a glimpse of that morning. Passionate, filled with more emotion and desire than she realized he possessed. It was as if she discovered a well after being parched; she would greedily drink each drop he offered to her. It's why she waited in the one place he'd definitely return to.

"There you are." Wyltam stood in the doorway, watching as Marietta crossed and uncrossed her legs, resting against the armrest.

"Long day?" she asked, turning back to her book once more.

"Very."

She hummed a response, her body tensing as he neared.

"That's all you have to say?" He walked to her side of the desk, looming over. "You are not one to be quiet."

Heat blossomed in her stomach at the expression on his face, the way he seemed to barely contain his emotions. She stood with a stretch and stepped away. "You ignored me for days. I do it for a few minutes and—"

Wyltam gripped the back of her dress and pulled her flush to him. His voice was a harsh whisper in her ear. "It's my attention you want?"

She sucked in a breath.

His laugh was deep and rolled over her skin, causing her to arch back. "I'm frustrated, Marietta. And hurt. You lied and lied deeply. What am I going to do with you?"

"It looks like you already have plans for me." She reached between his legs, her hand encountering his hardened length. "You appear quite *frustrated*."

"You make me feel as if I'm losing my fucking mind. I want to be angry with you." His nose skimmed along the length of her neck.

A shiver worked its way through her body. "But you aren't?"

"I don't want to talk." He pressed a kiss into her skin. "I've spoken enough for one day."

Marietta tilted her head to give him better access to her neck. "Tell me what you want."

Wyltam turned her to face him, his dark eyes wholly black, burning with desire. "You. On the desk."

Her lips curled into a smirk. "Then make me."

He gripped her body and shoved her back into the desk, lifting her to sit on top. Her pulse quickened, a deep ache forming in her lower abdomen. His fingers dug into her thighs as he slipped his hands between the slits in her dress. Wyltam's mouth hovered above hers, and when Marietta went to close the distance, he leaned away. "We're on my terms tonight. Do you understand?"

Marietta raised her hand to his face, but he seized her wrist, drawing her hand behind her back and pinning it firmly. While not aggressive, the surety in his touch sent her pulse thrumming through her body.

His voice was deep, guttural, abrasive against her ear. "Do you understand, Marietta?"

She nodded, only for him to grip her chin. "Use your words."

Her eyes met his defiantly as heat washed over her body. "Do your worst."

His lips hooked into a smirk as he gripped the back of her dress, the fabric falling away. He helped her shimmy out of it and let it drop to the floor. He grabbed both arms and placed them behind her again, her chest arching into him. As soon as he released her, she tried to move but found herself bound with nothing. A low whimper escaped her mouth.

Wyltam forced her knees apart and stood between her legs. When she felt his fingers lightly trace the inside of her thighs, the ache within her grew taut and heady.

"What I find amusing about you pushing me to madness," he said as she trembled underneath his touch, "is that you don't think I'll return the favor." His fingers neared her most sensitive spot, and she arched her back.

"There are many ways I could do this. Withhold information. Make impulsive decisions without consulting you. Make you sit in silence." His fingers neared again, and she moaned for his touch. "But the most entertaining way is like this. Making you want me so bad that you beg."

Marietta glared at him as a responding tingle cascaded through her body. "I'd like to see you try," she murmured.

With his free hand, he pushed back his hair, his laugh coming in a deep rolling sound. "I'm sure you would. But you so badly want control—over yourself, over everyone—and I took it from you in a matter of seconds." His fingers hovered over her center, her chest tightening as she longed for his touch, to experience him filling her. His finger flicked the spot, sending a jolt of pleasure through her body and drawing a moan from her lips. "It was almost too easy."

"You're enjoying this too much."

He stepped back, his stare locked between her legs. "As are you. I wonder if you'll make a bigger mess than last time."

Marietta tried to pull her arms free. She wanted him and she wanted him now.

"Aithyr won't budge." Wyltam rolled up the sleeves of his black shirt, revealing the risen veins that traced his skin. "But you are more than welcome to try."

She pulled again to no avail. One of his hands gripped her leg, the other teasing at her entrance. His dark gaze was liquid as he took her in. He squeezed her thigh as his touch brushed against her. Her stomach tightened as she gasped. The next swipes of his finger came slower and slower, the motion circling where she was most sensitive. A rhythmic throbbing started in time with his touch, Marietta tightening her core, feeling herself wound so tight that she could snap with a single breath. Then Wyltam pulled away.

"What're you doing?" she asked, her voice distant.

"What I promised." He slipped the fingers into his mouth before rubbing them against her once more. "You can come when I let you."

"Wyltam," she warned, her muscles tightening at the thought.

"Call me 'your king.' I rather enjoy that one."

She let out a frustrated cry through gritted teeth that earned a smirk from Wyltam. His movements sped, the sudden rise in her pleasure causing her to crest. Just as she was about to break, he pulled away again. "Call me 'your king.'"

Marietta ground her teeth, imagining they were digging into his flesh. Stubborn ass of a man.

"I love how resilient you are." Wyltam kissed her as his fingers touched her once more, her pleasure sparking instantly.

"Wyltam," she moaned against his lips, "make me come."

His hand moved faster. "Like this?"

Marietta nodded as her senses overcame her with the need to climax.

"Beg, Marietta."

"Please."

"Please what?"

Her back arched, as her body couldn't handle his touch much more. At the moment she was about to break, he pulled away again.

"Wyltam," she growled.

He tapped against her again, causing that gods damned jolt of pleasure. "You know what to call me when you beg."

She blew out a breath. "Infuriating."

His smirk was damning. "That's not it." He leaned over her, a line of saliva dripping to between her legs. He smeared it on her. "You know what will let you come."

Something deep and primal woke in her as he started again, his touch slipping over her with new fury. Within seconds, she was at the edge, her legs trembling as she was ready to fall. "Please," she said, her voice coming out sharp and wispy, "make me come, My King."

His fingers moved with renewed vigor, the already-built pressure bursting as her vision went white. She cried out, her body tensing and pulling against his restraints.

"That's it," Wyltam said in a thick, syrupy voice. "Just like that."

Marietta still trembled as he dropped to his knees, her thighs tightening around his head as his tongue licked along her still-too-sensitive skin. She heard his belt, the sliding of fabric, then the sound of skin on skin. She glanced down at him, a new ache forming in her as he touched himself while tasting her. His deep moan rumbled through and her mind grew heady with pleasure, knowing she couldn't take much more. Marietta wanted him, wanted to be filled with him.

"Please, fuck me."

Wyltam's mouth stayed pressed to her as he said, "You know how to beg."

She whimpered as his fingers slipped inside her. "Please, fuck me, My King."

With a smirk, Wyltam stood and grabbed the hem of his shirt, pulling it off his body. Beneath, his abdomen was toned and tightened. Suddenly, her hands were free. She reached for him, Wyltam instead grabbing her from the desk. He spun her around so her front faced the wooden top and his papers scattered about. "Is this all right?" he asked as he bent her over, his length pressing into her ass.

Marietta barely nodded as want surged through her body.

"Words, Marietta."

She placed her hands at the small of her back. "I want you to fuck me just like this."

Wyltam let out a shaky breath, the chilled touch of his hand pinning her as his cock nudged between her legs. He slid all the way in, slowly, torturously, her body going molten with the sensation of him deep inside her.

"You feel perfect," he murmured. "You feel absolutely perfect."

He slid out and back in, harder that time. One hand gripped her hip, pulling her along the length of his cock with rhythmic thrusts that sent her spiraling. The items on his desk fell to the floor as he thrusted rougher, Marietta's legs slipping as her body tightened and snapped. Wyltam groaned as he continued filling her. Marietta looked over her shoulder and met his gaze. Wyltam's voice was tight and deep. "Keep going, love. Keep coming for me."

Marietta did, losing herself in the feeling of Wyltam.

Marietta did not know what time it was. In fact, she cared very little for time at that moment. Her body was liquid, curled against Wyltam in bed. They had moved here at some point in the night. He drew lazy circles across her skin, interspersed with the occasional kiss. She finally broke their silence. "You continue to surprise me."

"How so?"

"All of that." She gestured with her hand. "You never struck me as the type to take control during sex."

"Why?"

"I don't know."

"I think I do," he murmured. "Because you normally don't enjoy the idea of me being in control of you."

She thought for a minute. "Maybe that's it."

"And you did enjoy it."

She gave him a look. "I was in the heat of the moment."

"Sure." His face fell, and he shifted away.

Her body went cold. "Don't leave tonight. Please stay."

Wyltam paused, his gaze fixed on the bed. "I need time."

"Time for what?"

"To process."

"Wyltam—"

"You chose Elyse and her magic over protecting Satiros. You chose it over being a ruler with me." He ran a hand through his hair. "I don't blame you for wanting to help her, but it was a choice you made. This is one of many consequences."

"I … don't know what to say."

Wyltam stood and dressed himself. "I need time."

"How long?"

He shook his head. "Enough to wrap my head around the fact fey exist. Enough to find out wherever Keyain is so we can plan. We have tens of thousands of soldiers putting down their lives for us." He pinned her with a stare. "It was your job to protect them and now …" He shook his head. "Good night, Marietta."

The door clicked shut behind her, and she gasped, the air fleeing her lungs as if pulled by an invisible force. She had messed up terribly. She knew Wyltam would be furious. The gravity of what she had done—putting millions of lives at risk—loomed large and oppressive in her mind. Yet, she had done it anyway, all because Elyse had asked her to.

Regret twisted deep inside her, heavy and unrelenting. She buried her face in the pillow, fingers tightening in her hair as the weight of her choice settled. A scream built in her chest, but all that escaped was a broken whisper.

Chapter Fifty-Three

KEYAIN

Time didn't matter. Neither did food nor sleep. Keyain didn't need to worry about those things when Choke took all senses from him and rendered him memory-less. In the moments of sentience when he dosed himself again, he managed to eat enough from the stores of food to keep his body going. His hair hung in greasy strands on his head and his eyes looked black beneath. He only needed to think of those for minutes at best before the Choke took its hold.

He danced in the empty ballroom with a dark-haired female with a sinister red smile. *"You would never survive without me."* How right she was.

Keyain tried to touch her multiple times, to slip his hands through the silky strands of her hair, to warm her cold fingers. No matter how hard he tried, he felt nothing where she should be.

Until one day.

Keyain cracked open his eyes, the light bleeding around Olytia as she shook him awake.

"You stupid fucking idiot."

He scrambled back, only to be caught by her hands. *"You think you could get away with it? That I would let you or Wyltam rest easy?"* Her sinister laugh rendered him motionless, even when a vial appeared in her hand and she poured it down his throat.

So this is how he died. Funny, he remembered the poison tasting bitter.

His eyes fluttered closed, her hands thumping on his chest. He supposed he deserved the hitting. After all, he had a hand in her death.

A sudden warmth came to his pants, and a slap struck him across the face. "Wake up!"

Keyain bolted upright at the sound of Ryder's voice, his head spinning with the sudden loss of Choke in his system. He turned to see his friend hovering over him, his face paled.

"You asshole," he cursed. "How fucking dare you scare me like that!"

The room tilted as Keyain pushed away from him. Then he remembered. He was in his manor, sent here by Wyltam. Wyltam, who was now marrying Marietta. Bile rose in his throat. "What are you doing here?"

"The fucking king sent me because you never arrived at the palace." Ryder slipped under his arm and heaved him up. "You look like fucking shit. I knew something was wrong. I kept telling Peryn we needed to check on you."

He shoved off him. "I was fine."

"Fine? You call this fine?" Ryder gestured to the littered living room they stood in. "What happened?"

"Tell Wyltam I resign."

"Oh no, you don't." Ryder got in his face. "We are in a *war*. While Hastyrn is suitable in the meantime, he even admitted all he knows is theory. We need someone who has fought and taken a life to lead us."

"Not happening."

Ryder wiped his face. "Look at me. I want you to use your brain for only a few seconds here, all right? We are sending inexperienced soldiers to fight other Syllogian elves and we cannot motivate them to kill. Want to know what motivates them?"

Keyain tried to shove past. He didn't need to hear this, and soon he no longer would. There was more Choke somewhere.

"A war hero! One who saved our city-state—"

Keyain turned abruptly and wagged his finger in his face. "I saved *shit*. Just ask Wyltam. None of us were in danger."

"For fuck's sake." Ryder shook his shoulders, making his head spin again. "Don't you hear me? We have Satiroans sacrificing their lives with a leader who doesn't know how to minimize the casualties. I don't care about what you actually saved—it's what they think you saved, okay?"

Ryder always knew how to hit him. Over the years, Keyain has tried to know many of his soldiers, understanding one day it could end with them giving the ultimate sacrifice. He thought that their attack on Olkia had been that moment, yet that was nothing compared to the war they'd have with Chorys Dasi and Reyila. Even so, Keyain knew he wouldn't return. He couldn't.

"I can't go back," he said. "No one will want to follow a disgraced minister."

"Disgraced? Wyltam said that you needed time to rest."

Keyain's stomach lurched. More nepotism. Worse was that it came from Wyltam's hand. After everything, he still protected Keyain. "That's more of a reason to not return. It means I'm a fraud."

"Fuck, Keyain." Ryder shook him again. "Wyltam sent me to get you to the palace discreetly. Everyone thinks you've been ill and you look the part. Go clean yourself up and let's get in that carriage to the palace."

"Ryder, I can't—"

"King Wyltam said that if you resisted, I should remind you of what happens when you disobey direct orders."

Dread coiled through his body, knowing exactly what the words meant. Wyltam would never let him go, not entirely. He hung his head and let Ryder guide him to his room to get himself together.

The Satiroan countryside sped by in a blur of villages and towns broken up by stretches of farmland heavy with this autumn's crop. Ryder was smart enough to say nothing as they made their way back to the palace. Even with scrubbing in the bath and putting on nice clothes, grogginess held Keyain by the throat. His sweat-slicked skin, accompanied by a pounding headache, made it all the worse. He closed his eyes and leaned his face against the glass.

When he opened them again, they raced by trees of varying heights standing as sentinels, their branches reaching toward the sky like outstretched arms. A lush array of foliage filled with life crowned them, unlike the occupants below. When did he last visit his family plot in the Ash Gardens? Not since their burial. Their deaths had been so sudden, feybarb striking them down in a merciful manner before the illness made them suffer. At least that's what he told himself for his sanity, the actual truth being too painful to remember.

His thoughts lingered on his parents and the wasted legacy they had passed on to him. He hardly took in the palace when they arrived, paid no mind as he navigated through the halls, ignoring his peers. He didn't come to again until his suite door snapped shut behind him.

The walls whispered all his failures from over the years, reminding him that he returned with another one added to his belt. He spotted the empty cabinet in the corner of the room, his instincts kicking in before his thoughts caught up. All the alcohol he had accumulated throughout the years, vanished. With a frustrated sigh, he raked a hand through his hair. In his peripheral vision, he noticed a figure standing in the living room, back turned to him as he gazed out the window. Despite not seeing his face, Keyain recognized him instantly. "What is this about?"

A devastating silence held the room as shame bubbled up inside Keyain's chest.

"Come sit," Wyltam called, not bothering to turn around. "There's much to discuss."

Keyain's steps were heavy as he met Wyltam, collapsing into the chair before the window. He followed his gaze out to the garden, where night came early with the cloud-covered sky.

"Your substance issues were worse than I realized."

Keyain went to speak, but Wyltam held up his hand.

"You are forbidden to drink any amount of alcohol, take any drugs besides for medical purposes, or use any mind-altering substances from now on," he said, his voice hushed. He never needed to raise his voice to project the weight of his words, something Keyain always admired.

"You can't enforce that."

"I use my power as king for little." He glanced at Keyain. "But I will use it for this. If you even have a sip, you will be placed into substance help from one of the temples."

Acid burned at the back of his throat. "I thought you were going to rule differently."

"And I thought you've learned your lesson over the years."

"Why couldn't you have executed me for treason and this would all just end?"

Wyltam turned to face him, half of his face illuminated by the graying evening light. "I could never bring myself to give such an order," he said, his voice soft, almost thoughtful. "That's how I know you never truly loved Marietta."

His words were a wound in his chest, striking true and leaving him pained and breathless. He never wanted to issue that order against Marietta. Dyeiter said it was the only way to save his position as minister.

Realization washed over him as Wyltam held his gaze. If he truly loved Marietta, then why did he choose this fucking position? Even if there was no hope of repairing what was between them, how could he send her to such an end?

"I need you to catch up with your team. Keep your head down and focus on the war." He leaned in close. "We might lose this war, Keyain. Even if we can produce enough aithyr objects by spring, there's a chance we—" He heaved a breath and closed his eyes.

Keyain stilled himself. "What happened while I was gone?"

Wyltam shook his head. "Chorys Dasi has more magic than we could have ever planned for."

Icy dread shot through Keyain. "Tell me everything."

Chapter Fifty-Four
KEYAIN, BEFORE

Regardless of his age, Keyain's parents insisted on treating him like a child. Despite garnering the title of captain—which he achieved before his third decade—his success didn't matter to them. While such titles were often effortlessly obtained by younger nobles leveraging their family's influence, Keyain had earned his position through hard work, free of any parental manipulation.

None of that mattered to them. They focused on his connections and what benefits he could bring to the family's status. His parents often alluded to the idea of befriending the aloof prince, insinuating it as a means of advancing. His mother even mentioned an attempt to coincide his birth with the queen's child, despite the evident three-year gap, which led to another recent fight of theirs. As Keyain distanced himself from his parents' grip, their aspirations for his importance through associations grew increasingly absurd.

Even now, fresh from practice, his hair barely dried, he abandoned his afternoon plans at his parents' demand. Another lunch with another influential family, perhaps Kally this week? Though it's been a few months since they made him talk with Shaye, so there was always that looming possibility. It didn't matter that he knew these females within the confines of court life. His parents insisted he spend proper time with his marriage prospects, despite the dreadful females and their parents' hunger for the Vallynte wealth.

Keyain turned onto a new path in the Central Garden, halting when he ran into someone. "Oof, apologies. I wasn't …" He trailed off as he took in who it was.

"It's fine," Prince Wyltam said, glancing over his shoulder, his chest heaving.

The last time Keyain had been this close to the prince, they were children at gatherings where their parents met with the queen.

A voice called from down the path. The prince swore and faced the canopy above. "Give me a lift."

"A lift?"

Prince Wyltam gestured to the tree boughs hanging overhead. "And hurry."

Confused, Keyain cupped his hands together and hoisted him up. As Keyain went to grab the prince's legs, he pulled himself the rest of the way. He had always been on the lither side. Did fencing do that much for his build?

As soon as Prince Wyltam moved back toward the trunk, one of the Queen's Guard appeared around the corner, panting. "Have you seen the prince?"

Keyain shook his head. "Should I have seen him?"

The guard sighed and took off down the path. A second later, Wyltam landed next to him on the ground. "Thanks." He turned to leave without another word.

Unsure why he was compelled to speak, Keyain asked, "You're an excellent fencer, right?"

He paused, barely glancing over his shoulder. "I don't perform for people."

Keyain laughed, having heard that. "Would you like to practice sometime? Just us and not as a spectacle?"

The prince fully turned around and stared him down. "Sure. I'll send an invitation."

"Do you need my name or—"

"I know who you are." He pivoted and made his way down the path.

Keyain stood across from Prince Wyltam, his knees slightly bent and body turned to the side, his head facing his opponent. Stretched out in front of him was his foil, a fraction of the weight of a real sword which he had grown accustomed to. Wyltam's instructor gave the signal, and they sprang into action.

Keyain stepped forward, Wyltam matching his movement with the grace of a dancer with his feet barely audible on the wooden floor. As the prince neared, Keyain lunged and thrusted his foil toward him but nearly missed. The instructor called the point. Keyain looked down to see that Wyltam's tip touched his padded abdomen.

Surprised, Keyain went to comment. "That was—"

The prince turned around and returned to his spot without a word. Irritation prickled down Keyain's neck as he resumed his starting position. Rumors had it that Prince Wyltam was a skilled fencer, but Keyain was no amateur either. The next point wouldn't be so quick.

The instructor signaled them to go again. Keyain gripped his foil and moved forward with deliberate movements as he watched his feet, ready to dodge Prince Wyltam. The prince surged forward and thrusted, Keyain stepping back before it made contact and parrying another blow. That did nothing to slow the prince as he pressed forward, Keyain sliding back to near where he started. Frustrated, he grunted and jabbed forward, only to feel the tip of the prince's foil touch his shoulder.

"Touch. Point to Prince Wyltam."

Keyain blew out a breath, flexing his hand on his foil as he watched the prince return to his position, unfazed and unimpressed. He swallowed his embarrassment and molded it into the anger that got him through his training.

"On guard," the instructor called.

Rage fueled Keyain's advancement on the prince. He'd have to land a hit before him, which meant he'd have to be brutal and hard. Keyain drew in a steadying breath and drove forward with all his strength. He let out a strained exhale as the tip pressed into his stomach.

"You're not as good as I thought you'd be," Prince Wyltam said, lifting his wire-mesh mask.

Keyain tried to rein in his anger as he ripped his own from his head. "You're faster than you ought to be." He quickly shut his mouth. Unbelievable. He finally had the prince alone—something no one else had managed to do in a decade—and he insulted him. "Apologies. I didn't mean to offend."

"No offense taken." His dark eyes wandered over his body, his expression blank as he took him in. "You're all strength and used to fighting with a cumbersome weapon. Like a sword, the foil is an extension of your arm, except that it requires more finesse than brute strength. Quick to yield, easier to handle."

"I grew up taking lessons, too," Keyain said, his cheeks heating. "I know the basics."

Prince Wyltam cocked his head to the side, a hint of a smile on his lips. "You're interesting. If you'd like to continue practicing fencing, I'd enjoy your companionship, I think."

"You think?" Keyain blew out a laugh before he remembered who he spoke with. He bowed and said, "It'd be an honor, Your Grace."

"One stipulation, though, Captain Keyain."

He met the prince's gaze. "What would that be?"

Wyltam leaned in close, his voice dropping to a whisper. "No titles while we practice."

There was a glint in his eye that Keyain couldn't quite place, his heart hammering harder in his chest than it ought to with the prince so close. "I can allow that."

Prince Wyltam laughed, the smile cracking his lips because he slid his mask back on his face. "Let's see if you can last more than a second this time."

Much to his parents' delight, Keyain's relationship with the prince developed beyond fencing lessons. While Wyltam had always been aloof, he now attended gatherings if Keyain was there. He accepted offers on outings to the city as long as Keyain was by his side. Court had labeled them as an inseparable pair.

While the parties were enjoyable, nothing beat the moments they stole away with one another. Without the prying eyes of courtiers, Wyltam became a different person. His laughs became more open, his smiles not hidden behind long hair. The more time they spent together, the more Keyain witnessed them.

"Where are we going?" Keyain asked, blindly following Wyltam through a darkened stairwell. Keyain had nothing to guide him but his grip on the back of Wyltam's shirt. They had to be below the ground by now.

"It's not a surprise if I tell you."

"A light to see where I'm going might help me not—"

Wyltam came to an abrupt stop, Keyain's body pushing into his. Despite the proximity, neither moved away, a position he often found themselves in as of late. A light appeared in Wyltam's hand, illuminating the handsome planes of his face. The dark of his eyes matched the surrounding tunnels that stretched out in either direction. Keyain smiled and Wyltam returned it.

"Tunnels sprawl beneath the palace," Wyltam said, slipping his hand into Keyain's as he pulled them along. "Sealed up centuries ago by my great-grandfather. Or at least that's what my mother said."

"Why though?"

"To keep them hidden." His deep voice echoed across the stone walls. "So the royal family has somewhere to flee."

"Morbid."

"A soldier abhorring death? That's ill-fitting."

Keyain's fist tightened around Wyltam's grip. "Who said I'm abhorring?"

His laugh was breathy and deep, causing Keyain's chest to constrict. "That temper will get you in trouble."

"It hasn't yet."

"*Yet.*"

Keyain huffed, half enjoying his teasing, half feeling that anger rise. "Where are we *going*?"

"Impatient too?"

"Wyltam."

"We're almost there." He glanced at Keyain for only a moment before leading him down another tunnel. Their footsteps echoed, amplifying as the passage ended into a craggy cavern.

Stalactites hung like chandeliers from the stone way above, casting elongated shadows that danced as Wyltam entered the space. Somewhere, water dripped, the echoes mingling with their own breaths as Keyain turned on the spot.

"This is it."

Keyain turned to Wyltam. "A cavern is fascinating, but not what I had expected. Why are we here?"

Wyltam tightened his hand, Keyain realizing they were still clasped. "I found it a few years back and have been trying to decide what to do with it. It's perfectly removed from the world up there that I can … be myself." His gaze met Keyain's. "With you."

A tense silence settled between them, Wyltam's words lingering in an impossible existence. There have been many similar moments over the past few months, though never spoken aloud, no moves ever made. Wyltam proved to be the missing piece in his life, already having the success he needed elsewhere. He was the only person who ever saw his true self.

Keyain's freehand traced up Wyltam's arm, his palm coming to caress his cheek and Wyltam's breath hitched. Tracing the curve of his lips with his thumb, Keyain leaned in to feel their fullness against his.

"Wait," Wyltam said, resting his forehead against Keyain's. "If you're going to kiss me, do it because you want to, not because I'm the prince."

Keyain slid his fingers into the hair on the back of his head, pulling him closer. "Since the first day we fenced, you have been more than just the prince. You are a solace, a freedom. I want to kiss you because I think I love you."

With his eyes closed, Keyain didn't watch for a reaction. Part of him knew he wouldn't be rejected, not outright. How many times had they lain together, close enough for their lips to meet, yet holding back? The only difference between then and now was that they were completely alone.

Within a moment, Wyltam's mouth was on his, their lips parting to taste one another. Keyain's core melted as heat flooded his body, a tension fused with longing. Wyltam pressed closer and tugged Keyain to the ground. At some point, the light rolled away, distantly illuminating their bodies as they slowly undressed one another.

His skin, soft under Keyain's mouth and tongue, added to the building ache inside him, his breaths growing desperate and echoing off the stone. He was a fevered dream, a reprieve from reality. And with no one as their witness, Keyain made sure Wyltam left that hollowed space below the city-state knowing Keyain loved him and not his title.

Keyain kissed down the column of Wyltam's neck, his pulse fluttering underneath his lips. How fortunate for him to be here, for them to find each other and remain together for almost a decade.

These quiet afternoons were his favorite. Alone with the male he loved, where they could be themselves. While relationships like theirs weren't unheard of, they were kept in the shadows of court, playing along with the need for only rightfully born children to inherit titles and lands. Many nobles had their affairs. They were open secrets that no one discussed. However, their relationship was unlike any of those.

Wyltam tilted his chin, guiding Keyain's mouth to his. He tasted like black tea, reminiscent of wintry evenings, cold outside but a warmth enveloped indoors. He bit Wyltam's lip and earned a moan.

If anyone knew about them—about how close they truly were—then his rise through the guard would always be overshadowed. People would've assumed it was their relationship that placed Keyain in his role, when the reality was that he worked his ass off to get it.

Even now, on the eve of their departure to aid in culling the orcs flooding into Syllogi, Keyain knew his moment was coming. The decades of training, the years of being careful with Wyltam to spoil nothing. It all came to a head now.

Wyltam's ever-cold touch traced the length of his ear. "Don't go."

Keyain sighed and pulled away. Not this again. "It is an honor to fight for Satiros."

"It's only an honor if the fighting is honorable."

Keyain bristled and sat up. "And what would you know about honor?"

The expression dropped from Wyltam's face. "How do you know the orcs are dangerous?"

"Dangerous?" Keyain laughed and jumped from the bed, hastily grabbing his shirt. "They rape mothers and kill children in the countryside. They burn our crops, attack without mercy. You would know this if you ever bothered in politics."

"You are only listening to indoctrination that's being fed to you." Wyltam lounged on the bed, propped up on one arm and barely covered by the blanket. His form was slender, not adorned with bulging muscles, but beneath the surface lay a subtle definition. His build spoke of agility rather than raw strength, a tautness that hinted at endurance. Keyain turned away as he imagined his mouth trailing over his skin. "The orcs aren't these bloodthirsty monsters. Ask yourself—what are they running from?"

"You are a fool, Wyltam." Keyain's fingers fumbled over his buttons, his anger rising quicker than it should have. "Your mother should punish you for such thoughts about our enemies."

Wyltam rolled his eyes. "My mother has punished me for less. And she's looking for any excuse to show the other Syllogian city-states how much her army has grown under her rule. This isn't some heroic journey; you're going in to slaughter innocent people."

"Innocent people?" Keyain dropped his hands and leaned onto the bed, towering over Wyltam. "You could do more to care for the elves of this city-state and less the orcs lusting after us. Where's your love for your people, Your Grace?"

Addressing him with his honorifics had done just the job Keyain had hoped. Wyltam lifted himself up, his quiet rage lurking underneath. "First, there are more than elves who live here."

Keyain sighed. "You knew what I meant."

"Second, I care about all people, including orcs. What do you know of the orcs outside of your military education? What do you know about their civilization? Or the problems they have in their lands? I ask you again—what do you think they're running from?"

"It's what they're running toward, and if I have to explain this to you, then let's hope your mother has a long reign." Keyain stood to his full height, glaring down at the male he loved, wishing he wouldn't be such a fool. "It doesn't matter where they live or their troubles. What matters is how it impacts us and our people."

Wyltam shook his head and gazed past Keyain to the window beyond. "That's where you're incredibly wrong."

Keyain ignored his comment and reached for his pants. When they returned victorious, then he'd understand the truth of what Keyain said.

Ever since he was promoted to the title illustris, his career had halted. Sure, he oversaw fifty captains and all their subordinates, but where was the growth beyond this? Only General Mylax and the minister of protection sat above him, and neither of those males would be leaving anytime soon. And if they were, there were his fellow illustris who had been in this position for decades. Could Keyain live like them and accept that's where he'd ended up? The answer has been and will always be no.

However, the queen was keen on pursuing the orcs. If Keyain could show his dedication and lead his legion to victory, then perhaps it would set him up to take a position one day. He could overshadow his peers and his superiors, putting himself in the eyes of the queen for his hard work.

"If you do this," Wyltam said, drawing him from his thoughts, "if you go, then I won't be here when you return."

Keyain scoffed. "You don't mean that." Wyltam's gaze was that of stone, unbudging and unforgiving. "You can't ask me to not serve my city-state."

"You can choose murder, or you can choose me." Wyltam stood and reached for his clothes. "But you can't have both."

"It's not murder when it's justified."

Wyltam turned his back to him. "Death is never justified."

His words left Keyain stumbling. "This is an empty threat. Orcs aren't even people, Wyltam. They're barbaric and have this inner urge to kill and destroy. If we do nothing to stop them—"

"You're dismissed." Wyltam kept his back to him, acting as if Keyain were no longer there.

"I leave tomorrow. I could *die*." Keyain's throat tightened. "Don't leave things like this."

"I have no interest in people who serve my mother's selfish motivations. Now go. Your prince is ordering you."

Keyain flexed his fists, wanting to punch something, anything. Instead, he lumbered to the door and paused. "I have no interest in people who keep me from my duty. My queen comes before anyone, including *you*." He enunciated his anger by slamming the door behind him.

Chapter Fifty-Five
ELYSE

Though they spoke through magic, Elyse knew Wyltam was angry. Maybe it was because she waited to tell him about Queen Octavya's strange offer, or maybe it was because she'd made it at all. Either way, she pushed it aside. Obsessing over it wouldn't help her get through the rest of their days in Amigys.

As she finished her conversation with Wyltam that evening, she took her time getting ready. Kurtys had arranged for her to dine with Layla and Assyl tonight. After discussing the plan with Seth, they agreed it was important for Elyse to build a rapport with them—something the Satiroan Ambassadors in Amigys had never managed. Seth then confessed that he was considering replacing one of them with Kurtys. While she wanted to agree, some small part of herself worried about who would join her at parties back home. The disturbing realization made her encourage Seth to give him that position.

Elyse slid her last ring into place when she heard the knock from her balcony. She stepped into the main part of her room to find Wynn lingering near the doorway. He stopped at the sight of her, suddenly drawing himself up straight and clearing his throat. "You look lovely."

She fanned out the skirt of her dress. At first glance, the thin material appeared muted black, but when it caught the light, it shimmered in iridescent shades of blue and green. It hugged her curves more than she cared for, but at least the color suited her. "I didn't know they could make such a fabric."

"The fabric, right." He closed the space between them and crossed his arms over his chest. "Kurtys gave me the location. Send a word if you need me."

"I always need you," she teased, heading toward the door. "But it's comforting knowing you'll be close by."

Wynn flexed his fists once, twice, then nodded. Elyse waved as left, finding Kurtys waiting for her at the end of the hallway.

The walk to the room was brief. Kurtys mentioned that ambassadors usually stay outside the palace, but suspected Elyse would prefer to remain nearby.

"I would rather see the city," she admitted as Kurtys knocked.

"I'll keep that in mind for—"

The door opened and an array of voices greeted them. "Finally, the Satiroans arrive." Layla hung against the frame, her smile loose and accent slurring. "Please, welcome to our humble party."

Elyse turned to Kurtys. "I thought you said this was just us with Layla and Assyl," she hissed under her breath.

"It was supposed to be." Kurtys grabbed Layla's elbow. "This was supposed to be a dinner with the four of us."

"Four of us and our closest friends with a liquid dinner." She gestured behind her. "And you call us serious. I promise that everyone here has been approved by me and no one will ask you to dance." She said the second part to Elyse with a mischievous smile.

Elyse watched as the drinks began to pour, and how quickly revelers downed them. In the corner, there was a group of people hollering and cheering as a male chugged from a bottle.

Layla slipped a glass into Elyse's hand, the liquid a light red and sparkling with green olives sunken into the bottom. "Try this."

"Oh, I don't know."

Kurtys took his and gulped it. Elyse shot him an incredulous look. He shrugged. "There's not much we can do now other than enjoy ourselves."

Layla encouraged Elyse to drink, and when the first splash of alcohol hit her tongue, she was surprised. Sweet and bitter with a touch of bubbles. She took another sip.

"See? Not so bad. Come, Satiroans, meet my friends."

Layla turned to walk away, expecting them to follow. Kurtys grabbed Elyse by the arm and dragged her in further.

Through her glasses, she saw streaks of aithyr illuminating in the air, with some strands flowing into the attendees. The thickest one, however, circled around a grand fountain at the center of the room. Layla took them past it. The creature had a feminine form, with seaweed hair cascading over its shoulders and webbed fingers weaving through it. The sculpture's gaze was fixed on its own tail, adorned with membrane fins that flared outwards with graceful elegance. Elyse nearly walked into someone carrying a tray of scallops served in their shells as she kept glancing back at it.

They reached the corner of the room and found a group engaged in a game, each participant taking their turn tossing a card into the center. They all groaned as a card showing an elderly elvish woman was laid down.

"Drink up," Assyl said Assyl said with a laugh. When he spotted them, he waved them over. "My friends, please play."

"Oh, I don't ..." Elyse shook her head and stepped back.

"She's never played Flick before," Kurtys said, taking a seat next to him.

"More of a reason to join," Assyl said, moving over so Elyse could sit with him on the couch. "But more importantly, more of a reason to drink. Come."

Assyl explained the rules to Elyse while the other players, three females and two males, chimed in with the details he missed. The game was based on chance, with each player hoping to reveal the highest-value card on their turn. The cards had different effects on the players, determined by their hierarchy, and the order of play would change with each round. Assyl shuffled the deck and doled the players five cards, instructing Elyse to keep her hand face down. The female seated on the other side of Assyl flipped their first card and tossed it on the table.

"Orange tree, not a strong start."

They went in a circle and a different female turned over an archer, which made the people who came after her swear.

"Archer shoots down the line, so if you go after her, you are going to drink. Unless"—the next person revealed a card with a suit of armor— "you have the armor. Rych, you bastard."

When it was Elyse's turn, one of the males said, "Get ready to drink."

Elyse tossed her card down, revealing a black drakon drawn onto its surface, its mouth spitting fire.

"Seriously?" Rych shook his head.

Assyl took a sip of his drink and said, "Black drakon defeats everything, even suits of armor. Lucky hand."

Elyse stared at the card, then back at Assyl. "What do I win?"

"Your sobriety," he said. "And the occasional bragging rights. Clear the table."

As they played, Elyse learned that the other participants were native Amigyans who had befriended Layla and Assyl over the years.

"You and Kurtys are more fun than the ambassadors," one of the females said as she tied back her dark curly hair. "Much more like the Satiroans I remember when I traveled there."

"You've been to Satiros?" Kurtys asked as he took his cards from Assyl.

"Many times. We love Satiros." Her expression grew serious and leaned in. "I know you're here because of the war and all the"—she gestured vaguely with her hand—"but no one holds ill will toward Satiros, even with your new treaty. Most of us just want to refrain from the fighting." The female flipped over her card and slammed it down on the table. "The scholar! Give me your hand, Michalys."

Elyse sipped her drink. The queen and king had said that to her among the group of Satiroans and to Seth in private. They were trying to stay uninvolved, which was why the Chorys Dasian ambassadors were present at events. Amigys wanted to position themselves as neutral ground. From what Seth had gathered, Chorys Dasi wasn't thrilled with that stance. They took a risk hosting them to further that point of neutrality.

After a few rounds, Elyse finished her drink, and the alcohol flushed her cheeks. Another appeared in her hand from Layla.

"I like to make a good impression," she said with a shrug. "Plus, you're the most pleasant person Kurtys has brought along, which doesn't say much, but you are better."

Kurtys glared, which made Layla laugh and fall into his lap. She wrapped her arms around his neck and whispered something in his ear that made his cheeks redden. When she stood, Kurtys joined her. "I'll be back," he promised Elyse.

"I'll keep an eye on her," Assyl said, shooing them away.

As Assyl dealt out the next hand, her skin prickled. Time slowed as she looked up to see Dominykas hovering behind Kurtys's empty chair. "Mind dealing me a hand?"

When their eyes met, Elyse quickly averted her gaze. In the absence of his mask, his features were strikingly handsome. His tousled brown hair framed his high cheekbones, his eyes bright and alert. He recognized her, but she acted as if she did not know who he was.

"This is the missing Dominykas from the other night," Assyl explained. "Dom, Layla said you were sulking."

"It was brooding, actually," Dominykas said as he threw down his card. "There's no better place to brood than a dark garden. Isn't that right, Lady Elyse?"

She offered a smile. "I wouldn't know." She tossed her card to the table and revealed an ornamental column broken in two.

Assyl hissed. "Shit luck. You automatically lose your next two hands unless you flip the unicorn."

"How do you remember this all?" she asked as she took a big sip, wishing her heart to ease. Dominykas claimed the seat beside her, their knees nearly brushing. He was too close, his gaze scorching on her skin.

"Years of practice," Assyl said. "And lots of practice within those years."

When Elyse's turn came back, Dominykas heckled a male whose card negatively affected Elyse. "She already has to drink," he said. "You didn't think once was enough?"

"As if I could control what cards I had."

"It's fine," Elyse said, cutting off Dominykas' response. "I don't mind drinking."

"Spoken like a true Kyaerie," Assyl said, clapping her back.

With the next hand, Dominykas leaned over. "Have I offended you?"

Elyse regretted looking at him, her mind numbing as she noted the color of his eyes—hazel with flecks of brown and green. She fidgeted with her rings, twisting them as she focused on the table.

"What is there to offend?" Elyse asked.

"You seem—"

She threw back the rest of her drink. "I'll return shortly," she said, shaking her empty glass.

Her legs couldn't move fast enough, her head was unable to clear itself. Elyse wouldn't have another drink, not when Dominykas's mouth was etched into her memory. She didn't know him. She had no reason to feel this way.

Elyse scoured the room, checking the opposite corner with no luck. Someone asked her if she needed help.

"Have you seen Kurtys? If you know him."

"Hope you're not a jealous lover because …" They wagged their eyebrows.

Elyse grimaced and took off, heading toward the exit. Of course, he was having sex when she wanted to leave. She thought of Wynn and his promise from earlier.

The hallway air felt considerably cooler. She contemplated returning to her room alone but dismissed the idea. It didn't matter what the Amigyans said about Satiros. She was the king's voice, which made her a target. Instead, Elyse closed her eyes and pulled aithyr into her body. Elyse imagined the scar across Wynn's face, the way his hair was always unruly in its tie. *"Come find me? I'm ready to leave."*

When she stopped, she kept her eyes closed for a moment and leaned against the wall, enjoying the quiet.

"Careful." It was Dominykas's voice, low and quiet, making Elyse open her eyes. "I'm beginning to think you're following me." He stood near the restroom and headed toward the door. The space narrowed between them, his hands tucked into the pockets of his pants.

"I could say the same for you."

"So you do remember me from the garden." His smirk was maddening.

Elyse laughed lightly. "The brooding, yes."

"The 'saving your life' was more like it, unless you weren't about to swim with the sharks." He was close enough that she could reach out and touch him. He leaned a shoulder into the wall, his gaze flitting to her mouth, then meeting hers again. "I don't think you ever thanked me."

"I was a bit preoccupied with my thoughts that evening."

"Hm, yes. A bit of brooding yourself." He smiled and tilted his head. "Are you trying to get out of here?"

"Desperately so."

A smoke appeared in his hand and he wiggled it between his fingers. "I could use some company."

Elyse's instincts urged her forward, the temptation to say yes nearly overwhelming. She wanted nothing more than to take his hand and leave with him. Blinking, she broke her stupor. Her promise to never pursue another Chorys Dasian echoed in her mind. Elyse pushed off the wall and took a step away from him. "Not tonight."

His gaze flicked over her shoulder, his brows furrowing before settling into a neutral expression.

Elyse turned to find Wynn in his guard uniform. "Ready, Elyse?"

She nodded and looked back at Dominykas. "Have a good evening."

"Don't make me say it again."

She paused and asked, "Say what?"

He tsked. "If it was a good evening, this wouldn't be the end of our conversation."

Elyse adjusted her glasses as she met his gaze. "Then just evening to you."

Dominykas's laugh made a smile come to her lips, and she hid behind her hand as she turned to Wynn. After a moment of walking together, he asked, "Who's that?"

"An ambassador," she said, hating the way her mouth naturally smiled.

Wynn hummed as he glanced over his shoulder. Then his hand slipped to her lower back as they reached the corner. When she went to question it, it disappeared.

Elyse sensed herself being drawn away from Dominykas, convinced she could still feel his eyes on her as they arrived at her door. As she unlocked it and stepped in, Wynn lingered for a moment. "Mind if I come in?"

"What happened to not wanting a soldier spending ample time with me alone?"

He rolled his eyes. "No one is here to see. Plus, I'm not in the mood to hop between balconies."

She held the door for him and let him through. Wynn continued to ask about her night, starting with where Kurtys was.

Elyse leaned out of the bathroom as she undid her hair. "I think he was having sex with someone."

Wynn scoffed. "And he just left you there?"

"With Assyl, the one from Kyaeri." Elyse ducked inside the bathroom and reached for the ties on the back of her dress. "He's friendly. I didn't mind." Elyse's arm twinged and she swore.

"You all right in there?"

"No, I can't get my dress. Do you mind helping?"

Wynn didn't answer at first. Then she heard the couch shift and found him waiting in the doorway. Elyse turned and waited for his help. When Wynn touched her, he paused for a moment, and she glanced back. "Is there a problem?"

His eyes darkened, his gaze dropping to his hands. "I'm figuring out how to undo it."

The dress loosened with Wynn's calloused touch grazing her skin. She held the fabric to her body. "Thank you," she murmured.

"I'll let the other guards know to stay up for Kurtys," Wynn said, taking a step back. "Afterward, I'll head to bed myself."

"Good night, then."

As he went deeper into the room, Elyse followed him. "I thought you didn't want to hop balconies?"

"It's easier going down than it is up," he said, smiling. "See you in the morning."

Elyse shrugged and readied herself for bed. As she did, she went over the list of meetings she had for tomorrow, not because she wanted to, but because her mind kept drifting to Dominykas. If left to think about him, she'd wonder what going off with him alone might have felt like and how much she might have enjoyed it.

Chapter Fifty-Six
MARIETTA

With everything else in Marietta's life spiraling, at least her plan with the temples moved forward. As she climbed the Temple of Oramytiz's steps, a controlled smile lingered on her lips, performing for the crowd at the base. Her influence was growing—favor for her was undeniable. But did it matter with Wyltam's cold distance looming?

Of course, it mattered. Still, the sting of his absence gnawed at her. His anger was justified, reasonable even. She knew it would take time—time to process, to accept. Gods, she'd be furious too if he had hidden something so monumental from her. Fey were real, and their enemies were all the more lethal.

"How are you holding up?" Coryn asked, his voice a low murmur as he walked beside her.

Marietta's gaze fixed on the pale yellow stone of the temple. "I'll manage."

He glanced toward her, his expression softer than usual. "Even without him here?"

She tensed at the mention, forcing herself to focus on the deity's statue ahead—their face shrouded by a veil, untouchable and distant, much like Wyltam now. The sight invoked an unease slithering through her chest. She rubbed against her breastbone, wishing it would still.

Coryn's gaze pressed into her, but he must have let it go.

Marietta paused at the top, sending the crowd gathered on the street to uproar. She waved and flashed a bright, hollow smile. Wyltam should've been there.

Their footsteps echoed in the entrance, joined by the ever-present scraping of the plate armor of her guards. The elven attendant bowed their head as they approached, their yellow tunic embroidered with a chimera motif in a glistening shade of deeper gold, marking them as an iros. "Welcome, Your Grace. Please, if you could follow me."

Trailing behind them, Marietta lingered in the entry as her eye caught sight of the inscriptions that stretched from the ceiling to the floor. The first read, *"Do not judge one's character by the guise they wear, for appearances deceive, but the soul reveals truth."* It gave her pause, wondering if this was just one of many reasons the elves mistrusted the temples.

"Are you from Satiros?" Marietta asked the attendant, turning to catch up.

"I am, Your Grace. Born and raised."

They fell into an easy silence as they continued down the hall and ended at a door. The iros turned, their voice firm. "Only Queen Marietta and Coryn of Therypon may enter beyond this point."

Marietta's brow furrowed. "Why?"

"The followers of Oramytiz restrict who may witness our ceremonies. At the end of yours, you will swear a vow of secrecy, Your Grace."

She faced the rest of her guard. "We'll be fine."

Ryder and Adalyn exchanged glances while Tolis gestured with his hands. "We'll be right here."

The prayer chamber appeared relatively plain with soft light drifting in from a window in the ceiling. A warm glow created by the sunlight bouncing off the yellow stone highlighted the altar. Beyond it stood a statue of Oramytiz.

"Queen Marietta, please have a seat up here. Coryn, we have a space for you to sit off to the side." The iros took them to their seats and continued. "You must not interfere with the ceremony under any circumstances, and we ask that you remain silent for the duration."

"That I can do."

"Very well." The iros clapped their hands and a dozen more attendants of Oramytiz came through doors behind the statue.

A familiar face stepped forward. Izzy took the space in front of the altar and said, "Lady Marietta, we are here today to have you witness the power of our deity, Oramytiz." One of the other iros brought over a chalice and set it on the altar. "In our world, truth bends into lies, and lies often expose hidden truths. Marietta, you're about to walk that line. To seek Oramytiz's claim is to bend reality to your will and to see beyond the meaning of one's words. You can't reach for the chalice without risking the trap of deception."

The iros lifted the vessel, its design plain and unordinary to the eye. "This chalice is a reflection of your motives, a seer of your heart's depths. Should your soul bear no dishonesty, the ceremony will begin. Do you vow to keep secret the truth of our deity's domains?"

"I do," Marietta said, her voice ringing through the chamber.

"And do you come to us with true intentions, using the power of Oramytiz for only altruistic reasons?"

She answered again. "I do."

"Then drink and reveal the power of Oramytiz."

The iros handed her the chalice and gestured for her to drink. The contents inside were the dark red of blood, the scent reminiscent of alcohol. She downed the liquid, swallowing the thick and pulpy wine. The iros of Oramytiz stared at her with blank expressions.

"Do I drink all of it?"

A dozen discordant voices sounded at once. *"It's already gone."* Except the voices hadn't come from the iros.

Marietta glanced down into the chalice, not only finding it empty, but the vessel changed. What was just stone turned to glass, the edges a rusty orange with a bright golden light emanating from its center.

"What happened to it?" she asked Izzy.

A hand pierced through their stomach, tearing a gaping hole through their center. A being emerged, their face shifting with every blink, never the same twice. Ominous voices echoed as the figure crawled through Izzy's body, which collapsed into a heap on the ground. *"You should ask what happened to you."*

Marietta shrieked and crawled backward, dropping the chalice. The glass broke into pieces that began to shake and slither toward her. She jumped to her feet and turned to run to Coryn, finding him with a knife at his throat. Behind him stood Azarys and Sylas, except they didn't appear as their normal selves. Sylas glistened with striations of gems streaking through his body. Azarys appeared exactly as he had in the *Lyken's Guide to Chorys Dasi:* two horns curved from his forehead, his nails elongated into claws sharper than the knife he wielded.

"Careful now," came the voices.

Marietta spun to find shards of glass crawling up her body as the shifting figure came around the altar. Panicked, she swiped at the shards, only for each piece to pierce her skin and stick to it when she tried to pull away. She screamed again, the glass dissolving into her body.

"Somebody help!" she cried out to the frozen iros.

The figure approached her, their head tilting as if they inspected her. *"Such a reaction is unexpected."*

Marietta blinked, trying to calm her heart. "Oramytiz?" Her voice shook more than she cared to admit.

"It is I."

"Coryn, he's …" Marietta said, turning to find him sitting peacefully in his chair. "I don't understand. There were two more people a second ago."

"Why are you here?"

Marietta steadied herself and examined her arms, discovering glowing golden veins beneath her skin. She lifted them, presenting the sight to the deity. "What is happening? Why is no one reacting?"

"What do you seek?" They approached, their appearance settling on no face for more than a second, beautiful and unbecoming, horrifying and glorious at the same. Their head tilted toward her arms as if they inspected them.

"I—I'm here for a deal."

"And?"

Marietta hated the shiver that worked her way through her body. She glanced at Coryn, finally noticing that his stare was far off and glossy. She turned to the iros, finding the same. Where blood and gore should have pooled from the torn-open corpse, only Izzy's serene form remained undisturbed.

None of it was real.

"It's all an illusion."

Their lips curved into a smile. *"Correct. Now, what do you offer?"*

Marietta thought of the inscription on the wall when she walked in. "Claim me as your iros and I'll help create a world where no one is judged by their appearances, like pilinos."

Oramytiz frowned. *"An impossible task, though I see the truth in your words. Do you understand what it is to be an iros?"*

"Being your champion."

Their laugh rocked through her skull. *"May I see your arms more closely?"*

Marietta nodded slowly and lifted them.

Oramytiz's touch was warm and gentle, like the afternoon sun on her skin. Their fingers traced the new veins along her forearms. *"They were right. You are of a dying breed, though not the last."*

"I'm what?"

"I accept your deal."

Oramytiz struck her, their hand piercing straight through her skull.

After a day of rest, the sharp ache in her head had finally dulled. Perhaps it was the result of being claimed by another deity. Oramytiz hadn't been kind in their claiming, the visions clinging to her mind like a persistent mayfly. Even in sleep, they lingered—Izzy collapsing, reminiscent of Valeriya's death. When the pain subsided enough, she seized the first distraction she could.

Outside, the sky was dark as Marietta paced the library in the Royal's Wing, her eyes skimming the shelves. Coryn trailed her, occasionally offering his opinion.

"Royal Pets and Their Peculiar Habits," he grumbled. "Who would even read these?"

"Royals with an affinity for animals," she answered as she finished reading titles on the shelf over. Nothing had pertained to fey or even hinted at anything useful. "Oh, how about this for you: *The Courtly Collection of Classical Literature: An Anthology for the Aristocracy?*" She held up the cover for him to see.

Coryn gave her a mocking smile. "You know me better than anyone."

"The very best," she replied with a hum, fingers pausing on a spine.

He glanced over her shoulder and read aloud, "*Divine Diplomacy: Royal Relations with the Deities of Duality.* That might be useful for both of us."

Marietta pulled the book from the shelf, her stomach twisting as she peeked at the small text inside.

Her face must've shown her displeasure. Coryn asked, "Did you want to talk about it?"

She cleared her throat. "Hard to talk about a book I've never read."

He pinned her with a stare, then sighed, gesturing to the narrow couch at the end of the aisle. "Being an iros to one deity is a lot to take on. Being an iros to multiple is unheard of. It's all the temples can talk about. They say you are a blessing from the gods."

Guilt knotted her stomach. "That isn't true."

"But it could be."

"Coryn, I saw the deities. I talked to them."

He nodded. "As with Therypon. See? You are divine."

She shook her head slowly, her brows knitting together. "I don't think that's it. Seidytar came to me, and we struck a deal. She offered it—mentioned that I would spread chaos."

Coryn's eyes narrowed in thought. "And the others?"

"Similar." She hesitated, running a hand through her hair before continuing. "But with them, I made the offer—it was my deal. They all said something strange, though: that I'm different. Oramytiz called me a 'dying breed.'"

His gaze sharpened. "What does that mean?"

"I don't know. It's … overwhelming." A beat passed, and she forced herself to continue. "I've been wanting to ask—do I have their abilities now?"

Coryn took a moment before answering. "Not yet. You'll need to complete their ceremonies, like you did with Therypon."

Her gaze fell to the floor as she absorbed the information. The tight knot in her chest loosened, if only a little. "I'll have to do those, eventually."

"Most likely after the wedding." He glanced toward the shelves, the silence stretching between them. "I'll search for any texts we have on deities and deals."

Her gaze snapped back to him. "Discreetly," she said. The memory of Wyltam's warnings tugged at her thoughts. "Keep this between us. For now."

Coryn's mouth twitched, as though he might argue. His eyes returned to her, searching her face. But after a long moment, he only nodded.

They wandered the remaining part of the library, both in silence. His expression was serious and pensive, as if he considered what she shared. Marietta tried not to think about it.

As they neared the exit, a faint melody drifted down the hallway. The sound wrapped around her, pulling her toward its source. Without a word, she quickened her pace, her heart racing with each step. When she reached the music room, she froze, breath catching in her throat as her eyes fell on the one playing.

Wyltam sat at the piano, the room lowly lit with a single light globe hovering over his head. His fingers moved gracefully across the keys, coaxing out a hauntingly beautiful melody. His brow was furrowed, his eyes closed. She recalled him mentioning that playing helped clear his mind.

Hesitantly, she stepped into the room, careful to not disturb his focus. The melody swelled and swelled, building to a crescendo before tapering off into a gentle, lingering refrain. There was a sense of longing in the music, a bittersweet yearning. Seeing him play stirred something in her chest, as if another piece of the Wyltam puzzle fell into her lap.

As the last notes faded into silence, Marietta clapped lightly.

"I don't enjoy performing for people," he said, glancing over his shoulder, his expression hinting at a tired smile.

She slowly approached him. "It sounded like you were performing for yourself. That's what made it beautiful."

"I had a few technical flaws," he admitted. He stared momentarily, then he moved over on the bench, offering the other half to Marietta.

She took the seat next to him. "I couldn't tell you were troubled, but I know you don't play just for the sake of it."

Wyltam studied her before nodding and turning his gaze away. "Another deity?"

"So you've heard."

He sighed as a translucent dome formed around them. "Whatever you're doing, it's dangerous."

"I'm not—"

He gave her a pointed look.

Marietta shook her head, her anger rising. "Were you listening?"

"I didn't know it was you and Coryn until too late."

She needed to walk away before her anger jeopardized their fragile truce. As she started to stand, Wyltam's hand lightly gripped her arm, halting her movement. "It's working."

"What is?"

"You're dangerous plan. The people love you. There are rumors that this is a divine sign that we'll win the war. Even nobles have taken an interest in the deities." He stared at his lap, then turned to Marietta. "I hope whatever you're giving in exchange is worth it."

She could hear the deities' voices, their commanding tones vivid from the moment the deals were struck. A faint smile touched Marietta's lips. "I think it will be."

"Power rarely is."

The dome dropped around them, Marietta taking it as her cue to leave. She stood and made her way to the door. She paused on the threshold, glancing back. "Will you come to bed with me tonight?"

His silence was deafening.

At last, he said, "Goodnight, Marietta."

Chapter Fifty-Seven

KEYAIN

"No one saw the person who did this?" Keyain swallowed his building anger as he glared at the crude drawing. It was of Wyltam bending Marietta over in a sexual manner. The king's ears were depicted as being clipped. Scratched above were the words 'Ever Elven.' A mockery of not just the crown but the entire city-state.

"It might've happened between shifts, sir," the captain at his side answered. His shoulders were tensed, and a flush of red crept up his cheeks.

Good, he should be embarrassed that it took half the morning for his guards to realize the drawing was even on the rampart. Keyain pinched the bridge of his nose and swatted at the groundskeepers. "Get it off as soon as possible."

Keyain strode away, his expression carefully neutral. He knew any display of emotion could fuel further rumors, that if he showed even a hint of anger, they would brand him as jealous. Yet, if he appeared too content, people would interpret it as disrespect toward the crown. After all his years in court, he was done being fodder for gossip.

Wyltam's words echoed in Keyain's mind, tightening his fists as he grappled with the revelation about the fey. The weight of his barely contained anger and anxiety pressed down on him. Wyltam's serious eyes and steady voice had left no room for doubt—this wasn't a lie. Keyain's gut twisted, the memory of their conversation making his heart pound. The threat was real, and everything had just changed. Yet here he was, having to make sure minute things were taken care of.

Keyain spoke through gritted teeth. "Give me a full list of names of who was on duty last night."

The captain fl inched. "It was dark in this section, Minister. I'm sure that—"

"Must I remind you it's their job to watch even the dark parts of the wall?" Keyain pivoted him, looming over the captain as he pointed to the guards' tower. "They were less than thirty feet away. They should have at least heard someone. The picture is quite … elaborate."

"I make sure my guards aren't sleeping. Every hour, I patrol the grounds and—"

"I'm not doubting their vigilance or yours as captain. I'm questioning their loyalty to the crown."

The captain stuttered, his breaths creating subtle plumes of smoke in the chilled morning air.

Without turning back, Keyain resumed his stride toward the gate. "I want that list." His anger simmered, barely contained. He couldn't understand why his day had to start like this or why he had to see them portrayed in such a way. If fate was a game for the gods, they seemed to take particular pleasure in tormenting him.

Slowly counting to ten, Keyain gestured for the captain to come along. "If your guards didn't see anyone," he began, his tone measured, "then how can we deter future vandalism? Will it embolden others to follow suit?" He paused, glancing at him. "Give people seeds and they will grow a garden. If I were in your position, I'd increase patrols along the rampart. Search for any dim spots, and we'll ensure they're properly illuminated."

The captain sighed and saluted him. "Understood, Minister Keyain. Again, I take full responsibility—"

"For their actions, I know. I want that list by the end of the day, regardless."

Keyain passed through the palace gates, weighed down by the familiar stress of his position. He craved something to dull the edge, something strong enough to carry him through his meetings. A whiskey with a sharp bite, one that would knock him out cold after a few glasses, was what he needed.

The unexpected longing surprised him, stirring both confusion and concern. He hadn't realized how deeply his reliance on alcohol had taken root until it was suddenly out of reach. Without that familiar crutch, he was left exposed and vulnerable, a stark reminder of his problem and how well Wyltam understood him. Keyain dug his nails into his palms as he made his way to his meetings.

As the morning wore on, a dull ache settled in his skull, growing more intense with Adalyn and Ryder's relentless bickering. Once more, they veered off-topic while delivering their updates. Adalyn reported that citizens in the countryside remained adamant about not relocating behind the city-state walls, expressing discontent with the new queen and the alliance. However, they had persuaded some to enlist in the army, though they still fell short of their recruitment targets.

Keyain glanced at the two sitting across the table from him, catching Adalyn rolling her eyes at Ryder with her arms crossed. Ryder, per usual, ignored Adalyn's growing irritation. Peryn sat to Keyain's left, watching them with a bemused smile. Normally, Amryth would've stepped in to stop Ryder at this point. Deyra would have told her to let them continue, that if she stopped them now, they'd have more energy to bicker later. The change in dynamics only made him want to focus harder.

"Anything else to report?" Keyain asked, pulling the conversation back to their meeting. "Still only trade ships leaving Reyila's port?"

"Correct, with no troopships being deployed," Ryder answered, running a hand through his fluff of auburn hair. "The only movement was that group hovering in the Ouresk Forest. Not enough for a war. Perhaps defending their borders?"

"Perhaps." Keyain set the papers aside. "Monitor their location."

"How many ships have left port in the last week?" Adalyn asked, lounging back to pick at her nail.

"As in trade ships?" Ryder asked.

"Well, you just said there weren't troopships—yes, trade ships."

"You don't need to be so—"

"Has there been an uptick in the traffic coming out of Reyila? We know they're using them to transport people to and from Reyila."

Keyain paused at that and flipped to the last page of the report. "Have someone pull the numbers."

"It's possible they're using trade ships to move troops." Adalyn sat back and raised a brow.

"Or it could be people fleeing Reyila because of war," Peryn said, crossing his arms.

"No point in speculating. Ryder, have your scout look into it. I'll work with King Wyltam if he gets an update from his mage inside Chorys Dasi."

"If he had one, he should've already shared it," Peryn pointed out. "I'm aware," Keyain said through clenched teeth. "But we had diplomats in their city, and we've heard nothing since we banned the Chorys Dasians from the palace. I want to know if they're alive."

"Likely not," Adalyn said with a grim expression. "You mentioned they were pretty gruesome during the Orcish Skirmishes."

Keyain's mind flashed back to the bodies—mutilated beyond recognition, left in pieces by Chorys Dasi's brutality. He forced the memory down, swallowing the fear that crept up his throat. "They could be alive, which means we could extract them."

"If a mage can't get in there, what hope do we have?" Peryn asked, his frustration growing evident.

Ryder leaned in, voice firm. "If we send anyone, it should be to retrieve the queen. Cut the snake off at the head."

Adalyn rolled her eyes again. "And if they don't know who the queen is? Not as if anyone has seen her."

The royals of Chorys Dasi have always been secretive, their queen never showing her face in public. Thought to be some weird family tradition, the other city-states of Syllogi tried not to question their ways.

"We've seen her brother," Keyain interjected. "Though he's a maniac like the rest of their lot." He glanced at his aithyr clock, his mind already shifting to the next task. "I want to speak with the prisoner before my next meeting," he added, turning to Peryn. "Take me to him."

As they made their way to the dungeons, Keyain's thoughts circled the half-elf they had captured—the one accused of the murders. Wyltam had tasked him with determining whether the prisoner had ties to the elven purist group he had somehow uncovered. Despite Peryn's success in capturing the suspect, Keyain sensed that Wyltam doubted his competence. The delay in the trial had only heightened his unease. But he couldn't afford to push back. Wyltam's warning was clear—this was his final chance.

"Anything I should know before I talk to him?" Keyain asked.

"He's an excellent liar. It's part of the reason it took so long for us to find him. He knew how to cover his tracks."

"Noted. Thanks for investigating this a few months ago. I know you typically deal with internal issues at court." Keyain clasped his shoulder. "At least you've been able to focus on that since you found the murderer."

Keyain sat in the interrogation room, waiting while Peryn escorted the prisoner. Peryn wouldn't be pleased about him speaking to the half-elf alone, but it was Wyltam's directive. Wyltam believed Jory might be more willing to talk to a minister, given his father's position. While most rumors held some truth, it still caught Keyain off guard to learn that Leyland had a bastard pilinos son.

When Keyain had first brought Marietta to Satiros, Leyland had hinted at his pilinos child, suggesting he might bring him to court one day. He had even thanked Keyain for setting a precedent. But Leyland never followed through, and as Jory was dragged into the room, Keyain understood why.

Jory's loose curls hung tangled around his face. Unsure if it was the sterile lighting of the room or from spending weeks underground, his brown skin appeared ashen. While all signs point to a weakened prisoner, his gray eyes were lit with a fire Keyain was familiar with.

As Jory sat, Keyain turned to Peryn. "I'll talk to him alone this first time."

Peryn's posture stiffened. "Are you sure?"

Keyain clenched his jaw. "An order, Peryn. Just him and I."

His subordinate nodded his head once before closing the door softly behind him. The isolated room was typically set aside for rigorous examinations, with no one able to overhear.

Jory's stare took him back. He thought the half-elf would be scared half to death after being confined in the dungeon and pulled into a room alone. Instead, his gaze locked onto Keyain with an unanticipated fury. In another surprise, Jory spoke first. "I have no more information to share. I would have never done that to fellow pilinos."

Keyain nodded and took out the leather-bound notebooks that were found in Jory's apartment. He drummed his fingers on the tabletop and watched carefully for any reaction in his expression, finding none. Remembering back to Peryn's warning, Keyain opened to a marked page and began reading out loud.

"'I seethe with rage at the sight of them, these traitors to their own kind, these fools who dare to forget their place in the natural order of things. They have grown too comfortable, too complacent within our city walls, and it sickens me to my core. They do not possess the elven look, with their clipped ears unlike my own. I'm nearly elven. Doesn't that place me above them? Their reign of arrogance will soon end. I will not rest until they are reminded of their inferiority, until they cower once more at the feet of their elven superiors.'"

He glanced up to Jory's furrowed brows, his lips parted. "Is an elven manifesto to scare me?"

Keyain remained quiet for a moment, observing the half-elf's unshifting expression. Silently, he flipped the notebook around to show the name written across the front. *Jory Green.*

Jory's furrow deepened, and he let out a dry laugh. "I have never seen that before in my life."

Keyain slid the notebook over to him. Jory hesitated and picked it up, his thumbs brushing over the cover. He shook his head. "You would be hard-pressed to find anyone in Rambler Grove with a journal covered in leather. A recordkeeping book, sure. But a personal journal?" He laughed. "This isn't something we spend coin on in the Weeds. Impractical." Jory tossed the notebook back across the table toward Keyain.

Keyain couldn't detect a lie in his posture or words. Stumped, he said, "Maybe that's why you despise your fellow pilinos. Your father has all the funds for you to live a life of comfort, and yet you're still stuck in Rambler Grove. Hard to have life's little luxuries when it makes you stand out from your neighbors too starkly."

Jory sucked on his teeth and sat forward, his gaze focused on the table. When he finally glanced up at Keyain, his eyes were piercing. "I appreciate all my father has tried to do for my mother and I. However, as much as he tries, he will never understand what we've gone through. He's an ignorant, well-hearted fool."

Keyain nearly got up to grab another witness, believing Jory was about to confess. But then he kept speaking.

"Minister Keyain, did you see my apartment? Were you part of that raid?" he asked.

"No."

He laughed dryly. "Thought so. The gold my father gave us always went back into the community. My mother and I didn't want his pity. What good was it for us to live comfortable lives while our neighbors and friends continued to struggle?"

His manacles rattled over the wooden table top as Jory slid his hands across. "My father made empty promises to my mother about bettering the city-state for decades. He insisted he wanted to help pilinos, that he understood us. Yet, he was missing something so clearly fundamental to the pilinos in the Weeds: none of us can succeed without all of us succeeding. That is the unspoken agreement. So, we gave away all his gold. To the schools, for more crops. Gods, even the refugee intake centers."

Keyain sat back and nodded. "You believed you were receiving favoritism from a father who didn't understand you."

"By a father who never *knew* me. And how could he? He had a bastard he could never live with as long as he wanted to be a minister."

"That's where you're wrong," Keyain said, shifting in his seat. He kept his voice level, pushing his emotions deep under. "He was planning to bring you to court around the time of Queen Marietta's arrival."

"Did you truly bring me in here to make me feel guilt for my father?" Jory pinned him with a glare. "It's not working."

Keyain observed the tightness in his jaw, the tired look around his eyes. He was bitter, but not toward his circumstances in life, but toward his father. It wasn't the jaded attitude he'd expected out of someone who murdered his peers. He decided on a more direct approach.

"Fine. We won't speak anymore of Leyland," Keyain said, changing topics to why Wyltam sent him down there. "Let's talk about the Battle of Sepeia."

Jory raised his brows with a mocking expression. "Do you need a history lesson, Minister?"

"Humor me. What do you think of it?"

Jory shook his head and stared at the corner of the room. "What do I think?" His voice was barely above a whisper. "During the peak of the murders, people worried the culprit sought to create a situation as devastating as the Battle of Sepeia—the mass murder part. We thought they were going to start by slowly picking us off until something changed. And then, something did change. The day your guards surrounded the Temple of Therypon, the day you ripped Marietta from those steps, it was the proof we needed. Another story of an elf controlling a pilinos and forcing them into marriage, a tale as old as time. The pilinos who believed the city-state was changing were devastated. Hells, even those of us who knew better were left hollowed out." Jory's eyes met his, the anger stark. "We said no more. We would not sit around and let ourselves be killed and controlled—we would not let it happen to anyone else. So, they took to the streets."

Keyain's pulse thumped in his temples, and his vision blackened on the edges. "The riots?" Keyain asked.

Jory gave a terse nod. "If you're going to arrest me for anything, let it be that and not for whatever bullshit you drudged up to frame me."

Silence stretched between them. At last, Keyain slid a piece of paper face down on the table between them. Before Jory reached for it, Keyain already had a hunch of how he'd react.

Jory flipped it over and stared at the blue flame printed in the middle.

"What is this?"

Keyain stood abruptly, thanked him for his time, and exited. The tightness in his chest made it hard to draw in air. With the wall there to support him, Keyain took a deep breath in through his nose and exhaled slowly. Once again, Wyltam was fucking right.

"We'll have to go about this delicately," Wyltam said. "Leyland wants his name cleared, but as long as people think we have Jory in custody, then it'll let down the guard of the actual murderers."

Keyain released a long sigh, his shoulders and neck tensing. "I can have Peryn look—"

"I'm taking care of this." Wyltam's voice was firm.

"This is under my purview as minister of protection."

"And under your purview, you apprehended an innocent civilian. I already have someone investigating it. Jory is to be removed from the dungeons immediately."

"And where is he going to go?"

"I said I'm taking care of this."

Keyain ground his teeth, his fists tightening. "So, you don't think we can handle this?"

Wyltam eyed him. "You have a war to focus on. You haven't been back very long."

"And the fey? Any updates?"

Wyltam closed his eyes, composing himself. "We still don't know how many fey there are or the scope of their magic, but we're working to find out."

"Why ... why trust me with it?"

The question had gnawed at Keyain since Wyltam first shared the truth.

"Because despite the selfish choices you've made over the years, I know you'll make the right one when it matters."

For all the times Wyltam had been right, Keyain hoped he'd be right about this too.

Chapter Fifty-Eight

ELYSE

"Stop dropping your hands," Wynn warned. "You're getting distracted again."

Elyse positioned herself, standing with her feet shoulder-width apart, arms raised, ready to face Wynn. He had made it clear—this visit wouldn't interfere with her training. She may have lost a week while they traveled, but Wynn was sure she'd not slack one bit, even though her mind was elsewhere.

The queen's offer echoed in her head, clashing with their commitment to stay neutral. Layla and Assyl, meanwhile, were determined to steer clear of any political talk with her. Seth had mentioned Kyaeri's decision to remain distant from both sides, a stance still undecided.

Those were valid reasons to be distracted, but they weren't what was really gnawing at her. Dominykas had become a constant presence in her mind, like a dull ache that wouldn't fade. She hardly knew him—he was a Chorys Dasian, a stranger. But emotions, unlike logic, paid no heed to reason. And so, despite everything, Dominykas lingered in her thoughts far too often.

Wynn threw a punch at her gut. Elyse gasped and collapsed forward. "You actually hit me."

"You raised your hands too high that time." Wynn brushed back the loose strands of his hair that flew free from its knot. "Something you haven't done in weeks, maybe longer. If you'd been paying attention, you might have noticed it before the punch." Elyse shot him a sharp glare, which only made him laugh. "Anything bothering you?"

She hesitated. "Yes—no. I don't know."

Wynn eyed her a moment, then sat with his legs crossed. "Let's hear it."

Elyse wiped her face with the back of her hand. "I can't."

"Why not?"

"It's embarrassing." Elyse plopped to the ground across from him.

"Sounds like a great reason to tell me."

"Remember that male that was waiting with me the other night?"

Wynn leaned forward, his expression serious. "What did he do?"

"I—nothing. He did nothing." When he didn't relax, Elyse threw herself back on the floor with a sigh. "During the ball, I panicked and headed to the gardens, down by the water. I was looking over the edge when my foot slipped—I nearly fell in. Dominykas caught me."

"Dominykas?" Wynn's expression darkened. "Convenient that he happened to be there."

"He was smoking. And brooding," Elyse said, covering her smile with her hand. "He seems nice."

"But?"

"But I know nothing about him besides that he's the Chorys Dasian ambassador, and he enjoys smoking Mage's Eye."

"Elyse—"

"I don't want to be with him," she said quickly, meeting his stern gaze. "And I can't stop thinking about him. It's frustrating."

Conflicting emotions flickered across Wynn's face before he extended his hand. "Come on."

She took it and rose to her feet. "Where are we going?"

He stepped toward her balcony. "Forget the parties tonight. Let's explore the city instead."

Excitement bubbled in her gut at the thought. "I'll have to ask if it's all right and then change if we're going in public."

Wynn shook his head. "Send a note stating you're feeling ill."

"People will see us leave and they'll know I'm lying."

He flashed a mischievous smile. "You forget we have magic."

Elyse hadn't bothered to change, keeping to her training clothes. It seemed unlikely anyone would recognize her in a casual outfit, especially with her hair braided neatly down her back. As they walked, her gaze never stopped moving. Statues stood at the center of the fountains, beckoning her to touch them. People of various shades of sun-kissed tan and brown squeezed onto narrow pathways along the canals and bridges, some opting to travel by push boat. They clustered in doorways to shops, expanding into pockets of larger markets just out of her eyesight. With her glasses on, she watched streams of aithyr flow into the water, the buildings, the people.

While pilinos and elves were both prominent throughout their walk, Elyse noticed a pattern. Elves would walk arm-in-arm as they perused stores with a pilinos trailing behind them, often carrying more than one bag. Pilinos operated most push boats, their occupants being elven. While Elyse didn't leave the Satiroan palace often, she thought back to the few times she had, not remembering the stark servitude of half-elves and humans.

Wynn slowed his steps as they walked under a verdant canopy of spiky fronds, and she inhaled the briny air mixed with something nutty and smokey. They came to a building at the corner of two canals. Tables filled with people lined the building's front, and as they passed, she noticed they all drank out of matching cups. Pulling aithyr into her body, discovering an aroma that was both sweet and bitter. She met Wynn's grin as he reached the door and entered the building.

Inside, the room buzzed with a lively crowd and a cacophony of voices mingling with the hissing and sighing of the brass contraptions that sat on the counter. Streams of aithyr flowed into the machines, drawing her closer with wide eyes. A worker placed a nozzle into a carafe of what appeared to be milk, the liquid sputtering as the machine whirred. Steam, she realized. Tilan and Fig needed to see this. Could they use a similar function in their own designs?

The machine across from it hummed until the worker toggled a switch and walked away with a powdered dark substance that she recognized. She turned to Wynn. "Coffee?"

He gestured toward the line of people waiting to order, guiding her along. "Coffee that is unlike anything that's available in Satiros."

Elyse watched as the workers danced behind the counter, exchanging cups and liquids and coffee before handing it off to expecting customers. "Why don't we have this back home?"

"Fear of magic," Wynn said. "Wyltam's mother polluted an entire population's mind with the idea that magic is dangerous."

"We still have lights and mages for carriages."

"But you don't have amenities like this." He nodded to the machines. "The world is much larger than Satiros. What you have seen and experienced is a fraction of what magic can be." Wynn smiled, then turned to the worker, ordering drinks and a pastry.

Elyse watched as they were made, mesmerized by the steps. Wynn bumped her with his hip. "I was like you once."

"Hmm?" She tore her gaze away.

"When I first came to Syllogi. We never had magic in Enomenos besides the rogue object for those who could afford such luxuries. My family never did. Magic looked and felt like freedom. Like endless possibilities."

"And that's why you became a mage?"

He shook his head. "I learned magic for the sake of being a carriage driver. The money was good, and it was the only way to learn in Satiros. The plan was to always move on to Amigys or Kyaeri to find where I could become a mage."

Elyse smiled at the thought of Wynn driving a carriage, shuffling around wealthy elves. "But you stayed in Satiros?"

He shook his head. "Passed my mage test and hoarded gold for two years. As soon as I could, I came here to Amigys."

She paused, noting his far-off stare, the slight smile to his lips. She kept her voice low as she asked, "Where did you meet Wyltam, then?"

"Circle of Mages. Sibylla and I found each other here, in this shop of all places. I was enraptured with the brewing machines as much as you are now and we started talking. After a few weeks," he said, shrugging, "she saw something promising in me and brought me into the fold."

Elyse imagined a younger Wynn and Sibylla sitting at a table glowing in the evening light. To think that a single conversation led them to be standing there together now.

When their drinks were called, Wynn took her back outside to sit along the canal with their legs dangling over the edge. Rainbow fish darted through the deep shadows cast by the setting sun. Elyse took a sip of her drink and her eyes bulged. Bitter but sweet, milky and creamy. She turned her gaze to Wynn, who laughed.

"What do you think?" he asked

"Incredible," she said, taking another sip. He handed her the pastry, an oblong biscuit that was hard to the touch, and told her to dunk it in her coffee. She did and took a bite, a faint sound coming from the rear of her throat. The coffee enhanced the lightly sweet and almond taste. "We need this in Satiros. I can't go back knowing we don't have this."

"We could. You have the money to open your own shop."

Elyse laughed. "I don't have time for that."

"One day you will," he said, eyeing her. "It's not wrong for you to think about the future, especially if you don't see yourself staying in politics after the transition to Enomenos."

She hadn't thought of what she'd do once Wyltam no longer needed her. "I'll be a mage like you. Doing whatever you do."

Wynn shrugged. "You could, but being a mage like me is inherently political. There's a lot of work left to do in Syllogi. I imagine a lot of it will be messy and dangerous. There's no shame in being a mage with roots, with family." He paused, his icy eyes searching her face. "I think I want to set down roots myself. I could help you with the shop, if you'd like."

Her heart hammered in her chest at the thought. She imagined her own place to sell coffee along Oak Boulevard teeming with elves and pilinos alike. She imagined it was her dancing behind the bar. She imagined Wynn at her side. "Do you mean to be in my life that long?"

"You're stuck with me forever." Wynn stood with a smirk and offered his hand.

She took it and asked, "As my mentor?"

Wynn's eyes sparkled with something she couldn't quite place. "Imagine how much more fun we could have if I weren't."

Elyse hesitated, unsure if his words were flirtatious. Given their recent fallout, she didn't want to assume anything. "Do you intend to stop being my mentor?"

He stretched, then met her gaze. "Wyltam meant it when he said he wished to take over your training. Once we return to Satiros, I'll no longer be your mentor." He pulled her to her feet. "But we'll still practice. We need to fix those dropping arms of yours."

Elyse rolled her eyes with a smile, dreaming of a future where they could be friends. Maybe even more, if given the time. The idea quickened her pulse.

They returned their empty mugs, and Wynn led her deeper into the city. The canals acted as streets, with some townhomes perched directly on the water, accessible only by boat. Bridges, crowded with foot traffic and small carts, connected the various neighborhoods.

They came to a statue of an amphibious creature with large, round eyes and fins fanning out from the head. As they waited for the cart to pass over the bridge, she rested her hand on the stone and pulled at the aithyr. The subtle shift beneath her touch caught her off guard. She didn't have time to linger, however, as Wynn pulled her forward and across the bridge.

She discovered something new at every turn. "I wish I could explore every corner of Amigys, though I fear that still wouldn't be enough. It's as if I'm drunk on it all."

Wynn's smile was warm. "We haven't even seen the best part yet."

They came to a square where a group of musicians played a fast-paced tune with a crowd of people dancing before them. Wynn offered his hand.

"I don't know this dance," she said, stepping back.

"Me neither." Wynn seized her wrist and tugged her into the crowd. He moved with natural grace, while Elyse struggled to follow. Her brow furrowed as she focused on matching his rhythm. Wynn's laughter rang out, and the fading sunlight cast a warm glow on his smile. As she took in the carefree scene around them, the weight of her apprehension lifted, and she let go of her reservations, realizing no one was watching them.

Wynn spun her and drew her back close to his body, tipping her back so her braid neared the ground. Her cheeks ached with her grin, unable to let it drop. Wynn swept her toward a stranger, who took her hands and pulled her into another dance. While normally Elyse would find herself withdrawn, she couldn't help but continue. She switched partners again and again, moving with the group as songs changed. Through it all, she always found her way back to Wynn.

They didn't stop until her feet throbbed, their bodies slick with sweat. Her grin lingered, but what struck her was Wynn's smile—one she'd never seen before. It suited him, as though his face had always been meant to carry that kind of joy.

As they stepped aside from the crowd, she glanced at the dark sky. "Should we head back?"

Wynn shook his head, a playful glint in his eyes. "There's one more place I want to show you."

He guided Elyse over a barricade and through the Forum, their steps echoing in the stillness of the night. The government buildings stood as ominous silhouettes against the sparkling city below, their imposing forms softened by the distant lights. As they descended a set of stairs, Wynn's hand brushed against Elyse's lower back, a subtle, yet deliberate touch.

At the base of the stairs, they arrived at a wide-open area. The entrance was barred by a gate, its ironwork creaking slightly as Wynn unlatched it. With a careful sweep of his arm, he held it open for her. Elyse stepped through and stopped short, her breath catching at the sight before her. Sunken pools dotted the ground like seeds of a pomegranate slice. As the clouds parted, the moon's pale light cascaded over the pools, making their surfaces glimmer. Elyse gasped as althyr streams rose gently from the water. Beneath the surface, a plant cast a soft, otherworldly light, illuminating the entire field with an ethereal sheen.

"A plant unique to these waters," Wynn said, his voice low. "They glow under the moonlight. The ashes of the city-state's dead are put into these family pools, some believing that's why they grow as they do. But no one knows for sure. One of the world's little mysteries."

She caught the awe and excitement in his voice, a spark she longed to share. But her thoughts drifted to the day she laid her mother's ashes to rest in the burial gardens. That time was a blur, nearly forgotten, yet every emotion lingered like the mourning veil she wore, thick with the scent of smoke from the pyre.

Elyse and her father never returned to visit. Perhaps this was her sign to do so.

The memory tightened around her chest, leaving her limbs heavy and her gaze distant. Wynn's hand hesitated before brushing a strand of hair from her face. "Is something wrong?"

She fought to suppress the ache, squeezing her eyes shut to bury the past. "I'm fine."

"I don't believe you," he murmured, his voice soft but firm. "But I think I know what might help."

He took her hand, his touch both reassuring and tender. They began their slow walk back to the palace, the warmth of the evening wrapping around them. Along the way, they paused at a small shop still open at that hour. It offered a frozen treat, a blend of cream and fruit, shimmering under the shop's soft light. Elyse remembered a similar treat from Satiros, but it had never tasted as exquisite as the one she shared with Wynn now.

With sticky hands entwined and the sweetness still on her tongue, her spirits began to lift. "Thank you," she murmured.

"For what?"

"For breaking the rules. For showing me how to live."

Wynn tightened his grip on hers. "There's much more of this to come," he said, drawing her nearer. The warmth of his body pressed against hers, a tangible reassurance. "I'll make sure of it."

They stood close, closer than they had since their shared night. Elyse counted the quickening beat of her heart to steady herself until she felt the gentle pressure of his finger beneath her chin, tilting her face to meet his eyes.

"Elyse, I want to kiss you."

"You could," she said, knees trembling. "But you won't. Because of the rules."

"You make me want to break every rule," he murmured, pressing his forehead to hers. "This trip has shown me how alive I am with you. The world takes on new colors, new sounds. Things I've never experienced before, though I lived here for decades."

Their breaths intertwined, the intense desire to feel his lips on hers almost palpable. The emotional walls she had built seemed to crumble, as if they had never existed. Wynn was here, holding her, wanting her. Elyse, her voice barely above a whisper, asked, "Then why aren't you kissing me?"

"Because I respect you, and you deserve a fresh beginning to whatever might develop between us," he said, his voice calm but laden with regret. He sighed deeply. "But mainly because if I kiss you tonight, then I will want to kiss you every night until there's no longer breath in my lungs."

Her heart hammered against her ribs. "That doesn't sound like a bad thing."

"It is when you're the king's orator and I'm just a guard."

Elyse protested as he pulled back. "You are not just a guard."

"But I'm playing the part of one." His lips tilted into a smile and he took her hand, pressing a kiss into the back of it. "When we return to Satiros, Wyltam will be your mentor. And then I promise you this kiss."

She committed his expression to memory, his face softened by the dim light that traced the sharp contours of his features. There was an openness in his gaze, raw and genuine. "I'm going to hold you to that promise, Wynn."

He ducked his head and smiled with a laugh. "Let's get you back before it's too late."

Chapter Fifty-Nine

AMRYTH

Deania joined Amryth the night she returned to the Honeysuckle. They sat at the bar, and Amryth couldn't help but notice Tanaly's absence. While they waited, Deania kept the barkeep engaged with easy conversation, her laughter filling the space between them. Amryth, however, scanned the dimly lit tavern. There had to be something she was missing.

She turned toward the tables. They were emptier than last time, though it was the afternoon. To the other side of the tavern, she found a pair of pilinos talking over drinks. As she turned away, she sensed their stares fall onto her. Odd.

A bright laugh sounded from the back of the bar, followed by Tanaly walking through the door with a barrel-chested man with olive skin. She came to an abrupt stop when she noticed Amryth and Deania and then made her way over.

"Up early for drinks, I see." Tanaly waved toward their cups, avoiding eye contact with both.

"We're here for you!" Deania leaned across the bar, pulling her into a hug. "Unless that's an issue."

It was subtle, the way she glanced back at the male she walked with, then stopped, hesitating before speaking. "Never a problem for you, darling."

Amryth stared at the male, drawing his gaze. Human with a full black beard, considerably taller than average. His right hand twitched under her stare, all senses becoming acutely aware of him. She had seen him before, on her first night at the Honeysuckle.

"Hi, Pelok!" Deania leaned forward and flashed a smile.

Something in the back of her mind connected with the name. Exisotis, Marietta's friend from Olkia. She blinked as the realization came over her.

Tanaly waved him over. "I don't think you've met Amryth," she said. "Deania's partner, if you could believe that."

Pelok approached and held out his hand, Amryth taking it, finding his grip strong. "Nice to meet you."

"Same here."

Tanaly leaned forward and dropped her voice. "He's digging into the same situation. Perhaps he could help you if you helped him?" She glanced back and Pelok, an unspoken conversation passing between their stares.

"Sure!" Deania answered. "We were at a dead end, anyway."

Amryth forced a smile, her frustration simmering beneath the surface. She hated making deals in the dark, and Pelok was nothing more than a name tied to Exisotis and Marietta. Trusting someone she barely knew felt reckless.

Her hesitation must have been clear. "Pelok is a dear friend," Tanaly reassured, resting a hand on Amryth's forearm. "He knows exactly what you've been working on, and he can help."

Amryth sat back, assessing. "What did you have in mind?"

Tanaly urged Pelok forward, and he said, "I need someone to get into a place that is known for not serving pilinos. Tanaly volunteered, but we could use some extra support from someone with a certain skill set.

"You have an observational eye," Tanaly added. "And you know how to be discreet when uncovering information. You've proven that much."

Deania turned to her with an excited smile. Amryth sighed. "I'm interested," she said, wishing she wasn't so easily persuaded by her. Though if it helped them free Jory, then it would be useful.

"The location is the Ladybird Inn," Pelok said. Amryth stilled the reaction from her face and thanked her past self for never telling Deania the name. "It was a known site for elves to go celebrate after another pilinos body was found."

Amryth's stomach dropped. Unsurprising, given their ties to the university professor who viewed the Battle of Sepeia in such a golden light. But to know that there were people who celebrated the gruesome murders made her tighten her fists.

"My thought is, the inn keep should have records of who stayed at the inn and when. If we can get our hands on that list, then we can match their names with the dates."

Not a bad idea, but one that left her uneasy. "Stealing is often accompanied by breaking in."

"Unless we stay at the inn," Tanaly said. "Then no breaking in is required. Just some gentle curiosity and roaming hands."

Her years of service in the guard made her want to say no, to not breaking any laws, but when she turned and saw Deania's hopeful face, her chest caved in.

"I'll help!" Deania jumped out of her seat.

"Absolutely not." Amryth crossed her arms.

"Elves have staff with them at times. I'll be there to assist."

"At the inn where they cheered when pilinos corpses were found?" Amryth shook her head. "It's too dangerous."

Deania planted her hands on her hips. "I can handle it."

"Well," Pelok said, his voice drawing their focus, "it would be less conspicuous if we only had elves involved. I'll provide a distraction so they can search, but it's something I'd prefer to manage alone."

Amryth went to question that, but was cut off by Tanaly. "We'll get separate beds, darling. Nothing to worry about."

The joke didn't lift the frown from Deania's face. Amryth rubbed the back of her neck, the knot of unease tightening in her gut. Every instinct screamed to walk away from this. The Exisotis might not pose an official threat anymore, but that didn't mean they were free of hidden agendas. Still, Deania trusted Pelok and Tanaly. She wanted to be part of this, even though she couldn't. That alone made Amryth ignore her better judgment. "I'm in."

As they left, Amryth offered to walk Deania back to the temple. Silence settled between them, heavy and uncomfortable. Deania, clearly upset at being excluded, kept her gaze averted. Amryth nudged her gently with an elbow. "It's only one thing."

She turned her face to Amryth, tears lining her eyes. "We agreed to do this together. A team."

"We are still a team. This part is too dangerous for you."

She shook her head. "Don't patronize me."

"I'm not."

"You are. You don't think I can handle myself."

"It's because if you were to get hurt, I would never forgive myself. If you died, I would be completely lost." Amryth hated the way her throat tightened as she spoke.

Deania's voice came out small, barely a whisper. "I'd rather die at your side than wait, only to find out you're never coming home. I thought you'd understand that."

Amryth stopped in her tracks, her chest tightening as memories of Deyra flooded back—days when things were simpler, when Deyra was still alive. She pictured Deania lying alone, a knife in her stomach, bleeding out.

"That wasn't fair. I'm sorry." Deania's hand cupped Amryth's cheek, her touch soft, pleading. "Come back to me."

Amryth swallowed hard. "Everything that I'm doing, it is to help Jory. But also …" She couldn't find the words.

"Remember what I said?" Deania pulled her forward. "You're a good person, always worrying about others. One day you'll have to learn to not worry about me."

Amryth questioned if that day would ever come.

Following Pelok's instructions, Amryth met Tanaly at her home on the west end of the Wooded Ward and they walked arm-in-arm to the inn. The night was cool and Tanaly pulled out a flask, encouraging her to drink.

She caught Amryth's weary stare and said, "Can't be a drunk with no alcohol on your breath."

Despite her better judgment, she took a swig and handed it back. The liquor burned all the way down.

Amryth inhaled deeply as they reached the correct street, forcing a giggle as she stumbled along beside Tanaly. Her companion slurred her words effortlessly, and Amryth matched her with a loud laugh.

They clumsily made their way up the inn's staircase. Once inside, Tanaly feigned a trip, yanking Amryth aside. She erupted into exaggerated laughter, straightening herself with a playful grin. "Oops."

A bald elven male stood behind the desk and waved them over with an amused smile. "Fun night?"

Tanaly placed her arm on Amryth's shoulder and pulled her close. "Just getting started."

"Not a lot of space tonight. Too many countryfolk behind the walls these days."

As the male turned to grab keys, Amryth noticed the mural above his head. A forest burned with ghastly blue flames on the left side, seemingly with people inside. Beyond the trees were people sprawled on the ground with blood pooling beneath them. Their foes, to the right, stood with bows and arrows, swords and dagger, cheering as a pilinos man fell to his knees in the middle of the scene with a sword jutting through his stomach. The elf who wielded the weapon smiled. The Battle of Sepeia, on display for everyone to see.

She shouldn't be surprised that it hung on the wall. Hells, they even named their gods damned group after the massacre. Yet seeing it presented as a sign of elven heritage almost made her lose focus on their task at hand.

Tanaly elbowed her sharply as she leaned across the counter to pay the innkeeper. "A little extra for the noise," she said with a wink.

The innkeeper rolled his eyes and dropped a set of keys into her hands. "Third floor, room five."

Keeping up the ruse, they staggered to the stairs, laughing as they went, and made their way to the room. The plan was simple: wait until late into the night, then sneak back down.

Once the door clicked shut, Tanaly whirled around, her eyes sharp. "Whatever's going on in your head, shut it down," she hissed. "You almost blew our cover back there."

"I wasn't expecting the mural."

Tanaly studied her for a minute and then tossed the flask. "We have a few hours. Take off the edge until then. Don't fuck this up."

Irritated, Amryth took another pull of the flask to placate her.

They fell into an easy silence, Tanaly staring out the window to the street. The only light in the room came from the golden light globe hovering above the roofline, painting bright light onto a dark canvas. She wondered what Deania was doing now. If she was still upset. After seeing the painting, Amryth was glad she wasn't here.

When the time came, Amryth and Tanaly slipped quietly from their room, descending the dim stairwell. The inn's light globes cast a faint glow, leaving shadows clinging to the corners. The first floor remained as brightly lit as before, but the innkeeper's desk sat empty. Tanaly motioned for Amryth to follow as she moved swiftly into the hall beside the check-in counter, stopping at an unmarked door. She tested it, finding it locked. As Amryth went to say something, Tanaly pulled out a set of lock picks with a smirk. Amryth gave her an unimpressed look. Of course, a thief would have tools to aid in stealing. Why was she even here if Tanaly had done this before?

Amryth kept a lookout while Tanaly worked on the lock, hearing a click a few minutes later. Silently, they slipped through the door and closed it behind them.

The office was small and simple, containing a few shelves filled to the brim and a desk that had stacks of paper across its top. Amryth's feet stumbled as she walked in. Before she could question it, Tanaly whispered, "Check the desk. I'll get the shelves."

Amryth got to work, sitting in the chair and began going through the piles of papers. Most of them were bills, many past due. Moving onto the drawers: the top two were locked. The bottom one opened for Amryth, finding neat rows of files. Flipping quickly through them, she noted they were only more bills. With a sigh, she knelt and explored beneath the desk, her hands probing for any hidden mechanisms or releases.

Amryth heard something slide from across the room and she glanced up at Tanaly, seeing her engrossed with the line of books on the shelves. Ignoring her, she reached back inside the drawer and felt around. Her fingers drifted along the smooth wood until she felt a notch. Curious, she pressed her finger into it and the door above popped open.

She looked up to call Tanaly over, her excitement gave way to surprise. Tanaly sat on the windowsill, a sneer on her face. Cold dread washed over Amryth, causing her to spring to her feet, her head growing dizzier and her limbs turning numb.

"Once a guard, always a guard. We'll be sure to comfort Deania." With a salute, she jumped out the window.

Amryth's legs felt heavy, her mind spinning with the bitter realization—she'd been set up. She stumbled toward the window, only to find the space empty, Tanaly already gone. A guard rounded the corner, his steps echoing loudly in the alley. Cursing under her breath, Amryth quickly ducked back inside, her heart racing. She had to get out—now.

She took one step toward the door when it was blown open; the innkeeper appearing with a snarl on his face. "Think you can steal from me?"

Amryth let her instincts take over, her body lurching full force into him and shoving him into a bookcase. Whatever had been in Tanaly's flask rendered her movements leaden and unsteady, as if her limbs were weighed down by unseen chains.

Years of training, and it had come to this—a betrayal she should've seen coming. Amryth cursed under her breath, her steps faltering as she stumbled into the hall. She barely made it two steps before someone slammed into her, driving her back against the wall.

Out of the corner of her eyes, she caught sight of a familiar green. Her body numbed and slacked against the hold, and she rested her head against the cool stone. She was utterly fucked.

The guard behind her yelled out to the room. "Go get the captain! He's going to want to see this."

Chapter Sixty

AMRYTH

The morning chill clung to Amryth like a blanket. The holding cell she was placed in last night did nothing to insulate her to the autumn air, though she shouldn't complain. She deserved everything that had happened to her.

Sleep eluded her. Every time she closed her eyes, she heard Tanaly's amusement as she said Deania's name and jumped out the window. She made a mistake by trusting Tanaly and Pelok. Why had she?

Because Deania wanted her to. Because Deania trusted them. Rage burned from her gut to her throat. Tanaly likely shared that the mission had gone wrong, painting Amryth as a casualty while conveniently omitting her and Pelok's role in the deception. Deania would be consumed with worry, blind to their deceit, a thought that made Amryth clench her fists harder.

In the cell opposite to her, a drunk lay sprawled across the bed, her snoring echoing in the empty cells. It drowned out the approached steps of the jailer who knocked on the bars to get Amryth's attention. "Stand up, turn around, and place your palms on the wall."

She stood, her limbs stiff and back aching. The cold of the brick numbed her hands. "Where am I going?" The jailer hummed to himself, saying nothing further. "I shouldn't be on trial already."

"So you do remember what it's like being a guard." His expression was amused as he slapped the manacle on her wrist. "If only you remembered before committing a crime." She ignored the jab and accepted her fate.

While thieving itself wasn't the most egregious offense someone could commit, Amryth was still only a few months out from her discharge agreement with the guard. While she was considered a normal citizen now, she was privy to a lot of information that was kept close to the crown. By committing a crime, she had proven herself untrustworthy in holding that information. Amryth didn't know what happened next because she had never heard of anyone being so stupid. Whatever would come couldn't be good.

Worse, though, was the regret that clung to her like her shadow. Deania would be fine. Her parents would need to cut back their spending, but would ultimately be okay. No matter what punishment awaited her, she would face it. But she failed Jory, and that was the worst of her offenses.

If the jail had been uncomfortable, the dungeons were unbearable. Despite breathing through her mouth, she could still smell the reek of bodies. It became obvious her case had been elevated when the jailer hauled her out at dawn and took her to the palace. Given her previous position, she'd have to talk to someone higher up. Unfortunately for her, she had a strong idea of who that was.

She passed faces pressed against the bars, their eyes following her as she was escorted to another section and tossed inside. Her cell had a proper door with a food pass through that the guard left closed as she slammed the door shut. Darkness overtook her vision.

Occasionally, voices drifted through from the other side of the door, accompanied by the faint glow of light as guards lifted the pass through.

"That is her."

"Serves her right for betraying us."

"I heard she'll be hung."

She rolled her eyes at the last one. She knew it wasn't her life that she needed to plea for, rather her freedom. If she were the king, she wouldn't let herself go. Her work grew sloppy and garnered attention, and he required her discretion. She'd no longer be of use to him.

After some time, the door finally swung open to reveal the silhouette of Keyain. Amryth stood on unsteady legs, not surprised to see him. She was more surprised to see him so soon.

He didn't acknowledge her as she walked into the hall, finding Peryn with an unreadable expression. She knew what he thought—that she had been snooping after warning her not to. To say he was disappointed would be an understatement.

They escorted her past the line of cells and into an isolated interrogation room, one typically reserved for sensitive discussions. Or, as she'd heard, for intimidating prisoners who refused to talk, offering no chance for eavesdropping.

Keyain shrugged off his jacket and slung it onto the back of the chair. "I'll handle this from here, Peryn."

Her senior glanced at him with surprise. "I should be here for the interrogation at least."

"I need you to be available for questions about the approaching army."

Amryth stood straighter. Which army?

"Don't make a habit of questioning me. You've done this twice now," Keyain said, his voice not having any of the bite it usually did. "Go before you piss me off."

Peryn held his ground for a moment before taking off, closing the door hard behind him. Keyain slumped into the chair and rubbed his forehead. "Really, Amryth? Stealing?"

The manacles clinked together as she sat. "I accept my punishment however you deem worthy."

He sighed and pinned her with his stare. "I just want an explanation, preferably before Wyltam gets here, so I can help you navigate this nightmare of a situation." The strain in his voice paired with the dark circles under his eyes was unsurprising given an army marched on them. His usual edge was gone, however.

"You seem off," she said, furrowing her brows. "No angry words? No yelling at me?"

He offered her a soft laugh. "Did you want me to yell?"

She thought about it. "Not preferably."

"Then I won't."

"What's really going on? Besides the war."

He shook his head, a wry smile tugging at his lips. "You are in the dungeons with your hands manacled together, yet you're still more concerned about me." He laughed again, the sound dry and hollow. "Deyra always said you could be bleeding out, and you'd make sure everyone was comfortable first."

Amryth winced at the familiar ache brought on by her late wife's name, yet she couldn't suppress the laugh that bubbled up from the memory. "'Selfless, even on your deathbed,'" she quoted.

A smile spread across Keyain's face, softening his features and making him look years younger. "Yes, that. I forgot …" He trailed off, his face sobering. Silence stretched between them, and he cleared his throat. "What were you doing at the Ladybird Inn?"

She shook her head. "It's confidential."

"Amryth, you're not in a position to have anything be confidential."

The door opened behind her, King Wyltam stepping in. "Odd circumstances to be meeting." He walked to Keyain's side and remained standing, his hands clasped behind his back. "She's here because of me."

"You sent her to the Ladybird Inn?" Keyain asked incredulously.

"Not directly," he said. "But I suspect it's involved based on the last report she gave me. Have any of your guards uncovered anything else about a group called the Blue Flames?"

Before he could speak, Amryth said, "Peryn was. I saw him at the meeting that I included in my report."

Keyain slowly looked up from the table, his brows furrowed when he turned to Wyltam. Keyain shook his head after a moment, as if they had a whole conversation without speaking.

"What did you find at the inn?" the king asked.

"We were searching the records of who stayed there. Allegedly, the inn housed people who were celebrating the pilinos murders."

"And how did you get to that?"

Amryth hesitated. "We spoke to the only witness of the murderers, a half-elf named Adira. They claimed their attackers had wings and horns, which sounded ridiculous. We searched the theater's costumes but found that would have worked with what they described." Amryth paused and met the king's gaze. "Adira believes they were fey, which sounds …"

"Insane?" Keyain offered, his stare far off.

King Wyltam placed a hand on Keyain's shoulder. "I recall that from your notes. It's not as insane as you would believe. But you said 'we.' I thought you were working on this alone."

"Deania from the Temple of Therypon had been helping me," she confessed. "Which led me back to the Honeysuckle Tavern—the very place you had directed me to initially."

"You sent her?" Keyain shook his head. "A little awareness goes a long way."

Wyltam shushed him. "Amryth, continue."

"Well, when we went back, Deania's friend who worked at the tavern introduced me to Pelok, who I know was in the Exisotis. They had a plan, and I agreed to it, only to be betrayed and set up to get caught."

The silence stretched before them, making Amryth glance between the two males. Wyltam and Keyain stared at one another again, Keyain nodding his head.

Then Keyain stood and King Wyltam turned to Amryth. "Do you know why they set you up?"

Her stomach curdled with the memory of Tanaly's words. "She said, 'Once a guard, always a guard,' so I assumed because of my service."

Keyain nodded once and walked to the door. "Wyltam will explain to you what's about to happen. I'll be back to check on you." Before she could answer, he was out the door.

Perplexed, she turned to the king who eyed her. "What's going on?"

"I think you stumbled into something bigger than you realize. Pelok isn't just part of the Exisotis—he's a leading member. His deliberate betrayal and reasoning make me question our alliance, treaty or not. I regret that you'll be underground for the foreseeable future."

She sighed, trying to not show her disappointment at having to stay in her cell. He stood and gestured for her to follow. Upon exiting, she saw no one was around, the dungeons eerily quiet. The king walked her past where her cell should be and took an adjacent hallway that led to a dead end. He didn't slow his pace as he walked into it, passing through as if nothing was there.

She hesitantly stepped through it, glancing back to see the low lit hallway they were just in. Confused, she turned to Wyltam, who held keys. He took her hands and unlocked the manacles, tossing them to the side. Without speaking, he turned and continued into the dark.

With a light globe lighting their way, Amryth refrained from asking questions. They were in the tunnels below the palace, but she hadn't realized that they intersected the dungeons. She tried to pick up details to get a sense of where she could be, but all the stone and dirt looked the same.

They passed through another hallway concealed by magic and walked until it opened up to a brightly lit cavern. At its center, two people waited with their arms crossed.

"Sibylla, Tolis—this is Amryth."

Chapter Sixty-One

ELYSE

"They're willing to meet with us," Kurtys said, voice calm but urgent.

Elyse glanced up from her seat, surprised by the words, but more so by his insistence. She had brushed off the idea earlier, knowing that no one would approve of this dinner. Yet here he was, pushing the matter again. Standing opposite her, Seth's posture stiffened, arms locked tight across his chest.

"We can't trust them," Seth said, shaking his head. "You're talking about the Chorys Dasians, the people we're about to go to war with."

Kurtys didn't waver. "That's why this is crucial. If we handle it well, we could avoid the war altogether. Without Chorys Dasi, Reyila wouldn't dare march on Satiros."

Elyse knew better. The dinner wouldn't change anything. Reyila's desire for revenge over Queen Valeriya's death ran deeper than diplomacy could touch. She'd sat in enough meetings reporting Satiros's unanswered attempts to ease tensions. What Kurtys didn't know was that the war wasn't their only threat.

Fey, dangerous and hidden, loomed as an unknown threat. At best, swaying Chorys Dasi might delay conflict; at worst, it could invite something far more insidious into their halls.

Seth's voice broke the silence, cutting through the false hope. "Optimism's one thing," he said dryly. "But they're still ambassadors, far from home."

"They're the only Chorys Dasians who will listen, who can send word back to their court," Kurtys countered. "Their message could sway the royals."

"They could poison you. Drag you out of there in chains, or worse. It's a trap."

"It's not a trap," Kurtys said. "I've spent years building trust with them."

"Then why are you and Elyse the only ones invited?" Seth's frustration seeped into his voice. "If they meant to stop the war, why not make this open to all us Satiroans?"

Kurtys met Seth's gaze evenly. "Elyse represents the king, and they trust me. Only me, at this point. Elyse had started to win them over, but our time here is short. We leave in a few days—we can't afford to miss this." His expression softened, voice quieter. "It's dinner. Nothing more."

Elyse, silent until now, weighed the risks. "If we go, we'll bring guards."

Seth's pacing slowed, his eyes locking on hers. "You're seriously considering this?"

She hesitated, weighing her words carefully. "We've prepared for war, yes. But if there's even the slightest chance of stopping it before it begins …"

Seth rubbed his temples, clearly frustrated. "This is not a good idea."

"Good idea or not," Kurtys said quietly, "it's an opportunity to avoid war."

The room fell silent, tension holding like a drawn breath. Elyse leaned back, her mind already running through the logistics—how many guards they'd need, how to keep things secure. Yet Wynn's absence gnawed at her thoughts. He wouldn't be there to look out for her. He had a task to do elsewhere on behalf of Wyltam that evening.

As Seth gave in to the idea, Elyse stood and went to find Wynn. When she explained the situation, his brow furrowed, concern flashing in his eyes.

"I don't like this," he murmured, leaning against the doorframe to the balcony of her room. His fingers brushed a stray lock of her hair, twisting it absently between them.

Elyse shifted closer. "You're nervous about me being around him."

Wynn scoffed, the ghost of a smile playing on his lips. "Of all the things I'm worried about, *he* isn't one of them." His gaze drifted beyond her, toward the glittering horizon. "I don't think this dinner will stop the war. But if word slips to the Amigys officials that Satiros tried to smooth things over ..." He shrugged, his voice turning quieter. "That might help. Our allies won't stay neutral for long. But I don't like that I won't be there to protect you."

"If I need you, you're a short message away." She hesitated, then leaned into him, her forehead resting against his chest. His arms circled around her, pulling her close, his chin lowering to the top of her head.

"You'll be careful?" His voice was soft, but there was a tightness behind the question.

"Always," she whispered, letting the warmth of him settle her nerves.

As evening descended, Elyse slipped into a black dress that dipped low at the chest, thin straps tracing her shoulders. The bodice clung to her frame, flaring out at the hips before cascading down to her ankles. She had grown to prefer this—simple, dark, unadorned. The gowns gifted to her by the Amigys royals were grand gestures, but they weren't her uniform.

They arrived at the restaurant just before sunset, a small battalion of guards shadowing them. The building itself was a testament to the city's ancient beauty, its facade adorned with fey creatures carved in stone, surrounded by thick foliage that clung to the walls. Through her glasses, Elyse saw faint streams of aithyr flowing into the rock—silent currents of power embedded in the architecture. She turned to Kurtys to comment when she noticed the tension in his posture, the tightness around his mouth.

"Are you going to be sick?" she asked, her voice soft with amusement.

"No, no. I'm fine," he said quickly, pulling open the door and gesturing for her to enter. "Just a touch nervous."

"You sounded so confident earlier."

"I have to be in front of my superior."

"And not me?" Elyse raised a brow, teasing the edge of his nerves.

He managed a strained smile. "Apparently not."

Inside, the dining room was sparsely populated, with only a few patrons scattered across the tables. A female attendant approached, bowing her head in greeting. "This way, please. You'll be eating in one of our private rooms tonight."

Elyse exchanged a glance with Kurtys before they followed the attendant up the narrow stairs, their footsteps echoing off the stone walls. At the top floor, the attendant knocked once before pushing open the door. Behind them, the clatter of their guards' armor halted at the threshold, leaving the two of them to step inside alone.

The room was bathed in the warm glow of the setting sun, long streams of golden light filtering through the wide windows. From this vantage point, Elyse could see The Cliffs district below, the palace rising in the distance with the bay stretching beyond it. It was a view designed to impress, but her attention shifted as a glass clinked against the table.

Nyran stood, his tall frame casting shadows across the room. "Lady Elyse, Kurtys," he greeted, his voice formal but edged with familiarity. "We appreciate you making the time."

Elyse bowed her head. "I appreciate the break from the parties, if I'm honest. They're a bit more raucous than I care for."

"'Raucous' certainly fits them," Nyran said with a hint of amusement. "I hope this setting is more to your taste." He gestured to the room.

Elyse turned to take in the space. "It's beautiful, especially the view," she replied, her gaze drifting to the expansive vista outside the windows.

"Indeed it is," came a voice Elyse recognized immediately. Dominykas stepped out from the corner where he had been leaning casually against the wall. He took a leisurely sip of wine, his eyes fixed on her as he moved closer. "Black suits you well, Lady Elyse."

Though the pull toward Dominykas remained, her recent night with Wynn had dulled its intensity. She accepted a glass of sparkling wine from a server, the coolness of the drink grounding her and easing her thoughts. "That's good to hear, considering I wear it often."

Dominykas took the seat across from her as she sat, his lips hinting at a smile. "Have you ever considered crimson?"

"Dom," Nyran warned. "This isn't—"

"Because you would look beautiful in it, especially paired with black."

Elyse set down her wine and leaned back. "Are you saying I'd look beautiful in Chorys Dasian colors?"

Dominykas's smirk widened. "Would you like to find out?"

"Dominykas, show restraint," snapped Nyran. "At least get through the first course before acting flirtatious with her."

A server placed a steaming tureen of herb-infused vegetable stew before her. "While I appreciate the compliment," Elyse said, her gaze steady as she lifted her spoon, "I'm currently seeing someone."

Both Kurtys and Dominykas went still. She noticed a slight tremor in Kurtys's hand, his fingers twitching at his side.

Nyran filled the silence with innocuous questions about her stay thus far. Elyse, keen to shift the focus, asked about their tenure in Amigys. But her question seemed to float unanswered. The conversation looped back to her, the interest unmistakable.

When they reached the main course, Elyse braced herself for the type of meat dish they'd likely serve. The week had been filled with stomaching what she could in order to not offend her hosts. When the silver lid was drawn back, she stared at the plate, surprised. Steamed fish with a side of pasta in a tomato sauce. She took a bite, the fish melting in her mouth. Looking at Kurtys's plate, she could see the grill marks and char on his food.

"We heard you have a taste for steamed dishes," Nyran said. "Kurtys was kind enough to mention it."

Elyse furrowed her brows. When had she shared that detail? Or had Kurtys simply picked up on it? She turned to him, noting the perspiration gathered on his forehead. "Are you sure you're all right?" she asked again, keeping her voice low.

"Are you still unwell?" Nyran asked.

"Only a minor chill."

Nyran pushed back his chair and set his napkin neatly on the table. "We've paid enough for the room. The restaurant should have something for you. Come."

Kurtys shook his head, his tone strained. "I'm fine."

"We insist," Dominykas added, leaning forward. "It's better to take care now than risk falling ill on your journey home."

Kurtys didn't hesitate; he stood and followed Nyran out the door.

"We're going to Kyaeri next," Elyse corrected.

Dominykas's smile widened. "That's right. How have you found the travels so far?"

"Exploring a new city-state is a nice change," Elyse said between bites of food. "I've always wanted to see outside of Satiros, so it's been exciting to finally experience that. I wish I had more time to explore Amigys, but I've heard great things about Kyaeri."

Dominykas sat back, his tone smooth and deliberate. "Kyaeri has soaring mountains, picturesque waterfalls, and cities built into the cliffs. It's truly unique in Syllogi. I would have loved to be the one to show you around."

"Is that so? You've visited enough to be a guide?"

"I've been to every Syllogian city-state. I've even been to Reyila."

Elyse took a sip of her drink, the wine warming her from within. "Which is your favorite?"

"Do you want an honest answer or a pandering one?"

She leaned forward, a playful smile on her lips. "Why not both?"

"If I were pandering, then I would say Satiros. It's where I've seen and explored the most beautiful sights," he said, his voice dropping into a deeper tone. "But if I were being honest with you, it'd be Chorys Dasi. Too bad there's a war. I'd love to show you there as well."

At the mention of war, Elyse straightened, wishing Kurtys were there to steer the conversation. "Wars are brutal, or so I've heard."

Dominykas raised an eyebrow, the faintest hint of amusement playing at the corner of his lips. "You're not wrong."

"Almost as if we should do everything within our means to prevent one."

A soft laugh escaped him, his tone far too light for the gravity of the topic. "Reyila sent their terms. There was a way to avoid it. Unless, of course, something's changed?"

Elyse set her silverware down, meeting his gaze with a measured wariness. "She's my cousin. I would never, under any circumstance, accept their terms of execution. But amending relations with Chorys Dasi? That's a conversation."

Dominykas studied her, his expression unreadable. "Our prince is married to the Reyilan queen. Unless Satiros offers something equally enticing, Queen Agnyssa's alliances to the north won't falter. Though … she does have another brother."

Elyse froze at the implication.

"One who might marry someone with ties to the Satiroan crown. Perhaps a cousin?"

"No." The word snapped out, reflexive, before Elyse could stop it. Her mind reeled, dragged back to the memory of Azarys, to the fey, to the threat they both carried. He was a liar. A murderer. Dangerous in ways no alliance could fix. Accepting this dinner had been a mistake, a naive hope that the war could be avoided when Chorys Dasi hid a darker secret.

"You said we should do everything within our means." Dominykas swirled his wine, watching her over the rim of the glass. "And yet you reject this so quickly."

A flush of heat rose up Elyse's neck. "Not him."

Dominykas chuckled, shaking his head in feigned disappointment. "My prince is a fool to lose such a bride. He should have held on to you." His gaze slid over her, slow and assessing. "You're as intelligent as you are striking."

Elyse's spine stiffened. "No amount of charm will change my mind."

His smile turned smug. "So, you do find me charming."

"That's not—"

"Perhaps Prince Azarys could learn from me," he mused, lounging back in his chair with a self-satisfied grin. "Tell me, what do you find my most charming trait?"

"I'm tired of this game." She cast a glance toward the door, wondering how long Kurtys could possibly take. The sooner he returned, the sooner they could leave.

"You wound me, truly." He crossed his arms over his chest, feigning offense. "A game? I thought we were having a thoughtful conversation about avoiding war. Yet, here I am, mistaken for a mere sycophant."

"Unfortunately, I don't know you well enough to judge otherwise."

"Unfortunate indeed."

Silence hung over them, thick and stifling. Elyse no longer had the appetite for the meal in front of her. At last, Dominykas spoke. "It seems our companions will be delayed. Would you care for some fresh air on the balcony while we wait?"

Elyse wished to refuse, but felt compelled to nod. As she went to stand, Dominykas gestured for her to wait. He swiftly moved to her chair, drawing it back with a practiced ease and extending a hand. She hesitated briefly before accepting it, noting the calloused texture of his fingers and the firm grip of his palm.

The humid breeze greeted her as they stepped onto the balcony, her eyes finding the farthest point on the horizon over the sea. In the distance, she could see creatures breaking the surface of the water. Her gaze followed the line from the shore to the canal below, where the people in the push boats seemed tiny from this height.

"I can't get over how beautiful it is," she murmured, her voice barely above a whisper.

"Neither can I." She turned to find his eyes fixed on her, their intensity undiminished. The weight of his gaze lingered as he drew nearer.

She shied away from his attention and focused on the fey carvings on the building behind him, noticing the lack of aithyr streams like the front had. Curious. Perhaps the entrance was enchanted.

Elyse glanced backward at the stone wall as Dominykas gently brushed a strand of hair from her face. She considered stepping away, creating some distance between them, but the urge to remain where she was held her firmly in place. It was as if he controlled her very emotions, drawing her in like a bee to nectar. She studied the features of his face, though he was backlit by the setting sun. The breeze came, blowing back her hair and carrying his scent—juniper and citrus.

Memories surfaced all at once. Strong arms beneath her grasp. Soft lips against hers. Silk sheets caressing her body.

She gasped and took a step back. Dominykas's features melted into pale olive skin, fluffy black hair, and russet eyes.

"Hello, goddess."

Chapter Sixty-Two

ELYSE

Elyse stumbled backward, Azarys's grip on her wrists unyielding. Not him. Not now. Her mind raced to process his presence. A crushing weight seemed to press down on her, anchoring her in place. She reached for the aithyr around her, except it didn't come. Her chest tightened. She focused and tried again.

"I'm here to save you." Azarys cupped her cheek. "I'm here to bring you home."

Elyse searched for aithyr in her line of sight, finding none—sensing *none*. It wouldn't come to her. In her panic, she lashed out with her fist with all her strength, connecting with his jaw. It was enough that he let her go. She turned and ran for the door. Within two steps, Azarys snatched her and pinned her to the wall, flipping her so they were face-to-face.

"You learned to throw a punch since we last saw each other." He lowered his face to hers. "And here I thought I'd be okay if I neutralized your magic. You broke my back last time, my powerful and talented goddess."

Elyse trembled and tried to catch her breath. "I don't want to go with you."

He tsked. "You need to be with your own people, and I need you by my side. Don't you understand?" He went to caress her face again, but she jerked away from his touch.

Her mind raced like a cat after prey. She needed to steady herself, to devise a strategy. She needed Azarys to talk and buy her time. "You're a murderer."

"I've taken many lives. You'll need to be more specific."

If she couldn't see or feel aithyr, they likely gave her magicsbane. "The pilinos in Satiros."

"Criminals, all of them. They fled their trials in Chorys Dasi and needed to pay." Elyse loosened the metal on her ring and forced herself to relax. Azarys's grip eased as she stopped fighting. "Alas, I was only involved in lessening the damage. Oryck took his duties a bit too far."

Elyse thought back to that day in the townhouse. Oryck had introduced himself as an emissary. "What is he, an executioner?"

"Of sorts." Azarys dropped her wrist and brushed the loose hair back from her face. "I've missed the sight of you, goddess."

As he leaned in to kiss her, Elyse feigned flinching and drew her arm toward her head. In a smooth motion, she flicked the top of her ring and splashed the liquid Mage's Eye onto her tongue, enough to counteract the magicsbane.

Azarys drew back with a frown. "I would never hurt you."

"I don't trust that."

"You've changed so much," he murmured. "More bold, more confident. Even these" — he grabbed her glasses— "are new. I can't wait to see all the ways you've changed."

She pressed herself to the stone wall as he leaned in again, the intoxicating juniper and citrus washing over her. She felt the tug of aithyr as she pulled, willing it closer. "Why were you with Oryck when he killed the pilinos? People saw you in your fey ..." she said, stumbling over the word, "fey form."

His smile sharpened. "I made sure the deaths came quickly and weren't drawn out. There was no need to be cruel. But you know my form." He leaned in close, holding her head as his mouth moved against her neck, making her shudder. "I wish to see what yours is. My guess is the last *lu"baiheòl*."

His body tensed at the same time Elyse felt the rush of aithyr under her skin, the trails of it circling around her. She released it all at once from her hands, sending Azarys backward with a gust of air.

She hardly registered the horns on his head and the claws that dug into the balcony tile as she turned and fled through the door. She needed to run, to escape. She heard Azarys behind as she made it to the hallway. "Goddess."

She tripped over something, her limbs numbing as she recognized the guards who escorted them there, all with their throats slit. A scream built in her throat and she pivoted toward the stairs. A server appeared in the stairwell. "Please, I need help."

The server closed in on Elyse, and in a flash of recognition, she realized she had seen her playing Flick at the party. A surge of realization hit her—Kurtys knew.

Elyse charged her, opening another ring that contained Mage's Eye and pulled as much aithyr as she could into her body. With a decisive motion, she unleashed it in a focused burst aimed directly at the server's gut. The female fell, and Elyse darted past and made it to the stairs.

Another figure ascended toward her. Without pause, Elyse launched herself into them, feeling the hem of her skirts tear. She leveraged her weight to slam into them with a satisfying crack as their head connected with the wall. She bolted down the steps, refusing to glance behind.

Below, the clamor of footsteps and raised voices echoed on the staircase. Elyse reached the nearest landing and focused, channeling aithyr through her, thinking of Wynn's bright blue eyes and the way they crinkled at the corners, sending him a message. *"Chorys Dasians. Az trying to take me."*

She turned a corner once, then twice, finding a dead end. The footsteps grew closer behind her. Elyse rushed to the window, discovering it towering over the canal. Too high to jump. Panicked, she opened the closest door to find a storage closet. Her heart sunk and she went to move onto the next as hands wrapped around her, covering her mouth as she was pulled backward into the closet. She tried to scream, stopping when she heard the voice whispering in her ear. "Quiet. Close your eyes."

Sylas. Sylas was here.

She thrashed against him, his free hand covering her sight. There was a grinding sound of stone on stone, then the muffled voice of Azarys. "Goddess?

There's nowhere to go."

Her breath hitched, and she relaxed against Sylas as she heard Azarys walk past.

The floor beneath her feet rumbled with a grinding sound, their bodies lowering. Sylas's voice whispered in her ear, "Door on the right leads to the side alley."

"Sylas—"

"Stop. If you want to save Wynn, run to the Forum. He's on the hill overlooking the burial pools."

"Why are you here? Why are you helping?"

"Elaborate plan to take you, but you need to escape, okay? Find Wynn and leave the city."

"What're you talking about?"

The space in front of them suddenly felt more open as the grinding sound stopped. Sylas answered by shoving her forward into the door.

Wynn. Elyse's stomach plummeted as she dashed into the kitchen and found an exit a few feet away. She tore it open and escaped through. Her muscles tensed as she channeled aithyr, propelling it through her body and into her legs. Wynn was in danger, and he needed her to save him.

The slit in her dress tore further as she vaulted over a stack of crates, her legs carrying her onto the street. She turned around, getting her bearings before sprinting toward the Forum.

People yelled at her as she sprinted; carriages coming to an abrupt halt as she moved, walkers shaking their angry fists. One of her shoes slipped off, and she continued, not stopping to pick it up. She tried messaging Wynn again. *I'm coming. Wynn, I'm coming.*

Over a bridge, down a path, up a set of stairs. Elyse did her best to recall how to get to the Forum, thinking back to the night Wynn took her out in the city. As she sprinted, more buildings became familiar. She could make it there in minutes if she hurried.

"Wynn?"

She ran a block.

"Wynn, are you okay?"

Her chest heaved, her blood pounding her ears as she started up a staircase to the Forum. She opened two more of her rings, downing the last of her Mage's Eye.

"WYNN?"

His silence was deafening as she reached the top. The bay turned to orange as the sun settled over the horizon. The Forum had closed for the day. Elyse slowed and caught her breath. She ducked under a barricade into the area and reached for her face, realizing she lost her glasses in the mix. That didn't stop her from seeing the swirls of aithyr. She paused and focused on them, pulling into her body as she let it flow to her ears. Panting breaths, the scraping of metal on metal. Someone cried out. Elyse darted in the direction, running full speed into a plaza above the city. Her heart stopped.

Wynn barely stood, holding a dagger in one hand, the other pressed to his side. Five mages circled him and he tried his best to deflect. Bright, bloody crimson stained his shirt.

Elyse didn't think. She didn't stop to consider how reckless it was or form a proper plan. Her mind was consumed by Wynn, by the overwhelming need to save him, and by a ruthlessness that made her want to kill.

She charged forward with a scream. Her fist met the first mage, her hand cracking with her aithyr-powered strength, sending him flying. Another swung at her with a dagger. She ducked and swiped a discarded dagger from the ground, using the momentum to swing up, the blade easily cutting across their abdomen. He fell to the ground with a cry.

"She's not supposed to be here!" one of them shouted as they dodged Wynn's attack.

"If we harm her, he'll kill us."

"She's going to kill us if we don't!" The attacker turned on Elyse. She charged at them, her body twisting to the side of their blade. She took her free hand and shoved it to their face and summoned fire. They screeched as the skin on their face melted, their hair scorched. They fell to the ground and didn't move.

Elyse redirected her focus to the rest.

"Run," Wynn grunted as he ducked. "Get out of here, Elyse."

She hardly heard him as the remaining three paused their attacks and assessed her. Elyse grabbed another dagger off the ground, her vision blackening at the edges.

"Subdue her!" one of them finally yelled. "The prince was supposed to hold her."

Two mages went in opposite directions, beginning to circle Elyse. She screamed as she pulled the aithyr into herself, darkness taking over her vision. A black shroud expanded from her body, entrapping them. Their bodies seized in the dark and she screamed louder as the energy ripped through her body. It was as if half of her was being torn asunder. It was as if this darkness inside of her would consume everything if she wished.

She didn't care. She wouldn't care. They would be punished for attacking Wynn, for drawing his blood.

A figure approached in the darkness, their body the hazy white of aithyr. They raised a hand and placed it on Elyse's forearm. Though they didn't speak, Elyse knew she needed to stop.

She dropped her aithyr, the black shroud shrinking back into her chest. She heaved a breath, finding the enemy mages all still on the ground. Black veins marred their skin around their mouths, eyes, and noses.

The last mage swore as Elyse approached.

"Go, Elyse." Wynn slumped to the ground, barely able to hold up his head as he spoke the command.

She would never. She could never leave him. The female mage twisted toward Elyse, her blades moving faster than Elyse could react. In a fit of frustration, she screamed, her vision going black. Through the dim, she saw the outline of the mage and stuck her blade into her chest, pushing her to the ground. With the power of aithyr, she jammed the blade further until her ribs crunched underhand.

Elyse's strength gave out, and she fell back with heavy and ragged breaths. Her vision cleared slowly, and she inched across the blood-soaked ground, crawling toward Wynn. Every movement was a struggle, a battle against the overwhelming weight of despair that pressed down on her. Wynn. She needed to get to Wynn.

At his side, her trembling fingers brushed away the tangled locks of hair that clung to his battered face, tracing the jagged path of the fresh wound that marred his features, a cruel twin to his scar. Blood flowed unabated, staining his cheek and trailing down to his neck.

"You need to leave," he whispered, his voice strained and barely audible.

"We need help," she stammered. "We can find a healer."

Hesitantly, she lifted the edge of his shirt, her stomach churning at the gruesome sight of his exposed organs. The reality of his injuries crashed over her, but she couldn't look away.

"There is no saving me," he said, his voice filled with resignation. "They're after you."

"No, no, no, no…" Tears pricked her eyes. "I won't leave you here."

Wynn's shaking hand cupped her cheek, his eyes filled with a love so profound it needed no words. He leaned in slowly and pressed his lips to hers. She held onto him, sobbing into the kiss. "Elyse, look at me," he said, his voice barely more than a whisper. "I'm sorry I won't be there to see the mage you'll become. Chorys Dasi wants you. The palace is compromised. You need to flee to the Circle of Mages in the mountains south of The Queen's Pass."

As tears blurred her vision, she didn't dare turn away. She needed to memorize every detail of his face. The lines around his eyes, his lips. The way his scar pulled at his mouth when he talked. The look in his eyes as he tried to save her.

"I won't leave you," she choked out.

Wynn removed his hand from her cheek and opened one of his rings.

"Don't!" she screamed, lunging too late to prevent the poison's release as it splashed into his mouth.

"Run, Elyse," he murmured, his voice weak as he slumped further against the wall.

"Don't leave me," she begged, shaking him. "I need you, Wynn. You said I would be stuck with you forever." Wynn's ragged breath slowed. "Wynn, please!"

He slipped his hand into hers. "I love you. I could've loved you forever. Choose life, Elyse." His grip slacked in hers.

"Wynn?" She shook him. "Wynn, wake up!" She shook him again, his body heavy, his blue eyes glazed over lifelessly.

A guttural scream erupted from deep within her, a visceral sound that echoed through the air and tore at her throat. He couldn't be gone. The world couldn't exist without Wynn. She pulled at his arm. "Wynn, please come back! I need you!" She pressed a kiss into his hand. "Please don't leave."

A sob shook her body. In the distance, she could hear voices. None of it mattered. If she had run faster, if she had realized it was Azarys sooner, Wynn would still be alive. She took a heaving breath; the tears streaming down her face and mixed with the pool of blood beneath her knees.

As voices drew nearer, Elyse felt a gentle touch on her shoulder. She tore her gaze from Wynn's lifeless form to see swirls of aithyr coalescing into a spectral figure. The aithyr being gestured urgently, guiding her toward the main Forum.

Leaving Wynn's body was like peeling the flesh from her own skin. She wouldn't—couldn't. The aithyr being held out its hand. Elyse hesitated, then placed her hand in its, the world suddenly slipping away.

There was no pain, no turmoil threatening to tear her from within, and though she saw, it was as if she looked at the world from someone else's body. Her legs moved to their own accord, running back up the stairs and toward the far side of the Forum. With it, Elyse drowned herself in the aithyr until she existed no longer.

Chapter Sixty-Three
MARIETTA

Another day, another temple, and still no Wyltam by her side. Marietta avoided Coryn's gaze as he sat across from her in the carriage, heading to the Temple of Zontykroi.

"I've never been inside their temple," Coryn said, trying to lighten the mood. "Do you think the interior is as menacing as the outside?"

Marietta shrugged. "Does it really matter?"

Coryn held her stare, unperturbed. "I know you're upset that Wyltam refused to come again, but try to see the bright side."

"And what would that be?"

"More time with me."

Marietta rolled her eyes. "Yes, because we don't spend enough time together."

"Sounds like you don't enjoy my company." He raised a brow and leaned back in his seat. "Shocking, considering most people love me."

"Don't you know most people have terrible taste?" she added in a mocking tone. "I would be more humble if I were you."

He tsked. "In the quiet of humility, the echo of one's own worth may be the only resounding cheer."

"Gods, don't get poetic." She pinched the bridge of her nose. "The echo of self-worth falls as an irksome drone for those who seek a modest silence."

"Not bad. See, all this time with me is rubbing off."

"Unfortunately."

"You don't mean that."

Marietta took in the curve of his smile, the light of amusement dancing in his eyes. No, she didn't. If anything, she appreciated his companionship now more than ever. She shrugged and said, "I enjoy you enough."

The carriage came to a halt, their destination a black monolith in the evening light. Marietta stood and smoothed the fine fabric of her skirts before taking Coryn's outstretched hand and exiting the carriage.

The Queen's Guard created a circle around her as cries came from the small crowd gathered, despite the time and weather. Her breath formed a puff as she laughed and waved before ascending the steps.

Statues lined the path and emphasized the heaviness forming on her chest. Some were of the elderly, of the pained and dying with their faces contorted. "They're eerier than I remembered," she murmured to Coryn.

"I guess they are. At some point, I must've grown blind to that," he answered as they passed the statue of Zontykroi with his close-cropped hair and missing ears.

The white banners with the deity's symbol—a crescent facing up stacked on top of a thin-lined circle with another crescent below facing down—blew in the chilled autumn air. Flurries of snow contrasted with the dark stone, and Marietta pulled her cape tightly around her body.

Black marble walls lined the inside as they entered, the dark stone swallowing the light from the globes that drifted above. While the dark should have been oppressive, it felt light, freeing almost.

"Good evening, Your Grace," Moira said. Stitched across the front of her white tunic was an ornate version of the pattern on the banners outside. "We appreciate your understanding with the time," she added. "It's always best to perform claiming ceremonies under the moon."

They followed Moira through the temple halls, finding more statues of what appeared to be ordinary people—elves, half-elves, humans. Even an orc with their jutting tusks and vast frame.

Reaching the prayer room, Marietta was taken aback by how simple it was. The other temples possessed impressive depictions of their patron in fitting form of their attributes, standing tall above their worshippers. The statue of Zontykroi was the same as out front but smaller, placed level with the rest of the chamber. Fungi of all kinds grew in the corners and at the base of the columns. Marietta went to inspect as the attendant pulled her attention.

"Death humbles us all." Moira faced the statue, her head tilted to the side. "It doesn't care about status or titles, of accolades or crimes. Death is the equalizer of everyone, us all meeting its fate one way or another."

Moira glanced over her shoulder, her white irises standing out in the dim. "I know it's not as impressive as the other temples, but it's special in its own way."

Marietta surveyed the unadorned nature of the dark room, comfort settling around her like a soft cloak. Above, a round skylight admitted the rising moon's gentle glow. "Simplicity doesn't diminish its beauty." She met the smile with her own. "I feel welcomed here."

Moira nodded. "A good sign. Zontykroi approves of you." The attendant turned and clasped her hands behind her back. "I asked for a private claiming ceremony this evening, if you don't mind. Given that you are our queen, the attention detracts from the meaning of today." She gestured Marietta forward and approached the statue. She noticed the immature heads of yarrow at Zontykroi's feet. "The moon is full as well. Another good omen."

"Do you believe in omens?" Marietta asked.

Coryn answered first. "Most do."

"That's true," Moira added. "The flow of the world is ever-changing. Certain signs indicate whether that change is positive or negative, giving insight to that which our mortal beings could never understand." Moira hesitated, then asked, "I know magic hasn't always been embraced in Satiros, but does Your Grace know of aithyr? Given your relation to Fulbryk, I'll assume so."

Marietta nodded, the ache of Wyltam's absence sharp in her chest.

"Aithyr flows through everything. Is it not the power of aithyr to give us such signs?"

"I didn't realize the temples were so closely tied to magic." Marietta tilted her head, previously thinking the two ideologies were opposites.

"Oh, we aren't." Moira stepped forward, her gaze focused on the ground as she crouched. "Just Zontykroi." She pressed on a stone, the floor retracting back to reveal a rectangular hole. "In order to commune with Zontykroi, one must experience death."

Her breath quickened. "I have to die for the claiming?"

"Of sorts. You will live, but not before you experience death." She waved Marietta forward. "Come."

She exchanged a glance with Coryn, who offered her a reassuring smile. Gathering herself, she approached Moira and clasped her hand before descending into the hole. Darkness swallowed her as she lay on her back, staring up at Moira.

"Zontykroi," the iros called out, "bless this being as she steps into your realm. Return her to us unscathed." The stones slid overhead.

In the dark, Marietta heard nothing, saw nothing. Even the padding beneath her back cushioned her, leaving her devoid of sensation. The air grew thick in the enclosed space, threatening to choke her. Perhaps that's how she was about to experience death.

Never one to fear the dark or small spaces, being trapped made her limbs tense, her body wishing to push against the stone above and inhale fresh air. Instead, she resisted the temptation. She focused on her breaths and closed her eyes. She imagined herself as the darkness, as nothing, and her mind slipped away.

She stood on a white, shimmering floor that seemed to shift under her feet. Darkness expanded all around her. In the distance, she saw a figure and started walking toward it.

"You've come." The voice came from everywhere, including inside of her. She turned, finding no one.

"Zontykroi?"

"Keep walking, chaidhleh sithfaìelph, and I will join you on your journey."

She saw the figure on the horizon and began again. "Seidytar also called me that. What does it mean?"

"It means you are a … chosen."

"Does that mean you'll claim me as your iros?"

"If you would like to be." She saw a shadow at the corner of her vision that disappeared when she turned toward it. When she faced forward, it returned. *"You always have a choice with me. I do not command the living nor make choices for you. I only usher your soul on once you pass."*

"Does that mean you know where we go when we die?" At his silence, Marietta sighed. "If being your iros means helping the people of Satiros, then I claim it."

"Just those living in Satiros?" The figure materialized more in her peripherals. *"Becoming my iros means accepting death. Death scares you."*

"Untimely death scares me," she corrected. "Death of those I love before their time scares me."

"Death claims all mortals. It should not be a fear, but an inevitability. You fear not having forever with those you love, that you leave things unresolved." A hand slipped into hers. *"You fear that you cause them pain, that death rests on your shoulders."*

I cannot say if your decisions lead to death, but I can promise you this: death is indiscriminate. Whether you're promised centuries of life or the few weeks of infancy, death will claim you despite if it seems unfair or just. Regardless of your actions, they will succumb to death. All one can do is make sure they pass on in peace."

She turned to the figure that came into view beside her. Zontykroi's face was austere though handsome, the point of his ears severe enough that she furrowed her brows. Suddenly, his features were gone, replaced with that of a skull. Marietta jumped back, but the bony hand held onto her tight. Her heart squeezed in her chest and she looked forward. The figure shifted at her side.

"If you accept your place among my iros, I task you with the responsibility of passing on the dying. Sparing life, while tempting, comes with grave costs. My iros may attempt it, but I only spare those who will be restless souls in my domain."

Marietta processed his words, coming to the shocking realization. "You can prevent people from dying—your iros can."

"A feature known to only those in our order, which I risk sharing with you

because I can sense you want to accept."

They grew silent as the person she approached took a more solid form. They slumped to the ground, Marietta hurrying her steps.

"Not everyone will accept the choice to live and the price it is to pay." Zontykroi kept pace at her side. *"Only those truly for the living are given the chance."*

Marietta slowed her steps as she neared the person, bloodied and beaten. Brown hair stuck to his face. Another shape appeared before them, ethereal and wispy, vaguely the form of a woman. It held out a hand to the side of the person.

She kneeled next to the fallen person, keeping a distance from the new figure. She took in the details of his face and gasped, her fear suffocating her. "Wynn?" Marietta grasped his arm, her touch turning his skin white and wispy, slowly spreading through his body. She watched in horror as he became devoid of color, his expression easing from pain to peace. He opened his eyes and blinked, then turned to the figure beside her.

She wanted to tell Zontykroi to save him, to spare his life, but her body grew heavy, her tongue stuck to the roof of her dry mouth. Wynn stood and placed his hand in Zontykroi's, his being shattering into thousands of streams of light.

Marietta took a heaving breath, her friend there one moment, gone the next. The figure off to the side extended its hand to nothing, then disappeared altogether.

"You've now seen death," Zontykroi said. *"Is it fear you feel or grief?"*

Marietta moved her jaw, tears streaming down her face. Wynn had looked peaceful, had gone to the deity willingly. Was that what happened when someone passed? She shook her head, an aching opening in her chest. Grief, with its recognizable ache, spread through her body. She glanced up at Zontykroi, the deity transitioning from skull to familiar face with each pulse of her blood. "I fear the feeling of grief, not death."

"Do you accept your position as my iros?"

She didn't hesitate. "I do."

A bright light flashed before her eyes.

Marietta was on her back once more, the stone pulling back from above her. The bright light remained, lighting everything she saw. Moira's mouth parted as she extended a hand to Marietta. As she stood, a gasp came from Coryn. She turned to find her guard with furrowed brows and a slack jaw.

Moira approached with a mirror. Before Marietta's eyes and curving above her head was the upturned crescent of Zontykroi.

Marietta's hands shook as she dropped it, her grief swallowing her whole once more.

"She's witnessed death," Moira said. "True death with Zontykroi."

"Wynn," Marietta said with a sob. "Something's wrong—he's dead."

Coryn approached, and she fell into his arms, a sob working through her. Coryn murmured something, but it was cut off by someone entering.

An attendant filled the doorway, Adalyn beside him, breathless and wide-eyed. Her face, drained of color, said more than words ever could. When she spoke, her voice trembled. "Word just reached us—Reyilan legions were spotted in the Dead Forest. They're advancing on Satiros."

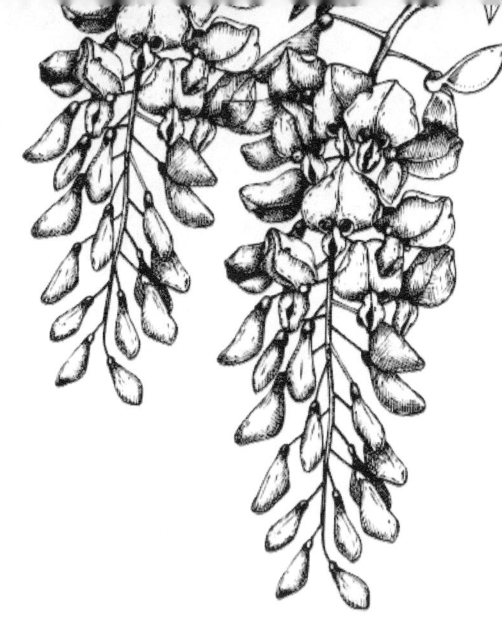

Part Three

"Aithyr is never made, never lost—only shifted, a power that moves from one force to the next."

-

Lyken's Third Principle

Chapter Sixty-Four
MARIETTA

Marietta closed the door behind her, leaning against it as her legs buckled. She sank to the floor, the weight of it all pressing down on her. Tears clouded her sight, but the image remained clear—the vision of Wynn unraveling into threads of light, replaying relentlessly in her mind.

Wyltam appeared beside her, crouching with concern etched across his face. "Marietta? What happened?"

Her voice broke. "Wynn—I saw him. He's gone, Wyltam. Dead."

Wyltam's brow furrowed as he gripped her trembling hand. "What?"

"I saw the god of life and death. He showed me Wynn dying." She heaved a breath, her voice breaking. "I watched him die."

Wyltam stared at her for a moment, then said, "The god could've been deceiving you."

"He wasn't—"

"Marietta, I warned you."

"Listen to me!" Marietta grabbed the collar of his shirt. "He is gone. The god didn't lie or manipulate me. Use your magic to talk to Wynn—send him a message."

Wyltam gently pulled her hand from his shirt, retreating a step as he sank back, closing his eyes. Silence stretched, one minute, then another, as if he could will away the truth. When he finally opened them, worry creased his features. "He's just busy."

Marietta's voice trembled, barely more than a whisper. "I'm sorry, Wyltam. He's dead. He's gone." His body tensed, but she pressed on, voice tight with grief. "And Elyse? Can you … can you see if she's alive?"

"I already did."

"And?"

Wyltam swallowed hard, his eyes darting back and forth. "I'll try again in the morning. In case they—in case he—" His hands shook slightly as he ran them over his face, letting out a deep sigh. When he lowered them, his expressionless mask slid back into place. He helped Marietta to her feet. "Come, I'll send for tea. We have some things to discuss."

Seated in Wyltam's office, Marietta poured herself a cup of the lavender tea, the herb unlikely to stop her body from shaking as grief threatened to take over. Wyltam sat in his chair, his head resting back. At last, he said, "I told Keyain about the fey."

Marietta's stomach dropped. "Keyain? The same Keyain who betrayed you?"

"He knows when I'm serious about a threat." He sighed, rubbing his brow. "I'm postponing the guild vote until after the wedding."

"But I gave them one month. The Vassals branch—"

"Reyila's legions have moved into the Dead Forest. They've crossed into Satiros's territory." His voice was tight, the words clipped. "My contact confirms Chorys Dasi is ready to march any day now. We thought we'd have until winter. We thought we had time." He finally lifted his head, locking eyes with Marietta. "We either focus everything on the war or the wedding."

Her stomach knotted. "Then we need to warn the ministers about the fey."

"No."

She blinked, caught off guard by the sharp refusal.

"Someone leaked Valeriya's death to the public—something only my ministers knew. If word gets out that Chorys Dasi holds stronger magic than we anticipated, panic will rip through the city."

Marietta thought of the riots a few months prior. "The population is swelling. It could be …"

"A disaster. We'll expect a surge over the next week. We won't have room for everyone." He sighed, pushed back his chair, and stood to pace behind his desk. "Keyain knows, and that's what is important. He decided against telling his troops. If they knew they went against a supernatural threat, how many would turn coat?"

"Hopefully none," Marietta said cooly.

"If only."

"And what of Enomenos?" she asked, thinking of how her father and the representatives from Enomenos would be in the city-state any day.

"We sent them a message as a warning but expressed the wedding will still happen, no matter what."

"Seems foolish to have a wedding now."

Wyltam paused his pacing and fully turned to her. "Getting a crown on your head is of the utmost importance. We need the promise of Enomenoan troops, the Exisotis' ability to gather intelligence." He shook his head. "The people need hope that a new queen will lead them to safety."

She swallowed hard. "And what if we still can't win?"

His hardened gaze fell on her. "Then you will flee the city."

"Wyltam, I'm not—"

"You will flee the city and get somewhere safe. The tunnels beneath the palace empty out into the surrounding countryside. If our defeat looks imminent, you will leave."

"You don't get to decide that. You just said that I'm hope for the people of Satiros."

He turned to Marietta with a somber expression. "And if you die, I will lose hope in everything."

His words hung between them, ominous but softer than anything he'd said to her since discovering the truth about fey. Marietta pressed the heel of her hands into her eyes as tears formed again. The weight of the war, the looming marriage, and Wynn's loss threatened to crush her. She would give anything to feel Wyltam's arms around her.

"Wyltam, I'm—"

"Go get some rest. It might be your last chance over the next few weeks."

Marietta woke to the pale light of dawn, her eyes adjusting slowly to the dim room. Wyltam sat at the edge of the bed, his expression heavy with something unsaid. Silence stretched between them, thick and unbearable, before he spoke.

"Amigys used a mage to deliver a message." His voice was hollow. "They found Wynn's body."

A fresh wave of grief hit her, sharp and sudden, but she forced herself to shift closer, laying a hand on Wyltam's arm. "I'm sorry," she whispered.

"Elyse—" He cleared his throat as he dropped his head. "Wynn spent his last moments to get her help. A few of our friends are searching for her."

"Searching?"

"There wasn't a body at the scene. She and a Satiroan ambassador are unaccounted for."

"What friends?"

"Allies I have in the area. They'll find her."

He rose without another word, his grief palpable. Marietta stayed quiet, giving him space as she lay in bed for hours, watching the first light spill across the room. Her mind drifted back to the chaos after Keyain caught her kissing Wyltam, to the lies she spun about a pregnancy that never existed. Those moments, once monumental, seemed so small now. Back then, she had Elyse. She had Wynn. She had Amryth before everything fell apart.

Her thoughts looped in circles, each memory sharp as it resurfaced. She paced the room, restless. The grief churned, gnawing at her from within, killing any chance of hunger. She needed something—anything—to ground herself.

As if in answer, Mycaub and Keya stepped in, the boy's excited chatter filling the space, pulling a laugh from the governess. They both paused when they saw her.

"Lady Marietta," he said with a bow, too formal for his age.

She knelt to meet his eyes. "Marietta, remember?"

His face flushed, and he ducked behind Keya's skirt, still bashful but with more energy than usual.

"Are you done with your lessons today?"

He shook his head.

The governess met her gaze. "He could be, if you have something in mind."

Marietta smiled, offering her hand.

The palace kitchens followed the same chaotic rhythm she remembered. Cooks and bakers, runners and servants all played their part as they danced across the floor to the chorus of chopping, sizzling, and laughter.

Marietta wore her new apron that Chef Emynuel handed her. "A gift from the king," he had explained. He must've planned that weeks ago, thinking she would've visited the kitchens again at some point. Perhaps she should've. She ran her hands over the simple but fine cotton. On her chest was embroidered her shop name, Rise Above Bakery, with the wisteria of the Satiroan crest below. She tried and failed to ignore the pulling in her heart.

As she gathered the ingredients and bowls with Mycaub, she noticed someone in the corner eating, making her steps falter. Tilan sat with a small plate of food, his expression revealing his surprise at seeing her as well. She considered approaching him, but the memory of their last conversation stopped her. She waved, receiving one in return. His arms were adorned with metal braces of some sort. While curious to know the details of them, she was content knowing that he had gotten help with his hands. Before her mind could spiral into the past, she dove headfirst into baking with Mycaub's help.

Standing on a chair next to Marietta, she steadied his hands as they measured semolina flour and placed it into a bowl.

"Would you like to do it yourself?" she asked while he scooped more.

He nodded eagerly, a mix of enthusiasm and caution in his movements as he leveled the flour. When he dumped it into the bowl, a cloud of white dusted the counter, and tears brimmed in his eyes. She hushed him, gently demonstrating that mistakes were part of the process. She swiped some flour and dabbed it on her nose. "Sometimes I even wear my mistakes."

Mycaub giggled, his laughter brightening the room as he threw his head back, a wide smile spreading across his face. Marietta scooped up more flour with her finger and marked his nose. "Now we match."

Her laughter was cut short as she sensed the hair on her neck prickle.

Glancing toward Tilan, she noticed he wasn't alone. He spoke, nodding as he exchanged words with another. Since when did they talk to one another? Both turned their heads toward her, her expression shifting to concern. Tilan said something to which Wyltam clasped his shoulder before striding across the kitchen.

Marietta turned away, unwilling to endure another update, another reminder of the world beyond the kitchens. "We should work on the syrup next." She led Mycaub to the stovetop, deliberately ignoring Wyltam. "These were my favorite as a child," she said, guiding Mycaub as he placed an orange half into the pot with water, sugar, cinnamon sticks, and cloves. "My father always made melomakarona around the solstice."

She kept the conversation flowing with Mycaub as they waited for the mixture to boil and the sugar to dissolve. Once it was ready, she removed it from the heat and added the honey, allowing Mycaub to stir. "Good job!" she praised, scraping the last remnants of honey from the jar. "I could've used a helper like you at my bakery."

He met her gaze, his dark eyes wide. "Me?"

"Absolutely." She placed her hands on her hips. "You're very helpful. I foresee many baking days ahead of us."

A grin broke across his face as he leaped down from the chair, dragging it back to the worktable where they would finish the dough. Unfortunately, Wyltam was already there. Marietta stilled, anxiety coiling in her stomach, unsure of the news he would bring and whether he would stay long enough to help comfort the swell of her emotions. Mycaub, however, bowed his head to his father.

Wyltam greeted him and asked, "What are you making?"

As Mycaub climbed back onto his chair, he began recounting every step they had done, including the number of scoops they had for each ingredient. Marietta furrowed her brows, both surprised that he could remember it all, but also how talkative he had grown with Wyltam. Much had changed in the past few months.

Marietta ducked down to Mycaub's level when he finished speaking. "Can you go see if they're done juicing those oranges for us?"

He nodded and jumped from the chair.

"Careful," Wyltam warned, earning a smile from his son. He turned his attention to Marietta, his words faltering.

She spun and began cleaning up part of the mess they made. "Can you explain what that was about?" She nodded at Tilan. He probably sought the familiarity of the kitchens. That, and the chaos. He always went to the loudest places to do his best thinking.

Wyltam's eyebrows twitched. "Tilan was telling me things I already knew." He walked around the counter and rolled up his sleeves. "How can I help?"

She glanced at him, half tempted to say they didn't need it, but thought better. Mycaub seemed to enjoy his father's presence more than he had prior. "Help him carry back the orange juice," she said, turning to find Mycaub walking slower than a snail with a cup in his hand. The kitchen workers were forced to maneuver around him.

A low laugh came from Wyltam, and she turned to see the half-smile coming to his lips. "He's so cautious. I was the same way." He took off before Marietta could respond, leaving her dumbfounded. She watched as he approached his son and ducked down to speak with him. Mycaub held the cup closer to his chest, making Wyltam laugh again. He stood and walked him back toward their station.

Never had Marietta witnessed Wyltam's humor spill so freely. Never in front of others, let alone in a crowded kitchen with his son beside him. The sight of their laughter struck a chord within her. For the first time, she glimpsed what could be if Wyltam chose to forgive her: the three of them together, a family.

Hours later, Marietta found Wyltam in his office, surrounded by piles of strange objects scattered across his desk. Before him sat a book. He only paused his tinkering to flip the page and continue reading. The low light made his features more haggard.

She knocked on the doorframe. "Can I bother you?"

Wyltam didn't look up as he answered, "Come in."

Marietta grimaced at his lack of acknowledgment, though she supposed she deserved it. Her nose crinkled at the overwhelming scent of sulfur as she entered the room. As she approached, she hesitated behind the chair while he joined glass and metal components. Wyltam's current indifference drove home that his presence in the kitchens was because of Mycaub and not because he forgave her.

"I'm sorry," she started, picking at the fabric of the chair. "It's understandable that you're angry with me, and I don't hold it against you. I should've told you or someone else sooner. But this?" She gestured to his head bent over a glass globe wrapped in iron strips, inside foggy with a clear liquid. "This rift between us? It helps no one but our enemies."

Wyltam took one of the globes and set it into an iron casing, taking a second half of iron and twisting it shut. The silence was deafening, forcing Marietta to focus on the sharpness of her breath and the relentless beat of her heart. She thought he wouldn't respond, but at last he said, "I need time to process how I feel. The greater the emotions, the longer it takes."

"What emotions are you processing, then?"

His dark gaze found her, his hands still working as he grabbed the next globe. "A mix of adoration and heartbreak." He glanced down as he placed the glass into the iron case. "Two conflicting emotions over one person."

Marietta furrowed her brows, her jaw moving, though she found herself speechless. Plopping herself into the chair, her face and chest warming. "Adoration and heartbreak, as in …?"

"I regret not warning you that becoming a royal would change not only how you present yourself but also the choices you make. Choosing Elyse's magic was selfish and served only Elyse. Now we're left scrambling for solutions based on myths." He lifted one of the globes, shaking the liquid inside.

"I didn't do it to be selfish," she whispered.

"I know," he said, "you thought you were helping. The same hubris as Valeriya, believing you were doing good, but your scope was too narrow."

Tears blurred Marietta's eyes and looked up to blink them away. Yes, she had made a mistake, but knowing such didn't ease the painful rift growing between them. Wyltam became colder and more distant than ever. While she didn't regret helping Elyse, she did regret pushing him away. Having had him so close only made the icy distance burn more.

"The difference between you and Valeriya," he said, drawing her attention, "is that she functionally died because of her choices. I would need to be dead for the same to happen to you."

She turned to him, losing the battle with her tears as they streamed down her cheeks. "You still care."

"I apologize if I ever made you feel otherwise."

She huffed a laugh and wiped her face dry with the edge of her sleeve. "Can we return to the adoration part?"

His gaze dropped again, his hands moving slower as he talked. "Your laugh, your very being—I'm helplessly drawn to you. I catch myself watching you, and when you're not beside me, it's like something's missing. Even as I try to explain these emotions, I don't understand them. I struggle to articulate how I feel." He twisted the metal shut around the globe and met her stare. "You are a song I can't get out of my head, and expressing how I feel is like trying to speak in musical notation."

Marietta's heart hammered in her chest, her throat thick. Throughout her life, she'd compared to many things, but never a song. Nothing came close to that comparison.

"But those feelings?" He shook his head and selected another globe. "I experience them when we're united, which is far from what we are now. The discovery of fey is no small secret. You risked the lives of so many after swearing to me and the citizens of Satiros that you'd keep them safe. As we stand at the brink of war, with a crown almost within your reach, I can't help but wonder if you would stay true to your oath or prioritize your loved ones." Marietta went to respond but he added, "And I question if I am one of those people."

She had wanted all of his emotions, but experiencing them now was too raw, too real. "I never meant to be divided. How could I trust you if I thought you'd take repercussions on Elyse? Never did I think you'd accept the existence of fey so easily. Their existence is absurd."

Wyltam sighed and sat back in his chair. "Everything I do for Elyse is for her protection, which removing her magic would do more harm than good. I'm not as cruel as you make me out to be. Not for the ones I care about."

Was that what she thought of him? Cruel? She shook her head. "You are many things, Wyltam Grytsier, but I don't think you are cruel."

He exhaled with a laugh. "You still don't know me enough. War will bring out my worst, but I promise to never turn it on you. You should go rest."

Marietta stood with a stretch, noting at the objects strewn around him. "Will you join me tonight?"

He kept quiet for a breath, then said, "If I finish these in time." He set another completed iron gadget and started the next.

"If I help you, will it get you to bed sooner?"

He glanced up. "I'm not sure if you'll want to help with these."

"Why not?"

He shook one of the globes. "Liquid magicsbane wrapped in iron with black powder and an igniter. It—"

"Combusts," Marietta said quietly, dread shooting through her body. "That's why you and Tilan were talking. More weapons."

"The goal is to cause wounds so that the magicsbane can take effect," he said, eyeing her. "All the other creations are tools. Equipment. Goggles to see aithyr. Devices that can locate persons drawing magic. Shields composed of aithyr for those of us who can use magic. Even stealth armor for select individuals."

Marietta nodded. A sudden heaviness settled into her chest.

"I also saw his designs for the Exisotis. We will use none of those," he said, raising his brows. "I promise."

"Will the Exisotis use them? Or Enomenos?" The items on his desk weren't the lethal creations Tilan crafted; they were tools designed to neutralize Chorys Dasi's magic. Instruments of assistance, not destruction.

Wyltam didn't answer for a moment, then finally said, "War exposes the worst in people. Do not judge them for protecting themselves."

"I judge them for being so eager to wield death." She picked up a globe. "Show me how to help."

Chapter Sixty-Five

ELYSE

The world appeared distant to her, as if seen through a blurred lens. The edges of her vision fuzzed white with aithyr. She could sense her body move, but not the life beyond her. If she hungered, she didn't feel her stomach growl. If her feet ached from the days of walking, she didn't feel the pain. The aithyr shielded her from her mortal body.

Elyse saw everything and felt nothing.

No physical sensations and no emotions, as if they were locked away, removed from her as well. If she felt it all, she'd crumble and never move again.

Mostly, she avoided people. She hadn't interacted with anyone until she reached a river and needed to cross by ferry. The ferryman had tried to help her by asking why she traveled alone. The aithyr had answered for her, insisting she only needed safe passage, the voices muffled as if she had a head cold. The ferryman said he didn't give rides for free, but he'd make an exception. He fed her, gave her shoes, for she had none until that point. When they landed, he told her to wait, that he'd get her a change of clothes as well. The aithyr knew he had alerted the guards, which was undesirable, so she fled.

Throughout the Amigyan countryside, she found hollows to sleep in, taking the occasional stable to shield her from the chilled nights. Elyse knew she needed to travel somewhere, but the aithyr took over. Where she went, she didn't know. Didn't care.

While she ate little, she tasted none of it. The stale water she drank satisfied her minimal thirst. Aithyr removed her mortality for the better. It kept her alive when she would choose death.

Time meant nothing. Hours slipped into days. She didn't keep track of the number of suns risen or the waning of the moon in the sky.

The land eventually gave way to hills, mountains towering in the distance. She traveled up and down until she reached the rocky base. At one point, she stayed in a single spot for a day, waiting for what she didn't know.

Then she heard the voices, an elven male with skin so olive it appeared green in the haze, and a human woman who towered above him. The aithyr pushed her toward the pair. They offered her a hand. She never reached for it, and instead, collapsed to the ground.

The first thing she became aware of was the piercing pain in her skull, followed by a wave of overwhelming nausea. Elyse rolled over, heaving though nothing came out.

"Shhh." There was a wet cloth on her forehead, a hand slowly rubbing her back. Her heart skipped a beat, her mind jumping to Wynn. She opened her bleary eyes to see Sibylla. "You're awake," she said breathlessly.

"Wynn," Elyse said, her voice harsh and dry. Then she remembered.

Tears welled in her eyes, blurring the room into an indistinct smear of colors as she grappled with the memories that threatened to swallow her whole. A sob built in the back of her throat as she lowered her head to the mattress, ignoring the pounding pressure in her skull. "He's gone, he's gone, he's gone ..."

"It's all right," Sibylla murmured, her voice tight. "You're all right."

Her chest caved open, his last moments burning into her mind. The blood caked to his skin, his hair, his clothes. The lifeless gaze in his eyes. Elyse punched the mattress once, twice, and sobbed. She couldn't get enough air, her throat closing, her chest too tight. "He said forever. He said he'd never leave. He said—"

Every shallow inhale she drew echoed the frantic beats of her heart, each pulse a haunting reminder of her failure. How did she not realize it was Azarys? How could she have trusted Kurtys? For if she hadn't, then she would've been with Wynn. If she hadn't, then maybe he'd still be alive.

Sibylla took a shaky breath next to her, and Elyse turned her watery gaze to see her head pressed into the edge of the mattress. The mage lifted her head, eyes red from crying. Elyse tugged her into a hug, burrowing her face into her hair. In return, Sibylla lifted a hand to the back of her head, pulling Elyse close as they continued to weep for the shared person they had lost.

They would never open a coffee shop. She would never complain to him about the laps around the Mage Pit. There would never again be more lazy afternoons in her suite where he napped, and she flipped through a book. Wynn was gone, and now she didn't know what to do. Didn't know how to continue.

Elyse wasn't sure how long they stayed embraced with one another, crying. It didn't matter. Not even the pain in her head mattered, even as the room spun. Eventually, Sibylla pulled away and took Elyse's hands in hers.

"How are you here?" Elyse asked.

"Wynn sent a message to me"—she took a deep breath—"that he sent you in this direction. To come and save you. I left Satiros within the hour." A tear trailed down her cheek as she added, "He loved you so much. He would be so grateful that you are here and not aithyrstruck. We thought—" Tears filled her eyes again, and she shook her head. "We thought we lost you for good," she whispered.

Her voice sounded raw. "I don't understand."

"When they found you, aithyr had choked out any bit of your personality, as if it took over," Sibylla explained. "It's rare to recover from that. People in that state don't wake up and remember who they are. How much aithyr did you use?"

Thinking back, Elyse remembered the Mage's Eye she took and how exhilarating it was to have her body completely filled with the energy. How she felt unstoppable. Elyse worked her mouth, shame washing over her again.

All of that power, and she still failed.

"A lot."

Sibylla's brows furrowed, her gaze roaming over Elyse. After a moment of silence, she said, "You should eat. I'll have someone deliver breakfast."

Her stomach turned at the mere mention of food. "I just want to sleep," she said, lying down on her side. "But I don't know if I can." Tears gathered on the pillow.

"Wait," Sibylla said, leaving briefly and returning with a cup. She lifted it to Elyse's face. Effects consumed her aching mind and heart, leading her back to darkness.

When she woke again, she heard a murmuring of voices. Elyse rolled over, her eyes heavy with sleep and her head still aching, though not as severe. Sibylla spoke in low tones to a male whose skin was the color of olive leaves. Propping herself up on one arm, she wiped her face to make her vision adjust. Yet the color of his skin remained. She took in other details, like the silky black strands of his hair, of the pointed tips of his ears. Two tusks peeked between his lips. When he turned, his ruby-colored eyes landed on her.

Sibylla came to the bedside. "How are you feeling?"

Pain lingered on the edges of her exhaustion, but she pushed her mind from it. "Well enough."

She offered a small smile. "Grab some water and a bite of food. We want to show you the compound."

Elyse, curious, nibbled bread and observed the room. The walls were of rough stone, as if the space formed naturally in the rock. A fire burned in a hearth, offering low light to the dark. She noticed a window behind her. Standing on shaky legs, she hissed at the stinging in her feet as she shuffled to it. In the fading light, the mountains and hills stretched to a sea in the distance. She turned with a question on her lips, finding Sibylla and the stranger staring at her.

"Welcome to the Circle of Mages," he said, his voice low and pleasant. "It's an honor to have Anthylia's daughter and our founder's granddaughter finally here." He bowed his head.

"Wyltam hasn't told you much. Neither did Wynn," she said. "If you can manage a walk, we could see the compound before it's too dark."

Mere thoughts of people or conversation made Elyse hesitate. As she glanced around the room, the edges of her grief threatened to crush her, and she accepted the offer.

Sibylla introduced the male as Mol, an orc from Sufiaard, which they explained was the true name of The Southern Wastes, contrary to what she was taught in Satiros. More evidence of her sheltered life.

They left the infirmary and came to a dining hall filled with mages. With their arrival, several members turned to the entrance. Some nodded, others kept their gazes locked to Elyse. Normally meeting others who could wield aithyr would excite her, yet as her eyes scanned across the crowd, her chest remained hollow.

Sibylla and Mol took her past the library overflowed with books and people clustered around various tables. Next to it sat the sanctuary, a place for mages to practice emptying their minds and centering themselves. Dormitories, forges, and workshops lay concealed within the mountain.

They guided her outside to a spacious flat clearing that served as both a practice yard and stables, where dirt, stone, and grass converged. A sweeping view of the mountains encircled the cliff, the surrounding peaks bathed in the golden hues of the setting sun.

Elyse turned, absorbing the sight of this unfamiliar terrain with its clusters of trees and scattered rocks. Her gaze trailed down the mountainside, capturing a glimpse of a meandering river etched into the valley. A sudden gust swept across, tousling her hair and bringing an unexpected vivacity to the surroundings, almost as if the pages of her books had sprung to life before her very eyes. She should be filled with excitement, her curiosity piqued by the newfound landscapes; however, all Elyse desired was to retreat to the comfort of a bed. A lump formed in her throat, a tangled mess of emotions threatening to overpower her, and she swallowed hard.

"Where are we?" Elyse asked to distract herself.

"Southern end of the Ekrixi Range, somewhere between the Evgeni Sea and Sufiaard," Sibylla answered. "Hidden among the rocks with the help of magic, of course. I trust you won't tell anyone?"

Elyse shook her head, her gaze finding mages sparring at the farthest point of the cliff. Sibylla urged her toward them. Their steps were a choreographed dance around one another, synced with ducks and dodges, lunges and swipes. The mage closest to her conjured wind to distract her opponent, then swept her leg under their feet. They jumped back just in time, though their stance was unstable.

In the center, two mages didn't hold back from one another, faces snarling as they moved in a frenzy of blades and punches. A male, with his hair pulled back into a knot that showed his rounded ears, lashed at the female, his body moving as graceful as a dancer. The half-elven female dodged his attack and yelled as she threw a punch, her fist erupting in flames before it made contact. The male fell, the female smearing the blood from her nose into her hair of a similar color. She glanced up at Elyse; her face going slack. She kicked the male at the ground. He glanced up, giving her a similar expression. Slowly, all the sparring ceased.

"Is that her?" the half-elven female asked.

"It is," Sibylla said. "Anthylia's daughter."

Whispers rippled through the gathered crowd, their curious gazes scrutinizing Elyse, making her feel uncomfortable, like a specimen under a magnifying glass. Anxious, she tugged at the sleeves of her shirt, wishing to evade their attention.

"I understand this has been overwhelming for you," Mol said, capturing her focus amid the prying eyes, "but the council wishes to speak with you tonight. It's been decades since we've had a Fulbryk at the compound."

Elyse turned away from the crowd, wanting to leave as quickly as she could. "Of course."

Sibylla and Mol guided her back inside, encountering a growing number of people lingering in the halls as they made their way. "They aren't usually this attentive of newcomers," Mol explained, holding a door open for Elyse to pass through. "Beyond being a Fulbryk, the circumstances of your arrival caused an equal amount of curiosity. Chorys Dasian mages attacked you and a Circle member. A member died and the mage left bodies that ..." He trailed off and cleared his throat. "They're curious."

Sibylla glanced at Mol, narrowing her eyes. "They have more information?"

"The council will provide further details," Mol answered.

They arrived at a nondescript door, Mol knocking before stepping back. It swung open, revealing three mages seated at a circular table. Mol gestured for Elyse to take a seat.

Elyse surveyed the council chamber and observed its lack of decoration compared to the rest of the compound. The walls were bare, the table plain and unadorned. She had expected a more elaborate setting for a council meeting.

Mol sat between the other three. "We are the Council of the Circle of Mages." He slid his chair forward as Elyse's lips parted. Alongside him were a human male, a half-elf, and an elven female. "Your grandfather founded the Circle of Mages to uphold his principles, which stand as a moral guide to practicing magic, preventing mages from using the power for ill will. Our role as the council is to rule in equal parts to ensure mages are held accountable, leading us to why we wished to speak with you. Could you please explain to us what happened with the mages you encountered?"

Elyse worked her jaw, her gaze dropping to the table. She focused on the weathered surface, the nicks and cuts carved into the top over time.

"Isn't this a bit too soon?" Sibylla asked from over her shoulder. "She only woke nearly an hour ago."

"That is why it's important we speak with her now," the human man said. "While her memory is fresh."

"Take your time, of course," Mol added, earning a glance from Elyse. "Tell us what you can. We'll interject with questions."

Elyse gripped the fabric on her thighs. She steeled herself, drawing the familiar comfort of aithyr into her body as she retold everything to the council—the mages who attacked Wynn and her experience with Chorys Dasi thus far.

"Are you sure it was the prince?" asked the half-elf. "No one has seen the Chorys Dasian queen and her brother in decades."

"Unfortunately, I'm sure."

"And how intimately did you know him?"

Heat came to Elyse's cheeks, and she stared anywhere but at the council.

"I knew him only a few months. What connects this to the mages?"

The elven female sat forward. "Was Sylas with them?"

Elyse stilled at his name. Amid the chaos of that day, she had forgotten his help and his warning. "Yes," she whispered. "Sylas was a member, wasn't he?"

The council members glanced at one another, though none of them spoke. It took Elyse a moment to realize they were using magic to speak in private.

Finally, the elf said, "A long time ago. I was still in my training when he was a member. He went rogue not long after I became a full member. How did you know he was part of the Circle of Mages?"

Elyse hesitated. "He told me. He also mentioned my mother's involvement."

She held Elyse's gaze, her stare flinty. "You are lucky to walk away whole from that conversation, then. Sylas is one of the most dangerous mages I have met in my lifetime."

Elyse tilted her head at that. "I have a hard time believing that."

The elf leaned forward and picked up her quill. "Can you explain what you mean?"

"Twice now he's helped me escape Azarys's attempts to capture me."

The council began exchanging glances with one another again, then Mol asked, "Can you share the first encounter? We were not aware of this."

"I was betrothed to the prince, though he went by a different name." Elyse pulled more aithyr into her, letting it curl around her senses, so she wouldn't experience the pain of her words. "Then I broke it off. He didn't accept my refusal and tried to abduct me, anyway. Sylas bought me enough time to escape."

The half-elf's stare landed behind Elyse. "How much does Wyltam know about the Chorys Dasian prince and his court?"

Elyse glanced over her shoulder at Sibylla as she answered, "Those details should come from him." She lifted her chin, holding her stance.

Tension pulled at their conversation, Elyse turning to the council. The half-elf kept their eyes on Sibylla while the others exchanged glances.

"We are simply gathering information," the elf said after a minute. "This is the first we've heard of the abduction part. Wyltam's a member of the Circle of Mages yet didn't reach out."

"We're trying to get a complete picture of what happened here," Mol added, "so we know how to prevent another member death in the future. We can't help if we don't know the whole truth."

"Again," Sibylla said, her steps approaching until her hand slid onto Elyse's shoulder, "Wyltam can explain if you are curious."

"Wyltam isn't here, Sibylla," the half-elf said. "And you are currently blocking our investigation. At this time, we ask you to wait in the hall while we finish speaking with Elyse."

"At this time," Sibylla ground out, "I don't feel comfortable leaving Elyse here without a mentor. Given my relationship with Wynn, I stand in as her mentor."

"Wyltam asked to be her mentor, no?" The human male flipped through a sheet of paper. "Yet Wynn had been the only mage to train her."

"Further, she is not an official initiate of the Circle. Unfortunately, we don't recognize her as having a mentor," the elf added.

"We don't want to cause a scene, Sib." Mol furrowed his brows and spread his hands wide. "Elyse will be fine for the rest of this conversation."

Sibylla's grip tightened on Elyse's shoulder. Then she spun and exited, the door closing forcefully.

"Now then," the human said, leaning forward. "Perhaps you can explain to us what Wyltam knew of Chorys Dasi?"

Aithyr shifted under her skin and over her heart, stilling her emotions. "He knew what I just shared. That is the extent of my understanding."

"And could you tell us about the magic you used to take out the mages that killed Wynn?"

Elyse sucked in a breath, her eyes clamping shut. She didn't want to relive it. "I don't remember."

There was a pause, then the human added, "The veins around their eyes, noses, and mouths were black when a Circle of Mages member arrived at the scene. Presumably, given your story, it wasn't Wynn who caused their deaths. So, unless someone else aided you, we can assume it was you."

She shook her head. "I don't remember."

"We're not accusing you of anything." Mol's voice softened as he added, "Whatever you did got you out of there safe while also taking out dangerous mages."

Elyse pulled more aithyr into her body, willing her trembling to cease. "I honestly don't know. I had Mage's Eye in my system and my vision went black—"

"Where did you get the Mage's Eye?" The elf paused writing to stare at Elyse.

She closed her eyes, dread pooling in her stomach. "Sylas. A gift for doing him a favor."

"What was the favor?"

"Does that matter?" Elyse opened her eyes to find the council sharing glances again.

"No, it doesn't," Mol said quietly. "We understand you haven't had the easiest life after your mother's death, facing much of your hardship on your own. What if we could promise that you'd never be alone again?" Mol sat back, pausing as he took in Elyse. "While you need no invitation to be here, we're offering you a position within the Circle of Mages. After all, it isn't right for the Fulbryk heir to not be in the Circle. You could stay here and train to become the best mage possible. For the next few decades, you'd live here in peace with fellow mages like yourself. You'd have a solid home, a chance to decompress from everything you've experienced. A chance to be free."

Elyse's grip on aithyr slipped for a moment. How did he know she wished for that?

"Through the program, we'd pair you with a mentor that works best for you," he continued. "Not just your mother's mentee or his friend. No disrespect to either of them, of course, but it's likely another mage is more compatible with helping you train. After a few decades, you'd be sent into civilization with your mentor to take on challenges, to see how you can better the world. We've sent people to Yirende Zemli beyond Ekrixi Range many times. Some ask to visit the mixed cities east of the jungles of Qathr. We've even sent people to Isvark—the frozen lands north of Chorys Dasi. If you're lucky, you could explore Sufiaard, though I'm rather biased." He flashed a smile with a chuckle. "You could have all of this and it could start today. You could settle here for a while. Put down roots."

A memory flashed in her mind, of Wynn telling her the same, that a coffee shop in Satiros could be their roots. It was tempting, to settle in the same place where she would train to be like him.

As she went to speak, Mol interjected. "Of course, Wyltam asked for you to return, though he added the choice was ultimately yours. He'd understand if you stayed. Honestly, Elyse, there is no wrong answer, but I can't help but sympathize with you. I made a similar choice years ago when I left Sufiaard to be here. Like how Chorys Dasi is posed to attack Satiros in a matter of weeks, if not sooner, my home was also under attack …"

Elyse drowned out his voice and dug her nails into her thighs. "Chorys Dasi is near Satiros?"

"Very close," the half-elf said. "If you return home, it'll be to a war."

She closed her eyes, feeling the aithyr flood her body as she took a steadying breath. If Sylas had known Wynn was being attacked, if the mages had been Chorys Dasians, then Elyse knew who was responsible for sending him to his death. She gripped her thighs harder, imagining it was Azarys's throat.

"I'm going home to Satiros."

Chapter Sixty-Six

MARIETTA

What should have been a joyous celebration of her people's arrival in Satiros for their wedding had devolved into a hollow gathering. Ministers and their aides wore strained smiles, their eyes betraying a weariness that clung to the edges of their expressions. The representatives from Enomenos were joined by her father and several prominent members of the Exisotis, tension rippling through the group.

As the welcome dinner dragged on, Marietta found it hard to choke down the food in front of her. The Head Defense Councilor of Enomenos sat across from her, having taken charge after Elector Alora returned to Olkia on news of troop movements. It was a cautious move—two leaders in one place during wartime made for an easy target—but it turned their conversation into a delicate game of diplomacy.

Her father was seated beside her, with Wyltam on her other side. The defense councilor engaged Dyeiter in tentative small talk, but Marietta barely registered it. She took a bite of her roasted lamb, yet it tasted like ash in her mouth.

"They're predicting a colder winter," Dyeiter said as he sipped his wine. "The cold settled in quick once autumn arrived."

Her father cleared his throat. "Cold weather makes for a poor wedding."

Marietta's head snapped toward him, her eyes wide with disbelief.

"Winter weddings are favored in elven culture," Dyeiter said, setting his fork down. "Longer nights are traditionally associated with conception."

"Interesting how elven tradition takes precedence," her father muttered, his voice low. "We've already traveled to your city."

As Dyeiter went to respond, Marietta placed her hand over her father's. "Could I have a word?"

"It's all right, Lady Marietta." Dyeiter leaned back, his tone measured. "We were having a pleasant conversation about personal beliefs."

Wyltam turned his ire toward his minister. "Perhaps you could explain where your wife is tonight, minister? It's unlike Lady Tryda to miss a dinner."

"She's feeling under the weather," Dyeiter replied with a tight smile.

"Now," Marietta insisted under her breath, urgency threading her voice.

Her father's gaze burned in the direction of the minister. As they stood and walked away, the defense councilor said, "The cold never bothered me. Grew up in the mountains north of Avato. Ice is practically in my veins."

Once in the dimly lit hallway, Marietta turned to her father. "What was that?"

His bronzed skin glowed in the low light, his eyes burning with barely contained anger. Dressed in a coat and pants more refined than she had ever seen him wear, he seemed a stranger, different from the father she remembered. "He led the charge to have you executed. Forgive me if I'm still feeling hostile."

"This is an official dinner for the treaty! If you can't control your temper, then you could have excused yourself. The Exisotis—"

"The Exisotis will always be there to protect *you*."

"Then protect me by making this dinner more a celebration of my marriage than a funeral!"

His gaze softened slightly as he placed a hand on her shoulder. "I should have fought harder to get you out. For not doing so, I'm sorry." He turned to walk toward the door again.

"Wait."

He turned back, and she searched his face, the memory stark in her mind that none of her features came from him. "I want answers."

He glanced at the door. "Not now. Tomorrow."

"Father—"

"They're waiting for us, Marietta."

Her father left her to stand alone in the hall. String instruments echoed from the small ballroom, drowning out the silence that held the table.

Today should be a celebration. A union. Two forces coming together.

A servant appeared before her. "Is there anything I can get you, my lady?"

"The strongest alcohol you can find."

She nodded and turned to talk away.

"Wait—a poor joke." Then she considered it for a minute. "Actually, could we get a few bottles of the firewater reserved for the wedding?"

Marietta returned as the last of the plates were cleared, each step slow, deliberate. The room quieted as she stood behind her chair, Wyltam's gaze steady on her, though the tension from the others pressed in. The Satiroans watched her warily, their eyes tracking every movement of the servants as they set down glasses with a faint clink. Across the table, the Enomenoans exchanged guarded looks, their skepticism clear.

"These are difficult times for a celebration," she began, her voice calm but weighted. "I won't pretend to feel celebratory—I don't think any of us do."

She accepted a glass from a servant, her fingers brushing the cool surface as she forced a polite smile. Holding the glass in front of her, she continued. "Thank you for being here, nonetheless. Dark days are upon us, and we all feel it. But," she paused, glancing around the table, meeting each set of eyes, "I still believe in brighter ones ahead."

The final glasses were placed, and as each person grasped theirs, Marietta raised her own.

"To mine and Wyltam's union, to the treaty that will be fully realized, and to a brighter future."

For a moment, the room hovered in silence, the clink of glasses delayed by hesitation. But Marietta held her glass high, unwavering, her words lingering in the heavy air, hoping they helped bridge the gap between doubt and hope.

Trailed by half a dozen of her guards in the Queen's Garden, Marietta held onto her father's arm as they walked. His body shielded her from most of the icy wind that had swept in overnight. "How's mother?"

"Upset she isn't here to support you, of course," her father said, the silver in his hair catching the light. "She misses you."

Marietta's chest constricted, missing her mother's warm hugs and the smell of herbs from her garden would linger on her fingers. She had been the one to teach Marietta how to voice her opinions, to tilt her head back and savor the sun. "I miss her." Emotion bit at her throat more than she wished to show her father.

He glanced at her, frowning. "She wanted to come."

"And you convinced her to stay?"

"She understood the danger. Neither of your lives was ever worth the risk. At least I had saved her."

With that, Marietta scoffed. "If you truly cared about saving me, you would've told me the truth from the beginning."

"Part of me wished I had. You would've never met Keyain nor ended up as King Wyltam's bride." He stared down the path. "But your mother's only wish was to give you the normal life, the one she didn't get." He sighed and closed his eyes.

Marietta frowned at him with suspicion. "What wasn't normal about it?"

"Once she met me, her life became the Exisotis. She knew what it meant, needing to hide in plain sight. She often worried if I'd ever make it home."

"Did you ever consider telling me?"

Her father let out a huff of laughter. "Every day. But I learned early on that if I told you to do something, you'd just do the opposite." He glanced out at the garden, a brief smile lighting his face before it faded into a frown. "I should have told you about the Exisotis when you came of age."

"I think it should have been sooner." Marietta stopped to smell a lilac bloom, still pristine despite the cold. "Honestly, there are a lot of things you should have told me—like that you're a fey and not really my father."

His posture stiffened. "I have been and will always be your father. As for the fey, whatever you think you know, you know nothing. Let it go."

"You already know I can't." Marietta met his gaze, her throat tightening. "I need answers. Chorys Dasi is marching toward us and we need to know how to stop the fey."

"Quiet, will you?" He glanced at the guards behind them. "The truth doesn't hold what you seek."

"It likely has more answers than we currently have."

Her father slowly turned to her. "We? Who did you tell?"

"Elyse brought it to me—we found the portraits in your father's book. We found all his books that Anthylia—"

"Does the king know?" Her father placed an arm on her shoulder, his stare burning into her.

"Of course he does."

"Who. Else."

Marietta pulled away from his touch. "Keyain, regrettably, but only us for now. There have been … incidents with information leaking. We didn't want to risk public panic, even if the ministers should know. At least tell *me* about the fey. I know Chorys Dasi—"

His body tensed, and his words came out clipped. "Marietta, they will— they have—" He swore under his breath, rubbing his chin as he avoided her gaze. "It was Chorys Dasi who attacked Elyse."

"How would you know that?"

"I have eyes and ears in all corners of Akroi. But I need you to listen to me—they cannot have her. Do you understand?"

"Of course, they can't have her."

"No, Marietta. You need to listen." Her father leaned in. "No matter what, keep Elyse away from the Chorys Dasians. Keep her away from their prince and their queen. They see her as a weapon, just like her mother." He swore and turned away, covering his mouth. "I need to leave. This changes many things."

As her father went to step away, she grabbed his arm. "You need to tell me what you know."

"And I need you to stay as far away from this city-state as possible. It seems neither of us will get what we want." He shook his head, frustration clear in his voice. "Tell your king this: magic isn't enough. My father didn't have all the necessary tools to stop them himself. This war will only end with the ground soaked in Satiroan blood."

Chapter Sixty-Seven

KEYAIN

"It's my fault this happened," Keyain said, sinking into the cushioned chair facing Wyltam's desk in his public office. "I left things to Peryn, knowing Adalyn and Ryder needed to be part of the Queen's Guard. There were too many moving pieces. I take full responsibility."

"While humility is appreciated, it helps no one right now." Wyltam slid a stack of papers across to Keyain. "My artificers promised to get as much done as they can. We're prioritizing the magicsbane devices, but …"

"But what?"

Wyltam grimaced and said, "The Shepherd told Marietta there is no hope in us winning against fey. While Marietta seems to believe his information is to warn us, I don't trust that he'd share the truth. I think he wants Satiros to fall."

Keyain watched as Wyltam closely. "Is he going to take Marietta and flee?"

He nodded once. "That, or have someone else get her out. I've doubled her guard from now until the wedding."

Keyain sighed and sat back, resting his chin on his hand. If the Shepherd managed to remove Marietta before the wedding, then Enomenos could back out of the treaty. They could abandon Satiros as Chorys Dasi and Reyila approached. If they knew their enemies were also an unknown number of fey, maybe they would retract on the treaty, anyway.

Keyain hung his head. That's what he feared. Fey, from what Wyltam had explained, possessed a multitude of advantages: magic of various kinds, strength no single person could match. With Enomenos, they would have the bodies needed to sustain the war for a time. But the hope of winning would still be grim. There had to be a way—one he wasn't considering.

A heaviness settled over him, but so did an idea. "Marietta has been claimed by all the temple deities, unless that's a rumor?"

Wyltam blinked slowly. "Another thing I've been trying to manage."

"She's grown close with them, though, correct?"

He furrowed his brow. "Yes?"

Keyain bit his tongue, barely unable to believe what he was about to suggest. "They could give us an advantage against Chorys Dasi."

Wyltam huffed a small laugh. "You're suggesting … You, of all people?"

"The way to win a war is to set aside differences with potential allies, is it not? See if Marietta can convince them to raise arms in her name."

Wyltam's eyes darted back and forth. "We need to know how many of them could wield magic."

"Something a meeting could fix."

Wyltam nodded. "I'll have it arranged."

Keyain left, the weight of his own suggestion settling heavily on him. The temples were a force they couldn't trust, yet their numbers and magic were compelling. But were they enough to counter the fey?

The thought hounded him into the night as he reread the reports that came in. His scout reported over one hundred thousand soldiers have left Chorys Dasi, heading southeast toward Satiros. Infantry. Cavalry. Siege engines. A month ago, Keyain anticipated them blocking the Halia that fed into the city-state, seizing trade from the rest of Syllogi. Thankfully, they had prepared for that. What they hadn't prepared for was how soon they would start the war.

Even as news of the war ripped through the court, his peers had acted exactly as he predicted. Tryda and her allies viewed Marietta as their biggest threat, as if it would change anything in the eyes of Chorys Dasi and Reyila to give them Marietta. Their enemies wouldn't stop until they took the city-state for themselves, likely wanting to execute everyone in power—himself included—and place Mycaub at the head with a regent from Reyila watching over him. At least, that's what he'd do if he were in their positions.

The division in court expanded beyond the palace walls. With the surfacing of the blue flame movement, hate for pilinos was at an all-time high. While Amryth's arrest had been embarrassing in that one of his former Elite Guard got caught thieving, it had more importantly been enlightening. The Exisotis were working on something, which in itself wasn't surprising. It made the Shepherd all the more dangerous to have nearby.

Keyain rubbed his temples. He'd had enough of court life and schemes. He'd had enough for a lifetime.

If they managed to survive this, he knew he'd step down. Not only as a minister, but as a lord as well. It would require him to still be in the palace, interacting with the people he had grown to despise. And if he could ever find someone to love him enough to have a child, he'd have to pass that curse on to them. The chances of that happening were slim, which meant he'd have to find a benefactor unless they were given to another elven noble. The thought of his family home passing to any of his peers felt sickening. While most were decent people, their money and influence had never gone where it was needed. Keyain wanted someone who deserved it, who deserved a break for the shit life threw at them.

All at once, the solution hit him, and he began to draw up the papers.

His manor was ever the same: dark and ominous, a shell of the lively home it used to be. Hopefully, his benefactor could breathe new life into it.

Legalizing the papers took only a few days, requiring both Dyeiter's and Leyland's approval before reaching Wyltam. His choice was unexpected and unprecedented, much like the rest of his career. She would be a fitting solution.

Keyain's footsteps echoed in the quiet hallway. Memories of his parents' parties rose in his mind, of laughter, of dancing, of happier times. Keyain had believed Marietta would return such energy to this home once upon a time, but that was a foolish thought in more ways than one.

Voices carried from the warmly lit kitchen. Irys, his housekeeper, sang a song to a giggling Emlyn. He made his footsteps loud as he approached.

"Hello?" Irys appeared in the doorway, her expression as stern as he remembered. He caught the twitch of her hand, a reminder of the weapon she always kept close.

Behind her stood Emlyn, her auburn hair glowing in the light, lips parted in surprise. She was barely past her first decade, still bright with the kind of joy only youth could grant. Mercy had spared her, mercy her mother had fought for, saving her from a life of pain. When Irys adopted Emlyn as her own, the half-elf had been at death's edge. That was the reason Irys worked for him. She understood the need for change, aware of the consequences that would follow if they didn't.

"Minister," Irys said with a bow of her head.

"None of that." He lumbered forward, hesitating as he neared. "I hope I'm not interrupting."

She studied him for a moment before saying, "Never. You seem better."

"Much."

She ushered him into the kitchen, where he took a seat next to Emlyn by the counter.

"It's not like you to drop by unexpectedly," Irys remarked. "Even last time, we had some warning."

Keyain flinched at the tone in her voice, the lingering hurt evident. "I'm sorry for what happened before. I wish I could say I wasn't myself, but that wouldn't be true. Because I couldn't control my own emotions, you were forced from your home."

"This is your home."

"I don't live here. Haven't in years."

She smoothed her apron and turned back to the stove. "You still own it."

"Not for long."

Irys dropped the spoon in her hand and pivoted to him. "Did something happen? I knew I should've contacted Ryder sooner."

Keyain furrowed his brows. "You reached out to him?"

"Who do you think left you food? Made sure you were still breathing?" She shook her head. "Emlyn, can you give us for a moment?"

The girl went to leave, but Keyain held out his hand. "She should stay; she should hear why I came."

Irys held his gaze, her mouth set. Finally, she nodded to Emlyn, who took a seat.

"I will not pretend I'm a good person," Keyain started. "In fact, the opposite is true. Even when I try to make the world better, I ignore those who care about me, often to their detriment. There's something broken in me, and I can't fix it if I have my current responsibilities."

"Keyain—"

"Please, let me finish. Sincerely, I regret what I did. I'm sorry for betraying you by promising that Marietta would join us one day, that she would set a good example for Emlyn. I truly believed she would have chosen to be here, but I had lied too deeply, causing pain to all of you." He glanced between the mom and daughter. "To make it worse, I threw you from your home and acted as if a sum of coin would make up for it. It was selfish of me and I will never forgive myself for it. This manor—these lands—will always be your home, and I want to ensure that will always be true."

Keyain pulled the papers from his coat pocket and handed them to Irys. She wiped her hands on her apron and took them, trembling as she read. Her warm eyes widened with disbelief. "Keyain, you can't."

He turned to the girl. "Emlyn, I declare you as my heir. You will assume all the rights and land to the Vallynte estate, acting as its sole provider. All privileges of the estate will be yours, including the manor and Vallynte village. Further, this adds you as a member at court and grants you the title of lady. Upon my death or incapacitation, all of my possessions will be yours."

Emlyn turned to Irys. "Mother?"

"What about your children one day?" she asked, pushing the papers back in his hand. "It'll make a mess with your family. And the lands should stay with the Vallynte name."

Keyain shook his head and pushed the papers back to her. "I'm not going to have children." Saying the truth out loud was like lifting a heavy weight from his chest. That dream was one so closely tied to Marietta that he doubted he could ever overcome it. Regardless, they deserved it.

"She doesn't know how to be a lady. She's barely a decade old, Keyain!"

"I'll teach her everything I know about being a noble. You've been running my estate for decades, acting as my proxy. You are more than qualified to teach her the responsibility of it all." Keyain went on to explain how Emlyn would be introduced to court. When she came of age, she'd manage the village in his stead and they'd work on the reporting together.

Irys stood with her eyes locked onto the papers, only lifting them to stare at Emlyn. "What do you say? Do you want to do this?"

Emlyn fidgeted with her dress. "I think I want to. Could my mother come with me?"

A smile came to Keyain's lips. "Absolutely. I've already secured an inn for you to stay in while a suite is readied. Space is tight at the moment. There's a chance they'll move my suite to one of the larger options, to include you both."

"Keyain," Irys started.

"Three separate rooms, of course. I work late, so you won't even know I'm there."

"Is the court ready for a pilinos lady?"

"They've already had one, so what's a second?" Keyain shrugged. "I'll protect her with my life."

"She's just a child. If someone—an elven someone, specifically a male— sees her and pilinos haven't been ruled as equals …"

Keyain followed her thought. "She has legal protections now," he said. "Not everyone at court will be welcoming, but there are plenty of nobles who won't take issue. Emlyn will have allies—friends, even."

"How soon? We've heard an army is on the way." Irys met his gaze, her expression pained.

He worked his jaw, his eyes burning with a warning he didn't want to voice in front of the girl. "Tonight, if possible."

Irys's lips trembled, her eyes turning glassy. "Okay," she said after a moment. "Okay. If Emlyn is okay with it, then so am I."

Keyain turned to his new heir and took in the panicked details of her face. Despite all the wrong he had done, he would do right by her and her mother. For all his family had taken to build their wealth, he would gladly give them everything upon his death. But most importantly, he would do anything in his power to at least protect them if he could no one else.

Chapter Sixty-Eight

AMRYTH

While free from the dungeon, Amryth couldn't shake the sensation of being trapped that plagued her. Even a third walk through the Temple of Therypon's gardens gave no relief. Restlessness stirred in her like an oncoming storm. She was supposed to stay within the Temple of Therypon after Wyltam explained the situation to their leaders. They agreed to let her live in the private acolyte spaces and to keep her hidden from Tanaly and the Exisotis, which beat living underground with the mages.

Part of her considered joining the temple to fully shed her guard reputation. As Amryth waved to a pair of attendants passing by, the familiar discomfort of alienation returned. Becoming an official member wouldn't change that. The temple was not hers, nor would it ever be.

Returning inside, she shook off the evening chill and made her way to Deania's office. She should be done working, so they could finally go eat. Amryth knocked on the door.

"Enter!"

Deania's smile greeted her, a warmth that sent Amryth's heart into a reckless flutter. The day Amryth left the underground and arrived at the temple, that feeling had only intensified.

"I grabbed one of the newspapers today," she said, gesturing to the print resting on the pile of papers covering her desk. "Look at page three."

Amryth took the paper and began reading her only window to the outside world. The first headline read, **'*Crown Critics Question Leadership as Danger Draws Near.*'** Unsurprising. *The Crown's Conservator* had always been critical of Marietta and Wyltam. She flipped the page, glancing through the articles.

Elf-Righteous: Elves and Pilinos on the Verge of Open Hostilities Amid Chaos

With the pilinos guild measure vote occurring next week, old wounds reopen in the elven fight to maintain tradition in the city-state. Tavern brawls broke out in numerous establishments in Bud Town and Greening Juncture, many elves being accused of starting the altercations, yet pilinos counterparts were not given the same punishment.

Magic or Mayhem? Citizens Clash Over the Role of Magic in Society

A growing new-age movement that gained momentum after the tragic death of the late Queen Valeriya continues to see growth. This, however, has led to many debates between progress with our city-state and those who worry about the continued loss of jobs.

All gossip and infighting that did nothing to help their fight against Chorys Dasi and Reyila. Amryth went to ask Deania why she hadn't picked up *Satiroan Press*, but stopped when she flipped to the third page. They drew her likeness behind cell bars while someone who appeared to be Keyain passed her a key. The title read, **'*Betrayal Behind the Breastplate. Scandal Erupts as Former Guard Leader Faces Charges.*'**

Authorities shared they arrested a former Elite Guard member, Amryth Sulyng, after breaking into the offices of the beloved elven establishment, Ladybird Inn. While they couldn't disclose why the accused was there, owner Tatyr Wylams was compelled to share his own thoughts with The Crown's Conservator.

"Among elves, the Ladybird Inn is celebrated for its dedication to preserving Satiroan elven culture," he explained. "Many pilinos and their kind see us as a threat, but in truth, we're merely striving to protect our heritage while our own government seeks to erase it."

Amryth glanced up at Deania, her jaw dropping. "This is a joke."

Deania gestured and said, "Keep reading."

While Minister Keyain Vallynte had been the face of the elven heritage movement only a few months ago, many elves now question his motivations. After he announced an unrelated pilinos as his heir, some argue that he's stripping away the valor of brave elves who march against their enemies, much like he did with his own familial legacy. This most recent scandal brought additional light onto the disgraced minister.

Palace nobles have described the Elite Guard as a sworn few hand-selected by Minister Keyain, or as his "inner circle." Soldiers who excelled through the ranks and pulled close to the minister's side to aid in special assignments, meaning the Elite Guard were on a personal level with Minister Keyain. However, the group possessed five members a few months ago and has now dwindled to three with Amryth's departure. The missing guard? The accused's late wife.

During Minister Keyain's seizure of the Enomenoan city-state, Olkia, the minister sent a specialized team to collect the soon-to-be Queen Marietta from her home, attacking and abducting her. Deyra Sulyng, former wife of the accused, met her death during that dishonorable mission.

Whether Amryth Sulyng holds a grudge against the future queen is a question only she can answer. However, we can all imagine the animosity we would hold if our loved ones died under similar circumstances.

Given the relationship between Amryth and Minister Keyain, some call into question if there will be a fair trial. Many fear that pilinos sympathies control the narrative of this cultural shift which will leave Amryth without consequence for her actions. With this new information brought forth by a credible source, fear of nepotism and mutual hate for our queen leave many to believe Amryth will slip through the fingers of justice.

The paper crinkled in her fists as rage washed over her. They dared to mention Deyra, to write about how she died, something she shared with—

"Tanaly is a lying bitch," Deania said, sitting back in her chair with brown eyes ablaze.

Amryth crumbled the newspaper and threw it to the ground, her throat growing tight. "Taking me and Keyain out with one hit," she said through gritted teeth. "After they had the nerve to set me up. Why me? Why, when I told Tanaly the truth, had told her I saved Marietta?"

"Because you represent everything that they hated for so long." Deania stood and walked to Amryth, pulling her into a tight hug. "I get her anger, probably more than she understands. You quit the guard after realizing the truth. Apparently, the Exisotis didn't care."

She shook her head, her body trembling as she tried to choke down her emotions and eased into the hug. She smoothed back strands of Deania's hair, silken beneath her touch. "Wyltam is going to know I spoke."

"I'm sure he already does."

"And Keyain."

Deania nodded.

"They're going to force me back into the dungeon."

Deania shrugged. "A possibility, but I doubt it."

"Why do you say that?"

"An elven newspaper painted Marietta in a positive light, albeit at the cost of yours and Keyain's reputations. But getting them not only to admit that she could be a victim but also firmly stating she was queen? Unparalleled." Deania sighed. "Tanaly did say she didn't want to tarnish the people's view of Marietta."

Amryth scrubbed her face and paced. "Instead, she ruined mine."

"And Keyain's."

She gave her a withering look.

"There is one fatal flaw in Tanaly's plan," Deania said with a gleam in her eye.

Amryth threw herself down in the plush chair off to the side of Deania's office. "What now?"

"Tanaly didn't know about the work you've done in the Weeds."

Chapter Sixty-Nine
KEYAIN

Tryda clinked her silver spoon against the rim of her cup and took a sip. "You should've left her in Enomenos."

Keyain turned his drink in his hand, saying nothing. Tryda had summoned him without explaining her reasons, claiming it was more important than his war council. He fought the urge to glance at his aithyr clock, the weight of his next meeting already hanging over him.

"We have her to blame for the war, for Valeriya's death. How many more will die because you brought her here? Misfortune clings to her like flies to spoiled food." She shook her head. "You are a son to me. I loved your mother and father dearly. When your parents passed, we made sure you were never alone. We honored them—" Her voice cracked and she paused, swallowing hard. "We honored them by keeping you safe. And while that never came at a cost, I'm asking for repayment."

Keyain laughed, though there was no real humor in it. "Just you? Not Dyeiter?"

She leaned in, eyes sharp with intensity. "Only me, Keyain. Mycaub needs to be on the throne."

His hand slipped, the cup falling from his grip. "Tryda, that's—"

"Treasonous? Hardly so. It is his birthright to rule, stripped away by

Marietta's inability to follow tradition. If we have Mycaub crowned over his father, Reyila could pause their advance. This is a tactic to win a war."

Keyain swore and scrubbed his face. "You want to let a toddler rule. And do what with Wyltam and Marietta?"

Tryda sipped her tea, her eyes locked on Keyain. "Wyltam has spent his rule handing out power to his ministers. They are primed to help a child king. As for what to do with them, we … have them walk away. Give up their ruling, and remain banished from not just Satiros, but all of Syllogi."

"You sound mentally unwell." He sat back, heart pounding in his chest. If it were anyone else, he'd have them arrested for even spouting the idea. There was no telling if Reyila would call off the war if Mycaub was on the throne, at least not without them having a strong influence over him. But he could see why Tryda would want to gamble with that. It meant less bloodshed.

"You've always had too soft of a heart. Caring for them as if they wouldn't stab you in the back at first chance." She took a sip. "The clip did just that."

"I will not tolerate you speaking ill of Wyltam's bride."

Tryda laughed and set down her cup, squaring up to Keyain. "You sound like a puppy trying to growl. I will speak ill of her in my suite if I damn well please. She is the reason this war is happening. All of this could've been prevented if she had been executed."

Keyain flinched, shame twisting inside his chest.

"I know you feel bound by duty to your king," Tryda said, her voice softer now. "You've always been loyal, Keyain. That's why you can't see what needs to be done. It's why you *served* Olytia as you did—as she made you."

Bile burned at the back of his throat. "Don't bring her into this."

"She was my closest friend for centuries. I'll admit she had grown paranoid by the end, but I know she cared about you deeply. It's why she chose you."

"Stop—"

"And clearly you've benefited from it, long after her early death." She pinned Keyain on the spot. "You have many people to owe for keeping your position, boy. Take that into consideration with this offer."

"I won't—"

"You will. Your position as minister of protection is to ensure the well-being and safety of Satiros. Right now, its biggest threat is the ignorance of our king and his bride. If I have your support, we could save tens of thousands of soldiers."

He drew in a shallow breath, then another. "You didn't say 'we.' Dyeiter doesn't know."

"How could he? All the power of his position and no results. I'm the one giving ideas to the male responsible for winning this war—that's you. I'm the one trying to save you, Keyain. To help you, as a second mother—as family. If you support the idea, we bring in Dyeiter and draft a motion to remove Wyltam."

"No."

"Once he's removed, we place Mycaub at the head—"

"No!" Keyain slammed his fist on the table. He pictured Wyltam's face upon discovering he'd been sleeping with his mother. He imagined his face at Marietta's trial when he learned that he betrayed him again. He thought of the moment when Wyltam had said he couldn't have possibly loved Marietta if she sent her to her execution. Staring down at the possibility of betraying him once more, he finally understood what he had meant. "I stand with King Wyltam, our rightful ruler."

Her dark eyes peered into his own, her brows twitching. "You're wrapped around the king's finger again, aren't you?"

Keyain took the jab without flinching. He had been and would always be, for better or for worse. "I won't lose King Wyltam's favor again."

"Well then," Tryda said, downing her tea. "That's disappointing."

He stood, keeping his gaze on Tryda. "You are going to leave the palace. Go stay with your son's family in Wisteria Heights. If I catch even a whisper that you've been talking to anyone—ministers or their wives—I will haul you back to the palace and charge you with treason. Do I make myself clear?"

Tryda stood, placing her hands on the table as she leaned forward. "You certainly do. Good luck, Keyain. You're going to need it."

Chapter Seventy

KEYAIN, BEFORE

Though a cunning queen, Olytia couldn't mask her emotions, often to Keyain's detriment. That morning, after receiving a note, she lashed out, shredding the paper in fury before turning on him. The sting of her slap paled in comparison to the pain of the note's contents.

Wyltam had returned.

As quickly as he disappeared, had he made himself known. Olytia covered for his decades of absence, painting him as an aloof prince unfit to rule. Mostly sharing rumors that Wyltam explored Akroi and beyond, planting his royal seed wherever he saw fit. Keyain knew better. He had been the one to push Wyltam away. Admittedly, it was an effect Keyain had on most people close in his life. Olytia never failed to remind him of that fact. Even his parents hadn't been spared by his unnerving effect of disappointing those around him. By never marrying and refusing suitors, he caused his parents to succumb to their feybarb illness.

If it weren't for Olytia, then he'd still be trying to claw his way up to general because he could never have made it himself. He became the minister of protection thanks to her. His gracious queen, who saw him when he was nothing and gave him a chance. Olytia never failed to remind him of that either, even when Keyain hadn't been questioning.

For years now, Olytia had invited Keyain to her bed. She placed him in a suite that connected to her room through the tunnels, all so she could discretely be with him. Not that her discretion mattered after she'd grown careless. Moryvan, the head of her Queen's Guard, had known for the better part of a decade. Thankfully, he recognized not needing to discuss it with Keyain, for such a matter of affairs was beyond what the court would understand. They would assume Keyain wanted to become the king, to take power for himself. Yet, the truth remained that he wished only to serve his queen, to thank her for all that she gifted him.

The palace buzzed with the gossip of the aloof prince's return. Some rumored that he had brought a girl home with him. Others claimed it was Lady Anthylia Fulbryk—daughter, heir, and prodigy of the infamous mage, Lyken Fulbryk. Ever since her brother, Anthys, disappeared from court, Anthylia had kept her distance.

If those rumors were true, then Olytia would be in an especially foul mood. The Fulbryks were the only noble family to not follow her six months at court ruling, and that had everything to do with Olytia's distrust for magic and its practitioners. With every new law passed about banning the practice and restricting the education of it, Keyain saw her grip tighten and her suspicion grow.

Part of Keyain questioned what made her so nervous. They could have mages close to her if she wished, and Keyain would even oversee them for her as part of his duty as the minister of protection. At least she had been persuaded to allow magical items as a growth in infrastructure. Losing draft animal waste in the streets was enough of a convincing factor for Keyain, as well as trading candles and gaslights for light globes.

Keyain sighed as he returned to his suite, wishing he had more than an hour to himself before Olytia would expect him in her rooms. While he appreciated being the minister of protection, the position meant long days filled with meetings and less of doing what he loved—being with his soldiers and guards. On days like today, he considered not answering Olytia's call and having a night to himself. Perhaps he'd even read a book. But that would be selfish. The least he could do for his queen was ease her tension.

Running a hand through his hair, he lumbered through the suite when someone cleared their throat, drawing Keyain's attention to the living room. He looked the same as the day he left, pale as a full moon, with a sheet of black hair obscuring half his face. His eyes, however, were like obsidian daggers raised at Keyain, making his heart flip.

"I see you've come leech off your mother," Keyain said, throwing his jacket onto the table, taking in the way Wyltam held himself. He stood with his shoulders back, hands tucked into his pockets with his gaze unwavering.

"A leech would know a leech."

Keyain tightened his jaw. "Why are you here?"

"You don't want to see me?" Mockery edged his tone, sharp and deliberate.

"Why are you in my suite, Prince Wyltam?"

Silence held him for a moment, tossing his title out as a barrier. They were no longer friends, no longer more than that either.

"I think the more interesting question is when did you become such a prig?" Wyltam stepped into the light unhurriedly. "I see your tastes have grown expensive. You throw your title around as if no one has a clue who you are, which they do. You enjoy the power."

A spike of rage shot up his spine, making him grind his teeth. "You've been gone for how long? What would you know?"

"This was only basic court gossip I garnered since returning." Before Keyain could question, Wyltam answered, "Oh, I've been watching. Occasionally, I'd check on the court's status, see if I should come back. Imagine my surprise when the male I knew so well, the one dedicated to helping others and spreading good, transformed into a self-absorbed prick in just a few decades. You've turned the person I loved into someone unrecognizable, hiding within a well-crafted shell of self-loathing and insecurity."

Keyain's anger snapped, and he hit the tabletop. "You know nothing."

Wyltam's head tilted in his annoying condescending manner that Keyain hadn't missed. He walked closer, the space narrowing between them as the air grew taught, as if it too remembered the history between them. His voice was low, his eyebrow twitched. "I know *everything*."

Sweat broke out over Keyain. He didn't mean … Of all the people who shouldn't know, Wyltam sat at the top of that list. After everything they had been through, after all those private moments between them. Acid crawled up his throat, choking out a response.

Wyltam stepped past him. "I think I'll go meet with my mother now. Surely she missed her only child." He paused at the door of his suite, glancing over his shoulder to add, "Take the night off, Keyain."

Keeping up appearances, Keyain mingled at a gathering in the Noble's Wing, flirting with a younger courtier who managed to get an invitation. She fluttered her lashes, making Keyain crave a stronger liquor. He wasn't supposed to bed any of them, just entertain the thought enough that people didn't suspect his and Olytia's relationship, if it could even be called that.

He kept one eye over his shoulder, waiting for him to appear. Without fail, he would humiliate Keyain or mock him at just the right time. Apparently, Wyltam sharpened his tongue during his break from court, gaining the ability to hold a group of people long enough to make Keyain leave. And no matter the size or place of the gathering, he *always* appeared.

Wyltam's gaze felt like the prickly crawl of sickness over his skin. Keyain's palms sweated, heat rising to his cheeks. His presence was a disease that his body tried to fight off. After years of successful politicking, Wyltam had to return and threaten it.

Even when the prince wasn't near, Keyain had to deal with him. Rumors of his return blossomed faster than spring Satiroan wisteria, each story more ridiculous than the last.

"The prince had a lover that his mother didn't accept—a clip, too!"

"Well, I heard he was a prisoner on a pirate ship in the Evgeni Sea."

"Actually, the queen ordered him to return and about time she did."

It didn't matter what he did while he was away. Olytia fixated on uncovering the reasons for his return, convinced he sought her throne. Ever paranoid, Keyain felt relief that she didn't force him to investigate. Yet her obsession only deepened her misery, making her unbearable to be around. Her already volatile moods spiraled further, often culminating in screams directed at Keyain. Though every moment grated on him, he couldn't walk away. Olytia was his queen. For all she had given him, she wielded the power to take it all away just as easily. Keyain listened to her, endured her fury, and fucked her the way she liked, regardless of his own wishes.

"Have you ever been there?"

"Where?" Keyain swiped a drink from a servant passing by.

"That new restaurant in Petal Row." She pouted. "I asked if you'd like to go …" Her voice trailed off.

"Don't stop on my account." A cascade of pins and needles washed over Keyain as he appeared at his shoulder, interrupting the lady.

She turned to Wyltam, her eyes lighting up as she sized up her new target. "I didn't think we'd be so lucky to see you tonight, Your Grace."

Wyltam's gaze flicked over her face in the most irritating manner. "I always find excuses to see Minister Keyain."

"Prince Wyltam," he said into his glass before taking a long sip. "Was there something you need? I was just talking to—"

Wyltam raised a brow as Keyain failed to recall her name.

"Lady Odyssa Pyrt, Your Grace." She turned her shoulder to Keyain to face Wyltam fully. "I was asking the minister if he's ever been to Fable Vine in Petal Row."

"I believe that's his favorite place to dine." He locked his dark gaze on Keyain. "Isn't that so?"

Keyain swallowed his agitation. "One of them," he lied. "If you'll excuse me."

"I could use some fresh air," Wyltam said, stepping with Keyain as he walked away. Wyltam glanced over his shoulder. "Would you like to join us, Odyssa?"

Petulant, arrogant prick. Wyltam kept small talk with the girl, making her laugh as they made their way outside. Keyain's shoulders wound tighter the longer Wyltam lingered, making him guess what he was trying to gain from this torment. Embarrassment? Likely. A moment alone to make some jab about Olytia? Also likely. Perhaps if Wyltam was in the mood, he'd do both.

They halted near a fountain. Keyain paused, searching for the quickest route to shake them off. Unfortunately, the evening air proved favorable enough that they garnered attention from other courtiers as they lingered.

"Keyain, tell her how beautiful she looks in the moonlight."

Keyain turned to Odyssa, her eyes wide and hopeful, but focused on the prince. He muttered, "So beautiful."

"The two of you make a fine pair," Wyltam added, making Keyain's stomach drop. "It is courting season."

"I am open for courting," she said, batting her eyelashes at Wyltam. "Courting and whatever else comes my way."

"Hear that, Keyain?" A smile hinted at Wyltam's lips. "She'd be open to anything that came her way."

"I'm not looking for a wife," he ground out.

Wyltam leaned in and murmured, "What about some fun?"

Keyain glared at him then. This was Wyltam's entertainment, knowing Keyain would turn anyone away because of his mother.

"I am looking for some fun, my prince." Odyssa stepped closer to him.

Bile burned in the back of his throat. "Wyltam, a word."

"Honorifics," he warned.

Glaring, Keyain snapped. "Prince Wyltam, a word—now."

Wyltam glanced down, his hair masking the triumphant smirk as he turned to the garden and motioned for Keyain to follow.

"What about me?" Odyssa asked, reaching for the prince.

He didn't bother to look back. "Wait here. I'll send Keyain for you when we're done."

Keyain's pulse thundered in his ears as he trailed him through the dense paths of the Central Garden. Taunting bastard, bringing up courting. "Are we just going to walk or … ?"

"Do you truly want people to hear our conversation?"

"I'm starting to not give a fuck," Keyain snapped.

Wyltam turned to face him suddenly. "What would you like to discuss, then?"

"What was that back there?"

"A young lady clearly wanted your affection, yet you refuse. From what I heard after I left court, you could barely keep your cock in your pants," he said, quirking a brow. "Now, you choose to be monogamous with my mother. Why?"

Keyain pulled his hand through his hair, staring anywhere but at him. "I will not talk about this."

Wyltam held his gaze. "Is she forcing you?"

He tightened his jaw, his teeth grinding. "I'm not talking about your mother."

"Because I'm right?"

"Because I used to fuck you and now I fuck her. Happy?"

"No, Keyain. I'm not happy." He stepped closer and Keyain refused to back down. "She's manipulating you like she did during the Orc Skirmishes."

"Don't start with that again."

"She convinced you to murder innocent people fleeing for their lives."

"This again? No," Keyain spat. "I killed brutes who'd steal land from innocent elves."

Wyltam leveled a stare. "And who told you that? My mother?"

"It's common knowledge. Surely a prince would know. Perhaps those who stay loyal to their people do."

"A prince knows many things. I was taught law policy since my first decade, as well as economics, war theory, social sciences, geographies, politics, and the lands beyond our borders—including those outside of the Akroi Region." Wyltam paused. "Tell me, what do you know of the lands west of the Ekrixi Range? Of the dynamics between Yirende Zemli and Sufiaard?"

Keyain shook his head. "This is irrelevant."

"Pilinos and elves are equals. However, it's because they united against a cause. Do you know what that cause is?"

"Pushing the orcs from their borders allows them to live in peace, similar to how it helped unite Syllogi."

Wyltam sighed. "Wrong. The orcs are brilliant smiths. Or they used to be before the elves and pilinos invaded their home in Sufiaard, aided by Yirende Zemli. The orcs had ships that could float across the sand, buildings that withstood the shifting, unsteady ground. They had creations that your imagination could simply not comprehend. These elves, these pilinos, they raided orcish homes, using fire and brawn to take down this great civilization, all because of *how* they thought they did it. They were searching for sandstone crystals."

Keyain waited for him to explain. Exasperated, he broke the silence and asked, "And those are?"

"Not real." Wyltam looked him eye to eye. "They couldn't comprehend the orcs being clever enough to figure out how to harness magic, assuming they needed some supernatural material to aid them. The orcs were hunted down, the mages tortured to tell them where the sandstone crystals were. Those who fled extermination tried to find safety in the east—"

Keyain's blood ran cold, and he bared his teeth. "That isn't true."

"—where the armies of Syllogi slaughtered them."

A piercing ache formed in his chest, remembering all the gore and viscera of battle. Was it all for nothing? He grabbed the front of Wyltam's shirt. "You're a liar."

"I am nothing of the sort. But do you know who is? My mother. She knew all of this. She knew why they fled and lied. How many of your fellow soldiers died in that battle?" Wyltam lifted his chin and suddenly a blast of air knocked Keyain back.

Keyain grappled with what he had just seen. "You know—You're a—"

"A mage? Yes."

"That's what you were doing all this time?" Keyain wiped his face. "Your mother will kill you over this."

Wyltam stared at him for a moment. "Do you honestly think my mother thinks highly enough of me that I could learn magic? Or would she only believe it because it came from the mouth of her courtesan?"

Blood pounded in his ears. "You know nothing."

"You are a fool if you don't think everyone knows." His voice grew quieter, gentler. "It's not a secret. It hasn't been in over a decade."

Keyain closed his eyes, his breath coming sharply. Did everyone truly know? "I deserve my position," he said defensively. "I have served your mother unwaveringly."

"If that's what you still think, then we need to talk about the untimely death of Minister Tryke." A transparent dome went up around them, dulling the garden sounds. Keyain struck it with his hand, cursing as it met his palm with the solidity of a stone wall. "How did he die, Keyain?"

"Feybarb."

Wyltam shook his head. "It was strychnine."

Keyain furrowed his brows, noting the name of the poison that was rare to find in Satiros these days. Before he was born, strychnine was a common powder used to kill vermin in the city-state. The expense to ship it from the south made them seek alternatives. A less expensive substance replaced it over a century ago. "Rat poison?"

"My mother killed him with her signature toxin," he said. "Just like she did with my father and your parents. Mimics the effects of feybarb perfectly."

The ground seemed to tilt beneath his feet. "What are you talking about? My—my parents and Minister Tryke died tragically from feybarb."

"All within a year? When all three stood as obstacles for you?"

Keyain's throat grew thick at the thought of his parents buried in the Ash Gardens. "You're insane. My parents were never obstacles."

"Karyna. Lillyth. Isybel. Tarylie. How many of your parents' marriage proposals have you turned down over the years?"

"To be with your mother," he hissed. "The stress of never marrying was too much for my parents." He paused, swallowing the emotion that threatened to choke him. "Olytia even said so."

Wyltam grew quiet and placed a hand on Keyain's arm. "Repeat what you just said. My mother told you that *you* killed your parents from stress, which ultimately she caused. You refused to marry because of my mother. My mother is very simple to understand: she wants power and control." The sympathy in his expression made him want to pull out his hair. "She took advantage of you."

"I'm only a minister because of her," he said, his breath coming in sharp gasps.

"Because she murdered the person who previously held the position."

"I'm not an idiot. I would know …" He closed his eyes, shame washing over him.

"My mother knows exactly how to wrap around your heart and squeeze until there's nothing left," Wyltam said. "Deep down, I believe the male I once loved still exists. It's never too late to right your wrongs."

"Wyltam—"

"Are you happy?"

The question was a slap in the face. Keyain had everything he ever wanted—power, a good position, influence. But was he happy?

He thought of all the nights Olytia demanded his presence in her bedchamber, of all the times his cheeks stung from her violent touch. At one point, Keyain had a plethora of people in his life that were close to him. These days, he only had her, and that thought was more damning than he realized. He sucked in a breath, not having enough air.

Wyltam placed his other hand on Keyain's shoulder. "What you have with my mother needs to end."

Keyain tugged at his hair, panic bubbling from his gut. "She'll punish me if I deny her. She has before." His eyes welled and he would be damned to cry in front of Wyltam. He bit his tongue, the pain helping him gain control.

Wyltam looked him in the eye, his voice a touch above a whisper. "I have a plan that could set you free."

"I should get rid of him," Olytia hissed as they passed through the door next to the ballroom. "What purpose does he serve other than being an insufferable pain?"

Keyain refrained from rolling his eyes. Rymos only made sure the entire palace ran smoothly, so her lifestyle wouldn't be disturbed.

Olytia glanced at him. "Oh, please don't tell me you have a soft spot for him. The minister of protection, leader of our army, wants to defend the minister of schedules and meetings?" Her laugh grated his ears.

Keyain swirled the glass of wine he held, glancing around to make sure they were the only ones present before he spoke. "Do you ever wonder how many people think you're an insufferable pain?"

Olytia's slap stung across his cheek. "Unworthy dog. Don't bite the hand that feeds you."

"Apologies. I despise these things."

She hummed to herself, her fingers finding the front of his shirt and toying with the buttons. "So do I, but if you play nice tonight, you will be rewarded."

Nausea churned in his stomach as he raised the glass. "Liquid courage?"

Olytia narrowed her eyes at it, sending a wave of panic down his spine. They had expected she'd be suspicious.

"You first," she said with a smile. "Sounds like you need it, too."

He brought Olytia's fingers to his lips and pressed a kiss before sealing his fate. The sweetness of the wine covered the bitter taste. He handed the glass to Olytia.

For a moment, he thought she wouldn't take it. That Keyain had damned himself for no reason. But at last, she took the cup and downed the contents.

Keyain kissed her cheek before turning from the room, trying to keep his gait steady as his nerves began to take hold.

"Keyain?"

He swallowed hard and faced her once again. "Yes?"

"Do you ever wonder if your peers hate you because you're a sorry excuse for a male? Even they know you're nothing without me. Remember that."

He released a breath, his guilt absolving with it. "Yes, Your Grace."

She smiled at the honorific and turned back to the ballroom entrance and walked out.

Keyain left the way they had come, slipping into the crowd, his skin slick with sweat and his neck stiff as the poison took hold. The dosage had been high. Olytia likely sensed it too, but she would dismiss it as nothing more than a headache. The crowd swirled around him as he navigated toward the other ministers huddled near the dais where Olytia sat. Gambling a glance at her, he noticed her rolling her neck with a scowl.

Behind the throne stood Wyltam, his head bowed while he listened to someone speak. His expression, as always, was unreadable, but Keyain knew exactly what he felt at this moment.

Royir clapped a hand on Keyain's shoulder. "There you are. Unlike you to be late."

"Throbbing headache," he muttered as his lip began to twitch. He only needed to stay long enough to be seen.

"Used to get frequent headaches myself … then I annulled our marriage!" Royir barked a laugh and left Keyain to grimace alone.

The pounding in his heart pulsed in time with the sound of the crowded room. By now, several people had noticed him; he could easily leave to seek help. Yet a twisted part of him wanted to see it happen, to witness the world rid itself of one more monster.

Keyain's back arched with a powerful twitch, shaking him from his stupidity. Taking one last glance at Olytia's scowl as she sat upon the throne, Keyain made his way to the hallway, dodging servants and courtiers alike. He didn't remember entering the storeroom as his breathing became labored, but he must have, because there was a voice.

"Didn't think you'd make it."

Keyain slumped down as a convulsion racked his body. A vial pressed into his lips. He tasted nothing as the liquid slurry slid down his throat. It took a moment for his muscles to ease and he finally looked at the male helping him. His curly brown hair fought against its tie and even in the low light, Keyain could see the shocking blue of his eyes. A thick scar forked from the top of his left cheekbone to the corner of his mouth. He held out his hand. "Wynn."

Keyain took it. "Pleasure."

Behind them, a cry erupted from the ballroom, followed by a cacophony of panicked voices. Keyain smiled, his head falling back against the wall. A mixture of laughter and tears bubbled up from deep within him.

"Seems like you and Wyltam were successful," Wynn said, clapping his shoulder. "Long live the king."

People dashed down the hallway as the screams erupted. Despite the poison coursing through him, his chest felt light and his mind remained clear. He smiled as he said, "Long live the king."

Chapter Seventy-One

MARIETTA

Marietta paced on the veranda, swearing under her breath. "She was supposed to be here half an hour ago," she complained to Coryn. "She made a big deal about the Queen's Court's presence at the wedding, but then didn't bother to show when I asked for her ideas."

"You're better off without her here," he said, earning her glare. "What? You can't stand her."

"Doesn't mean I like when she stands me up either."

Marietta threw herself down in a chair and picked up one of the pastries. She tested the bounce of it between her fingers before popping it into her mouth. Another one of her recipes used by the palace kitchens.

The doors opened abruptly, Marietta turning to make a snide comment to Tryda. But she paused when she saw Wyltam. His mouth thinned into a thin.

"What's wrong?"

"There's been a small feybarb outbreak."

Marietta stood slowly. "Within the city?"

He shook his head. "We need to hurry."

Wyltam wouldn't answer her questions as they rushed through the halls, her guards running behind them in a crashing, ominous sound. They reached the infirmary, all the nurses and physicians wearing long metal masks over their faces.

Panic, true and sharp, shot through her very core. "Wyltam?"

"It's your father."

The air left her body. Holding his hands, she led him toward the door.

"His grace isn't permitted," a nurse said as they came running up. "No elves are allowed beyond this point, kings included. Too contagious for you. Come, Lady Marietta."

Behind her, she heard Wyltam order Coryn in after her.

The infirmary cots were arranged in a row, the room in chaos as people ran back and forth between two beds. A nurse appeared with a few masks, slipping one over Marietta's face and guiding her forward.

One bed held Minister Dyeiter, his body twisted and breathing raspy. Panicked, she approached the other to find her father, his face contorted in agony. His skin, once flushed with life, now looked pallid and waxy. Beads of sweat glistened on his brow. His body convulsed in erratic spasms, his fingers curled into claws.

Marietta dropped to his side. As she bore witness to her father's pain, a raw ache consumed her, seeping into every thread of her being. She took his hand in hers despite the nurses's protests. "Father?"

Each breath he drew was a ragged gasp.

She turned desperately to Coryn. "Heal him. Coryn, heal him please."

With a solemn expression, he shook his head. "The feybarb moved too quickly. There's nothing they can do."

"Marietta." Her father's voice came faintly.

She faced him again, tears streaming down her cheeks. His sunken eyes contrasted with her memory of him. She was a kid on his back, walking into town. They were in Kentro, and he let Marietta steal her first taste of ale. Each memory hit her, making her tears fall harder. She raised her shaky hands to his side and reached for the power of Therypon. She couldn't lose him—she refused to.

Someone gripped her shoulders, and she turned to find Coryn, his eyes wide with concern. "You'll only prolong his suffering. I'm sorry."

Realization crashed down at her all at once, her breath coming sharp as she repeated, "No, no, no …"

"Marietta," her father said again.

She took his hand and pressed it to her cheek. "Please, stay with me," she cried. "Don't leave us."

His eyes rolled open, his gaze finding her. "Marietta, my darling girl. Escape while you still can," he whispered.

As he collapsed to the mattress, Marietta felt the life slip from his body. As she shook with her sobs, the sensations crowded her chest, warring between warmth and unease. The latter won. Marietta rocked back and forth, gripping his hand. A foreboding voice resonated from the depths of her mind. *"With life comes death. Take solace, knowing he has no pain."*

Wyltam appeared in the doorway of his bedroom, worry lining his face. "How are you feeling?"

Marietta hugged the pillow tighter and clamped her eyes shut. The pyre burning for her father had happened that morning, Marietta to numb and raw from it still. Wyltam had offered to arrange a service to have him placed in the Ash Gardens along with the other Fulbryk members. Instead, she sent him home. While he grew up in Satiros, Enomenos was where he belonged.

"As good as I could be."

He nodded and walked toward the bed, hesitating before he sat on its edge. "I have some good news, though."

"Hm?"

"Elyse will be home tomorrow."

Marietta lifted herself up. "Tomorrow? You're sure?"

He nodded. "I was going to let it be a surprise that she'd make home a few days before the wedding." He ducked his head. "I figured you needed the surprise now."

Tears welled anew in her eyes, and without a word, she pulled Wyltam to her. They sank to the mattress, Marietta clutching him as if he were the only solid thing in a crumbling world. Her sobs came in waves, muffled against his shoulder, while his hand moved in slow, soothing circles on her back. For a brief moment, she let herself lean into his strength, feeling the steady rhythm of his heartbeat against her own erratic pulse. The world outside could wait—right now, all that mattered was the quiet comfort of his embrace.

The frozen ground resisted Wyltam's efforts as he tried to dig a space for Wynn's ashes. With no family ties or plot in Satiros, Wyltam struggled alone with the unyielding soil. Marietta stood with Elyse, holding her chilled fingers and feeling the weight of the moment as they watched Wyltam solidify Wynn as his family.

Behind him was a tangled garden sown with the ashes of the Grytsier line. Generations of their ashes had been buried in the ground, nourishing the plants that lingered per Satiroan tradition.

Tears welled in her eyes, tracing a path down her cheeks. Beside her, Elyse remained frozen, her nose reddened at the tip, eyes glistening, yet her face stayed stoic, devoid of any emotion. Since arriving in Satiros the previous night with Sibylla, she had barely uttered a word. She conveyed to Wyltam what had occurred but had since fallen into silence. Sibylla pulled Marietta aside, expressing how devastated she was and emphasizing the need to give her space and time to heal.

So Marietta tightened her grip on her cousin's hand, a silent gesture of support as her mentor's ashes were presented. Wyltam gestured Elyse and Sibylla forward, the three of them joining in burying his remains. They each took a fistful of dirt and placed it over the top. One day, his remains would sprout a new life, a remembrance of the one he had lived.

A sob overtook Marietta. While she hadn't known Wynn long, he impacted her life. From the first day of meeting Marietta on the streets of Satiros when she stormed away from Keyain, he had a smile on his face, as if he always found something amusing. He stayed positive, and that was the type of person Marietta gravitated toward. She had thought she'd have more time to get to know him.

Coryn's armor poked through her cloak as he slid an arm around her waist. She leaned her head on his chest, not caring that Keyain, Ryder, Adalyn, and the rest of Queen's Guard stood behind them. She hastily wiped away her tears as Wyltam placed his weight on the shovel. His head hung low, his knuckles white against the wood. He would never shed a tear, but that didn't mean he didn't grieve.

Elyse rejoined her side, searching for Marietta's hand. Instead, Marietta pulled her close, placing a kiss on her shoulder. Elyse would eventually share her emotions, and Marietta would be there for her when the time came.

Wyltam packed the dirt and paused one last moment before dismissing everyone. The three Queen's Guards on duty dispersed into the garden to give them privacy. No one uttered a word, for what was there to say? Wynn was taken too soon.

Marietta took Wyltam's face in her hands, gazing into his eyes. "I am so sorry," she whispered.

He brushed a tear from her cheek, swallowing hard before pulling her into a tight embrace. "I thought that maybe while we were already here that we visit the Fulbryk plot," he said, his voice thick and he cleared his throat. "Might be your last chance to see it for a while."

Marietta agreed and turned to Elyse. "Will you join us?" Her stare focused elsewhere, but she nodded, slipping her hands deeper into the pockets of her cloak.

Ornate iron fences demarcated the plots, each adorned with twisting gates bearing the family name above. As she perused the names, some were familiar from court, while others, nestled in verdant chaos despite the frigid cold, belonged to families entirely unfamiliar to her.

In the distance, an old oak pierced the sky like a spire with thick vines wrapped around the trunk. Usually, with plants, the tree would be choked out by its twining. Yet, with whatever magic existed in the soil of Satiros, the tree towered over everything else in the gardens. As they walked toward it, she read the name above the plot's gate. *Fulbryk.*

Elyse's hand found hers and she pushed it open, the metal squeaking with age. Whether from the cold or grief, Elyse shook next to her, and she pulled her closer.

Amid the intertwining greenery of the surrounding gardens, the Fulbryk plot stood out as a deliberate burst of colors. At its heart stood a mighty oak tree, its branches almost extending to the neighboring plots.

"*Maryna Fulbryk.* Lyken's wife," Wyltam said, reading the plaque before the tree. "And next to her resting place is Lyken." The ivy originated in that spot, twisting up and around the trunk. At a distance she had considered the vines to be choking, but now she saw them for what they were: a husband's lasting embrace.

As she shifted her gaze toward Elyse, she found her standing above a mesmerizing array of anemones in shades ranging from deep red and soft pink to vivid blue, rich purple, and pristine white. Elyse gasped, and her frame trembled as she sobbed, emotions breaking through. "My mother," she whispered. "I haven't been here since … since …" She fell to her knees, her tears dripping into the soil.

Wyltam approached her side and sunk to the ground, pulling Elyse close. The moment between them felt intimate, one needing to be shared alone.

Giving them space, Marietta wandered back to the vines. A memory surfaced from her childhood, of when she went searching through her mother's things for one reason or another, and she uncovered a stash of notes. There must have been a hundred of them, possibly more, all in her father's handwriting. They were little things, comparing her to the sun, thoughts of what reminded him of her. The gesture was romantic, and now Marietta understood where her father had gotten it from. Like father, like son, apparently.

She exhaled a puff of air and stared into the swirling ivy. As a frigid breeze cut through the plot, the leaves shifted, revealing something white near the base of the tree. Marietta gave a silent apology as she stepped onto the vines and dug through them. Her hand met cold stone, and as she cleared it away, she realized it was a pedestal.

She hurried and ripped the rest of the vines, uncovering a bronze bust of a man, his skin lined with age, his nose wide. Wavy hair was brushed back from his face, but the similarities between him and her father were glaring.

So this was what Lyken looked like.

Marietta checked the placard underneath, thinking it would share some accolade from his life. Instead, her heart seized at the single symbol etched into the metal surface—an upside-down crown. The same one from *Goodnight Feyries.*

Unroot my secrets where I quietly repose.

Marietta trembled as she kneeled down and dug through the greenery at the base. The cold earth numbed her chilled fingers further, not caring about the dirt that'd get under her nails. Within a few inches of digging, she hit something solid, and she began moving the soil away, revealing a stone top sunken into the earth with the same symbol. She burrowed her fingers along the side, feeling for a lid that didn't exist.

"Wyltam, Elyse," she called out, her blood thrumming in her veins. "I found something."

They appeared at her side and crouched down next to her. She turned to Wyltam, then to Elyse. "It was here the whole time. Wyltam helped me break the code in the books—he had the others."

Elyse sucked in a breath.

"*Unroot my secrets where I quietly repose,*" Wyltam murmured. "Of course, it was the Ash Gardens."

Wyltam took a moment to explain to Elyse how her mother had passed the task onto him to find the books, but he believed it to be aithyrstruck nonsense.

Elyse stared at the stone, new tears trailing down her cheeks. "She never knew how close she was this entire time."

"We don't even know what *it* is." Marietta felt around the edge again. "There's no top."

Wyltam hummed, then held his hand over the symbol, but it didn't budge. Without speaking, Elyse took a dagger from gods knew where and slid it across the tip of her finger. The deep red of her blood dripped onto the stone and sunk into the symbol. For a moment, there was nothing. Then the top slid up, creating an edge for Marietta to grab and slide out of the way, revealing a hollow. Wyltam reached in, pulling out a pile of packages and a sealed letter. He blew the debris off the surface and read, "To my daughter, Anthylia."

Chapter Seventy-Two

ELYSE

After the exhausting journey from the Circle of Mages to Satiros, Elyse almost convinced herself she hallucinated the hidden box buried beneath her grandparents' graves. But the letter Wyltam had pressed into her hand was all too real.

"You should be the first to read it," he murmured.

Grief and curiosity battled inside Elyse, wondering if she'd begin crying anew or tear into the letter. Her curiosity won. Sliding her finger along the edge, she broke the seal and unfurled the paper. In her hands, she held her mother's unfinished goal, hidden not even ten feet from where her ashes rested. Elyse took a breath, then a second, and pulled aithyr into her body as she read.

My dearest Anthylia,

If you are reading this, then I have passed on and hopefully my ashes are buried beside where you stand now. I'm proud of you, little blossom, for solving my last puzzle as I knew you would. My dear, I need to tell you why we left the fey court all those years ago.

While in Chorys Dasi, I believed Agnyssa simply hated the pili descendants for existing. It'd be fitting of a bheithaìchìn *self-named queen whose heart and compassion have been missing before the days we were made* Aonseelì. *What I* uncovered was much more sinister than I could have imagined.

We all questioned why a fey would crown herself a queen on this plane. At last, I have discovered what she planned to do with her new subjects: open a gate between this world and Seelìthe. Agnyssa believes creating an opening and controlling it will give her the power to supersede the archfey who cast us out all those millennia ago. She is a fool to think the Seelì would allow it.

If she were to succeed with her plans, it would mean dire consequences not just for us, but for every being on this plane. Her aim is domination—fey, elves, and pili descendants all bent to her will, while anyone outside the fey bloodline is seen as fit only for subjugation. This ruling would be cruel and unforgiving. You know how little she views those with short lives.

Her ideas are immoral and I refused to aid her any further. This is why we left, why we entered the elven societies, rejecting our fey forms altogether. I gave this plane the knowledge of magic to help deflect Agnyssa so that one day they could defend themselves from her hungering power.

However, Agnyssa didn't want to lose control of us—of me. She feared I would foil her plans aided by other domain leaders, who at the time were still disgruntled in their oaths to her. Especially after the eilymaìdeach's relationship with the bheithaìchìn turned rocky (the pun was not intended but acknowledged all the same). Agnyssa thought they'd band together and fight her for control.

Daughter, blood of my blood, little blossom—power is the most addictive drug and I fear those who have had a taste, ever to crave more. You must succeed where I failed. You must stop them. The key is to not let them know you are aware. I urge you to burn this message upon reading. For once Agnyssa learns you have this knowledge, she will not spare you. And while I love Anthys dearly, I fear your brother cannot save you from her wrath despite his promises to me.

It is time you learn the truth of your mother's death. May the knowledge I hid from you and your brother guide you steadfast in the face of our enemies, for the pain of knowing the truth must come with a reason. Your mother, her beautiful luìbaiheòl self, was murdered by Agnyssa for my refusal to aid her ambitions. I will never forget the burning defiance in your mother's eyes, the deep red petals of her fey form, or her bronze skin paling as the blood left her body. In the end, she knew her death was to protect the people of this world. I will not toss aside her sacrifice.

Agnyssa and her kin must be stopped. Never would I pass such a burden on you, but I must. The fate of this world rests on your shoulders.

I hope you received this in time, that Agnyssa hasn't dug her claws into you yet. If she catches you, my child, you must do the unthinkable. End your life before she can use your abilities for harm. Agnyssa wants full control over <u>all</u> the domains—you and Anthys are the last luìbaiheòl *and out of her reach. Have it remain so. I understand being the last, feeling Agnyssa's grip trying to control the final* tìdglaidh *of this plane. Fight it. Escape it. Defeat it.*

These are the words I leave you with, little blossom:

I have always been proud of you—for what you have done and all you have yet to be.

With all the love in my heart and my being,
Your father

Tears spilled down Elyse's face, rendering her unable to convey the message to Wyltam and Marietta. She handed them the letter, sobbing once more. Her mother never had the chance to discover its contents—her father had taken her life. Elyse had witnessed the tragic event, capturing her mother's final moments before the fatal fall. Memories flooded back, recounting her childhood following her mother's demise, tearing open her heart once again.

Hate, which already festered inside her, took on an additional form. The only salve for the pain was retribution—for Wynn, for her mother, for all those she held dear. Elyse would get her revenge.

The dungeons were dank and cold, with a stench of unwashed bodies hanging in the fetid air. As Elyse hurried past the cells, their occupants' lingering stares compelled her to tug her hood lower over her face. Keyain trailed behind her, his heavy footsteps echoing ominously and causing the prisoners to retreat to darkened corners. A few hours ago, they had laid Wynn's ashes to rest. Upon returning to the palace, they met with Keyain to share their discovery. She had inadequate time to prepare mentally and emotionally for the torment of the task ahead of her.

The old metal door squeaked as they passed through to another section, the odor of prisoners replaced with stale air mixed with rust. Keyain hung back by the entrance, giving Elyse space to handle the task alone. The conversation was hers to have, knowing that he would never speak if anyone else were present. Countless doors lined the hallway, making it difficult to tell which ones were vacant and which ones were already occupied. Following Keyain's directions, she made her way to the third cell on her right, its iron handle cold to the touch. Pausing there, she unlocked the door and cautiously stepped inside.

Surprised, Elyse's father blinked at the sudden burst of light from the globe in her hand as she locked herself inside. Even with Keyain's warning, he was worse than she expected. With his hair hanging in stringy, matted strands, and his body gaunt and face hollow, he had become a ghost of his former self. The sight should've made her stomach churn. Instead, she smiled.

"Who's here?" he called out in a frail voice.

"Hello, father."

He paused a moment. "Elyse."

"We need to talk." Behind her, the door's pass through disengaged, allowing Keyain to overhear the conversation.

Her father laughed, the sound hoarse and sending him into a coughing fit. "How long has it been?"

"Tell me about the fey."

"You do not deserve to know," he hissed. "Turning on your kind. The queen's brother *chose* you when that was never your purpose. I knew you'd fuck everything up."

His insults no longer held the sting that they used to. "Tell me what I am."

"Broken," he said, "just like your ungrateful mother. She was the key, yet she threw her potential away … Everything I promised my queen, just gone to aithyr before she could complete it."

"What about opening a gate between worlds?"

He crawled toward her, limbs moving in a jarring, uneven rhythm, as if each joint had forgotten how to function properly. Golden eyes glimmered in the dim light, vacant and wandering, seemingly searching for something not there. "Has Agnyssa come for you yet? She will. You were promised."

"Tell me about my fey heritage," Elyse said, her tone flat. "What am I? Why don't I look fey? If I'm as important as they claim, then you must be fey, too."

Her father laughed himself into a coughing fit again. "Mortal forms. Curses of this world. Things you would never understand."

Elyse dug her nails into her palm. "Tell me then."

"We cannot stay in our fey bodies long, if you even have one at all." His tongue flicked over his lips. "While it is our most powerful form, we are limited. Choked. Not enough aithyr to sustain."

She furrowed her brows. "What do you mean by fey body?"

"You saw the portraits, you idiot girl. Could you not infer?" He sat back, his gaze fixed above her head. "I'm *bheithaìchìn*—the word sounded pinched but euphonic—"like your beloved prince. Beastial in this world's bastardized translation. I never liked your grandfather, even before ..." He trailed off and dropped his head, pausing before adding, "Your mother had hair of purple asters and the most beautiful bark for what this world calls skin."

Elyse trembled, unable to conceal the overpowering emotion that consumed her. She had never once heard her father describe her mother as beautiful—he didn't deserve to say it. "What am I?" she ground out.

"A mistake, you miserable child."

"That's not an answer."

"But it is—your mother began letting aithyr take over while you still kicked in her womb, don't you understand? She ruined herself and you simultaneously."

"She wouldn't have," she answered too quickly.

Her father's lips curled into the cruel smile she despised. "Oh, she intentionally made you susceptible to aithyr. Your mother ensured you'd succumb to it before Queen Agnyssa took you. She tried to run, but I caught her. She tried to kill you so many times, but I stopped her. Look at how I'm paid for trying to save your life."

Elyse pulled at aithyr, letting it wrap around her emotions and help steady her breath. "What did Agnyssa promise you in exchange for betraying your daughter and wife?"

"Everything. I should've let your mother kill you. Agnyssa will punish me to see the disappointment you've become. Years of trying to fix you, just gone."

"Do you think she would spend the time to save you?"

"My queen collects what's hers one way or another," he said. "She will have you, Elyse."

"Unlikely. How many fey are in the Chorys Dasian army?"

"Heed my words, you useless girl. Queen Agnyssa will have you. Save yourself the trouble and surrender."

Elyse lowered the globe so her father could see her expression. "When she comes, I will kill her. Do you understand?"

As he laughed, another round of coughing gripped him. "I hope I live long enough to watch that disaster."

"How many?" Elyse snapped, her aithyr slipping as exhaustion snagged her mind. Her patience grew thin, and she wanted to be near him no longer than necessary.

"I have a feeling that you will become intimately familiar with them soon."

"Enough with the veiled answers." Elyse tightened her grip on the glass globe in her hand. "How do you kill a fey?"

Her father tsked. "Your mother read you all those feyrie tales, yet you don't remember?"

"Answer the question."

"Why should I?"

Elyse tilted her head, taking in his surroundings. "I'll get you fresh food. A change of clothes. Maybe, if you answer well enough, something to bathe the wretchedness from your body."

He contemplated for a moment. "Your grandfather disclosed our secrets to the masses. I thought he made it pretty clear." He began to sing. *"Ash wood and iron's deadly play. Feyries' laughter fades away."*

In the depths of her mind, an old memory rose to the surface—a book that held a special place in her heart from her childhood. Until now, she had forgotten it. "Ash and iron ... is that true or just a children's poem?"

"True, though it only slows the healing, not dealing a killing blow."

"What other vulnerabilities?"

His smirk returned, the expression unsettling on his gaunt face. "Tell me, do you feel him? Even now?"

She furrowed her brows, waiting for him to explain.

He sighed, exasperated. "I wanted your mother to, but she never gave in. The prince is a fool. His demise might be yours as well. Do you even understand?"

"Understand what?"

"The claiming."

Elyse blinked, not comprehending.

A deep furrow formed between her father's eyebrows as he frowned. "Yet somehow he did it."

Gods, her father lost his mind, and all it took was a few months in a dungeon.

"Why did you kill her?" Elyse asked, her voice breaking. Remembering her grandfather's letter, a wave of devastation crashed over her. The weight of knowing her mother had never fulfilled what he had started settled heavily in her chest. "I saw you that day. Why?"

"I told you, idiot girl. She tried to end your life, don't you remember? Years of suffering your abhorrent mother. I would not let it be for nothing, though ..." His gaze darted around the cell and he shook his head. "She'll come for me."

"Why did she try to kill me? What did Agnyssa have planned?"

Her father slumped back. "You are a weapon; I was tasked with your creation and delivery."

"A weapon?"

"You were supposed to be more powerful than your mother, more powerful than Lyken," he said. "You shall be her key that turns the lock."

A coughing fit took him again and did not stop this time. He reached for his cup, dipping it into a pail of water. "If you had any decency, you'd give me that fresh water and food now."

Elyse crossed the room, forcing her father to sit back. She kicked over the bucket, letting the water spread across the floor. "If I had any decency, then I'd kill you now, but I fear if I did, then you wouldn't suffer." She leaned forward, stilling all the emotion from her expression. "The pain you caused me will return to you tenfold."

She spun toward the door.

"It's started, hasn't it?" he asked.

She glanced over her shoulder.

"Broken, just like your mother."

Elyse had enough, ripping the door open and slamming it shut. She turned to Keyain, who had latched the pass through. "Happy?"

"Kicking the bucket was unnecessary," Keyain hissed.

"He'll get fresh water now, won't he?"

He shook his head. "We aren't cruel to prisoners, understand?"

She ignored him and shoved past.

"And if you held your tongue, then we could've gotten a little more information out of him."

She turned on him. "Instead, you got to hear my trauma."

Keyain opened his mouth, then seemed to reconsider.

"I never want to see him again." Turning abruptly, Elyse stormed toward the exit, her breath coming in rapid gasps. She stumbled upon a dimly lit passage and she paused for a moment, crouching down as she buried her face in her hands. Memories came rushing back, and she could distinctly recall the sound of her mother's voice, brimming with warmth and joy, as she sang to Elyse.

Ash wood and iron's deadly play,
Feyries' laughter fades away.

Silver blades in shadows dance,
Steel–wrought nets, their last chance.

Mortal whispers weave their bane,
Pixie wings, a fragile chain.

Herbs and rings, a safeguard's boon,
Guard from the feyries' haunting tune.

In these verses, somber lay,
Feyries' laughter fades away.

She tucked her head between her knees, the weight of longing for her mother pressing down on her. Two decades had slipped away, and her memories had grown faint, blurring with time. That realization sent tears streaming down her cheeks. She missed her voice, her touch. Even with her father's words, she refused to believe her mother had tried to kill her. He had to be lying. She didn't—couldn't—remember it that way.

Drying her tears, Elyse stood and remembered what had sent her to her father. This was not the time to cry. That would come later. Right now, she needed to work with Keyain and Wyltam and Marietta, and they needed all the ash wood and iron they could find.

Chapter Seventy-Three

MARIETTA

Lyken had left behind his notes on fey, a collection honed over the years. Among them were early drafts that eventually shaped the principles of magic. The fragile pages contained some of the first feyrie tales, each inscribed with native fey names alongside his translated versions of them.

"*Luìbaiheòl*," Marietta said out loud, and not for the first time in the past hour in the suite's dining room. They still wore their burial clothes, not wanting to waste time changing. Following Lyken's pronunciation notes, she repeated the words over to herself, the language melodic as it slipped over her tongue. In his letter, Lyken claimed her father was *luìbaiheòl*, which they now knew was botanical.

Recollections flooded her mind of her father's reverent voice reading Marietta feyrie tales when she was a child. Why would he share fragments of his history with her back then, only to vehemently insist she avoid it? Grief ripped through her once more. She swallowed it down, focusing on the present and what they needed to do.

Wyltam glanced up at her from the notes he flipped through, Elyse working silently at his side. "Your pronunciation is getting better."

Marietta smiled weakly. "To the best of our judgment."

He nodded, then returned to his work. Ever since he took it upon himself to read Lyken's notes, he had grown contemplative. The single silver lining was that they knew how to injure them thanks to Elyse.

"More people need to know," she said.

"Keyain is aware, but this new threat they pose for the world is …" Wyltam's eyes darted back and forth as he searched for the word. "Catastrophic. If there's another plane where fey exist, then there are more all-power beings that could break through to here, regardless if Chorys Dasi can control the portal. Fey beasts, dark creatures, things we have no defense against."

Marietta plopped back into her chair, pushing her thumbs into the center of her brow bone. "We can't do it alone."

Wyltam eyed her. "The more people know about this, the more panic it will cause."

"That's preferable to all of us being ruled by fey."

Elyse glanced at Marietta and said, "We could find a few people to trust with this information."

"Should we bring in the ministers?" Marietta asked.

Wyltam shook his head. "Not yet. I need to share this with a select few I can trust. I'll summon Keyain, and we'll devise a plan."

When Keyain arrived, they compiled a list of allies and strategized. Wyltam planned to request their audience the following day.

With the furniture rearranged to fit the entire group, Marietta stood with Wyltam and Keyain in the small room off of the Mage Pit. Tilan and a half-elven mage named Fig stood next to Elyse. She knew the mage enough to hug them, Tilan enough to shake his hand now that the braces eased his movement. To Elyse's other side stood Sibylla, Tolis, and Andyr, who all possessed grave faces that matched Elyse's. Losing Wynn had cast a dark cloud over the group, one that Marietta felt with the heaviness weighing on her chest and wished she could ease.

Adalyn and Ryder wore serious expressions. Marietta seldom witnessed that side of the latter. Perhaps that reflected their demeanor during meetings with Keyain. In that moment, she became acutely aware of her limited understanding of Adalyn and Ryder, despite the time spent together. She knew they supported pilinos, but the depth of her knowledge about them remained shallow. Yet, seeing them standing here, ready to work without knowing the specifics, proved their unwavering dedication and willingness to cooperate.

Coryn, Amryth, and Deania stood at the other end. Her gaze kept finding its way to Amryth, to the friend who abandoned her when she needed her the most.

Wyltam cleared his voice and stepped before the assembled group. "Thank you for coming at such short notice. While this team seems random, all of you have proven yourselves as trustworthy over the past few months. What we're about to share is dire news that will cause mass panic in the city-state and must be kept between us."

A few exchanged glances, some accompanied by furrowed brows, while others simply crossed their arms. Despite this, no one dared to interrupt him.

"Through Elyse and Marietta, we have uncovered a secret of Chorys Dasi, one that changes the severity of this war. Elyse, if you will."

Elyse approached, her face solemn. Marietta handed *Lyken's Guide to Chorys Dasi* to Wyltam, the pages already opened to the center. Pressing the tip of a dagger into her finger, Elyse's blood dropped to the book. The group gasped as the portraits appeared.

"Fey are real," he declared firmly. "They aren't stories or myths. They aren't a distant history that we learned about. They are here and they march toward our city-state. We need your help to defeat them."

Deania's hand gripped Amryth's forearm, their eyes meeting. Ryder blinked and began to smile, only for it to drop and his brows to furrow. Only the mages remained unfazed by the news.

Wyltam went into detail about Elyse's history, how she had discovered the books, finding Lyken's letter, and the details within it. As he explained the consequences of Agnyssa's plan, the room held in utter silence. It was as if no one could move, let alone breathe. When he finished, Fig sat, holding their head in their hands. Wyltam mentioned they were unsure if the portal was already open somewhere. It only added layers to why they needed to thwart Agnyssa before she grew too powerful.

"If that portal opens, if it hasn't already, it could unleash things we could never defeat with our current army and arsenal." As Wyltam continued, Tilan shook his head and took a seat next to Fig, his face creasing in the way it did when he needed to mull over something.

"I'm still gathering information," Wyltam added, handing the book back to Marietta. In turn, she handed it to Tilan and Fig, motioning for them to pass it among themselves. "In the coming days, I will detail everyone's role. The reality is, Chorys Dasi and Reyila will reach our walls. We only have Lyken's notes and old feyrie tales to go on for the abilities of the fey. We confirmed ash wood and iron can deal dire blows, though not outright kill. If we assume their army has fey, then our troops stand little chance. Tilan and Fig—the recent change in the designs was to counteract this front."

They nodded and handed the book off.

"Stifling Chorys Dasi's magic will be our most promising tactic. Also, we will use Elyse as bait because they seem keen on capturing her. Several of you, including myself, will be assigned to guard her when the time comes to enact the plan, which won't be until the Chorys Dasian prince, queen, or their mages show themselves."

The book made it to the end, Deania and Amryth suddenly whispering to one another, making Wyltam pause. At the attention, Deania lifted her chin and bared her teeth. "He's the murderer—the one who killed all the pilinos."

Wyltam paused, then stepped forward to see who she pointed to. "We know."

Marietta's stomach dropped as she took in Amryth's glower.

"How long have you known this?" Amryth asked.

"Brynden, the Chorys Dasian Emissary, was actually Prince Azarys. At the time, I didn't know what he was doing—what he was capable of. It wasn't until Amigys that he admitted his crimes," Elyse said, her voice quiet and far away. For a moment, her eyes blinked back tears, then she seemed to gather control of herself. "But I've suspected he was the murderer since Marietta's trial, when I found the portraits."

"You've had this for months!" Amryth's sudden yelling caused Marietta to jump.

"I—I didn't mean ..." Elyse stammered.

Amryth stepped forward, her hands curling into fists. "People have been agonizing over these deaths. Families and friends wanting closure. And you decided to what, hide it because the murderer was a male who gave you attention?"

Elyse recoiled, and a surge of protectiveness washed over Marietta. "You left!" she snapped. "When were we supposed to tell you?"

"Don't even start with me." Amryth's gaze pierced through Marietta like a dagger, full of accusation. "You have the nerve to treat fellow pilinos this way when—"

"No one would have believed us!" Marietta jabbed a finger accusingly at the damning evidence in the book. "How would you react if we came to you with this?"

"What if Jory was found guilty and executed? He's been sitting in a cell for weeks when you could've exonerated him sooner!" Amryth heaved a breath, only calming when Deania placed a hand on her arm.

Marietta started to yell at her when Wyltam interjected. "Enough. Jory isn't going to trial—he's already been released. The evidence was planted."

"By who?" Amryth snapped.

"We don't know," Keyain answered. "But this is all a distraction."

"A distraction?" Deania threw the book, Coryn barely catching it before handing it back to Wyltam. "Your guards are the ones who failed to investigate this properly!"

"I understand," Keyain said, his voice strained. "But more pilinos will die if we don't work together."

Deania clenched her fists, her knuckles white with anger. "Work together? Your incompetence has cost us too much already."

Amryth ran her palm across her forehead and turned to Deania. "If we have a chance to kill this bastard, then we should take it. We can yell at Keyain for his ineptitude later."

Hesitating, Deania nodded with a sigh and leaned her head against Amryth's arm.

They were right, of course. Withholding the truth about fey hurt everyone and Marietta felt that guilt threatening to swallow her whole. "We'll make it right," she said, catching Deania and Amryth's stare. "We'll get that closure."

With the outbursts settled and every detail laid bare, Keyain outlined the plan, assigning roles to each person. He distributed sheets that detailed everyone's expected part, assuring them he would dispose of the papers after today.

As Marietta scanned through hers, she couldn't help but be impressed. For every scenario—be it the battle atop the walls or within the nearby villages—Keyain had devised a strategy. Even in the event of the armies splitting to encircle the city-state, the tasks were adjusted to adapt to the changing variables.

Before the attack, Marietta, Deania, and Coryn were to gather the temples, to see who would take up arms to defend against their enemies. Amryth aided by Sibylla would lead efforts in the Weeds to help disperse pilinos throughout the city-state, fearing that Chorys Dasi would focus on Rambler Grove. When the battle began, Elyse would get into position as a distraction to draw in the prince or queen. The mages would hide nearby in the shadows, while Adalyn and Ryder would wait with special cohorts fitted with the gear Fig and Tilan created. And until that day, the crafting duo would complete as many devices as they could.

Keyain turned to the group. "Our primary goal is to secure Marietta and Wyltam. If they fall, so does the hope of our soldiers."

Marietta observed her companions' faces, each etched with a mix of uncertainty and determination. An eclectic group of mages, soldiers, iros, and crafters united with a common cause.

She could only hope that it wasn't too late, that could still stop Chorys Dasi and its queen.

Chapter Seventy-Four
MARIETTA

With everything happening, it hardly seemed real that in two days Marietta would be married to Wyltam. The night before the religious ceremonies—a precursor to the legal vows—she stood on the balcony, a glass of wine in hand. Her breath swirled in a fog as she exhaled, the piercing cold slicing through her clothes. The chill never bothered her. Not that she preferred it over the warmth of the sun, rather, she appreciated how winter nights existed as the antithesis of summer days. Dark, brisk, often spent in solitude. It mirrored her recent life all too well.

The door opened behind her, footsteps sounding. "Aren't you cold?"

"I think it's going to snow tonight," Marietta said, glancing over her shoulder.

Wyltam peered at the sky and the dark clouds hovering over the city. "More of a reason to come to bed."

"My mind won't stop." She shifted her gaze back to the still-green garden below.

Wyltam slipped beside her and wrapped an arm around her middle. "Do you need to be alone?"

She shook her head. "I need a distraction. Care for a walk?"

With cloaks around them, they ventured to the Queen's Garden without her guards. Wyltam had no plans of leaving her.

The world lay encased in frost, the oak fountain shimmering in the light as they passed. Underneath the lattice of wisteria, Marietta paused to examine the leaves and petals that remained. "I don't understand how they're still blooming."

"Botanists wondered the same thing. Many have compared plant life from Satiros to elsewhere in the region, all coming to the same conclusion. It isn't the plants that are special, rather the soil itself. Mages come all over to research it," he murmured, leaning in so that the heat of his breath ghosted over her ear. "It's aithyr-rich, meaning it's completely unique to here."

Marietta's heart fluttered at his closeness after missing it for so long, and she leaned further into him. "Tell me more."

"Walk with me and I will."

She nodded and pulled him closer.

They stepped onto the path circling the garden. "Botanists have experimented with soil samples," Wyltam continued. "Used to grow plants both from and not from Satiros, to see if they could replicate the phenomenon. Do you know what they found?"

A gust of wind blew back the hair from his face, his pale skin tinged pink on his nose and cheeks. His dark gaze softened, her stomach tugging at the sight of him. There was a familiarity with how they moved together, an unspoken understanding that had begun manifesting months before, only coming to its full fruition now. It felt right, like she had finally found her place.

"Marietta?" Wyltam quirked a brow, a smile hinting at his mouth that left her breathless.

Standing up on her toes, she kissed him and tangled her hands in his hair, desperate to draw him nearer as if she could merge with his very being. Her frozen lips thawed against his warm ones, her tongue venturing into the heat. His embrace enveloped her, offering a sanctuary from the frigid wind.

Something cold touched her cheek. Her eyes fluttered open to find large, fluffy snowflakes falling lazily around them. One landed in Wyltam's hair and she smiled, wiping it away.

Wyltam gripped her chin gently, garnering her full attention. The light cast a halo around his head, making him appear almost ethereal. He opened his mouth to speak, then closed it and dropped his gaze. She couldn't bear the thought of him hiding at such a time, determined to hold on to this precious moment. Marietta kissed him again with the entire heat of her body that his touch caused. "Take me right here," she murmured.

"Marietta," he said, his voice low.

Her laughter mingled with his lips as she tugged at the front of his jacket. They lay on the path, their clothes becoming a hindrance as they eagerly tried to fit together. The cold air nipped at her skin, a stark contrast to the heat of Wyltam as he entered her. Marietta's eyes were fixed on him, surrounded by a mesmerizing flurry of bright snowflakes as she found her release. But he was more than a distraction. Always had been.

Home was never a place or location for Marietta, rather the warmth and comfort of love. It emerged in moments of safety, when everything fell into place. Now, on the precipice of the world shattering around them, she found the unthinkable against the curve of his lips. She found it in the pressure of their bodies pressed together, in his breath skating across her cheek when he sighed. It was in his voice when he whispered her name, drawing out each syllable as if it were a prayer. As if she was sacred in his eyes. Marietta wasn't sure when it happened, but Wyltam became her home.

Her skin flushed, her breath hitching with each of his thrusts. Her ecstasy soared higher and higher, teetering on the precipice, until she could only whimper. With Wyltam's forehead pressed against hers, his face agonized with her pleasure, Marietta plummeted over the edge, her body clenching as her climax shot through her in waves. Wyltam's murmurs turned to groans, and she sunk into his touch. She tilted her head back as his grip tightened in her hair, wishing that he felt that same, that she brought that comfort to him.

When they both stopped moving, sharing the same air with breathless gasps, Wyltam took her in with a liquid gaze. His eyes were like the night sky, an endless abyss. Except instead of the expanse of nothingness, she found tenderness and compassion, devotion and desire. In the eyes of the man who cared for her beyond any logical sense, she found a place for herself. Wyltam didn't need to speak a word because at that moment, she sensed it. He, too, was home.

"What did they find?" she asked as he went to move away.

Wyltam braced his arms next to her head and lifted himself up. "With the soil?"

"Yes."

He laughed then, a full smile coming to his face, and he tried to hide it by hanging his head. Marietta grabbed his chin and tilted him back so she could see her favorite sight.

"The plants grew faster and bloomed longer for a time. But the longer the soil had been away from Satiros, the less effective it was in aiding plant growth." Wyltam tucked a strand of hair behind her ear, his touch lingering at the tip.

"How sad," she said. "The longer it was away from home, the less like home it became."

Wyltam furrowed his brows. "I suppose that's one way to look at it." He sat back and offered his hand. "But I'd much prefer to escape this cold and settle into a warm bed with my soon-to-be wife, if that suits you."

His words ignited a flutter in her stomach, a smile breaking across her lips. "Please."

As they made their way back to the entrance, Wyltam came to a sudden stop, his eyes growing wide.

"What is it?" she asked, his grip tightening on her arms.

"Keyain called an emergency meeting. The army is racing back to the walls, with Chorys Dasi and Reyila in pursuit." He faced her, the whites of his eyes stark against the shadows. "The war has begun."

Chapter Seventy-Five

KEYAIN

Sweat trickled down Keyain's back as he checked his aithyr clock again. He couldn't move forward without Wyltam. The first task was to get everyone in place, but that clearly hadn't happened yet—Keyain was still waiting. Only Marietta would be late to the start of a war.

"I can go find them," Peryn offered, rising from the table. Keyain eyed him carefully. Amryth's inquiry had linked Peryn to the Blue Flames meeting, and even his explanation—something about investigating Jory—hadn't held up. Still, it was Peryn who had been sent from the city walls to warn him of the attack.

The report had been grim. The onslaught was swift, taking out nearly half a legion in minutes. No one saw the army coming or heard them until it was too late. Hastyrn had called the retreat to the city walls. Keyain's worst fear was now reality—they didn't have enough soldiers.

He studied Peryn, trying to ignore the nagging voice that warned him not to trust the male. Peryn wasn't supposed to be at that meeting, but with his forces struggling to stay alive, Keyain set his suspicions aside. "Go," he ordered. Peryn quickly left.

Keyain grabbed a report from earlier, scanning it for anything he might've missed. Oddly, the day's intel had been quieter than usual—nothing new spotted, no signs of escalation.

The door opened again. Keyain looked up, ready to unleash his frustration at Marietta, but stopped short. His confusion deepened as he recognized the figure.

"Tryda?"

Her condescending expression sent a wave of unease through him.

"You shouldn't be in the palace."

"And you have some nerve to disgrace your parents continually," she said calmly, walking closer to him. "You even disgraced Dyeiter after he worked tirelessly to help you. Did you even mourn his death?"

"Again, you should—"

"Despite all that," she said, speaking over him, "I still want to help you, especially on the eve of our freedom."

Dread tightened in his stomach, rising slowly until it clenched his throat. "What is this?"

Tryda gave a casual shrug, a hint of a smile playing on her lips as she stepped closer. "I did what any rational elf would. I don't kneel to pilinos queens—those two words don't belong together. So here's the plan: you sit here with me, wait for the Chorys Dasians, and surrender. I'll negotiate for your life. If not, you die tonight." Her smile faded as her voice softened. "I don't want to lose you too."

Keyain's fists clenched, knuckles whitening as he stepped toward her, his voice low. "What did you do?"

"I did what Olytia would have wanted," she spat, her tone sharp with fury. "I'm the only one trying to save our city-state!"

"All you've done is condemn us," he growled. His anger cooled as realization settled in—he had to hurry. If Tryda had sold Satiros to Chorys Dasi, Wyltam and Marietta needed to know. He pushed past her, but her grip closed around his arm.

"This is your last chance, Keyain."

His mind flashed to Wyltam, Marietta, and the soldiers retreating behind the walls. His last chance was here, but not in the way Tryda thought. Keyain shook off her hand and strode into the hallway, only to hear Wyltam's voice sound in his head.

"In Glass Gardens. Peryn said we're no longer meeting—send reinforcements."

Chapter Seventy-Six

MARIETTA

As Marietta stepped beside Wyltam, the fountains of the Glass Gardens did nothing to ease the creeping dread settling over her. There would be no temple ceremony. No vows. No wedding.

She wasn't going to be queen of Satiros. Not tomorrow. Perhaps not ever.

"This is treason," Wyltam said sharply as they approached the guards, his voice echoing off the glass walls. "As your king, I command you to let us through."

The only reply was the gurgling of the fountains.

A guard walked forward, his hand resting lightly on the pommel of his sword. "Your Graces, for your own protection, Minister Keyain has instructed me to escort you both to safety. He's in charge while we're under siege. Frankly, you're a distraction."

Marietta saw the flicker of fury on Wyltam's face as he stepped toward them, the tension in his jaw clear. "Let me speak to you. Alone," Wyltam ordered, the edge in his voice unmistakable.

Before the guard could respond, Peryn entered the gardens, his boots muffled on the stone. "Your Graces," he greeted them, bowing his head.

Wyltam remained fixed on the rogue guard, but Marietta turned to Peryn. "What's happening?"

"Keyain didn't have time to meet with you." Peryn's voice was firm as he moved closer, his arm slipping around hers. "His orders were to get you both to a safer place. We'll regain control of the situation soon."

She jerked her arm, trying to free herself, but his grip only tightened. His eyes locked on hers, and for a moment, everything slowed. A sharp pulse shot through her temples. Something twisted in her mind, as if a foreign thought was pushing its way through.

A dozen discordant voices crept into her consciousness.

"Lies."

She pulled out of his grasp and took a step back. From the other side of the room, the guard raised his voice.

"Lady Marietta, I insist we leave immediately." Peryn grabbed her forearm as the pulse in her temples returned.

Multiple forces tore at her mind, dragging it in different directions. She staggered sideways, hands braced on her knees as a sharp ringing filled her ears.

From across the room, she locked eyes with Tolis. "Friend?" he said in hand speak.

She shook her head and signed a single word: "Foe."

Without warning, Wyltam lunged forward and brought the guard crashing to the ground. Another guard rushed ahead, sword drawn, but Coryn was faster—his blade met the guard's, deflecting the strike aimed at Wyltam.

Marietta didn't hesitate. With the distraction giving her just enough time, she gripped Peryn's arm and summoned the black energy of Therypon, channeling it through her fingers and unleashing it into his skin. He screamed, releasing her as pain wracked his body. Marietta spun away, sprinting toward her guards.

A dagger sailed past her, the blade cutting through the air. Behind her, a guard cried out, falling with a heavy thud.

The others advanced, armor clinking in unison. Wyltam dodged their blows with ease, his magic surging in a violent wave that knocked them off their feet. Without a second's pause, he and Coryn charged for the exit.

Marietta reached Andyr and Tolis just as Wyltam's eyes found hers.

"Run!"

Chapter Seventy-Seven

ELYSE

Elyse tugged her cloak tighter to her body, trying to shake both the chill and exhaustion from herself. She had been asleep for maybe half an hour before Wyltam's message came through. Upon arriving at her meeting point, she sent a cornicular for tea, fidgeting with her rings filled with Mage's Eye. For good measure, she kept a full vial on her as well. Half a dozen daggers were hidden on her. She was stretched thin, a thread pulled tight across fabric. Any more pulling, she would snap and break.

Her task was simple—arrange a meeting with the ministers while Wyltam strategized with Keyain. She knew the ministers would be disgruntled by his absence, some already bitter about being kept out of war discussions. They would have to sort that out themselves. Now wasn't the time to coddle city-state leaders. Minister Royir hadn't even bothered to show.

Elyse sipped her tea, savoring the bitter taste, as her eyes drifted over the ministers huddled in quiet groups, whispering. Their wary glances flicked toward her. A cornicular appeared at her side.

"My lady, someone is at the door for you."

She frowned and stood, following them to the entrance, her irritation spiking when she saw who was waiting. "Grytaine, this is hardly the time."

Grytaine's face was paler than usual, eyes wide, darting nervously over her shoulder. "Elyse, what's happening? A message came for Royir, but he's gone. It said I should come here."

"You should go back to your room," Elyse said sharply, but was interrupted by another messenger. He gestured toward her but handed the note to Leyland. "Now."

Leyland shared the note with Rymos, their eyes snapping to Elyse as she approached. Before she could ask, Wyltam's voice echoed in her mind: *"Palace under attack. Forget the ministers—secure aithyr items. Get to the tunnel. Trust no one."*

She halted, looking around the room. Already, a whisper broke out over the table as another messenger arrived. She turned toward the door, heart pounding. Someone grabbed her arm.

"It says to go to the throne room. Do you know what this is about?" Sethyr asked, concern plastered over his face.

Elyse felt uneasy. Wyltam had said to trust no one. "I don't."

"Come with us," he urged. "I failed to keep you safe before, and I promise I won't fail you this time." His guilt weighed heavily in his eyes, a painful reminder to Elyse of the loss of Wynn.

She shook her head. "I have someone I need to find."

As she moved toward the door, Grytaine stepped in her path. "Something's wrong. Tell me where to go and don't say my suite. This isn't just about us." Her hand rested on her pregnant belly, and for the first time since Elyse had known her, tears filled her eyes. "Royir doesn't care about me or the baby. Where do I go?"

The ministers were beginning to file down the hall, casting furtive glances their way. The air thickened with tension, as though a storm was about to break.

"I don't know," Elyse admitted. "If you won't stay in your room, hide somewhere safe. Don't come out until you see someone you trust."

"Elyse, wait—"

But she was already running, nerves urging her limbs to move faster. She slowed as she reached the garden doors, hearing the crash of metal and hushed voices. Through the window, she spotted a group of soldiers in red and black, their bronze armor gleaming in the low light. Fear surged through her, quickly overtaken by something hotter, something rawer. She clenched her teeth. The rage she'd held since Wynn's murder rose to the surface—since the male who lied and tricked her broke her heart.

Elyse unstoppered the vial, chugged the Mage's Eye, and kicked open the doors. The guards abruptly halted at her arrival. She pulled aithyr into her body and jerked her arms toward herself, imagining the air being ripped from their lungs, visualizing them asphyxiating to death. The Chorys Dasians collapsed, their legs kicking as they clawed at their throats. She waited until they stopped moving to bolt into the garden.

She needed to reach the library on the other side of the palace. Her legs pumped as she sprinted over the dark path on frozen ground. The light globes hovering above the garden paths ignited as she passed, creating an unfortunate trail behind her.

"Chorys Dasian soldiers in the garden," she sent to Wyltam. *"Did you know?"*

Elyse diverted from the path, remembering her secret hideaways and shortcuts from her childhood. She sprinted through the meadow with her favorite pixie statues. As a group of Chorys Dasians rounded the corner, she skidded to a stop.

"Is that her?" one of them yelled.

Elyse ducked back into the foliage, branches smacking her in the face as she made her own path, hearing the wood snap behind her with her enemy's approach. She waited to see if Wyltam sent anything back, refusing to allow her mind to assume the worst.

Passing through a thicket of lilac bushes, Elyse followed the pull of aithyr, a familiar comfort drawing her closer. She stopped when she came upon a hulking statue of a canine creature. She remembered, suddenly, when she had been fleeing from her father this statue had called to her—just as it did now. The enemies closed in behind her, but Elyse steadied herself, taking a breath. Above the statue, a thick stream of aithyr drifted. She focused on it, willing it to shift, to descend into the stone. Her body trembled, and something wet trickled from her nose, but she kept her attention locked on the tendril. Slowly, it responded and flowed into the statue.

For a heartbeat, nothing happened. Then, with a sharp crack, beams of aithyr erupted in all directions. The pressure in the air shifted, her ears popped, and fissures spread across the statue's surface.

"She's straight ahead!"

Elyse cursed under her breath as the soldiers stormed into the clearing. A wave of dizziness passed through her, a sharp headache following close behind. Somehow, she managed to turn and sprint in the opposite direction. She knew they would catch up soon, yet she refused to give in without a fight.

As she reached the edge of the clearing, a deafening crack split the air, followed by a monstrous roar. The soldiers' screams cut through the din as metal clashed, and the wet, sickening sounds of tearing flesh filled the space. Elyse's steps faltered, and she was instantly thankful the bushes hid the grisly scene. Fear jolted through her, pushing her legs into motion as she fled across the garden. *Almost there,*" she messaged Fig as she raced through the palace entrance.

Inside, the halls were unnervingly quiet, as if this section did not know Chorys Dasi had invaded. Each step echoed, her boots striking the tiled floor in time with her rapid pulse. Sweat slicked her skin as she reached the library, jamming a banner stand through the door handles. It wouldn't stop the soldiers for long, but bought seconds could make a difference.

The office door was open when she arrived. "Grab the artillery design," Tilan ordered Fig as he loaded prototypes into a bag. "The less they know about black powder weapons, the better."

Elyse joined Tilan, her hands moving swiftly to help pack the items.

Fig glanced over their shoulder. "What happened to you?"

"Chorys Dasi infiltrated the palace," she said between breaths. "Had to fight them off. They're in the gardens."

Tilan and Fig exchanged a glance. "Just grab the remaining bags of black powder and any schematics, then," Tilan said, turning away from the items. "They'll be useless without the firepower."

A rhythmic pounding echoed from the main section of the library. Elyse stood, her heart leaping to her throat. "They're here. I'll buy you two time. You need to reach the tunnels."

Tilan clapped her shoulder, and he slid the knapsacks onto his back. "Find us, all right?"

Elyse nodded, retrieving a vial she had hidden in her desk. She had consumed enough Mage's Eye to see the aithyr streams clearly. Ignoring the potential consequences, she sealed her fate and downed another vial, enjoying the calm that washed over her body. She pulled aithyr into her and it sung along her senses, humming in time with her pulse. Nothing felt more natural than this, than the power of magic under her skin.

Fig paused, lifting their aithyr glasses up then down over their eyes. "How much of that shit do you have in you?"

Elyse stepped into the main library, removing the daggers from their hiding spots along her body. "Run," she demanded and took off into the rows of bookcases.

Despite the drug's calming effects, one emotion swelled as she raced toward the front of the library. The glass doors shattered, and enemies surged into the space. When her gaze landed on the first Chorys Dasian soldier, a smile twitched to her lips, her chest heaving with each breath. Hatred, potent and powerful, carried her feet forward. She wouldn't leave until she bathed in their blood.

Chapter Seventy-Eight

ELYSE

Elyse moved with the grace of a dancer, her steps assured and fluid as she stalked toward the soldiers. Like the others she had encountered, they wore black and red fabrics beneath bronze armor stained with blood. Their helmets, however, were adorned with crimson feathers down the center, leaving their faces bare. Purposefully catching the eye of one soldier, Elyse lured him away, diverting his attention from Fig and Tilan in the opposite direction.

"Someone's here!"

Sharp clinks of metal echoed off the vaulted ceilings, shattering the stillness of her sanctuary. For two decades, this had been her refuge. Now, their presence defiled it. She would reclaim it with their blood.

Elyse's swift movements drew the attention of another soldier, his eyes scanning for her through the bookcases but quickly losing track. In the center of an aisle, she stilled her breath and imagined herself as nothing—thin, invisible, a shadow in the air. Her body vanished, and she shattered the silence with a scream.

Predictably, the soldiers rushed toward the sound. Eight Chorys Dasian guards gathered as Elyse darted back through the aisle, slipping through the maze of shelves. With a fleeting thought of apology to the books, she focused her rage, letting the heat simmer beneath her skin. It built and coiled inside her, ready to strike.

The soldiers turned, startled, as she dropped her invisibility. "It's her!" one shouted.

A few charged forward, but Elyse unleashed the stored aithyr. A fireball exploded in the middle of the group, consuming them in a blaze. She smiled at their agonized screams, briefly savoring the sound before ducking back into the shelter of the bookcases. But this time, the soldiers learned. They scattered, encircling her in a deadly, tightening loop.

She met the first soldier with an arc of electrical energy crackling around her fist as she forced a dagger into their gut. Surprised by her attack, they let out a cry and stumbled backward, leaving her hand coated with blood. Spinning, Elyse grabbed the arm of an approaching soldier, using aithyr to freeze their limb solid. His scream pierced through the library. Her body continued to pull aithyr, as if she could live off it like food or water, imagining the energy turning into all the ways she could avenge Wynn.

A guard swore and yelled, "Don't harm her!"

Good. That would make things easier. They wouldn't meet her strikes with the same force. Elyse's body moved on its own now, her mind slipping away as she lunged, swung, and drew blood. A fist slammed into her cheek, forcing her back a step. She responded with a burst of wind, sending her attacker stumbling.

"I said don't harm her!"

"But she's killing us!"

The blow jolted her from the trance, her limbs trembling, teetering on the brink of exhaustion. But stopping wasn't an option—not yet. Tilan and Fig were still too close.

She bolted to the side of the library, the soldiers following in close pursuit. As she moved, she opened one of her rings and dumped magicsbane onto the blade just as she reached her old alcove. Turning invisible once more, she hid behind the curtain and waited.

Elyse pressed a hand over her mouth, the metallic tang of blood sharp in her nose, muffling her ragged panting as the sound of footsteps neared and slowed.

"Spread out," a soldier ordered.

The curtain drew back suddenly. The details of the soldier's face came into clear view. The arch of his nose, the dark hair plastered to his forehead. His bright eyes stared through her. As soon as he turned away, Elyse plunged her dagger into his neck with a spray of blood and vaulted over his body.

As the fight continued, Elyse understood she couldn't possibly kill all of them, yet would have to continue drawing them away from Fig, Tilan, and the tunnel entrance. She'd make her way down there eventually, unless Wyltam had another order for her.

She bolted across the library, noting that the guards spread out once more among the stacks. While they wouldn't group together again, perhaps she could attack them all at once another way. Aithyr flowed freely into her body, and she channeled the energy, feeling it surge through her limbs, amplifying her strength. With a sharp push, she shoved a towering bookcase. It toppled with a deafening crash, slamming into the next, setting off a chain reaction. The shouts of confusion echoed around her, and a fierce grin broke across her face.

Turning toward the tunnels, Elyse's path was suddenly blocked. A figure loomed before her. She screamed, slashing with her dagger, but the assailant's grip was iron, twisting her arm and sending a sharp sting through her skin as their blade found its mark. In an instant, the power drained from her body, the aithyr retreating, leaving her hollow. She slumped against her attacker, fury rising—until she saw his face.

Sylas eased her against him, his body clad in soft black leathers, his expression unreadable.

"Let me go," she pleaded. "Don't do this."

His eyes met hers as he called out, "She's secured."

A scream tore at her throat, and she thrashed against his hold. What happened to the male who helped her escape Azarys not once, but twice?

Sylas twisted her arms behind her back, half carrying her toward the group of soldiers. A little more than half remained.

"Where is he?" Sylas's voice was a growl. "I was the only one assigned to grab her."

One of the guards approached, their face covered in sweat and blood as they panted. "We had it under control."

"Answer the question."

Footsteps reverberated through the library entrance, each step grinding shards of glass beneath heavy footfalls. The thud of armor grew louder, punctuated by the harsh scrape of metal dragging across the floor. As the figure advanced, soldiers fell to their knees without hesitation, their heads bowed in wordless submission. The bronze armor gleamed under the low lights where the metal wasn't dulled by blood, the torso ribbed to be reminiscent of abdominal muscles. Their grip was loose on the blood-soaked battle-ax, its weight scraping along the floor.

It was the helmet that truly marked them—a striking bull's head crafted from bronze, complete with massive horns and razor-sharp teeth. The mouth gaped open, allowing the person within to see. A wave of panic washed over Elyse as she faced the fabled warrior from *Lyken's Guide to Chorys Dasi*.

The Bull of the North.

They moved closer, and though Elyse couldn't see their face, an irresistible force pulled her in as their gaze fixed upon her. She strained against Sylas's grip, her heart racing as her pulse quickened. She lifted her chin, knowing who was underneath the helm.

He stopped when his pointed sabatons almost touched the tips of Elyse's boots. Her lips quivered as she raised her eyes. Her body turned to ice. A pair of red eyes stared back at her with a smile so achingly familiar that she wanted to scream.

His voice was low and pleasant, possessing the Chorys Dasian lilt. "There you are."

Chapter Seventy-Nine
MARIETTA

With Wyltam beside her, Marietta sprinted after Coryn, her legs heavy and unresponsive. It was as if she watched from a distance, disconnected from her body. Their footsteps rang out as they fled the Glass Gardens, Andyr hurling something over his shoulder. Moments later, an explosion shook the ground, nearly toppling Marietta. Wyltam steadied her with a firm grip as they entered the next corridor—a long, unbroken stretch ahead.

"Oh, thank fuck. This way!" Keyain appeared from the stairs, motioning for them to follow. "Chorys Dasians just left this area, heading toward the library. We need to reach the entrance by the temple."

"The Blue Flames?" Wyltam asked.

He answered with a singular nod. "Tryda orchestrated this." He glanced around the corner and signaled for them to follow.

"And Peryn as well," Ryder growled, charging up the stairs.

Keyain shot a look back. "I gathered that."

As they arrived at the top and prepared to turn, a pounding surged in Marietta's temples. "Duck!" she shouted in a voice that wasn't her own.

Instinct took over. She reached out, unleashing a bolt of lightning from her hands, striking the hidden Chorys Dasian lurking around the corner. The guard staggered back with a shout, his eyes narrowed like daggers.

Andyr turned to Marietta, surprise etched on his face as he drew his sword. The assailant screamed, thrown off balance by Andyr's gust. "Run!" he urged, brandishing his weapon.

Wyltam pulled her along, though a part of her wanted to turn back, to tell him they needed to help Andyr. But her lips wouldn't move; her body wouldn't respond to her will. A wave of crippling fear washed over her as a sharp voice echoed through her head, reverberating like a crack of thunder. *"Chaìdhleh sìthfaìelph, we had a deal."*

A sudden wave of sensations crowded her chest just as a soldier burst through the doorway. Marietta shoved Keyain aside and unleashed flames from her palms, engulfing the enemy in fire. She turned from the screams and spoke in a deep, terse voice. "Keep going."

Wyltam and Keyain exchanged a glance, then took off again. The stirring in her chest intensified, and she glanced back to see one of the downed enemies struggling to rise, a hand reaching out. Marietta raised her own, sending a bolt of lightning arcing toward him, silencing the threat.

Her temples throbbed again, but the pressure in her chest eased. Suddenly, Coryn was thrown aside as another soldier charged from a doorway. As the enemy swung his sword toward Marietta, Tolis lunged, plunging a blade into the soldier's neck.

She sputtered at the spray of blood across her skin as she heard the fighting all around her, watching as Keyain and Ryder hacked at their assailants. Wyltam hurled a dagger, striking one soldier squarely in the eye, sending him crumpling to the ground with a scream. Keyain's sword followed, plunging into the man's back, silencing him for good.

Marietta raised her hands, calling upon the deities' abilities to return. But before she could harness their power, Coryn yanked her forward.

"No!" she screamed as Tolis squared off with the remaining soldiers, the rest of their party close behind her. She struggled against Coryn's grip, desperation clawing at her until she heard Wyltam.

"Trust that he can fight and find his way back to us. We need to keep moving."

She fell silent as she took in the wide panic of his eyes, his pale face splattered with blood. His hand was covered in it. A sudden terror sliced through her. Wyltam's mortality, which she never questioned, suddenly became a real thing he could lose. She nodded, bracing herself, and started running once more.

Approaching the temple doors, they directed themselves toward a tapestry hanging on the opposite wall. Keyain pulled it back and waved them forward. Marietta furrowed her brows until she watched Ryder walk through the brick illusion.

They raced down the hidden stairwell and into the tunnels, which were as she remembered them: dark and dirty, with stone walls and dusty floors. They ran as quickly as the space allowed.

"If we get separated, head to the escape route," Wyltam said, not slowing as they came to an adjacent hallway. "Peryn knows about the tunnels, likely told Chorys Dasi. Time is our only advantage. Hopefully they don't realize we're down here yet."

They moved in silence, no one speaking as their feet clattered across the ground. As they neared their escape route, Marietta slipped her hand into Wyltam's for a moment. She squeezed, her aching heart easing as he squeezed back. He glanced sideways and offered a small smile. Then, everything shifted into slow motion.

One moment, she was gazing at her partner's face; the next, they were knocked to the ground as Chorys Dasian soldiers erupted from an adjacent tunnel.

Marietta's ears rung as she glanced around, dazed. Wyltam already moved to stand, daggers in hand. Coryn grabbed a soldier by their throat and sent Therypon's crackling energy into their skin. Keyain stabbed another through the neck as Ryder gutted them.

A rush of sensations ignited in Marietta's chest, compelling her to rise and gather them all at once. Their voices clamored in her mind, each vying for dominance.

"Aìltbuith thudhìa guleòo'n bhàsmor."

"Tàch bhàsmor dh'iòm!"

"Sfhènel'dhia!"

Shoving past Wyltam, she faced the approaching enemies. A stirring started in her chest, followed by a crackling heat that snapped and popped like fire. The energy flowed down her arms to her fingertips as she lifted her hands. The enemy soldiers charged, weapons drawn, and Marietta unleashed the fire that simmered beneath her skin.

Heat surged through the tunnels, the flames whipping into a swirling tempest that engulfed their enemies. Their screams were swiftly extinguished as the heat flared and then vanished, leaving nothing but their charred corpses.

She collapsed, her head spinning and vision blurring. She sensed Wyltam grasping her arm, someone cursing in the background.

"Marietta." His deep voice pierced her fog. "We need to move—the escape route is just ahead."

As he pulled her forward, soldiers in Satiroan green rounded the corner led by one they had already confronted. With a smirk, Peryn raised his sword.

Chapter Eighty

ELYSE

Elyse thrashed against Sylas, not to escape but to wrap her hands around Az's throat, to feel the heat of his blood on her skin. Azarys stood in front of her and she wanted to watch the life leave his body. She bared her teeth.

Azarys's low laugh echoed in the helmet, abruptly stopping as he narrowed his eyes. His gauntleted hand rose to her cheek. She jerked away from his touch.

"Who?" he demanded.

At their silence, he turned to the soldiers. "Do not make me repeat myself."

"Ryho, Your Grace," one of them answered.

Azarys stalked forward, the soldier visibly shaking as the space between them narrowed. Azarys ripped off Ryho's helmet and wrapped his hand around his neck, lifting his feet off the ground. He sputtered as Azarys growled, "What did I say?"

The soldier tried to speak, his lips moving with no sound.

"Louder."

"She was killing us," he managed. "I had to."

Azarys squeezed and the male's neck snapped as easily as a twig beneath his touch. He threw him to the floor. "When I said do not touch her, do not *harm* her, I meant it."

When his attention turned to Elyse, her hearing deafened by the pulse in her ears. She stepped back into Sylas, feeling the solid bulk of his body.

"Let her go," Azarys demanded.

Her wrists were free. Despite her fear, despite watching him kill that male with next to no effort, she charged forward and used her momentum to push into him, except Azarys didn't budge. A low, rumbling laugh came as he wrapped his arms around her. He gripped the back of her hair and tugged so she was forced to stare him in the face. "I have you, goddess. You're mine now and always."

"I'm going to check the library," Sylas said behind her, his footsteps walking away.

"You do that."

Elyse sensed the surrounding magic, could look at the swirls in her peripherals. She had enough Mage's Eye in her blood that she could still see aithyr, but could she channel it?

Azarys murmured something to her. She didn't hear him as she focused on pulling the energy into her body, imagining herself a leech, sucking in all of it within her vicinity. The urge to kill Azarys overcame her as he took off his helmet, his black hair flattened against his skull.

Normally, aithyr flowed into her as a stream. However, with the magicsbane, it slowly seeped like sap flowing from a tree. Azarys talked, but she heard nothing, feeling the energy vibrating under her skin.

"Goddess?"

She lashed out with flames, hearing him grunt as he ducked out of the way. Grabbing a dagger hidden on her thigh, she lunged forward, only for Azarys to grab her wrist and twist her onto her stomach. His knee dug into her back, the metal threatening to pierce her skin. Gripping the hair on the back of her head, he lifted her face off the ground. "How did you manage that with magicsbane?" Instead of anger, he sounded in awe. Another blade bit into her arm, the energy fleeing her once more.

Azarys pulled her head back farther, Elyse hissing with the pain. Her eyes met his as he loomed over her. "You are always full of surprises. One of the many reasons I love you."

His words fueled the burning hatred in her veins, despising the way his lips twisted into a smirk above her, triumphant in his control. "Your love is rotten," she spat, "vile and cruel, ruining everything it touches. I do not and will never again love you."

He leaned as close as his armor would allow him. "Hate me if you wish, goddess, but your disdain does not hide your desire." His other gauntleted hand caressed her chin. "Your love is alive and well. I can sense it, the way you crave me deep down as I do you. Given time, I'm sure I can resurface it."

Her breath quickened as she felt a pull toward him, noting the curve of his lips, remembering the pleasure of his touch.

Never again.

She thrashed against him.

"Found something interesting."

Sylas's voice drew Az's attention, his face melting further into a smirk. "Well, what do we have here? Friends of yours?"

Time slowed as Elyse turned her head and saw Sylas restraining Tilan and Fig, forcing them to the ground. Azarys released his grip on her and lifted her upright by the back of her cloak. She lunged at him, attempting to shove him away while desperately reaching for aithyr, but it remained elusive. He couldn't take Fig and Tilan.

Azarys pulled her flush to his body so that she stared at his bronzed chest. He began smoothing back her hair. "And who are you two?"

"Fuck off, racist shit," Tilan growled.

She heard a thud followed by Tilan's cry.

"I can do this all night, couldn't I, goddess?" He glanced down at her, and in response, she spat defiantly in his face. Instantly, his expression turned dark, and he yanked on her hair, forcing her to meet his piercing gaze. "So desperate for my attention," he said with a tsk. "While I enjoy your newfound feistiness, please wait until I have time to play with it."

Elyse narrowed her eyes. "And if I refuse to comply?"

"Then it'll only take longer." He pulled her back into his chest, speaking over her head. "Again, why are two little clips running through the library at night?"

She heard Fig sigh. "Do you really want to know?"

There was another thud and Fig's muffled cry. "Just answer the question," Sylas said.

Fig laughed. "Only if you answer mine. Why is the Prince of Chorys Dasi such a driveling prat?"

She heard Tilan's laugh next to theirs as Azarys's grip tightened.

"Someone has been talking," he said, his voice strained. "What else did you tell them, goddess?"

"Nothing. Just let them go."

"They mean something to you then. Interesting." He was quiet a moment, then added, "Bring them to Agnyssa. There's a chance Elyse may have overshared, so we can't have that, now can we?"

She heard shuffling behind her, her heart racing as panic seized her. The Chorys Dasian queen would kill them both, if not worse, when she realized who Tilan was and what they'd created.

"Wait," Elyse said, placing her hand on Az's chest.

Azarys pulled back. "You have something to add?"

"Let them go and I'll do whatever you want." She searched his gaze, watching his brows rise. "Release my friends and I'm yours, okay? But if you don't, I will fight you on everything until my dying breath. I will make sure you never know peace."

"What if all the peace I need is your presence?"

"You've only just scratched the surface of what I'm capable of."

A grin hooked his lips, and he slowly released her. "All right, I can live with that, but I need you to make a deal."

"A deal?"

Sylas started to speak. "Azarys, don't you dare—"

Az only raised his hand at the mage, silencing him. "Get on your knees, hold my hand, and state the agreement of our deal. Then seal it with a kiss on my palm."

Elyse's heart raced in her chest. She cursed her own foolishness for striking a deal with him. But if it bought her friends' freedom, it was a price worth paying. Slowly, she sank to her knees as he removed his gauntlet and extended his hand.

"I promise to listen to whatever you have to say and won't resist any longer, if you promise not to harm my friends and to release them." She leaned forward, ready to kiss his palm, but the gleam in Az's eye settled like a stone in her stomach. She knew her promise had to hold—had to keep them safe.

She quickly added, "But they must be freed in a place of my choosing, and I need to see that they're safe."

She waited for Azarys to accept. Though he ground his teeth, his eyes narrowing, he eventually nodded. Her lips pressed into his palm with a warmth radiating between them. Surprised, Elyse pulled back abruptly.

"Let's make this deal finalized." Azarys turned to Sylas. "Grab the clips. Where are we going?"

Elyse stood, jerking away from his outstretched hand. "To the Temple of Therypon."

Chapter Eighty-One

KEYAIN

"Peryn," Keyain growled, removing his sword from the dead soldier at his feet. He shifted his attention to the male he had considered a loyal companion for decades. "Why?"

Peryn gestured toward a patch on his uniform, the blue flame sending a chill through Keyain. "You had everything, and you gave it all away for a clip."

He steadied his voice. "That is not what happened."

"Isn't it though? A young minister, a champion of your people. You fought to preserve elven land, which is why we looked up to you." Peryn gestured to himself and the surrounding soldiers. "Our greatest warrior turned into our greatest enemy." He spat on the ground.

"I don't want to fight you."

Peryn gave a grim smile and said, "Well, I do." He lunged at Keyain.

Fighting erupted around them, the narrow tunnel restricting their movements. Keyain's concern grew with each clash of steel; a single misstep could injure one of his allies. Peryn seemed aware of this, using the cramped space to his advantage. Keyain parried each blow, stepping back deeper into the corridor with every swing of his sword. Beside him, his allies engaged the remaining soldiers, their efforts a frantic dance against the onslaught.

Keyain ducked and threw a dagger at Peryn's face, following the throw with a jab of his sword. Peryn turned from the dagger, barely lifting his weapon fast enough to block Keyain's attack. Keyain held his sword against Peryn's chest, using his other hand on the flat part of the blade to push it in further. "I trusted you."

"And I trusted you, but look where we are." Peryn head-butted Keyain, sending stars dancing before his eyes.

Keyain stepped backward, his sight still swimming when he felt someone at his back. He spared a glance, finding Ryder. His friend grinned, and he turned back to the soldiers who confronted him. Even when they were fighting for their lives, Ryder still had that damned smirk. The familiarity bolstered Keyain.

Peryn thrusted forward with his blade, which Keyain parried and shifted away. Sweeping low, Keyain sliced up toward Peryn's groin. Though he blocked it, Peryn staggered and lost his footing, allowing Keyain to press the advantage. Keyain twisted and pivoted his sword, making Peryn's clatter on the ground. Without a second thought, Keyain drove his blade through his gut, hating the sting in his eyes.

Peryn had been with him for decades, had been his most trusted. Now the life faded from his eyes at the end of his sword. Keyain withdrew it, watching his friend slump to the ground.

Marietta's screech pierced the air. "Wyltam, no!"

Keyain turned, finding Wyltam staggering over a dead body to get to Marietta, the hand at his side slick with blood. Keyain's breath slowed, his mind with it, as he surveyed the surrounding carnage. The ground became muddy from the dirt mixed with blood. His allies, now exhausted and bloodied themselves, were beginning to lose their fight. They were so close to the escape route. Marietta and Wyltam just needed some extra time.

Stepping up to where Coryn fought beside Ryder, Keyain said, "Get them out of here."

Coryn grunted as he swung his sword into the throat of his foe. "There's a dozen or so behind them. You can't beat them all."

Keyain attacked the next soldier, shoving Coryn behind them. "Then make my sacrifice count." He turned to Ryder. "Go with them."

His friend laughed, his smile splitting across his face. "Not a chance."

"Ryder," he warned, taking a slice to his upper arm.

"Not a chance, brother." He drove his sword into the side of an enemy soldier, making them topple before slicing off his head. "Together, all right?"

Keyain's chest felt hollow, a sickening gratitude washing over him that Ryder would give his life alongside his. From behind, he heard Marietta scream. At least her voice grew distant as they made their way to the escape route.

Suddenly, a new wave of soldiers clad in red and black surged down the passage, flanking the contingent they battled. In that moment, the weight of inevitability settled over him—he would die fighting. Fear, raw and immediate, gripped him, not for the approaching death, but for the regrets he carried. Marietta and Wyltam would have a chance of escaping, but was it enough? Would he leave the world better than he found it?

As the next round of soldiers hit, Keyain tried to focus on the calm of his sword in his hand. He ducked and dodged, sliced and thrusted. Someone caught him on the cheek. Another blade nicked his upper arm. A third swung toward his neck. At the last second, Ryder's sword blocked its blow.

At the same time, a blade connected with Ryder's throat. His friend didn't even cry out as he fell. Whatever dam held Keyain's emotion back cracked with a wave of anguish. Keyain screamed as he hacked at the soldier in front of him.

A deep rumble shook through the tunnels, followed by a gust of air and dust and rock. Keyain lost his footing for a moment, but remained sure-footed over the corpse of his dead friend, knowing this was the end. Ryder's sacrifice would not be in vain; neither of their deaths would go without meaning. Instead of pushing aside his emotions, Keyain sunk himself into them as his weapon grew slicker with blood. Tears blurred his vision. His scream tore at his throat.

A sword pierced his shoulder. Keyain cut down the soldier attached to it. Another caught his calf, and he nearly severed their arm. Another soldier tried to press him back, but Keyain ducked and found a gap in their armor. He lifted with the full force of his body, knocking him back into the two remaining soldiers.

Noting the number of bodies piled below him, he stumbled forward with a hysteric laugh, using his bloodied hand to wipe the tears away. The remaining guards took off in the opposite direction as Keyain took another step.

His breaths were too shallow, the pain in his shoulder unbearable. But he still stood on his two feet, his grip tight in his hilt. He closed his eyes and inhaled deeply. The tunnel was clear—Marietta and Wyltam would get away. There was a chance, perhaps, that he would find them after this.

His brief bit of hope vanished as he heard the clamoring of armor. A moment later, more than a dozen guards spilled onto the path. Their approach came in slow motion. A blur of red and black through his tears. The air felt electric, thick with the metallic scent of blood and sweat. Keyain remembered it well.

As the soldiers neared, Keyain steadied himself. For his king and almost queen, for his city-state, Keyain raised his sword for the last time and charged his enemies.

Multiple swords pierced him at once, the metal bone deep, and he screamed out and threw his body into them. As they retracted, Keyain wielded his weapon and parried a single blow. A few more blades plunged into his back, his arms, his legs.

Blood bubbled in his throat, yet he still swung his sword, catching a soldier in the gut. More piercing pain led to his chest becoming slick and heavy. Coldness crept into his limbs, his vision spotting. Faintly, he was aware of the soldiers now running past him. In the tunnel, he exhaled one final time, feeling the familiar sense of loneliness that had never left him. Even as he died, Keyain was alone.

Chapter Eighty-Two
MARIETTA

Marietta screamed as Coryn hauled her away. She had watched the sword carve into Wyltam's abdomen and knew how deep it went. His steps were slow and unsteady, his body leaning to one side as he struggled to keep his balance. Peering around Coryn, she could see Keyain and Ryder holding back the enemy soldiers. "No! No more! No!" Her voice cracked into a cry as Coryn pushed her along.

As they reached the escape route, Marietta shoved away from Coryn. "We need to heal him."

"I can't," he said, raising his arm covered in blood. "Bastards had magicsbane. I can't heal."

Marietta controlled her breathing and cleared her mind as much as she could. She called upon the deities, the pulse returning to her temple as her chest came alive with multiple sensations. She tugged on the stirring sensation, focusing on the stone behind them. A crackling laugh shot through her mind as the rock crashed down. The dust sent them all into a coughing fit, but the tunnel entrance was completely blocked.

The voices returned, their tones reminiscent of bickering. Her head rolled back as the forces raged within her.

She was vaguely aware of Coryn swearing as he pulled out a light globe.

Wyltam slid down the tunnel wall, his eyes closed when he rested back against it. Marietta pushed herself forward and dropped to her knees before Wyltam, lifting his shirt. The gore snapped her back into herself, pushing out the voices. "Coryn! Stop the bleeding. Make it stop!"

"We don't have time," he said, appearing over her. "The wound is deep. Without my magic—"

"I don't care!" Marietta screamed.

"Take her and run," Wyltam said, his voice strained. "Marietta, I need you to look at me."

Tears trailed down her cheek. "I'm not leaving you."

"Truth for a truth?" he asked, his smile pained.

"What?"

"Truth for a—" Wyltam winced as he spoke.

"You need to stop moving."

"I should've told you this weeks ago. I wish I had a lifetime to say it to you." He took her hand in his own. "Please know I died saving the person I love."

"No, no, no …"

"I love you, Marietta, but I need you to keep on living. I need you to have blood in your veins and air in your lungs. Promise me you'll run."

The tears flowed freely now, unsure if it was her hand that shook or Wyltam's. She pressed her forehead to his as a pounding started on the rocks behind them. "I love you, Wyltam. Please, stay with me. I can't face a world without you. "

"You must, my love." He cupped her cheek. "For I refuse to know a world where you don't exist."

Heaviness and warmth battled in her chest, and Marietta gasped as a calm sensation pulsed out from her temple and warmth spread to her fingertips. Without controlling her hand, she hovered over Wyltam's wound.

Coryn grabbed her shoulder. "Marietta, don't!"

Marietta pulled at the warmth, at the energy itching under her skin, a scream coming from both Wyltam and Coryn. Bright light glowed from her hand, the flesh beneath her touch repairing. "I refuse to live in a world without you," she said through the tears. "I refuse to leave you behind!"

The energy left her body suddenly, Marietta falling back into Coryn.

"You had no right!" Coryn yelled. "There's infection and internal bleeding and flesh not healing correctly! You've had no training!"

His words fell on deaf ears as the color came back to Wyltam's cheeks, his breath suddenly deeper. His eyes, however, didn't open. "Wyltam?" She shook him.

Coryn pulled her back with a snarl. "We need to run. Do you understand?"

"I'm not leaving him!"

Coryn wiped this face and bent down, grabbing Wyltam's limp body and throwing it over his shoulder. He took two steps before bowing over. "I can't, Marietta. We have to leave him."

As he eased Wyltam down, Marietta slipped her shoulder under one of his arms. "If he stays behind, then so do I." Her voice quivered.

Coryn sighed and gripped Wyltam's other side. As the ringing of metal grew louder, rubble started to fall down over the rocks. The enemy soldiers' voices were so close that she could almost hear the words they spoke. Panic surged through her, but seeing Wyltam unconscious focused her mind.

They were going to escape; Marietta would make sure of it. Without another word, they ran as fast as they could.

Chapter Eighty-Three

AMRYTH

Amryth mustered her most neutral expression as she worked in the Temple of Therypon. Everything had gone to shit. It'd been less than a couple hours since Wyltam ordered her and Deania to find Adalyn and Sibylla to help secure the pilinos. Chaos ensued as they went from building to building in Rambler Grove to tell them to either go to the temples or hide elsewhere in the city-state. Many chose the temples.

Deania attempted to get the temples to go help the palace, only appealing to Therypon and Zontykroi. The others claimed they didn't have enough people to watch over the pilinos in their temple. Just one of the many grievances of the evening.

The news came not even twenty minutes earlier. The Chorys Dasian army began flooding the city-state. Amryth was grateful they grabbed as many pilinos as they could. Whether Chorys Dasi would fight the temples was beyond her, but at least they had ways to defend themselves. She already expected to use her old skills from years in the guard. Thankfully, they weren't to that point yet.

Amryth handed a blanket she found to a young human mother with a baby at her breast. "Is there anything else I can get you?" she asked.

"My husband?"

"What's his name?"

Amryth wrote it down and located the temple worker who kept track of people on the premises. Her heart sunk when she couldn't find him on the list.

"There are still a few more rooms to check," she said, clasping Amryth on the shoulder. "Thank you for being here."

How odd it was to be thanked for something so obvious to her, as if she wouldn't be the first to volunteer.

As she turned to help the next people, a male stood in her way. His black hair hung in loose curls around his head, his skin a rich, warm brown. "Amryth Sulyng?"

She planted her hands on her hips. "Can I help you?"

"Heard you were arrested trying to clear Jory's name."

She nodded and began walking. "Matters little at the moment."

"Matters a lot to me." He held out his hand. "Jory."

Amryth halted and turned to study his face more closely. He bore a slight resemblance to Minister Leyland, yet it was not enough for her to recognize him as his son. "Well," she sighed, "shit."

"I know you're busy helping, but if you could find the time later, I have some information I think you'd be interested in hearing."

Amryth nodded as she noticed Adalyn hovering and motioned her to come over. "I'm curious to know what about."

He took off as Adalyn approached. "Seidytar is at capacity and Kystrorgiste is nearing theirs," she murmured. "Any update from Sibylla?"

"Not yet. Have you heard any updates from the palace?"

Adalyn shook her head. "Maybe Deania or Sibylla have?"

A moment later, someone called their names from down the hall. Deania marched with Sibylla toward the entrance, beckoning them to follow. When they caught up to them, Amryth asked, "What's going on?"

"Chorys Dasi soldiers are approaching the temple with pilinos," Deania answered.

They hurried to the entrance, Deania suddenly coming to a stop. "I need you three to stay out of sight. No matter what you see, no matter what you hear, keep to the shadows. Understand?"

Amryth frowned. "Not without an excellent reason."

"If the Temple of Therypon is seen harboring two active guards close to Lady Marietta and the king, along with a former military leader, they might see it as an opportunity to attack." Deania wiped her face. Amryth wished to pull her close, to tell her it would be okay, even if she didn't know if it would be.

Sibylla and Adalyn agreed, stepping off to the side of the entryway, still inside the building. Amryth remained rooted in her spot, even when Adalyn called after her.

She stared at Deania, grinding her teeth. She'd been here before, on the precipice of someone she cared for deeply about putting themselves in the face of danger. Amryth couldn't go through it again—she wouldn't. "Promise me you'll be safe."

A sad smile came to Deania's face. "I can't promise that."

"Then I can't promise I'll stay out of sight. If someone even lays a hand on you—"

"Amryth, come here." Deania pulled on the front of her shirt and kissed her.

It was soft, powerful, and over far too quickly, leaving Amryth's lips tingling in its absence.

"Bravery isn't just about facing danger. It's about trusting those you love when they have to face it. Be brave for me, Amryth." She kissed her again. "And stay out of sight," Deania warned before exiting the temple, lining up along the hoplite paladins, protecting the front with shields and spears.

Amryth stumbled her way over to Adalyn and Sibylla, her eyes locked on Deania.

"First time you two kiss?" Sibylla asked, her eyes trained on the steps.

"I didn't even know she liked me." Amryth shook her head, a sudden fear cutting through the warmth her touch had brought. She couldn't lose her. Not now, not ever.

Adalyn clasped her hand on Amryth's shoulder. "She's tough. She'll be okay."

Amryth swallowed the emotion in her throat, her hand gripping Adalyn's for comfort. She, of all people, would know.

A whisper rippled through the crowd as the guards neared the top. Sibylla gasped and stepped forward, only for Adalyn to grab the back of her armor. Confused, Amryth shifted where she stood and saw who came up the stairs. Confusion washed over her when she saw Elyse, but dread dropped to her stomach when she saw who gripped the back of her neck.

Chapter Eighty-Four

ELYSE

Wind whipped at Elyse's hair as she climbed the stairs to the Temple of Therypon, Azarys's grip digging into the skin of her neck. She cursed inwardly at the loss of her rings, the poison gone along with them.

"You can let go of me," she hissed under her breath.

"Not until my end of the deal is fulfilled."

In the dawning light, Elyse could scarcely make out Therypon's statue, but she caught Azarys rolling his eyes at it. As they neared the top, the rows of temple fighters with their raised shields came into view. An elven woman approached, one Elyse had met in previous palace meetings. Nosokyma held up a hand. "That's far enough."

The guards behind Azarys halted as they came to a stop. Sylas pushed Tilan and Fig forward, the latter bringing their pointer finger from their temple and flicking it back at Sylas, the insult seeming to have no effect on him.

"My dear temple friends," Azarys said, fanning out his free hand. "My betrothed wishes to see safe harboring for her clip companions here. Surely, you're no stranger to such accommodations."

"Lady Elyse Norymial is not your betrothed," Nosokyma said, stepping forward, gesturing to Tilan and Fig to approach the top of the stairs. "I offer her safety as well as per the will of Therypon."

Azarys's grip tightened on her neck. "I've claimed her as mine." A murmur came from the Chorys Dasian guards behind them. "There is no safer place than at my side."

"I'm okay," Elyse said, holding up her hands. "Take them and keep them safe."

Nosokyma nodded, motioning Fig and Tilan behind the line of acolytes. At the last second, Tilan turned around. "Can we say goodbye?"

"Only if you tell me what the braces on his arms do," Azarys said, his brows raising with curiosity. It was then that Elyse realized Tilan and Fig didn't have their bags, sweat breaking out over her body.

"They help ease my movement and stiff joints, powered by aithyr," Tilan said, waving to Elyse.

Azarys let her go and she shoved away from him, her heart racing. Elyse ascended the stairs to Tilan and Fig, aware of all the eyes locked on them in that moment. As she pulled Fig into a tight embrace, Elyse whispered, "After I hug Tilan, all three of us run for the temple."

Fig cupped the back of her head. "Clever girl. I prefer it over the self-sacrifice."

As Elyse went to Tilan, there was a commotion at the line of temple guards. "You're the bastard who killed the pilinos!" Deania stepped forward, her finger pointing at Azarys.

Fig clutched Elyse's hand as they turned to flee to the temple, but her feet remained rooted in place.

"You came to our city-state, butchered our people," she spat, "all because they sought a better life! Chorys Dasi is the worst layer of hell and Prince Azarys stands here as its archdevil!"

A murmur broke through the crowd. Tilan grabbed Elyse's other arm and pulled. Her heart started pounding with fear as the sudden realization washed over her in a single, overwhelming wave. She couldn't step forward, only backward to Azarys. She exchanged a panicked glance with Tilan.

Azarys laughed as he climbed the stairs, the metallic rattling of his armor accompanying his every movement. He removed a gauntlet and tossed it to the side. "You," Azarys growled. His other gauntlet clattered to the steps. "He was searching for *you*. Did it feel good? Killing Mathyas?"

Deania's smile sharpened. "His daughter felt better."
Azarys snarled as he neared the top, reaching out to grab Deania, except a blue dome rippled at his fingertips. The blue extended around the temple, encasing it from all sides. Nosokyma joined Deania. "This is the sanctuary of Therypon, and you are not welcome here."

Azarys hit the dome with his fist. "I'm going to catch you and let Oryck skin you alive like you deserve. Your death will be sweeter than the others." Azarys rolled his neck, Elyse trembling as his features shifted. His ears and cheeks took on a sharper angle, and his canines lengthened, transforming his face into something distinctly predatory. His fingernails twisted into vicious claws, and from his brow, two formidable horns spiraled outward and wrapped around his head. "That I promise you."

Accepting her fate, Elyse shoved Tilan behind the barrier with Fig and faced Azarys. "You kept your end of the deal. I'm yours."

Azarys turned his red gaze to her, sauntering with a smile that emphasized his canines. He gripped her forearm and pulled her close to his body, leaning down with a kiss.

A thousand thoughts raced through her mind. Disgust, rage, and terror should have surged through her, but instead, a deep tugging gripped her gut—a primal need that demanded attention. When he pulled away, she was left reeling. Azarys drew his clawed thumb along her lips, a smirk playing at the corners of his mouth. "Let's go show you to Agnyssa."

Corpses lay strewn across the palace stairs and the entryway, their blood staining the once pristine white stone. Elyse couldn't bear to meet the gaze of the lifeless forms of her peers, her emotions unraveling. From her peripheral vision, she noted that not all the fallen wore armor.

Pain sliced through her skull and Azarys, no longer in his fey form, urged her forward, his touch restricted to her lower back. He acted as if he knew she couldn't escape, even when she had the intention of doing so at the temple. She was completely and utterly bonded to him in a way she couldn't quite comprehend.

Her head grew dizzy, her heart racing. She focused, searching for a hint of aithyr, but encountered only emptiness. The sweet taste of Mage's Eye sounded tempting, and she glanced at her fingers once more, only to remember Sylas took her rings.

Elyse stumbled on the stairs to the throne room, steadying herself by placing a hand on her thigh, her breathing labored. A tremble worked its way through her body.

Azarys rubbed her back in small circles, his voice soothing. She shook her head—it shouldn't be soothing. None of this should be soothing. Opening her eyes, she turned to the side of the stairs, coming face-to-face with Drystan's lifeless form. She sucked in a breath, then another, and collapsed back into Azarys.

"How many did you butcher?" she asked, her voice shaking.

"As many as it took to get to you, my goddess." He supported her as she stood, wrapping his arm around her to bear the weight. "We're almost done. Get through this and all will be better."

With each measured step, Elyse ascended the stairs, the doors of the throne room swaying slightly on their hinges. Inside, clusters of people stood in tense conversation, the crowd parting as they approached to reveal the dais and throne. An older man, gray streaking his rough, tied-back hair, stood with his hands clasped behind him—Azarys's uncle, she recalled briefly. On the throne, a woman with glossy black hair lounged, a smirk curving her lips. Her legs were crossed, bare feet resting casually. No introduction was necessary; Queen Agnyssa's portrait had captured her perfectly.

Cowed before her throne was Lady Ymorea. Her sobs echoed throughout the throne room.

"Please, she has nothing to do with this!" Minister Rymos sat on his knees off to the side with a Chorys Dasian soldier gripping his neck.

Agnyssa snapped her fingers, and a crossbow shot out at Ymorea. Its bolt crackled with magical energy. Her blood added to the pool beneath her.

Rymos screamed and flung himself forward, the guard hitting him on the side of the head to silence him.

"Add her to the others."

A soldier dragged her body to the pile of corpses next to the throne.

Elyse trembled as Azarys held her shoulder. Sylas walked past and approached the fey queen. He bent over to her ear, the Agnyssa's brows raising as he took in Elyse and Azarys. When she made eye contact with her, Elyse moved her gaze and caught a glimpse of the crowd. Other politicians stood in attendance, including some ministers with their arms bound behind their backs. Sethyr turned to look at Elyse, his expression dropping at the sight of her. He was tied up next to Leyland, Adryan, and Rymos, all covered in blood and possessing haunted expressions.

She tore her gaze away as guilt overcame her. If she had gone with them earlier, would she have been taken without drawing attention to Fig and Tilan?

Elyse steadied herself and glanced to the other side. Rage, fierce and searing, sliced through her core. Kurtys stood among a cluster of Satiroans, a satisfied grin on his face, though a new scar marred his features where his left eye had once been. Her lips curled back in a snarl as she staggered a step toward him. Azarys's arm tightened around her and he hauled her forward.

A moment later, the sound of a child's crying sounded and she turned to find Tryda walking into the throne room, unbound, with Prince Mycaub clutched in her grip. Agnyssa raised a finger to Sylas as Tryda approached.

"My gracious Queen," Tryda said. "How wonderful it is to see a proper elf on the throne. While I could not bring you Wyltam or his clip, I could apprehend his son, Prince Mycaub." Tryda urged the boy forward, and he began crying harder.

"Whinier than I had hoped, but nothing Auryon can't break." Agnyssa's voice didn't fit her. It was soft and pretty, almost lyrical with the Chorys Dasian lilt. Something too pure for the vile creature Elyse knew she was.

"You said the prince would sit on the throne." Tryda's voice was sharp. Agnyssa waved her off. "Your help has been wonderful, both you and your elven allies."

"I trust that we will be rewarded for our aid. After all, you would not be in the palace if it weren't for me and the Blue Flames."

"Is your life not enough of a reward?" Agnyssa asked, her amusement echoing through the throne room. "Move before I decide you are undeserving of it." She turned to her uncle. "Grab the boy and ready a carriage for Reyila. Auryon promised his wife her nephew."

Their uncle moved down the dais and grabbed the crying prince as Agnyssa called out, "Let me see her."

Azarys dragged Elyse forward. The queen's stare bore into her as if she could see every mistake that led her to this moment. Her gaze narrowed. "She resembles you, Gyrsh."

Elyse's heart plummeted when she heard her father's voice. "Don't let her appearance fool you. She's all Anthylia." He leaned against a soldier for support, his skin pale and drawn from his time in the dungeons. Apparently, his queen did come for him.

Agnyssa's eyes turned brighter. "Good. How's her aithyr control?"

"Wouldn't know," her father said. "She's been doomed to succumb since Anthylia gave herself to aithyr. Elyse is starting to show the same cracks."

"You know nothing," Azarys growled over her shoulder. "He was determined to let Elyse rot alongside an elf, to never learn magic or her potential. Not until we found her."

Agnyssa nodded her head. "That's what Sylas said. Any explanation, Gyrsh?"

"Her spirit needed to be broken, so we didn't repeat what happened with Anthylia. Not even to her third decade, and she's losing her fight. Attempts to get her to shift as a child failed. At the very least, I could make her compliant before she completely lost her mind to aithyr."

Elyse glared at her father. What could he possibly understand about her aithyr use? After one visit to the dungeons, he presumed she was succumbing to its power.

"What you're saying, Gyrsh," Agnyssa said, her voice sharp, "is that you didn't hold up to your end of our deal?"

Her father's throat moved as he swallowed. "A complete loss in terms of conscious magical ability, but based on what little you've told me, she might be of better use."

Agnyssa tapped her finger against the arm of the throne, glaring down at Elyse. After a moment, she stood and began walking down the dais. Her bare feet padded silently across the stone. "I need to know whether she's fey first."

"She can't shift—"

Agnyssa rolled her neck, a pulse shooting through the room. Elyse felt a tug in her gut that threatened to topple her. All at once, Agnyssa's form changed like Azarys's—her cheeks suddenly sharper, her canines longer, horns curled up from her forehead to the ceiling, and her feet became hoofed. Elyse stepped back into Azarys. Seeing his clawed hands wrapped around her made her scream and thrash away. She spun around and saw that a majority room transformed—people made of fire and ice, some with antlers and animal ears, others with scales and gills. Her breath caught, and she stumbled backward onto the dais.

Her fellow Satiroans yelled in surprise. Adryan received a swift smack to the back of his head from a woman whose skin shimmered like shifting water, her hair a flowing current cascading down her back.

"If she was fey, that should have worked."

Elyse slowly tipped her head back to look above her, finding Agnyssa pulling her lips back in a snarl.

"I can prove she's fey." Azarys offered Elyse his hand. She trembled away from his touch, her eyes clamping shut, wishing she'd wake up from this nightmare.

"Have you made her transition?" Agnyssa's tone dripped with sarcasm.

Azarys growled and grabbed Elyse, hauling her to her feet. He brushed the hair away from her neck, Elyse realizing too late what he was doing. His teeth dug into her neck, her body swirling with pleasure and pain, suddenly limp in his hold. Elyse's head rolled to her chest. Azarys turned her face away from the dais to show Agnyssa.

A rumble began through the crowd. "Quiet!" Agnyssa ordered, the room obeying. Elyse glanced up through hazy eyes, watching as the fey queen slowly approached. "You knew her how many weeks?" she asked, her voice quiet. "How did you claim her? What does she know of it?"

Elyse pushed off Azarys as the feeling came back to her limbs. "What does claim mean? He said it before, but I don't understand."

The rumbling returned. Agnyssa raised her hand, silencing them at once. From the close distance, the red in her eyes swirled with energy, her face similar to Azarys's but also so different. Soft where he was sharp. Power almost seemed to radiate from her. "It means he took you as his mate—claiming you as his—which he could not do without your acceptance. Azarys, explain yourself."

His body pressed into the back of Elyse, pulling her close to him. "I asked if she trusted me and she said yes. What else did she need to know?"

"And how did she claim you back if she can't shift to her fey form?"

Azarys hesitated. "We're working on that."

"Come here," Agnyssa hissed, pointing to the ground before her feet.

Azarys walked around her to his sister. A crack echoed off the walls with her slap across his cheek. "That was for claiming without my permission." Her hand met his cheek again. "That's for lying to me about it for months—Sylas told me, you fucking fool." A crack sounded again with a third slap. "And this is for knowing she couldn't claim you back. You will be just as useless to me if you lose your sanity."

Azarys worked his jaw and faced his sister once more. "I refuse to let you use her for your project."

"Project? Azarys, it was her *purpose*. And if you think I still won't use her for the fear of losing you, then you are an even bigger fool than I realized." She snapped her fingers and pointed to the ground. "Beg for forgiveness and I'll consider an alternative future for her."

Azarys dropped to his knees, taking her palm and pressing it into his cheek. "Forgive me for my impulses. I knew she was fey the moment I saw her. I fell in love with her and need her near me at all times, sister. In turn, I give you our offspring to use in her place."

Offspring? As in a child? Bile rose to Elyse's throat at the thought of being with him, at the thought of carrying his child only to give them away.

Agnyssa pushed her brother back. "Conception could take centuries."

"But think of how much more potent our bloodline would make the Fulbryk's? Wasn't that your biggest hesitation in using Gyrsh?" Azarys stood, raising his chin. "Our child could be even more powerful."

Agnyssa thought it over for a moment until Sylas drew her attention as he came to stand next to Elyse. His body seemed formed of rock with bright crystal striations tracing down his arms that caught the light. The beauty of his form took Elyse back a moment.

"Elyse's aithyr abilities surpass all that I've seen," he said to Agnyssa. "It's not a question of if she'll surpass her mother, but when. As I've told you, I watched her fight. Her ability to concentrate on aithyr is astounding, and what she can conjure is unbelievable for someone who hadn't known about aithyr until a few months ago." He stepped forward and bowed his head. "If given your approval, I'd like to train her underneath me. Elyse trusts me, so I can get her to shift. There's a chance she's *luìbaiheòl* or even *eilymaìdeach* after Lyken. If she is, how much stronger is your claim to the *Seelì*?" He raised his head and glared at Azarys. "Plus, he's the reason Wyltam and Marietta escaped. If he had followed your orders and gone to the tunnels instead of finding Elyse, they would've had enough strength to subdue them."

Elyse's chest tightened as the floor seemed to tilt beneath her, a mix of relief and a rising tide of pain. Marietta and Wyltam were alive, but what of the others?

Agnyssa's expression darkened as she glared at her brother. "Very well. Sylas, for your unwavering allegiance, I grant you responsibility of Elyse Norymial under the pretense that you can reveal her fey form. If she proves useless to us, we proceed with the plan to use her as a catalyst. If she is *luìbaiheòl* or *tìdglaidh*, you will aid her in producing a fey child I can use in place of her."

Sylas froze, his body going rigid before he lowered his head in acknowledgment.

Azarys growled and stepped in front of Agnyssa. "She is my mate!"

"And you can't follow the rules." Agnyssa pushed her brother back and took in Elyse. "Perhaps if you're fortunate, Sylas will share. Unless you let history repeat itself. What was her name again? Simi?" A wicked smile came to her lips.

Azarys snarled, his voice rising. "Don't you—"

Agnyssa silenced him with a raised hand. "Azarys, as punishment you will remain with me in Satiros to continue cleaning up and stabilizing the city-state while Sylas takes Elyse home."

"I've already spent months without her," he said, his eyes wide with panic. "I can't handle more."

"Perhaps you should've thought about that before you claimed a fey who can't transition." She stepped back onto the dais and faced the crowd. "I won't hear anymore. This is but one loose thread to tie before we can move on. Sylas, take your boon. Bring forth the witnesses."

Sylas in his rocky form pushed Elyse along as the bound ministers were dragged forward, Tryda and Royir standing behind them. She jerked away from his grip.

"*Stop fighting,*" his voice said in her head. "*You don't want to see what comes next.*"

Elyse furrowed her brows and Sylas pulled her close, turning her so her face pressed against his chest. She struggled to look back, but his grip held firm. Voices clashed behind them, sharp and tense, followed by a woman's cry—was it Tryda's?

"Welcome Satiroans to a pivotal moment in history!" Agnyssa's voice silenced the murmuring of voices. "You are the fortunate few to witness fey in our true forms." Elyse forced her head to the side, catching Agnyssa's reflection in the polished stone behind Sylas.

"Satiros has been wasting its resources," Agnyssa continued. "The magic coursing through these lands is palpable and useful to our ambitions. Far too long, fey have hidden in the shadows. Today, we stand in the light. Bow to your fey queen!"

Agnyssa gestured for someone and they were brought forth, the form of Royir struggling against a soldier. "But perhaps we only need a few witnesses." Her hand jutted out and wrapped around his neck. He gasped sharply, his breath turning into a wheeze. There was a resounding snap, then the dull thud of his body hitting the floor. "Keep the female—she's still useful. Kill the rest."

Elyse pressed her face into Sylas's chest, the clash of steel and dying screams etching themselves into her memory—Sethyr, Adryan, the ministers. Her chest tightened, lungs straining for air, as Sylas's hand moved gently across the back of her head.

"Go into the city, my fey!" Agnyssa screamed. "Let them know about who rules this world! Tell them their new fey queen's name and kill all who resist!"

Chapter Eighty-Five
MARIETTA

Sweat soaked Marietta's back, her shoulders burning from Wyltam's weight. Minutes into their escape, a deep rumble shook the ground, followed by a gust of wind. The soldiers weren't behind them—or if they were, they hadn't come through the tunnels. For now, they had bought enough time. The path started to climb, offering a sliver of hope.

The tunnel abruptly ended, leaving Coryn breathless as he pushed open the wooden hatch, revealing a bright sky above. He helped Marietta up before lifting Wyltam's limp body for her grab. She placed him gently on the ground, checking his pulse again. He still breathed, but he wouldn't wake. A sharp gust of wind blew past, chilling Marietta to her core.

"We should be about half a league outside the city-state," Coryn said, scanning the road next to the hole they just crawled out of. "We need cover. Provisions. Weapons."

"We should get off the road too," Marietta added, brushing back the hair from Wyltam's face.

"We'll need to disguise you two." Coryn wiped his face and dropped into a crouch. "We need a plan."

"We need to get Wyltam help," Marietta said, warming his fingers in her hand. "We could sneak back into Satiros—"

"Absolutely not."

"Or find the Enomenoan army, then march back to Satiros with them."

Coryn shook his head. "We don't know where they are and can't afford to wander during winter."

"Then where? Olkia is a lot farther than the army," Marietta snapped. They didn't have much time, let alone did she know if they could help Wyltam. She watched the steady rise and fall of his chest and begged the goddess again to fix him.

"There's an old Therypon temple on the coast." Coryn stood and stretched. "They have healers there who might be able to undo … whatever this is. And also someone to teach you what the fuck you're doing."

Marietta's gaze hardened, her voice low and steady. "I'd rather have him unconscious in my arms than dead in that tunnel."

Coryn's jaw tightened, a flicker of frustration crossing his face. "I've spent the last few months protecting you. And for what? I thought you were dead back there! The most important person—" He cut himself off, shaking his head as if to clear his thinking. "We need to move forward. My vote is we go to this temple."

The wind stirred, lifting strands of Wyltam's hair across his still face. Marietta glanced down at him, her hands tightening around his arms. "You're sure they can help?"

Coryn stared to the south. "It's the original Temple of Therypon. If there's any place that can save him, it's there."

Marietta rose slowly, casting one last look toward the tunnel they'd escaped. The sun edged over the horizon, painting the path ahead in a soft glow. "Then we go south."

She paused, setting her jaw. "We'll find that temple. We'll save him, gather our strength. And when we return, Chorys Dasi will regret ever setting foot on Satiroan soil."

Chapter Eighty-Six

KEYAIN

Darkness stretched endlessly around him, the white floor beneath his feet rippling like liquid. Keyain turned, scanning the void, but found nothing on the horizon. His knees buckled, and he collapsed, memories flashing through his mind—every fight, every strike, the moment Peryn fell, Ryder's death beside him, and that final sight of Wyltam and Marietta fleeing.

Had it been enough? For all the harm he had caused, he could only hope his sacrifice had bought their freedom.

He curled forward, resting his head on his knees as his chest tightened, silent tears slipping down his face.

"You grieve, but not for your own life."

A voice came from beside Keyain, making him jump. He turned to the sound, finding the spot empty. He glanced behind him.

"Most who visit my domain wish for a second chance at life, claiming they have more to live for, yet you are asking if you have done enough."

Keyain faced forward, his pulse thrumming as he saw the shape in the corner of his eye. Turning toward it, it disappeared again. "What is this?"

"Your judgment, Keyain Vallynte. You are a curious case, hence why you wait in my domain. I should usher you on, yet your soul remains incomplete. Despite

sacrificing your life, you believe you haven't done enough. Why is that?"

His shoulders slumped as his head dropped. "I've made so many mistakes, and even now, I don't know if I've undone my wrongdoing. Marietta and Wyltam may have escaped, but what about what's coming?" His throat tightened, and for a moment, he saw them lying still, their bodies entwined. "All I ever wanted was to keep people safe."

"From death? I come for everyone."

Keyain stiffened at the voice, the shape becoming more material at his side.

"No, you don't fear dying. You are the administer of it, the Praetor of Death. You've killed more than most and you understand the cost of a life. How curious."

Turning his head toward the figure, his stomach dropped. The faces on the figure changed from a skull, to an orc, to Alyck, and Olytia. So many faces, ever-changing.

"Keyain Vallynte, Praetor of Death, I offer you an exchange. I will grant you temporary life imbued with my domains in exchange for a death. You will know closure, your soul at peace when I take it, for this death will save those you care about. Swear to take the life of Agnyssa Vynz and you will be granted enough time to carry out the task and aid your friends. At its completion, you die once more. What say you?"

Keyain blinked. He could walk the world once more if he promised to kill the Chorys Dasian queen. Not just any being could grant that. As he furrowed his brows, he shifted his attention back to the being, becoming acutely aware of the sheer power emanating from him. Then he realized—he sat next to a god.

A part of Keyain longed for the tranquility of oblivion, a wish to lay his head down and escape. A few months ago, he sought that release in bottles of alcohol and the haze of drugs. But now, something within him had shifted.

The god's face stilled into that of a male with a stern but handsome face, his hair cropped short, cheekbones extenuated with sharper tips to his ears.

Keyain lifted his chin, staring into the aching, deep chasm of his eyes, and nodded. "I accept."

Chapter Eighty-Seven
AMRYTH

The Chorys Dasian patrols began just before sunrise. Fey in their monstrous forms swept through the streets, injuring and killing anyone who dared question their authority. The victims's screams carried through the muted halls of Therypon's temple. Pilinos clung to one another—some weeping, others staring blankly into the distance.

Deania refused to answer her about what Azarys's outburst meant, instead shutting herself into her office. Frustrated, Amryth spent hours doing what she knew best: making sure everyone had what they needed. She kept herself distracted by working until her feet ached and back twinged.

Adalyn had convinced her to stop and eat, sharing a meager meal with her, Sibylla, Tilan and Fig. They recapped everything until that moment. Elyse had bought them enough time to hide their prototypes and designs, but then they were caught by the Chorys Dasian mage. Everything after that made Amryth want to break something. She had to be a hero and sacrifice herself, now in the literal claws of their enemies.

Though part of her was thankful Elyse had given herself up. She understood her worth to Chorys Dasi and ensured Tilan and Fig left with their lives. Based on the reports they heard from the paladins guarding the temple, the fey walked freely, slaughtering at will. The name of the Chorys

Dasian queen spread like wildfire, whispered as a curse beneath the breaths of the pilinos.

Agnyssa, the fey queen.

By the time the night fell, Amryth dressed in all black, not bothering to tell anyone where she went before slipping into the dark. She stole one of the temple's swords, figuring they wouldn't miss a spare. Sticking to the shadows, she ran along the river in the chilled evening air, thankful no more snow had fallen, though it meant the red stood out more starkly. Bodies lay in piles, the cobblestones slick with blood. Amryth kept herself steady and crossed into the Wooded Ward.

Never had she seen so many buildings without lights. She prayed to the goddess that most people were hiding from the fey and not one of the corpses in the streets.

Jogging across an alley, she slipped into the shadows of the park. Her parents were smart; they would know to stay inside.

The trees loomed tall and still, their branches stretching toward the sky as if watching over her path to the townhouse. A sudden crunch in the snow made her freeze behind a tree. The wind picked up, sending the branches swaying and cutting through Amryth's layers. She gripped her sword tighter until the sound faded. When nothing else followed, she moved on.

What would happen to Satiros now that Chorys Dasi had taken control? Sibylla couldn't confirm if Marietta or Wyltam were still alive. She had tried to reach Wyltam a dozen times, with nothing in return. But Amryth refused to believe silence meant the worst. Until she saw their bodies, she would hold on to the hope they lived.

Amryth neared where the park let out onto Oak Boulevard, the glass globes lit and hanging low above the frozen landscape. A voice shouted from ahead. She ducked behind a platform that usually held a statue of a griffin, now empty, as two males entered the park.

"She wants it alive," one of them snapped. "If you kill it, she'll kill us."

"How the fuck does she want us to catch it?"

The first snapped into a fey form just as Azarys had, their nose and mouth replaced with a beak, their arms now white wings. He screeched and took off into the night. The other male swore and ran after them, his body becoming scaly with a forked tongue slipping between his lips.

Amryth fell back onto her hands. Having seen Azarys do it had been one thing, but to watch as others shifted cemented how dire their situation was. They couldn't take the city-state back, not without reinforcements.

She scrambled backward off the path and into the street, the laughter and murmurs of voices drawing closer. She swore under her breath and retreated to the base of the statue.

A rush of wings sliced through the air, followed by a heavy thud just above her. Amryth squeezed her eyes shut, frustration mingling with dread. How could she possibly face two fey on her own?

She thought of Deania's smile and her warm brown eyes. The scent of her hair. The softness of her lips. It steeled her spine. Amryth took a deep breath and drew her sword as she jumped up. The weapon clattered to the ground as she saw what was perched on the platform.

The creature had an eagle's head, front legs, and wings, its body reminiscent of a lion. It spread its wings wide, the beak splitting with a piercing screech that made Amryth cover her ears. She ducked in time as the griffin took off above her head and into the night sky.

Chapter Eighty-Eight

ELYSE

Elyse felt nothing but the numbness of shock as her body lolled along the carriage. Sylas had her blindfolded and placed her inside hours after Agnyssa sent her ilk into the city-state. Most of the day was spent sleeping after Sylas gave her something for her growing head pains. While the drugs had mostly helped, the ache remained an echo in her skull.

She had once dreamed of visiting Chorys Dasi, of walking along the black sand beaches, to see the ocean stretched out in front of her. She had thought Azarys would be with her then. What a fool she had been.

Her mind tried and failed to wrap around the implications of what he had done. Azarys had called her his mate, yet she didn't understand. What did it mean to be Azarys's *mate*? Instead of providing answers to her questions, Sylas assumed the role of a silent overseer as the carriage crept along the path.

At long last, he told her to take off the blindfold. She blinked once, then twice, her eyes adjusting to the tight space lit by a small globe. She pushed back the curtain, finding a darkened sky and the rolling countryside beyond.

At that moment, the gravity of her situation crashed down on her. She inhaled shakily, attempting to stifle the rising sob, but it emerged as a gasp, followed by another. After escaping twice, she was finally caught and dragged to Chorys Dasi. While Azarys wouldn't be there at first, he would return. As would his sister. Elyse was being forced into the very court her grandfather had fled.

Although she was aware of what happened to Marietta and Wyltam, as well as Fig and Tilan, she did not know of anyone else's fate. Was Keyain all right? What of the Queen's Guard? Amryth and Sibylla had been in the city-state. Did they manage to seek shelter before the fey tore through the streets? Each question spiraled her deeper into despair, the crushing weight of her situation making it difficult to think clearly.

"Elyse, look at me."

She lifted her head and narrowed her eyes to slits. "I hate you."

"Elyse, please."

She tried to pull at aithyr and still felt nothing, releasing her frustration as a scream, thrashing inside the carriage. She was helpless, useless.

"If you ever want to see your friends again, I need you to listen to me."

That got Elyse to pause, turning her watery gaze to Sylas. He leaned forward and rested his forearms on his knees, narrowing the space between them. A translucent dome formed around them. She stared into the patchwork of greens and browns in his irises.

"My friends?"

Sylas's stare locked onto hers, searching for some sign of understanding, his mouth curving into a sorrowful frown. "I tried to stop this from happening," he whispered, his voice thick with regret. "I tried to spare you. Elyse, I'm so sorry."

"Then you should have let me go."

"I did," he said, his voice rough. "Twice."

He hung his head with a sigh, wiping his mouth. "I know you understand you're in danger, but you don't know the extent. Do you remember the song you sang to Azarys? Back at the townhouse?"

Elyse blinked, and she scoured her memories. "The one that my mother sang to me?"

He nodded, lifting his head again, a sad smile softening his features. *"Brìsdplèan Òraboèdhl.* The Planesbreaker's Hymn." His eyes searched hers, the silence thickening. "The song is about you."

The Planebreaker's Hymn

In a land lush with magic and life,
our old family keeps.
With open ears and open hearts,
we can hear their weeps.

Lives of thrall and hailing calls,
urging to fight that which binds,
us to a land that will never be home unless
we search our like kind.

Through moonlit trees and beachy seas,
by twinkling star at night,
we wander a–through strangers' worlds,
by vigorous will and might.

Call thee who lost,
on thee who fight,
on thee who set worlds alight,
and draw on the spirits of the fallen
to set our worlds a–right.

Of fey descent shed elven blood,
one guided by self and a heart of gold.
We sing these mourning songs
so our stories ought not untold.

Rise shall be the favored,
a champion for a world lost.
One whose choices preferred the bold,
free us for that of life cost.

Epilogue

The cold already started to blow down from the mountains, the bite of wind like a familiar song on her skin. Home, Valeriya often thought, or at least similar to.

For months, Valeriya and Katya lived in a small village outside of Avato under new identities. Katya now went by Hanna. Valeriya had adopted the name Alyna. It didn't matter if Wyltam changed her hair, now straight, chopped to her collarbones and colored a dull blonde. Her former husband apparently possessed the magical skills to even do such a thing. Her eyes were the same icy blue, her skin still freckled in the same pattern. There was a slim chance anyone would recognize her, but the possibility lingered.

Much of her time in Enomenos had been spent living in Marietta's shadow. Only recently had the whispers about the new pilinos queen begun to fade, offering a reprieve from the constant reminders of her missteps during her reign. Valeriya harbored no resentment toward Marietta's rise. After all, how could she when she saved Valeriya's life, even if the pain of the healed wound remained debilitating at times?

A pilinos queen ascending to power was a significant milestone for Satiros, undoubtedly historic. What truly grated Valeriya's nerves was the stark contrast in their paths. Marietta stumbled into the right place at the right time, merely existing to seize the dream Valeriya had relentlessly pursued her entire life. It was the bitter realization that while Marietta basked in the glory of her newfound status, Valeriya's own aspirations for immortality and lasting remembrance had crumbled into obscurity. Instead of leaving a memorable legacy, Valeriya was destined to fade into anonymity, her recognition forged by the weight of her most notable failures—a fate more damning than being forgotten entirely.

She would forever be remembered as the queen who died for Marietta, not as a sacrifice, but as an obstacle to this historic moment. And those who knew the truth would remember her for her foolish trust in her sister, for the blind hatred she held for Wyltam. For it, she lost everything. Her throne, her life, her son. The last hurt the most. Though she would see him one day, she'd miss the most precious years of his life, watching him grow from toddler to adult. Wyltam had better hold his promise, to be a father like he had failed to do in the past. It was all she asked for besides a new life with Katya.

Valeriya had waited seven long years for their reunion, but it was far from what Valeriya had envisioned. They did everything they were supposed to do—lived together, ate together, slept together—yet it all felt *different*. Where there used to be interwoven threads remained only tangled knots. They needed to unravel to move forward, but where could they start? Where did the knots even begin?

One particularly chilled morning, Valeriya prepared a simple breakfast of fried eggs and toasted bread, timing it just right for Katya's departure to the fields. A small triumph, considering Valeriya usually cooked the eggs either too early, leaving them cold, or too late, forcing Katya to scarf them down. Yet, regardless of the timing, Katya's reaction remained unchanged.

When Valeriya placed the plate down in front of Katya, she turned to her with a slight smile. "Thank you."

"You're welcome."

Valeriya took a seat across from her, mindlessly tearing at her bread as her brain completed the routine. Next came the strained silence. It was either a sign of their dwindling connection, or Katya's deliberate choice to keep her distance. A compliment would surely follow before she left for the day.

As one minute stretched into the next with neither speaking, Valeriya's stomach began to churn. Was it always going to be this way?

Katya's raspy voice broke the silence. "You should get out more."

"Excuse me?" Valeriya's heart fluttered.

"You're holed up in here too much. It's not good for you." Katya fidgeted with her fork before setting it down. "Having been alone for so long, perhaps a walk through town could help. Maybe stop and meet a few people."

"I do that every morning when I fetch water."

Katya attempted to speak but halted, ultimately nodding. Standing up, she leaned over and kissed Valeriya. "The eggs were perfect. I'll see you tonight."

By seeing her tonight, she meant having a stilted conversation before deciding to go to sleep. It felt similar to catching up with an old acquaintance rather than a past lover.

Valeriya had everything she wanted, yet none of it at all.

Many of the villagers hailed from Syllogi, encompassing both pilinos and elves, and accents from all over Akroi. Regardless of origins, they all shared an unwritten code, a mutual acceptance. Here, amid this community, the past held no sway. It was a fresh start, a place where everyone was welcomed without judgment. It was an unexpected solace for Valeriya, one she hadn't realized she desperately needed.

Their new home was cozy and tucked away on a hill that overlooked the central market square. It was easy to heat and stayed cool on the warm days. Even cooking had been more enjoyable, Valeriya slowly learning how to cook. The home they paid for with their money from Wyltam came with a vegetable patch, just ready for harvest. The old man who had lived there prior to them planted the seeds earlier in the year, not making it to see the efforts of his labor. With each meal, Valeriya found herself thanking him for gifting her another task to fill her days. Gardening had a purpose and Valeriya learned to relish the soil between her fingers.

The only downside was the lack of running water, not just for their home, but for the entire village. There was one central well for the denizens who lived there, meaning Valeriya got to know the faces of her neighbors quickly.

On her first week in the village, Valeriya happened upon an elder elven lady bent with age. She struggled to grip the rope as she drew the water up from the bottom of the well. Not thinking twice of it, Valeriya took over for her, filling her containers. When the lady turned to leave with her buckets, Valeriya offered to carry them back, only for her to decline.

Every morning had been that way since then, Valeriya hauling her water, offering to carry it back to her home, only for the elven lady to thank her and go her separate way. She became part of Valeriya's routine. Wake up, eat breakfast with Katya, go to the well, help the elven lady, then head home to tend to the garden. What little purpose there was to tending dirt and pulling weeds fulfilled her for a time. Yet it didn't take long for her restlessness to start once again.

As a way to change her routine and keep her mind fresh, Valeriya asked the elven lady for her name one morning.

"Beverly," she said, smiling. "And you are Alyna."

Valeriya cringed at her rudeness. Of course, she would know who she was, being that Katya came acquainted with a few villages through her work in the fields. Valeriya had kept to herself for the most part, not offering her name to anyone. Perhaps that's why Beverly never bothered introducing herself as well.

The following day, Valeriya greeted Beverly by name and asked her once again if she needed help to carry the buckets back to her home. Anticipating a no, Valeriya failed to hide her surprise when she said yes.

"Are you busy this morning?" she asked, leading Valeriya down the street.

She hesitated, ignoring the twinge in her shoulder. "Not quite."

"We need a few extra hands to help knit clothes to sell in Avato before the winter hits."

Her heart sank, staring down at her feet. The downside to being a royal was the lack of transferable skills. Once again, she proved useless. "I don't know how."

"We can teach you."

Valeriya shook her head. "It's best if I didn't."

"There's no glory in misery. Whatever you left behind, you can leave in the past." Beverly placed her hand on Valeriya's. "Accept the mistakes, let go of the what ifs, and find peace with what you have. That's the best advice I can give."

As Beverly began to walk again, Valeriya remained rooted in the center of the street, her knees locked in place. She said it as if it were so simple, as if they were easy things to forget.

"Everyone starts over here. You deserve no less." Beverly stepped up to one of the houses, beckoning to her.

Valeriya worked her jaw, thinking of her son, her mistakes, and the lingering worry of her sister. Did she deserve a new life after all that she did?

"If you don't like it," Beverly said, drawing her from her thoughts, "you don't need to help again. No questions asked, no assumptions made."

She could do that, barring no commitment. "You'll have to start with the basics," Valeriya said, steeling her spine and following her up the steps. "I haven't the slightest clue of how to knit."

There was a glimmer in Beverly's eyes as she took the buckets. "That's all right. It's never too late to learn something new."

The morning slipped into the afternoon as Beverly and a few townsfolk gathered around her. They were patient as she learned to spin wool, welcoming her myriad questions about the dyeing process. When it came time to try knitting, she grew frustrated by her slow progress and returned to spinning on the machine.

All the while, they talked. Beverly and the villagers filled Valeriya in on what went on in town, not necessarily gossip. Thankfully, they seemed devoid of that. Instead, it was stories they heard, problems people experienced. They even shared with Valeriya their local folklore, like how some believed there was a beast in the woods north of town. Beverly assured her that it was just the wolves stealing chickens, that no one but old man Hermyl had seen such a beast.

Through it all, Valeriya didn't have to answer one question about her life, and for a time, it was a distraction. She forgot who she was and where she came from. It was liberating, each step growing lighter as she rushed home at the end of the day. The sun set quickly, meaning Katya would be home soon.

When Valeriya arrived at the house, the inside was already lit. She half-expected Katya to be frazzled or panicked at her disappearance. Instead, she found her at the stove, standing above something that smelled incredible.

"You can cook?" she asked instead of greeting.

Katya faced her with a smile, one that crinkled her eyes. How long had it been since she'd seen it? Too long. "Learned it after I left Reyila. But I want to hear about your day."

Valeriya paused. "You knew."

She smiled and turned back to the skillet, deftly stirring the mixture as it sizzled. "The whole village talked about it today, how Beverly convinced Hanna's wife to break out of her shell."

Valeriya blinked in surprise. "Wife?"

Katya shrugged. "That's what I refer to you as in town." At Valeriya's stunned silence, she added, "if that's all right."

"More than all right," Valeriya managed. "It's fitting."

Katya looked down before glancing up at her. "Tell me about your day while I finish this. I'm curious to know what you think."

As Valeriya began to set the table, she told Katya the events of the day and all that she had learned, the conversation extending into dinner and thereafter. What had happened didn't fully dawn on her until she was curled around Katya in bed.

The distance between them might not have been Katya's fault, but rather Valeriya's doing. Perhaps things weren't as bad as she thought.

Valeriya nuzzled into Katya's hair and murmured three words she always thought but never shared. "I love you."

Katya shifted closer, pulling Valeriya's arm to her abdomen. "I love you too," she said, her voice heavy with sleep. "It's good to have you back."

Hours slipped into days, days into weeks, and slowly Valeriya could knit a scarf. She held up her first one that didn't drop a stitch, showing Beverly.

She clapped her hands and smiled. "From learning how to spin wool to creating your first scarf. You should be proud, Alyna."

Her old self would have laughed at the menial task becoming a source of pride. The new version of herself relished in the praise.

Every day, Valeriya met Beverly at the well and followed her to her home where they would make yarn and knit clothing. A few days a week, other villagers would join them. Meryn the half-elf with a face that echoed Chorys Dasian features. Ezra, who looked vaguely reminiscent of the half-orc Valeriya knew in Reyila. Emil. Anya. Yelena. And at least half a dozen more. They became her friends, the ones that gave her tips on cooking, who taught her the art of baking. When Valeriya's clothes began to fray, they showed her a practical stitch instead of the colorful embroidery she hated as a child. They didn't just stumble into her life, they were a complete landslide.

Most afternoons she left Beverly's with a smile on her face, her chest light. Katya savored the transformation within her; their lives finally settled into a comfortable harmony. Whenever the past did creep in, Valeriya accepted its truth and let it slip by. What was the point in dwelling when there were clothes to knit? When there were developments on Anya's ongoing battle against the foxes taking her hens? Or Ezra's never-ending search to find someone to love them?

At times, they would ask her for advice as well. What should they say? How would she interpret this? Secretly, those were her favorite moments, when she had something to offer them in return for their camaraderie.

But that all changed when news of the war reached their village.

The day that Valeriya learned Chorys Dasian troops hovered on the Satiroan border was the day she retreated to the walls of her home, struck with grief. Her fault. It was her fault. They were waiting for her sister's troops, and when they arrived, countless innocent lives in Satiros would be at risk. Because of her decisions, her lack of insight.

Katya tried to convince her to let it go, but Valeriya saw the lingering guilt in her eyes. Katya's friends were there as well, coming to care for Wyltam, Andyr, and Wynn like the family she never had. Now, their lives were threatened.

Determined to avoid Beverly, Valeriya waited until nightfall to fetch water from the well. The frigid weather worsened the ache in her shoulder. The season had just begun and already her body had forgotten how the cold whipped crossed the mountains from the north. Seven years in Satiros, and she even lost that.

Valeriya crested the hill of their home, scanning the horizon. They'd get more snow tonight, meaning she and Kat would need to chop more wood to stave off the chill.

She turned back to the house when a flicker of light caught the edge of her vision. Thinking her mind conjured it, she glanced back, not expecting it to still be there. Focusing her mind and calming her breath, Valeriya reached for the few wisps of aithyr trickling in this part of the world. She pulled it into her, focusing the energy on her vision. What she saw made her drop her buckets, water scattering all over the stone.

"Kat!" she screamed, coming into the house. "Kat! Grab your knives. We need to go. There's—"

Katya grabbed her by the arms, her brows furrowing. "What are you yelling about?"

"Reyilan soldiers," she said, fear taking her breath. They were turning on Enomenos, turning their blades to the friends she had made here. "A century on the hill just outside town. The village doesn't stand a chance!"

Katya paled, her hands slipping. "We can't fight a hundred soldiers alone."

"Two regular people can't, Kat." Valeriya took her hands. "Two mages could."

Moving as quickly as possible, Valeriya and Katya changed into their old tight clothes, strapping knives to themselves before rushing out the door. Running alongside Katya in the shadows might have sparked a sense of nostalgia, if not for the fear that quickened their hearts and tightened their throats.

They slipped through town and into the woods beyond, stalking through the trees until they broke into a clearing. The soldiers sat in groups around meager fires. Only a handful of tents were erected. If that wasn't already sufficient evidence of the lot's dilapidation, the myriad of injured soldiers would confirm it. Katya gestured for her to go left, Valeriya following the path along until she was in position.

"How much farther?" someone asked.

"Until they can't find us. It's unlikely that they will search this area, but it's better to go to the other side of Avato to make sure we're a safe distance away." A half-elven male stepped into view, a bloody strap of fabric over his one eye. Valeriya's stomach dropped at the sight of him.

"Wait!" Valeriya tried to message Katya, but her message didn't reach her in time. A fire burst at the back of the group, erupting in screams. Propelling herself forward, Valeriya pulled aithyr into herself as she sprinted toward the flame, the opposite direction from the Reyilan soldiers.

"Katya!" she screamed as more fire came, Valeriya summoning wind to blow snow over top. "I was wrong. Kat, stop!"

Her partner appeared in front of her, the soldiers turning on them. She tugged on Valeriya's arm. "What are you doing?" she hissed.

"It's Vasily!"

Katya's mouth dropped, and she pivoted to the oncoming soldiers. "It can't be."

"Who are you?" one of the soldiers demanded, pointing his sword at them. A few others closed in, forcing them closer to the flames licking at their backs.

"It is—I saw him." She turned to the crowd and shouted, "Vasily?"

A murmur broke over the group of soldiers. Some bared their teeth and raised their swords, murmuring something to the allies beside them. Slowly, a half-elven male approached. There was considerably more gray in his hair, the wound over his eye changing his face as well. Nonetheless, Valeriya and Katya would know him anywhere.

Vasily's remaining eye widened at the sight of them and he stumbled forward. "Lower your swords, you fool. You dare take up arms against our princess?" He dropped to his knee, awestruck.

A few of the soldier's expressions mirrored his and they, too, took a knee. A slow rumble broke over the group and suddenly they all kneeled before them.

Valeriya's chest rose and fell sharply, panic surging. They knew where she was. Auryon and his ilk would find her and use her. She turned to run when Vasily spoke.

"Princess Valeriya, your presence is the most beautiful blessing we could've asked for." A tear broke free from his eye. "The years have been less than kind to us back home, the past few months being the worst. King Auryon controls the city, controls the army. The city is terrified. No one has seen Queen Nystanya in a year. We know she lives, but for her to remain silent as we go to war?" He shook his head.

"We were forced to march upon Satiros, but we do not wish to fight. We abandoned our post only to be met with Enomenoan resistance. We sought freedom; we sought a new life. Many of us wish to return home, or to save it. But we are but a hundred in number. Until now, I have given up hope. Until seeing you, I thought I'd never hear the snow sing between the peaks again. King Auryon took our freedom. He took our queen. Please, help us. Help us take back our home, princess."

Valeriya's feet numbed, her bile rising with the request. Vasily had one of the highest honors in the Reyilan military. As she examined his uniform, she noticed a single badge—a striking red against the navy fabric that only the other pilinos bore.

She shook her head. "I can't. I have to remain dead."

Katya slipped her hand in Valeriya's. "Say yes."

Valeriya turned to her, bewildered. "What?"

"Look at them." Katya's voice choked as she took in the soldiers. "What have we done, pretending to live a domestic life while our home suffers? They need us. Nystanya needs us."

"Wyltam said—"

"Forget him." Katya dropped to her knee. "Fuck your anonymity. *Fuck the Chorys Dasians.*" Her eyes burned like the fire behind them. "We have one hundred impassioned people here. How many more are willing to fight in Reyila? The forces are sent to Satiros, so they're distracted. They are fractured. Let's go home, Val."

Valeriya's hands trembled as she took in the troop, as she took in Katya's stern expression. *Accept the mistakes, let go of the what ifs, and find peace with what you have.* Beverly's advice from all those weeks ago rang in her mind. She had started to build a life here with Katya. They had known peace for the first time since they were children. Why would she give it all up?

Because now she knew the truth. The soldiers standing in front of her were hers, her family's, her sister's. Born of royal blood and born to serve, Valeriya had promised to protect the people of Reyila. Seven long years had passed since she left her home, yet after a century of her life, how had she forgotten her vows?

Valeriya raised her chin, she raised her fist, and she raised her voice. "No more running. No more hiding. Together, we are going to free my sister. Together, we will take back Reyila!"

Glossary

Marietta Lytpier Fulbryk *mare-ee-et-ah lit-peer*

· Half-elf from Enomenos. Daughter of the Shepherd. Grand daughter of Lyken Fulbryk.

Amryth Sulyng *am-rith sool-eeng*

· Elf from Satiros. Former Elite Guard member.

Keyain Vallynte *kee-ein val-en-tee*

· Elf from Satiros. Minister of Protection.

Elyse Norymial *eh-lees nor-eh-mee-al*

· Elf from Satiros. King's Administrator and Orator.

Wyltam Gytsier *will-tahm grit-see-er*

· Elf from Satiros. King of Satiros.

Wynn Styrmer *winn stir-mehr*

· Elf from Satiros. Originally from [redacted]. Circle of Mages member.

Deania Dinke *dee-ahn-ee-uh deenk*

· Half-elf from Satiros. Originally from Chorys Dasi. Cleric to the goddess Therypon.

Adalyn Pryce *add-duh-lihn pr-ice*

· Elf from Satiros. Elite Guard member. Part of the Queen's Guard.

Ryder Dye *rih-durr die*

· Elf from Satiros. Elite Guard member. Part of the Queen's

Guard.

Peryn Kryoss *pair-en kree-oss*

· Elf from Satiros. Elite Guard member. Part of the Queen's Guard.

Coryn Niershade *core-inn neer-shaid*

· Half-elf from Satiros. Originally from Amigys. Iros to the goddess Therypon. Queen's Guard Captain.

Andyr Kryto *an-deer kree-toh*

· Elf from Satiros. Circle of Mages member.

Sibylla Marsyas *sah-bil-la mar-see-as*

· Elf from Amigys. Circle of Mages member.

Tolis Wigram *toe-lis wih-gram*

· Half-elf from Kyaeri. Circle of Mages member.

Tanaly Tyburs *tan-ha-lee tai-burs*

· Elf from Satiros. Barmaid at Honeysuckle Tavern.

Fig Willoby *fig wil-low-bee*

· Half-elf from Satiros. Artificer.

Tilan Reid *till-ehn reed*

· Human from Enomenos. Former blacksmith. Former Head Artificer to the Exisotis.

Royals, Nobles, & Courtiers

Olytia Grytsier *oh-leet-ee-ah grit-see-er*

· Deceased. Elf from Satiros. Late Queen of Satiros. Late mother to Wyltam Grytsier.

Mycaub Grytsier *my-cub grit-see-er*

· Elf from Satiros. Prince of Satiros. Son of Valeriya and Wyltam Grytsier.

Tryda Tywik *tr-ee-dah tie-wihk*

· Elf from Satiros. Former Lady in Waiting to the Late Queen Valeriya and Queen Olytia. Married to Dyeiter Tywik.

Dyeiter Tywik *die-ee-ter tie-wihk*

· Elf from Satiros. Elf from Satiros. Minister of Law. Married to Tryda Tywik.

Gyrsh Norymial *gee-ursh nor-eh-mee-al*

· Elf from Satiros. Former Minister of Foreign Affairs. Father of Elyse Norymial. Husband to the late Anthylia Norymial.

Anthylia Norymial *ann-thil-lee-uh nor-eh-mee-al*

· Deceased. Elf from Satiros. Lady of the Court. Late mother of Elyse Norymial. Late wife to Gyrsh Norymial. Mage mentor to Wyltam Grytsier.

Grytaine Romyn Lasyda *grih-tayne roh-minn lahs-see-duh*

· Elf from Satiros. Lady of the Queen's Court. Married to Minister Royir Lasyda.

Royir Lasyda *roi-eer lahs-see-duh*

· Elf from Satiros. Minister of Coin. Married to Grytaine Lasyda. Formerly married to Lyna Pinyl.

Leyland Fedyr *lay-land fehd-eer*

· Elf from Satiros. Minister of Vassals.

Rymos Batyst *ree-mohs bah-teest*

· Elf from Satiros. Minister of Conduct. Married to Ymorea Batyst.

Ymorea Batyst *eh-mohr-ee-ah bah-teest*

· Elf from Satiros. Lady of the court. Married to Rymos Batyst.

Adryan Pytts *ay-dree-an pihts*

· Elf from Satiros. Minister of Commerce.

Sethyr Calsyn *seth-eer kæl-sin*

· Elf from Satiros. Minister of Foreign Affairs.

Kurtys Valtyrs *kur-tis val-ters*

· Elf from Satiros. Member of Foreign Affairs branch.

Drystan Tassatys *dris-tan tas-sat-tis*

· Elf from Satiros. Member of Resources branch.

Lydia Rynts *leh-dee-uh rintz*

· Elf from Satiros. Minor lady to the Court of Satiros. Former friends of Elyse Norymial.

Enomenoans

Pelok Fairweather *peh-lock fayr-weh-thehr*

· Human from Olkia. Owner of the Lonely Dog Tavern. Friend of Marietta and Tilan. Head Diversionist of the Exisotis.

Alora Lunalis *al-lore-ah loo-nal-is*

· Human from Kentro. Elector of Enemenos.

Anthys Fulbryk *ahn-this full-brik*

· Elf from Notos. Goes by the monikers, "The Shepherd" and "Markys Lytpier." Former lord of Satiros. Father to Marietta Lytpier Fulbryk.

Chorys Dasians

Azarys Vynz *ah-zar-ris vinz*

· Fey from Chorys Dasi. Went by the moniker "Bryndan Vazlyte." Prince of Chorys Dasi. Twin brother to Queen Agnyssa.

Agnyssa Vynz *eg-nys-sa vinz*

· Fey from Chorys Dasi. Twin sister to Azarys Vynz. Queen of Chorys Dasi.

Auryon Vynz *or-ee-in vinz*

· Fey from Chorys Dasi. King of Reyila. Married to Nystanya Ruuyl, Queen of Reyila. Younger brother to Azarys and Agnyssa Vinz.

Sylas Tygenbrook *sie-lus tie-gehn-bruhk*

· Fey from Chorys Dasi.

Temple Acolytes

Nosokyma *no-so-kee-ma*

· Temple of Therypon.

Rafayl *rah-fale*

· Temple of Seidytar

Cyrus *sie-rus*

· Temple of Kystrorgiste

Izzy *ih-zee*

· Temple of Oramytiz

Moira *moi-ruh*

· Temple of Zontykroi

Deities of Duality

Therypon *thair-ih-pohn*

· Goddess of Healing & Pain

Seidytar *say-dih-tahr*

· Goddess of Chaos & Order

Kystrorgiste *kee-strowr-geest*

· God of Creation & Destruction

Oramytiz *or-am-mee-tisz*

· Deity of Reality & Deception

Zontykroi *zohn-teh-kroi*

· God of Life & Death

Terms

Aithyr *ay-thur*

· Naturally occurring, invisible energy used to perform magic.

Pilinos *pihl-len-nohs*

· Any persons containing human descent, including humans, half-elves, and half-orcs.

Pili *pihl-lee*

• The first humans formed from earth by the old gods.

Iros *eer-os*

· Elite warriors who serve a single deity. A highly respectable position within a temple.

Cornicular *kor-nik-ue-lar*

· A secretary or clerk. Includes scribers, specialists, assistants, and schedulers.

Mage's Eye

· Substance that has a relaxing effect when ingested. Helps see aithyr streams.

Magicsbane

· Substance that, when it enters the bloodstream, prevents the affected from accessing aithyr.

Drakon Root

· Illegal substance that is lethal to pilinos.

Feybarb

· A quickly onset illness that only affects elves.

Leecher

· Derogatory term for magic users.

Aithyrstruck

· When a mage succumbs to aithyr and loses control of their mind.

Pouskyai

· A sparkling wine named for the Satiroan town it hails from.

Illustris

· Title of Marshalls, serve directly under the Commander or General

Fey Words

Bheithaìchìn *bih-tay-shah(n)*
Luìbaiheòl *lwee-bey-awl*
Tìdglaidh *teehd-glai(d)*
Eilymaìdeach *el-lee-may-deech*
Seelìthe *Seh-leet(h)*
Seelì *Seh-lee*
Aonseelì *ahoh(n)-seh-lee*

Region

Akroi *ah-kroi*
· Region between the Mavros Sea and the Evgeni Sea. Extends from the Ekrixi Range to the Tefra forests. Includes the city-state collectives of Syllogi and Enomenos, as well as the Queendom of Reyila to the north.

Subregions of Akroi

Enomenos *en-no-mehn-nohs*
· Collection of city-states in eastern Akroi. Known for is mixed populace of elves and pilinos. Society built without the use of magic. Ruled by the Enomenoan Unification Council, which is a democratic group selected by the citizens. Includes the city-states Olkia, Kentro, Notos, Rotamu, and Avato.

Syllogi *sill-oh-ghee*

· Collection of city-states in western Akroi. Ruled by the elven. Pilinos are considered lesser citizens. Society relies on magic. Monarchial societies.

· **Satiros** *sah-teer-ohs*: Eastern most city-state in Syllogi. Known for its lush gardens that bloom all year despite the weather. Surrounded by farmlands that supply food for the rest of Syllogi.

· **Chorys Dasi** *kor-es dah-see*: Northern most city-state in Syllogi. Main trading port with the Queendom of Reyila to the north.

· **Amigys** *ah-mihg-gess*: Southern most city-state in Syllogi. Major port to the rest of the world.

· **Kyaeri** *kai-air-ee*: Western most city-state in Syllogi. Settled on the waterfall that feeds the Halia River in the Ekrixi range.

Reyila *ray-eel-lah*

· Queendom in northern Akroi.

The King's Council of Ministers

THE CITY-STATE OF SATIROS

King or Queen

Currently held by King Wyltam Grytsier.

Crown is passed on to the first born child regardless of gender.

The Ministers

Minister of Law

Currently held by Lord Dyeiter Tywik.

Oversees the court of law. Provides order to the city-state.

Minister of Protection

Currently held by Lord Keyain Vallynte.

Oversees the city guard and army.

Minister of Foreign Affairs

Currently held by Sethyr Calsyn

Oversees the foreign relations with other city-states.

Minister of Vassals

Currently held by Leyland Fedyr.

Oversees the populace of Satiros and maintains relationship with the temples.

Minister of Conduct

Currently held by Lord Rymos Batyst

Oversees court conduct and palace procedures.

Minister of Health

Currently held by Galyn Mydeus.

Oversees overall health and well-being of citizens.

Minister of Commerce

Currently held by Adryan Pytts.

Oversees businesses, guilds, and the economic welfare of the city-state.

Minister of Education

Currently held by Lord Redwyn Horsyn.

Oversees education and educational institutions.

Minister of Infrastructure

Currently held by Gordyn Donyr.

Oversees maintenance of roads, bridges, buildings, and more in the city-state.

Minister of Resources

Currently held by Lord Asyn Teryp.

Oversees the production of resources for the city-state.

Minister of Religious Affairs

Defunct.

Oversaw the relationship with the Deities of Duality.

Minister of Mages.

Defunct.

Oversaw common magic practitioners in the city-state.

Acknowledgements

This book took me through countless frustrations and setbacks, but through it all, there were a few key people who kept me moving forward.

To my husband: your patience is a gift. Thank you for calming me when I wanted to panic and for pushing me forward when I was ready to give up. For all the late nights, the endless idea sessions, and for taking care of the house and Bella while I was lost in this world—New Worlds Wake wouldn't exist without you.

To my alpha reader, Lindsey: your feedback brought this story back to life. Without you, it wouldn't have reached its final form—or have such a great title.

To my beta readers, Jade and Lauren: the book has changed a lot since your first read, and that's because of your thoughtful insights. I'm incredibly grateful for your time and guidance.

To my writing group: for every weekend we spent writing together and every idea you helped shape—thank you for seeing me through to the end.

To Bella, who can't read: thanks for being my late-night writing buddy, always curled up under my chair.

And to the readers who picked up this book: I'm deeply grateful for your time, support, and love. Thank you for reading.

About Eri Leigh

Eri Leigh brings her wildest daydreams to life through her writing. Her debut novel, *A Queen's Game* , launched the *Aithyr Uprising Series*, full of court intrigue, dark secrets, and a touch of anxiety to keep things real. The series continues with *New Worlds Wake*, and Eri's imagination is always brewing up something new.

When she's not plotting her next twist, Eri is with her D&D group, which has been going strong for nearly ten years. A former cosplayer who brought Fire Emblem and Monster Hunter characters to life, she now channels that same creative spark into her writing. Her husband even built her a custom bookshelf, packed with fantasy novels from authors like N. K. Jemisin and Sabaa Tahir, who continue to inspire her. And through it all, her loyal dog Bella is always close by, usually curled up under her chair while she writes.

With a style that combines intricacy and depth, Eri Leigh is carving out her place in the fantasy genre. Her worlds offer rich, immersive escapes, perfect whether you're seeking epic adventures or simply curling up with a gripping book.

Stay connected with Eri!

Instagram: @author.erileigh

TikTok: @authorerileigh

Threads: @author.erileigh

Scan the QR code below to sign up for Eri's newsletter: